VIOLENCE & VIGILANCE

Turesia Untamed

book 1

BOOK ONE *of* TURESIA UNTAMED

VIOLENCE & VIGILANCE

DAVID T. LIST

to UGA

don't feed the birds

(or the tigers, elephants, gators
or insects)

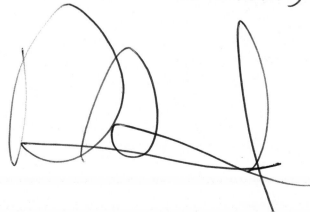

VIOLENCE & VIGILANCE
1st edition 2023

to Evie

I would have fought all of Turesia for you

Prologue
Painting a Crime Scene

FOHRVYLDA
the Wastelands

Captain Jeret rests against a shade tree on a hill to watch the ambush unfold. Wastelands patrol is monotonous, but today may prove eventful. His position overlooks the dusty path between Ingston and Ariheim, two dried up lumber towns just this side of death. Both parties below, the hapless caravan approaching from the east, and the bandits tucked behind bushes preparing to waylay them, are unaware of him and his soldiers, and Jeret intends to keep it that way. He's got no battalion or even company today. He's got what he prefers when painting a crime scene: an orcane arrowteam. Fleet, stealthy, effective. While enhancing an arrest with extra charges piled on your perpetrator, it's good to have as little help as possible. Keeps stories straight. Good bowmen keep your hands clean when that's what you want. And these should be some of the best damn archers in Marshal Zander's force, despite being greener than shat grass. His orcanes, which are essentially four-legged sharks with wiry black and white fur and a mean temper, are the quickest mounts in Fohrvylda, and double as charging teeth if an arrest goes to shit. Gods willing, it won't today.

The doubly ignorant caravan comprises a wagon drawn by two oxen and six armed individuals walking alongside. Upon the driver's perch are two lumpy figures wearing hooded shawls, one holding the reins. From the look of them, they've spent more time slumped on that wagon than anywhere else. The mercenaries are cheap—plain swords, mismatched leather plates if any armor at all. One of them is barefoot. One is digging in his nose and gazing at the northern horizon. Another wears a distant troubled look as if he's filled his pants and is trying to determine which pant leg to shake the shit out of. None appear spry enough to help in a fight. Based on their facial expressions, some aren't even aware they're on duty. Jeret would consider their sloppy appearance a ruse if it weren't for the wagon itself. The blanket strapped over the cargo is hole-ridden. The contents it's failing to conceal are cases made of unfinished wood, emblazoned with a white moon over a black sea. Ale. And not good ale, but shit ale from the eastern bluffs, where everything tastes like a mixture of seawater and piss, even the air itself. Pirate ale.

In the wastelands, it's important to declare the value of your haul with the competency of your protection, conveying to your potential ambushers that their gains will not justify their losses. Jeret considers today's pairing a nice fit. But that cheap ale and its accompanying cheap guard has attracted the inebriated attention of Captain Jeret's true quarry—Kraus the Thirsty Bandit, an apparent master ambusher. He is wanted by Promontory for acts of violence such as the one he's currently poised to commit. It's rare to have any warning on Kraus' strikes, especially considering he himself barely seems to. His assaults are sporadic in timing, unpredictable in location, and somehow equal parts inebriated and effective in their execution. By the time a patrol can respond, the elusive drunk has escaped, either having slunk off into an alley or passed out directly under their nose. Today, though, Jeret has turned the tables. He was tipped off about Kraus' intentions by a reliable source. *Today, he will fall to me.*

It's unclear exactly how many bandits make up the ambush. They're hidden well. Two besides Kraus, maybe more. The first two mercenaries of the convoy stroll by the black-clad ambushers hiding under shrubbery and could not be more oblivious.

"Shouldn't we warn them?" comes a hiss from behind Jeret. "I can hit those bandits from here."

Jeret turns and examines the bowmen who spoke long enough to memorize his peach-fuzz face. He's young. A terrible quality in a soldier, however accurate a shot he might be. Fresh soft skin, not yet mauled by blade or broken bottle. Round eyes, eager to know what the hell is happening. May as well be blind.

"Is that a fucking recruit?" Jeret asks his second, Mourt. He knows the boy is, but failing to comment on it may give Mourt the impression Jeret's willing to accept unproven meat in place of real help. Second Mourt vets Jeret's troops but can only do so much when chaff is all he has to sort through.

"Stores are low," Mourt says. His oily voice has no emotion attached. "The navy's in great demand. *Heathen Tide* and all that." He's taller than Jeret. Gangly but strong. His black eyes lurk beneath a cavern of a brow. He's got no ambition, an excellent quality in a second.

"And we're left with the chum," Jeret says. "Imagine if Marshal Zander had the spine to demand more soldiers. Do you know the lanista has a higher seat than him at Vretos' table?"

"In the boy's defense," Mourt says, without looking at Jeret or acknowledging his tirade, "he's right. He never misses."

"He damn well better not." Jeret returns his attention to the coming attraction.

The caravan is deep in range of the ambushers. Jeret's pulse is quick. *Would I have called the action already or been patient?* Kraus might be perpetually sloshed, but he's infamous for his ambushes. Little does he know, today Jeret will share his fame.

"Hyah!" rises a shout from the ambush, and Jeret starts despite himself. The centermost two of the six mercenaries drop without a sound. Jeret can't even tell what hit them, but there they fall, unconscious or dead. Two cloaked men spring from the bushes brandishing knives. One of the mercenaries shrieks and makes a run in the direction from which the caravan came. It's a girl. Probably sister to another mercenary. The two ambushers forget all else and run after her. Nose picking boy starts to give chase—maybe that was his sister—but the cart driver yells him back. Kraus the Thirsty Bandit has come out of hiding and is blocking the road by himself, nothing but a hefty stick in his hog-thigh fist. He's a huge lump of a man. Nothing small about him from his sloping shoulders down to his massive boots. "Get back here, you sops!" His black mane is as oily as his thick beard.

The remaining mercenaries have had time to ascertain their situation and apparently decide splitting their wages three ways instead of six is worth risking a dance with this hulking brute. It surely helps that Kraus has no blade and is already staggering drunk. The two on the wagon are yelling at each other. One is struggling to load a crossbow. The oxen seem appreciative of the rest.

"Ready arrows," Jeret whispers to Mourt. "Only Kraus needs to survive."

The mercenaries bare their swords and approach Kraus, but Jeret can tell there's no unity among them. Kraus lumbers toward one, stick raised high, making the mercenary flinch and protect his face. The barefoot fellow takes his chance to advance at Kraus' side. Kraus changes course, jabbing the barefoot fellow in the throat, then swinging a mighty arc, thunking the man's head and sending him cartwheeling into the bushes. Meanwhile, on the cart's perch, the bolt is nocked and the crossbow is leveled at Kraus.

"Take out that crossbow," Jeret says.

There's a *thump* and the whisper of an arrow's farewell. The crossbow wielder doubles over and the weapon clatters off the side of the wagon. The driver grabs his partner's cloak, trying to heft him back to his seat, as if that will remove the arrow. He stops when an arrow pierces his own back.

Kraus has flattened another mercenary. It's down to him and the nose picker.

"Got no beef with you," Kraus says. "Just here for a drink, if you don't mind."

Nose picker is trembling. Kraus barks and stomps at him and the boy throws his sword down. He scrambles alongside the cart and flees in the direction the others ran.

"Stop him," Jeret says. *Maximize casualties*, that's today's agenda.

An arrow punches a tree a couple of feet premature of the running boy. Seems he heard it, because he turns his head toward Jeret's patrol while he runs. The next arrows don't miss.

Kraus is making his way to the rear of the cart, humming loudly, unless that's the sound of his breathing. He's not noticeably concerned or even aware that the two manning the wagon have lain down for good.

Captain Jeret's orcane, standing tense beside him, is generating a whistling whine, straining its furry snout against its reins. Jeret turns and twists its leather muzzle, lest it forget who's in charge. Hackles bristle across the beast's shoulders. Its glassy black orbs are fixed on Kraus.

Kraus has ripped away the blanket and is trying to pry open a crate with his bare hands. The lid comes loose with a squealing crack. Kraus unstoppers a misshapen bottle with his teeth, spits the cork away, and dumps the ale into his face. His two partners are returning holding the limp body of the woman by her arms. They lower her to the road, where she groans faintly. She's not dead. An idea occurs to Captain Jeret.

"Come back for the payoff, I see. You worthless mutts," Kraus slurs. Judging by the passion he shares with the bottle, his two helpers have no further relevance.

"On my mark, take care of the help," Jeret says, raising a single hand. "Spare the girl."

One of the ambushers joins Kraus and helps himself to a drink. The other bandit has made his way to the wagon's perch and is digging in the pockets of the two deceased. When he discovers their cause of death he pauses, confused. He looks at the other bodies.

"Hey. Which one of you's got a bow?" He gives the arrows a closer inspection and realization dawns on his features.

Jeret points at him. Two arrows fly. One sticks in his chest, the other punctures his face, between his ear and his eye. He spasms, bites at his shoulder while spitting blood, falls backward off the wagon. The other ambusher is alerted, backing up wide-eyed, knife in hand. Kraus smashes an empty bottle on the path and goes for another.

"Uh, Kraus. We ain't alone." The ambusher trips over the unmoving woman, lands on his ass. This motivates him to make a break for it. He scrambles to his feet and achieves about three strides before arrows embed in his arm and lower leg. He howls and tumbles into bushes. This rouses the woman mercenary, and she sits shakily. Her hood has fallen, letting loose a trampled flower of yellow hair. She takes a long squint at Kraus, who is gripping the wagon with one hand and emptying a bottle into his bearded mouth with the other. She stands up, rubs the back of her head, looks over her shoulder. That last ambusher is taking his time dying in the bushes.

"Quit with the godsdamned yelling," Kraus calls back, without bothering to look. "Gonna bring Promontory down on us."

The girl has drawn a dagger from inside her cloak and approaches Kraus' back like she wants to stick him with it.

Jeret sighs. He wanted her alive. He raises his hand once more. Bowstrings creak as they draw tight behind him. Before arrows can loose or the girl can lunge, Kraus turns and heaves his bottle at her face. She has no time to react. It ricochets off her forehead so hard her feet leave the ground, and flies straight into the air. She skids on her shoulder and flops down in a motionless heap. Again. Kraus unleashes an outlandish combination of swear words at her, and plants himself up to his waist in the wagon, scrounging for another bottle.

Jeret laughs.

"What are we doing here if we're not even going to stop him?"

It's that fucking pink recruit again. His cheeks are all flushed like something's got him riled up. Jeret stands, stretches, walks over to the lad.

"Lahuvot's cock! Don't you ever shut up?" Jeret says.

The boy looks up at Jeret and his resolve visibly diminishes.

"Listen well, scab. You're a Promontory archer. Talking is a luxury you haven't earned and probably won't. You loose when Mourt says so. Meanwhile, tame that tongue or I'll cut it out and let the orcanes fight over it."

The recruit shrinks down and eyes the dirt.

"Alright, Fohrvylda's finest," Jeret says to the rest. "The thirsty bandit is in our grasp. He's been a canker on Promontory's ass for a good, long while. We'll get a fat sack for this." There is some nodding and affirmation. "I think we can do better than silver though, thus our meticulous strategy today that Pinky is so fond of." Jeret points at the recruit, who clearly regrets talking. Maybe even enlisting. "I want to get out of wastelands patrol. But for that we'll need more than a thirsty bandit's bounty. We need someone meaner." Jeret is met with mischievous grins and dark chuckles. The fact is, if Kraus the Thirsty Bandit kills a soldier today he'll double his bounty. But losing a soldier would blemish Jeret's perceived worth as a captain. And although that pink recruit is pleading for a bleeding, it's not worth the trade. Today all eight archers live, so long as they can coordinate their tale. Even the one who missed. There are other ways of inflating Kraus' bounty.

"Second," Jeret says. Mourt approaches, his gaunt face stretched long. "Kraus just killed everyone down there, particularly that girl." Mourt nods, and his tongue flicks over his lips. His eyes are glistening coals. He takes a step before Jeret catches his arm. "Make a mess."

~

Daylight leans on Kraus' eyelids like molten lead. A smithy is at work in his temples. His mouth and nose are full of sour ale and his tongue is plastered to the roof of his mouth. There's talking. Something sharp prods his leg. He attempts to spring to life. Except for some reason his wrists and ankles are bound. So instead he writhes and grunts in the dirt. *Dammit.* Must have got careless. Clearly his help wasn't worth what he'd paid them. Or wait ... did he pay them?

A cool shadow eclipses his face and he is able to pry open his eyes. A silhouette in a helm with a single stubby spike on top. Hard to see much else, especially considering everything is doubled. But that helmet spike says enough. A Promontory soldier. The worst kind of ruffian you'll meet in the wastelands.

"You must be Kraus the Thirsty Bandit."

It's never good when they already know you. The stink of orcane shit climbs through Kraus' mustache, making his nostrils curl. He can hear one of the beasts snuffling around. They must be close. Maybe a bottle of that pirate ale is close too. It was vile but it did the trick ... and then some, judging by his current state.

"Never heard of him," Kraus says. "Gimme something to drink and I'll tell you my name."

He turns his head in time to watch a boot heel converge with his forehead.

"You little shit," Kraus says. "Cut my ropes and try that."

Laughter.

"Let me give it a go," comes the voice of an enthusiastic boy. Kraus blinks away the blood and squints toward his assailants, trying to place his attacker, maybe make some sort of defensive—

"*Uff!*"

A toe buries in his guts. More laughter. That cheap ale threatens to take its leave.

"Damn, boy," Kraus says, swallowing bile. "I've been kicked harder by a passed-out whore. Put your spine into it if you got one."

"You want more?" The boy's voice is shrill. Kid's probably never been in a fight. Fucking archer. Kraus spots him. He's dressed in blue like the rest of them, prancing forward on skinny legs, prepping what could be a decent kick. Kraus clenches his teeth. The kick lands in his ribs, hard this time. Vomit erupts onto the boot and the boy's laughter becomes a scream, followed by swearing as he drags his boot through grass.

Kraus spits out a chunk and cackles. "Dumbass."

"That's enough."

The command stifles the laughter like piss on a candle. Kraus makes out the sheen of a plate metal cuirass. "You must be the boss," he says.

The soldier squats beside Kraus and pulls his sweaty head out of his helmet. He's got a clean-shaven face and a punch-me smirk. His chin is as pointy as his black widow's peak.

"Hello, Kraus." The man places a black-gloved hand on Kraus' shoulder, a move that would normally earn you no less than a broken wrist. "I'm Captain Jeret, of His Might's Domestic Patrol."

"I give a shit, why?"

"You've had a busy day. Look over there." Captain Jeret points.

It takes some blinking, but Kraus' eyes eventually unite on a tangle of naked legs protruding from a shrub. In the shadows beneath, a girl's face is pressed against the dirt, her yellow hair hung in branches, her eyes cloudy.

Kraus has a bad feeling and it's not just the shit ale. "That your mother?"

The captain chuckles. "No, my mother died a long time ago. This girl died about an hour ago while you raped her."

Ice fills Kraus' guts. "I didn't rape nobody." Except ... *did he*?

The captain *tsks* and rises to his feet. "You." He points at the soldier with puke on his boot. "What happened to that girl?"

The boy snorts. "That drunk right there stabbed her and raped her."

Kraus' teeth are clenched. He doesn't remember doing it. But he doesn't remember not doing it either.

"And you." Captain Jeret points at another. "What did you see?"

"I saw the thirsty bandit stick that girl's belly with a knife and then have his way with her."

The belly? Kraus stares at the girl. Why would he have stabbed her belly? That's not how to shut folks up quick.

"I didn't do that," he says, with no conviction.

"So says the drunk. Witnesses say otherwise, as does the evidence itself." The captain folds his gloved hands behind him and paces. "Assault, ambush, murder, rape—I could go on. And may I just say, thank you for your services."

The soldiers chuckle some more. Kraus can't take his eyes off the dark pool beneath the girl's chin. Ants are forming a circle around it. A fly lands on the side of her tongue. Kraus shakes his head, fanning his headache into life, trying to remember. He was nearly drunk while he hid in the bushes. Still is. He gave those mercenaries a few bumps with a stick. Didn't even kill any, probably. Then he got the ale. Why would he have done ... that? He only wanted a drink.

"Why didn't you stop me?" his mouth mutters. But the captain has moved on from the conversation.

"Collect the girl," Captain Jeret commands. "Carefully, so we can return her to her family. They'll surely want to have the body, despite its condition. Get this rapist up."

Kraus is hauled to his feet. The pressure of the bonds on his ankles releases as someone pulls a blade through the rope. It's less of a comfort than he'd expected. He can't take his eyes off the girl. "I need a drink."

"I think not," Jeret says. "I prefer my soldiers unraped."

One of the young soldiers boxes Kraus' ear. "Walk."

They stood him up too quick, pushed him too hard. Kraus' feet jumble with one another. He teeters, falls forward with no means to catch himself. His left knee lands on a pointed rock and he flops onto his face beside the girl's corpse, applying a fresh burst of dust to her. Sweet, sweet pain saturates his leg, rolling through his bones, cutting off his breath. His eyelids flicker. Fractured kneecap? He utters an ecstatic grunt.

Pain'll fix everything.

A valuable lesson taught by time and blood. For when your own skin's too tight, or too loose, or you can't stand the sight of it and the godsdamned liquor is all gone. It helps that he's always sorta liked hurting. Matches his outsides to his insides.

Through a pale tunnel her eyes are staring into his, toward where his soul should reside. It's not only because she's dead that she sees nothing.

Distantly, Captain Jeret is scolding someone. "Well done, lout. Pile him on your orcane. You can run alongside."

Kraus grinds his knee into the sharp stone. Feels like his kneecap is separating. The agony is comprehensive, a hatchet exploring his bone. His mouth stretches into a silent scream.

It's a good thing, pain. Pure. Honest. Nothing else like it. Not watching a fight. Not bouncing on a whore. Not gazing at the ocean or filling up on drink. Pain's better than the drink. It's a primal thing. A language impossible to misunderstand. What do you have going on? Doesn't matter, pain's here. Kraus has always believed pain says something different to him than it does to others. Most folks don't want it around and when it shows up they prefer it gone quick. So much so they'll act stupid. Put a torch against a man's arm and he forgets all about his bottle or his coin bag. Jam a knife in his boot and hell, you can make off with his shirt.

When the tide recedes and his vision returns, Kraus realizes he's drooling and groaning. The soldiers are watching him, transfixed. Or maybe that's disgust.

"I'd heard about you." Captain Jeret shakes his head. "Crippling yourself isn't the best habit, is it?"

"It ain't my worst one."

"I can imagine. You'll be glad to know where you're going, pain flows deeper than the Faithless Sea. Your chance to repay your debts is at hand."

Crunching his knee into the stone bears no more fruit. It's gone numb, like the rest of him. Kraus is forced to acknowledge the captain's face. "Do your worst, cunt."

"Happily." Jeret smiles, making his mouth all the more punch-me. "I hope you like feeding birds. You're going to Keswal."

1

Don't Feed the Birds

FOHRVYLDA
Keswal, Promontory

The ceiling of the Last Room trembles as the twenty thousand spectators above rumble, stamp, and yell. Dust snows down, hovering and swirling in the air between Irdessa and today's convict warriors. Beside her, Torvald observes them, his straight, black hair bathed in the gold of oil lanterns.

The sand glass indicates there's an hour until they fight.

There was a time when that relentless glass scared Irdessa. She'd tremble and fight back tears. That was long ago, but she hasn't forgotten. Now the muffled roar from above turns her blood into lightning. Torvald's presence keeps her energy static.

There are ten fighters total, including herself and Torvald. The other eight are new to Lanista Udiari's company. Three are proven, five wet; almost as shitty a way to start a day in Keswal as you can ask for. Wets are still searching through weapons, trying them, finding them unsatisfactory and dropping them, rubbing their sweaty hands on their legs, casting glances at one another. They won't find the confidence they're searching for. It's not in that arsenal. The proven mostly stand out of the way, trusting the rusty steel and dry-rotted leather that has kept them alive thus far, be it through one fight or several. Irdessa holds two javelins. She wears layered, dirt-stained linens and light, knee-high leather boots. But it's not her trusted gear that steadies her, it's the Tactician.

Torvald clears his throat. "We have an hour to devise a strategy."

All rattle of weapons ceases, and every eye turns to him. Wet and proven can all benefit from Torvald's words. In fact, their lives depend on it.

"I am Torvald, Lanista Udiari's trustee," he says. "Some know me as the Tactician."

The inevitable applause from the prisoners makes Irdessa smile. Torvald has refined his speech over these last two years. Irdessa finds herself silently filling in the unpleasant bits he leaves out.

"This will be the first time fighting for many of you."

And the last.

"If you are proven, there are many possible reasons you've survived thus far. But for those of you who intend to prey on a fellow combatant to survive ..."

Then you won't.

"... I do not offer my protection in the arena."

The room is without response as Torvald somehow meets every eye, all at once.

"But then, I can't guarantee my protection to any of you."

A hollow, raspy chuckle from one of the fighters. "You think we need your protection?"

The crowd parts to expose a hulking, oily wet with a pitch-colored beard and a banged-up face. He has one hand on the low ceiling and the other grips an axe's handle like it's a cane.

A scowl takes Irdessa's face. What an idiotic way to draw attention to yourself. Who could be stupid enough to act so haughty? This man is either supremely ignorant, mentally unfit, or done with life. There's a stained bandage wrapped around his left knee. He favors his right foot. Injury is the first thing Torvald perceives while weighing his fighters. Besides fear, it is the most important detail. This ugly brute will die today, Lahuvot willing, and word will spread to anyone else who might interrupt Torvald.

Torvald matches the man's gaze. "I'd recommend it. But it's not up to me what you need."

The man nods his shaggy face. "I'll say."

"We're fighting orcanes." Torvald says it like he's ripping a bandage off a wound.

Mouths fall open. Gasps escape. Irdessa's pulse spikes. The last time they fought Promontory's orcanes she almost lost a foot to one of the bastards.

"Good," the brute says. "Always wanted to kill a barkshark."

Torvald continues, "These aren't the cavalry striders making rounds, the ones that perhaps caught you. They're retired. Possibly injured. But they aren't much less of a threat for that. Perhaps more if they band together.

Irdessa smirks. They don't typically do that. Luckily for fighters of Keswal and outlaws of Fohrvylda in general, Beastmaster Grimmet beats all camaraderie out of orcanes at a young age.

A couple of people whimper, which in turn brings some chuckles. Irdessa has fought orcanes multiple times in her two years in Udiari's company. There's not much she hasn't. And all fights have their similarities. Those who, in this moment, expect to die today probably will. They'll manage to catch their trembling breath. Maybe even still their hands for a time. They'll absorb some encouraging words, be bolstered by the bloodlust of those who stand beside them. Then the gate will ascend and their fear will truly introduce itself. Without meaning to, Irdessa begins singling out individuals who will die before the sun sets.

The warriors who have no intention of dying come in different forms. Those who've known violence are more likely to keep control of themselves. Some will see the orcanes and fly into a fury. They have a better chance of surviving than wets who shit themselves, but not by much. Rarely can a man match the speed of an orcane, even a wounded one. Only collectively is victory assured.

"This will be a hard fight," Torvald says.

Half of us will die. Irdessa is able to keep her face from showing it.

"There are three of them," Torvald says. "So we'll make three teams. Two will misdirect, distract. The other will strike. Those wearing steel will catch the orcanes' attention, not unlike a fish lure."

A convict drops the rusty helm he'd been considering and backs away from it.

"Strikers will wear little armor. We must hit fast and avoid direct attack."

Throughout the room several wets are visibly nervous. But other faces have hardened. Those people press forward to ensure they miss nothing. Even the scruffy brute has shut his mouth and squared both feet toward Torvald, standing as if he's forgotten his injury. Or was he faking?

What Torvald says is partially true. One group will strike. One will run, maybe strike. The third will almost undoubtedly fill orcane bellies and provide an opportunity for the other two groups.

"While you studied your resources, I studied you. And in each of you I've witnessed strengths."

And weaknesses. It takes effort for Irdessa not to mouth the words.

A few dark looks communicate displeasure at the comment. It's well known that the Tactician can weigh a man in a glance. Wets and proven alike get downright uncomfortable when faced with the fact that Torvald knows who'll die.

"Those who misdirect must be fast, like you ..." Torvald points at a tall lanky boy with hair the color of straw and a purple bruise under his right eye. Irdessa noticed him earlier. While others hefted swords and axes, he examined the knives. They'd pried at armor and steel-reinforced boots, and he'd quickly snatched the pliable leather shoes. His eye is not swollen shut. It's not a debilitating injury.

"What's your name?" Torvald asks.

The boy straightens his shoulders. "Pinprae."

The ugly brute cackles. "Piss spray? Damn, boy, I see why you got your eye blacked."

The boy's chest deflates.

Torvald ignores the brute. "You were a thief on the outside. Better at fleeing than fighting. That's why your knuckles are so clean."

The boy turns down his chin and tucks his hands away to hide the incriminating evidence. Maybe he was alright at fleeing. Not good enough. He's here.

"Keswal is about survival, and survival is not always about fighting. I need runners." Torvald pauses long enough for Irdessa to notice him flick his eyes in her direction. She sighs inwardly and braces herself.

"Beside me stands Irdessa the Undying."

Convicts hoot and applaud. Irdessa lifts a single hand in response. When they celebrate Torvald it's because he's earned it. He is the Tactician. When they cheer for her, she feels like a fraud. She's done nothing but follow his instructions. Any adoration aimed at her is misplaced. She fights the urge to hide behind Torvald.

He aims a smile at her. "If you've heard she is fast and cunning, you only know part of the truth. There's a reason she's called the Undying. She'll long outlive me."

She hates when he says that.

"Pinprae, you'll be a runner. Team with Irdessa. She'll put your speed to use. And get a new name."

"If you're gonna be prancing, how 'bout *Prancer*?" says the brute, rousing up some laughter. There's no ill will in the look the boy returns to him. He must like it. He turns hopeful eyes toward Irdessa. She gazes disinterestedly at the far wall. You can't let in wets. Not on fight day. Not until they're proven. Not even then if you're smart.

Torvald proceeds to the next convict, a wiry woman with frizzy black hair. She's kneeling beside the vases of used arrows, filling her quiver. Her deeply lined face speaks of stale bitterness, the look of a mother who's watched her children fall asleep hungry too many times.

"You're a poacher. Any good with a bow?"

Of course she is. Even Irdessa spotted how expertly she vetted the bows.

She stands and clears her throat. "If I hadn't run out of arrows, I'd not be here now." It's a strong voice coming from so thin a frame.

"Oh, I like her," says a fellow with a closely shaved scalp.

She responds to him with a look that could curdle water.

"You'll strike," Torvald says. "With me."

She nods.

Torvald continues sorting. The shaved man has scars all over his hands and a couple across his chin and cheek. Small eyes peer from under a notched, hairless brow. He's a proven, already fought in Keswal but newly acquired by Lanista Udiari. The leather cuirass he wears sits comfortably on his shoulders and the spear is at home at his side. A soldier, probably convicted of some war crime.

"Soldiers are the best and the worst to stand beside you," Torvald explained once. *"Though their crimes might be particularly heinous, they usually acted so in consenting company. It's likely they regret their actions, assuming they even acknowledge them. They're trained*

and can follow orders. They've seen combat and won't quickly lose their nerve."

"And what makes them the worst?" Irdessa had asked.

"Ambition. If a man decides he can do my job better than me, there's nothing stopping him from trying to supplant me."

"That hasn't happened yet."

"None have understood my job."

"And what is that?" she'd asked.

"Keeping you alive."

The soldier is to be a runner. He doesn't seem happy about it, but happiness comes in scant portions in the Last Room.

Torvald comes to a thin fellow with skin the color of driftwood and bright red tattoos over his exposed arms and his face. The crescent moon tattooed on his cheek tells Irdessa he's been initiated into a tribe from the southernmost bluffs. The tattoo is a reward for ritual murder. The man's glistening eyes meet Irdessa's and he pointedly licks his lips. Two years prior he might have intimidated her. But since then far worse than him have threatened her in Keswal and ended up in the dirt.

"Runner," Torvald says crisply, "with him." He points at the ex-soldier. Irdessa notices a finality in his voice no one else could have caught. That man will die today. She puckers her lips at him.

"And you ..." Torvald says to the ugly bastard.

Finally, thank Lahuvot.

The man's scrubby brow collapses under Torvald's stare.

"And you ..." Torvald says again. It sounds like a challenge. All has gone quiet as the two lock eyes from across the room. Irdessa realizes she's holding her breath.

"How long since your last drink?" Torvald asks.

The man's grimace stretches over his entire face. Irdessa has a good look at him for the first time. He seemed grimy before. But something in his eyes is downright ghastly. Keswal is a place for outlaws, and although Torvald has some influence on filtering the shitbags Lanista Udiari purchases or acquires for his company, sometimes something foul creeps in. Irdessa has seen her share of cutthroats, rapists, highwaymen, pillagers, even those who tamper in the dead. They enter Keswal thinking their skillset will avail them, not taking Torvald into account. In Udiari's company, he is your first and last hope.

Something about this man's visage tells Irdessa he's no simple thief or drunk. Even the lowest thug has passion for something, the thrill of killing, or the chase, or the rape, or a bite to eat, or just a shirt. This man's eyes are a void. Emptier than an orcane's. Something happened to him. Such apathy in Keswal is a death sentence, for you and anyone near you.

"What's your name?" Torvald asks.

"Kraus."

"This is your first fight in Keswal."

Kraus doesn't move.

"It helps me to know what my fellows were up to before joining our ranks." Torvald's eyes are as sharp as crushed glass.

Kraus still says nothing. He's become a gargoyle disguised as a man, glowering, his knuckles white.

Irdessa's stomach churns with anticipation. *Gods' sake, put him with the damned and move on.*

"We don't have to discuss what landed you here," Torvald says. The walls themselves sigh in relief.

"That's best for everyone," the brute says.

"What's your plan for Keswal?"

"Seems like a good place to die," Kraus says.

Irdessa needs no closer observation to know he is serious, and is not afraid. What an anchor. He'll feed many birds.

"I think you'll make a good striker," Torvald says. "You're with me."

Irdessa's mouth falls open. She shuts it quickly. Survival for the group relies on the front that all is going as planned. But this can't be the plan. An injured man with no will to live may as well be a boulder tied to Torvald's neck.

Torvald proceeds to sort. There's a deserter, the one who considered armor and chose against it, who will run with Irdessa, and a heavy-set butcher who will strike with Torvald. The last fighter's an elderly woman with small hands and grey in her hair. She was a jeweler on the outside, caught buying stolen merchandise. She is complimented on her dexterity and placed with the doomed runners. Not because of her crime. Torvald does not presume to judge his combatants. It's more likely because there's no evidence the woman has ever run a step or lifted a weapon.

Once all are accounted for, Torvald offers some finer points to the convicts: how to exploit a wound, tells that orcanes give before pouncing, the signs and calls he and Irdessa use during a fight and what they mean. All the while, a gap surrounds Kraus that no one seems willing to step within. Irdessa is smart enough to know not to express fear, but she keeps Torvald's shoulder between herself and the man. Since Torvald mentioned his past, he's been brooding like he's wrestling with an unpleasant decision. She preferred him loud and ugly.

There comes a muffled trumpet blast, followed by the thunder of kettle drums. The commotion above the Last Room intensifies and thin lines of sand shower from the rafters.

"It's time," Torvald says over the ruckus. He walks to the ten-foot-tall wooden gate and stands in the archway, facing the convicts with a half-smile. His eyes have sharpened to pins. "Look around you." He points with the sheath of his long, curved sword. "We're an unlikely alliance. But in an hour's time, there will be no wets among us. If I've learned nothing else in my time here, there is no family like one forged in Keswal. Decide now if you'll join."

Irdessa's jaw clenches. Thoughts of her father, Andelsior, lead her to believe that Keswal is more likely to destroy a family than forge one. Andelsior was arrested alongside her and Torvald two years ago. Unlike them, he didn't survive his first fight. Irdessa must stow away the thought.

The ground rumbles. The portcullis outside the wooden gate is lifting. Irdessa's blood rushes. Her chest heaves. Her javelins—her fangs—grow light.

"Now is the time to live forever," Torvald says. "Join me and make a mark never to be forgotten!"

Pinprae raises his dagger and hoots, making the little old jeweler start. The brute throws up both hands and yells, as do the deserter and the ex-soldier. The murderer's tongue flicks over his lips. The heavy butcher takes a backward step, jowls aquiver.

The gate ascends, grinding upward so that blinding sunlight creeps over the sand and up Torvald's ankles. His words, void of any other purpose than to incite bloodlust, do just that. Irdessa bounces lightly on the balls of her feet. Keswal cannot reach her fast enough. Her javelins are extensions of her arms. Among her stand not men but meat. Some will avail, some will die terribly. They are all tools at the disposal of herself and the Tactician. Her eyes are fire, her muscles wings. She rolls her head on her shoulders and the bones of her neck loosen and snap. Beside her Torvald has turned to face the rising gate. He's still. Calm. He gives her a sidelong glance, and the corner of his mouth curls in a secret smile.

With three feet of hallway exposed under the gate Irdessa can contain herself no longer. "I'm tired of all this dust," she yells to no one in particular. "Let's wash it off with orcane blood!" She is met with battle cries from the convicts which merge with the encompassing roar from the arena's stands. She rolls under the massive gate into the corridor and stamps toward her destiny.

At the tunnel's mouth, across the highest point in the arch, hangs a placard. On it is etched the phrase:

ERST YYS HAEDISUA

Irdessa raps it with the butt of her javelin. She strides onto the packed earth and sand of the arena, thrusting her weapons high. The response from the masses is deafening. Flower petals rain down from the northern and southern stands.

"What's inscribed there?" Pinprae yells, close behind her.

"Just hit it," comes Torvald's voice. "I'll tell you after."

Irdessa struts toward center arena from the Deceiver's wall. The battleground is a pentagon, roughly eighty yards across at its widest. To her left, above the two southern walls, are the two sections of unadorned rows for the convicts and for the general rabble. To the right, above the northernmost wall, are the plush booths and shaded seating for His Might Vretos, who'll never miss a fight; his court, who compete for his favor in all things; and wealthy Promontory citizens, including business owners, merchants, and high-ranking military. The westernmost edge of the arena has no wall—instead an expanse of open sky and a vertical drop of several hundred feet to the ocean. Beyond, iron-colored clouds band across the sky, leaving a crimson sunset visible in strips out over the Faithless Sea.

Arriving at the center of the arena, Irdessa lifts her weapons in the sun and turns slowly, to the audience's rabid delight. She holds twin hardwood javelins some five feet long, thin and tipped in sharpened steel, flanged down their length to facilitate the liberation of blood. She spins them in her hands, loosening muscles and joints, to the gratification of her fans. Thousands of people chanting your name has a way of boosting your spirit, but that's not why she scans the audience. Her eyes search the stands not for the individuals quivering for her attention, but the opposite. She wants to see those more concerned with what life they've paused to be here, however insignificant. She wants to see people inconvenienced and annoyed. Bored even. These are the sparse moments when Irdessa can observe people not enslaved by Promontory, as she has been these last two years. It's a glimpse into a life to which she hopes to return one day, however unlikely that might be. From her view little seems to have changed. Those with money and influence on the north are ever garish. The southern seating is drab. Both are equally thirsty for blood.

Irdessa's fellow combatants have joined her.

"What now?" Pinprae yells over the crowd. His bruised eye darts all over. The dagger shakes in his fist. Irdessa considers giving his face the butt of a javelin, maybe knock some nerves out of him. She's no longer infected by the anxious energy rampant in fresh convicts. Now it's more an impatient buzzing that borders on irritation.

"The orcanes will be released all at once, from three points around the arena," Torvald says. "Form teams. Stay alert."

Irdessa scans the gates lining the battlefield on the northern and southern walls. Lanista Udiari's company relies on the Last Room exclusively, but beasts and other convicts utilize most any of the other twenty-odd arched openings of varying size. The birds have their own doors. If she's learned nothing else, this deceptive still is a perfect time for apprehension to encroach if you let it. So don't. The fight has already started.

"Be ready to run," she says, for Pinprae and the deserter.

As always, while riding the energy of anticipation, Irdessa's eyes stray to the Deceiver's wall on the east, which is the actual cliff face from which Keswal was carved. The Deceiver himself is a fifty-foot-tall statue. A hewn relief of a giant man, half trapped in the stone. He seems to have kicked one foot through the wall and gotten stuck in the process of squeezing from the cliff. His right arm extends upward toward His Might Vretos' booth, which is perched high in the northern seating.

From his fingers hangs a thin chain, that would probably be imperceptible at this distance were it not for the gleaming crystal that adorns it, reflecting the setting sun in a brilliant pinpoint. The statue's surface is smooth. His hair defies gravity, rising upward like torch fire, and his face wears a look of anguish, as if the chain brings him great pain and he yearns for Vretos to take it back.

There's a *thump* from the southern wall and Irdessa's guts heave. Then two more *thumps* from the northern walls. A thunderous howl tears through the shouts of the masses, tapering up at the end into a raspy squeal. It's as healthy an orcane call as she's ever heard. The tattooed murderer drops his sword and falls to his knees, gripping his ears.

Godsdammit, Torvald, you said they'd be retired. She meets his eye. He offers an apologetic smile and a shrug. She bares her teeth. *You knew. Son of a bitch.*

Irdessa feels the pounding of their paws before she sees them. Two orcanes are closing in from the north, one from the south.

"Thief, deserter, your fate is now." Irdessa sprints directly toward the southernmost orcane. "Hug my heels if you want to live!"

~

Pinprae runs behind Irdessa the Undying. What fuels his feet is a true mystery, as if he's not bordering on pissing himself. As if this path will end anywhere besides inside an orcane's belly. They're running in a line to crash head-on into what appears to be not a wounded, retired orcane, but one at the peak of its vitality and mad as all hell. It looks like a massive wolf, but stumpier, as tall as Pinprae's head at its shoulder, with a trunk-like neck and a pointed snout prime for cutting through water. They're supposed to be more suited for swimming than running. As this one bears down on them, he cannot believe that's true.

Pinprae throws a panicked glance backward to see the armored deserter some ways behind him. Farther back still, Torvald the Tactician runs west toward the cliff edge with his strikers. The other team hasn't moved. The bald soldier is shaking the tattooed man by the neck, perhaps trying to jiggle some use out of him. Both northern orcanes— neither of which look injured—are en route to converge on them. Those "runners" might as well be rabbits in a snare. Did Torvald predict that? The jeweler woman seems to be considering abandoning her team.

Ahead, Pinprae can see the beady, black marbles that are the orcane's eyes. Its claws kick up gravel and dust fifteen feet in the air. *What did Torvald say?* Attack the white part. That'll be a feat, considering it's black across its entire back, and outside its legs and the top half of its head. Impact will occur in moments, and the only white Pinprae can see is its belly, maybe its throat.

"I thought we were only supposed to distract it," Pinprae cries.

"Shut up, Prancer," yells the deserter.

Irdessa points with her javelin and banks to the left abruptly, back toward the Deceiver's wall, her feet impossibly agile. Pinprae follows, nearly turning his ankle in the process. It takes all his fortitude to run behind her, to match her pace rather than outrun her, although he's tempted to make a break for the Last Room and attack the gate with his knife. His thoughts are a steady, jumbled stream of swearing, mostly at himself for ever wishing he could witness the Undying and the Tactician at work.

A bloody shriek from behind. The stands erupt in cheers. *The deserter?* Pinprae's bowels liquefy.

"Keep running," Irdessa yells. "Don't look back."

She's making a tight arc to the right. Pinprae is holding his place behind her. But he's unable to keep himself from looking. The orcane rolls to a stop on its back, gripping the bald deserter's head in its mouth, forelegs wrapped around his shoulders. The man's free hand plucks at the beast's massive paws, to no effect. His puckered lips are protruding from between the animal's clenched teeth. The orcane's hind legs rise up and kick, raking the man's stomach like a brutally effective mousing cat. With that one attack, the bald man becomes a flailing sack. The hind legs kick again. This time, red viscera bursts forth, gleaming in the golden sun, arcing high and spattering in piles over the ground. Pinprae's feet stop responding.

The two other orcanes are fighting over the woman jeweler, tugging her in opposing directions. Her body separates in a crimson splash, ceasing her scream. The orcane that won her legs throws away the limbs and trots panting toward the soldier, who left the tattooed man to his whimpering fate and stands there shooing the orcane with his spear.

"Prancer!"

It's Irdessa, and she's at full sprint, closing on the orcane that's gnawing on the bald man's emptied torso. Pinprae watches her launch a javelin. It flies too fast for him to follow, but the orcane spasms, its spine arching. It gives a piercing bark, disentangles itself from the remains of the deserter, flounders onto its feet. Its shark eyes fall on Pinprae. The orcane rears its head, giving a whistling howl that ends in a harpy's shriek. Doesn't that mean ... *it has found a target?* All the heat flees Pinprae's body in a single instant and the hairs on his arms and neck turn to icicles. *Oh shit, oh shit, oh shit, oh shit.* He was supposed to do something, but what? His dagger feels like little more than a sewing needle. He's considering running it across his own throat when the orcane charges, running hobbled, its white lower jaw soaked entirely in the blood of what was a functioning teammate until moments ago.

"*Run!*"

Pinprae doesn't see Irdessa, but the command hits him like a bolt of lightning. He flees on feet powered by naked dread. The orcane's stride is compromised, thank the gods. Enough for him to stand a chance? He runs toward the southern wall, away from the northernmost skirmishes. There's no telling where Irdessa is. Over his right shoulder, distantly, Torvald's team is in action. The black-haired woman with the bow is kneeling, firing arrow after arrow into an orcane that is charging at her. The large, oily-bearded Kraus is pacing, yelling, axe held high, cursing the beasts for damn cowards and inviting them to a one-on-one. The other orcane rears, slinging a dark-skinned body into the air. A flash of silver. One of its black paws flies free. There's Torvald, his long sword gripped in both hands.

The orcane on Pinprae's heels is gaining on him. He can hear its strained whimper, like a salivating hound chasing a cat. Against all common sense, Pinprae looks back. The orcane is within twenty yards and closing. Its massive head remains level despite its trampling feet. Its red teeth are bared, black eyes round. Pinprae's toe hits something and he tumbles. He's on his ass, scuttling backward like that'll help him. It's all over. His ma's words return to him, the ones she uttered after socking him in the eye.

"Thieving's gonna get you killed, boy. You're gonna end up in the belly of a monster in Keswal."

The orcane gives a stabbing squeal so bright and high he's shaken from the thought. The earth rumbles beneath Pinprae. It's going to eat him, and no memory will make it any more pleasant. He lifts an arm in a pitiful farewell to his life.

The orcane's body flinches, rocked by an invisible impact. Its forelegs sprawl and it faceplants into earth. The beast flips end over end, crashing lifeless in a blast of dust, sliding to a stop with its cold, black snout against his crotch, which is soaked for some reason. It seems someone pissed in his pants.

The roar of the crowd surges until it fills Pinprae's head and all he can hear is:

"Ir-dess-ah!"

"Ir-dess-ah!"

"Ir-dess-ah!"

"Get up." Irdessa is inexplicably standing above him. "We're not done."

She jerks him to his feet and darts over to the fallen orcane. It takes only a moment for her to find a javelin. She yanks it out and blood chases the weapon from the wound.

"Can you run?"

"Can I ..." His eyes are bound to the massive fallen orcane. "... run?" He's never seen a dead one. It's said their dorsal fins are clipped at a young age to make room for the leather saddle. Indeed, there's a puckered, hairless line amid the short black fur on the thing's back. Its triangular teeth and shark eyes are a mess of blood and sand.

A sharp sting rocks Pinprae's cheek. His ear is ringing. Irdessa is in his face. Did she slap him?

"We're not done!" she says, and runs. Pinprae follows her numbly, rubbing his face. *What use could I possibly serve besides diversionary chew toy?*

Ahead, the ground is littered with the fallen and their loose parts. The three-footed orcane is thrashing on its side like a speared fish, trying to dislodge the axe embedded in its eye socket. Kraus clings to the axe's long handle, getting jostled around like he's netted the father of all marlins. It sounds like he's laughing.

The last orcane drags itself growling toward the poacher, who is advancing to meet it. The beast's fur is striped with blood from half a dozen arrows. A spear extends from its stomach. The woman shoots an arrow directly into its snout from five feet away. The orcane sneezes tremendously, expelling a red cloud on her, and rolls to its side, giving a tremor then moving no more.

Keswal's stands explode in applause.

Irdessa slows her pace and walks toward the arena center, where Torvald runs a surprisingly clean cloth down the length of his sword. He's so composed you'd think he bloodied his blade divvying out steak dinner. The archer shoulders her bow and joins him, her face dripping red. Black-bearded Kraus is trying to pry his axe out of the orcane's skull, swearing at full blast.

Pinprae hesitates several yards away. Four survivors. Five counting himself. But why would someone count him? Those are warriors, the likes of which he's never seen. He is not worthy to stand among them, or even be alive for that matter. Irdessa looks back and gestures for him to join her.

You did well, she mouths, as he comes to a dazed stop beside her.

I did? He takes in the crowd in a slow circle. They're bouncing on their feet, cheering and yelling, commoners and the rich alike. All manner of valuables, trinkets, and detritus shower from the seats, scattering over the earth. The sun has sunk low enough on the western horizon to cast eerily elongated shadows over the floor of Keswal. The shadow extending off the heap that is the jeweler's legs stretches all the way to the Deceiver's wall.

Pinprae is now a proven, no longer a wet. It's less validating a feeling than one might think. The sound of the crowd is dying slowly, or he's going deaf. He gazes over the scattered dead. Ten went into the fight. Five remain. He tries to remember the faces of the deceased. All that's coming back is the deserter from his own team. *How did I outlive him?*

Pinprae finds himself unwilling to look to the northern spectators. The seating on Keswal's southern side is divided. Half for commoners, half for convicts belonging to a lanista. Commoners have the barest accommodations, nothing more than stone hewn into seating terraces. Jugs of wine, vendors, waving fans, and spread blankets intersperse that mass. Convict seating is marginally better. A perk of being arrested and sold to a lanista is that you watch fights for free, in cushier seating than the general rabble. Minimal shade above, functioning cushions below. Seems those luxuries are lost on this crowd. Of all the audience, they're the most somber. The obvious downside of their position is that they'll probably soon die on the battleground they are observing. Those who meet Pinprae's eye offer little more than a nod, if anything. Maybe Pinprae's survival is heartening for them. If he can do it, then who the hell can't? Then again, they've likely seen far more deserving than him fall in Keswal. Probably even friends of theirs, or family. What gave him the right to survive? Pinprae looks at his feet, which waver beyond the sheen of tears. *Godsdammit, Pinprae, not now.*

"Behold!" a voice booms from the northern seats and startles him sober. It's the infamous Bloody Portent, the chronicler of Keswal, yelling into his blossom-shaped loudphones. His large cheeks are clean shaven and his long robe is a gaudy patchwork of bright colors, as if sewn by a color-blind tailor. "Torvald the Tactician and Irdessa the Undying."

A surge in the applause.

"Among the triumphant are Pinprae the thief."

Pinprae's heart thuds. He holds a single hand in the air. Perhaps the crowd acknowledges it. He can't tell.

"Jasmin, a poacher of His Might's own boars."

The poacher watches the crowd with the same bitter annoyance she's worn since the Last Room, only now it's painted red.

"And finally, Kraus the Thirsty Rapist."

The cheers are interspersed with a heaping of angry boos. Kraus, who managed to pry loose his axe, scowls toward the Faithless Sea. Rotten vegetables hurtle from the stands and burst on the arena floor. None are close enough to hit him, but their message is delivered even so. His white-knuckled grip on the axe and the shudder of his shoulders convince Pinprae he'd use his weapon on every member of the crowd one by one if he had the chance.

"Meanwhile," the Bloody Portent continues, "joining the glorious dead: a deserter of the Domestic Patrol, a cultist from the southern bluffs, a black-market jeweler, a poisoning butcher, and a soldier gone berserk. Rejoice. They have paid their debt to Fohrvylda."

The cheers are less enthusiastic, and rightfully so. Everyone saw it happen. This reminder serves little purpose. The crowds are filing from their seats.

"Time to move," Irdessa says, turning briskly and making for the archway of Last Room. Jasmin the poacher follows her. Kraus limps after them. Torvald faces the northern wall and bows low with unerring grace, tickling a few more cheers from the crowd. "Let's go, Prancer," he says.

Pinprae follows him, considering the appeal of the name Prancer over his own. The Deceiver has taken on an amber sheen in the sun's final rays. The crystal hanging from its stone fingertips shines fiercely.

As Pinprae and Torvald near the walls, gifts cascade down around them. Flowers, coins, articles of clothing. Shoes, for some damn reason. The second pointy heel to ricochet off Pinprae's forehead draws blood. How sad is it that this will be the most significant of his injuries? Covering his head fails to convince the crowd to relent.

When they arrive at the tunnel to the Last Room, Irdessa raps the placard again with her remaining javelin. The poacher taps her bow against it.

"Um, what's inscribed there?" Pinprae asks again.

"Shut up, ya fucking wet," Kraus calls back, slapping the flat of his axe against it.

"I'm not a wet anymore," Pinprae mutters.

"Then you should know," Kraus says.

"It means 'Don't feed the birds,'" Torvald says. He gives it a tap with his sheathed sword.

Pinprae's lost his dagger and he's not sure his spent legs will let him jump high enough to hit it. He jumps and swings at it. Misses. "Wouldn't we rather be feeding birds?" He jumps again. Misses again.

Kraus chuckles. "Still a fucking wet."

Torvald has reached the gate and turns to watch. "Might want to get a move-on."

There are several distant *thumps*, the same as when the orcanes were released.

Pinprae jumps once more, this time grazing the wooden plank with the tip of his fingers.

"I got it!" he says.

There comes a flurry of feathers and shrill clucks and squawks from the arena behind him.

"Get in here, you dumb wet," Kraus calls.

The sun is aimed squarely at the hallway opening now, so that the shapes pouring out into the arena are silhouettes. Pinprae can tell they're two-legged, taller than a man, and approaching rapidly. He runs down the hall and scrambles under the gate. As it lowers the skittering of nails follows him down the hallway. The gate closes with a muffled boom, silencing the pursuit.

"What the hell were those?" Pinprae asks.

"You ain't ever seen dreadhops?" Kraus is chuckling, prying off his leather plate and releasing a uniquely abhorrent odor. "Must be a city wet."

"Those are the birds," Torvald says. "And today, you didn't feed them."

2

Born for a Time of War

FOHRVYLDA
Keswal, Promontory

Irdessa lounges in the shade of Lanista Udiari's seating in the southern stands of Keswal. Around her are the rest of Udiari's motley company. The sky is cloudless, but the air is mercifully bearable, thanks to the canopy overhead. Torvald is to her right, and beside him, Kraus. The rapist is not so hopeless as he was when he arrived. Quite the opposite. Seems being a prisoner who's subjected to death matches has put quite the spring in his step. It's the opposite for the sane, but that goes without saying. To Irdessa's left is the insufferable Prancer, who has hardly left her side since their fight with the orcanes. All that remains of his injury is a thin greenish crescent running along the bottom of his eye. As long as Pinprae is the best name he's got, she'll call him Prancer like everyone else does. In the row below them, Jasmin sits with some other archers. Seems she has impressed the company's bow enthusiasts. The rest of Udiari's convicts are untested as far as Irdessa's concerned. She'll learn their names if she has to. A wooden partition stands on either side of Udiari's seating, separating them from the shabby commoner stands on the east, and other lanistas' convicts on the west.

The preceding fight was all convicts, no beasts. These are necessary to appease certain audiences, particularly gamblers. Seven errant mercenaries faced off against nine soldiers of the Domestic Patrol who were all convicted of desertion, a charge which can mean almost anything. The mercenaries won, with few injuries and only a single casualty. As usual, Torvald and Irdessa analyzed and commented on their strategies, pointing out which actions benefited them, which did not. There wasn't much to be learned. Fluid tactics are superior to static formations. Deception is your friend. Don't run into a spear with your face.

She has observed that Torvald, despite his mood being subdued of late, creates something of a dilemma for the convicts. They want to be nearby, to absorb his wisdom and longevity by proximity, and yet they're guarded in speech and movement, as if that might prevent him from extricating their secrets and stamping them either damnable or damned. Torvald has taught Irdessa to assess people in all ways, especially those details they give freely: what they wear, how they wear it, if they turn away when the killing stroke falls, whether they cheer and for whom, whether they're bored, afraid, excited. Most importantly, whether or not they can learn.

Dreadhops are scouring the arena floor, ever insatiable, cleaning up for the headlining fight of the evening. Meanwhile the musicians work their horns and flutes and kettle drums and cymbals, stirring up an accompaniment so cheery it feels like an outright lie. Irdessa, like most who'd call themselves mentally fit, has no desire to watch the birds clean up. It's disturbing to witness dead men rendered to bird shit. But it's more unsettling to witness the faces of those who are excited by it.

The great birds devour whatever they can bash to pieces, rip up, and shake down their long throats, including weapons and armor. Whatever they can't digest, they'll eventually vomit back up, even if it kills them. Their plumage of lively shades of red, orange, yellow, and purple, give them a deceptively innocuous appearance. This is offset by their daunting height, their piercing red irises, and their battle axe-beaks that curve to a chisel point at the tip, perfect for hammering through steel and skulls.

There are always too many dreadhops released. Maybe it's to keep them competitive. Two of the birds are fighting over what appears to be a bloody scrap of leather. Their stunted wings beat the air as they tug at it. Spectacles like these produce their own side games for the gamblers. At length, the taller one loses its grip and the stouter bird scampers off, throwing its head back and wriggling the object down its throat. When Irdessa sees fingers disappear into the huge golden beak, she realizes it was a leather-clad arm.

The gong begins to clang, summoning the dreadhops back to the tunnels. The enormous birds charge for the exits, leaving vibrant plumage trickling in the air behind them.

"They're so obedient," Prancer marvels.

"Beastmaster Grimmet," Irdessa says, pointing toward the plush northern seats where Vretos' throne is a centerpiece and the members of his court each have their own luxurious booth. "He has a way with murderous animals."

Grimmet, red-haired and round-bellied, is looking overly smug today, gorging himself on some sort of roast leg and flanked by two curvy women wearing thin-strapped bits of cloth. His bloated mannerisms are contrasted with his son, Pappu the falconer, who stares longingly at the Faithless Sea. The boy is black-haired and considerably darker-skinned, attributes he acquired from his mother, a native of Ausgan. The island nation Fohrvylda, and its capital city, Promontory, in particular, attract a range of visitors and cultures, mostly tourists interested in the world-famous Keswal. But being descended from

Ausgan—Fohrvylda's eternal enemy—earns you little popularity here, even if your father is a member Vretos' court. Rumors are the boy's slight size is due to an injury suffered during his birth, wherein his mother died. His perpetually apathetic expression suggests he might not be concerned with or even aware of what's happening around him. But his ability to train sprakes is a feat of legend. Before his work with the birds, the falcons were useful for hunting and little else. Keswal fodder if they were injured. Now Promontory employs the birds for a range of jobs, including spying, communicating to the far corners of the mainland, even seeking and attacking errant outlaws.

The dreadhops are gone and their gates have closed. Men in grey clothes are raking sand and shoveling whatever scraps and meat the birds failed to finish onto carts to haul over and dump off the western edge of the arena.

"People of Fohrvylda," the Bloody Portent booms into his flower-shaped loudphones. He's located low in the northern seating, far below Vretos' throne or his court's booths. Even at this distance his brass instrument makes his voice sharp in Irdessa's ears. "This is the moment you've all been waiting for. By the gods, the sand will blush today."

Applause punctuates the general din of the crowd. The musicians proceed happily as if they're the attraction. The Portent clears his throat into the loudphone until the song skids to a nearly functional conclusion.

"Finally," Kraus says, cranking a pinky finger in his ear.

"Introducing first," the Bloody Portent booms, "from the southern bluffs, come savages of stone and the sea, snatched from their strongholds for crimes too gruesome to speak of. I give you ... marauders from the Silvercliffs!"

Several gates raise on the northern and southern walls. Out pours a leather-skinned mob covered in whirling tattoos of crimson and slate. All wear long black hair that's knotted into thick, dusty plaits. Two dozen are on the floor and they're still coming. None wear more than animal skins, black with white spots, perhaps harvested from seals or young orcanes. Hard to be sure at this distance, but there appear to be as many women as men, if the chest-covering skins are any indicator. Their bronze scimitars flash in the sun as they fan out across Keswal. Some scurry along Keswal's border, at the base of the walls, searching for weakness in the stone or a handhold on the cliff.

"Fucking pirates," Kraus says. He leans over and gives Torvald an elbow nudge that nearly unseats him. "Don't drink their damn ale. I'll tell you that."

Some of the marauders notice the crystal hanging from the Deceiver's rock-hewn fingers and take special interest. They begin to scramble at the Deceiver's leg. One gets as high as the statue's knee, from where he grips the stone tree trunk of an arm and reaches out for the gem. A handful of arrows sprinkle down from the north wall. Half of them clink off the stones. The rest thump into his back and leg and neck. Enough pierce him to keep him from uttering even a single cry as he topples down and flops onto the sand. The rest of the pirates lose interest in the crystal.

"You'd be wise to stay clear of the Deceiver," the Bloody Portent opines.

"That's debatable," Irdessa says, "depending on what's in store for them."

"There are so many of them," Prancer remarks.

"Fifty," Torvald says. "Well, forty-nine."

"What could they possibly let loose on fifty pirates that'll stand a chance?" Prancer says.

"Maybe your stupidity." Kraus snorts. "You're wetter than the ocean's slit."

"I'm not a wet anymore," Prancer says, as if anything short of violence will prove that to Kraus.

"You're gonna die a damn wet," Kraus says.

Prancer purses his lips and shakes his head.

Irdessa cuts her eyes at Kraus. There's more dirt in his beard and in the wrinkles in his sweaty neck than on Keswal's floor. What a human stump. A good punch to his throat would relieve everyone of his commentary, at least for a moment. Torvald gives her a flat expression, his hair hanging around his shoulders like a black curtain. His look says, *Be patient.*

Irdessa's eyes widen in surprise. Appears this rapist is under Torvald's protection for some reason. She spits. Soon as that protection's up, she's going to kick some respect into Kraus. Then let Prancer do it.

"Four dozen pirates," the Bloody Portent bellows. "By now you're surely asking yourself, why so many? What can stand against so formidable a force?"

Irdessa is way ahead of him. The ferocity of the marauders will be severely compromised on land. No lines to swing on, masts to launch from, water to paddle through gripping their scimitars between their teeth like hounds with sticks. It's doubtful they were given access to their black powder either. For the sake of everyone present and the arena itself.

Give me a dozen archers to pick them off at a distance. Her eyes flick down to Jasmin. She hadn't meant to learn the archer's name. *We'd benefit from something loud and scary to break their morale when they get up close.* Irdessa frowns. Some Krauses would be perfect.

She reckons she could turn back that force with twenty well placed warriors. Even still, fifty experienced scimitars can paint some sand. These pirates won't fight men though, not today. It's time for a beast fight, and she doubts Admiral Garr or Marshal Zander are giving up more orcanes soon.

"Fifty dreadhops," Irdessa says to Torvald. "That would be an interesting fight." Except, if that were today's card, they wouldn't have stuffed the dreadhops already. Maybe coal shucks? Maybe something from Tiasa or Halandor? The beastmaster had an excursion recently. "Oh, what about grindbears?" She's always wanted to see a grindbear.

Torvald doesn't respond. He wears a troubled look. He's so tense lately. Everything's serious. Nothing's fun anymore—not that there was ever much fun to be had here. Irdessa huffs.

"Your wily beastmaster has outdone himself," the Portent bellows. "He has caught the uncatchable."

A kettle drum thuds into life, initiating a rumbling roll. The din of the crowds subsides in anticipation.

"No words I can offer do justice to what you are about to witness."

"And yet, on you bleat," Kraus says, shifting his massive ass on the stone. Irdessa never foresaw herself feeling sympathy for a bench.

"Never before captured—never tamed—not until now."

"The Portent's full of it today," Irdessa says, more to elicit a response from Torvald than anything else, to get a hint of what he's thinking. Chances are he has guessed their opponents and the outcome of the match. But Torvald doesn't seem to hear her. He's sitting forward with elbows on knees, watching the northern audience closely, particularly Vretos and his court. He did mention a unique fight card coming up. This must be it.

Massive, ornate stone columns are planted throughout the northern seats, and from them hang silk canopies of light blues and greens. Trickling water glistens like crystals through narrow aqueducts and thralls pump the air slowly with wide fronds. Flowering plants shift in their wake, surely relieving the nearby noses of Keswal's ever-present aroma of old blood.

His Might Vretos sits straight on his majestic stone chair, alone, halfway up the northern seating. There's no shade covering him. The orcane skin draped across him makes his shoulders appear as broad as most men are tall.

In the booths below Vretos are his court—the beastmaster, the marshal, the admiral. Marshal Zander, commander of the Domestic Patrol, is preoccupied by something a captain is whispering in his ear. From their gestures, they're debating the attentiveness of the archers lining the northern seating. That's rarely a concern unless the combatants are winged. There's a tightness in the marshal's mannerisms lately. Anxiety, if Irdessa didn't know better. According to Torvald, however prim Zander appears in his black greatcoat with its angular shoulders and crisp collar, he's in trouble. He currently occupies the lowest chair at Vretos' table, which apparently rivals a public toilet in its ability to catch shit.

Admiral Garr, commander of the navy, wears a sour grimace under his massive golden mustache, like he might have better things to do. But his eyes move quickly, from Vretos, to Beastmaster Grimmet, to the battleground. His wine goblet never travels far from his frown. He's nervous. Why? He's in the second chair. He and Vretos are tight as tick asses. What's he got to worry about?

The Bloody Portent draws a breath visibly and belts on, "From the jungle mountains of North Halandor. An ancient beast, born for a time of war, a time of chaos ..." He has captured the attention of the entire arena.

"You'd think he's snatched Lahuvot's mount right out from under him," Kraus scoffs.

"You get used to it," Torvald says. His expression is unreadable. He hasn't relented in vigilance.

"Part man," the Bloody Portent booms. "Part beast. Two legged children of Vostuar from the Gygus tribe. Weapons of a forgotten era."

"Impossible," Torvald whispers. A trick of the sunlight makes it seem his face has gone paler.

"Tonight, for your enjoyment ..." At maximum volume, the Bloody Portent's voice is a chisel rattling in Irdessa's ears. It is Torvald's reaction, though, that has chills rising up over her arms and neck to squeeze her throat. "Prepare to witness ... Uergatas!"

"Goatmen?" Kraus says. "How the hell'd he catch those?"

Torvald's head is shaking slowly in disbelief. Irdessa racks her mind to remember what a uergata even is. A child of Vostuar the Impenetrable. A defender of the world. They have three tribes and they're all in Halandor. As if any of that translates to instructions on how to kill one. Irdessa hates being the least informed. It brings to memory her time before Keswal, when Torvald and her father worked together assembling strategies for Vim's Vanguard and rarely involved her.

"Are you ready?" The Portent's voice rivals the volume of a Faithless Sea thunderstorm.

The crowd's response isn't noticeably livelier than it is for any other fight. Perhaps they, too, find themselves uninformed about uergatas. The consequence of capturing too rare a beast is that no one knows to give a shit. But a weight has settled in Irdessa's gut that keeps growing heavier, to the point that she's uncomfortable sitting still. Torvald stares at the gates as if one's going to grow teeth and dash over the arena.

A trumpet's peal startles Irdessa. The bubbling thunder of kettle drums has grown to resound off the cliff face. Finally, the band concludes their accompaniment with three orchestrated blasts.

The tallest gate on the Deceiver's wall ascends, spilling fine sand as it rises. Within the exposed shadow stands ... nothing. The pirates had been oblivious to the Portent and the crowd and most everything else. Now an apprehension falls over them and those closest to the massive gate scurry away from it like startled puppies from a clanging metal pan.

The hush that has encompassed the arena is like none Irdessa has ever known here. Her fellow convicts, the general rabble, the northern spectators, all lean forward watching the gaping hallway.

Nothing happens.

Irdessa looks to Vretos' court. Beastmaster Grimmet pushes a woman off him, holding her at arm's length and shifting his eyes between the gate and His Might Vretos, whose expression is unreadable. Grimmet's son Pappu is intent on the fateful opening. Anguish is written over his smooth face. The Portent is chatting with a slim fellow by his side, idly tapping his cane on the wooden wall of his booth.

The northern crowd begins to murmur. That's never good. If they grow bored, Vretos will see to it that blood spills. And not always that of a combatant. Vretos leans over the edge of his booth to speak to Marshal Zander, who seems all too eager to be called on. The marshal confers with his captain, who gives a flick of his hand. Several archers nock arrows and aim at the black hallway.

"Seems our visitors are shy." The Bloody Portent's tone is unconcerned. "Perhaps our beastmaster exaggerated?"

Beastmaster Grimmet's cheeks burn darker than his red hair.

There comes a yelled insult from someone in the northern seating. Some chuckles from Udiari's company. The marshal nods at his captain, who points a finger at the tunnel. A single arrow is loosed. It disappears into the hallway without a sound. Several of the pirates have grown bold enough to advance within fifteen yards of the opening, holding their scimitars before them like torches.

"Perhaps we'll watch pirates become pincushions?" the Bloody Portent says, and stifles a yawn. Some of the responding laughter is markedly nervous. He turns lazily toward Vretos, awaiting instruction.

There's a shriek from within the nobility seating. Prancer gasps. Irdessa looks in time to see a two-legged, man-shaped monster stoop from the corridor and rise to its full height. It's huge. If the gate is ten feet tall at its capstone, the beast is all of nine, and that's not counting its massive, ribbed horns. The horns curl back and out before bending upward and terminating high above its head. Udiari's company has fallen deathly silent, as have the commoners on the other side of the partition, or at least those who aren't blind drunk. Even the can't-be-bothered rich in the north seating have forgotten their fans and thralls and gape at the monster. Beastmaster Grimmet scarfs on his roast leg with a boyish giddiness.

"By the gods," Prancer breathes. "They're real."

The thing takes several strides, turning its massive, horned head left and right, eyeing Keswal's audience with deliberation. It is covered in brown fur with black streaks along the outsides of its arms and legs, its eyebrows, and its short, flicking tail. In its hand, or paw, or hoof, is what appears to be a sapling, stripped of limbs and bark, whittled to a point on the top like a ten-foot skewer. Below the beast's waist all semblance of humanity ends. Its brawny legs bend like a goat's, terminating in massive cloven hooves.

It's not any observable ferocity, though, that makes Irdessa's blood cold and her breath shallow. It's the creature's face. Its snout is long, not unlike a goat's, extending from broad brows to end in flared black nostrils and a taut mouth. But its gaze is sharp, its pupils are too discerning to be a beast's. Its jawbones are prominent and a long black beard hangs from its chin, to stand out against the ashy, brown mane around its neck.

"Well, that's ... unnatural looking," Kraus says. It is the most reverent tone Irdessa's ever heard from him, and possibly the first time she's ever agreed with him. Torvald is frowning, as if he's witnessing a brewing storm. Prancer's gaping mouth could catch a pelican.

The uergata looks far cleverer than anything that furry should. If it opens its mouth and speaks, at this point Irdessa won't be surprised. She's uncomfortable staring at it, and yet she can't rip her eyes away. It's too big to appear so human.

"How did Grimmet catch that?" she whispers to Torvald behind her hand, in case the thing might overhear her or read her lips.

Torvald shakes his head. His frown has deepened. What is the beast telling him by simply standing there? What has he already deduced?

"I don't think it belongs near humans," Prancer hisses. "Or humans near it."

"They don't," Kraus says. "That's why giant hunters in Halandor drove them back north of the mountains."

Irdessa tries to picture that creature being driven anywhere. She's never bought into the hype of the so-called giant hunters, but if they're able to push around towering goat fiends maybe she'll reconsider.

The pirates jabber at one another, crouched in low stances with scimitars gripped at the ready, like a pile of bone ants watching a lurking mantis. Two of them are closing on the goatman, hunched so low they look like crabs as they near the beast's ankles. One of the pirates scurries ahead of the other, holding the scimitar in his teeth and moving on all fours. Irdessa's heart pounds against her ribs. She's covered her mouth with both hands. The monster turns its head to watch the pirate draw close. If there is any malice or even tension, it doesn't show. One of its ears flops twice, making it resemble a common goat seeking respite from a fly. The pointed staff in its hand stands so idly, Irdessa wonders if the pirate might not simply snatch it away.

The pirate is within five feet, and he's stretched his scimitar out toward the goat's cloven hoof, which looks all the larger in comparison.

"It uses that staff for support," Torvald says, but not specifically to anyone. His tone and posture and glassy eyes tell Irdessa he's actively analyzing. "Its hooves aren't enough to balance on the sandy arena floor without assistance."

"Look at the size of its legs," Kraus says. "I bet it's got a hell of a kick."

Indeed, considering how lithe are the beast's torso and arms, its legs appear overstuffed.

"It looks sad," Prancer says.

Kraus gives a snorting chuckle. But Irdessa sees it too. If the set of its furry eyebrows and the droop of its shoulders translate to mankind, the uergata is downright forlorn.

The pirate at the beast's ankle is trembling, his blade fully extended. At last, the tip of his sword grazes the thing's hoof. The uergata snorts and slides its hoof away from the man. Two more pirates join the curious one, perhaps emboldened by the lack of consequences. Soon, half a dozen pirates are advancing. The beast stamps. Irdessa feels it in her stone seat. The marauders scramble backward over one another. But now they're reassured. That stomp didn't hurt. Ten are pressing forward in an unorganized line, forming a wavering wall of scimitars. The uergata watches them.

"They about to finally fight?" Kraus says.

From the tunnel marches another uergata, then another, then two more side by side. Each of the beasts carries its own pointed staff. The pirates back up but do not break their untidy formation. It seems they're set on blood. The uergatas stand side by side, staring down at the pirates. Pound for pound, this face-off has become less one-sided. At last, the massive gate falls shut, and Irdessa's never heard so lonely an echo.

"Five of them," Prancer says, eyes round.

"What would we do without you, wet?" Kraus says.

The uergata are all of similar coats, but not alike. The most notable variance is in the thickness of their horns and how far out they extend. The longer Irdessa stares, the more obvious their differences become. One is brawnier than the rest, and its black coat is pocked and stripped bare here and there, as if scarred. One is greyer than the others and grips its staff with both hands, if those are hands. The fur around its face and ears is glazed with white and its beard hangs far down its chest. One is nearly charcoal colored, with sand-colored lines running the length of its limbs like lightning. They all tower over the pirates, the tallest uergata being nearly one and a half a man's height.

And yet the pirates are no longer afraid. Their numbers present too sure an advantage. They've scratched a hoof and felt no punishment. Now they're pushing each other toward the uergatas, moving to encircle them. Scimitars had an advantage over staffs as it was, in lethality if not in range. Now that the beasts are outflanked, that advantage is complete. The best the tall uergatas can hope for with those sticks is to knock pirates away and keep their backs against the wall. But even then, sticks can't defend against steel for long. Not that much steel.

"Theirs is an ancient race," Torvald whispers so only Irdessa can hear. "Older than the gods the Ausgan monks worship. Their homeland is far away. I don't know how the beastmaster managed to capture them, but I'm sure they yearn to return home. They will grow weaker away from it."

The pirates are within five yards of the uergatas. A pirate could leap forward right now and draw blood. The goatmen don't seem to stand a chance. But they lower on their haunches, holding their staffs beside them, still making no sound. Preparing to defend themselves? Do they even understand what's about to happen? Irdessa realizes she's gripping Torvald's shirt. He's too fixated on the goatmen to notice.

"Those goats better make a move sooner than later," she hisses.

As if because of her words, one pirate lunges at the uergata on the edge of the line, swinging his sword at a downward angle. Before the stroke can fall, the five goatmen spring straight into the air all at once. Above the pirates' heads they soar in a mounting wave. The apex of their jump brings them high above the level of the arena's wall. There, they seem to suspend, long enough for the entire arena to draw a breath, long enough to turn their staffs, grip them in both hairy hands, and plummet, spikes first.

They fall on the pirates, spearing them, crushing them under hoof, flattening them. By the time the pirates can even react with swinging swords the uergatas are in the air again. Two of the beasts have pirates stuck on their skewers. They swing their staffs midair, slinging the punctured bodies, then aim downward again and fall.

Keswal's audience erupts in riotous approval, stomping, jumping, yelling. The arena trembles so hard Irdessa wonders if the entire thing might break off the cliff face and fall into the Faithless.

Some of the marauders throw down their swords. The goatmen crunch down on them, piercing pirates like they're frogs. The marauders were never organized, but now they're in utter chaos. The uergatas jump and jump again. One of the goatmen slings a body clear over the northern wall to land among the rich. There is screaming and scrambling as a broken shade drifts down to envelop a colorfully dressed couple and their bloodied, uninvited guest. This causes a panic in the archers, who loose arrows at another uergata at the crest of its jump. The arrows miss. One particularly poorly placed shot flies clear across Keswal to clink off the lanista's stone seating inches from Kraus. He jumps with a hoot and bursts into laughter.

"I fucking love Keswal!" he roars.

Half the pirates are dead or dying. Irdessa watches the uergatas adjust their tactics now that their opponents aren't so tightly gathered. They pounce shallowly, targeting individuals, jabbing with their skewers over and over. One uergata's stick impales a woman and breaks in half. The goatman drops it and resorts to kicking and headbutting. Every direct hit levels a pirate, likely killing them on impact, occasionally bursting their head outright. One uergata lands in range of a scimitar. For a moment it appears the pirate's blade might score a hit, free some goat blood. But the uergata grips its stick by the end and swings in a broad arc. The pole hits the man at the waist, folding him nearly in half. His lank body soars over the western cliff.

"I thought you said they'd be weak," Irdessa says numbly.

"Imagine them in their homeland."

"I think I'll not." This is turning her stomach.

Several of the surviving pirates run or stagger to the cliff and, without hesitation, throw themselves over the edge. It's not the first time Irdessa's seen it happen when all hope is lost. Perhaps some will miss the jagged stones. None will survive the impact on the ocean's skin from several hundred feet.

"There's one way to keep from feeding the birds," says some wet.

"Right," Jasmin says. "Now they can feed the fish instead."

"Fish feed the birds too." Kraus' grin carries as much hilarity as a coffin.

Prancer hasn't spoken since the uergatas first jumped. His face is frozen in that horrified expression of his that makes Irdessa want to slap him.

Without ceremony, the last pirate standing is skewered, through his shoulder and out his belly, by the shortest uergata—the hefty black scarred one. It lifts the man, turning him upside down, inspecting him while he breathlessly wriggles on the stick and leaks his life down the beast's wrists. The other uergatas scan the twitching bodies. For a moment Irdessa expects them to finish off the dying. Instead, they cease all motion, just as before the fight. The moans of dying pirates underpin the receding clamor of the audience.

The uergatas gradually turn their golden eyes on the crowd. Irdessa has the bowel-clenching realization that if the goats choose to leap into the stands there's not a damn thing she or anyone can do to stop them. The crowd at large seems to have arrived at the same conclusion. The cheers fizzle out and all movement becomes tension. Irdessa fights the urge to hide behind Torvald. The uergata with the impaled man holds him aloft like a lizard on a spit.

"Gnats of Alesuariil ..." The uergata's deep, rumbling roar echoes off the walls with a vibrato like a goat's bleat. "Is blood what you crave?"

"They *talk?*" Prancer whispers.

A hush engulfs the crowd and a frown creeps over Irdessa's mouth. It was bad enough before they spoke. The beast has an accent she's never heard and never wants to hear again. Torvald's eyes flick to the broken arrow several rows down. *Right, Torvald. Stick them with that.* Then again, she has no plan.

No one has an answer for the uergata's question. Irdessa's not entirely sure what it even meant. Alesuariil is supposedly the god who populated the world with mankind. To her knowledge, no one in

Fohrvylda gives much thought to him. Some of the rich are throwing furtive glances toward Vretos. This is his arena after all. The beastmaster has forgotten the roast he'd been eating. His son suddenly looks interested. Excited even.

"You want to watch your brothers and sisters taken apart?" the uergata asks.

Still no response. Now even Vretos' court is looking up at him, as if he alone has some solution for this. The uergata takes notice in their attention, or perhaps Vretos' enormous throne.

"You." The goatman aims its stick at Vretos, whose expression suggests he's witnessing a dog pissing on his boots. "Is that your god?" The uergata points a stubby digit at the statue of the Deceiver. "Suppose I kick it down and grind it to sand? How will you like that?"

There is still no answer from the crowd. Vretos sits as still as the Deceiver itself.

"Looks like the goats took this whole thing personal," Kraus says. As usual, he makes no effort to dampen his voice, so it feels like it resounds across the entire arena. His head cranes to the side. "Well, maybe not personal but ... *goat*-onal?"

The scarred uergata winds the stick back like a lumberman's axe and heaves it at the Deceiver. The skewered man soars soundlessly, flaps against the statue with a meaty smack, falls boneless to the arena floor. The northern seats gasp. Pirate blood paints the Deceiver's hair and face, accenting the anguish the sculptor chiseled therein.

"Goat!" Vretos yells. By the time Irdessa's eyes find him, he has leapt over the front of his booth. There's a collective inhale from the rich and the military and the convicts and the commoners alike as His Might plummets sixty feet to the arena floor. Vretos' feet smash divots in the packed earth and he bounces, falling into stride as if he's merely stepped off a curb. He's closing briskly on the talkative uergata. The other goatmen stir to life, stepping toward their shorter comrade, who squares hooves at Vretos. All along the northern wall, bows creak as strings stretch, no less than one hundred arrows drawn and aimed at the uergatas.

"Damn." Kraus chuckles. "He's lost his mind."

Irdessa begrudgingly agrees with Kraus once more.

"I am no child of Alesuariil." Vretos' voice is impossibly loud as he marches. He raises a hand up behind him, palm out. To stall the archers?

The stocky uergata glances back toward the others. Some grunting communication happens. Permission? The goatman issues a blasting bark and trots toward Vretos, lowering its horns. Vretos is an enormous man, but that beast makes him look like a child. The uergata runs, hooves stamping the ground like boulders falling. It's going to flatten Vretos. Despite all the times Irdessa has fantasized about His Might's demise, she finds herself terrified. Why would these creatures stop at him?

Vretos raises both hands at the last moment and catches the uergata's horns right where they sprout with a loud *slap!* The beast's momentum is nearly halted. Vretos' maintains his stance and his heels dig furrows as he's forced back toward the wall. He shifts his weight, twists the goatman's head on its thick neck, flips the beast onto its back.

"Mine is the crown to be taken!" Vretos roars down at the blinking uergata. He slices his hand through the air, backing away from the stunned creature. Arrows slip loose of their bows. The uergata scrambles to recover but is blanketed in pointed steel. One arrow thunks into Vretos' left shoulder. The goatman coughs dryly and writhes, kicking up dust, quickly turning glossy black in the sun. Its comrades cease their approach. They stand still and watch.

Vretos faces the remaining goatmen as the first bleeds out. There's a noticeable lack of blood from the arrow embedded in his shoulder. Doesn't seem he's noticed it. He points at the eastern wall. "The Deceiver is no god."

The surviving uergatas are statues.

"*I* will grind him to sand," Vretos says. "In due time."

The goatmen don't look impressed. Irdessa's never heard Vretos mention the Deceiver. Apparently the statue is a depiction of the immortal being responsible for the war between Fohrvylda and Ausgan. Some atrocity he committed hundreds of years ago ruined the peace on the northern island of Redemier, cursing it and forcing Vretos and his hunters east to Fohrvylda, Intemrus and his monks west to Ausgan.

"Go back in your cages," Vretos says. "Or meet your own god." He turns and stalks toward the northern wall, even as the gongs begin to sound. "Don't let those dreadhops at me or I'll break their necks," he yells up at his own people.

"Fuck's sake," Kraus says. "He's a madman."

Irdessa seen enough of His Might's antics to have long-since established that fact. "You sound like a wet," she says.

Kraus laughs, nods approvingly at her insult. That's not the response she was going for.

It's time for the Bloody Portent to wrap this up but he appears to have run out of words. He looks from Vretos to Admiral Garr, who hides an amused smile, to Marshal Zander, who is yelling at a soldier and shaking him by the collar. Beastmaster Grimmet looks nervous. His son Pappu watches the sunset, forlorn once more.

"People of Fohrvylda, what a glorious day for Keswal," the Portent says into his loudphone, giving a nervous laugh. "I'd say the marauders paid their debt." He sweeps his hand in the air awkwardly, then steps from his booth and smooshes himself into the throng of people hastily filing from the arena.

The tall gate on the Deceiver's wall rises. The uergatas don't move. Their horns cast long shadows over the floor and up the Deceiver's legs as they watch Vretos leave with the neglected arrow sticking out of his shoulder. One of the smaller gates along the north wall rises and Vretos disappears through it.

The goatmen take in their surroundings a moment longer, particularly the sunset, the ocean, then solemnly make their way back to the gate on the Deceiver's wall, leaning heavily on their staffs. They're stoic once more, seeming to have forgotten the melee and their comrade, who lies motionless beneath a covering of arrows.

The dreadhop gates open. Feathered carnivores flood the arena. The brightly colored birds all give the goatmen a wide berth, flocking instead to the fallen marauders. Seems they're not even interested in the dead uergata. Then again, perhaps the multitude of arrows ruined that dish even for them.

Torvald is watching Vretos' court, studying them as they file out. Kraus stands up, stretching mightily. "Who'd have thought it? Pirate tastes better than goat," he says, and limps up the stairs toward the exit. "I figured they'd taste like piss."

Lanista Udiari's company rises in small groups and follows Kraus, talking in subdued voices. The fight has created a somber mood.

"Learn anything today?" Irdessa asks Torvald. Maybe now that there's no one nearby to overhear he'll let on what's eating him.

"I can only speculate ..." Torvald says, not looking at her. Doesn't seem like he's talking to her either.

"Think they'll try to fix him up?" Irdessa says, pointing at the fallen uergata. Keswal's surgeons have means of bringing back those on the brink of death with an elixir called *hush*. It's rare, made from sap of the Sun Tree they say, and Vretos reserves it for the prematurely dispatched—for the crowd favorites, or those who have not yet received their due punishment.

"No. That would undermine Vretos' lesson," Torvald mumbles. It seems he's sinking deeper into glumness. Irdessa wants no part of it. She doesn't need him in a good mood, only to work out the strategy and translate it into instructions. In the meanwhile, she'd be happy to forget what she's seen today. She stands to leave.

Torvald grabs her wrist. "Do you trust me?" he asks. He's planted his most piercing gaze on her.

"Why would you even have to ask?" She jerks her hand away. The intensity of the fear in his eyes makes her breath shorten.

"I won't let you die in Keswal," Torvald says through clenched teeth. His eyes chisel into hers, making her turn away.

"I know," she says. "How many times are you going to say that?"

Torvald turns his attention back to the dead goatman. He's not usually indecisive, unsure.

"Unmanned by blood, Tactician?" Irdessa sneers at him. It seemed like a good way to lighten the mood, but it came out crueler than she'd planned.

Torvald shakes his head slowly. Is he ... about to cry? Irdessa gawks. Whatever she needs right now, it is not this. She needs Jasmin to be sarcastic, or Prancer to be hopelessly naïve. She'd even welcome Kraus' disgusting jokes. Irdessa sometimes forgets Torvald is her age. He rarely displays anything resembling weakness.

"Torvald," Irdessa hisses, heat rising in her cheeks. "Snap out of it. Cry in Keswal, die in Keswal."

"You're right." Torvald fails to catch the tear before it runs down his cheek.

Irdessa gasps. She huffs in disgust and stomps away, nearly tripping on the stairs. They've gone all blurry. *Brilliant move, Tactician. Destroy all my trust in one sweep.* His dread has infected her. This is why you can't be weak. You can't be afraid. How did Torvald forget that? It's as if he thinks those uergatas represent some personal threat. As if Keswal would feed its top-earning prize fighters to foreign monsters. Never. She wipes her eyes. *Can't let the others see.*

At the doorway, Irdessa unwillingly glances back. There he slouches, still watching the dead goatman. Dreadhops gorge themselves comfortably on punctured pirates. Seems Torvald will sit there until the guards come through and make him leave. He looks like just some boy. Alone. *Pitiful wreck.* Irdessa's lips curl down at the edges. Her answer has changed.

I did trust you. Not anymore.

3

The Pinnacle of Savages

FOHRVYLDA

Vretos' Lodge, Promontory

Beastmaster Grimmet makes no effort to suppress his smirk as he saunters into the dining hall of the highest lodge in all Promontory. Today, thanks to the shining success of his uergatas, he'll be taking third seat at Vretos' table.

The oak-built chamber is spacious, with stone hearths roaring on three walls and rough-hewn rafters as thick as Grimmet's waist crisscrossing up to the smoke vents. The western wall is open, allowing for a view of the Faithless Sea and the clamor of sprakes cavorting out on the cliff and the ocean below. The floor and benches and chairs are blanketed in layers of animal skins. Skulls and skeletons of all sorts, immortalized in threatening poses, hang by chains from the rafters and decorate the northern wall.

In the center of the room is the table, a six-sided conglomeration of halved trees, smooth on top and rounded below. The center of the table is open, and one of the six sides can slide aside, allowing thralls to enter and move dishes around the table. The other five sides are for Vretos and his court. This is Grimmet's first time earning the third seat. It is an enviable position. It puts only Admiral Garr between Grimmet and Vretos himself.

Lanista Udiari is already in the fourth seat, early as always, leaning on the armrest and holding a stein in his thin hands like a spider holding a gnat. His narrow face is doing a fine job of hiding the contempt that Grimmet knows is there. Until today, the third seat was his.

"Lanista," Grimmet says, "how's the new chair?"

"Feels ... temporary," Udiari says, eyeing his mead.

"I thought the same thing," Grimmet says, and pulls out the oaken chair to Udiari's left. He plants his ass upon it. His initial impression is that it feels exactly like the fourth chair. A hefty stein awaits him, filled to the brim with the crimson froth of Draconis cherry mead. "And maybe you're right. The marshal would be glad to give up fifth chair."

Lanista Udiari gives a smile that resembles a wolf baring its teeth. His worth to the court is perhaps more fragile than anyone else's. His prisoners, namely Torvald and Irdessa, can only hold the crowd's heart for so long. It is a true mystery how the young Tactician has avoided death for two years in Keswal. He's just into his twenties but possessing the insight of a seasoned veteran. The best fighters last no more than a handful of fights. And no one lasts forever. No one is above mistake. Once Torvald falls, and Udiari's usefulness diminishes, there is no telling who might take his place. Until then, no other lanista in Promontory comes close to providing the entertainment and coin Udiari does.

Grimmet is sprawling himself out over the third chair, trying to convince himself it's more comfortable than fourth, when Marshal Zander walks briskly into the room, pressing the door closed quietly behind him. His face is a picture of annoyance, as if it pains him to break his work to attend this tiresome event. Maybe Grimmet would look as unhappy if he were stuck in the least envied chair in the room. If Zander's Domestic Patrol spent more time enforcing laws and less time inventing charges, perhaps he'd maintain a better position here. Though probably not.

The marshal thumbs loose the buttons of his black coat with a twitchy hand, takes his seat, and rubs his eyes for several moments. His job took a downward turn two years ago when he arrested Andelsior of Vim. Unrest blossomed across Fohrvylda and has shown no sign of taming itself since.

"Have some mead, Marshal," Grimmet says. "You look tired."

"Don't be so smug, Beastmaster," Zander snaps. "What's the lifespan of your goats, anyway?"

Grimmet chuckles. Not so long ago, he was ensnared in political pettiness with the marshal. No longer. Third chair need not worry over fifth, only second and fourth. Grimmet's new position places him between Udiari and the admiral. It is Udiari he must thwart to keep him from regaining third. How he'll deal with Admiral Garr is trickier. Garr has been entrenched in second for years, helped surely by the marshal's gradual decline. He is Vretos' preferred because the navy is his. And, as Vretos will remind anyone, anytime, for no reason, *"The Heathen Tide is our highest priority."* Perhaps it's true and yes, Vretos needs Admiral Garr's navy to span the Faithless Sea and assault Ausgan, but he won't win that war without Grimmet's beasts employed as mounts, spies, and weapons.

The door bangs open and Vretos strides in alongside Admiral Garr. From their raucous laughter, one of them has told the joke to end all jokes. Thralls in kitchen whites scurry behind them, carrying an entire boar on a serving plate the size of a wagon wheel.

His Might marches for the table, wearing the skin of an adult orcane across his shoulders and its skull as a hood. Beastmaster Grimmet has confronted beasts of all sizes. He's captured them all, trained some, and disposed of those that won't take training. None have ever intimidated him the way Vretos does. He's a hulking bronze behemoth of a man, with forearms the size of Grimmet's thighs, and shoulders so broad he has to walk through most doors sideways. His eyes are black beads and his nostrils are perpetually flared, making him look like he's always on the verge of violent acts.

Two thralls pull back Vretos' huge chair as he unclasps the orcane skin and slings it onto the antlers of a mounted skull. Of course he's wearing no shirt. Pale scars zigzag through the wiry black hair of his chest and shoulders and back. The roasted boar is placed on the table before him.

"Lanista," Vretos says, taking his seat. His voice is immense yet smooth, like a bottomless river. "I hoped Keswal spectators would see the unfurled intestines of a convicted rapist last week." He pries a hind leg from the boar with a juicy, cracking squelch and waves the dish away. The thralls heft the dish over to Garr, doing their best to stifle grunts. "You know how they love such things. Did you forget to pass that instruction along to your Tactician?"

Lanista Udiari is a master of remaining level-headed, despite how dire the situation is. This hardening is probably a skill he acquired years ago while learning to survive Keswal himself. But when he clears his throat and sits up straighter to respond, Grimmet smiles. Udiari's not used to fourth chair.

"Torvald was informed," Udiari says. "It seems the rapist was more resilient than even he planned for."

"Perhaps the rapist should have been hobbled," Admiral Garr says idly, while folding his coat and placing it over the back of his chair. He sets his naval hat on the table at his side, pats down the remnants of his greying hair. He's a stout man with heavy sun-spotted arms and stumpy legs perfect for perching on a heaving deck. He rolls up his sleeves and takes a seat. It requires both his hands and a thrall with a serrated knife to dislodge the boar's other hind leg, and when the deed is done Garr has to catch his breath and smooth his mustaches. The thralls slide the dish in front of Grimmet.

"The marshal had me believe he *was* hobbled," Udiari says silkily. When referring to the fifth chair, Udiari's disdain has no need to hide. "That's why I got him at a discount."

The roast boar is aimed at Grimmet, filling his nostrils with savory pork, pepper, and the sweet compote dissolving around it. He cranes his head and eyeballs it, trying to determine how best to acquire a meal short of hefting a battle axe and forfeiting dignity.

"My captain assured me the thirsty rapist had a broken kneecap." Marshal Zander's cheeks are burning, and veins stand out on his neck. It's too early in the meal to be that emotionally unstable. What an easy mark. "I saw his bandages and his limp. The mongrel apparently did it to himself. Maybe he fashioned a splint within your lax custody."

Udiari snorts. "A splint? For a broken kneecap?"

"I don't care," Vretos says, chasing down a mouthful of hog with a voluminous pull from his stein. "Next time he fights, he dies. Understood?"

"Absolutely," Udiari says with an oily smile, no doubt happy to have redirected some amount of blame onto Zander. "We'll sever a leg if need be."

Grimmet sees no obvious angle of attack on the boar. What an impractical dish for a dining table. Every meeting it's something new, only serving to remind everyone that Vretos is the pinnacle of savages. A month prior they were served wings of wild dreadhops, which were barely wings at all. You'll find more sugar in a honeysuckle than meat on a dreadhop's wings. Before that it was leapshark flank, which might as well have been steaks of blubber. Grimmet gestures at the nearest thrall and points at the boar. The thrall jumps to attention and produces a serrated knife to saw at the boar's rump. Grimmet is pleased to note the thralls are quicker to attend to third chair than fourth.

"You've elevated your position, Beastmaster," Vretos says. He shifts focus from his meal to Grimmet. "I hope you appreciate it."

"Thank you." Grimmet flushes with pride. "I aim only for my efforts to avail you."

"Your efforts avail more than me," Vretos says. "The pirates had become a nuisance. Spread all over the harbor like chokewort. Apparently if you butcher fifty of them, the rest quieten down." He chuckles, plucking remnants of meat from the bone with bared teeth.

"It was an amusing card," Udiari comments, as a thrall cuts him a plank of boar. "Until then I was convinced your excursion to North Halandor was an incredibly expensive holiday."

Grimmet clenches his teeth. Heat rises to his cheeks. *Amusing card?* That's one piss-poor assessment of the most spectacular slaughter Keswal's ever seen. But Grimmet remembers himself before rising to the bait. He inhales slowly. He takes a sip from his stein and assumes a nonchalant expression. Truth is, Udiari is beneath Grimmet now. Grimmet owes him no explanation or even acknowledgment. This elevated position earns Grimmet a higher stipend. Of course the lanista would attack that.

"Not your business how I use my coin, old man. And not mine how you waste yours. If I were you I'd have bought a complete set of teeth by now." He lifts his stein to Vretos. "How is the mead, Your Might? It came highly recommended from the nobles in Draconis."

"I've had worse," Vretos says. "Too sweet, isn't it? Like the easy lives of that bloated mishmash of a city. Next dish," he tells the door.

Grimmet fights to keep his smile from withering. It's a gamble to ask Vretos anything.

"Speaking of, I've begun to wonder if I'm not too easy on you all. Spies tell me that my enemy, the sovereign of the monks, is plotting yet again. I'd love to launch the Heathen Tide at last and crush him before he gets too deep in his song. We've got about as many ships as we can man. Isn't that right, Admiral?"

Garr straightens, his thick golden mustache animating like a conscious mop. "Indeed it is, Your Might. Excursions to purchase lumber from Tiasa proved quite useful since domestic resources have diminished."

Beastmaster Grimmet eyes Garr. Those are all facts. An unmentioned fact is that Tiasa lumber mills are collectively inflating prices on exported lumber to the point that Garr's excursions will soon require more than simple coin to remain productive. He'll need to tap into Zander's resources, namely men willing to swing steel. Grimmet's heart races. This might be as solid an opportunity as he gets to deprecate second chair while boosting fifth. But the talk of spies and monks stalls his tongue. It's not below this court to baselessly accuse Grimmet's son Pappu of being one or both of those things, all because of his appearance. Ridiculous charges, especially considering Pappu's contributions to Fohrvylda as sprake trainer. More ridiculous since Pappu's never set foot on Ausgan and has no reason to undermine Fohrvylda. But the accusations send Grimmet into an uncontrollable rage and the whole court knows it. Throwing a tantrum will not improve his status, but the chance to take Garr down a notch can't be ignored. Grimmet clears his throat, but before he can get to besmirching, two thralls burst through the door carrying an upturned terrapin shell the size of a washbasin. A third thrall follows with wooden bowls and pewter utensils. Vretos is served a ladle of steaming liquid and the thralls back away.

"You all remember that veal pie from several meetings ago?" Vretos asks no one in particular, eyeing his soup suspiciously.

Grimmet scowls. His moment has passed.

"You mean the one textured like baked maggots?" Admiral Garr leans back from his cleaned boar bone and dabs at his golden mustache with a cloth napkin. "How could I forget?"

"That fateful dish resulted in some changes in the kitchen staff." Vretos shakes his head. "Seems our new chef thinks turtle soup should follow hog meat." His grimace suggests he finds this idea akin to having someone vomit into his mouth.

"Chef Bel can explain, Your Might," a thrall says, bowing low with his hands squeezed into one another at his waist. "This dish is a—"

"A chef who's worthy of his title need not explain a damn thing," Vretos says. "Give me a spoon."

Vretos tests the soup, smacking his lips and working his teeth. The thralls are holding their breath. Even the wind coming in through the west hesitates. The chamber has become a veritable court hearing.

"It'll do," Vretos says at last.

The thralls nearly collapse with relief. One laughs nervously, wiping a tear from her eye.

"I'll tell Chef Bel," says the only thrall bold enough to speak.

"Keswal numbers are bolstered," Vretos says, between mouthfuls of soup, which must be better than he let on. "They haven't been this high in some time. The spectacle that is the uergatas brings new interest, domestic and foreign. Seems the uergatas have enemies all over the world. And thanks to the eastern seaport being liberated of its marauder infestation, Fohrvylda's tourists can return. I'm proud of my admiral and beastmaster."

Grimmet beams shamelessly. Garr takes the compliment in stride, lifting his goblet and tipping his head as if to say, *"It's nothing."* The thralls do their best to remain invisible as they heft the large soup shell over to the admiral.

"I'm curious," Admiral Garr says, twisting the tip of a mustache as his bowl is filled. He looks down his cheek at Grimmet. "Those goatmen of yours are quite lively when worked up. How did you manage to subdue them? That must have been no small feat."

Grimmet hides his smile behind his stein. That's a question he'd been hoping for. "Indeed, it was not. When we arrived at the Bay of Idir, between North and South Halandor, we witnessed the uergatas in their native element, hopping all over the forested mountain sides like so many fleas. I knew at a glance we'd need special accommodations for such beasts. We disembarked under the guise of parlay, asking to simply rest on their land and refill our provisions for a return trip to the south. They obliged us, once convinced we had no affiliation with their real enemies—the giant hunters—which was quite a rigorous vetting. Then we devised our strategy."

Grimmet's bowl is filled with soup. He pauses in his story to slurp from his spoon. It is indeed delicious, despite being little more than broth containing bits of leaf. It's bittersweet, like dark wine, but with a lingering heartiness of beef stock.

"Our apothecaries produced a numbing poison, made from mandragora root harvested from beneath Keswal," he says. "They'd grown listless anyway. Until that point, they'd only squeezed lemon into water to treat scurvy, and seen to those of our crew who couldn't keep down food."

Zander gives an exaggerated *hmph*. "We could have used those apothecaries here, seeing to our men," he says. "What with the riots and—"

"Marshal," Grimmet snaps. He wouldn't have tolerated interruption from the fifth seat even before his promotion. Definitely not in the midst of this story. Apparently Zander has not yet modified his strategy, or simply doesn't understand Vretos' table. It's pointless to attack two chairs up. Udiari should be Zander's target, not Grimmet. "The apothecaries gathered many herbs and resources on our trip. Perhaps even enough to help protect your men since you're clearly incompetent. I already provide you with obedient orcanes and sprakes. Do I need to train your soldiers as well?"

Marshal Zander's eyes bulge. "You take too much credit for your trained monsters. It is your son Pappu that has the touch. All you have is a whip."

Lanista Udiari snorts laughter.

Grimmet's vision reddens and tunnels on the marshal. He stands, flipping his chair onto the blanketed floor with a muffled clatter. "Mention my son again, Zander, and I'll show you what I can do with a whip."

Zander's jaw muscles clench. Whatever he wants to say, he's smart enough not to. His roast boar sits neglected on his plate. The soup ran out before it got to him. That's what you get for being fifth chair. Udiari is wearing an amused smile. The admiral is chuckling. Grimmet knows haranguing Zander made them both look idiotic, and benefited Udiari. *Instigating buzzard.*

Grimmet eyes a thrall, who scurries over and rights his chair. Once Grimmet has sat and smoothed his napkin, he has a long drink of mead to cool his cheeks before continuing. "As I was saying, the apothecaries made a poison and put it in the wine. Uergatas had no interest in our food, as you might imagine. While we were getting ready to ship out, I asked the uergatas to join us in a toast, to their hospitality, and to new kinships."

The admiral is acting confused by the beastmaster's words, as if Grimmet isn't capable of coherent speech. It's truly a repulsive habit, and he employs it on everyone but Vretos. His Might has turned up his bowl to slurp down the last of his soup.

"And so we served five uergatas the adulterated wine," Grimmet continues. "They became so groggy we were able to bind their arms and legs and restrain them below deck before they recovered. We had to modify the hatch to accommodate their horns. It was that or saw them off, which, of course, was out of the question. They recovered during the ride and were less than happy to learn of their plight. They never spoke. Not to us, anyway, but if I'm to believe what they told us before their capture," and he lowers his voice to emphasize the detail, "one of them is the son of the chieftain of the entire Gygus tribe."

Udiari's spoon clatters into his empty bowl. "You sedated and kidnapped the heir of a uergata chieftain," he says. "How noble. I hope we didn't have plans to return to that part of Silexare, ever."

"I wasn't there to be noble," Grimmet says. "I went to catch monsters that can turn the enemies of Fohrvylda into bird shit." He takes a breath. "Besides, our flags and sails were emblazoned with the emblem of Draconis. Another reason we made that stop on the way." He winks at Udiari and taps his temple with a fingertip. "If the goats want to wage a war, let the Halandor giant hunters handle it. Again." He gives a laugh, notices he's the only person entertained, and reins in the mirth with another drink of mead.

"Casualties?" Garr asks, as if it's his place to demand report.

Grimmet doesn't mind sharing. "Only one. A fool who partook in the tainted wine. It proved too strong a dose for a man. He fell into a nap that has yet to end."

"Impressive," Garr says, although his concerned expression suggests he is something besides impressed. Probably jealous he can take no credit.

Grimmet leans back in his chair and interlaces his fingers behind his head. "I know."

"Next," Vretos says.

Thralls enter the room once more. This time, their platter holds what appears to be steaming, roasted legs of lamb, piled over a bed of greens and skinned potatoes.

"Finally," Vretos says, as a thrall tops off his stein with a ladle from a wooden cask.

Grimmet tactfully undoes the wide belt at his waist. These meetings last hours and serve to demonstrate important points to Vretos' court. Take what you can. Earn what you get.

Admiral Garr leans forward, fixing Marshal Zander in a bushy-browed stare from across the table. "Regarding your wounded men," he says. "I'd have thought you'd be better off now that I've thinned the ranks of marauders. What exactly are you struggling with?"

Zander opens his mouth to respond but Udiari beats him to it.

"I hear private arenas spring up in the east like weeds in a garden." The lanista shakes his head. "The people have no discipline."

"Private arenas are illegal," Vretos says, his cheeks stuffed with potatoes and lamb. "What are you doing about those who break the law, Marshal?" He chews noisily while Zander stammers. "Clearly not enough. Maybe you've grown too comfortable in that chair. I can adjust the comfort."

"We fight tirelessly," Zander blurts. For what little it's worth, the exhaustion in his eyes testifies to his words. "The seating of the convicts in Keswal has never been so full."

"Tirelessly, eh?" Udiari says. "I hear your captains spend their time inventing charges. How tireless a job is it to breed corruption?"

The marshal looks like he's going to choke. It certainly doesn't help that his stein has run dry and no one's seen the need to fill it.

Vretos speaks again. "Seems everyone's doing your job except you, Marshal. Last time your excuse was pirates. The admiral's vigilance and the beastmaster's goatmen have dealt with that. So what is it now? What will it take to eliminate rogue arenas that are leaching revenue from the Tide?"

"*I'll set an example*," the marshal hisses through clenched teeth, gripping the side of the table with shaking hands. "One to end it all. I will burn an arena to the ground and all those who partook in it."

The lanista chuckles, rotating a bare lamb bone between his finger and thumb. "Wage war on the populace. That's your idea?"

"Not just anyone," Marshal spits at him. "This place has it coming. They've rebuked His Might's law for long enough."

"And gotten away with it?" Lanista Udiari shakes his head.

Grimmet smiles and sits back with his mead. Not so long ago, the lanista was administering this edged rebuke on Grimmet. It's nice to be out from under it. Zander's referring to the city of Vim most likely. It's been a brewing shitstorm ever since Garr tricked him into arresting Andelsior, Vim's leader. Until then Andelsior's mercenaries, known as Vim's Vanguard, collected outlaws and delivered them to the marshal, who sold them to Keswal lanistas. Andelsior's arrest sparked a revolt from the otherwise orderly city. Now Zander is forced to do his own job, Vim feeds Promontory soldiers to its own illegal arena, Andelsior is dead, and his daughter and right hand, Irdessa and Torvald respectively, profit the lanista.

"No longer." Marshal Zander is trembling with rage, or fear. The dish that held the lamb is placed before him. It has been emptied of everything but wilted greens and lamb bones.

Grimmet sucks the grease off his thumb. "I must give credit to your new chef," he says to Vretos. "The lamb was succulent."

Vretos ignores him. "I'm curious to read the report when it's done." He leans back and throws a bare leg over the arm of his massive chair. It seems a brief respite from food is in order. Grimmet is glad for it. He's overworking the buttons of his shirt as it is. Admiral Garr places a battered tin on the table and lifts the lid to begin his arduous ceremony of packing a pipe.

"As for you, Lanista," Vretos says. "You're quite critical of our marshal, considering your demotion. Rogue arenas aren't the only threat to Fohrvylda's revenue. Your prizewinners are losing their glamour by the fight. This time last year their names filled Keswal to capacity, and then some. That orcane card should have brought twice as much coin as it did. What will you do when the Tactician loses all appeal, and the Undying's name betrays her?"

Udiari dabs a cloth at his mouth with deliberation. A smile plays at the edge of his lips. It seems he was anticipating this question. "I have plans that will advance Keswal. Plans that will usher in a new era of combat." He sits back and folds his thin hands over his black coat, wearing an even expression.

Garr lights his pipe, gives it several puffs.

"Go on," Vretos says.

"You're right about Torvald and Irdessa," the lanista says. "Their popularity wanes. Therefore, I'm shifting Torvald to fight designer. In that position, he will use his tactical expertise to assemble fight cards such as Keswal has never seen."

"How's that?" the admiral asks, teeth clenched on his pipe. By his perplexed expression you'd think Udiari spoke gibberish.

"He will put his knowledge of skirmishes to use, arranging fights that are evenly matched for the first time in Keswal. Real competition, even if the combatants are utterly diverse."

Grimmet frowns. That's a halfway intelligent notion. He *tsks* and shakes his head as if it's the stupidest notion he's ever heard.

"Cards like what?" Vretos asks Udiari. "How do you propose to advance Keswal?"

Lanista Udiari leans forward, his bony elbows on the table. "First, Torvald will make a fight card for the beastmaster's uergatas. One that makes for an *actual fight*." He enunciates the last words slowly, as if twisting a dagger.

Grimmet and Garr arranged the card the lanista is criticizing. Grimmet brought the uergatas, and Garr brought specifically fifty pirates. It was a play on the uergata tradition of bringing no more than fifty heads and one hundred hands to a conflict. They both agreed it was quite clever, although the deeper meanings were lost on the entire audience and the Bloody Portent failed to mention the number's relevance. Udiari's insinuation is a stab at them both.

"Last I checked," Grimmet says before he can stop himself, "that uergata fight is the talk of the entire nation. The next two events are selling out. Maybe you should focus on invigorating your aging convicts rather than repairing something that's not broken."

Garr's furry red eyebrow is arched high. He works his pipe in his teeth but does not offer comment.

Vretos, however, does not seem to share Grimmet's anger. "You have my attention," he says.

"Thank you." The lanista clears his throat. The way his eyes dart between Garr and Vretos suggests he's less than confident about what he's going to propose. "Obviously, in his new position, Torvald will no longer personally be a fighter. He'll work alongside me, learn the ways of lanista, then eventually take my place at the time of my retirement." The volume of his voice is decreasing by the word. "And if he is pulled from the fights, I'd imagine he'll prefer that Irdessa joins him. In this way, their names need not end with their death and be forgotten, but continue profiting Keswal for some time."

Grimmet gawks at the lanista. Of all the nerve. Udiari was asked for good news, and his response was an elaborate announcement of how he'll pull his two prize fighters, effectively taking a steaming shit on Keswal's income.

"And what if I'm not done watching Torvald fight?" Vretos says. His tone is level. But the question carries as much threat as a sword unsheathed.

"Obviously, this will revolve entirely around your timing," Udiari says quickly. "I hope you can agree that no one is more suited to carry my legacy than the Tactician himself."

"Ha," Garr blurts. "Legacy. That's a lofty assertion considering your current position."

Udiari looks him straight in the eye. "Yes, my legacy. How many other lanistas have ever graced Vretos' court?"

"Retire the money maker?" Grimmet says. Best to kick Udiari while his footing is shaky. "How's that good for Keswal?"

The air in the room is thick, despite the salty sea wind blowing from the west. The lanista is without pithy response. Silence hangs like a miasma.

"Your legacy ..." Vretos says, eyeing the lanista. To his credit, Udiari has assumed his most stately posture and matches Vretos' gaze. Vretos has a drink from his goblet and shrugs. "We'll see." He turns his eyes to Grimmet. "How do your goatmen fare, Beastmaster?"

Grimmet fights the urge to squirm in his chair. He was hoping to avoid this subject altogether.

"They're as fit as the day they were captured," Grimmet lies.

"Rumor has it they're as cooperative as an orcane in rut," Garr says, striking a match to relight his pipe.

Bastard. Grimmet's ears burn. He adjusts his cuffs. It was only a matter of time before the admiral aimed one at Grimmet.

"I'm no fool, Grimmet," Vretos says. "I appreciate your goatmen. I was glad to have the chance to wrestle one. Especially since the people have named them the Unstoppable. Glad to crush any rumor that I might be diminishing. Thank you for that."

Grimmet dips his chin in grim anticipation.

"Speaking of ..." Vretos turns eyes on Zander. "I was shot." With a single finger he taps his shoulder. The only evidence of the wound is a pale puckering welt on his skin, surrounded by less-pale puckering welts.

"The archer responsible will never shoot a bow again," Zander says immediately.

"He had no business shooting a bow in the first place," Udiari says. "Of what use to you is an archer with no bow?"

"He's no longer an archer of mine. His debut in Keswal is next week. He'll be equipped with a single arrow."

Vretos smiles. "That won't be necessary."

"He's already in the care of Lanista Crowe," Zander says resolutely.

Vretos returns his attention to Grimmet, to his dismay.

"I know about the uergatas. Garr's right, they aren't taking to gentling. They brood and sulk. What is your plan for them?"

Of course Grimmet has thought about this. His plan was to eventually replace them, after he'd squeezed all the fight out of them.

"Their next match is to be against cliff barghests," Grimmet says with no certainty. "As long as they're promised a return trip home, they'll perform."

"Beast on beast. Sounds ... riveting," Udiari says, containing a yawn with his fist.

"Promised by whom?" the admiral asks. "You think they'll believe you?"

Grimmet's collar squeezes his neck. He clears his throat, but that doesn't put a response in his mouth. He'd considered splitting the uergatas up, pitting one against several men or beasts. It would promise four more fights, yes. But at their current rate of decline, segregating them may be their deathblow. Alone, they'd surely be even more hopelessly dismal. The first time a uergata stood passionless and let itself die, word would spread. For all Grimmet knows, people might even start pitying the monsters. It wouldn't be the first time. And last time a beast of his grew to be sympathized, it resulted in a boycott of Keswal and Grimmet's ass teetering on the far edge of the fifth chair.

"You should get another good fight out of them," Udiari says. "Go out with a blast, not a whimper. It would be more tragic than entertaining to stretch out the inevitable."

Grimmet turns to Udiari with clenched fists, thoughts of lanista strangulation dancing in his head. "As should you," he says, "with your fading prodigy, Torvald, and his javelin-slinging partner. What a selfish request, to retire Keswal's favorite fighter for your own dignity's sake. Serve Fohrvylda or yourself, lanista. You can't do both."

"By the gods." Vretos gasps. He's smiling, eyes distant, nodding, and scaring the shit out of Grimmet. "You two, together, through ankle-biting pettiness, have birthed a brilliant idea."

Grimmet's mouth falls into a deep frown. He doesn't know what idea he or Udiari birthed, but its conception seems anything but consensual. Vretos only smiles like that when something horrific is underway.

"The Tactician and the Undying ..." Vretos proclaims, holding up his left hand, palm out, as if what he's saying is being stamped upon the clouds. "Versus ..." He lifts his right hand and looks to it. "... the unstoppable."

Grimmet's lungs fail him. The heat falls out of his cheeks. He looks at the lanista, who doesn't appear any keener on the proposition.

Marshal Zander bursts into snuffling laughter. "Now *there's* a fight card."

"I'd pay to see that." Admiral Garr puffs his pipe enthusiastically. "Hell, everyone will pay to see that."

Vretos pounds both fists on the table, making the dishes and steins hop. "We'll have to extend the seating."

"I can organize that," Zander says, as gleeful as a dreadhop covered in guts. And why wouldn't he be? The fifth chair benefits from anyone's suffering. If Torvald and Irdessa die, Udiari will lose all relevance. Zander will be promoted to fourth chair.

Problem is, Torvald has never lost a fight. Not a one. And if Grimmet loses the goatmen ... His head is shaking against his will. In the uergatas' state, there is no telling how many more quality fights he can get out of them, if any. For all he knows, they'll offer their throats to Torvald's blade, taking an honorable death to a fellow prisoner over remaining imprisoned far from their home for the entertainment of their enemies. If they do die, he has no backup plan in place. Torvald killing the uergatas will cost Grimmet this chair. *And I'll be godsdamned if I give it up without a fight!*

"It is a great idea," Grimmet says, hauling a grin onto his face and turning to Udiari. "That is, assuming you can postpone Torvald's retirement."

"No one's retiring," Vretos says.

Udiari's mouth is an icy grimace. He seems to have no more confidence in Torvald than Grimmet does in his goatmen.

"Here's your offer, Lanista, and by Vostuar's balls, you better appreciate it." Vretos' eyes are as wide as Grimmet has ever seen them. "Come up with a card to fight four uergatas. It will include Torvald, Irdessa, that walking dead rapist, and whomever else—your entire company if you need to clean house—with whatever tools they need. The usual restrictions lifted. If your precious Tactician wins, he is free to retire from Keswal."

The lanista's eyes flicker like embers reinvigorated by a breeze. "All restrictions lifted?"

"All."

He watches Vretos for an uncomfortable moment before wetting his thin lips with his tongue. "May I retire Irdessa as well?"

Vretos' smile cracks into a snarl. Then he chuckles. "You better be happy I like you, Udiari. Yes, keep your Undying. She'd be useless without Torvald anyway."

Udiari nods. His eyes are distant now. Chances are he's already calculating how to bury the goatmen.

Grimmet's mind sprints furiously. The uergatas cannot lose this fight. He must enliven them, if only for one last fight. But for that to happen, they need to believe they will be set free; they will return home. The admiral is right, Grimmet's promises mean nothing to them. If their grunts and glares are any indicator, they'd just as soon stomp him into a smear than buy anything he's selling. He will not earn back their trust.

Vretos clacks his wooden stein on the table, shaking the thralls into life. "Now, who's hungry?"

"Oh, I am," Zander says, markedly cheery to not be the sponge of all scorn, however momentary it is.

Grimmet is not. How can he motivate his goatmen to sling Torvald's bones all over the arena? They won't listen to him. He needs something. He needs ... *the touch.* A crooked smile finds its way onto his face. The uergatas don't have to listen to Grimmet. They need only listen to his son, Pappu. All animals listen to Pappu.

4

Never Know the Grave

FOHRVYLDA
Udiari's Manor, Promontory

Udiari shuffles the papers on his dining table and shifts his weight in his armchair. Every last document—records of transactions and fighters, notices of debts, incriminating correspondences—has plagued his desk for time immemorial. For each, he invents an excuse not to throw it in the hearth yet. You can always burn a thing. Harder to unburn it. The morning sun tortures him through the ceiling-high windows across the dining hall. He could pull the thick curtains. But that might set the wrong atmosphere. Worse, and more accurately, the right one.

The door opens and the hinges squawk, making Udiari's heart hiccup into his throat. It's only a thrall. Shanto, if memory serves. Lost an arm to Keswal and has been a reliable helper ever since, or at least part of one.

"Master Torvald to see you," the thrall says.

"Send him in," Udiari says, sitting upright, despite his crooked spine's protest. He pushes the papers away. Finding his hands itchingly empty, he snatches the papers up again. "And relieve him of weapons," he calls out.

"Of course." The door closes.

The lanista taps his toe on the lacquered hardwood. He crosses his legs. Uncrosses them. Fans himself with the papers. There's a sheen of sweat across his forehead. He snatches a kerchief from his vest and dabs at it. *Nothing is the matter, why?* he practices saying. His armpits are swamps but that shouldn't be obvious. Except it's Torvald we're talking about.

The door opens again. Udiari leaps to his feet. Torvald walks in. He's wearing simple shoes and a loose grey outfit. His long black hair is unbound, framing his face and hanging over his shoulders.

"Lanista," he says as he approaches. Those steel-grey eyes puncture any façade Udiari constructs. It is unfathomable that this man is a third Udiari's age. The lanista sighs heavily, letting his shoulders fall.

"Torvald," he says. "Please, have a seat."

Torvald sits in the chair across the massive table from Udiari and throws one leg over the other. "How'd your dinner go?" Torvald asks. He has an uncanny control over his outward temperament. Surely he knows what Udiari must report to him but he acts like he was summoned frivolously.

"Well enough, thank you," Udiari lies. "Nothing to sweat over. You know I prefer our meetings to theirs. How's Irdessa?"

"She's well, thank you."

"She's become formidable with those javelins, hasn't she?"

"She's become formidable all around. I'm more impressed by her every day."

Udiari nods, tries to appear engaged. He needs a drink. "Whiskey," he says. "Marintha Select. And two glasses."

A thrall dislodges himself from the wall beside the embroidered violet curtains and hastens across the rug to an ornate cabinet with glass-paneled doors. Udiari's thralls are all converted Keswal fighters. They're retired and typically unwhole, but able to work and happy to be out of the fight. Some lanistas expend their every convict in Keswal. Udiari prefers to get his money's worth. Helps him sleep at night too.

He folds his hands and settles back in his chair, trying to ease the pressure on his stiff back. The glasses and whiskey are delivered. Udiari unstoppers the crystal bottle and pours two fingers for Torvald, three for himself. He slides Torvald's glass across the table. Torvald places his hand in its path, halting it in a sliver of sunlight that refracts through the glass to waver over the wallpaper and the paintings.

"It's a bit early, isn't it?"

Udiari downs his glass and refills it. The whiskey is smooth. Its heat feels almost like life inside his old ribs. He clears his throat. "Vretos wasn't happy," he says.

"Is he ever?" Torvald says.

"He wanted the rapist dead."

"That man didn't rape anyone."

"You think Vretos cares about that?"

Torvald shrugs. "I like him."

Udiari clenches his jaw but a smile leaks through. "You know who you remind me of?" he asks.

"I expect you'll say you," Torvald says.

"Yes," Udiari says. "When I was young and thought I'd never die."

"Oh, I know I'll die. And I have a feeling I know where. But I've been wrong before." Torvald winks, and it feels like a dagger entering Udiari's heart.

"Kraus can't survive another fight."

"Noted," Torvald says.

"That fight last week ..." Udiari says, more to redirect an awkward silence than anything else. "The pirates and the uergatas ..."

"Yes?" Torvald sips his whiskey.

"Hell of a show, eh? The people have named the goatmen *Unstoppable*. Not sure how Grimmet can top that one."

"Let's not tempt him." Torvald smiles.

Udiari chuckles. Aside from their voices, the room feels deathly quiet. Is this the last laugh he'll share with Torvald?

"Any insight on how Grimmet managed to catch them?" Torvald asks.

"He tricked them. Sedated them. Apparently one of them is heir to the Gygus tribe."

"Grimmet tricked a uergata chieftain?" Torvald's arched eyebrow registers disbelief, and some amount of disgust.

"A son of a chieftain," Udiari corrects.

"That won't bode well for any human civilization near where it took place."

That's not Fohrvylda's concern, it's Halandor's. And they're a vast ocean away. Udiari lifts his glass. "Not a problem either of us will ever need concern ourselves with, eh?" He attempts a smile.

Torvald meets his eyes but does not return the smile.

Udiari clears his throat, takes a drink. He forgets too easily that Torvald is originally from Halandor, not Fohrvylda. "Regarding that fight, what would you say the pirates did wrong?"

Torvald leans back in his chair. His eyes lose focus. "I've put some thought into that."

Of course you have. Udiari smiles.

"First of all, I don't think the pirates ever had a chance. Especially not knowing the uergatas' unique tactics. The pirates were surprised by the initial attack. By the second pounce, they'd lost nearly a fifth of their forces. That's enough to crush the morale of even a seasoned militia, especially in a box like Keswal. Marauders are little more than sword-bearing citizens, albeit lacking any inhibitions. If they'd been fighting for their homes, and on their own turf, the outcome may have been less one-sided."

"So, how would you have fought back the uergatas?" Udiari asks.

"With fifty pirates?" There's a smile in Torvald's eye, if not on his lips.

"Let's assume you have about fifteen."

Torvald's jaw clenches. He stares at the window. Outside, grey clouds are encroaching, devouring the blue, shifting steadily eastward to wrest the sky from the sun. A wind whistles at the windowsill and a leafless limb trembles and scratches the glass. Udiari anticipated an uncomfortable conversation today but he knew better than to think the fight card would surprise the Tactician. In fact, he's probably anticipated this since the uergatas were first introduced.

"There is no unstoppable force," Torvald says.

"I'll buy that."

"I can't tell you how I'd have stopped them before knowing their strategy. And, to be honest, no matter how intimidating a show they put on, an advantage will always exist for those who have more knowledge of their opponents."

Udiari drinks whiskey in lieu of a response.

"The uergatas have several weaknesses," Torvald says. "During their leap, they are locked in a path for several moments, unable to pivot or dodge. They can block or deflect, but in limited directions."

"During that time, to what are they vulnerable?" Udiari asks.

"Piercing weapons. Spears, like those they use. Arrows."

Javelins? Udiari doesn't ask. If he's thinking it, Torvald already has.

"Perhaps slashing weapons as well," Torvald says, "but not knowing more than I do, I couldn't say. For all I know, their coats turn away blades. We both know they can't turn away arrows."

Udiari nods, easing deeper into his chair. The whiskey's heat runs through his arms and legs now, lending him false youth and vigor, and with it the laughable delusion that he himself could hope to lead battle in Keswal again. Amazing how distance in time can erase the darker details and leave you only the sweet aftertaste of glory. These conversations are, hopefully, the closest he'll ever be again to the fighting.

"Their horns," Torvald continues, "fearsome though they may be, don't appear to be a primary weapon. When the uergatas ram, it's with their forehead, the base of their horns. I imagine they don't want to skewer something awkwardly and lose their balance due to a wriggling, impaled opponent. Perhaps the horns themselves could be ensnared in nets, tied down with ropes. Leveraged against them." Torvald shakes his head. "It's a shame ropes aren't allowed in Keswal."

Hope sparks in Udiari's chest. "Let's assume, for the sake of a uergata fight, that nothing is forbidden. Including ropes."

Torvald arches an eyebrow and nods approvingly. "Interesting. Are we also assuming the uergatas will employ identical tactics and will be armed the same as last time?"

Udiari's glimmer of hope fizzles and he *hmphs*. He has a drink. "Seems an unwise assumption."

"Agreed."

"I doubt they'd ever be armored," Udiari says. "You can't get near enough to fit them. They're not even exercised. It's not safe to let them out of their pen."

"Their *pen*? They're caged with the beasts?" Torvald asks.

"They are."

Torvald's lips curls downward. "Insult piled on injury."

"What did you expect? You've seen the size of them. They won't fit in cells."

"What about Beastmaster Grimmet's son?" Torvald says.

"The falconer? What about him?"

"Suppose he attempts to work with them to get them armored. Feasible?"

Udiari sighs and pushes back in his chair. "Let's assume so. Worst case."

"Then maybe we can get in front of that. Influence it. Zander has an armorer the beastmaster might choose to employ. Does Zander owe you anything?"

"Everyone owes me something." Udiari ponders a moment. "Perhaps Zander's armorer will approach the beastmaster with a discounted offer. That may forestall any suspicion. Grimmet has expended himself to acquire those goatmen and is in some debt. He desperately needs them to survive."

"And what is it you need?" Torvald asks. His eyes are shards of glass.

Udiari sighs heavily. "I need to retire."

"And for that, you need me alive."

"You're my beneficiary, Torvald. You and Irdessa. You'll inherit this all." He waves his hand at everything. At nothing.

"Irdessa will want to return home to Vim," Torvald says.

"She'll be free to do as she wants," Udiari says. "But under its new leadership Vim isn't what it was."

That's an understatement. Ever since the arrest of Torvald, Irdessa, and Irdessa's father Andelsior—Vim's unofficial leader—the town has been on the edge of utter disorder. It's on the far side of Fohrvylda, across the wastelands, where towns largely govern themselves independently of Promontory, so long as they do nothing to threaten the nation's productivity or the coming Heathen Tide.

"I know. And maybe it's beyond saving. But there's something there that needs doing. She's the one to do it."

Udiari knows what Torvald refers to. Betrayal is what led to their arrest. The one responsible still runs free, and despite Udiari offering to arrange a serving of justice to whomever that is, Torvald won't give him further details. Says it's not Udiari's burden to bear. Apparently he's decided it's Irdessa's. "Does Irdessa know that?" Udiari asks.

Torvald gives a melancholy smile. "Not entirely. There was a time I thought it was important to keep her informed about Vim. But if the news isn't good, and there's nothing she can do to change it ..." He trails off, shaking his head. "It seemed crueler to tell her than not to."

Udiari doesn't respond. It's rare for Torvald to be unsure of anything, and seems to only happen when he's talking about Irdessa.

"Do you think Vretos will let me leave Keswal?" Torvald asks, watching his glass.

Udiari shifts his weight. Torvald isn't asking that in the hopes of being enlightened. He's already sure of his answer.

"I'd hoped so," Udiari says, sounding much more naïve than a man his age should. Especially one who's survived Keswal.

Torvald lifts his glass and gives it a twist, making the whiskey swirl. "You lost your seat."

Udiari says nothing. For any other fighter, the politics of the court are little more than distant noise. Maybe Torvald was the same when he first arrived in Udiari's company. It's impossible to even imagine now. Torvald concerns himself with everything. Nothing surprises him.

"Will my success get it back?"

"I don't give a damn about the seat, Torvald. You're my ticket to retirement, with Irdessa at your side. Once you inherit my house, you and she are out of Keswal."

"Once I stop the Unstoppable," Torvald says. His inflection suggests the deed is impossible.

Udiari's cheeks burn. *After all I've done for Keswal, this is the thanks Vretos gives me. Kill my best man. The only fighter I've ever cared to protect.* He lifts his glass to his lips, then slams it down without having another drink. Thunder rumbles faintly. The naked branch at the window taps more insistently. Time is running out. For everyone, perhaps.

Torvald straightens in his chair. "There may be a way to level the field."

Despite himself, Udiari allows a glimmer of optimism.

"You said nothing is forbidden," Torvald says. "I'm not keen on this idea. I have more respect for the uergatas than this. Unfortunately, obligation overrides honor. Besides, I hope I never find myself in a fair fight, if such a thing even exists." It isn't a question, but he seems to await response.

"More respect than to do what exactly?" Udiari says.

"Pit traps," Torvald says. "Dug into the floor of Keswal before the fight, then concealed."

A frown makes its way onto Udiari's face. Torvald has never lost a fight in Keswal. There are many reasons for that, some more respectable than others. But this ... this seems beneath him. Besides, tampering with the arena before the fight is reserved for special occasions, and by a select few. Never convicts. "That's asking a lot."

"Yes."

"Beastmaster Grimmet would certainly cry foul," Udiari says, although the beastmaster's crying is barely a concern.

"Grimmet imprisoned Children of Uar and brought them to Keswal to be killed. If the uergata tribe discovers Fohrvylda was behind the treachery, it could bring an entirely separate war to the cliffs of Fohrvylda. He has no room to complain."

Udiari works his lips around his teeth, pokes the holes in his gums with his tongue. "Vretos did promise me freedom to set up this card," he speculates. "And Marshal Zander owes me."

"I want to be there to install the traps."

"Of course you do. Any other demands?"

"Yes," Torvald says. "I pick out who will help me place the pits. No one else can know. Surprise is the only way this will work."

Udiari's few teeth are clenching. "By the gods, Torvald. You're putting me in an awkward place."

"I'll swap with you."

Udiari chuckles while refilling his glass. "You'll want Irdessa's help, I imagine."

"No," Torvald says. "Kraus."

Of course. Kraus has the look of a man who's had to dig a hole. "Tell me this will give you an edge," Udiari says.

"Everything gives me an edge."

Udiari stands and raises his glass. "Well, then. A toast."

Torvald joins him.

"To the brave," Udiari says.

Torvald responds, "May they never know the grave."

5
A Leap of Faith

FOHRVYLDA
Keswal, Promontory

The morning is so chilly Irdessa's breath is vapor even within the torch-lit refuge of the Last Room. A frigid, salty wind cuts through the sandy slits in the wooden gate. Thunder rumbles in the distance. It's cold enough to warrant the extra layers of leather Irdessa's wearing, but she'd prefer to be without them. Torvald insisted though, and today, of all days, she is giving him no arguments.

Today, Udiari's company fights the four remaining uergatas. The Unstoppable. With anyone besides Torvald at her side, she'd have abandoned hope completely. Those monsters are like nothing Keswal has ever seen, or at least not in her time here. Try though she might, she could determine no exploitable flaws in their tactics, none that use the tools at the company's disposal anyway. Torvald claimed to have found their weaknesses but refused to disclose them to Irdessa. Perhaps it's for the best. She'd have picked his strategies apart in her mind and worked them down to nothing and then found herself with no faith in him today. Luckily, Torvald has a way of helping her suspend disbelief.

Their strategy is specific. Four parties, one per uergata. The idea is to flank them and taunt them into separating quickly. Torvald will lead a group of three proven strikers, quick and deadly. Some wet farmer named Riner leads a group of five other wets. If they don't know they're feeding birds today, then they're as dumb as they look. Jasmin leads a group of four surefooted archers. Kraus leads the last group, which includes Prancer, Irdessa, and a proven named Callen, who was a seller of stolen goods on the outside. Inside, he's proved handy with whips. He promised to be an expert on knots and snares.

Why she isn't leading a group is a mystery that had better undo itself after the fight. She assumes it's because Kraus knows the specifics of the traps, having helped Torvald dig them. He was chosen for the preparation over Irdessa, a fact which might have caused her concern if the task had entailed more than hacking at Keswal's packed floor with a pickaxe under the Fohrvylda sun.

"It's a daunting day," Torvald says. "Most of you saw the uergatas fight the pirates."

"That was no fight," says a woman's voice.

"More like a slaughter," says a proven with a wrinkled scar where his nose should be.

Kraus stomps forward from where he's been brooding against the wall. "Shut your mouths or you'll never see the arena floor."

Something dark has come over him today. There's no humor whatsoever, disgusting or otherwise. No mirth. It's not the apathy that took him when Torvald mentioned his past, more like anxiety for a fate to which he is bound. It's odd, because he was the only convict excited about fighting the uergatas. When Torvald initially brought the news, several days ago, everyone else clenched up to keep from shitting themselves. Kraus dropped ten years in age, giddy as a child with a pot of honey.

"It is my intention that you all survive," Torvald says to the convicts, with none of his usual charisma.

But some of you won't.

"But you won't."

Irdessa's eyebrow arches. Wasn't that supposed to be a secret? *Torvald, where's your game face?* To his credit, he didn't point directly at the wets when he said it.

"If you have a god, I suggest you make peace with it."

Irdessa fights the urge to kick him. Is the idea to strike fear into everyone?

"Speak for yourself," she says, raising a javelin. "Tonight I'm eating goat."

A couple of convicts offer muted affirmation. It's such a lackluster response she regrets saying anything. She rolls her head on her shoulders, bounces on the balls of her feet, stretches out her arms, but she can't shake the chill from her bones. Torvald ... has he truly not climbed out of the funk that took him? He promised her he's devised a foolproof strategy. Hell, he and Kraus were even given unimpeded access to the arena to set up traps for the goatmen. Despite herself, she searches his eyes. He isn't projecting fear. But behind the splintered grey glass, there is the same grim anticipation Kraus elicits.

Out in the arena, the Bloody Portent can be heard, albeit muffled by tons of earth. With some effort, Irdessa has learned to search the faces of the convicts, listen to Torvald, and eavesdrop on the Portent at once. She can only make out details here and there. Words, sometimes phrases.

The Portent's voice is on a rise, and ends abruptly on the words, "... *Falconer Pappu.*"

The declaration is over and the crowd's response is a dreary applause that translates through the ceiling into a low rustle, like water flushing through an aqueduct.

"Our enemies are outnumbered," Torvald says. "They're far from Halandor and are forlorn. They're down one since they arrived, and are sentient enough to know this arena is where their lives will end. The lore of the Children of Uar tells us uergatas cannot thrive away from their homeland."

Jasmin is checking the bows of her archers. Prancer adjusts the sack on his shoulder, his eyes locked on Torvald. He's grown more somber in the days following his first fight. Keswal has that charming effect on people. Kraus rests his tower shield on the toe of his right boot and secures the hatchets hanging at his waist. He too has a sack over his shoulder. Their group will rely on his protection, Callen's knots, and Prancer's speed to ensnare the uergatas. Irdessa will make them bleed. If Kraus' group can kill two of the beasts, Torvald promised to take care of the others.

The Bloody Portent's voice seeps through Torvald's intermission. "... *handywork ... Zander's own blacksmiths.*"

Irdessa frowns. If blacksmiths are involved in this fight, it surely wasn't for the benefit of Udiari's company. Whatever armaments the combatants of the Last Room come into are secondhand.

"Some of you have already grown to trust me," Torvald says. "The rest of you must take a leap of faith."

He looks at Irdessa and she cringes. He could have chosen a better word than *leap*, considering today's adversaries.

"Our lanista has been gracious to us all and allowed me to pay a visit to the uergatas in their pen."

Irdessa's game face breaks in a gasp. Torvald's eyes declare it is no lie. *Why didn't he tell me that?* The whole room reacts in surprise. Except Kraus, who stares at the floor.

"They're withering. They've lost the will to fight, or even eat. Grimmet has done all he can to muster them and it's failed." His eyes sweep the convicts. "The uergatas have outlived their usefulness in Keswal. Why else pit them against the Tactician and the Undying?"

Some chuckle. Some nod in agreement. But Irdessa hears the hitch in his voice. A lie hides in his words. Grimmet may have done all he can. But why did the Portent mention his son Pappu?

The horn of Keswal chops the damp air like a dull axe, and the chill in Irdessa's bones spills out over her skin, making her tremble. She clenches her teeth. *I will be godsdamned if fear is what kills me.*

"The birds don't eat goat meat," Irdessa says. "So let's make them go hungry."

"Fuck the birds," Kraus says. This brings nods from the convicts, and some beating of steel on steel.

"No fear," Irdessa says.

"No fear," Prancer responds.

"*No fear!*" Irdessa yells, stabbing the air with both javelins.

This time they all respond—Torvald, Kraus, Prancer, Jasmin, the proven, the wets. Irdessa turns to face the inevitable. The chills that ride her skin feel more like the fire that she needs. The gate trembles into life, ascending to let a toothed wind bite Irdessa's knuckles and her cheeks. Outside, the crowd's enthusiasm is a rushing windstorm, roaring down the corridor, shaking the ceiling, electrifying her blood.

Torvald turns his back on the convicts, moves alongside Irdessa. "You're stronger than me," he says, only loud enough for her to hear.

Irdessa glances at him. He's motionless, with drops of moisture gleaming in his hair, holding it static around his shoulders despite the wind. That discreet smile alights on his lips.

"Without you, I'd have never survived my first fight," he says.

It's a sweet lie. The truth is opposite that. She'd have died without him. Every time. Thinking of their first fight reminds Irdessa of her father. At least he died quickly. But the memory strikes her differently with each visit, and each is painful in its own way. Irdessa grits her teeth and blinks quickly to regain focus. The gate disappears into the ceiling, exposing grey earth and grey sky.

"You'll be a better leader than I," he says, despite the irritation Irdessa is intentionally conveying. "Your heart's lighter."

"Torvald, shut up," she says. "It's time to kill, not puke cheese."

Torvald chuckles. Irdessa steps forward. Torvald's hand clamps on to hers, halting her, pulling her aside. "Kraus is leading your party," he says.

"Fuck you," Irdessa responds. But she stops long enough for Kraus to shoulder past, bumping her out of the way with his enormous shield. She rubs her shoulder. This'll be the last time she follows him anywhere. Supposedly the commoners root for him. Why, she's not sure, but they don't matter. The rich want him dead, and they don't pay for their lush seating to watch rapists thrive. Kraus pauses at the threshold before the gate, before the crowd can see him. Maybe there is something he fears.

"Irdessa." A peacefulness has taken Torvald's eyes, and now both corners of his lips curl into an earnest smile. "*I love you*," he whispers. "Always have."

The words hit her like a slap to the face. She yanks her hand away but can't move from the spot. Torvald leaves her, walks under the placard into the arena. He draws that curved sword of his but doesn't rap the swinging wooden plank. "Strikers, with me. Kraus, stick to the plan, at all costs."

"Aye-aye," Kraus rumbles. He spits a grey wad up onto the placard and limps under it. Irdessa stumbles after him, with barely the presence of mind to knock the placard with her own javelin. She doesn't buy into the superstition of it, and she knows Torvald doesn't, but those watching need all the encouragement they can get. Why'd he fail to strike it? *Torvald. So tactical about everything but this moment. Son of a bitch.*

Out in the arena, it takes all Irdessa's strength to put a swagger in her stride rather than a shiver. The stands are full to bursting. It might be the largest crowd Irdessa's ever witnessed here. On the northern side, the onlookers wear heavy furs and have fires blazing in their braziers. The seats have been reinforced with wooden scaffolding, extending out over the arena and lined with sharpened wooden stakes not unlike the uergatas' weapon of choice. It won't necessarily keep the rich from being battered with slung bodies of convicts, but the goatmen won't be jumping in that direction. The tempest of the audience is indistinguishable from the thunder rumbling in from the west. Out over the Faithless Sea, the clouds are black-green and roiling, and their bellies smear downward at a sharp angle.

"Come on, Undying," Kraus yells, lumbering toward the cliff, toward the coming storm. He's still favoring his right leg. Irdessa follows, not quite able to muster confidence. Something is wrong, besides that she's following this clod. It's not the uergatas. Somehow, they're not the apex of her concerns, and that is a problem. She can't help but notice the lack of evidence of pit traps. Stained earth, dirt, flattened clumps of grass, same as most fights. Surprisingly little detritus. Maybe that's for the better. The last thing they need is the goatmen seeing the traps and the surprise being ruined.

The northern gate thumps open. It's too soon. Kraus' group is not in place yet. Looks like none of the groups are except Torvald's. He has moved directly under the Deceiver's thigh and is crouched with his team, as if the beasts won't see them there.

Irdessa looks to the black opening of the massive gateway. If the uergatas start off as timidly as they did in their first fight, she still has time to—

Out march the uergatas. One after the other, the goatmen exit the tunnel with heads lowered, horns forward. They rise to full height, steam blasting from wide nostrils, twisting horns towering over the arena floor. They're taller than she thought, but that isn't what drags Irdessa's feet to a stop and pulls her jaw swinging wide. They're armored. Every one of them is clad in unpolished steel panels at their thighs, their furry chests, their sloping shoulders. Gone are the rough wooden spears. They carry long-bladed halberds whose handles are nearly twice Irdessa's height. The earth rumbles under their hooves. Black eyes pierce the field to single out the scurrying humans.

Irdessa's heart is kicking against her ribs. The space separating her from the giant goatmen is not nearly enough. They are not withered or complacent. They weren't supposed to be armored. Her javelins might as well be sticks. With some effort, she closes her gaping mouth. How can Udiari's company stand a chance? Because Torvald said so?

Irdessa fights the urge to slap her own cheek. She has to trust him. He's never failed her. Do the job. Do what she's good at. She takes a deep breath, as Torvald loves to remind her to do. A Keswal breath. She rolls her shoulders, bounces on her toes, dissects her enemies with her eyes. She's seen phenomena she'd consider magic, or at least unexplainable. These beasts, however outlandish, don't seem to be. Yes, they're large, sentient, and imposing. But they breathe, like her. Their eyes dart about, perhaps to isolate targets, assess the threats, if they even perceive any. If they don't, perhaps she'll surprise them. And if she does, she knows Torvald will.

The uergatas charge, and Irdessa sees a chance. That armor they're sporting seems to be plates layered on flapping plates, all stitched into some vest or shirt—more cobbled than custom. This is surely how they were fitted so quickly. The design is ideal for repelling attacks from above, but near useless for a javelin from below. Or a sword. Or arrows. Or honestly any attack her party might bring. She almost smiles. Did their armorer truly fail them so utterly? Or was even that somehow a part of Torvald's strategy? They'll certainly be no faster carrying all that steel.

The uergatas are splitting up rather than remaining grouped. Another miscalculation. As one, they could likely overpower any single group, then move on to the next. It's not like their time is limited. Split up, their chances aren't so assured. A goatman for the wets, one for Jasmin's group, one for Torvald's party under the Deceiver, and one dashing straight at Irdessa.

"Dess, come on!" It's Kraus. He's been calling her that despite her complaints. Before this moment, that annoyance seemed significant. Kraus and Prancer and Callen have made it to the edge of the cliff, closer to the drop than Irdessa's ever dared to go. Seems like an awful place to be caught by that stomping giant goat and so she stands her ground. If she draws attention to herself, maneuvers it between her and Kraus, perhaps they can pincer it, her occupying it with some semblance of threat while Callen readies his snares. Irdessa lifts both javelins in defiance and yells at the uergata, ignoring the yelling from her guts that Torvald is human and capable of error, and this may be the end of Lanista Udiari's company.

Off to Irdessa's right, the archers form a crouching line with Jasmin standing behind them. They launch tentative arrows at their target, but at that distance and angle, the beast's armor turns back their attack. Irdessa wants to shout at them to wait. *Hold out until it's upon you then loose in force.* But her own fight is at hand.

The black-furred beast leaps at her while still thirty feet off. This is what Irdessa had hoped for, but rather than darting in with a quick fatal attack from below, she freezes, stupefied. How can something that large jump that high? She barely manages to dive aside. The ground shakes as hooves plant where she stood. Irdessa rolls, scrambles, gasps, watches the gargantuan halberd chop a divot in the earth. She leaps up, considers replying with a test strike of her own, but ducks instead as the halberd's blade cuts the air within an inch of her head. *Fuck, it's fast.*

The thick clanking of its metal armor suggests each plate weighs as much as an oak shutter, but the damn monster is failing to be encumbered. It's giving her no breathing room.

Kraus is yelling something. Trying to get the beast's attention? Trying to get hers? He should be battering the fucker with that tower shield, not talking, the dumb shit rapist. She throws herself backward as the halberd dashes the ground again, then again. No window for her javelins. But she is alive and the fire in her veins is finally searing away the chill. She may not have hit it yet but she's dancing with the goat. It needs only to make a mistake. Never mind her fate if she does.

The uergata gives a grating bleat, frustrated if Irdessa is any judge. It stomps toward her, each stride covering four of hers, slashing left, right, left, right. Each attack is over-powered, telegraphed from a mile off. Dodging is requiring less effort. If she didn't know better, she'd think it's going easy on her. Still no opportunity to attack, but is the beast tiring? The dull look on its furry face matches that of any grazing goat Irdessa's ever observed, so when it lunges with an abrupt stab at her chest, she's almost caught by it. It's close enough to piss her off. She falls left, jabbing as she goes. Not the strongest strike but her weapons are sharp and its arm is moving fast. The tip of her javelin punctures its forearm. Blood sprays its goat face as the tip punches clean through. The uergata jerks, black eyes widening in surprise, and a rattling roar escapes it.

The southern stands thunder their approval. A thrill fills Irdessa. *Was I the first to draw goat blood? Before Torvald even?* It's almost enough to make her laugh aloud. Too late, she notices the approaching hoof. She tries to roll aside but it clips her hip, nearly pinning her. She groans, the searing pain momentarily stealing her strength. Felt like a slap from a sledgehammer. She regains clarity in time to see a descending blade. No time to even block, not that it would save her.

"Shit," she thinks aloud.

There's an ear-splitting rasp of steel tearing steel. Kraus stands above her, straining under that tower shield, the uergata blade embedded a foot deep through it, having stopped almost against Kraus' scalp. Irdessa knows opportunity when she sees it. She makes like a rat and scurries between the massive hooves while the goatman wrenches at its weapon, nearly lifting the shield and Kraus off the ground. She drops a javelin, grabs the other in both hands, scrambles to her feet and strikes, piercing no less than three inches into the uergata's hip. Its massive legs waver. It releases its weapon, spins around, yanking her javelin from her, but she's already retrieving the other. Kraus topples, the shield too heavy for him to support with the goatman's enormous weapon still attached. The uergata kicks at Irdessa, but it's lost too much stability. She lets the trunk-like hoof pass by her, its wind lifting her hair. She thrusts, this time stabbing with all her might. The javelin punches up into furry armpit, then through, its fluted tip grating against the underside of the metal plates of the uergata's shoulder armor. The nightmarish sound it responds with is different this time. Pain. *Rage.*

For the first time the beast backs up. It's lost its weapon and she's lost hers. She draws both her knives.

"Not so tough now, are you?" she yells, stalking toward it. *Don't give it a fucking inch! Not 'til it's dead!*

The goatman has lost all resolve. It looks back toward the others. Irdessa dares not follow its gaze. She must strike when the opportunity presents itself, and here it is. A perfectly exposed swath of goat neck. She draws back the knife that will end this enemy. Before she can throw it, Kraus is there, blundering her attack aside. The uergata recovers, charges them with horns down, bowls them both over, and for some reason, rather than stamping them out of existence, it flees.

Irdessa rights herself before the pain of her injuries can lock her joints. "What the fuck, Kraus? Whose side are you on?" She reaches for her fallen knife, but Kraus pulls her away.

"It's part of the plan," he huffs. Standing on his shield, he's able to wrench the uergata's weapon loose. He slings it aside, grunts as he heaves up the shield, then shuffles toward the cliff, limping. "Torvald's orders. Now come on."

Irdessa chooses not to kill him. But by the gods it was close. She doesn't chase the wounded uergata either as it lopes toward Jasmin's archers—not that she could stop it now. She follows Kraus numbly, stashing her other knife away. She's never let confusion prevent her acting according to Torvald's directions, and his plans have never failed her. But something's wrong here. Kraus should have let her finish that beast while she had the chance.

Toward the cliff's edge they run until they're dangerously close to the precipice. Below, the Faithless Sea is choppy and angry, with house-sized swells rolling over its surface. Kraus is propping the massive shield toward the northern wall, not toward the uergatas but toward the rich, as if they pose some threat. Callen and Prancer work furiously at the contents of their bags. Irdessa sees ropes but no nets. Do they mean to assemble nets on the fly? Why now? It's too late. What have they been doing all this time? Kraus clearly misunderstood Torvald's commands.

"Why'd you stop me?" Irdessa yells. "I could have killed it."

"I don't doubt it." Kraus reaches out and grabs her upper arm before she can react. His grip is a vise. "Stay behind the shield, love," he grunts, holding the door-sized plank tight against his left shoulder and peeking through the crack at the top toward the north wall.

She's too surprised to fight him. A surge in the crowd's fervor turns her head in time to see a uergata descend from the air blade-first into Riner's wets. Yells of anguish. The clash and scrape of steel. The beast hacks through the convicts as if stirring a big vat of stew.

Jasmin's archers are focusing their shots on the quicker of the two beasts running their way, ignoring the injured one. Most arrows miss.

Some clink off steel plates. Those few that find their way to furry flesh do so without the notice of the raging uergata. At the last moment it drops to all fours and dives horns first into their midst. The line breaks. The uergata assumes a wide stance. A single swing of its massive halberd scatters the archers.

"Down we go." Kraus pushes Irdessa toward the cliff's edge. Her breath seizes up in her throat. She snatches his beard out of sheer reflex, locks her grip. Something is knocking against his shield. An arrow punctures the earth at Kraus' foot. Shot from the northern wall?

"Callen, if you're all set, hold up this shield," Kraus says.

"Got you." Callen stands up, too high apparently, and catches an arrow in his eye. His head rocks like a kicked thistle and he falls over the cliff's edge.

"Well, then," Kraus says. "Prancer, you hold it."

Kraus is squeezing Irdessa's bicep, holding her at arm's length, trying to wrench her fingers out of his beard. Prancer kicks his emptied pack out into the wind. He has pulled a knotted hemp harness up around his legs and secured it at his waist. There are more harnesses on the ground. There is no net.

"*What the fuck is this?*" Irdessa yells. She digs at Kraus' wrist with her free hand. His arm might as well be a tree limb. Prancer relieves Kraus of the shield and is almost crushed under it. He grunts, trying to steady it as the hail of arrows intensifies.

"Kraus, stop! They think we're trying to escape," Irdessa says.

"Imagine that." Kraus is hauling one of the rope-made harnesses up around his own thick legs with one hand. Something bangs into Irdessa's shin. She looks, afraid an arrow found her. It's a steel pulley, configured into Kraus' hemp belt.

Over the battlefield, Jasmin is running toward them at a crouch while arrows from the north wall chase her heels. Her archers lie in pieces and the uergata responsible is bounding toward the southern wall, the injured one close behind.

"It's time to go, Dess," Kraus growls. "You need to put on your belt." He grabs both her arms and extends his, freeing his beard of her grip. She's able to rip out a good fistful of it in the process but he doesn't seem to care. She's wanted to hurt him since the first time she saw him and now, after besting a uergata, being made powerless by his filthy grasp is filling her with incandescent rage. She maneuvers her legs around his thigh, locking her heels behind his leg. If she goes down, he's coming too.

"You bastard," she roars through gritted teeth, trying to free her arm. "Torvald saved you. You were supposed to die."

"I know what he did," Kraus says. "Quit fighting me."

The crowd surges again, a unified roar of disapproval if Irdessa's ever heard one. The arrows on the tower shield relent.

"Ah, shit," Prancer says, peeking around the shield toward the Deceiver.

Across Keswal, beneath the titanic stone statue, two uergatas are engaged with Torvald's team. Some fighters are lying flat. One of the goatmen is visibly injured, its arm limp at its side. The other one is fighting Torvald ... who has dropped his sword. He's staggering.

"Why ...?" Irdessa's strength abandons her. The cold wind breaks through her skin into her blood.

The goatman yanks back its halberd in a bloody spurt. A coiled red rope follows it from Torvald's stomach. Torvald falls to his knees, wide-eyed, holding his belly, reaching for the halberd. The uergata shakes the weapon, but it's entangled in glossy crimson cord. It raises a hoof and delivers a mid-air stomp to Torvald's face. Torvald cartwheels backward over the arena floor and comes to rest in a heap. But that can't be him. He's never ... looked like that.

"Torvald?" Irdessa's hands have gone numb. Her fingers won't respond.

He's a motionless lump, as lifeless a body as Irdessa's ever seen. The uergata steps over him and strides for the southern wall, as if Torvald the Tactician means nothing to it.

"No," Irdessa says.

"Dess ..." Kraus is hauling her over the ledge.

The wounded uergata swings its weapon. The final standing member of Torvald's team bursts open and falls like a sack. The uergata bounds away, leaving Torvald where he lies.

"No," Irdessa rakes her nails down Kraus' arm. "*Torvald!*"

Kraus' grip is beyond negotiable.

"Prancer, help." Her voice cracks. "Help, please. You have a shield. We have to help him."

Prancer won't even look at her.

The archers on the north wall are largely concentrating arrows on the uergatas, who have taken a dubious interest in the un-scaffolded southern wall. Jasmin is five yards from the tower shield when an arrow appears in her right shoulder. Her mouth opens in surprise, but she keeps her feet. Another arrow hits her hip. She squeals, falls to all fours, grabs the shaft in time for a flurry of arrows to wash over, flattening her.

Kraus is squeezing Irdessa, shaking her, trying to get her heels unlocked. "Godsdamnit, Dess, Torvald wanted this."

"Wanted *death*?" Irdessa's rage boils over. She releases her heels and swings her shin into his groin. Considering he's holding her, there's not a lot behind the kick. But he grunts. She kicks his throat, sloppy at first, but with the point of her toe on the next try. His grip loosens. She's able to tug one hand free, finally. She grabs the knife in her belt and heaves it from its sheath, swinging it at Kraus' face in one motion. He flinches, which is all that saves his eyes. His nose opens across its bridge and blood curtains down his cheeks. *Quick fucker*. She swings for his eyes again, this time to bury it in his fat skull. He blocks this one with his arm. The knife plunges into his forearm up to its hilt. Now he drops her. She's able to catch a handful of his leather cuirass, enough to keep from plummeting into the grey gale. She swings onto her feet, freed.

Prancer never sees her coming. One flying kick to the side of his knee is all it takes to break it and claim the shield. He crumples down howling and she wrenches it from him, but the massive plank weighs more than she expected. She grips one handle in both her hands, hauling it, carving a line in the earth. It's impossible to block the arrows and move the shield. She'll have to risk it.

Along the south wall the uergatas leap like grasshoppers clear into the stands, landing among the convicts and the rabble. Men and women run, shriek, dive away or get trampled, but the uergatas aren't there for them. Up the stands they flee. The longbows on the north are loosing, and their rain of arrows shows no discrimination, clinking off uergata armor and nailing people to their seats. The goatmen do not slow. They bound up the stands, toward doors built for man. Soon they'll be out of arrow's reach.

Something impacts the back of Irdessa's head, ringing her ears like a bell. She doesn't register falling but now she's crawling on swaying earth, blinking away stars. Someone yanks her up by the belt. Smells like Kraus. She's over his shoulder and he's hobbling back toward the cliff. Her eyes focus on the massive stone statue of the Deceiver across the arena. At its foot, Torvald is an unmoving pile of grey and red.

"No ..." Irdessa mumbles. She grabs at Kraus' neck but her fingers may as well be made of grass.

Kraus spins around and leans backward over the edge of the cliff. Irdessa's guts seize up into her throat as the empty, stormy expanse monopolizes her view. They fall. But instead of plummeting, they jerk to a stop. She is hanging from his shoulder facing two flailing ropes, hundreds of feet of whirling mist, and so distant it can't be real, black stone teeth with white peaks tearing through them. Kraus kicks off the wall, plunges several yards, swings back against the cliff, landing on his boots. He kicks off again.

Blood seeps through Irdessa's hair, down her temples, drips off her eyebrows, her nose, her lips. His blood or hers? She can't tell by its taste.

Kick, plummet, halt.

The roar of the crowd grows distant.

Kick, plummet, halt.

Her chill is ebbing. Numbness engulfs her.

Kick, plummet, halt.

This isn't happening. It's all a nightmare. It will soon end, then she and Torvald will arise and battle the uergatas, as they planned. Kraus will be the one to die. *Murderous raping piece of shit.* To wake up, she needs only rise from this dream. Her eyes slip closed and she sees Torvald's smile, then his guts wound around the monster's blade.

She pries her eyes open as panic sears through her veins. Hot tears mix with blood. The waves crashing below ram violently against Fohrvylda. They're not so dizzyingly distant as they were. Kraus is saying something. Swearing. Something thuds off Irdessa's back, knocking the breath out of her. It falls past, screaming. It's Prancer, and he's full of arrows. Irdessa's vision is tunneling. Icy needles stab her neck and lower back. *Rain.* Prancer shrinks away until he abruptly wedges into rocks, a mishmash of arms and legs. Waves rush in to rinse the blood away.

Torvald wanted this.

Irdessa can make out Prancer's face. He looks surprised. His brains vacated his head without telling his face where they were off to. Why would Torvald want that?

Kraus ceases his organized descent down the wall. He's fussing with something. His feet scramble at the cliff. "Dammit ... what the—shit!"

He kicks off the wall once more, wraps both heavy arms around Irdessa, and in the time it takes her stomach to climb into her ribs, she realizes the rope has abandoned them. They rotate, spiral, descend. Now she's watching the cliff face rushing by like a waterfall. The wind's melody prevails over the rain, the crashing waves. Drowns out almost everything.

I love you.

She feels Torvald's arms tighten around her. This time she presses her face into his neck. The Faithless Sea arrives.

6

The Forever Basalt

AUSGAN
Basalt Tier, Erudition

Basalt Kale rinses his pruning stones in the water basin in the corner and puts his anxious hands back to work on the decorative liana vines on his windowsill. There's little left of it to safely cut away. His nerves refuse to subside and so he's already barbered his window dressing so mercilessly it's likely to not survive the day. That's alright. If all goes as planned, he won't either. Andesite Culver is on the way, unwittingly bringing the key to Kale's end. But for some reason he's late.

Kale pokes his head out the square window. Outside is the narrow, neglected cobbled street and Erudition's imposing stone-block city wall, adorned in leafless, thirsty vines. It's tall, featureless, close enough to spit on, always seeming inconvenienced by Kale's dorm and Basalt Tier in general. Still no sign of his friend. The sun isn't high enough to peek over the wall and provide direct light. That won't happen until around noon, and then it will hurry off, quickly eclipsed by the higher dorms, leaving this entire tier in shadow again.

Culver's martial arts lesson ended a quarter hour ago. He should be here by now.

Kale withdraws, takes a deep breath, smooths his dele, tries to still his tapping toe. This might be the most excited he's ever been, which is a curious development. If only he'd known. When life fails to entice you, consider alternatives.

He rinses his pruning stones yet again. Considers opening a scroll to read, if only to occupy his hands and mind. But he can't focus on those now. He barely can at the best of times. They're all regarding consonance, the magic of Ausgan, and as time has taught, they have nothing to offer Kale the amusical. He could prune his neighbors' shrubbery too. If he doesn't, it won't get done. But then he might miss his friend's arrival. He huffs, drops to the stone floor for more exercise.

Kale lives in Ausgan's capital city, Erudition, a stone-built monastery draped over the eastern face of Mount Adenhelm. His dorm is in Basalt Tier, the lowest tier, wedged between the foot of the mountain and the city wall like dirt under a fingernail. In this cubicle dormitory, just large enough to let him lie out straight, Kale's existence involves biding his time, exercising, maintaining his and his neighbors' plants, and questioning his purpose.

Initiates to Erudition usually spend only one or two years as basalts down in this dismal tier—introduced to martial arts, supersensory perception, singing consonance, all while negating in combat training. When you graduate to andesite, you do so without a backward glance. Andesites learn to summon the Imala, the deity responsible for the physical laws of existence, while serving as porters, cleaners, apprentices to clothiers and artificers, always looking upward to Rhyolite Tier. Once in rhyolite, you finally learn the channeling of the Imala, which is the cornerstone of consonant battle magic. Those who excel at it become mancers-in-training and move up into Stravhelm, the shining tower perched high on Mount Adenhelm's shoulders, where they develop their specialty. From there you can, and are apparently encouraged to, look down your nose on Erudition and the entire jungle island of Ausgan.

Kale will never graduate to rhyolite, or even andesite. Years ago, when the exemplars of his class moved on from basalt, he stayed behind, not having grasped even the faintest notion of supersensory perception. A year passed, then two, as he tried and failed to learn the basics of consonance and his classmates progressed through andesite, each gradually forgetting Kale or purposefully distancing themselves from him. By the time exemplars his age had mostly graduated to Rhyolite Tier, they'd all moved on from whatever friendship they'd had with Kale, the forever basalt. He's been in basalt for ten years. A decade of struggling to be something he's not. If he were ever going to learn consonance, he would have by now. Accepting that has taken time and work. A lot of disappointment and anger. Introspection in the night. Questions. Why can't he get it? Are his proctors failing him? If so, is it on purpose? Why has no one intervened? How has no one important noticed he's the only basalt who requires a shaving shell to keep a smooth face? Does the Triumvirate even know he exists? Why has he never suffered negation sickness? What's wrong with him? All his questions inevitably lead back to one: Why was he inducted in the first place?

Induction happens shortly after you're born. Exemplar chaplains travel to the native villages south of Erudition within weeks of a native baby's birth. They test the newborn for an affinity for consonance. Depending on the results, the baby is inducted and is taken as an exemplar intrant to train in consonance so that he may one day defend Ausgan. The birth mother and her village receive an endowment of rain and food. Kale has decided that whatever chaplain took him from his native birth mother made a mistake. It's the only explanation. He should be out plowing a field under the sun, or whatever it is that natives do. Instead he's here, where he will forever age in stasis while new exemplars come and go, either graduating past him or dying in training from negation sickness. He will never learn consonance.

With that acceptance came freedom. He's no longer angry or sad or bothered by his loneliness. Time bleached away those emotions, leaving Kale faded like the stone outside his window. Now he feels almost nothing. So he deliberated and planned, and tonight, Imala willing, he will take his own life.

Running footsteps approach, scrambling Kale's thoughts and making his heart bounce. He climbs up from the floor, peeks out the window. Can't see anyone yet, but that has to be Culver. It's no basalt. Their sandals aren't so crisp sounding as that, and they never run. It's not rhyolites patrolling either. They rarely travel this low in the city, and when they do they're in pairs. Kale straightens his dele, sits straight-backed on his cot, and folds his hands in time for Andesite Culver to clatter into the room huffing and sweaty.

"Got held up," Culver says, leaning his large frame on the wall to catch his breath.

Kale attempts to mimic a bastion of patience but can't still his hands. He's not used to excitement.

Culver draws a silk kerchief and pats his cheeks and forehead, makes an effort to collect his black hair out of his face. He's Kale's only friend in the tiers, but why the andesite chooses to associate with a basalt like himself is and has always been a mystery to Kale. Despite being two years younger, he's taller and heavier than Kale, his cheeks bearing the fuzzy promise of black facial hair. The life of a porter involves hours of walking under direct sunlight, delivering messages and trinkets and artifacts and packages throughout Erudition, which has left his exposed skin as dark as polished mahogany. Kale, on the other hand, is no darker than raw honey.

Kale can wait no longer. "Did you get it?"

Culver smiles. With a final deep breath, he straightens his shoulders and tugs straight the lapels of his dele. His is more colorful than Kale's, an auburn shade with a thin collar, full sleeves, and hems descending to his knees. The thin embroidery lining his cuffs and hem and collar were probably white at one point. Now they've taken a pearlescent sheen, despite Culver's obsessive fussing over his clothing. He reaches into the fold of his dele and withdraws an object far smaller than Kale expected. It's a stained disk, not unlike a cross section from a barkless tree limb, with four irregular black beads embedded on one surface. "You mean this?"

Kale accepts the disk and it nearly slips from his hands. Smooth as porcelain, dense as a stone. "It's heavy."

Culver nods. "It's endensed whaletusk, which isn't exactly light to begin with."

Kale is familiar with endensing. It's an artificer technique that summons the Imala to manipulate hydration. It works on most natural materials, condensing all pockets of air into hardened liquid, thereby shrinking and strengthening an object.

"These here," and Culver indicates the black protrusions twinkling in the light of Kale's lamp, "are lodestones. Don't ask me how they're tuned. What I do know is this ..." He lowers his voice, gently plucks the object from Kale's hands, and turns it over to expose the disk's flat underside. There's a complex engraving artfully chiseled into the center. "... that's the master artificer's signature. He puts that on keys made for the Triumvirate. You wanted into Stravhelm. This should do it, and more."

Kale can hardly believe it. *The Triumvirate.* Magus Kalderys. Magister Obsydia. His Presence, Sovereign Intemrus. Stravhelm is where mancers become named and where the Triumvirate resides and rules, all with their respective silent adherents and their chitin-clad sentinels. In that shining palace are the barracks, the nursery, the library, the cells, and Kale's destination: Lahuvot's Lake. He tries to still his racing emotions. *This is it.*

"How did you get it?" Kale asks.

"The usual way. Some adherent brought it to us to be dismantled for the lodestones. Usually, they're cracked or broken or at least chipped when we get them. This one ... well, look at it. It seems flawless."

Indeed it does. "But if it's not broken, why was it sent to be dismantled?"

Culver shrugs. "My best guess is a lodestone is out of sync. I wouldn't be able to tell either way. I don't tune lodestones or interrogate adherents when they visit."

"So then this might not work?" Kale asks. The sudden hope this thought brings is unwelcome. He planned for this, anticipated it, waited for it. There is no room for second thoughts.

"Might not," his friend says.

Kale's nerves are rattling, his fingers trembling. He doesn't trust himself to speak too much. He hasn't told Culver his intentions. There's no way his friend would have gone through with this if he had.

"So we're clear ..." Culver's expression is stern. "... you're going in there for some medicine. Then you do what it takes to get rid of that key."

"Yes," Kale says, without meeting his friend's eyes. The pretense he used was that he'd collect healing remedies, particularly ginger tonic, for his neighbors who suffer from negation sickness. It's a lie, and one he's not proud of. The truth is that he hasn't provided his neighbors that sort of help in some time. The young residents of Basalt Tier assist in training, negating consonant attacks and taking unspent energy upon themselves. This leaves them incapacitated and bed-bound, feverish and throwing up. A good many die in this process, particularly those who linger in Basalt Tier too long, never managing to graduate to Andesite Tier. The ruling body in Stravhelm considers this acceptable loss. There was a time Kale did everything he could to ease his neighbors' suffering. He'd empty their sick bowls, swap their sheets, clean their dorms. But as time passed and he watched one young exemplar after another die despite his care, he withdrew from the effort. It became too painful to observe signs of improvement one day only to return the next and find them stiff and cold. Kale couldn't save them. And being immune to negation sickness, he couldn't join them either. Now all that remains of those duties is Kale's maintenance of the liana vines he planted years ago in their windowsills. He can prune and water the lianas without being seen, without ever meeting or speaking to the residents. The plants serve to freshen the air and hopefully provide a more comforting view than the plain grey rock of their dorm or the city wall. In the end, it means little more than anything else Kale is capable of. They still die.

"I'll get the medicine, then get rid of this key in the jungle," Kale says. Also a lie. He'll navigate the underbelly of Stravhelm until he finds Lahuvot's Lake, the subterranean pool of molten earth where enemies of Ausgan are given their final bath, and he'll join them, leaving not a trace of himself or this contraband key. He meets his friend's eyes. "Nothing bad will come to you, I promise."

"You either," Culver says and smiles. "I don't have a lot of friends."

Kale returns as authentic a smile as he can. Truth is, he's not sure if Culver has any other friends. Other andesites are deep in studies of channeling Imala, and reluctant to include Culver. Kale assumes it's because Culver associates with a basalt. Unlike Kale, Culver shows promise in summoning, and has some skill at supersensory perception. Maybe if Culver didn't spend time with Kale, he'd have a brighter future. Kale won't live to see it, but he hopes for it.

Culver's still watching him, and Kale becomes aware that he's let the silence slip on for an awkward amount of time. The quiet of Basalt Tier is broken by the muffled moans and retches of Kale's sick neighbors. A lonely breeze whistles through something sharp, something broken. Kale used to envy his neighbors. They're at least acting to plan. They have a distinct future in front of them, if only death. Today, at last, so does he.

"I don't know how you stand it." Culver shivers, rising to his feet, averting his eyes from the window.

I don't. It has broken me once and for all. Kale doesn't say that. Culver wouldn't benefit from that much truth.

Kale stashes the key within the bedding on his cot and rises as well. "I'm off to the Elucidatorium," he says. "Proctor Alika has new exemplars today."

"Ashmancer Haik is joining the class, isn't he?" Culver asks with a dour expression.

Kale groans. "You had to remind me."

Culver chuckles. "Just do your invisibility trick so he doesn't see you."

"You know it doesn't work like that."

"How exactly does it work?"

Kale shrugs. "I don't know." *... and it looks like I never will.*

Culver dons a smile. "Chin up, Basalt. Keep that key in mind. Find solace in it."

Kale smiles back without meaning to. "I will."

7

A Demonstration of Consonance

AUSGAN

The Elucidatorium

Proctor Rhyolite Alika stands with hands folded, smiling while watching the young initiates fill the rows of the Elucidatorium by twos and threes. They're a flurry of red deles, red cheeks, black hair, youthful energy. This is their first week as initiates, which means that for most it's their first time outside Erudition since induction. They'll be new to the jungle and experiencing some amount of overload, particularly if they've learned the basics of supersensory perception. Proctor Alika never tires of witnessing the ravenous curiosity of the young. They express it in comically exaggerated responses to nearly any stimulus, craning their heads this way and that, jumping at every howl and chirp and caw from the canopy, marveling at the line of bone ants transporting a dismantled fish. He smiles patiently, allowing them time to take in their surroundings.

Alika is vaguely aware of the green eyes of a score of lehua setuar watching from above. They're tree spirits, and quite skittish. Nothing draws the inquisitive spirits like the wonder of the young. They observe with eyes like orbs, hair-like tufts the color of lehua flowers rising from their small heads. It would do the students no good to try to see them. With this many present, they'd blend into the leaves before being spotted, becoming more like flowers than they already appear. As Alika understands, the spirits are more amiable toward Ausgan natives than exemplars. If that's true, Alika envies natives. It's taken him years to earn the setuar's trust. He hums to them when he's alone and they enjoy it. That must remain a secret though. The accepted stance of Stravhelm is that communicating with setuar is native magic and borderline blasphemous.

The Elucidatorium is a memorial to a more violent time. It's a jungle amphitheater ten miles east of Erudition, halfway between the holy city and the coast. The amphitheater is comprised of a massive pyroclastic boulder which was thrown from the volcanic Mount Adenhelm in one of her more violent fits. The boulder split the clouds like a comet, impacted the jungle, and cracked cleanly in half. In the centuries since His Presence Intemrus put the volcano to sleep, the two symmetric boulders settled, sank, and the jungle forgave the stone's offense. Today, one half of the boulder still stands straight as ever, while the other rolled onto its side and has all but been inhaled by the earth. Etched across its vertical side, the standing half has a mural portraying curling lofty clouds, lines of driving rain, edged earth, and a sun glaring down over all. These represent the basic elements an aspiring consonant exemplar might one day manipulate. The other boulder half has been chiseled into rows for seating, all cut semicircle to face the mural and the stage at its foot. Cloud sweeper trees—acacia bolds, titan myrtles, sagacious mahoganies— tower over the amphitheater, forced by the surrounding jungle to press inward and intermingle their vine-laden limbs overhead, offering their shade. Aside from the seating and the mural, the trodden footpath is all the evidence of mankind for miles in any direction.

Basalt Kale is the last to arrive, exiting the jungle in his threadbare grey dele and taking his place in the front row, sitting head and shoulders taller than those around him. Alika gives him a greeting nod, but Kale looks distracted.

"Resonations, students," Alika says. "I am Proctor Alika."

The responding "Resonations, Proctor Alika" is a discordant mess, but they'll have plenty of time to improve that.

"You are consonant exemplars," Alika says. "That means you're chosen by the Imala. You were discovered and gathered from among the native population shortly after your birth. Our chaplains brought you to Erudition to train in consonance. To fulfill your blessing. Your purpose."

The dull expressions of the young initiates demonstrate how little his words impressed them.

"Now, what is that purpose? Why were you brought here?"

No one attempts an answer. *Good.*

"Let's start at the beginning. Generations ago, before Stravhelm and Erudition, a civilization inhabited the northern island of Redemier." He stretches a hand northeastward—not that the distant landmass can be seen from here. "You might have heard it called the cursed island. This was before the curse.

"In that civilization, a young enthusiastic student of nature uncovered secrets never before known by mankind. He determined that the right melody, sung at the right pitch, and at the right place and time, could produce unexpected effects. To outsiders, it looked like magic. In fact, it still does."

That perks up Alika's audience. All but Kale, whose mind seems to be far distant.

"I refer, of course, to Sovereign Intemrus, the founder of consonance. Around that time there was an unfortunate event that split the population. A malicious inhabitant of the island deceived the people, turning them against one another in an attempt to destroy them. For that Deceiver's purposes, his curse worked. The population split. The sovereign fled west from Redemier, bringing with him his pupils and their families and all who valued enlightenment and believed in the potential of consonance. He made his way to Ausgan, where his songs impressed the native population. In short order he founded the city of Erudition. Now, would anyone care to guess who led the population who fled east, to the island Fohrvylda?"

Hands leap into the air. Alika points at an initiate in the back row with slumped shoulders and hair nearly covering his eyes. He doesn't know the youth's name yet, but that will come.

"Vretos the heathen," the boy says.

"The heathen *king*," Alika says. "His weak mind was corrupted entirely by the Deceiver, and he's spent every moment since plotting our sovereign's demise. *Our* demise. Only the eternal vigilance of our timeless sovereign has protected us, our city, the natives, and the entire island of Ausgan. But the day will come when Vretos gathers his fleet and sets out over the Faithless Sea toward our shores, with our annihilation as his sole purpose." Alika speaks reverently. "Does anyone know the name of this event?"

This time the hands rise slowly, the initiates almost cowering beneath them. Alika points to an initiate.

"The Heathen Tide," the exemplar says in a low voice.

"The Heathen Tide," Alika confirms. "And *that* is why we are here. As I mentioned, you and I and every other exemplar in Erudition were chosen from the native population because we showed receptiveness to consonance. We were inducted as exemplars into the nursery in Stravhelm. And now you sit before me, initiates. You will learn to sing, learn martial arts, learn trades. In time you will move to Basalt Tier, where your study of consonance can truly blossom. You'll practice supersensory perception, to observe nature in greater detail than is possible with empirical senses alone. You will negate during consonance training. Some of you will graduate to andesite, where you'll learn summoning and channeling. Some will graduate from there to rhyolite, where you'll combine your learned skills and even fashion your own song. As rhyolites, you will take on a specialty, earn a title, rise up to support our mancers. You may even move to Stravhelm to become a mancer, assisting and supporting the Triumvirate: Magus Kalderys, Magister Obsydia, and Sovereign Intemrus himself. But no matter what rank we achieve, the sovereign has a plan for each of us. We *all* have a place in Ausgan's defense against the Heathen Tide."

The initiates are spellbound, excited, surely imagining themselves decked in armored carapace and chitin, weaponizing nature against the bloodthirsty heathens. Alika smiles at their excitement, but as always finds it awkward to mention this path and stir their imaginations in front of Kale. The truth is, some of these initiates will never progress beyond basalt, just like Kale. But unlike him they will die young. Kale is the first and only basalt to not succumb to, or even be affected by, negation sickness.

Alika paints a studious expression on his face. "Would anyone care to see a demonstration of consonance today?" he asks nonchalantly.

The young initiates nearly fall over themselves in excitement, raising their hands and shouting affirmation. Kale gazes at his own feet, starkly immune to their fervor. Oblivious even. He plucks at a strap on his sandal. Something is troubling him. Considering how much older and larger he is, his fidgeting would be more of a distraction to the class if it weren't for his disappearing trick. Years back, he figured out how to reduce his imprint against perception, making him less tangible to the observable spectrums of light, sound, smell. Alika isn't sure how he does it but has come to learn self-loathing is a key ingredient. He employs this talent while tending to his basalt neighbors, to hide from their perception. Alika, who knows Kale better than most, has learned what to look for and so the effect is lessened for him. Besides, you don't spend as much time as Alika does outside the city walls without sharpening your supersensory perception. Not if you want to live.

"I thought you might." Alika smiles at their youthful passion. "First, please indulge me for another moment. Consonance is a song to the Imala. You've heard of the Imala. They're responsible for all order, and therefore life. Using supersensory perception, we observe, recognize, and glorify their accomplishments with our voices. They repay us by loaning us temporary command of their power. To help illustrate their place, imagine a bowl of water on a table. Inside the bowl are fish, crabs, and sand. For the bowl's inhabitants, this may as well be the ocean. The Imala are represented by the bowl. If you remove the bowl, everything in it will cease to exist as is. The ocean becomes a puddle. The fish and crabs die. In the same way, remove the Imala and most every organism, planet, and even star will cease to exist as is."

Judging by their expressions, the analogy is marginally effective at best. One hand climbs carefully into the air. Alika recognizes her as Initiate Gallis, already notorious among proctors for her curiosity and attention to detail. Particularly details disclosed unintentionally.

Alika points at the initiate. "Yes?"

"You said, *most* will cease to exist?" Her voice squeaks in her attempt to be heard.

Alika smiles. "Yes, most. That is another lesson for another day. Life existed before the Imala. But it wasn't humanity, nor any friends of ours." The class does not return his smile, least of all Gallis, who seems to be contemplating her next questions. Alika considers the details he could afford to omit for younger audiences. He continues before she can derail further. "We sing to attract the Imala. This is summoning. Skilled summoners use supersensory perception to determine the exact barometric pressure, the specific composition of the air, the percentage of feldspar in those benches and what temperature they need to reach to melt. They can identify the plant life that lives under a shrub and predict the breeze before witnessing evidence of it. Some can even determine your emotional state from a distance by your body's imprint.

"Next is channeling. Channelers use the summoned energy to make a specific change to their surroundings. Heating a dish, cooling water, drying a dele, sparking a fire to life. This is how His Presence Intemrus shifts clouds, wind, and moisture and directs rain away from Mount Adenhelm and toward the native villages in the south. That's why the volcano has never awoken—"

"Is Intemrus the strongest of all?" a voice calls out. Alika didn't see the source, but they interrupted him outright and failed to use any honorific. Before he can reprimand them, chattering erupts.

"Of course he is, he's immortal." From another initiate.

"Magus Kalderys is stronger than him. He controls lightning."

"But Magister Obsydia controls Kalderys."

Laughter ensues.

"Enough," Alika bursts, louder than he intended. "Use honorifics when referring to the Triumvirate. Don't be vessels for idle banter. That's for the natives."

Kale jumped at Alika's outburst, which startled the initiates to his left and right. He must have been deep in his disappearing. This irritates Alika further.

"Summoning, channeling, these are why we sing. We train with batons and staves and fusils, but our enemies bear steel. However ungrateful an act that may be, steel is stronger than carapace, scale, or chitin. Even endensed. The heathens have spies in Ausgan. We must quell rumors and gossip with discernment or we give our enemies footholds. Be patient. In time you will build wisdom. With wisdom you earn truth. But truth without wisdom can be turned against you."

The class sits browbeaten, only a scattering of initiates risking eye contact with Proctor Alika. Kale gazes off into the boughs of the jungle, entirely detached from the class once again. Alika smooths the front of his dele, has a clarifying breath. Enough wasted time. He stoops to collect a stone then stands and holds it aloft. "Suppose we'd like to heat this rock to twice the temperature of its surroundings. The summoning will be simple, as this requires a relatively small amount of summoned energy, and therefore minimal attention from the Imala. The channeling will proceed as long as we want to maintain that change of temperature. When the summoner stops singing, the channeler expends the available energy and balance begins to return. With every action a channeler calls into being, its resolution has the opposite effect. If done correctly, the stone simply cools. But if channeling is interrupted before the summoned energy is spent, the return to balance is abrupt and unpredictable. Does anyone know the name of this reaction?"

The class is markedly less enthusiastic now. This part is less pleasant. And it seems no one is going to offer an answer.

"Basalt Kale?" Alika says.

Kale clears his throat. "It's called atavism," he says without looking up.

"Thank you," Alika says. "Complications arise when there is asymmetry between energy summoned and energy spent. This asymmetry is dissonance. If the energy doesn't suffice for the intended channeling, it simply fails. But when more energy is summoned than needed and the channeling fails to expend it, atavism occurs. These are rarely pleasant. Sometimes dangerous. Sometimes catastrophic. You will learn that dissonance is common during training, particularly because our younger summoners and channelers are entirely different parties. Channeling during high stakes or high intensity situations is also ripe for error. Luckily, our sovereign discovered a means to control dissonance and minimize its effects."

At this, Kale reduces his imprint drastically, becoming nearly imperceptible even to Proctor Alika. Alika can't help but marvel over the ability. When he first observed Kale negating his own presence, he assumed it was some advanced technique. But no. Kale doesn't sing, summon, or channel. He can't use supersensory perception. And so he throws his efforts into martial arts and not existing. Aside from being impervious to negation sickness—another anomaly of his—Basalt Kale is below average. He, like other basalts, used to negate with the intrants and adepts. That came to a stop after an incident that happened years ago wherein, by some freak accident, one of the adepts training with him abruptly ceased to exist, or *went missing* as the report goes. Kale was relieved of his training duties during the ensuing investigation. It was deemed an accident with no malicious intent. But since then Kale has not been assigned any significant role. It seems most of Erudition has forgotten about him. Excepting of course the portion of the population that knew the other exemplar and believe Kale owes some restitution.

"We resolve dissonance with negation," Alika tells his class. "Basalt Kale?"

Kale's shoulders droop and he reluctantly rises to his feet, rubbing his palms on his dele. He positions himself beside Alika, facing the class but watching some point far behind them. He's taller than even Alika, and is noticeably uncomfortable under the scrutiny of the class, despite that he's been assisting in Alika's classes for years. The initiates watch him closely. Some lean over to their neighbors and whisper behind cupped hands. Proctor Alika scowls at them. So much for quelling rumors.

"Initiates, please offer Basalt Kale the same respect you would me. He's a most gifted negator. The best I've ever seen in fact, despite his humble title." Alika smiles at Kale. Kale tightens his lips, as if that is the furthest thing from a compliment he could ask for.

"Kale if you would, please expound on negation for today's class." Alika must swallow his annoyance at Kale's perpetual sheepishness.

However bad he thinks he has it, he's still an exemplar in the holy city and there are still duties for him. It could be worse. He could be a native.

Kale clears his throat again. Anticipation thickens in the air. *Just talk about negators, Kale. You've done it a hundred times.* In the lengthening silence, one of the students hisses so loudly her words reach Alika, and inevitably Kale. "Maybe he's negated his voice." Hushed laughter trickles out.

A frown passes over Kale's face. His chest rises and falls as he takes a silent breath. Just as Alika worries he'll sink deeper into his own mind, his lips curl in a momentary smile, as if something nice occurred to him. Kale lifts his chin and eyes the young exemplars.

"Negation is the act of offending the Imala," Kale says, "which is surprisingly easy considering they put order to all of existence."

An exemplar lets slip a chuckle at this. Another couple smile. Unease melts from Kale's shoulders.

"Unlike summoners and channelers, negators aren't supernaturally enlightened about our surroundings. Negating doesn't require supersensory perception. In fact, it's better that we're essentially blind, stuck knowing what our animal senses alone can tell us. Such as ..." He swings his head to and fro. "... the sun's out."

More snickering from the students. Alika cocks his head to one side. Whatever occurred to Kale has him in a better mood. In fact, he seems to nearly be enjoying himself.

"Whereas summoners draw the Imala's favor by observing the sanctity and beauty of the natural world, negators offend the Imala by not caring." Kale smiles at his class. "And let me tell you, practice makes perfect."

Alika raises an eyebrow. This is a side of Kale with which he's not familiar. Perhaps he should consider a script.

"Kale, please tell us about atavism," Alika says.

Kale sobers. "Atavism is ... complicated. It's the opposite of what the channeler had in mind and it uses up whatever energy's unspent. But unlike channeling, it's nearly impossible to predict. The negator must absorb that unspent energy. Otherwise, it can become sudden driving hail, or a toxic steam burst on the far side of Mount Adenhelm, or a tremor under the Faithless Sea that causes a tidal wave to rise up and crush fishing villages—"

"Or any other calamity," Proctor Alika cuts in, hoping to curtail the horror now evident in the round eyes of the exemplars. "All of which we'd obviously prefer to avoid—isn't that right, Basalt Kale?"

Kale blinks, collects himself. "Of course. The unspent energy ideally goes to negators, who then get sick." He trails off, as if hearing the words himself for the first time, despite that he is finally back on track. "Nausea, dizziness, fatigue, breathing problems, skin problems. Always a fever. In fact, the more energy a negator takes on, the hotter the fever." Kale stops, watching the ground with a troubled expression. Judging by the faces of the students, Kale's unease is infecting them. Kale turns concerned eyes on the class. "Some of you will learn the hard way. This is why Basalt Tier is full of the sick and suffering. It's why we—"

"Die young?" The brassy voice comes from the path, where Ashmancer Haik strides into the amphitheater flanked by two andesite sentinels. He wears a dele made of hand-sized plates of pyromollusk chitin, ranging in color from magenta at his knees up to burnt crimson at the angular shoulders, and the short, tight collar. His spiky black hair could pass for a wayward sea urchin nestled on his head. He's taller than his sentinels who flank him on either side. They wear long-sleeved dark grey deles, black vellum boots, and chitin helms. A ridiculous choice of outfit in Alika's opinion. Haik doesn't even wear a helmet out here. After their miles hiked from Erudition, they cannot be comfortable.

The leather straps over all their shoulders tell Alika of the fusils on their backs. Imala forbid they walk anywhere without lethal weaponry. Alika needs no sensory pulse to observe that the setuar above fled outright at Haik's arrival. Meanwhile, his class of impressionable initiates grow reverent, their wide eyes shining. Why do the young so adore destructive arts?

"Ashmancer Haik. Welcome to our lesson." Alika tries to be deferential despite his seniority over the mancer. Haik, contrary to Kale, is overburdened with inflated self-worth. Allowing him the illusion that he is what he'd like to be makes for the smoother path.

Alika recognizes Haik's sentinels, despite the horn-rimmed conch helms overshadowing their faces. Sentinel Bronn and Sentinel Ilbres. They took his class not seven years prior. Since then, their improved status seems to have gone to their heads, as evidenced by their jutting chins, their condescending gazes.

Alika says, "We were just discussing—"

"Negators," Haik says, stopping beside Kale. He smiles knowingly down at the basalt. "And those who wish to be them."

Kale doesn't acknowledge Haik, instead focusing on the distance. Any mirth is gone from his demeanor. Looking at them, you wouldn't guess Haik and Kale are almost the same age. The two have little in common.

Haik turns to the students. He passes his gaze over the class, who sit spellbound with anticipation. "A demonstration, was it?"

The exemplars nod eagerly, rapt.

Haik squats, collects a pebble, then stands. His two sentinels begin to hum in harmony with each other.

"Summoning doesn't require words," Proctor Alika explains to his class. "Not words that could be understood anyway. Each song is improvised because every situation and demand are unique." But however unique a song must be, Haik's pebble song is about as colorful as a cloud.

"Thank you, Proctor," Haik says. "The secret to channeling is recognizing that everything is already full of energy." He squints at the pebble, turns it over, puzzles for a moment as his sentinels maintain their drab harmony.

Haik's concentration relents and his expression softens as if he's found an old friend in that rock. He looks back at his two sentinels, who cease their song. Haik lets the pebble rest on the flat of his palm and exhales. The pebble fizzes, throwing off white sparks. A persistent flame appears upon it, not unlike a tiny oil lamp. Haik says, "You need only unite and excite it."

The initiates gasp and clap their hands.

"Well done, Ashmancer," Proctor Alika says.

Haik ignores him, holding the flaming pebble toward the class as if this trick is something special. It does not warrant the pride he is showing it. He's a named mancer with a dwelling in Stravhelm. The youngest exemplar in Stravhelm, unless Alika's mistaken. The accepted story is that Haik excels at his craft and graduated to mancer early. Alika doesn't buy it. Haik is two years older than Kale. And as far as mancers go, he's barely noteworthy. He is favored by Magister Obsydia, which leads Alika to think his promotion was gained by some other means than his merits in consonance. Why the magister would have promoted him as she did, above those who show promise, he couldn't guess.

Alika allows Haik his moment, while the initiates marvel at the dancing white flame. But this lesson is not about channeling. If it were, he'd have invited someone more gifted than Haik. Alika addresses Kale, "Please demonstrate negation for the class."

Kale shifts his attention to the pebble, with none of Haik's melodrama. A shiver runs up him from knees to shoulders. The flame disappears and a needle of smoke slithers upward. The pebble frosts over in Haik's palm and cracks in half. He drops it as if it nipped him. The fragments clatter to the ground, frost quickly becoming condensation. The initiates cheer as Kale returns his gaze over their heads into the jungle beyond.

"Negators," Haik begins, rubbing his palm on his armored thigh. Judging by the disgust in his tone you'd think he's referring to Fohrvyldan spies. "How would our young exemplars ever train without them? How would they not destroy themselves each time their song is out of perfect resonance?"

Haik lets the question linger. Alika hides his distaste. He doesn't invite Ashmancer Haik to speak to his class. Haik's barely qualified. But sometimes Haik invites himself. He's one of the few channelers willing to work with Kale. The last time Alika politely told Haik his help wasn't necessary, the ashmancer ran directly to the magister, who made a private visit to Proctor Alika to inform him that Haik goes wherever he wants, whenever he wants. Since then, Alika determined that the smoothest course is to tolerate the young mancer while trying to bore him into leaving.

Haik paces in front of the class. "Negators take the damage upon themselves, isn't that right, Basalt? They get sick and scamper off to their beds, sometimes forever."

Kale doesn't respond. He's pulled his hands around to grip them behind his back. It doesn't prevent their faint trembling.

"Except you, Kale," Haik says. "You don't get sick, do you? In fact, you're not much of a martyr at all. Honestly, I'm not sure why Proctor Alika chooses you for his demonstration, you being so odd. So unpredictable." Haik pauses to conspicuously steal a glance at Kale's hands. "You feeling well? A little shaky?"

Kale says nothing. The air has grown still.

Alika clenches his teeth to maintain a pleasant face. He employs Kale for demonstrations specifically because he doesn't get sick. Why needlessly incapacitate exemplars for demonstrative purposes? It's inefficient, never mind cruel. Unless of course you believe basalts are inferior and deserve ailment. Also, Kale has too much free time. The more of it Alika can occupy productively, benefiting rising exemplars, the better. Usually.

"You've never gotten ill," Haik continues. The glint in his eye and his crooked smile warn Alika where he's going. "But one time you got angry, didn't you?"

"Ashmancer Haik," Alika says, trying for his most disarming smile, "you and your sentinels came a long way to be here today and we appreciate it. Demonstrating channeling and negation have been helpful to my class." He faces his students. "Can we all thank the ashmancer for his presence today?"

The class gives a half-hearted ovation, perhaps caught off guard by the abrupt dismissal, hoping instead for more demonstration, or to see Kale and Haik trade blows.

"I'm always happy to oblige, Proctor. Especially in case our young exemplars were of the wild notion that negating was an enviable profession. But while I'm here, I thought the basalt might explain why someone as gifted as himself is merely teaching, rather than combat training with his peers who are younger than him." Haik leans in close to Kale, who hasn't moved since negating. He whispers as if he intends only Kale hears him, but the hiss encompasses the amphitheater. "It's related to the incident, isn't it?"

"I don't know what happened that day," Kale says through clenched teeth.

"Neither do I," Haik laments. "And neither does Adept Thran I'd imagine. Not that we can ask him."

"Thank you, Ashmancer." Alika places himself between Haik and Kale. "Today's demonstrations are complete." It's the kindest way he'll put it. He doesn't want to take Haik down a peg in front of the entire class, but he will.

Haik turns to Alika, taking a step back. "That's a shame. I'd like to one day put him to a test. See how much negation he can withstand. Would you initiates care to see that?"

Of course they would. And they let him know with excited cheering.

"I thought so," Haik says. "We should see how much fire he can extinguish. How much is too much."

A snort escapes Kale, which surprises Alika and apparently Haik. Kale matches Haik's gaze, and there's an unusual energy behind his eyes. "I'm ready when you are," he says.

Haik's eyebrows climb high. He wasn't expecting a response, and definitely not compliance. Alika's never seen Kale do more than weather Haik's derision in frustrated silence. There's something going on with Kale today.

Alika interjects himself before the situation can devolve further. "Thank you for the education, Basalt Kale. Please sit. Perhaps we'll arrange another demonstration soon."

With anyone but the ashmancer.

Kale does as he's told, returning to his place between the expectant initiates.

Haik watches Kale incredulously for another moment. He clears his throat and addresses the class. "I would encourage you all to focus your energy preparing to fight the Fohrvyldan heathens rather than your fellow exemplars." He glares at Kale one final time. "Because all threats to Erudition will be eliminated. Wait and see." He turns and leaves, with his silent sentinels in his wake.

Proctor Alika watches him long enough to collect a neutral expression. Haik was friends with Thran, the initiate Kale allegedly disappeared. Despite the sovereign deeming the event an accident, those who were close to Adept Thran have not forgiven Kale. Far from it. Haik isn't careless enough to be perceived questioning the sovereign's ruling, but torturing Kale for it is never beneath him.

Alika turns a smile to his class. "I think for our next demonstration I'll invite Cryomancer Hyrala, who is known for ..." *Being the opposite of Haik.* "... her professionalism."

He hoped to get a smile from Kale, but he's not paying Alika any attention. He's already reduced his imprint to near-nonexistence, rendering him little more than a thought. Looking directly at him, you'd get the impression he's a memory you're seeing, of a time he was there, insubstantial at this moment.

Alika continues his lesson but without much heart. He's worried about Kale but unsure how to help. For the duration of the class, Alika never garners the initiates' attention again, but that's alright. He's long since learned to discourse without concentrating on what he's saying, and a day like today is perfect for such an exercise.

The sun has receded behind the sheer boulder of the amphitheater when Alika releases the class. Kale is among the first to stand, his presence snapping abruptly into focus and startling the initiates around him again. He's two steps from the jungle when Alika calls to him.

"Basalt Kale."

Kale stops but doesn't face him. The initiates file out, giving him a wide berth, eventually leaving the two of them alone. Kale's shoulders lower and he turns.

"Never let someone else tell you who you are and who you will be," Alika tells him.

Kale looks at Alika blankly. There's an odd light in his eyes. "Why do you try to help me?"

Alika is taken aback and momentarily without response. "Because I care about you, Kale. Of course. You know that, don't you?"

Kale gives a humorless laugh. "Sure. I do. But how do you see this all ending for me?"

Alika's puzzlement gives way to confusion. "Ending? What do you mean? I'm considerably older than you. I won't be around to see your ... end." The conversation has taken a dark turn. "What's going on, Kale? I've never known you to stoop to Haik's taunts."

Kale shrugs, and a hint of a smile lifts the corners of his lips despite his empty expression. "Maybe I never actually disagreed with him."

"And today?"

Kale shrugs again and his smile reaches his eyes. "It doesn't matter anymore."

Alika wants to be relieved at Kale's apparent optimism. But something is bothering him and he can't put his thumb on what. Before he can formulate any inquiry, Kale nods at him, making to depart.

"Thank you for caring, Proctor Alika. I mean it. You didn't—you don't have to be nice to me, but you are."

Alika can only shake his head dumbly. This seems like a farewell. "Are you feeling alright, Kale?"

"Better than I've been in some time." He turns and sets off at an energetic jog, disappearing around a bend in the path.

A pang of panic washes over Alika, confusing him further. There is something vacuous about Kale's good mood and it's making Alika anxious, as if there's a detail he missed or something he should have done. "I'll see you next week?" he says.

At first Kale doesn't respond, and Alika finds himself hoping the basalt simply didn't hear him. Then Kale calls back a single word.

"Resonations!"

8

Never Again

AUSGAN
Erudition

Kale ventures out of his dorm like a mouse, into the pale light of a waning moon. There are no strict rules about being out past the dusk count. In fact, for most exemplars it is encouraged. One should experience and learn all the intricacies of wind and weather, day and night. Unique interactions between animals and weather can be observed at every hour. Exemplars seeking to strengthen their supersensory perception should get intimately acquainted with the world the Imala tamed for them. But not negators. Ignorance is their purpose.

So Kale avoids the main street—the fourteen hundred wide, shallow stairs that cleanly intersect the tiers of Erudition, beginning at the eastern gate and ascending Mount Adenhelm all the way to the pale granite fortress that is Kale's destination. That route is under watch day and night by sentinels on Erudition's wall and Stravhelm's towers. Considering how pristine are the bleached stones, even the cracked ones in Basalt Tier, a wandering exemplar would stand out in the moonlight like a wharf rat on a beach. If Kale were surer of his self-negation, he might test the patrol by striding directly up the main stair. But not tonight. Not with what he's holding or where he intends to go.

Kale tries not to think about his invisibility trick. It feels like unexplored potential, still, after all this time. He justifies this, his final journey, by accepting that all he will ever accomplish or explore is behind him. He expected to experience some doubt tonight. Maybe even regret. But one night's hesitation is easily overcome when he considers how many days and months and years of disappointment led to this point. It's over. This sensation is normal. Only a mentally unfit person could march toward their death without some melancholy.

Kale weaves his way up and over the Basalt Tier dorms. The stone cubicles are piled atop one another, with crumbling stairs and a semblance of walking space outside their doors. The whaletusk key weighs down Kale's breast pocket, not letting him forget it for a moment.

Even still, each time it bounces off his chest his heart flutters. This is his last walk. These are his last steps.

Soon enough, he's ascended to Andesite Tier and the difference is immediate. The stone is freckled and smooth. Unlike Basalt Tier, which was carved directly into the mountain's feet, this stone is imported, perhaps from Adenhelm's western face, then cut and stacked to form houses with stone roofs and pronounced edges. A breeze brings to life the vines curling over these dorms' eaves and carries Kale the scent of flowers. Some andesites are still awake and their lamplight spills from windows, creating obstacles of illumination in Kale's path. Melodious voices carry faintly from some windows. You don't hear songs like this from Kale's basalt dormitory. Exemplars on this tier study to be clothiers, boatwrights, artisans, all while working as porters and lower-level sentinels. Their deles are made of fine silk with flowing sleeves and bright sashes.

He arrives at the upper border of Andesite Tier and notes that while it is luxurious in comparison to Basalt Tier, the next one up, Rhyolite Tier, may as well be a different world. On these streets, Mount Adenhelm steepens and the dorms of lower tiers are replaced by multi-floored manses with colored-tile roofs and doors that close. Potted flowers and fruits line the exotic, marbled stone paths. By daylight, hummingbirds and macaws consort on the intricate perches and feeders mounted on each corner. Rhyolites where whatever sort of dele they can dream up. Silk, hide, shell, vellum. Capes and sashes. Necklaces of dazzling chitin, brilliant gems, serrated shark teeth. They study to be sentinels and mancers. Only the most gifted of them will transcend this tier and enter Stravhelm to work toward their own unique name.

Kale's favorite feature of Rhyolite Tier, and one he does not often enough get to enjoy, are the massive windows that are sealed by colorful mosaics. The windows are murals made of translucent fish scales conjoined by thin lines of grey cement, and each one tells a story of Ausgan's history. He's always wanted to experience them all. Yet again comes that disappointment. That regret. Kale's steps slow. If this is his last chance, he can at least savor it.

The first window Kale stops before is taller than his own dorm and as wide as three of them placed side by side. It's lit from within, and the mural's level of detail is striking.

The scene is of two opposing forces. On the left is Sovereign Intemrus atop the East Rostrum, standing tall and thin in a white dele with embroidery the color of a shallow sea. His hands are outstretched. Above him are grey clouds that reach down with claws made of twisting cones of wind. On the right, across a depiction of the Faithless Sea, is a beast standing on a mountain of skulls. Vretos. He's red-eyed and hunched. Jagged brown fur covers his chest and arms and legs. Behind him is a frothing army with long, pointed weapons colored the grey of bleached obsidian.

"*Steel*," Kale whispers. Forbidden art. What advantage it gains in strength, it loses in elemental resistance. Besides, only the terminally malcontent would stoop to hack open the earth and harvest its veins when chitin, bamboo, and stone are so available and the Imala have revealed the secret of endensing.

The image predicts the Heathen Tide, wherein Vretos and his bloodthirsty warriors and beasts will sail over the ocean and the eternal vigilance of His Presence Intemrus and the exemplars of Erudition are all that will protect Ausgan from violent ruin. Or so it goes.

Kale moves on. The next window bears a map, complete with polished wooden plaques with etched words as labels. The image is mostly comprised of the blue of the South Sea, with jagged masses representing an island archipelago shaped like a crescent with points aimed downward. The westernmost landmass is labeled *Ausgan* and is green with rainforests. Above it are sporadic islets and lagoons that wind north and eastward toward the northernmost, central landmass. This one, the largest, is labelled *Redemier*, the cursed island. Apparently it's the home of the Deceiver, an immortal who will set his wild beasts, enormous wolves and birds, after any human who visits his island uninvited.

Continuing eastward and south, connecting the northern and eastern landmasses, is a land feature Kale doesn't understand. It looks like a piece of ceramic was dropped flat and shattered into hundreds of pieces, each one separated but the piece loosely retaining its formation. That section is labelled *The Towers*.

Finally, the easternmost landmass is an ugly grey splat, lifeless as clay. *Fohrvylda*. The heathens' homeland. It apparently stands hundreds of feet above sea level and thus is frigid and unwelcoming. If that's true, no wonder the heathens plan to invade Ausgan. In the middle of the map, separating Ausgan and Fohrvylda, is the Faithless Sea, thus named for its unreliable current. A serpent is portrayed in the middle, the peaks of its long body rising from the surface as dark-green semicircles. Its plaque reads *Tidamora*.

Again, the pain of loss stings Kale's heart, as if staying alive would mean he will one day be able to observe all those locations. Redemier with its mysterious threats. Fohrvylda with its cliffs. The Towers, whatever they are. As if he'll get to experience the fated Heathen Tide and witness Intemrus leading all consonant exemplars in the defense of Ausgan and the total destruction of their enemies. Or their own bloody demise. He knows better. That won't happen in his lifetime. Nothing happens, ever. And this procrastination is serving no purpose but to erode his resolve. He squeezes the whaletusk key and moves on.

Kale arrives on the highest street in Rhyolite Tier, whose upper edge borders the fortress Stravhelm—the pinnacle of the holy city, with its pearlescent towers thrusting skyward like limbless trees. From here he looks down over all of Erudition. He's level with the brink of the city wall and can make out the black silhouette of jungle canopy beyond, shifting beneath the stars. Basalts never get such a view as this. The longing pain strikes again. Is this his last observation of the wider world? Why didn't he sneak up here more often? Was he afraid of getting caught out of Basalt Tier? Why? As if some punishment could compare to what he has in mind tonight.

Kale shakes his head. He anticipated this doubt, but that doesn't make it easier to deal with. Indecision crawls through him, telling sweet lies. He could spend every night like this, exploring the city and appreciating views and wonders that other exemplars never seem to even notice. Is death necessary? He'd remain alone. Culver would continue accommodating him out of the kindness of his heart, and therefore never graduate to rhyolite. Proctor Alika would keep inventing excuses to put Kale's pathetic skillset to use, attempting to educate exemplars who'd rather be anywhere else. Eventually tension with Haik would escalate to a fight. Alika would step in to mediate and probably earn Haik's wrath—which seems to mean the magister's wrath as well— and the gentle old proctor would pay some undeserved price for Kale's sins.

Kale sighs, his resolve solidifying. His future in Erudition is pointless at best, more often a scourge on anyone who fails to reject him. By the time his absence is noticed, it will be appreciated. Erudition and all within it will have improved.

With heart pounding and hands clammy, breath coming in shallow gasps, Kale arrives at that fated slice of shadow between two rhyolite manses. He found this alley several weeks ago on a similar night run. He'd followed it down, expecting the same dead end he finds at the end of most every alley, but had found a hidden locked door instead that clearly led under Stravhelm. From that moment, this journey began to take form in his imagination. This solution. *Tonight it concludes.* Excitement trills within him, nearly making him chuckle.

A gust of saline wind howls abruptly, invading Kale's dele, snatching loose leaves from a nearby stone vase and blowing them toward the stars. Kale watches as they rise and spiral and flutter down over Erudition, toward that pond of stagnant shadows that is Basalt Tier. Never again will he skulk there missing sunlight, pruning weeds. Never again will he grip his ears and long for sleep as his neighbors whimper and moan. Never again will he rack his mind, trying in vain to invent some solution to their suffering. His eyes sting and his chest trembles. *Never again.* Is this relief? Fear? Anger?

The alleyway is shorter this evening. Before Kale's ready he stands facing the vertical granite expanse that is the base of Stravhelm. The moon, while bright, isn't in a position to illuminate the indentions of the door's lock, but Kale finds it quickly enough. Four indentions, irregularly set and at varying depths. He presses the key against it, rotating to find the fit for the lodestones, trying to prevent it from clattering in his shaking hand. What if it doesn't work? What if he came all this way just to have to return to Basalt Tier?

The whaletusk key clicks into place with the sound of a chitin boot on marble. A narrow rectangle of stone smoothly disassociates itself with the rest of the wall as if by magic, angling inward with a hiss. Kale presses the door. It offers no more resistance than a shell curtain. It must feature korundite hinges, like Erudition's main gate, because despite surely weighing hundreds of pounds, it moves silently and with minimal effort from Kale. Utter darkness lies beyond, and dry, frigid air assaults his face. Chills run down his neck. The blackness is so complete he nearly backs away. Instead, he plucks the key from the lock and breaches the dark. He'd leave the key in place, but for Culver's sake the key must share his fate.

Once inside, he turns and presses the stone door. It clicks as the lock seals again, pinching off the whistling wind and plunging Kale into perfect darkness. The chill air on his wide eyes is the only evidence they're open. Every scrape of his sandals on the grit of the floor echoes, multiplies, the sounds scurrying all over and throwing off any sense of direction. He forces regularity to his breathing. He would attempt one of those odd meditative poses he's always seeing other exemplars do—the rhystics, as they're called. He would attempt rhystic clarity or calmness or something, but he doesn't know them. All a basalt knows is rhystic subservience. He stashes the key against his pounding heart and reaches for a wall. With one hand against it and one shielding his face, he takes a cautious step, then another.

Kale can't help but relish the icy suspense gripping him, the horror of being trapped, being caught, maybe even being tortured. It's not purely fear running through him. There's something else as well. *Excitement.* Night runs always contain a number of thrills. Though never like this. He's not felt this alive since ... well, maybe he's never felt this alive. Why not? Has he simply been living wrong? Is there a better way?

When Kale was young, a couple years older than Proctor Alika's typical initiate, Alika had sat him down one day after some exemplars had treated him roughly. He'd felt bruised, upset, powerless, and not for the first time.

"Do you know what I do when something's bothering me?" Alika asked Kale.

"Sniff flowers?"

"I send a prayer up to the sovereign."

Kale had dwelt on it a moment. *"Does it work?"*

"It helps. You know, Intemrus sees all. And it's not his will that his exemplars suffer. Any of them."

Kale never had prayed because he'd never believed himself to be an exemplar. If the sovereign truly saw all, Kale figured, he wouldn't allow

Kale to stagnate in Basalt Tier. Besides, young negators suffer all the time. So either Alika lied, or Intemrus' Will is inconsistent.

But tonight, sidling along in the darkness beneath Stravhelm, headed for his own death and somehow displaced from his body as if watching from a distance, he feels an undeniable urge to try. And so he closes his eyes, for all the good it does in this lightless corridor, and whispers a prayer to the one whose stronghold he is invading.

"Sovereign Intemrus, if you truly see all, then please show me something. I don't know what. If you care about the suffering of your exemplars, prove it. If you care at all about me, stop me."

He has no expectations of the prayer, but it comforts him. It feels a fitting goodbye. Lahuvot's Lake is supposed to be on the far side of the cells, where enemies of Ausgan are imprisoned. Apparently it stinks of rotten eggs. Kale will either find that pool of magma or he won't. If he doesn't, maybe he'll eventually find something worth living for—not that he can imagine what form that could possibly take. If he does find the pool, perhaps Ausgan will thank him for bathing in it.

9

His Damning Secret

AUSGAN
The Cells under Stravhelm

Rathyn awakens in his prison cell under the holy city. He's on his side on warm rock, wedged against a carven stone wall. He knows he didn't sleep long. You can't down here in Stravhelm's cells. Not when the heat of the air suffocates you and the stench of sulfur gags you.

His neck is stiff. Maybe stiffer than before. His shoulder and hip ache. But those pains pale compared to the stump where his left hand used to be. Remembering it sends him into shivering sobs. And losing tears make him conscious that he can't remember the feel of water on his tongue.

It takes effort but he turns his head. Above is the hexagonal opening for his cell, fifteen feet above. It might as well be one hundred. Beyond it, so distant it shimmers in the dim light, is reddish stone ceiling. He presses his lips together and works his tongue. Slowly, surely, he is able to hydrate his mouth enough to swallow nothing. He clears his throat. Feels like gargling gravel. Pain brings more tears to his eyes. He squeezes them shut. He cannot afford to lose any more water. Although, if dying of dehydration means the end of this, part of him welcomes it.

The scrap of wool from his cloak has slid from his mouth and nose and is bunched around his neck. He doesn't know if it relieves the chore of breathing toxic air. Probably makes it worse. After several shallow breaths he slowly releases his grip on his arm's stub. The throbbing is immediate, as if someone is prying apart the bones of his forearms rhythmically. Again, he pinches his eyes closed and grits his teeth. He pulls the wool over his mouth and nose and readies to pinch the stump again. With his thumb he's able to determine where the bones prod from the cauterized skin. He grips below that. Not so tight the tips of bones grind together. He vomited the last time he accidentally squeezed that hard. Hopefully just tight enough to keep the rest of his blood inside him.

The monk who severed it used a chitin axe and did the deed in one swift motion. The impact of the blade against the red-stained chopping block echoes in Rathyn's head. It set him to chattering, speaking nonsense rather than screaming or groaning as he might have expected. He had urged them to fix it. Begged them. *Look, the fingers are still moving. It's not dead yet. Not dead yet ...*

Then, judging from the searing pain, the hissing, the smell of cooking meat, he's fairly certain they cauterized his wound in molten earth. The act was made ruder by his own hunger, which caused his mouth to fill with saliva at the smell of roasting flesh. He'd gone mad after that. His memory is tainted by nightmares of red-cloaked demons whose hands popped off to fly at him.

Rathyn settles onto his back and tries to control his breathing. If nothing else, the wool offers other smells to distract him from the stench of earth fire. His own sour breath is most obvious. Then sweat. Then a hint of spice, perhaps some broth he spilled on it before he was arrested. It's oddly comforting that all the tasks he's invented to pass time take significantly longer with only one hand. As if the passage of time could fix anything. At least it leads to some perversion of sleep. Eventually, peace.

He turns his head, checks the stone floor for new contents. Nothing. He's not seen water or food since they severed his hand, whenever that was. They're probably done with him. But if so, why not take him to the lake of fire? What purpose did it serve to leave him alive in the cell? They'd questioned him over and over. He'd tried to be strong at first, for all the good it did. They'd dripped molten stone on his palm, causing him to squeeze his fist, which caused the flesh on his fingers to fuse with his palm. And when he'd stopped screaming, they did it again on the back of his hand. At some point during the process, words began to bubble out of him. His failing senses managed to protect his damning secret. He did that by hiding that secret behind a mental image of his daughter who, along with his entire village, the monks may have punished because of him. Instead, he implicated Hargrim, a village far from scrupulous but not deserving of whatever hell his allegations will bring down on them. But then, even after he told them all he could think of or make up, they had not stopped the interrogation. Not until his hand was gone and his consciousness and sanity ebbed and flowed like the ocean's tide.

Maybe he's here as an example for someone else. Whoever follows him into this cell will see what becomes of treacherous goat farmers like Rathyn. And then what? They cooperate? Meet a better end? Maybe he's here to observe whatever cruel judgment the monks administer to Hargrim's citizens because of his words. Maybe then he will break.

It is pointless to think about. He can't change it. He stares upward. The monks used some sort of ladder to access his cell. They did something with a bone disk and the rungs of the ladder disappeared into the stone itself. Rathyn tried to find it when he first arrived but he only saw the outlines of the rungs, a circular impression in the stone, as if something was to be placed there. Until he lost his hand, Rathyn examined the circular impression, tried twisting it or poking the small indentions inside. It never budged. The ladder would not extend for him.

He's arrived at his final task. He works his tongue in his mouth some more. Tries to hydrate his lips and gums. Once he's tested his lips to determine they won't crack when he opens his mouth, he calls out.

"Hey."

It's more a croak. He clears his throat.

"Hey!"

It's louder. And the vertical stone certainly carries his voice up and out of the cell. He doesn't expect sympathy from the monks, or even a response if they're there. They already proved they're the demons he suspected them to be. But maybe there's another cell next to his. He doesn't wish this suffering on anyone else. Or he didn't before. Now he longs for anything. Anyone to talk to, even if only to torment him. Something besides the resounding quiet of this chamber, with always that vaguely audible hint that somewhere, something is burning.

"*HEY!*" he shouts.

It hurts so bad tears well in his eyes once more. He considers dabbing them with the wool and sucking it dry. He doesn't have the energy to yell again. If only the monks would drop a length of rope or just a sharpened shell. He'd do the rest.

Through his tears, something out of place appears above—a shadow in a shape not unlike a person's head is leaning out over his cell. A desperate energy takes him. He's reaching upward. His heart tells him it is no monk. This person's too curious.

And now the shape is gone. Rathyn's outstretched hand wavers beyond a sheen of tears. The shape was probably never there in the first place.

"No," he calls, feeling the despair close in. "Come back. Please."

He has no control of himself. He's weeping uncontrollably, squeezed into a ball on his side. Damned hope. Desperation doesn't seem so dark without it.

"Who are you?" says a voice. The dialect is a monk's. The voice is a boy's, maybe Rathyn's daughter's age. Rathyn is too filled with manic craving to control himself.

"Please, water. Water. There's a cup ... a rope ... please!"

The ceiling grows dim. Too much exertion. Maybe he's hallucinating. Either way, he's burning what little energy is keeping him conscious. Perhaps hope has its merits after all. He closes his eyes. It is time to try to sleep again. He can't afford to waste this momentum. Unconsciousness is your only respite in hell.

He gets tucked against the corner once more. He's wrapped his fingers around the stump of his forearm when he hears a wooden object strike the stone behind him. He turns over before the stiffness sets in.

It's too dark to be sure. But it looks like a bucket, at the end of a thin rope, and surrounding it is the sheen of something spilt.

Rathyn is on his knees. He thrusts his hand into the bucket. Cold water. He splashes his face and gasps. He does it again. Then again. He cups some and soaks his lips with it. Oh, sweet relief. He tries to ignore the demon in the back of his mind reminding him all his misery will simply start anew. Satiating his thirst will compromise his voyage toward release. Not that he could stop himself from drinking if he tried.

He's laughing. Choking down water, trying not to gag on it. Soaking his face, his head. A third of the bucket is gone when he hears the voice above shushing him.

"Be quiet," says the visitor.

Rathyn composes himself. He embraces the bucket and wraps his legs around it. In that moment he knows two things as facts. If someone tries to lift that bucket, they'll have to lift him too—not that the rope will support him. And, whoever sent this down is not his captor.

He clears his throat. For the first time in a long time, it doesn't hurt.

"Who are you?" he says, looking up at the silhouette. He is surprised by the saneness of his voice. And with his new lucidity, he wonders what else of himself he's lost besides a hand.

His visitor is silent a moment before answering. "My name is Kale. I'm ... passing through. Who are you?"

"Call me Rathyn. Thank you for the water." He watches the shadowed guest. "Passing through? I take it you're no keeper. Where are you going?"

Another silence. "Lahuvot's Lake."

Rathyn's heart pangs in alarm. Everyone knows that's where executions take place. The spies, blasphemers, disruptors, and whomever else the holy city grows tired of. Is there an execution soon? Is it his own? Rathyn tries to keep his voice free of fear. "The magma bath, huh? What's happening there?"

Yet another silence. Rathyn is starting to suspect either the boy is reluctant to tell the truth or making up answers as he goes. "I thought I'd have a dip." His low voice carries neither dishonesty nor humor.

Rathyn's responds carefully. "There are simpler ways to kill yourself."

The words echo.

Kill yourself.

Kill yourself.

Kill yourself.

Silence stretches. The monk speaks at last. "It's important to me ... that I disappear completely."

A chuckle leaks from Rathyn, surprising him. A self-loathing monk? Surely the first of his kind. "By the gods, monk. Do they torture you, too?"

The slight movement in the monk's head conveys that he's dragged his attention from within his mind and onto the prisoner who's interrogating him. "They torture you?"

Rathyn is struck by the apparent innocence of his guest. "Don't you know where you are?"

"Beneath Stravhelm. These are surely the cells. I'm guessing ... you must be a spy?"

Rathyn scoffs. "Imala's blood. I had no idea they keep their own more ignorant than they do us."

The voice offers no reply. Rathyn leans back on his elbows and watches the silhouette, his forearm pulsing anew. He's over the shock of the pain. Self-preservation, that pest, warns him to stall the boy as long as possible. Like rainwater, he'll surely be gone too soon.

"What day is it, boy?" Rathyn asks, despite the dread that question brings.

"I'm not a boy. I'm ... an exemplar." The stranger's confidence wanes with that claim. He doesn't sound convinced. "It's the seventeenth of the fifth moon."

"Seventeenth ..." The word slips out of Rathyn as a wheeze. So he's been imprisoned for over a month. It is at once longer and shorter than he'd thought. The realization puts painful pressure on his heart. Of course he's thought of his daughter since being arrested. But only now does he feel how much he misses her, how much she must be worrying about him. He's missed so much. The boy's innocence, his utter naivety, make Rathyn's teeth clench. He was a baby when he was taken from a village. How quickly the monks brainwash their captured young. Anguish gives way to rage.

"What's so exemplary about you? You training up to be a proper fiend so you can raid our towns and steal our babies? Want to stifle the rain like your precious monk sovereign when you get good and grown?"

Stop talking. He'll take the water away. He'll leave you here alone.

The monk flinches. "I didn't mean offense by that. I only meant ... I don't know what I am."

Rathyn sighs. He doesn't have the energy for anger anyway. "In that case, you picked one hell of a solution, wouldn't you say?"

The monk doesn't respond. Seems he's sinking back into his own thoughts. Rathyn can't make sense out of this visit. But it beats solitude.

"You give me too much credit, exemplar," Rathyn says. "I'm no spy. I might be a blasphemer. Not sure what that is, come to think of it. I'm here because they think I know a dirty secret. If that secret is true, am I still a blasphemer? And if it's false, then why do they care? Why'd they take my hand?"

The boy is quiet. But he hasn't backed away. Was it the secret? Did that get his attention?

"You want to know it, don't you?" Rathyn asks the boy.

Still air is his response. Rathyn could share it. But if the secret is what earned his place here, why would he wish that on anyone, especially a child?

"What secret?" the boy asks quietly.

It reminds Rathyn of his daughter, when the rest of the village has killed their torches and the insects play their song and she brings him some mystery from her day that she's sure only he can resolve.

Tears run down Rathyn's cheeks. "Why do you want to die, monk?"

He hears the boy exhale.

"You can tell me, boy," Rathyn says. "I'm going to die too. Soon enough."

"I've tried everything else."

"I doubt that! You're a damn child, locked in the holy city. What can you have possibly tried?" The boy doesn't move. Rathyn swallows his frustration. He was too harsh. Monks are softer than villagers. "Listen, monk—Kale. Here's an idea for you. Get the hell out of the holy city and have a look around. Go down south and pay my people a visit."

"I'm not allowed to do that."

"Are you allowed to be here?"

Kale exhales in what might be a snicker. "That's different. To visit a village you need permission from the magister."

"Then get her permission."

The boy's head cocks to the side like a curious puppy. He stays motionless so long Rathyn starts wondering if he's still there.

"I don't know," Kale says.

"What are you afraid of? That she'll kill you?"

Kale laughs. "I guess not. So, what's your dirty secret anyway?"

Rathyn shakes his head. "No. I won't do that to you. Maybe there's still some good I can do." *Assuming that saving the life of a monk can amount to good.*

"Down there?"

"Were you planning on getting me out?"

"I don't know how."

"Then yeah. Down here. Maybe I'll save your life."

"Thanks?"

Sounds like Kale is smiling again, which is a damn sight better than when he arrived.

"How about this," Rathyn says. "Forestall your swim in Lahuvot's Lake. Instead go visit a village. If you return and still fancy a dip, I'll tell you my secret. That should guarantee you a swim."

"Alright, Rathyn," Kale says.

"Just know," Rathyn tells him. "You're gonna have your eyes opened when you meet my lot. Once that's done, there's no shutting them back."

"Is that worse than swimming in magma?"

It's Rathyn's turn to laugh. "I couldn't tell you."

The monk's head whips around like something alarmed him. "I've been here too long," he says. And it strikes Rathyn's heart like a chitin mattock.

"No, don't leave yet." He didn't intend it to sound so much like a plea. "I'll tell you the secret."

"I have to go." He's not paying Rathyn attention, instead looking around the chamber.

"I can tell you how to stop them," Rathyn hisses.

"Stop who?"

"The entire Triumvirate."

Kale's attention snaps back to Rathyn. "Why would I want to do that?" he asks guardedly.

Rathyn closes his eyes, rests his head against the stone. "You have no idea, Exemplar."

"*That* is no secret." Kale's smile is audible. He startles. "Untie that rope!"

"... what?"

"On the bucket. You want to keep the water? Free the rope so I can pull it back up and out of sight."

Rathyn tugs at it. The hemp feeds through holes on either side of the wooden bucket, and although it is ratty and worn, he doesn't have the strength to break it. He fiddles with the knot but can't loosen it with only one hand.

"I can't," he says. "Just drop the rope down. They won't find it. And if they do I won't give you up." He wraps the rough hemp around his fist and his legs around the bucket. He will not let go, however this boy responds.

The echo of chitin boots resounds off the high ceiling. Kale's head disappears. Soon the rest of the rope slithers down, coiling into a bulky heap. Rathyn gathers it and stuffs it between himself and the wall, beneath what's left of his shirt.

"Thanks for that," Rathyn whispers. "Now go open your eyes."

He doesn't understand what obligated him to try and help the boy. Maybe monks aren't inherently devious. Maybe they're not beyond redemption.

The hemp rope is thin but strong. Rathyn sighs and leans back on it. The next time he runs out of water, and hope, it'll do just fine.

10

Obsydia's Will Be Done

AUSGAN

The Magister's Tower, Stravhelm

Magister Obsydia reclines beneath the morning sun on the roof of the third-highest tower in all of Stravhelm. She wears nothing but a breeze on her skin and the occasional drop of mango juice on her chin. Gentle fans, stitched of hundreds of sunset honeycreeper feathers and wielded by silent adherents, maintain a perpetual refreshing breeze. Her adherents wear mid-sleeved deles, sequined with glimmering fish scales the color of the sky. They wear vellum slippers to mute their steps. Their job is to keep her young and cost her nothing, not even attention. Obsydia strives to improve daily, but without aging a day. The time will come when she'll need more intensive help with such an endeavor. She looks over at Syvea Tower. Until then she must pamper as aggressively as she trains.

The adherent on her left is struggling to maintain a consistent breeze, despite being warned. Seems she's having problems with her wrist, maybe due to injury sustained while sparring. If fanning proves too complicated a task for her, perhaps she's more suited for a flight off the tower's edge. Obsydia's adherents are vetted carefully. They must be of a particular caliber to meet her needs. They can't stink or be distracting to look at. They must obey without hesitation or reluctance. Their personality should be no more colorful than the polished granite tiles upon which they stand. Their fans must excite the air no more or less than enough to keep sweat from Obsydia's skin. They must be no more watchful than the clouds, yet aware enough to move when she moves, aim their breeze where it is needed, dab away mango juice if it falls.

One of Obsydia's consonant gifts is perception of emotion. It is a rare gift and was crucial to her ascent through the ranks of exemplars. There's never a moment she's not aware of it, even while relaxing. Those adherents who harbor resentment end up scrubbing the exterior of Erudition's wall. Those who gawk at her take the magma bath. Envy and lust are sins. The mancers who competed alongside her during her climb through Erudition underestimated her perception. They all focused on their destructive arts, hoping to impress Intemrus with their ability to sing death to the enemies of Ausgan. Obsydia knew better. She couldn't compete with Intemrus in dealing destruction, and even if she could, that can't be turned on your peers. She could, however, manipulate. Now she makes up one third of the holy Triumvirate, and all who scoffed at her are in their rightful place, beneath her.

"Bring fresh mango. And skyseed. Hand the fan to him." She indicates the adherent standing beside a column with his head forward, his eyes toward the north. The adherent hands off her fan and scurries down the steps. It's pointless to learn their names. Not her business.

Her replacement quickly provides a more strenuous breeze. Obsydia watches the muscles of his forearms as he works the fan. She pours coconut oil from a slender conch pitcher down her chest and over her thighs, then works the oil slowly into her dark, glistening skin. The replacement's eyes remain forward but his pulse spikes. Obsydia considers toying with him further. But he might fail, and he's doing a good enough job. She observes him with a supersensory pulse. His heart is racing and his jaw is tight. He is excited to serve, even if his expression indicates indifference. He'll suffice.

Magister Obsydia's rooftop is a flat hexagon with four tall marble columns on the easternmost corners. Connecting the crowns of those columns are taut ropes of braided liana fiber, and from the ropes hang layers of brightly colored starsilk curtains, able to be pulled closed if Obsydia so desires. This morning she wants the sun on her skin. There is a conch tub that can be filled from the aqueduct system with hot or cold water. A drinking fountain with clean water boiled off subterranean pools then cooled by a duct network the mancers devised. A bell system for summoning adherents or her sentinels, who inhabit lower levels of her tower. Right now her daybed faces east and provides a view of Erudition, the city wall, then over the jungle's canopy all the way to the Faithless Sea. The tall East Rostrum—Intemrus' pulpit—is just visible some eighteen miles away on the sea's edge. South of it, not visible from here, are boatyards and fishing villages. Like a distant blue-grey spire, the East Rostrum stands taller than all around it, lest anyone forgets who holds the power. Or at least, who holds it today. Obsydia smiles. You're only immortal until you're not.

Forty yards to the northeast is the second-highest tower of Stravhelm. It's the sovereign's, from where he sees all. His windows are sealed with large translucent scales. They are angled such that one can see out but not in. Perhaps Intemrus watches the magister now. She assumes he does and has long since gotten comfortable with that possibility. He can't see her thoughts.

South of her tower is Stravhelm's lonely capital tower, Syvea. Tallest and thinnest of all, topped with a pointed spire, none visit that tower but Intemrus himself. His unique key sees to that. The tower is apparently named after someone he lost long ago. A loved one, if that's possible to believe. By Obsydia's observations, Intemrus doesn't suffer the same emotions that define humanity. Maybe he did once.

To the west, behind her daybed, the view is blocked by an impossibly large semi-translucent clamshell. At thirty feet wide and at least that tall, it effectively obscures Mount Adenhelm's jagged pinnacle and the black clouds beyond. Adenhelm's western face is a pocked hellscape of fumaroles and calderas. It is apparently by Intemrus' Will alone that those noxious clouds do not cross the summit and creep over Stravhelm and Erudition. An unfortunate byproduct of that weather manipulation is a perpetual lack of breeze above the holy city, a stagnation of air at the tops of the towers. Luckily, the magister has fans to spare.

Obsydia discovered the gargantuan clamshell deep beneath the Inner Sea and vowed to make it her own. Cryomancer Hyrala orchestrated a song like no other, using her two finest mancers and ten adept summoners. Together they froze a tunnel in the ocean all the way to the sea floor, allowing countless natives passage to tie up and procure the seashell. The song took its toll. Two summoners died of exhaustion, five never sang again. Apparently, there were casualties among the natives as well. Obsydia had the shell mounted upon her tower, calling it a tribute to those exemplars who perished in the effort. Now it's the standard for any who seek to impress her. An exemplar's promotions are merited exclusively by their abilities and consonant progress. But it's not beneath Obsydia to give a slight edge to those who flatter her with gifts. Now and again she'll see a trait in an exemplar she can exploit, even if such an endeavor takes years of cultivation and guidance. Such was the case with Ashmancer Haik.

Her weak-armed adherent has returned with mango and skyseeds on a thin, polished wooden tray, along with a goblet of blood grape wine. She replaces the tray on the granite pedestal beside the daybed and pads away quietly. Obsydia observes her. She's frustrated, but at herself. If she's given another chance at the fan she will try to make up for her shortcomings. The wine was a good start toward redemption. But no need to return her to a task she's already failed once. Perhaps her name will be Fetch.

An adherent in a messenger-orange dele has ascended the staircase and fidgets with her hands anxiously. It is too early for Obsydia's morning engagement. The adherent is nervous. She expects her message to interrupt Obsydia's meditation.

Obsydia heaves a sigh. "Yes?"

"Resonations, Magister. So sorry for the interruption. The negator Basalt Kale seeks an audience. He wishes to discuss ... um, improving himself? I told him you weren't seeing anyone but he ... wouldn't leave."

Obsydia cocks her head. It is her responsibility to monitor and supervise the rhyolites and promising andesites. She makes no effort to keep up with individual basalts. Most have no future. They ascend or they die. Basalt Kale, though, hasn't managed to accomplish either. Lacking any obvious function, he is an anomaly. And not only because of the incident with Adept Thran. He marked himself an enigma early on as far as Obsydia's concerned. She can ascertain anyone's feelings with no effort, even those of the sovereign himself at times, but either Kale is perpetually without emotion, or gifted in keeping his feelings obscured. That's no small task. Perhaps some entertainment will come of this. She stretches her arms over her head, her toes beyond the edge of her daybed, straightens her spine and holds for several long moments.

"Send him up," she sighs at last. "No sentinels necessary."

Obsydia sits up and crosses her legs on her daybed. "I'll only need one fan. You," she says to the adherent with the thick arms. "And you, my hair. Use vitality butter."

The second fanner hangs her fan and returns with a bowl and an endensed driftwood comb. Her pulse has quickened by the time she returns to Obsydia's side. She mixes coconut oil and vitality butter in a heated stone mortar, excited for the opportunity to brush the magister's hair, as well she should be. But she's frightened she'll make a mistake. It's hair brushing, what's to get wrong? At times, Obsydia could stand to mute her perception.

Basalt Kale appears on the landing of Obsydia's roof on unsteady feet. His wide eyes range over the surrounding landscape as he splays both hands out to steady himself. The staircase he ascended spirals upward around Obsydia's tower, circling it several times before arriving here at the top, giving any visitor with a weak stomach plenty of time to lose their nerve. Obsydia had the handrail removed when she took up residence here some fifteen years prior. She doesn't personally need one. And if an individual would fall without one, perhaps it's best they do. She doesn't want sand-gutted klutzes for sentinels or adherents—or even visitors.

"Resonations, Basalt Kale," Obsydia says.

Kale's head whips around and he looks at her. His eyes were wide when he arrived, and seeing Obsydia they stretch even wider. He drops to one knee in rhystic subservience—a stance that involves crossing your forearms on your upright knee and lowering your chin—but not before his eyes dance over her naked body.

"Resonations, Magister," he says to the floor.

Despite his bewildered reaction, his voice is without inflection, and even at close observation his imprint does not betray his feelings. Obsydia senses a challenge. She straddles her daybed and leans forward, her hair-brushing adherent adapting to her new position.

"What brings you today, Kale?" She runs her tongue along the edge of a peeled slice of mango.

"Magister, I humbly request to place my services in the service, um … of Magus Kalderys." His voice shakes but he shifts his eyes from the floor to Obsydia's face resolutely. "I'd like to offer my gift of negation and accompany him during a trip to the southern villages."

Obsydia almost lets her surprise show with a laugh. What a peculiar request. It is bold of an exemplar to request promotion before earning it. Most accept their place. But then, what is his place? He's too old for Basalt Tier. He does exhibit what appears to be immunity to negation sickness, but few other redeemable traits. Except bravery. Because here he is. He would make some mancer a good adherent—he's suitably inept in Consonance—if it weren't for his unpredictability. That's a horrible trait in an adherent. Perhaps she'll toy with him, figure out if he has any use. There's time to kill.

Obsydia leans back on her daybed and places one heel on the corner. For Kale to look in her eyes, he'll have to take in the most intimate details of her anatomy. For those stubborn exemplars who think they can mask their feelings, this typically undoes them. Male or female. She bites the mango and lets juice drip from her chin onto her breast. An adherent appears with a moistened sea sponge and gently but thoroughly cleans the juice away.

"That's an ambitious request, exemplar," Obsydia says. A sheen of sweat has risen up on his forehead and his cheeks have reddened to near burgundy. But his eyes give away no emotions. If his heart is beating she cannot observe it. *Impressive.* "Tell me what you'd offer the magus' campaign."

"I'm proficient in martial arts. I'm gifted in negation. I make a suitable substitute for several negators since I don't succumb to negation sickness. I bet I could even ... perform as well as a prime negator."

The gradual lilt in his voice suggests that his confidence, if that's what this is, waned with that last part. And rightly so. He has never seen a prime negator in training. They belong to the sovereign alone. Perhaps Kale is as gifted as a prime negator, but there's no way he could know that. Ability to negate alone doesn't give him value.

"That's a tall claim." She can't sense his breathing, or his temperature either. Is he attempting to prove his worth? She'd be more impressed if it weren't so annoying. Perhaps she should offer him a few skyseeds. Those aren't allowed to exemplars, as they supposedly promote lustfulness. They do lower inhibition, but she won't resort to that unless she has to. Spoils the fun.

"The magus has a crucial role in our struggle against Fohrvylda and must be accompanied by a select few," Obsydia says. "Those who journey with him have bold hearts. And perhaps you've proven your heart by coming before me today and avoiding my perception. Tell me ... how are you at martial arts? How is your training?"

Now he falters. For a moment he struggles for a response. "As a basalt, my training has not been the strictest. But I train on my own as often as I can. Occasionally with andesites."

Obsydia watches his eyes closely. It is frustrating that she can't read his imprint. No one should be able lie to her. But, aside from general unease, he gives no indication of dishonesty. He is fit. She's heard reports of him training alone, or with that one big porter, Andesite Culver. She could put him to the test by sparring with him. But the effort … not worth it.

"Being a basalt, you've had no formal training in higher rhystic stances, have you?" She knows the answer. Regarding the rhystic stances, basalts need only subservience and negation. Tranquility is a luxury. Dominance, aggressor, and defender are none of their business.

"I have not."

"And summoning? Channeling? Have you trained in these subjects?" He hasn't and she knows it. He's pitch deaf and his musical timing is nonexistent.

"No, Magister. I haven't."

Obsydia sits up once more and observes Kale deeply, yet again to no avail. "Basalt Kale, I'm remembering an incident. Were you, several years back, responsible for the death of a fellow exemplar?"

Kale's eyes drop to the floor and his jaw clenches. For the briefest moment, he fails to keep up his guard. *Shame. Regret. Self-loathing*, even. He's suffered for that ever since it happened and feels doomed to pay for it forever. Worse than that, he doesn't understand what actually happened. And then, just as quickly, his emotions evaporate. He responds in a low voice, "It isn't confirmed that Adept Thran died."

"It certainly isn't confirmed he's alive either."

Kale works his fists. "I have learned from my mistake and can assure you it won't happen again."

He's surely lying. No one knows what happened that day, except maybe Intemrus. And if he knows, he isn't telling. Obsydia stands, shooing away the adherent combing oil into her hair.

"Walk with me, Kale."

Kale rises from his knee. He seems to be having trouble with his dele in the area of his groin. Obsydia approaches the south edge of her tower. The stone beneath her feet still holds the morning's chill, and goosebumps ascend her ankles and calves as she walks. The starsilk curtain, nearly as light as air itself, hangs from between the two southernmost columns. The thin cerulean veil rides the breeze, presenting a shimmering blue sheen that makes the floor appear to move. Kale joins Obsydia reluctantly, sliding one foot forward at a time and stopping several paces from the tower's edge.

Past Syvea Tower the jungle extends to the far horizon, where it is obscured in mist. The jungles of Ausgan stretch all the way to the marshes on the island's southern peninsula, deep in the Untamed, where there are cannibals and Fohrvyldan spies who use steel and conspire against Ausgan. In the sky several miles distant from Erudition are heavy-looking grey clouds, the smear beneath indicating that rain is falling onto those acacias and myrtles and mahoganies. Barely discernible in the jungle thin ribbons of smoke rise from the swaying canopy, from the fires of southern villages. It's in those establishments that natives with no consonant gifts toil and sweat to provide sustenance and materials for Erudition and the nation's defenses at large. It's in those obscured gatherings that native men and women engage in carnal activities. Obsydia's never witnessed the act, only heard the returning chaplains talk of it. Read texts. Viewed the descriptive paintings and murals of it. Imagined it. Kale's guard is neglected once more as he takes in the view. Obsydia senses his longing, and she recognizes it as some version of her own.

"The magus' campaigns are dangerous," she says. "He and his escort are at great risk among the villages. His party is small—so they can travel quickly and escape if need be. But they are also strong, in case escape is not an option. Magus Kalderys appoints prime sentinels from the most elite among us. They cannot match the caliber of his channeled song, obviously. None can."

Kale glances at her and quickly diverts his eyes. But his intended question was obvious. *Not even the sovereign?* Such a statement as that is heresy, punishable by death, if that's what she were implying. *But no, Kale, I don't think even the sovereign can match Kalderys.*

"His sentinels are proficient enough to harmonize with him—summoning as needed. They're superior martial artists, in case they must defend themselves. They're also astute in practical arts, in case they must provide sustenance from the wild. By the time Kalderys trusts an exemplar to join him in the field, they have trained together long enough to sing, fight, and operate as a single entity."

"Why is it so dangerous?" Kale asks, as if saddened by the fact. "Aren't they going to meet chaplains or deliver news, or scout? I thought the villages were subservient to us."

Obsydia turns to Kale. Again, his imprint does not suggest he's being duplicitous. But if he's truly this clueless to the magus' campaigns, why is he in such a hurry to join? "What do you know of the Untamed?" she asks.

There's a childlike naivety in the look he turns toward her. She resists the urge to punch him. Ignorance, in all its forms, might be the most unattractive trait in a person.

"Of course the villages are subservient to us. They benefit from our protection and our knowledge. They rely on the sovereign to keep Mount Adenhelm tame, rather than it bursting and poisoning the whole island of Ausgan. They yearn to produce offspring who bear consonant gifts, so their families and villages can receive our generous dowry. If they're smart, they understand that one day exemplars of Erudition are all that will protect them from the dreaded Heathen Tide.

"The Untamed, on the other hand, can be viewed as an infection. One that we have been fighting back for the last three centuries—ever since Intemrus first established our monastery on Mount Adenhelm. Since then, Vretos, the heathen king of Fohrvylda, sends his spies to the southern tip of our island. They bring steel weapons and lies, with the intention of rousing our own people against us, shifting our focus inward rather than toward the eastern horizon from whence they will attack. And although our roving chaplains are vigilant and informed, our enemies do occasionally manage to slip past our notice, travelling ever northward toward Erudition, spreading lies and inciting unrest. Unfortunately, once a community has been Untamed by such lies, Erudition's response can only be annihilation, administered by Magus Kalderys and his entourage, Prime Sentinel Calomancer Arc, and Prime Sentinel Aridimancer Selu. Do you truly think you could offer anything to their quest?"

A ridiculous notion, and Obsydia makes no effort to hide that fact.

Judging by Kale's dull expression, his resolve has melted away, or at least his attention. "Maybe I can be reassessed," he says, gazing out over the swaying green forest. It's not apparent he's hearing her. "Study to become an andesite. It's been at least … a couple of years."

Vitality butter has dripped down Obsydia's neck and is coating her shoulders, running down her back, her arms, between her breasts. She needs to clean up for her next visitor soon, and she's lost all patience with this sad, overgrown basalt. "Kale, you can't sing. You can't summon. You can't hold a stave against a prime sentinel. There is no future for you beyond your current purpose. You know this."

He looks at her, startled by the conversation's sudden edge. Her comment hurt him, as if what she said isn't a glaring fact. She presses on before he can muster defense. "I don't think you want to campaign with the magus or else you'd have some notion of what he does. You want to leave Erudition. The longing is obvious, however well you tuck away your emotions."

Kale's face blanches. His ruse is failing.

"Something happened to you to make you so restless, and I bet I wouldn't approve of it."

His breaths are shallow.

"I'd imagine it happened recently, maybe even last night?" He can tell the truth or take a plunge, and she barely cares which. His rapidly blinking eyes tell the tale of his facade breaking down. *Fear.* She can't let him gain his footing or he'll retreat into his shell. "Tell me what happened, Basalt."

"It's … I don't know what … Nothing happened. I …"

His terror is palpable. She almost has him. She moves toward him, making him inch backward. In an effort to crush his defense once and for all, she grabs his shoulder. He freezes, his wide eyes darting all over her. Contact outside combat is not allowed. For a fraction of a moment he seems to consider defending himself. If only. She'd show him martial arts.

"Kale, those who lie ..." She indicates the expanse around her tower with her other hand. "... fly."

He exhales in defeat, shoulders drooping, and his emotions are laid bare. But instead of some miasma of terror or guilt for her to relish, she perceives fatal resignation, as if this is the outcome he hoped against but anticipated—apathy so comprehensive she can taste it. Corpses have more agency. Chills ride up her arm, emanating from her contact with Kale. She withdraws her hand, surprised.

"I don't have a future," he says.

She agrees, and is about to shove him off the roof for scaring her, when the click of chitin boots draws her attention to the stairway. One of her sentinels tops the stairs and stands at attention.

"What is it?" Obsydia snaps.

"Resonations, Magister. The Magus Kalderys, at your request."

Obsydia's heart flutters in her chest. He's early. There's no time to rinse. She's not ready!

"Basalt Kale, you're dismissed. Resonations."

She steps quickly to her wardrobe to inspect her looking scale. Gifted from an exemplar, it is an acacia-framed oval made of layered scales of a crystal tarpon, polished to a reflective sheen. Her reflection glares at her. She's a mess. Oil from her hair has drawn streaks all down her. She looks like she's been wallowing in it.

"Help," she commands. Two adherents are upon her, toweling her off more roughly than she'd normally care for. The adherent who'd been combing her is now behind her tugging oil from locks of hair with bare hands, the excess pouring off in strands. She draws Obsydia's hair back, twists a purple towel into it and coils it on top of Obsydia's head, securing it with a lacquered fish bone. Once she's marginally less slick, Obsydia waves away the adherents and rifles through the deles in her wardrobe. Clothiers see to it that she has a wide wardrobe of different hues and styles. They are each fitted, some formal, some extravagant, some armored, some practical. Today they are unanimously failing to impress.

She chooses a violet dele with shimmering white embroidery, flowing sleeves, and a high slit along each side that accentuates her legs. She wriggles into it and straightens her breasts in the looking scale. It's too formal. Can't breathe. She'll be sweating like a hog. Plus, it's already stained with oil. She wrenches it off and throws it at a nearby adherent, who wisely catches it without complaint. A robe is what she needs. Light. Absorbent. Dark green. That one. The color of shadows in a jungle. Silksedge, as smooth as silk but less likely to bake her inside it. She throws it around her shoulders and wraps herself in it, inspecting her reflection again. Her cheeks are flushed. Her hair looks like washed-up driftwood. There's nothing for it. She takes a full breath and addresses the sentinel without looking at him. "Send the magus up, please."

He descends away.

"Lower the curtains," Obsydia says. "Then leave. All of you."

Her adherents shuffle to the columns in pairs, handily untying and arranging the curtains across those expanses. United, the layers of silk hang heavily, wavering faintly. Their shadows throw an aqueous atmosphere over the rooftop as if everything is submerged underwater. The adherents file out. All but one.

"Um, Magister?"

"What?"

The adherent motions toward the south edge of her roof, where Basalt Kale stands idly peering over the edge of her tower. She'd completely forgotten he was there.

"Leave, Basalt. Didn't you hear me?"

He looks at her with that dead expression. For a moment she thinks he'll disobey. "Resonations, Magister," he mumbles, with a final glance at the expanse beyond her gazebo. Did he want to die? Is that the real reason he came? Because she'd be happy to grant him flight with a kick. He walks to the stairs and makes his way down.

He's gone. They're all gone. Obsydia is ready. She can observe the impending aura of resolution before even hearing Kalderys' steps. Those heavy boots greet each stair like it's done them wrong. When Obsydia can contain no more anticipation, Kalderys tops the stairway, his frame obscuring the distant East Rostrum, his visage nearly taking her breath. He wears a decorative armored dele. The outermost layer, extending from his shoulders down past his hips, is stitched of turquoise carapace plates, each a different shimmering hue, as if they're being viewed through trickling water. Under it is a layer made of smaller scales of a burnt amber sheen. This layer ends at his heavy chitin boots but is slit up the sides to expose starfish vellum winding up his thighs. A white silk cape drapes from his left shoulder, rimmed with bleached crab claws hanging from cloth strips. Intemrus, despite his sovereignty, can never have ascended a staircase the way Kalderys does. Never. Not hundreds of years ago in his physical prime. Not ever in his over-extended life.

The magus removes his conch helmet. Sweaty black hair is plastered to his tanned forehead, always, as if he's been working. His eyes are dark. His chin is squared as if by a mason. He stops before the magister and looks down at her.

"Resonations, Magister." Kalderys' voice is deep, with a brassy quality that suggests it can either trumpet or not exist at all.

"Resonations, Magus."

She called this meeting. There are issues to discuss. Her plan must proceed at a careful pace. There are many moving parts after all and the magus is among the most important. But just like that, having witnessed him with her eyes, observing his strength of purpose, she's entirely run out of things to say. "Sleep well last night?"

"I rested well, thank you. Hopefully you did."

"I was restless in anticipation of our meeting today." Sometimes her words aren't weighed or considered until moments after they've already been said. Typically, those are her least favorite.

"I'm flattered," Kalderys says hesitantly. "You should know the basalt still lingers on your stairway."

Obsydia smiles through gritted teeth. Raunchy little sneak will hear about this. If he'd left when he was told to she'd have let his oddities slide, as if he's capable of any harm. She'll get the truth out of him even if it leaves him in pieces. There are ways to accomplish that, and they're not limited to molten earth and sharpened stone.

For now, however, composure is key.

"Basalt Kale?" she calls, like he's a pet bird.

"I'm sorry, Magister. I got dizzy." His voice wavers from over the edge of the rooftop.

Flailing idiot. "I know my staircase is intimidating. Feel free to consider alternate means of departing. I can assist." Smiling at Kalderys while saying it surely replaces any unpleasant edge with light-hearted humor.

The basalt's sandals clonk quickly but far from steadily until Obsydia can hear them no more. She returns to the shade, embarrassed. Embarrassment seems to come easily when Kalderys visits. He stands patiently, as still as a hidden pond, one wide, dark hand hanging at his side, the other clutching his helm.

"Has the basalt gone now?" she asks after a quiet moment.

Kalderys blinks, unfocusing his eyes. The strength of his supersensory pulse hits her like a wave, unsteadies her, gives her a giddy smile. That pest can't evade the magus.

"We are alone, Magister."

"Thank you," she breathes. Something about that statement, coupled with the pulse he sent outward, makes her cheeks flush. She pulls her robe tighter, keenly aware of how translucent the fiber is upon her otherwise naked body. "What's the status of Intemrus' replacement key?"

"It's in the final stages, endensing and tuning. It should be finished in the next three days unless there are complications with the lodestones. I can visit the artificer and expedite production if the sovereign wishes."

"No need. Intemrus is happy to be without it for now. Otherwise he'd have sought a replacement before discarding his old one."

"There is talk his old key was lost."

"Rumors. I'd have told you if so. It was sent to the andesites for deconstruction by Intemrus' own adherent."

"I didn't believe the rumor, Magister," Kalderys says, exhibiting a jolt of emotion. *Shame.* He'd not meant to give the impression he'd believed it. He'd only meant to make her aware of it.

"There is something I've not mentioned," she offers. "Intemrus told me he welcomed an excuse to break from regularly visiting Syvea."

The magus exhibits a pang of anxiety without moving a muscle.

Obsydia continues. "I think it's for the best. I can see the improvement in his demeanor and his pallor when he distances himself from the tower."

"But ... Syvea. How long can he be away?" Kalderys' concern is genuine. He fears for Intemrus' immortality. Obsydia doesn't. She loathes it and intends to undermine it. Take it for herself. Never mind that now.

"Intemrus will endure," Obsydia assures. *Until he doesn't. And we would be smart to prepare for that day.* She can't say that. Talk about Intemrus' mortality may send the magus into conniptions. He is too dependent on the sovereign. That must change. She has to shift his reliance onto her alone. But how? Kalderys is not the first exemplar she's groomed to this point, but with him it feels like she's hit a wall. For some time, she's refused to call Intemrus *sovereign* while discussing him with Kalderys, instead calling him by his given, mortal name. That indirect strategy means too little. For her plan to advance, he needs to accept the possibility of a world without Intemrus. An Ausgan in which she reigns with Kalderys at her side.

But here she is at yet another moment of truth, and no segue she's rehearsed feels natural. If she botches this, Kalderys will turn on her, report her to Intemrus as a usurper, ruining everything. The magus watches her, perhaps impatient—she can't tell. On the surface, his black eyes reveal nothing. Annoyingly, Kale comes to mind. His vapid emotional state and his propensity to linger and disappear. She shakes thoughts of him from her head.

"Would you like to sit?" Obsydia asks, indicating a chair of intricately carved petrified driftwood.

"No, thank you."

She swallows irritation and has a seat across from the chair regardless, making him at least turn to face her. She throws one leg over the other, knowing that as her robe settles in place her thighs are exposed. Kalderys doesn't look.

"There *is* something troubling Intemrus," Obsydia says.

Kalderys frowns at her. "If it troubles His Presence, it troubles me."

"No need for you to be troubled," she says softly, observing his pulse, his heat. "You are judgment."

"As you say, Magister." A hound-like impatience, made of eagerness to salve the sovereign's trouble.

"He is troubled, but I'm not." Obsydia's voice is low. "Because I know the might of the magus. I know your strength."

Now he's watching her intently. *Intrigued?*

"The first and last contender. The Consonant Fist," she says.

"If the sovereign commands it."

"I have observed it," she says. "He trusts me, and I trust you. You are absolute. The holy city need not fear."

His cheeks glow. He's flattered. Nearly bashful. Then it passes, like a splash in a river, and he's back to his perpetual sense of duty. Obsydia wishes she'd not sent out all the adherents. Some wine would be welcome. She sighs audibly. She'll make little progress today.

"The prisoner from Napiri. He has confessed."

As she expected, Kalderys' heart quickens. His free hand forms a fist at his side. "I should have been informed of his interrogation." Kalderys' knuckles are white. "I will pay him a visit myself."

There's the vehemence Obsydia sought. Burning, pulsing. "No need, Magus. He gave us all he had and then some." Obsydia watches Kalderys another moment, savoring the strength of his emotions.

"I'd long been uncomfortable with the village of Hargrim, south of Napiri. Turns out its residents freely harbor and conspire with agents influenced by Fohrvylda. They've become untamed. Our response must be quick and comprehensive to prevent weeds taking root and spreading northward."

"Then send Intemrus' Judgment, Magister." Kalderys' words hammer the air, his voice pinched by fury. "Where weeds choke the land, white fire avails."

Obsydia observes him, and observes herself observing him. What is it about his blind sense of duty that affects her so? Yes, he's mighty. Energy tenses his shoulders and sets his jaw to trembling. His power is undeniable. It is unimaginable that Intemrus—ancient, frail, cold— wields such might as him.

Obsydia rises to her feet and looks up into his black eyes. "I call a Campaign of Cleansing on Hargrim," she says. Her heart is pounding. His heart is pounding. Those are words that cannot be unsaid.

"Intemrus' Will be done," he says with fiery excitement. Perhaps someday, Obsydia's Will be done. "And Napiri?" he asks, "The prisoner's home village. Is it, too, untamed?"

"Napiri remains devout," she says. "Their fate rests on one villager who still prays fervently. She encourages others into penitence, sometimes using force. They'll not soon turn away from Erudition with her as their leader. It was her father who was imprisoned, and she is quite passionate about earning his freedom through good deeds."

Kalderys raises an eyebrow. "You aren't concerned that her faithfulness is motivated solely by wanting her relative returned?"

Obsydia suppresses a scoff. Imagine judging goats by their fleeting fancies rather than the taste of their meat. "It's not their motives that the faithful should be judged for, it's their acts," she says. "Fervency such as hers should be rewarded, not punished, wouldn't you say?"

"If that is your wish."

Obsydia smiles. *Her* wish. *Her* plan. And for her plan to work, all Kalderys need do is remember that. Worry less on Intemrus until the day he departs for good. All is underway and too late to stop.

"You are excused, Magus," Obsydia says.

His heel stomps the stone and Obsydia feels it in her bare feet.

"Resonations, Magister."

"Resonations."

He dons his helm and leaves. Obsydia stands there feeling hollowed out by his absence. She pulls the pin from her hair and the towel falls. Her robe slips away. The power she commands in Kalderys is unparalleled and growing stronger each passing day. She'll have her daybed angled toward Hargrim, deep in the southern jungle. Tonight's is not a show to be missed.

11

For the Best

AUSGAN
Andesite Tier, Erudition

Andesite Culver lays out the evening's dele on his silksedge mattress and inspects it. It's an attractive shimmering teal while under shadow, capable of dazzling turquoise in the sunlight, and it's in good condition if not for a couple of snags that he should be able to resolve presently. He dealt with its mild sulfurous odor by turning it inside out, dabbing with elima petal extract and airing it out in sunlight. Maintaining fine clothes isn't mandatory, especially for a porter. It's tedious and time consuming. But there's something therapeutic about fretting over the individual threads and stitching and seams and embroidery and embellishments. Not everyone looks as presentable as Culver. Far from it. No other andesites do.

Tonight, his duties have him cleaning the residence of Calomancer Arc's adept mancers. Culver has forgotten their names, but he'll learn them before he arrives. Theirs is a respectable three-story manse in upper rhyolite. He wants to look forward to his time there but thinking of it makes him nervous. Adept mancers are proud. In most cases, mancers ignore porters, and andesites in general. Occasionally they show gratitude for his efforts and are conversational. But there are always those who are condescending, as if Culver's rank is something infectious or shameful. As if they were never andesites.

Culver is overdue for a promotion. He isn't sure how to prompt one though, and until he figures that out he'll emulate the next tier up, which is rhyolite. To do that well, it helps to spend time up there. That goes better if you dress the part. Promotions are usually timely and prompted by the magister or whomever is gauging your progress. Once Culver proved his worth as initiate, he was trusted with his new home on Andesite Tier and the occupation of porter. He's since mastered his duties—carting packages, copying and updating maps and documents, cleaning Erudition—and has been practicing supersensory perception and preparing for the basics of summoning by studying scrolls and eavesdropping on rhyolite. But it's been years and advancement is not forthcoming.

Culver pinches a loose thread with bamboo tweezers and carefully runs the sharpened edge of a shaving shell along its base, severing it from the garment. He gently massages the fabric until there's no evidence of the errant snag. He doesn't like to dwell on his inability to advance in rank. What if andesite is as high as he ever gets? What if he ends up like Proctor Alika? Teaching the same tired lessons to intrants and initiates while his peers move on and time hunches his shoulders and wrinkles his face. Granted, there are worse fates. Poor Kale. Stuck on Basalt Tier forever, to merely assist the proctor and bide his time, forever harassed by Ashmancer Haik and his ilk.

One day Culver will move up to Rhyolite Tier. He'll no longer have the free time to spend with Kale, sparring or running or eating or just talking. Culver isolates another snag near the left shoulder on his dele. He frowns. It might be his association with Kale that has stunted his progression. That's another train of thought he hates following. Their friendship is a rare bit of reprieve from the ruthless competitive rigor of Erudition. If he has to give that up to advance, would it be worth it? A mallet whomps his heart as the contraband key he gave to Kale invades his thoughts. *Intemrus sees all.*

By Imala, if he does ...

Culver dabs the sheen of sweat from his forehead.

That key came to him under unusual circumstances. Typically they're visibly broken or at least cracked by the time they arrive for salvage and disposal. Not this time. An adherent dropped off this key, never introduced herself or said whose adherent she was, but she told Culver to finish the job quickly and quietly, as if key disposal might ever be slow or loud. He assumed she meant for him alone to see the job through. He was the key's intended final destination. And assuming the sovereign doesn't see all, he was. He broke it down and recycled what could be reused. No one can prove otherwise ... unless Kale gets caught. A weight has developed in Culver's guts. Was the risk worth it? If it weren't for Kale's relentless skepticism, he'd accept that Intemrus sees all, never even question it.

Culver realizes he's digging frantically at the fibers of his dele with a fingernail. He stops.

His bamboo door swings open and clatters against the wall, startling him so badly he gasps. It's only Kale, and he's wearing an utter sack of a dele.

"By Imala, Kale. You couldn't have knocked?"

"I'm sorry," Kale says, smiling. "I didn't know you were ..." He leans to look over Culver's shoulder. "What are you doing to that dele?"

"I was distracted," Culver says, looking away from his friend and back to his dele. It's hard to be mad at Kale when he's showing his dimples. "Tell me you lost the thing."

Kale moves to the edge of Culver's cot and sits down. "Funny you should mention it. That's what I came to talk about."

Culver's cheeks go frigid. He turns to Kale. "You still have it?"

Kale nods apologetically, those dimples at the edge of his smile still defending him. "I do. *And it opened every door it touched,*" he whispers. "But don't worry. It'll be in the jungle soon."

Culver arches an eyebrow. "Thanks for the reassurance. But for the sake of my nerves, spit it out, whatever it is that brought you."

"I need to borrow a map. And a dele." Kale smiles wider, certainly to take the edge off the request. He shifts, then adds, "And some sandals."

Culver studies him. The key Culver gave him was supposed to facilitate some assistance Kale could offer his neighbors. This seems like something else. Culver's starting to feel duped. "You haven't told me how your trip went. Did you get the ... what was it again? Medicine?"

Kale's shoulders droop and his smile devolves to a sigh. He shakes his head. "I wasn't completely honest with you." He glances at Culver fearfully. Sighs again. "I wasn't going for medicine."

"Then what?"

The smile collapses entirely. "It's complicated. What matters is that I was in a bad place. I needed something. I'm not even sure what. But this feels like it."

Culver faces Kale squarely, leaning back against the wall of his dorm and crossing his arms over his chest. He speaks slowly. "What are you trying to say?"

Kale's eyes unfocus, his eyebrows furrowing in thought. Finally he heaves yet another sigh and meets Culver's eyes. "I met a prisoner under Stravhelm."

Culver gasps. "That wasn't part of the plan. Did it infect you?"

Kale shrugs. "*He* gave me an idea. And I'm going through with it."

"By Imala. It infected you." It's known that prisoners under Stravhelm are usually untamed natives who were turned by Fohrvyldan spies.

Kale smiles. "*His* name is Rathyn. *He's* a native from Napiri. And unless I'm mistaken, I've seen that name on a map of yours. Along with another name. *Hargrim.* I might have ... um ..." Kale suddenly looks sheepish, eyes darting to Culver then away. "I might have eluded the magus' supersensory pulse and eavesdropped on a conversation between him and the magister wherein she sent him off on a campaign." He blurts the words, eyes pinched like he's expecting a rap across the knuckles.

Culver's mouth swings open and the wind falls out of him. He nearly gives Kale a rap across the skull. That was *not* in the deal. Culver plops onto the cot beside Kale, staring at his feet with wide eyes, his thoughts a jumble. "On second thought, I don't want to know. For the love of Imala, don't tell me anything else."

Kale chuckles. "Don't be so dramatic."

Culver feels betrayed. He delivered the key because Kale promised to get rid of it. This is the opposite of that. Kale wants to layer more offenses on top, at Culver's peril. He turns to his so-called friend. "Are you a spy?"

Kale laughs, then apparently notices Culver's expression. "Culver ... of course not. I just need to—"

"You lied. I don't know what you really wanted that key for, or what you plan to do with a map or sandals. And I don't know why you lied to me." He's reminded of all those cautionary tales proctors tell initiates about the demigod living on the cursed island. The Deceiver. It's from him that all lies ultimately flow, including the lies that untame Ausgan natives.

"I'm sorry for lying. Can we leave it at that?"

"I don't know. What are you trying to gain from this?"

Kale shakes his head. "It's not what I'll gain from doing it. It's what I'll lose if I don't."

"And that is?"

Kale looks away from Culver, pursing his lips. "I didn't want to lie to you. And I don't want to burden you with this either. Please."

Before Culver can respond, there's the clatter of sandals outside the window. An exemplar runs past, their dele a yellow flash. Then comes another, and another. The accompanying chatter is excited. Seems something's happening in the direction of the main stair. Andesite Mari appears at Culver's window, black hair sticking to her sweaty forehead and cheeks.

"Resonations, Culver," she says excitedly. She notices Kale. "Oh."

"Resonations, Mari," Culver answers, trying to work a smile onto his face and certainly failing horribly.

"You should know," she says, "Magus Kalderys and his two primes are leaving for one of their missions. They're coming down through Rhyolite Tier now, so if you hurry you can watch them go."

That's always an exciting event, sending the armored exemplars on their way, watching the flash of the sun on their polished chitin, feeling the hammer of their boots, yelling encouragement and cheers with arms crossed overhead in rhystic celebration. Culver has watched their passage countless times with Kale, who enjoys it even more than he does. But he can't help noticing the proximity of this uncommon event to Kale's unprecedented requests. He also can't help noticing that Mari's announcement elicited no reaction from Kale. In fact, he's looking off to the corner, dodging Culver's eyes as if he's somehow involved with her announcement. "Thanks. Maybe I'll see you there," he says, without taking his eyes off his friend.

"Sure. Resonations," she says flatly, and is gone.

"Kale," Culver begins, his eyes growing wider.

"I'm sorry," Kale says. "There's no time to explain. A dele, sandals, and a map. Please. I'll never ask you for anything else, I promise."

Culver blinks. Then blinks some more. Why did that sound so much like a goodbye? He doesn't understand. But does he want to? There's something ominous about this visit. Kale doesn't appear to be in trouble. Troubled maybe, but also more excited than he's been lately. Until this key business, he's never done anything devious. Not on purpose anyway. And now he's treating this request like the pinnacle of importance.

"I don't know what's going on," Culver says. "Maybe that's for the best. Just tell me, are you alright?"

Kale smiles. "Better than I've been in a long time. And I have you to thank."

Somehow that fails to reassure. Culver stands up. He'll take a leap of faith and help his friend. Never mind that he's convinced Kale plans to break even more rules.

As a porter, Culver has no shortage of old sandals, and even the worst of them is better than what basalts are issued. He finds the least worn and dusts them off. He has maps to spare as well, all outdated but still relevant as far as Kale's needs. Northern villages don't change often. Culver's always kept the old copies after reproducing them. Something about owning a collection of maps, or even scrolls in general, lends his position an amount of prestige. Truth be told, reproducing and editing maps is among his favorite duties. It feels dignified to sit and toil, dipping quill in ink and drawing lines under a slanting sun ray, preserving and prolonging Erudition's collective wisdom. When there is progress against the Untamed, a map must be updated with the new border. He rummages for one that delineates Napiri and Hargrim, settling for a large map that includes the northern half of Ausgan, from the lagoons and islets north of the main island all the way down to the ever-shifting border of the Untamed. "I'll be expecting an explanation when you return."

Behind him, Kale heaves a great sigh. "By Imala, Culver, I owe you. Thank you."

Culver presents Kale the sandals and the map. "When might that be, by the way? If that's a question I can ask."

Kale responds with a melancholy smile. "As soon as I can."

A niggling thought is growing within Culver and with it a tinge of guilt. Something may happen to Kale because of this. He may leave for good, or be taken away. And while that in itself isn't something he'd ever desire, it ties back to a previous train of thought. Will Culver end up better off? What if ending his relationship with Kale prompts his promotion? That doesn't feel important right now. Maybe it should. He's committed to this path now, helping Kale leave. In time he can convince himself it was for the best. Not everything that *feels* wrong is wrong.

Culver opens his floor chest. He knows exactly the dele. It's attractive, unique, but it's never quite fit Culver, and honestly he's tired of pretending it ever will. Heat rises in his cheeks. Does that description also fit his idea of Kale? He shakes his head before turning back to his friend. What a weird turn this day has taken.

Kale has already switched his sandals out, testing Culver's old pair. "I should have asked you for sandals long ago." He's wearing his smile again, treasuring the sandals Culver considered garbage. Culver can't return a smile. He drops the folded blue dele on his cot.

"No hurry on getting it back. It doesn't fit." Even his own words sound ominous now. He can't meet Kale's eyes.

Kale collects the dele, faces him. Culver feels there's more to be said between them, but the silence is too thick. He forces his attention back onto his evening's dele, which in this moment has lost all opulence. It looks dull, old, and unable to impress even a native.

"I should go," Kale says.

Culver doesn't respond or look up.

Kale shuffles his feet. The silence has become an oppressive force. At this point, Culver would prefer that Kale just disappear. He's usually so good at it. Instead, he shifts closer to Culver.

"I sure hope," he begins slowly, "that someday this will all make sense to you."

There's a dull pain growing in Culver's chest. Kale is trying to tell him goodbye. As a friend. Culver does not approve. But it's his fault. He gave Kale the key to begin with. Feels like he's already terminating the loose strands of this relationship, the same way he deals with lose threads on a garment, and Kale's not even out the door yet.

"Culver," Kale says. "I won't incriminate you, I promise."

"You think that's what's bothering me?" Culver snaps. He didn't mean to say that, or anything.

"Then what?" Kale's tone is tentative.

Culver huffs. "If you don't mind, I still have work to do before my duties tonight. A moment ago you were in a hurry." He turns a glare on Kale. "Something change?" By Imala, that wasn't necessary.

A frown flickers over Kale's face then is gone, washed away by an emotional void, not unlike when he's enduring public humiliation from the ashmancer. He steps backward, holding the dele to his chest. "Sorry," he says. "I'd hate to linger where I'm unwanted." And he walks out, heading southward, opposite the direction Mari went.

Culver's eyes close and his head falls back. That's not what he'd meant. And now ... was that goodbye? Forever? His heart thumps and he steps quickly after Kale into the sunlight. As he expected, Kale's gone. No sign of him. He's so good at disappearing.

"It's for the best," Culver says, trying to take big enough breaths to keep rising emotions from squeezing his throat. He forces himself back to the dele but can't focus on it. Kale wanted to leave. There was nothing Culver could do to stop him, let alone withholding vital gear. He helped his friend.

I'll never ask you for anything else, I promise, Kale had said, as if that's a good thing.

It's for the best, Culver thinks, watching his dele through a sheen of tears. *I'll be promoted now. Become a named mancer, or a clothier or artificer. It's for the best.* Over and over he assures himself, but with each recital believes it less. In time, he will believe it. Evidence will support it when he's packing his possessions to move up to Rhyolite Tier. Tears roll down his cheeks.

It's for the best.

12

Immolation for All Vulgarity

AUSGAN

The road to Hargrim

Intemrus' Will be done.

Kalderys and his two prime sentinels warmed up, hit their pace, and are holding it comfortably. For two hours they've run on the wide, worn road leading south, the three of them sensory pulsing in unison with every synchronized footfall, bolstering one another's awareness collectively. The jungle is a blur to Kalderys' eyes, yet the world is his to observe. There are sloths and constrictors hanging from lianas, koa setuar glaring down from acacia bolds, lemon finches and honeycreepers flitting and singing in the canopy, rainbow crickets thrumming on the jungle floor, crab ants crunching beneath his boots. He perceives gatherings of squat masses that are distant huts and dining halls and medicine lodges, distant crisscrossing aisles that are intersections cut into the jungle, pinpoints of combustion that are community wood fires and the fumes they produce. He feels the movement of the clouds, knows their heading and who's pushing them. The sunlight's pressure tells how the sun manipulates the air moving over and through the canopy. The flavor of the air tells him how much moisture must be displaced for the cleansing.

The more you understand and appreciate your surroundings, the more you can alter them. The Imala, who create the perfect painting every moment of every day, reward those who open their eyes. It is for their glory that Kalderys takes nothing for granted because without them the world would spiral into disorder. For as long as he can remember he's been aware of the Imala's subtle vibrations around him. And as he trained his own supersensory perception, he discovered the harmonies necessary to excite those vibrations.

The subtle influence of Sovereign Intemrus is evident all around, particularly where moisture collects to become rain. It is such a delicate, perpetual touch. Kalderys can distinctly remember his own awakening to the truth of Intemrus' power. He realized that it is everywhere, affecting everything. The sovereign's song was so broad, so comprehensive ... how could one person know so much? Control so much? Everywhere Kalderys looked, His Presence stared back.

The knowledge nearly defeated Kalderys, forcing him to give up his own studies knowing he'd only ever be inferior. But he stayed his course, studied the Imala and the jungle, the ocean, the mountain, the lagoons, streams, rivers, tide pools, marshes, beaches, skies, clouds. Long after his contemporaries exhausted and quit for the day he persisted. Always one more repetition, one more hour, one more note. Then one evening, sitting alone in the shadow of the East Rostrum, observing hermit crabs harvesting seasonal algae clouds in the shallows, Kalderys had his second, equally vital epiphany. It was as if the Imala were bent over whispering in his ear, "*It is limitless. And it can be yours.*"

And so Kalderys set himself even further apart, weathering his mind and body and awareness in the storms of sacrifice, devotion, study. He determined that although no other exemplar has ever exhibited the sovereign's mastery, if one were to study long enough, they could. The sovereign did not invent consonance. He merely discovered it, is still discovering it, and has done so for three hundred years. He is its first excavator but will not be its last. Intemrus maintains that no one can live forever. Whether Kalderys eventually carves his own path or forever follows in Intemrus' steps is a matter of how long he is able to continue learning. What sets him apart from a younger, less experienced sovereign is that Intemrus affiliates with water and wind. Kalderys has a mind for lightning.

While running, Kalderys passes natives who scramble to clear the path. He does not share the magister's abilities of perceiving the thoughts and desires of others. He knows it would be wasted on him. By the time Kalderys has been called to act, sentiment is obsolete. These natives make their emotions plain on their faces. Awe, fear, curiosity, occasionally resentment. Sometimes hate. Perhaps the hateful are discontent with the amount of rain they receive, as if it's retained out of spite. As if they've earned more. Perhaps their family produced an exemplar and they were loath to turn the infant over to Erudition. Natives do at times resent relinquishing their offspring to chaplains, despite the generous dowry they and their village receive. Some turn downright feral, despite knowing their progenies have a higher calling than their life of labor. Shortsightedness, all of it. Animal instinct. Like a goat ramming the fence that protects it from predators. The worst possibility is that their faces wear hate because they're agents of Fohrvylda; spies, disruptors, instigators, crept northward from the Untamed to insidiously undermine the sovereign's rule, as they've attempted for generations. Whatever the case, their truth will be known in due time and they will answer for it. Intemrus sees all.

Halfway to Hargrim, Kalderys lessens his pace. Prime Sentinels Arc and Selu maintain formation off his left and right shoulder. It's for them he slows. They can sprint and sing, but not like he can.

He sings. Slow and deep, searching. His prime sentinels join in, adding harmonies, first Arc then Selu. He and his sentinels explore with their melody discordantly, probing for the moment's unique response. Summoning songs must tailor to their environment such that they elicit sympathetic vibrations from the surrounding world. Once resonance is found they burst into song. Stamping feet marking the rhythm. Perception guides the pitch, the harmonies. They split their voices, reaching into the moment and exploring like a tree's roots. The forest returns their polyphony, as does the earth and the sky. Consonant songs transcend words, relying instead on force of will to translate intentions. His sentinels sing of the splendor of the moment. Kalderys sings of the moments to come. He sings of a white fire birthed to sweep the jungle like a comb, removing tangle from the forest with teeth made of lightning, so fast they make time irrelevant, so bright all else is dark. The Imala are pleased. The moment sings back. Power magnifies. The destination approaches.

Hargrim, named after the builder of its central lodge. Today will tell the story of its demise. It is by Intemrus' Will that Kalderys' campaign will occur. That is sufficient motivation. But the rebelliousness of the natives strikes Kalderys' heart and makes his fists tighten. How ignorant of their place in the world, blind to their frailty. How utterly treacherous. A people who rely on the holy city for medicine, rain, guidance, protection from the volcano ... all in dissent, abetting spies, spitting in the face of the sovereign. They are given prosperity, life, voice. And in return they aim those gifts against the gifter? Today's campaign simply impels the inevitable.

Kalderys is gritting his teeth. This thought process is dangerous. Consonance is not bolstered by anger. Emotions are impediments. It is never Intemrus' Will that the children of Ausgan should perish. Kalderys' duty is to carry out the sovereign's will, even when he doesn't comprehend it. Despite the praise that the magister pours on him, Kalderys knows he himself is not immaculate. He has a significant journey still ahead of him toward quelling invasive feelings. The magister herself proves that whenever he's in her presence.

It is mid-afternoon when Kalderys calls his party to stop. The sentinels are crimson-cheeked, sweaty, but their voices hold strong. He raises his hand and his sentinels bring their summoning to a close. The energy is sufficient. Kalderys observes with all his focus. The Imala's energy weighs heavy above him like an invisible cloud, at once sharpening his supersensory perception and spreading it far wider than he needs. Kalderys observes with eyes and ears and senses no longer his own. This narrow path bends out of sight then widens as it opens into Hargrim. The dining lodge is the largest construction, composed of a stone wall, a chimney on its windward side, and a wide roof of clay tiles held up by timber posts. Dried fruits, salted meat, firewood, and cooking utensils are stored there. Spiralpine mats blanket the spikerush spread across the floor. Surrounding the dining hall are thatched huts with flagstone floors. Within the huts is evidence of enough regular bedding to accommodate some thirty individuals. This is indicated by silksedge mats, made dense with masses of shed skin and hair, residue of oil and sweat, and other leavings. Thirty-two matches the chaplain's last census. *Satisfactory.*

Kalderys scans for life. The imprints of humans are distinct from goats and hogs in their shape and posture and habits. They grunt and sigh, throbbing with heat from their labor. They sprinkle the soil with sweat, fill the air with breath. Dirt is turned over in rows. Straggling weeds are singled out, uprooted and tossed away. Meat is seared over wood fires. Native children poke in mud with sticks and chase one another. From behind the northernmost hut, a pair of natives lie together as one, trying but failing to stifle their panting and huffing.

He expands his observation to the jungle around Hargrim. At least two individuals roam the western forest, hefting traps and bait, satisfying the count. Surrounding it all, within every shadow and hollow is some source of movement. Beasts of all sizes, crawling, climbing, flying. For each of those is a thousand insects, skittering and buzzing.

These observations present as ideal a stage as Kalderys could ask for if it weren't for one detail. Something odd stands out back north, a hundred yards distant, just off the path Kalderys and his sentinels traveled. A dense, lifeless mass, not unlike stone. Except they passed no rock of that size. It's not a carcass either. Death attracts attention of its own sort, and this mass attracts nothing, exudes nothing. Kalderys turns to it, craning his head, narrowing his eyes, as if any part of this observation derives from empirical senses.

That is no rock or carcass. It doesn't appear to be natural at all. It's like a void, immune to his supersensory pulse entirely, a cavity that repels the Imala. And, despite being neither dead nor alive, it seems to be moving. Kalderys takes a step toward the abnormality. There's something familiar about it.

"Magus," Prime Sentinel Arc says. "We've been seen."

Kalderys turns his attention back to the trail leading to their destination. In the middle of the trodden path, an old native leans on a cane, watching Kalderys' party from under grey eyebrows. A slender youth helps support him. They approached without Kalderys noticing, which in itself is unacceptable.

Kalderys assumes rhystic focus, chin up, shoulders back, hands clasping his wrists in front of his sternum. That oddity is threatening the entire campaign. Not that the villagers could ever hope to contend with the magus and his sentinels. But if they attempt to flee ...

Losing focus is not a habit of the successful. The sovereign would not have been distracted so easily. Inner turbulence, insecurities, they have no place here. As much as Kalderys wants to investigate that void, this song cannot be stalled.

"It is time," he tells his sentinels, and marches for the village.

Intemrus' Will be done.

~

Kale lies on his back off the side of the beaten path, wheezing and rubbing his poor feet. As soon as the magus slowed, he fell to his back, kicked off his sandals, massaging his toes and heels, not that he can undo what those straps have done to him.

This pursuit started so calmly. Then half a mile outside Erudition the magus and his primes picked up speed. Kale kept up, but not without struggle. When he could barely draw breath, he convinced himself to keep running. By the time he could no longer feel his legs and his face was etched into a scowl of despair and each breath felt like something far sharper than air coursing through him, it was too late to turn back. He was lost.

The Imala reward suffering. That's a tenet proctors and mancers recite to younger exemplars. It never meant much to Kale, who lacks the supersensory observation to even recognize the Imala's presence. Besides, his own torment never resembled the suffering it seemed they referred to. Aching muscles, long days, injuries sustained from sparring, those never felt like suffering to him. Being alone did. And now, by his own choices, he's truly alone. Was this a mistake?

He can scarcely believe it was earlier this very day he'd fled the magister's tower while she and the magus wrapped up their conversation. She'd nearly extricated that he'd met with the prisoner, which would have damned Culver if she'd learned of the key. He almost threw himself off her tower to protect the lie and his friend—and even the prisoner, with whom Kale feels a connection for some reason. Then the magus had arrived. Kale had felt Kalderys' attempt to observe him, the waves of his uncanny perception, not sight or hearing but something more invasive. At first the magus' awareness seemed too complex to even understand, as if it latched on to and cried out at his presence. Then something occurred to Kale. Negating the Imala as he does during training uses the same muscle as reducing his imprint. He'd always known it but never tested it. And, much like negating, his ability to reduce his imprint is directly proportional to the observation aimed at him. It's a matter of focusing on the *observer*, not himself. Determine what they'd observe if he weren't there. The more energy they use, the more he has access to. And so, under the magus' supersensory glare, Kale stepped aside and let the waves of observation pass him, disassociating his body with the Imala, who otherwise dictate all existence. Standing there on the magister's staircase, he expected to be perceived. He expected the magus to report him, and the magister, having spent the last of her patience, to punish him. To death maybe. Instead, the magus said, *"We are alone, Magister,"* and Kale, for the first time, had truly appreciated his gift. After that, there was no way he'd let it go to waste.

The magus was to leave for a Campaign of Cleansing, which meant annihilation according to Magister Obsydia. Kale had no choice but to follow them. He'd gone to his dorm and stuffed bedrolls from empty neighboring dorms under the sheet on his cot so his bed won't appear empty. In other tiers the night count involves supersensory pulses to verify counts. The exemplars who administer Basalt Tier's count can barely be bothered to glance in a window. All more evidence of how little Kale will be missed.

From there he went to see Culver. That whole encounter stirs up regret in Kale. Of course Culver would ask more questions than Kale wanted to answer. Yes, Kale lied to him, but he certainly never meant to hurt him. The opposite in fact. Kale's mission was to improve Culver, among other things. He could have anticipated awkwardness, but there's nothing for it now. If that was goodbye … Kale shakes the thought from his head.

He'd fled to a locked door beneath a tower on the south wall and silently eased through. With his new key and his new understanding of sensory elusion, it was a breeze. All eyes were on Kalderys. Once outside, he hid the key and got in position to trail the magus. But if he'd known how long they'd run and the merciless pace they'd set, he'd have at least brought a bite to eat. His feet are chafed to near bleeding everywhere the unfamiliar sandals gripped him. When the trio he followed began their song of summoning, he hoped they'd slow to a walk. They did not.

They ran on, singing at full volume, each of them producing an array of melodies that somehow lifted song from everywhere and everything, even the ground. Still they failed to observe him. Kale marveled at this. How can the energy they summon be so comprehensive—a direct product of their supersensory observation—even while he remains unseen to them? Kale's always known understanding consonance was outside his grasp. But he believed that if he could figure out his own role in it, maybe life would be more worthwhile. At one point during their song, Kale could pick out seven distinct harmonies, coming from Imala knows where, and all to the pace of the trio's stomping feet. Kale knew gifted mancers use polyphony, singing more melodies than one, but had never heard it so vividly before today.

Now they've stopped and so has their singing, its echoes fleeing into the jungle and leaving a hollow ring, which is gradually succumbing to the jungle's own unending song. Kale sits up, pulls out the vellum map that Culver gave him. He inspects it until he finds the word Hargrim scrawled beside a dot in the middle of the expanse that is surely this jungle. He thought the distance from it to Erudition would be indeterminable, given how little he knows of this jungle and the villages interspersed therein, but now he's learning that's not the case. Topmost on the sketch is Ausgan's northern coast, with Mount Adenhelm dead center and Erudition depicted as a series of squares and spires on its eastern side. To the right of that, on the jagged line that is the east coast, the East Rostrum is depicted as a wilted triangle, rising up and bending to overlook the Faithless Sea. Kale shakes his head, cursing himself. Considering that Erudition is known to be eighteen miles from the East Rostrum, he had every chance of determining that the sprint to Hargrim would be over twenty.

"*Idiot*," he whispers, as if knowing the distance would have changed his mind about coming. Despite his ravaged feet, his burning lungs, his questionable safety, Kale is awash in a sense of freedom like he's never imagined. No matter what today brings, he'll not be the same. He has changed just by fleeing the walls, by being out from under the stare of Intemrus' tower for once in his entire pointless life. If he wants to never return to Erudition, that is within his power. Whether or not he'd survive a single night in the jungle is a different matter. And, curiously, surviving matters to him. He's not quite as ready to die anymore. Kale smiles. Was the prisoner right after all? Was Culver right? Is this what being infected feels like?

On the map, in the area around Hargrim, are more villages, though none within five miles. East is Sandspot. West is Redris. North is Napiri. And to the south is Brina. He can't imagine that information being relevant to this trek. Then again, what will this trip entail? He stashes the map.

The magus and his party are stopped, presumably making their final preparations for the so-called cleansing. *Annihilation* echoes in Kale's memory. He can't see his quarry, but he can feel a renewed surge of supersensory pulse from Kalderys. By now minimizing his imprint is second nature, but the pulses have sharpened. They were everywhere and observing everything, and now they've focused, giving Kale the feeling of standing in the middle of a crowd of people who all turned at once to point at him. He freezes. Has he been spotted? The observation fumbles at him, fingers scrabbling in darkness. Kale closes his eyes and concentrates on himself, his impact on the world, his worth. All nothing. The tide of observation recedes, unfocusing again.

Kale exhales, cleans the last of the grit from his sandals and their straps, winces as he pulls them back over his ravaged feet, tries not to think about the return trip. Maybe he'll ditch the sandals, walk barefoot, taking his time. It's not like he'll be missed back home. Then again, maybe after this he'll continue south.

There's a distinct odor originating nearby. Something ripe and fertile and utterly awful. Through a thin wall of malva brambles Kale makes out a bright clearing in the otherwise shaded understory. There appear to be large mounds of reeds or rushes. A closer inspection proves they're huts. They must be dwellings. This must be Hargrim.

His heart bounces off his ribs. *Annihilation*. What's about to happen? Is he safe here? Will they see him? What if Kalderys and his primes are overrun? What if the Untamed natives try to escape and run right into Kale? He's in no shape to fight anyone, what with his feet like this, and besides, if they're Fohrvyldan spies they'll have steel weapons … won't they?

Kale approaches the village, making his way over and through the perimeter of malva branches and the vines clinging to them. He's made it this far. The least he can do is observe the so-called cleansing. The abysmal odor is stronger the closer he gets. It can only be livestock and their muck, or death itself. As the jungle he's navigating thins out, Kale arrives at a wattle fence. The enclosure contains a shaded stretch of churned earth and several enormous bristly hogs, grunting and rooting about, spattered in the mud they're trodding through. He pulls the hem of his borrowed dele up around his nose and mouth. Imala willing, that's mud. Hogs are considerably larger than he'd thought. Infinitely dirtier. Kale, thinking of a juicy slab of ham with an abrupt lack of appetite, notes that this is not an awakening he'd anticipated.

Beyond the enclosure, between it and those sedge huts, are young natives, older than intrant exemplars but not by much. Some are the age of Proctor Alika's first years. Out here they're not exemplars. They're *boys and girls. Children.* They're dressed scantily, in woven straps or bits of animal skin that serve little obvious purpose other than to protect their nethers. Their arms and hands and feet and cheeks aren't much cleaner than the hogs. Three of the youths huddle together, their ruffled heads almost touching, concentrating on something on the ground, perhaps hidden in the dirt. Kales deduces it's the dirt itself holding their attention.

"*Filthy,*" he whispers unintentionally. But he finds himself enthralled, unable to look away. At times one child reaches over and touches another, sometimes a push, sometimes a pull, or a slap, or a squeeze. Now on the shoulder, now on the knee. Some of the touches are accompanied by smiles, or smirks, or grimaces. What the touches signify, Kale cannot fathom. It is almost like communication, except he can hear their voices accompanying it. They're capable of speaking. Are they too primitive to communicate solely with spoken language? Must they also handle and cajole one another? Or, and Kale nearly gets lightheaded at the thought, what if exemplars are the primitive ones? What if that physical contact enhances natives somehow, however simple and base it appears? The unwelcome idea blossoms like a flower, nearly knocking Kale back on his rump. Those children could have been him. He could have been raised alongside children like these rather than being collected at birth, taken to Erudition and isolated to serve his high purpose of languishing in a stone dorm. He slumps down, holding the wattle fence in his fists and squeezing his eyes closed. What a pathetic life he's lived. His first glimpse at a native village is of mud and what does he feel? Not disgust. Not judgment. Not even educational curiosity. No. *Jealousy.* Of grimy children poking mud. Kale grits his teeth. Opens his eyes. Thinks of that prisoner, Rathyn. Is this the eye-opening he predicted?

The children hum tunes, occasionally even singing words Kale can't make out. He chuckles. Of course the little brats are better singers than him. His mesmerization is broken by the sight of Kalderys and his primes entering the village. A couple of natives accompany them. One is old and leaning on a stick, the other looks hungry. Come to think of it, they both look hungry. As do the children. The old man's skin is nearly as dark as rich earth, and is as leathery and wrinkled as his back is bent.

The younger native gestures with his hands. More natives begin to assemble, moving cautiously toward the magus. He and his pristine primes look ridiculously out of place. They stand taller than the gathering natives, and their deles are mud-free. Kale considers his own appearance. If it weren't for the nice dele Culver loaned him, he could nearly pass for a native. What marks him apart is the lightness of his skin, dry soil at the darkest. He's spent more of his life in the sun's absence than its smile.

The old man is addressing the huts, the village at large. Kale can't hear him, so he creeps closer, edging along the hog fence. If that man's words are a call to arms, it isn't effective. But that doesn't seem to be the case. He and his younger companion appear to be cooperating with the tall exemplars. Villagers poke their heads from huts, abandon their field tools, detach from shade trees, approach warily. Kale scoffs. Those aren't spies.

Annihilation.

The magister's word sends a jolt through Kale each time he remembers it, but despite his mounting anticipation, everything he's witnessing suggests she drastically overstated the danger of the magus' mission. The sun is high and bright. The villagers appear unconcerned. The hogs are utterly unbothered. What if the villagers just turn over the spies? What if they're not even aware of any spies? What if the ominous sounding Campaign of Cleansing turns out to be a battle of water and scrub brushes against dirty natives?

One of Kalderys' sentinels calls something out over the village. It's Prime Sentinel Selu, her voice bright and commanding. Maybe it's meant to reassure the gathering. It has the opposite effect on Kale. Selu seems to always be looking for a fight, even now, with her hand in the air gesturing for everyone to gather round. Prime Sentinel Arc, standing by Kalderys' other shoulder, looks impatient. He's always inconvenienced by something. Kale's never had any use for either of them, however awestruck the rest of Erudition is in their presence. They're unpleasant. Boringly dutiful.

The natives continue to approach, any concern on their expressions or posture devolving into curiosity or annoyance. But Kale's apprehension is intensifying. Something's wrong with the air. It shouldn't be so dry or still or ... dense. He needs to hear what's being said but it's hard with the unnatural pressure in his ears. He navigates out of the shadows beside the hog fence, creeping between patches of sedge at a crouch and focusing intently on not existing. He's never tested his little invisibility trick on those ungifted in consonance. This would be one hell of a time to learn it doesn't work. He considers the consequences of being caught out here, and once again is surprised to learn he's no longer in such a hurry to die. If the villagers' attention wasn't aimed at the magus and his sentinels, he'd be in plain sight. Surely, even if he can disappear, lessening his imprint can only accomplish so much in the afternoon sun with an audience of dozens.

Kalderys is still talking, and Kale can almost make out his words. The natives don't appear to expect confrontation. If Kale's any judge, they're more confused by what he's saying than afraid or offended. It appears the last of the adult villagers have arrived. Some of them are carrying long-handled tools of wood and bone and shell. No steel. Some wear wide-brimmed straw platters on their heads that cast shadows over their faces and shoulders. Some of the adults carry small children on their hip, or herd them. Each child is more indecent than the last. Kale smiles. Aside from the dirty skin and unruly hair, the naked magister would fit right in. Decency is lacking out here. But if that's the worst of their offenses, Kalderys' hike seems excessive. What will they do with all the summoned energy when they determine this lot to be innocent?

Tension is melting from Kale's shoulders. He's disappointed. Had he expected violence and blood and battle? Had he hoped for it? He surely hadn't expected the Untamed to look so ... boring. Assuming this place is even Untamed. Even after meeting the diminutive prisoner, Kale had imagined painted faces, daunting weapons, maybe even clothing lined in steel. He shakes his head at his naivety. This is a village of laborers.

Kale looks at his feet. They hurt, but somehow the layers of dirt and dust are dulling that to a throbbing numbness. There is dried blood from cracked skin or puncture wounds from some bastard jungle plant. He can't tell how bad the wounds are. What are his plans from here? This was far from the great eye-opening adventure he'd hoped for. Was this promise of a new exotic purpose for his life a lie? He frowns. That would be cruel. Are the children as bored as he is? Kale turns to them. Most are looking at Kalderys and the gathered people. Except one boy. He's hunched on the ground, head askew as if nearly asleep, looking directly at Kale with disinterested eyes. Kale sucks in a breath. Imala-be-damned, he let his guard down! He tries to lessen his imprint further but it's no use. That boy's attention is stuck on him. Kale places a single finger against his lips and exhales a slow, "*Shhhh.*"

The boy smiles, his lips parting to reveal a gap where his upper two front teeth should be. Kale unintentionally smiles back, surprised. *Natives lose their teeth too.* Of course they do. Why wouldn't they? He marvels at his stupidity. What exactly was he expecting out here?

Raised voices draw Kale's attention back to the gathering. The hungry man who'd been supporting the old villager is yelling, gesturing wildly with his skinny bare arms, now and then pointing a finger directly in Kalderys' face. The magus and his primes stand like bleached statues. Kale edges closer, barely able to believe his eyes at this native's gall. A woman grabs him, tries to pull him back, but he jerks his arm free of her. His next words are shouted so loudly there is no misunderstanding them.

"Intemrus' holy hound is all you are! Why ain't he here? Got no teeth of his own?"

Magus Kalderys' shoulders rise and straighten. His chin dips as if this was the affirmation he'd hoped for. He throws a glance back at Selu to his left. She nods at him, meets eyes with Arc, who also nods. Kalderys assumes rhystic dominance, placing the fingertips of each hand on the wrist of the other directly in front of his sternum. Kale's ears pop and the hair on his neck stands on end. The air is squeezing in on the entire clearing. The townsfolk murmur, begin to edge backward. Kale rubs his ears. It feels like his skull is endensing his brain. The temperature hasn't changed, but at the rate the air is compressing it will soon. There's a high-pitched ringing coming from somewhere, maybe inside Kale's head. It feels like thumbs are invading his eye sockets. What is Kalderys considering that requires this much energy? That's one skinny man, couldn't they just hit him with a stave? Kale covers his ears, which does nothing for the pressure. The townsfolk seem to be considering running, but none appear to be as affected as Kale.

"*Intemrus' Will* ..." Kalderys' voice is magnified, riding compressed air and booming over the clearing. A suffocating stillness follows it, leaving Kale wondering if the outburst deafened him. Then his voice rings out once more. "... *be done.*"

Lightning rips out of the blue sky with a resounding *crack!* Kale falls, stunned, rolling backward and blinking furiously to regain sight. He scrambles up. Through the haze of the flash, he's able to see the man who'd confronted Kalderys. Or what was the man. He's now at the terminus of the lightning and engulfed in white flame. A net of lightning bolts streak from him and ensnares more villagers. The man disintegrates like tuft from a dandelion. He's gone. Someone screams. It isn't Kale, because both his hands are plastered to his mouth. Natives turn and run. They're snatched by lightning, cocooned in hissing, flickering light. More and more bolts of lightning are spawning, reproducing with each target they snatch. With sharp *pops!* men and women become nothing more than ascending ashes.

Kalderys and his primes are stone-faced statues posed in rhystic dominance. The villagers fall over one another, crying out, but the lightning is too fast. Kale scurries backward toward the jungle. He's about to leap to his ragged feet and make a break for it when he remembers the children. The boy who spotted him has turned his attention to the flaming tendrils. Kale stops retreating. That fire isn't slowing. It will ingest the entire community. Did Kalderys not see the children? That boy is no spy.

Kale gains his feet and runs for the child. Got to get him to lie down and maybe the lightning will pass over. The boy's cheeks are lit up by the coming fire.

"Hey," Kale calls, wishing he knew the boy's name. "You have to lie down!"

The boy doesn't hear him. He's enthralled. Probably not even aware of what's happening. The lightning will dismantle him like it's doing to everyone else.

"Kalderys, wait!" Kale screams, but his voice is buried under the deafening crackle of white fire, the cries of the horrified. He's running for all he's worth but might as well be standing still. Distance is inconsequential to the lightning. Before Kale has covered a third of the expanse, he knows he'll never make it.

The children don't cry out. They don't have a chance. They watch with round-eyed wonder as blinding fire seizes them. Kale shields his eyes, but not before witnessing a sight he knows he'll carry until his death. The lightning has its way with their small bodies much quicker than the adults, shaking them apart is if they were never made of flesh to begin with. Kale can barely see it through the bright flame, the blur of tears, but the pops of the children bursting into ash drives him to his knees.

He punches the dirt, unable to comprehend the violence he's witnessing, aghast at this sudden emotion. He's crying. Nearly sobbing. Why? He doesn't know these people. Doesn't owe them. It's hard to breathe. The air is scalding hot. The lightning, now branched out in all directions and surrounding him, is nowhere near satiated. Kale never intended to die this confused. But it seems to be time. At last.

~

Kalderys rides a supersensory trance while channeling the almighty Imala. He's aware of his own body only because it elicits signs of life, as do those of his sentinels. The white fire does not hunger for them. This is Kalderys' will. This is his judgment, sizzling through the village. Kalderys speaks to his lightning and it speaks back. It will find them all. It has no choice. It exists to end their existence, as breathing entities anyway. And today they burn so hot not even their breath remains.

His consonant song is a litany of lightning, which draws all the atmosphere's heat and aridity into unified strands, bound to his bidding. The Imala respond by exciting the air itself into plasma. Every collision accelerates it, magnifies it to collide faster in an electrical avalanche. Its targets are the only objects tangible to the fire. Plasma inhales the guilty and gifts the sky with their carbon remnants. This song is a plea to a gracious Imala, who will reward the discipline of a devout exemplar with immolation for all vulgarity.

The lightning is alive, stretching and breathing to serve its purpose. Slight deviations are to be expected in its path, as well as inaccuracies in the chaplain's census. Natives visiting from other communities picked the wrong day. All who are present will die. Kalderys does not need to know the exact count of recipients for his lightning. It is clever enough. If energy needs to spread thinner to reach more, some will simply burn less brightly. There is plenty of death for all.

It is not Intemrus' Will that citizens of Ausgan's jungles should die. But if they choose a path leading to death, he is no tyrant. His will does not supersede their freedom to disobey. They can become corrupted if they must. And in response, Kalderys cleanses. Because when the bloody beasts of Fohrvylda spill from their high cliffs, cross the Faithless Sea, and carve into Ausgan's beaches, there will be no room for rebellion in Ausgan's response. No safe nooks for barbarians to take harbor in Erudition's own yard. Not if consonance is to survive the Heathen Tide. The Untamed must be fought back.

Screams run thin. Lightning has branched to the edges of the village, plucking out remnants. There are always remnants. But Kalderys is prepared. His fire has jagged, white arms that intersect huts and scorch holes in the thatching. The arms flash into the jungle, reaching after the miscreants who think they can outrun consequence.

Suddenly, the net of lightning collapses, utterly disobeying him. It rushes inward, converging on a point beyond a low hut. In an instant, every bit of it is gone. Too soon. His vision darkens as if the sun was eclipsed. Kalderys rocks backward, staggers, falls to his knees as his earthly consciousness hammers prematurely into place.

"Stragglers," says Prime Sentinel Selu.

Kalderys hasn't regained balance enough to stand, hasn't regained sight enough to survey the village or even plant his eyes on Selu's face, but her surprise is evident. She's afraid she or Arc is to blame. She thinks the song was not powerful enough. That is not what this is.

"None can live," Kalderys coughs out, and his sentinels are away, chitin-tipped staves in hand. No native can outrun them. And once caught, no native can defend against them.

Kalderys rises to his feet by pulling himself up on his own stave. Sight returns gradually, making darkness recede. The energy had been plenty enough. They'd not under summoned. It was as if he'd been negated. Kalderys sends a pulse over the village. Something behind that hut still lives. It must be what inhaled his lightning. A powerful negator? Surely not sent by the sovereign, and therefore not intended to be there. Whoever or whatever it is, the primes ran right past it. But its mass seems to be identical ... to the anomaly. Kalderys tries to walk and lurches forward onto his knees in the mud.

"Show yourself!" he roars so hard he grows lightheaded. Channeling sickness? Kalderys has not suffered it for years. He's never had his guts tugged violently from his stomach, but that can't feel much worse than this.

There's a speck of movement ahead. On the far edge of the clearing foliage shakes where something has penetrated the jungle. The individual Kalderys observed behind the hut is gone. He shakes his head, attempting to regain clarity. Nothing is that fast.

"Primes, to me," Kalderys calls out, trying again to make his way to the hut. This time he falls forward onto his face. His eyes are not serving him. But the sensory pulse he'd managed to send told him enough. This was shaped like a man. Whoever it was is escaping and there's nothing Kalderys can do. He got a split moment's glimpse so brief it hardly registered, but it looked like the perpetrator wore a colored garment. That detail eliminates nearly any native.

Kalderys presses his knuckles into the mud and rises to crawling position. He has to see the footprints. Has to find a clue of who did this. His vision spins and a sharp ache pumps to life behind his eyes. His training should have made him resilient to nausea and yet he's crippled by it. It feels as if he's been attacked, and yet in all his years it's an attack that no one in Stravhelm ever warned him of, not even the sovereign.

His sentinels return one at a time. Prime Sentinel Arc is out of breath, his hands on his knees, watching Kalderys from under his heavy chitin helmet. He's been herding the remnants for Prime Sentinel Selu, who is, as always, tall and composed, despite the blood soaking into her stave and gloves. Blood paints the right shoulder of her armored dele. It's spattered across her ruddy cheek, contrasting the paleness of her eyes. She is the hardiest runner out of all Erudition. A physical paragon, proficient in consonance and martial arts. But even if she weren't, Kalderys would have acquired her. Her devotion to training, to the sovereign, and to consonance are fierce, unshakable.

"The stragglers are dealt with, Magus," she says. It pains Kalderys to hear the fear in her voice.

"This isn't your fault. I was negated. The offender went that way." Kalderys points to the jungle, simultaneously pulsing. The negator is already a quarter of a mile away. Soon they'll be out of Kalderys' pulse range. But they're slowing. And they left a trail, a linear imprint forming a path that burns deep into the jungle. If the jungle continues to slow their movement or provide the means to track their path, then hope is not lost.

"You were *negated*?" Arc asks. His inflection suggests that he doesn't believe it. As if he blames Kalderys for this failure. And why shouldn't he? Who could have done what Kalderys is suggesting? He grits his teeth.

"Arc, follow them," Kalderys says. "Nothing moves that quickly without leaving a mark. Find the tracks. They are slowing."

Prime Sentinel Arc runs after the negator immediately. Selu watches him, fists clenching her stave. Kalderys attempts to regroup. Darkness falls fast out here. The bodies that weren't immolated must be burned with the rest of the village. Kalderys climbs to his feet, steadies himself with his stave, watches Arc breach the jungle. If he's out there when the sun falls, he'll be in danger. Nocturnal jungle wildlife has a particular appetite for errant exemplars. Hopefully he has the sense to seek shelter in a village.

Selu still gazes toward the jungle where Arc disappeared. She's probably thinking something similar. She's who Kalderys would have preferred to send. Less likely to tire, to grow complacent, to grumble. But he needs her here. And if the jungle claims one of his primes, there's no question which one he'd rather it be.

Kalderys needs answers. But he can't let Prime Sentinel Selu see weakness. The sovereign's own prime negators aren't strong enough to accomplish what just happened. Not without dying on the spot. And yet this single exemplar became the vacuum that undid Kalderys' song.

His head spins, making it hard to focus on anything besides the mud seeping up around his boots. This is far from the outcome he'd hoped for. Is this the consequence for not examining the anomaly? For letting it so close to him without knowing its identity or intentions? Was this a test? He frowns. Is this the consequence for considering the magister human rather than divine, albeit briefly? Anger washes over him, pushing the nausea away.

Kalderys sends out a vigorous pulse. There are six unburned bodies. Four lie where they were corralled on the western edge of town, and two lie with shattered skulls bleeding out in the nearby fields.

"Sentinel Selu, I need you to finish the job," Kalderys says.

"At once." And she's off to collect the bodies.

It will be late before they finish the incineration. Past midnight when they arrive back at Erudition, with or without Prime Sentinel Arc. When they return, Magister Obsydia will have to be informed. That is, unless she already knows.

Intemrus sees all.

13
Eyes Opened

AUSGAN
The Jungle

Kale is bodiless, flying upstream in a roaring waterfall. The world is a river of green. He is pummeled with water but is not wet. Maybe it's wind. Maybe he's falling. The green gale screams at him, pinning his extremities flat, except he doesn't feel bound by physical existence. He tries to lift an arm but can't figure out how. Perhaps he's become immaterial. There is a quaking movement in his core, pounding, as if his legs are being clubbed by staves. Lightning is all he smells and tastes. It's in his mind but not burning him. He opens his mouth to scream but instead there's a burst of light, flickering, then gone in an instant.

The vague rumbling is becoming embodied in his lower extremities. Globs of rushing energy ping off his face and shoulders, turning to sparks then disappearing. He can move his eyes, or at least his attention, enough to observe flashes of white above, flashes of black below.

There is a familiarity to his feelings. He's not felt it for some time. Not since the days he negated for adepts. It is the strange trembling sensation that exists when he should be experiencing negation sickness. Only this is far stronger.

Sounds are beginning to infiltrate the roaring wind. Squeals, growls, insect-like creaking. Sounds of solid impacts as if exemplars are training nearby with batons. His journey becomes more tumultuous. Kale jostles and shakes. Flashes of recognizable objects pierce his consciousness. Broad leaves. Liana vines. Smooth bark of deep buttress roots. All disrupting his flight. Rhythm becomes evident in his pounding legs. He isn't flying. He's running. A grim memory surfaces like a punch to the face.

Kalderys.

He'd sung consonance. And Kale had stood by while it consumed most every villager in Hargrim. Then it tried to consume him.

His senses are enhanced. His veins are wide tunnels. His rushing blood sends sparks over his skin, from scalp to hands, to toes, then back again, over and over. His arms are stretched behind him and he leans into the wind. His feet tear through the underbrush on their own volition, leaping, flailing wildly, somehow not sending him crashing end over end.

This is not negation sickness. There are a dozen different manifestations of that, and Kale's seen them all—seizures, nausea, vertigo, muscle spasms. Kale stood by once as Basalt Reina took on more energy than she could handle. She gagged and heaved until she suffocated. She died on the beach with her eyes wide and bloody, her cheek mashed into a puddle of sandy bile. Kale escapes the vision to find it replaced with the boy from the village, smiling at him with dirt on his cheek, then flashing into surprised light, drifting away as ash.

Kale's feet are pushing harder than should be possible. His skin is impenetrable. He runs with the energy he stole from Kalderys' song. But the jungle is vaster than his endurance. Its limbs and leaves are slowing him. Something furry and arm-like darts out as if to catch him. He passes through it like it was made of smoke. A shrill cry flares up, the hint of burning hair touches his nostrils. Warm liquid seeps over his shoulder, tickling his back. He's aware of his dele flapping in the wind as his feet beat the earth. Still he has no control over his path.

Kale searches his thoughts, trying to figure out what is happening and why. He'd been struck during the white fire's dance. But unlike the people of Hargrim, he didn't burn. He could have. The energy was plenty enough. But Kale observed its approach and somehow, without conscious effort, without physically moving, he sidestepped it, exactly as he did the magus' supersensory pulses. He watched the lightning contact his skin, and in that moment created an alternate path for it. A path that led not somewhere else. *Somehow* else.

The lightning didn't inhale him. It vanished. Time grew slow. The huts around him wavered in heat, succumbing to fire. Sentinels glided past him as if they ran underwater, their voices low rattling growls. Screams of burning natives like unearthly beasts, ripping their throats and sustaining almost forever, until the staves of the sentinels resounded off their heads like boats banging against docks, crumpling their burning bodies into piles.

At that point, having unexpectedly survived, it occurred to Kale to run away. That's when he'd become kinetic energy. It was like Kalderys propelled him, as if gravity itself bent and Kalderys was up and Kale, sheathed in energy, fell through the jungle.

Kale had never put a face to the idea of spies or blasphemers until he met the prisoner beneath Stravhelm. The prisoner wasn't who he expected when he thought of spies. And neither were those laborers, or the children who played in the dirt. The boy with filthy cheeks. Did Intemrus want that child dead? Why? How much threat could he have represented, smiling on the ground and waiting for his new teeth? As much as Kale doesn't understand, he knows that was not the first time Magus Kalderys and his sentinels used consonance to execute a collection of people. It was not the first campaign the magister ordained. And the sovereign most definitely knew it happened.

"You're gonna have your eyes opened when you meet my lot. Once that's done, there's no shutting them back."

Is this what Rathyn meant? He knew this happens?

Kale's foot twists on a root and he loses balance. A tree hits his shoulder, spinning him as he staggers, sending him thumping to the ground on his back. He's finally stopped moving but his vision hasn't. He rolls onto his side just before the vomit comes. He retches. Then again. Then again and again until there's nothing left to throw up except strained whimpers.

Kale's emotions are a storm, which is, in itself, too alien a sensation for him to try to grasp. He'd been convinced that years of empty time had decayed his ability to feel anything. How wrong he'd been. He never could have predicted what he witnessed at Hargrim. That boy shouldn't have died. Kalderys shouldn't have done it. Kale should have done more to stop him. What, he's not sure. But something.

Tears burn his eyes. His teeth chatter and a deep shudder runs down his spine, making his back muscles squeeze involuntarily. It's with a dull dread that Kale feels his own unique variant of negation sickness encroaching. Tremors. With simple negation, it amounts to his hands being unsteady for a couple of hours, as with the ashmancer's pebble song. But Kalderys' song was far from simple.

Kale's hands are bleeding. But they can't be as bad off as his feet. His sandals are gone. Where, who knows? Obliterated by his electrified sprint if he had to guess. He's run his last. His legs and knees and shins and ankles and feet all feel as if he's tumbled down the western face of Mount Adenhelm. He's drenched with sweat and chafed from his dele and shaking like a leaf in a breeze. In the jungle's dying light, he has no way of assessing his injuries. But what's the point of assessing injuries if he's not done collecting them? Besides, he has no water to rinse his wounds, no ointment to clean them. He didn't think to bring any medicinal supplies. Even if he'd had the time and means, that would have been the last thing he packed. He knew he might die out here. Perhaps hoped for it. Medicine would only forestall that. How clueless he'd been to the degrees of suffering that exist between boredom and death.

"You idiot," Kale whispers, wedging himself between great buttress roots, trying to keep his rattling skeleton from falling apart completely. High above, the forest's black canopy is silhouetted against an azure sky. Darkness in the jungle makes the leaves, vines, and trees meld together into a flat ceiling. Insects and frogs and night birds produce a reverberating cacophony. Bioluminescent insects and fungus illuminate the forest in blue flashes and orange pulses. Exemplars are warned from a young age about the many creatures of the night jungle who crave the flesh and blood of mankind.

Kale isn't safe here. But he can't make it any farther. Not in this darkness. Not on these feet. He pulls his knees to his chest and presses his forehead against them and closes his eyes, wondering if bleeding out would be worse than being consumed a bite at a time. He tests reducing his imprint. Immediately he can tell his abilities are stronger. Whatever energy shot him through the jungle and reduced him to a shivering wreck is also strengthening his negation. He's invisible. Less alive than a stone, despite his shivering. Less odorous than air, despite his sweat and blood. Less noisy than a tree's heart, despite the pounding of his own, despite the seizure that rubs his back raw against the bark of the roots.

In spite of the events that led Kale to where he sits, there is a barely audible voice within him whispering out from behind pain and dread that is undeniably thankful for this opportunity. Whatever happens, even if that includes dying in the next several hours, he is glad. If he were back home, he'd be readying for sleep right now. He'd be flat on his back on his stone cot under a thin sheet, anticipating the night count and the moans of his suffering neighbors. Or maybe he'd be planning to creep around Erudition. Alone. Again.

Kale takes a wavering breath, exhaustion tugging at his consciousness. He will die out here tonight. And of all his cycling, spiraling emotions, regret is not among them. Culver will forget him, finally going on to be the exemplar he was meant to be. Alika will have to enlist other basalts for his negation demonstration. But that should pull them from their duties of negating for the inexperienced and often vicious rhyolite mancers in training. Ashmancer Haik ... well, he'll have to find a new target for his cruelty. And while the thought of a Haik deprived of a tormentee nearly brings a smile to Kale's face, it is closely followed by another series of more troubling thoughts.

What if Haik could have been stopped once and for all? What if Kalderys' campaign could have been prevented? And what if Kale is the only one who could have done it?

It doesn't matter now, he thinks, but isn't quite able to believe it. *Damn prisoner*. This speculation is his doing. Kale's had his eyes opened. And soon enough they'll be closed once and for all. It's just like he wanted. Isn't it?

14
When All the Good is Gone

FOHRVYLDA
Below the Towers

Frigid saltwater slaps Kraus' face and invades his nostrils, dredging him out of a forgery of sleep. Consciousness arrives gradually. He's on his back, soaked through and through, and suffering from a ferocious thirst. The air smells like fish. Maybe the water's been slapping him for some time. It wasn't a hassle until it tried to drown him. He pulls air into his battered chest, seals his lips, and forcefully expels water, snot, blood, and sand out of his nostrils. The action nearly makes him chuckle. Probably resembled a whale surfacing. The grey light pushing through his partly open eyelids makes him aware of a stamping headache. But that's nothing new.

Kraus blinks away the gunk crusting his eyelids and cranes his head toward the light. A giant serpent's eye is staring back at him with a pupil like a blade. *Except ...* He squints, allows reality to get its footing. *That is no eyeball.* He's within a cavern on the edge of the ocean, lying in shallow water, looking at the cave mouth, whose opening is reflected in the water, forming a circle. What he mistook for a pupil is the silhouette of Irdessa standing some thirty feet away in the entrance as rain falls on the ocean. Kraus groans. If only this were his first time waking up beside the ocean. Or fifth. A wave smacks his face. Water seeps into his ear. He tries to sit up.

"Shit!"

His entire body protests the movement. Now he remembers. *Irdessa, you feisty fireball.* He touches his face and finds a straight cut along his right cheek that travels through the cartilage of his nose. That's what he needed, more scars. It was a tactical strike on her part, almost got his eyes. His forearm is throbbing. The knife through the arm ... it hurts plenty good, but that was uncouth, like being served a plate of steaming shellfish but instead of your host setting the dish before you, he throws it in your lap.

Kraus' bones hurt all over. His impact on the sea is probably to blame. Breaking Irdessa's fall couldn't have helped. There's a stabbing pain deep in the back of his left shoulder, as if there's an extra bone in there. He tests his arm. Can't lift it over his head, but his shoulder's not out of its joint. Nothing seems broken.

Kraus stands slowly, feeling a lot like any or all of his limbs might give up and fall off in the process. He's amused to learn his feet are the only part of him not slathered in glorious pain. His poor cracked knee almost seems jealous to no longer be the worst of his wounds. He shuffles through the shallow water over uneven stones toward the cave's mouth, snorting out the rest of the snotty sea water.

"Looks like you made it out alive," he says, stopping beside Irdessa. The sound his voice makes is so gravelly he's surprised she doesn't scream, or jump, or react at all. Her bloodshot eyes are on something distant. Her face is haggard, splotched with dirt and dried blood. Her lips are pale and chapped. Kraus has seen two-day-old corpses that looked more vibrant. She's standing though, so there's that.

Kraus stands beside her and stares forward, as if that's the thing to do. What's visible of the sky is soot grey. A sharp wind slings rain along the face of the cavern. Occupying the ocean before them are natural pillars of earth and stone, some hundreds of yards in diameter, rising out of the choppy sea to stab straight into grey clouds high above. He and Irdessa are among the Towers, the distinct land feature that flanks the northern perimeter of Fohrvylda. A current must have brought them here, and while it's impossible to know how far they drifted, this is better than he could have hoped for. Promontory is surely scouring the rocks below Keswal, and probably Fohrvylda's entire western coast, looking for their bodies.

The Towers are massive columns, their forested caps level with Fohrvylda's mainland. Observed from the mainland, they extend northward as far as the eye can see, supposedly all the way to Redemier. From down here they look like enormous earthen stilts. Admiral Garr's ships can't safely traverse them, meaning only the falconer's sprakes or orcane patrols will be hunting them here, if anyone is. Hopefully the storm and the Towers themselves are enough to keep them hidden.

"That was a wild one, wasn't it?" Kraus musters his best impression of a smile.

Aside from a tremble of her lips, Irdessa does not move. It's probably for the better. His smiles usually have the opposite effect than he intended.

Kraus reaches back to scratch at the pain in his shoulder. Can't quite reach it. He's not sure what to say but that's not new either. "Haven't seen my pack, have you? I had some water in there."

Her shoulders droop further, as if his voice is leeching the life out of her. Maybe he should keep his mouth shut. Except orcane patrols will be searching soon if they aren't already, even if Kraus and Irdessa are presumed dead. The cover of rain will help them remain unseen, but it won't last forever, and it certainly won't protect them from sprakes.

"I guess we ought to move on," Kraus tries. "I figure we get our bearings then go east. Skirt the mainland until we find Ivolde Bay." The idea was to escape Keswal and hit the rocks running. While that didn't happen exactly as planned, at least the current pulled them in the right direction.

Still no response. Irdessa shivers. Hopefully not due to a fever.

Kraus forces out what hopefully comes off as a harmless chuckle. "Well, if it makes you feel any better—"

"Why did he die?" Her voice is thin and high, like a whistle in a cemetery. It paints in Kraus' imagination a single candle in an unlit room. After that fight, she could be talking about any number of people. But Kraus knows.

"Squaring off with the uergatas was part of his plan," he says. It isn't the best answer, but what is?

"Then why aren't we dead?"

Kraus scratches a scab on the back of his hand. *I've asked myself that a hundred, hundred times.* "Part of the plan," he says, feeling a lot like a parrot.

Her shoulders rise slowly, then fall even lower. A sprake cries distantly, and the sound is so lonely that Kraus wonders if anything is alive down here at all.

"What plan?" It's little more than a whisper.

Kraus takes a deep breath. "The plan was—well, it is—*Irdessa lives. Get her home to Vim. Nothing else matters.*"

She's shaking her head. Tears rolls down her bloody cheeks. "I don't want to be alive." Her voice breaks as she says it.

Kraus frowns. It's fucking wrong is what it is. Irdessa is the strong one, not the one who cries. Except now. She is pitiful. *Torvald, you son of a bitch. We should have all died together.* Her face is pinched by silent sobs, hands empty at her sides, shoulders trembling.

Kraus' mind goes to violence. But whose blood will make this right? Torvald should have picked someone else for this job and let Kraus die as the diversion. Except no one else would have distracted the archers the way Torvald did, least of all some rapist. It was only because he fought the goatmen and died, and the arena watched, that Kraus could free Irdessa.

That fact doesn't help in this moment. Someone smarter than Kraus would know what to say to make things better. They'd touch Irdessa's shoulder or hug her and then she'd stop crying. Kraus looks at his hands, as if they can accomplish something besides gripping bottles and choking men. Maybe someone smart would cry alongside her. Make her less lonely maybe? Kraus has never been one to cry, but this seems a prime time to start. All you need for that is a heart, right?

Then we're shit out of luck. Guess I'll just stand here like a two-legged cow.

Except ...

Pain'll fix everything.

His hands twitch. Wouldn't take much to open up a wound. And there are plenty to choose from. His fingers find the crusty opening of the new knife wound on his right forearm. *Pry it open.* The scab cracks. It wasn't much of a scab yet anyway. The hole in his skin grows warm and slick. His heart thumps quicker. She cut him good. He has yet to thank her for that. If he pushes hard enough, he can probably force a pinky finger down in—

"There were never any traps, were there?" Her voice drags him back down into the frigid cave mouth. His heartbeat punches his temples.

Kraus clears his throat, spits a red clot into the ocean. "No."

She snorts. "Did Torvald know everyone else would die?"

"He knew they might."

"They did," she says. "Everyone died. Fucking Prancer died. For what?" There's anger in her voice now and that comforts Kraus. If he's learned anything about survival, anger pumping in your veins is the next best thing to blood itself.

Irdessa turns her red eyes on Kraus. "Everyone died so that I could live."

It seems dangerous to affirm, however obvious the statement is.

"They didn't agree to it," she says. "They had no idea. For—" A gasp steals her breath. "For two years. All those lives ... my survival at their expense." She shakes her head. The tears are gone, but they left their tracks on the sodden mess that is her face. "His name wasn't Prancer. It was Pinprae. He told me that was his grandmother's sister's name."

Kraus looks at his boots through the shimmering water. His toes aren't getting any warmer. Who the hell names their boy after their mother's sister? He doesn't bother trying to muster up sympathy for Prancer, or Pinprae, or whoever. Never had much of that to offer.

"It could be worse," he says. Seemed useful right up until it fell out of his mouth.

Something between a laugh and a sob breaks free of her. "I can't imagine how."

Kraus scratches his temple, finds a clot of blood, chips at it with his fingernails. For a long time neither of them speak. The truth is, it could always be worse. Don't tempt fate by saying it couldn't. Kraus has learned that enough times.

"Why me?" Her whisper is barely audible over the shushing of rain, the waves breaking on the grey cliff walls. Out between the towering islands, silhouettes of upright spears stride across the rippled surface of the Faithless. Orcane patrols, ranging in groups of three. The riders stand atop their swimming beasts, reins in one hand, long spears or tridents in the other. There's no telling how long they've been circling these waters looking for bodies while being pummeled by the storm. They probably don't want to be down here any more than Kraus does.

Suppose they come this way and find us, will they arrest us? Kraus pictures it in his mind. They'll be excited first, thinking of their reward. Eager to tie wrists and ankles. But there will be no capture, because there will be no surrender. *I'll give them no choice.* They'll have to put him down. The idea is like a ray of sunlight in his mind, infiltrating the itchy scabs and soggy leather and exhaustion that entomb him. Hell, if he called out loud enough, he could probably initiate that rendezvous.

"Enough bodies have fallen there to attract an audience with a particular hunger." Irdessa's voice is lacking life, her eyes distant. Sounds like she's quoting someone. Torvald? Referring to a fall from Keswal? Without expounding, Irdessa wades forward. The water is at her waist and rising.

"Um, Dess?"

She gives a trembling exhale and sinks entirely beneath the surface, then sits still. That water's got to be painful. It's cold on Kraus and he's got meat on his bones.

"Hey, uh ... Dess?"

Irdessa's hair drifts like seaweed. Bubbles rise through it to the surface.

"Oh no you don't." Kraus plunges a hand into the water and hauls her up by her arm. She gasps for air, hacking and coughing.

"Can't let you do that," Kraus says. "I promised Torvald I'd get you to Vim."

The grief in her red eyes turns to rage. Kraus doesn't see her draw the knife, but he was ready for it. Once you've been greeted by a blade enough times, you come to expect one even in the unlikeliest situations. Sometimes even hope for it.

He catches her wrist before the blade can plunge into his neck.

"You didn't stop him from killing himself," she says. "What's it matter to you if I die?"

He strips the knife out of her hand by its blade. Hot blood slicks his palm. She aims a kick at his bad knee. He's able to pivot away before it lands.

"Let me die! Don't you like them that way?"

"Don't I ... what?"

"What kind of trade is a rapist for the Tactician?"

Kraus' face becomes a scowl. Turns out Irdessa doesn't need a blade to cut him. A deathly chill invades his gut, colder than the blustery wind or the icy water. He squeezes the handle of the knife. His thoughts turn bloody again, this time toward her. Usually, if he's not drunk, this sort of thinking leads to a helping of shame. It's worse when there's no shame. Worse for everyone.

"I didn't ask to live," he says.

"Neither did I," Irdessa says. "But I'm not too sandgutted to fix that."

He works his tongue in his aching mouth. "Someone told me once that no matter how bad you've got it, there's a person out there who needs you." The sentiment feels hollow. He did hear someone say it. That part's true. But they certainly weren't talking to Kraus the Rapist.

"How's that my problem?"

He opens his mouth to answer but there isn't one.

"Give me my knife," she says. Her eyes look manic.

"Hell no."

She takes a sloshing step toward him and glares up at his face, one hand extended. "Give it!"

A smile comes over Kraus. "Dess, you look like a fox barking at a—*hurg!*"

He gags. She's jabbed him in the throat. He's too surprised to keep her from snatching his wrist and twisting with both hands. She's not strong enough to get the knife from him. But now she's maneuvered a foot behind his and she gives a solid kick to his bad knee. He can't correct his footing. As he falls he flings the knife out into the ocean.

"Bastard," she yells, throwing a knee into his nose with a crack, making stars dance behind his eyelids. Blood flows over his cheek and out his nostrils. He's on his ass, nearly debilitated by the stabbing pressure in his shoulder, blinded by tears and blood, scrambling for a rock big enough to clock her with. How in all hell does she still have so much fight? He finds one and pulls it up, but Irdessa rips it from his hand like he collected it for her. He doesn't have time to guard his head. The rock hits his skull like it was lobbed by a catapult. His ear is ringing, the world tilting. He's gone under. Saltwater invades his nose and eyes and ears. He swallows a mouthful and vomits bubbles. She's holding him down by his hair in a stance stretched too wide for her legs to be caught by his grasping hands. All her weight's on his head.

Drowning is less fun than bleeding. Isn't much fun at all, based on the limited education Kraus has at it, and it isn't a subject he has any intention of mastering. The aches in his skin and muscles and bones focus to a pressurized panic.

Before he knows it, he's standing up, holding Irdessa's throat in one hand and punching her head with the other. The thumps ring out in the narrow cavern like nails being driven into a coffin. He slings her toward the rear of the cave. She tumbles through the shallows and lands in a gasping heap.

Kraus retches up seawater. "Godsdammit, *stop!*" His scream fills the cave like a dying orcane's roar. The pain closes in on him again from every direction, and by the gods it is welcome. "I'm taking you to Vim," he groans as his vision wavers between darkness and light.

There's his pack, half-buried under black silt in the shallows. He splashes down onto a submerged stone next to it, blinking away stars.

"You could kill yourself," says the pile of heaving leather and black hair.

Kraus chuckles. "That never seems to work." He retrieves his bag. It should still contain stitching and bandages, unless they fell out. Antiseptic tincture unless the glass broke. Lahuvot willing, the water skin is intact. "This'll be easier if you work with me. But I'll carry you if I have to."

"Why do you even care?" she says. "Torvald's dead. Go home."

"I don't have one of those."

"Then go fuck yourself, Kraus. I don't care. Leave me alone."

The stitching and needle is in the bag. So is the tincture, and Kraus has half a mind to down it. A godsdamned drink would hit the spot.

"I'm not worth much," Kraus says. "That ain't no secret. But Torvald trusted me. And people don't ... do that so often." *No one has ever trusted me.* "I made him a promise." *Like some great big stupid child.* "And he died ... while I went free. The least I can do is try."

She sits up slowly, sucking air through her teeth and holding her side. Blood runs from split skin on her left cheek. She gives a harsh laugh. "You think this will undo what you are? You're delusional."

"You've got a sharp tongue on you," Kraus says. "I didn't promise Torvald you'd get there with it."

She takes a palmful of seawater and splashes her face, then snorts and spits out a wad, her red eyes stuck on him like ticks. "Is that a threat?"

Somehow, even as a soggy beaten wreck, she intimidates Kraus more than most any mercenary, soldier, or outlaw he's ever trounced.

"You're going to Vim," Kraus says. "Conscious or not."

"After all this time ..." Irdessa's face has turned somber. "Why would he leave me with you? Of all people."

Kraus shakes his head. It's customary, people expecting the worst from him. But for some reason Torvald didn't. Torvald treated Kraus like he had something to offer. That's why Kraus never even considered telling him no.

"You have nothing to fear from me," Kraus says. "I didn't know Torvald as long as you did. But one thing's obvious. He ain't the sort of person to be surprised. By anything. Where we are right now? This cave? Cut to fucking shreds and at each other's throats? I'd wager he didn't just expect it. He intended it. And even if I'd known how it would all go down, I couldn't have told him no. That's just the kind of person he was."

Irdessa's lips curl downward at the edges, tears fill her eyes, and a cold hammer strikes into Kraus' breast right where his heart's supposed to be. Irdessa covers her face with both hands, but not before a pitiful gulp escapes her. Kraus sighs, scratches his head, feeling like more of a bastard than he did for punching her. "I'm sorry," he mutters.

She is weeping quietly. Kraus turns back to the sea. The rain is letting up. There are no patrols visible at this moment. But that doesn't mean they're not right around the corner or hiding among the Towers. Death by spear is feeling more and more welcome.

Irdessa sniffs. Kraus risks a look at her. She's staring at him, and despite how pitiful she is, Kraus gets the same feeling he had when Torvald stared him down before his first Keswal fight. He averts his eyes. Somehow it's more threatening when she weighs him. At least Torvald's intentions were obvious. She's probably looking for the quickest way to gut him.

"What landed you in Keswal?" she asks.

"Got too thirsty, I guess." He says it before a more honest response can form. "What about you?"

She rises to her feet and pulls her hair back into a knot, sniffling. "Long story."

"Well, we have a long walk. Somewhere around fifty miles depending on where we are."

She's still eyeing him. "You'll do better without that arrow in your shoulder."

Kraus chuckles. "That explains it." He aims a hopeful grasp over his shoulder. Misses again.

"Give me a knife," Irdessa says. "I'll get the arrow out."

Kraus stares at her. All signs, and most of his wounds, indicate that giving her a knife might be the last thing he ever does, besides bleeding out. Except, would it be stupider to try to haul someone as dangerous as her all the way across Fohrvylda against her will? He promised Torvald he'd do it, but like she said, Torvald is dead.

There was a time Kraus' word meant very little, and it wasn't so long ago. But, aside from his word, there isn't much of him that can be used for good. And although very little scares him, he is afraid of what'll happen when all the good is gone.

Kraus pulls a bone-handled skinning knife from his pack and takes it from its sheath. The narrow, curved blade reflects glimpses of the stormy sky. It's sharp enough to open up most anything that bleeds, and quickly. He aims the handle at Irdessa, watching her. She takes the knife and tests the edge with her thumb. Her eyes stray toward something distant. Kraus turns around and lowers himself onto his good knee.

If Irdessa kills herself, maybe he can borrow her technique and try it on himself. If she kills him, he's earned it a hundred times over. Better to let her do it right now than take another step.

"I'm in your hands," he says.

15

I Took You for Granted

FOHRVYLDA

Below the Towers

Irdessa drags her boot from one seawater-slicked rock to the next. It's hard to focus. Hard to inhale. Hard to justify breathing at all.

I love you.

She drags her other boot, moving forward but unsure why. She can't see the sun, or any evidence of it. Sunlight has no interest in being down here in the sharp wind of the alleys between the Towers. And who can blame it? The rain has congealed into amorphous, grey-green clouds.

"Step it up, Dess."

It's Kraus, the human cutting board, and he's determined to call her Dess. He is limping along at her heels. He blunders every third step and falls down swearing. But he does not relent. Irdessa has never hated anyone more than she hates him. If she turned to find him flayed open with gulls and crabs eating his meat, perhaps then for a single moment her lips would remember how to smile. He is oblivious to pain. He has no heart, and although what leaks out of him when he's cut looks like blood, it can't be. No one bleeds that much without lying down for good. Irdessa is begrudgingly coming to believe Torvald did choose him. She bears the Undying as title alone. This thing embodies it.

Torvald.

Encompassing Irdessa's throat is an iron shackle, making each swallow a painful, arduous task. The tears running down her cheeks are acid that by now have surely carved permanent canyons in her face. Her nose burns from the wind. Her cheeks ache from the grimace that mercilessly grips her face. The stones beneath her are a blur. Time must be passing. She's never known it to stop. But how can it ... without him? With each step she takes, the space between her and him expands, the realization looms darker and more dreadful. The realization she'd rather run to her grave than accept ...

He's gone.

At least he planned it all. He meant for it to happen exactly as it did. Right? She rubs her eyes and there is Torvald, alert, watching as a horned monster from a nightmare twirls his guts on its massive fork like noodles in red sauce. Torvald's eyes are wide, surprised, fearful. He never looks afraid. He did not intend this. And before he can make it right, untangle his innards and get them back in place, the beast has devoured them. It punctuates its feast by raising a hoof and kicking Torvald's face so hard his skull explodes.

Irdessa falls. But her knees don't meet the stone. Someone has caught her by the arm. She prays to any god that might hear her, *Let it be Torvald*. She's holding her breath. Surely she can pray hard enough. The monks in Ausgan pray and the rain falls, the wind blows, the lightning strikes. All she wants is one thing. She turns to the one who saved her.

"Gotta keep moving."

It is nothing like Torvald. Torvald's eyes are glittering, his face smooth, his hair a black lake. The one who caught her arm is a walking slab of the cliff itself, stained rusty brown. He is saying something to her but she doesn't understand it. His voice is the rumbling of Keswal's drums, muffled by the ceiling of the Last Room.

Her feet plod for so long that movement no longer feels voluntary. She tried to stop. Kraus hefted her up and threw her over his shoulder. The same shoulder she stitched up, right before stitching his arm, his hand, his face. He put her down only after she promised to walk. Surely this man is an animated corpse, and so is she. The sounds he made while she ran that curved needle through the bridge of his nose and tried to pull his face back together with catgut will plague her nightmares.

A lifetime is passing, one year for every step. Now and then Kraus' voice growls. A comment. A question. A snort. A swear. The grey light from above fades, slowly crushing Irdessa's idiotic notion that it couldn't get darker. There will be no moon. Surely Kraus will let her stop walking soon. All she needs is to lie down and go to sleep. This can still be a nightmare within a nightmare. Kraus didn't let her keep the knife. But he'll sleep eventually and then she can take it and be done.

A nudge at her shoulder. "Just a little longer."

She's become a sheep, and Kraus a shepherd. Except sheep have the slaughter to look forward to. She trudges on. Her feet have long since gone numb. There are no stars. The alleys beneath the Towers have tightened around her. With her eyes closed she can see Torvald dying. With her eyes open, she sees almost nothing. She makes out rocks just before her feet land on them. To her left the water laps at the stones, sometimes close enough to lick her ankles. To her right the cold cliff wall slides against her raw fingertips.

Her feet persist. The darkness grows deeper still, until her eyes no longer matter and every footstep carries the threat of a broken ankle. From the left corner of her eye, distant torchlight flickers over the water. She turns to see it, desperate to know something somewhere is alive, but it's gone. Kraus says it's orcane patrols, searching for their bodies.

Irdessa hears him fall again. Hears him curse then scramble up again. She's lost count of how many times it's happened. Enough to convince her he won't stay down, despite her wishes.

"There," Kraus says. "Told you." He must be pointing. He grips Irdessa's arm, and once again he's dragging her. He should get a staff, clack it at her ankles the way you do stubborn sheep. It's not like she has the strength to resist.

She is no longer walking over uneven stones, but a nearly flat surface. The waves are behind her. The air closes in. This must be a cave. Each sound is contained around her head, reverberating, making the silence that much more stark. The darkness is complete, or at least that's what her eyes tell her. She's always hated caverns, or anything like them. It figures she'd end up in one.

Kraus drives her to walk quicker now upon this slippery, echoing surface, despite the hitch in his gait, made obvious by his shoulder bumping hers with every labored step he takes. She tries to lift an arm, protect her face from the unseen, but a searing pain below her armpit tells her she's injured a rib.

She can no longer tell if she's walking or floating. Perhaps she's not moving. Perhaps the darkness is a tomb from which she will never leave, and Kraus' panting and shuffling is him having his way with her corpse.

Time passes. Hours, maybe. Kraus is offering her something, rumbling out words and pushing an object against her belly. A sack, by the feel of it, made of rough animal skin, stitched together. It's sagging, bulbous from a weight of liquid. An animal lost its life and its skin was stripped off so that Irdessa could shamble through a seaside cavern, directed by a walking, quilt-skinned carcass.

For me to live something must die.

She's supposed to drink from it. She refuses, despite the desperate voice crying out from deep inside her. Somewhere, a girl who looks a lot like Irdessa is thirsty. Maybe she's dying of thirst. If only Irdessa could care.

Ahead is the hint of a grey haze. It is growing, and it brings the whisper of wind and waves, the scent of the sea. The blackness before Irdessa cracks open and the night sky appears, slim at first, like a knife, and speckled with glittering points. The dismal clouds have gone away. Irdessa misses them immediately. The cavern's floor becomes soft and soggy, and her bootsteps give the squelch of wet sand and broken seashells.

"Finally. Thank the gods," Kraus says as they step out onto a wide beach. Irdessa can think of no reason to thank the gods for anything. In fact, if they even exist ... fuck them all.

They're still amongst the Towers, but these stone columns are more spread out. Irdessa's eyes have no safe place to fall. Everything she sees terrifies her, reminds her that she is alone and the one she relied on will never come back. *I took you for granted.* If she closes her eyes she sees

Torvald, smiling. Her fingers are without feeling, but she can almost imagine Torvald squeezing her hand.

Kraus is leading now. That's what Torvald said. He knew. Then why not warn her? Why didn't he say goodbye?

Fuck you, she told him. Irdessa cannot contain her trembling chest long enough to take a breath. He was trying to say goodbye. Why was she so cruel to him?

Tears in her eyes make the stars above smear. Her boots crunch the beach like old teeth chewing raw carrots. Between her and the sea is ever-hobbling Kraus. Onward he marches, as if fueled by Irdessa's grief. In the stars' dim light she can see his face, and it looks anything but human. His eyes are wide to take in what little light there is. With every footfall he flinches and sweat drips from his nose and his beard. Surely it is pain alone holding him together. Maybe they're not so different.

Torvald.

A memory approaches Irdessa, one she'd been subconsciously searching for ever since Kraus mentioned Vim. She had been strolling alongside Torvald under the sun, watching Udiari's company spar from atop the wooden balcony in the lanista's training yard. They'd been discussing their hometown, Vim, and Torvald's plans for it upon their release. The city needed order restored, since her father's arrest. It needed a healthy relationship with Promontory, one that benefited them both.

"How will you change Vim if you inherit this?" she'd said sarcastically, indicating the lanista's manor.

His response had been that sidelong smile, the one that bolstered her and yet infuriated her. Did he know then he'd never inherit Udiari's manor? Did he know then that he would die for her to escape?

"There," Kraus says, shaking Irdessa from her walking dream. He tugs her hand and she stumbles against a half-buried stone. He's peering over it, watching. She joins him.

Out past two hundred yards of flat beach the cliff wall breaks into huge steps and ledges, with edged boulders and angular trees jutting out. Turf houses and log buildings checker the terraced hill, ascending up and up into the darkness. Some of the earthen-roofed houses have torchlight winking from small windows, through overgrown, shaggy grass. Smoke rises from stone chimneys and is swept up the steep hill by wind from the ocean.

Tucked against the cliff, scattered along the beach are squat fishing huts on wooden stilts. At the seashore are piers made of smoothed stone, for the fishing vessels that surely work these waters. Ivolde Bay is closed off from the outer sea by the encompassing Towers, which are vaguely visible lining the bay out over the far horizon. Irdessa has heard that wise sailors do not attempt to navigate through them.

"We've made it to Ivolde," Kraus says. "The hard part's behind us." She can hear the smile in his voice, as if this is some reason to celebrate.

If he wants to celebrate, he can do it alone. She places her back to the rock and closes her eyes. She has to dream of Torvald before he escapes for good.

"Come on, Dess. We'll rest soon enough." He's tugging at her but she's done walking. She told him not to call her that. And at the time she said it, it seemed so important. The salty wind running over the beach sends a chill through her that refuses to leave. She draws her knees up to her chest and holds them tightly.

"Let's go," he grunts, and scoops her up. He's walking quickly over the beach, and her head falls into his neck. Her nose and cheeks are raw. Her lips are numb. She can't hold her eyes open, and sees little reason to try.

The wind relents abruptly and Kraus' boots thud hollowly over what must be sodden wood planks. He's tucking her against a log wall and speaking in a hushed voice. She's inside what must be a cabin. Silence suggests Kraus is gone—or dead, finally bled out. She surrenders to fitful exhaustion.

And awakens in the convict seating in Keswal. The sun is shining. Torvald is sitting next to her. The arena floor itself and the bloodthirsty northern seats have been replaced with a view of the shimmering Faithless Sea. She and Torvald watch like they did so many times from Udiari's training ground while the setting sun paints the horizon orange and red and gold. Irdessa has the lucid awareness that this is some warped fragment of a memory. A time not long ago while she and he oversaw Udiari's company training.

Irdessa is afraid to look at Torvald. Afraid this will all shatter. But what if it's his final goodbye? What if this is her last chance?

"You saved that boy," Torvald said, referring to Pinprae, who was currently throwing knives at a target and missing.

"I took an opportunity," she told him.

"You took a chance. If you'd waited until the orcane caught him, you wouldn't have missed." He wasn't angry. Speculative.

"I didn't miss."

"You've got something I don't," he told her.

"And what's that?"

"Heart. You're better for this world than me. You have more to offer."

Irdessa cringes at the memory. Was he trying to tell her something? *Asshole*. What gave him the right to leave her all alone? Is this what doing good deeds brings you? She saved Pinprae's life. Then he died worse.

"Why didn't you take me with you?" she whispers.

"I told you, you won't die in Keswal."

The ice encasing her heart melts into seawater. Or tears. She'd somehow forgotten the smile that his voice carries when he talks to her. How long before she forgets him entirely?

"You never told me you would. Why didn't you warn me?" Even in her godsdamned dream she's crying.

"I said you'd outlive me."

"Is that supposed to make it easier?"

"You're stronger than you know," he says, but he's wrong and she knows that now. Her strength was him. When he died, she broke.

The sun is sinking quickly. But for some reason, as it does, it grows brighter. And Irdessa knows in her heart that its searing light will soon make the truth inescapable.

"You said we'd help Vim together," she says. "You lied to me." She releases the accusation and is left with nothing. What did she expect? As if remarking on his affront to her can undo death.

"I told you it needed help," he says.

"Why?" The anger she clings to so desperately is crumbling into ache.

"Because it's your home."

"No it's not," she says. "It's *our* home. Yours, mine, and my father's. But he died. It was only us. You were supposed to go back with me. That's the whole reason we talked about it. It's the only reason." Irdessa is sick of crying. The sun's light has burned away the ocean. She can no longer see Keswal, or Torvald.

"It's still your home." His voice is growing distant. "And it needs you."

"But I need you."

It's no use. The light has enveloped all. He is gone. The sun is burning her. Irdessa raises an arm to shield her eyes and the grinding pain in her ribcage hauls her out of sleep.

She's on a hard floor in a derelict cabin smelling faintly of decaying fish and brackish water. Sunlight pours down on her through a largely collapsed ceiling. She can hear nearby waves sweeping over a beach. The angle of the sunbeam spilling through tells her noon is within a couple of hours. *How long did I sleep?* Her leather armor is gone, as are her boots, her woolen socks and undergarments. All that covers her is a stiff blanket smelling of mildew. She draws it to her chest and sits up, blinking.

Ruined nets hang from the rotten timbers that make up the walls. There's a low table with rusted tools hanging above it. In the far corner, Kraus lurks like a persistent shadow. Their eyes lock. Sunlight does his face no favors. He's as ugly as he ever was, but now he seems to have cleaved the hair off his head and face. It was done unevenly, leaving patches and tufts, as if from an encounter with a burning building. He's hunched in such a way that if he chose to, he could spring on her. She is without defense. But his eyes harbor trepidation rather than malicious intent. Irdessa touches her cheek. It's been stitched. If she slept through that, she was more exhausted than she realized.

"Looks like you shaved with a fish knife," she says.

He grinds a palm over his scalp. "I did."

"Where are my clothes?"

"Drying in the sun," Kraus rumbles. He goes to say more, hesitates, then comes out with it. "What happened to your father?"

Irdessa watches him for several moments, trying to work out what it is about him that makes her feel simultaneously murderous and at ease. "What do you know about my father?"

"You were talking in your sleep."

Of course she was. She has reached the pinnacle of shame. Beaten and battered, naked, stripped of everything she considered an identity. "Keswal welcomed him by feeding him to the birds in his first fight."

Kraus peers through a crevice between the logs in the wall. "Fishermen are all over. We should go soon."

"Then bring me my clothes, dry or not."

He does, then stands in the cabin door with his back turned while she achingly dresses herself. Her leather garments are in better shape than she'd expected, considering their exposure to seawater. He must have oiled them and her boots.

"I know how to get to Vim from here," Irdessa says, tightening the bootstraps up her calves, tensing as they contact flesh worn raw from too many miles waded. There are many miles yet to go. Ivolde Bay is on Fohrvylda's northeastern border. Vim is halfway across the wastelands, no less than thirty miles south. It's not close. It won't be easy. "You're free to go."

Kraus squats beside his pack. "I appreciate that. But I made—"

"I know the promise you made, Kraus. I'm no threat to myself. I'll go to Vim. If there are patrols searching for us, we'd be wiser to separate."

He's nodding, squinting upward as if in thought. "Thing is, no. I'm taking you."

Stubborn ass. Carved-up side of auroch. She grits her teeth.

"We've got a good bit of wastelands between us and Vim," Kraus says. "Can't be sure who's watching for us. The road up out of this bay cuts straight through Ivolde. We need to skirt around it, make our own path up the bluffs. That means we've got a climb ahead of us. I found some ropes in case we need 'em." He's rummaging in his pack. "Also, I figured we'd better get some food down."

Irdessa can smell the stockfish before he even draws out the hardened planks. Her mouth fills with saliva. It's one of the first signs of life she's experienced since the fall.

"Want cod?" Kraus asks nonchalantly.

Irdessa has crossed the room and snatched it from him before she even considers doing it. She rips off a piece with her teeth. It's the texture of bark, but softens quickly under her assault. There's not a lot of flavor to it, but hunger helps.

It's only when Kraus chuckles that Irdessa realizes how much noise she's making.

"You going to eat?" she asks, bits of dried fish escaping her stuffed mouth.

"Already did," he says.

"When?"

"While you slept."

She points at his water skin. "You've been busy," she says.

He throws it to her. Something shifts his pocked and stitched cheeks. Maybe it's a smile. Seems to have an amount of pride attached, which takes the edge off his face's ruined state about as well as a dandelion on a gravestone. Irdessa unrolls the top of the skin and has a long pull. She pauses to breathe then has another.

"Glad you know how to get to Vim," Kraus says. "Best I got is a guess."

Irdessa nearly chokes. "How the hell did we make it this far?" It probably sounds nothing like what she intended, what with the fish lining her cheeks.

"Torvald told me how to get here. Easy enough. Follow the bank, take that underground shortcut. Twenty or so miles from Keswal to Ivolde. Figured I'd ... I don't know, ask directions once we got out of the bay."

She scoffs, spitting fish across the mossy planks. "You need me more than I need you."

He chuckles. "Maybe I do."

"Your promise to Torvald is just an excuse."

He stares out the cabin's doorway for a long moment. "Maybe it is."

She finishes eating, watching Kraus all the while. She can tell her scrutiny makes him uncomfortable. He's not so frightening as she first thought. He's tragically ugly, and made worse by puffy scars running across most of his exposed skin, including his lumpy head. That knife across the nose she gave him failed to improve him. He's got a penchant for violence that would sour the stomach of a pirate. He is as nimble as a schooner in a swamp. But there's a simplicity in his eyes, not to be confused with naivety. He doesn't want much. Doesn't expect much.

"I'll cooperate with you," Irdessa says, "but you have to tell me why you got arrested."

Kraus turns his black eyes on her. "You first. You already agreed to it."

The thought of talking about it sends panic through her. Torvald's story is intertwined with her own. But his story ended and hers is staggering along like it was mugged and left for dead. She doesn't want to accept it, let alone talk about it. But Kraus' eyes tell Irdessa that perhaps his story hurt him too. Which is curious considering his relationship with pain. He's ashamed of something. Ashamed of what she'll think of him.

"Then let's get climbing, oaf," Irdessa says. "I'll tell you my story once we're clear of this bay."

Kraus' smile makes the patchy stubble on his chin flare out like a bristling hedgehog.

16

Keep Your Hand by Your Hilt

FOHRVYLDA
The Wastelands

Kraus has wandered the rocky plains and evergreen forests of Fohrvylda for as long as he can recall—not that that's saying a whole lot. He's trudged the pirate ports to the eastern, wind-blasted cliffs; to the southern bluffs that face the edge of the world; and up west to the outskirts of the capital city; Promontory itself. Hasn't ever had a need to go near the Towers, whose ankles he just crept around. Hopefully he won't again. But today, in garments that chafe him until his skin cracks and bleeds, wanted by the law, in the company of a girl who may or may not loathe his existence, walking with a knee that grinds with each step and with more wounds than he cares to count, his spirits are inexplicably high. Perhaps because of his current mission. It feels noble, or at least more noble than anything he's ever embarked on.

He and Irdessa scale the crags alongside Ivolde with little incident, other than the torn fingers and the banged shins Kraus acquires hauling his ass up a cliff face that is sometimes vertical. Once topside, they flee the vicinity of the bay using what sparse cover the collections of evergreens provide. After an hour of picking through spiky trees and climbing over sharp boulders, they find a beaten path that leads southward into the wastelands. There is little cover in that direction. The majority of the forests that once populated inland Fohrvylda were harvested as lumber for Admiral Garr's fleet of warships. Now the wastelands are comprised of lumpy earth, stumps, shrubs, and pine saplings. Any town that once relied on Fohrvyldan lumber has long since been deserted and ransacked. Despite that, Irdessa determined this is still their best option. It's easily the quickest. If they keep a brisk pace, they should make Vim within a few hours of the sun setting. The alternative would be to travel the eastern perimeter of Fohrvylda around the cliffs and port cities, to approach Vim from the south. Those cities and highways run deep with Promontory soldiers. Deeper now, possibly, because of their escape. Not worth the risk. Hopefully, Promontory isn't hunting them here in the wastelands. They might dodge an orcane patrol—given enough warning—but if sprakes are in the skies they have shit chance no matter what.

Traveling in the wastelands is a treacherous ordeal. There are rules to follow, and straying from them may cost your life. If you meet passersby, you surrender the road only if their group is larger than yours, or if they're riders. Or if they're from Promontory. It's up to you to convey you're not an easy target, preferably without bleeding in the process. You should carry a weapon and it better be showing. Don't grab the handle. That isn't polite. Definitely don't draw it. That's an invitation for everyone to do the same. But keep your hand by your hilt. There can be no guessing how comfortable you'd be drawing and using a blade. If it looks pricey, though, someone might decide to try to make it theirs. Another rule, one Kraus has never had any problem with, is *don't show fear*. Most passers have a single look at him, then turn their heads away quickly, as if hoping to forget what they've seen.

But Kraus has never traveled the wastelands with a pretty girl.

Irdessa has pulled her blanket up over her head like a hooded cape and walks behind him. She's tucked a stick in her belt and lets it poke against the blanket, not unlike a hilt and a scabbard. Kraus has no weapon, instead relying on his gods-granted good looks to thwart the curiosity of anyone they pass. So far it's working.

"My father, Andelsior, was the warden of Vim's Vanguard. They're the—"

"I'm familiar," Kraus says. He's had a couple of brushes with them. "Organized bounty hunters. They can hold their liquor."

"They're not bounty hunters," she says sharply. "Bounty hunters take a bounty. The Vanguard's only payment was to keep Vim free of Promontory's soldiers. Andelsior turned his prisoners over to Marshal Zander, who sold them to the lanistas. Vim was never harassed or raided by the patrol. That's not bounty hunting."

Kraus holds up both hands. "I got it. I had never observed that ... distinction." Because there is no distinction for an outlaw. Get popped. Do time. Doesn't matter how or if your captors are paid.

"Vim's Vanguard is a model of how the law should act if they weren't so corrupt." She eyes him a moment longer while they walk.

"Noted," Kraus says. *Shitpickers* is another of the Vanguard's colloquial nicknames, since they apparently handle Vim's garbage control as well as cleaning up local scum. Kraus smiles to himself. There's a term Irdessa will never hear him say.

"Torvald and I came active in the Vanguard around the same time. We were friends by then, and when he joined there was no way I was staying back. He rose in rank quickly. Mostly because he was such a keen strategist. Something about being a foreigner made people inclined to listen to him."

"Foreigner?"

"He's not from Fohrvylda. Must have been around thirteen when he arrived in Vim."

Kraus laughs. "Alone? And folks let him in the Vanguard?"

Irdessa glares at Kraus. By the venom in her eyes, Kraus wagers she'd have paired the look with another stab if she had the energy. "Not at once, obviously. He made an impression on my father. You knew him. You saw him work. Don't act so surprised."

Fair point. "I'll stop interrupting."

She shakes her head, as if trying to clear away extraneous details to get on with the point. "The night we went down was mostly like other raids. Twelve of us, including Andelsior and Torvald. I wasn't supposed to be there, but that's never stopped me. Our target was wanted for poaching. We learned he was in Cornelis. We surrounded the brothel he and his cohort were occupying. Young lad, but wealthy. Important maybe, because we weren't to kill him. We knew his entourage included hired blades but figured if we surprised them with an advantage in numbers he'd put up no fight. It's worked a thousand times."

She glances up the road and falls silent. Kraus sees a loaded convoy headed their way. It's not Promontory. Doesn't appear to be bandits of any sort either. Kraus and Irdessa step off the road, he making sure he's between her and the passersby. When the dirty-faced man holding the oxen's reins expresses interest toward Kraus' hooded companion, a baring of his teeth and a growl dispel it quick enough. On they go.

"So there we sat, awaiting an easy score," Irdessa says. "Imagine our surprise when we found ourselves surrounded by half a battalion of Promontory's finest."

Kraus grunts. "They have a bad habit of doing that, don't they?"

"Turns out we'd surrounded a brothel full of corpses. Someone beat us to the place, probably someone in league with the source that gave us the location. Killed the lot of them. Framed us. Turns out ..." Her jaw hardens. "... our target was Admiral Garr's nephew."

"Hopefully whoever set up that job got stripped and strangled."

She shakes her head. "It was one of ours. A Vanguard advisor named Dhovoi. Not much of a fighter but a friend of mine. My father trusted him. His younger brother was training to join up as well. Vyker, a promising spear-fighter. Neither of them had anything to gain from treachery against the Vanguard." Her voice is passionate. Kraus gets the feeling she's had this conversation before, maybe while trying to convince someone. Maybe trying to convince herself. "I think he got bad information," Irdessa says. "Torvald didn't agree with me, but he didn't know Dhovoi as long as I had. He never trusted him."

Kraus wants to ask if Torvald had ever been wrong before. But that would imply her father was. Instead he says, "Bad information?"

"Planted by some political enemy of Marshal Zander's. My father made the marshal rich. Elevated his position in Vretos' court. Considering the nature of the court, everyone always cutting each other's throats, that alone earns you some enemies. It's not a stretch to assume someone meant to diminish the marshal by taking down Andelsior and the Vanguard."

"Someone?"

"The beastmaster maybe, or Admiral Garr himself. His nephew was a disgrace."

Kraus continues to walk, trying to digest it all. "That seems overly complex."

"You don't know much about Promontory politics, do you?"

"I try to stay as ignorant on the subject as possible."

A momentary smile comes over Irdessa. "You're smarter than you look."

Kraus isn't sure he agrees. But Irdessa's smile alongside her lighthearted comment feels like more approval than he's gotten since burying a battle axe in a barkshark in Keswal. He keeps his mouth shut so as not to ruin it.

"So we all went down," Irdessa continues. "Arrested by the marshal's Domestic Patrol, ironically. The Vanguard should have been untouchable. We thought we were. But charges of conspiracy and assassination against the admiral's nephew were too much for them to overlook. Keswal was our sentence. No trial. We were all sold to lanistas. Lanista Udiari outbid all the others and managed to purchase Andelsior, Torvald, and myself. He and my father had done business before. I never saw the others again."

They've walked some ways before Kraus decides she's not just paused in her telling. That may be as far as she's willing to go.

"I suppose," he ventures, "the rest is history?"

Irdessa gives an exhausted sigh. "Lanista Udiari sought to protect us while exploiting us. Create a spectacle the crowds would pay for. In the end it worked, I suppose, because our successes eventually earned us names, and him a chair in Vretos' court. But my father didn't survive his first fight."

They're silent for a while, walking, the sun inching over the sky. Irdessa's story helped the miles of brisk, hilly terrain melt beneath them. But Vim is still a ways off.

Kraus clears his throat. "Guess I owe ya a story."

For a moment Irdessa says nothing. She's probably determining the kindest way of telling him she's not interested in hearing about a drunk rapist's crimes.

"That you do," she says eventually, and the waver in her voice suggests she's still thinking about her father. And Torvald, probably. Maybe she'd do well with some distraction.

"I was enlisted once. In the Domestic Patrol. Joined up when I was young, before Zander was the marshal."

"You worked for Promontory?" She sounds incredulous.

"I did. Seemed like I'd be good at it."

"Taking orders or wearing the blue?"

"Well, none of that. Hurting people. I ain't scared to fight."

"Is that a fact?" Her delivery is so deadpan he doesn't recognize the sarcasm until he glances over and sees the smile in her eyes.

He grins. "Hard to believe, I know. Getting yelled at though ... that's something I've never taken to. Makes me think about hurting the one yelling. And that makes me smile. And lieutenants hate when you smile. Makes them yell more, which only made me want to hurt them more."

"I can relate."

"Well, between that and having to keep clean boots and orderly clothes and shut my mouth and do exactly what everyone else was doing ..." He shakes his head again at whatever youthful idiocy convinced him he'd be a good fit at such a role. "It didn't work out. I was discharged."

"Discharged?" Irdessa cuts in. "You got lucky. Promontory prefers to charge ex-soldiers with a crime and sell them to lanistas. A message to future recruits to do better."

Kraus shrugs. "Just postponed the inevitable."

"True enough. Then what?"

"I joined a crew. Worked for a man named Loklin. Mostly we guarded transports crossing the wastelands. Easy work, but boring. Turns out crews are like Promontory patrols, only smaller and less organized. Better money, but the job is always *shut up and march.* They hate when you ask questions or make a suggestion. And since Loklin was a fucking idiot, I suggested a lot. He never listened. Dumbass. I wasn't *compliant* enough, according to him. What did he expect? I've never met someone with their head deeper up their own ass than that bald, bloated fucking ..."

Kraus notices he's ranting. He stops, shaking his head.

"Let me guess ..."

"It didn't work out," Kraus says, before she can. He hates talking about himself. Always gets stuck in old thoughts. Regrets. But Irdessa is clinging to the conversation like it's all that's saving her from something worse.

"I'm sensing a pattern," Irdessa says.

Kraus ignores that. "So I went out on my own. I was worth a pile of other men in a fight, and I was cheaper. So I stayed busy. I'd hire help when the jobs demanded it. I earned a name. Not one you'd have heard, I bet. My work never took me near Vim. Vim had its own protection."

The Shitpickers, he doesn't say.

"Yes we did," she says. "I take it that's the work that taught you about ambushes."

"It contributed to my education. The busier I got, the more I had to hire help. And the more I had to work with hired help, the more sick of it I got. You wouldn't believe the kind of lowlife cunts you have to rub shoulders with in that line of work."

Irdessa interrupts him with a hearty laugh. "The irony is stunning."

Kraus heaves a sigh. He's nearing the part he'd hoped to avoid. But they have miles to walk yet.

"I got bored with it," he says. "And it occurred to me I was wasting steps. I'd do work, get paid, get liquor, do work, get paid, get liquor, and so on. One day, maybe not my brightest moment—I was probably drinking at the time—but I decided to cut steps. Spice things up. Kill two shits with one squat. Decided to try my hand working the other side."

"Doing the ambushing," she says.

"Not yet. I accepted jobs as usual, then turned on them mid-trip. Took my pick of their haul. Protection tax, I'd call it. Transport tax. Whatever. Eventually, I just took their entire haul." He pauses, leaving only the scrape of their footsteps and the sawing of crickets in the late sun. He used to laugh when he'd tell that part. It felt clever. Folks listening would laugh. Today it doesn't seem funny. It doesn't seem clever. And it seems like anyone who would laugh at that idea might be a lowlife cunt. Kraus scowls, wondering what's changed. He continues his tale. "That ruined my name pretty quick. Folks stopped hiring me."

"Go figure."

"So I simplified further. Had no choice. Kept watching the same job postings. When a post caught my eye—some tasty haul of imported Draconis brandy or Ariheim lager—I'd wait for the post to disappear off the board. Then, knowing the haul and the destination, and having an idea of the protection they'd hired or at least what they spent on it, I'd make a plan. Set up camp. Blindside the convoy and take what I want. Honestly, I'm surprised it took me so long to figure that out."

"All that for a drink."

"A *free* drink," he says, smiling. "There's a difference."

"And raping? Was that an added perk?"

His smile falls away. That felt like a kick in the stomach. For a moment he has no response. He looks down. The moment stretches until it's more than a moment. He watches his boots, knowing the longer he fails to defend himself, the less defense there ever was. What defense could there be?

When it becomes obvious she's not going to break the silence, he does. "I never intended that. That's never ... been a priority of mine." He'd been looking for a response that wouldn't make him hate himself more. *Oh well.*

"Then why'd you do it?"

Kraus' shoulders fall farther. He clenches his teeth. She's referring to the charge levelled at him. Unfortunately, that's the only side of the story he knows. "They say I raped that girl." He's barely able to speak the phrase without spitting. Feels like a lie to say it like that. He saw her body. "They say I stabbed her in the belly." That's an assertion that the jagged, gory puncture wound on her smooth skin cannot argue. "I don't remember doing it," he says. "We were just there to hit the caravan for Silvercliff Ale."

How fucking heroic.

Irdessa's hood is low enough that Kraus can't see her expression. She's probably even more disgusted with him than he is with himself.

"The marshal is as corrupt as he is inept," Irdessa says. "Word is, in the years since he lost the Vanguard's support, he's had to resort almost exclusively to inventing charges to make arrests." She doesn't look at him. Probably because it would make it too obvious she doesn't believe it applies to his arrest.

"You didn't see her eyes." His voice betrays him, cracking as he says it. He gives his throat a rough clearing.

"Is that something you do? Stab and rape?" She sounds annoyed.

Suddenly Kraus doesn't want to talk to her. He doesn't want to talk at all. Doesn't want company, especially someone who'd tolerate a piece of shit like Kraus the Rapist. He just wants a godsdamned drink.

"Who the fuck knows?" he says.

Irdessa says nothing more. Kraus shakes his head. Her story is adventurous and tragic and fails to incriminate her of any atrocity. His is tragic as well. One long, continuous spiral into depravity.

The sun rests low in the western sky when they close in on the turf houses and fields that skirt Vim. Vim's a large city, maybe second only to the capital, Promontory, far to the west, but Kraus has never visited it. Too many people, and Vim's Vanguard is notorious for cleaning up trash. That doesn't bode well for a man like Kraus. Approaching the city gates, his unease blossoms. The setting sun, his soon to be concluded quest, this looming collection of torch-lit longhouses, cabins, and squared-off stone buildings, they all serve to sour his mood. It doesn't help that he confessed his crimes to his companion and surely turned her against him once and for all. Any time now she'll cut him loose. He will have officially served his purpose. *And yet I'm still alive.* He needs to get a drink. The rest will sort itself out. Or it won't.

"The fields are barren," Irdessa says, scanning the horizon, shading her eyes with a flat hand.

"They aren't supposed to look like that?" Kraus asks, but he can't take his eyes off the tall, spike-tipped gate they're approaching.

"They didn't before. They were cared for. And these homes were all inhabited."

Indeed, the only inhabitants of the houses they pass are ivy and shadows. But that revelation isn't nearly as pressing as the three men standing guard at the gate. They're all armed, with mismatched weapons and gear. Red sashes at their waists. They're not soldiers, thank the gods. Kraus would be more relieved if it weren't for their gaunt frames, obvious from fifty yards out. Hungry fuckers.

"I'll do the talking," Irdessa says.

They're a stone's toss away when one of the fellows marches forward and holds up a hand. "That's close enough." He's wearing a leather cap and a mail vest, secured in place by the red sash that's trailing in the wind. The blade of his spear is notched and rusty. This man, whoever he is, ain't a fighter. "Got the toll?" he says.

Kraus snorts laughter.

Now the tall skinny one pries himself from the wall to stand beside the first. "Someone tell a joke, ugly?" His airy, red tuft of a beard extends wider than his neck and his egg head. His pale right hand squeezes the sword hilt at his waist the way a toddler grips his mother's finger.

Irdessa's hand falls lightly on Kraus' shoulder in time to forestall the *Go fuck yourself* on the tip of his tongue. She hobbles forward as if her feet might fail her. "How much is the toll?" she asks in a raspy voice. Only the line of her jaw is visible from under the hood.

The third man rises from where he'd been crouching against the wall. He's older than the other two, with hunched shoulders, rusty streaks in his beard, and a scar down his face from an injury that claimed an eye. His functioning eye is fixed on Irdessa. Kraus' guts roil in anticipation.

The man in mail eyes Irdessa up and down. "More from you than the ogre," he says. There's an animal hunger written all over him. The appearance of weakness seems to have enticed him. "You two clearly ain't got the coin. He's free to go back the way he came, or we can finish the work someone started on his face. As for you, we got some questions that need answering."

"If you got questions, aim them at me," Kraus says. "You'd be surprised how resourceful ogres are."

The two foremost guards tense. The tall one shoots a glance at the one with the cap. Fucking sops. They expected no resistance. Kraus rolls his head on his shoulders, loosens his arms, clenches his fists to work some blood into them. Cap's gotta go first. Maybe a rock to the face will stun him long enough to knock him down and get that spear. Then poke skinny a few times and try not to get cut. Old man'll probably hobble off. If not, he gets stuck. Then stick everyone some more for good measure. Kraus' eyes are scanning the area around his feet for a good, fist-sized rock when Irdessa steps past him, all pretense of injury gone.

"Who is in charge of Vim?" she asks loudly.

Cap and mail looks like someone slapped him.

"Alderman Dhovoi," says the tall one, eyeballing Irdessa. "What's that to you?"

She removes her hood. "I want to see him."

The old man's mouth falls open. "Irdessa?" he croaks, brushing past the other two, using his beaten sword as a cane. "By the gods, it is you."

"Hello, Old Fent," she says. "Lost some more teeth I see."

Fent shuffles forward and takes Irdessa's shoulders in liver-spotted hands. "Who needs 'em?" he asks through a gapped grin. "Got no food."

The old man appears to pose as much threat as a downwind fart. Kraus sidles past Irdessa toward the spear fellow. "So, about those questions." He gives his prettiest smile. "I'm all ears."

The man glares at Kraus, works his jaw, shifts his grip on the spear. Skinny red beard wears a disappointed look, like someone snatched the meat off his plate.

"Dhovoi will be elated," the old man is telling Irdessa, shaking his head in disbelief. "I mean, *Alderman* Dhovoi. I heard—we all heard— about Andelsior. I'm so sorry." His eye is shiny, as if he might cry. "Is it true? About ... Torvald?"

Irdessa's chin juts forward as if she might cry too. If Old Fart makes Irdessa cry again, someone is getting broken. And it's leaning toward the mouthy, capped fucker. Kraus steps closer to the man. He needs a few knocks anyway. Just for being all bark. The capped man averts his eyes.

"News travels fast," Irdessa says, composed at once. "Promontory's sprake network never benefited Vim while Andelsior was in charge. Does it now?"

Fent shakes his head. "Alderman Dhovoi maintains a contact in Promontory."

"Who? And what do you mean by *Alderman* Dhovoi?" Irdessa asks. "And why are you watching the gate? Shouldn't you be at Cornerstone?"

Old Fent smiles, giving a wheezing sigh. "I had to get away for a bit. A lot has happened. Let's walk, shall we?" He pulls Irdessa by the arm.

"Come on, Kraus," she says. "Leave them alone."

Kraus is not one to excuse himself when violence is on the table. Far from it. But Irdessa's summons is like a summer breeze, conveying that perhaps his usefulness is not yet spent. Besides, if he can't find a drink in this shithole, then surely all of Fohrvylda has run dry.

Kraus leans so close to the capped man he can smell his teeth. "You got lucky, cunt."

17

The Best a Parent Can Do is Try

FOHRVYLDA

The Aviary, Promontory

The squawks and shrieks of sprakes grow louder as Beastmaster Grimmet makes his way down the long, wide corridor to the aviary. The salty sea wind rushing up the subterranean passage carries a ripe scent, curling his nostrils. Sprake droppings have a particularly sharp odor, not unlike a mixture of rust and putrefying vegetation. Orcane shit, he can deal with. At least it's mostly solid.

Grimmet arrives at the massive archway that is the threshold of the aviary and the ruckus is comprehensive. Most of the birds are content to cluck and chirp and trill. But now and then one of the larger raptors feels the need to release a shrill wail that resonates throughout the stone chamber and makes Grimmet's temples rattle and his eyes squeeze shut.

He stuffs a pinky finger into his ear and tries to jiggle his hearing back into place. *Thank the gods Pappu loves these birds. I don't.*

The aviary is a massive cleft in the side of the cliff that overlooks the Faithless Sea some three hundred feet below. Blinding sunlight floods the chamber, illuminating flashing feathers, stick-built nests, and spattered surfaces. The craggy walls rise ninety feet before meeting high above. The cliff's unfinished surface is full of crannies perfect to hold the nests of the oversized preening birds. In fact, the only work masons had to do here was to fill in and smooth the floor up to the wrought-iron cage. The brown, flaking bands are riveted to the floor in a huge semi-circle, and rise a dozen yards before bending back into a sealed half-dome, enclosing guests, segregating them from the birds and the threat of falling. Inside the cage are Pappu's training implements, wardrobes for blinds and tethers, perches of all sizes, mounds of hay, upturned bloody barrels for transporting food. Outside are hundreds of raptors, with way more freedom than Grimmet would prefer. The birds are in a constant uproar except in the dead of night, cavorting and flapping from perch to cage to the wind, or worst of all, just sitting there glowering down at Grimmet.

He pauses in the archway, and not only to catch his breath. Once you step out there, you're surrounded by oversized, feathered predators. Despite the cage, it's not a comfortable sensation.

When the boy showed interest in the sprakes some four years ago, Grimmet encouraged him, gave him a free leash. It was the first sign Pappu had any penchant toward animal-taming, having never shown interest in orcanes or dreadhops or even Grimmet's oversea excursions to hunt exotic beasts for Keswal. One of Pappu's first orders of business was a significant overhaul of the aviary, particularly the sprake's cage. He inverted its design so that the birds flew free rather than being caged. He promised Grimmet the ones they could use would return, and that this was the way to advance their training. He'd been right. Pappu made messengers of the birds, then watchouts and alarms, and finally attack beasts. They facilitate communication across all Fohrvylda, particularly the seaports, thereby making themselves irreplaceable. Vretos asked Grimmet to instruct the boy to teach his sprakes to spy on the Towers, the broken landmasses north of Fohrvylda. Apparently there are communities living out there in seclusion, people who oppose the Heathen Tide. According to Pappu, that project is still a work in progress.

Whenever Grimmet visits this new aviary, it feels like he's the captured spectacle while the birds come and go as they please, judging him freely. It will remain this way as long as Pappu's work is above reproach. Grimmet swallows his own discomfort and gives his son everything he asks for—not that the brat appreciates him.

Pappu is facing off against a particularly large sprake that bears all the markings of a full-grown adult. A black crest splays upward like a crown off the back of the raptor's head, and its mantle, wings, and train hold the hues of the ocean, from azure to sage to smoky slate. The greeting Grimmet planned sticks to his tongue as he realizes the raptor and his son are both on this side of the cage.

The damn thing is massive. Perching on a block no higher than Grimmet's ankle, the bird's head is level with Pappu's. The boy's head is forward on his thin shoulders and his straight black hair covers the tops of his tanned ears. He's almost nose to beak with the fucker, and Grimmet will be damned if it's not one of the most macabre-looking sprakes he's ever seen. Angry eyes peer from under furrowed feathers, white gashes along its hooked grey beak, shiny crimson talons longer than Pappu's fingers. There is no tether or lead or collar in sight. There doesn't seem to be anything keeping the damn bird from knocking Pappu over and harvesting his guts except the force of the boy's stare, which has never seemed like much force at all to Grimmet. Frankly, he didn't know until this moment that his son had a pair of stones on him.

"Thought I'd find you here," Grimmet risks. Maybe the bird didn't know he was there. It does now. He doesn't draw his whip or his cleaver, but his hand doesn't stray far from their grips. Neither of the two acknowledge him. A bucket-load of sprake droppings spatter down beside Grimmet, making him jump. He cranes his head and finds an obese bird perched on the rusty cage directly above, peering down. Grimmet stomachs a swear and moves to the side, but his boots are already speckled white.

As if by some signal that eludes Grimmet entirely, the raptor opposite Pappu visibly relaxes, diminishing in posture, clicking its beak softly, adjusting its claws on the wooden block. Pappu blinks, takes a step back from the raptor. Grimmet exhales.

Pappu pulls what appears to be a halved rabbit from a bucket and hauls open a squealing cage door. The large sprake leaps from its perch and struts along behind him, its claws clicking on the stone floor. As it reaches the cage door, it pauses to turn both gold eyes on the beastmaster. There it ceases all movement. Grimmet grips his whip. Direct eye contact with no apparent expectation of reprimand? Were that an orcane it would already be bleeding. The bird clicks its beak and hops through the door. Pappu slings the scrap to it.

"Hello, Father," he says without looking, clinking the cage door shut. The sprake stretches its massive wings and leaps up to a hemp-wrapped perch, where it tears into the meat.

"I'm impressed," Grimmet says, still not quite willing to take his gaze off the birds. "That bird looked gruesome. You're quite the beastmaster's son. I'm surprised you haven't taken to the orcanes yet."

"Orcanes are right where you want them, aren't they?" Pappu says, nonplussed by the compliment.

Grimmet chuckles. "It would be better if they didn't need to be tied up."

This is an understatement of legendary proportions. It would be better if they were allowed their nose, their ears, their inborn cooperation. Their strengths. The employed muzzle-bits are designed for orcanes to respond to the slightest touch. This is crucial for their riders to take advantage of their fleetness, but also irritates them to no end. Try though he might, Beastmaster Grimmet hasn't been able to beat the memory out of orcanes that if nothing holds their reins, the world is theirs to devour. Once an orcane's shoulders reach the height of a man's hip, its reins are either held or tied until death.

"I don't have enough time to undo what's been done to those creatures," Pappu says, as he straightens up some leather implements on a table. "Maybe if you give me some pups freshly broken from their mother, I could have a go. But I'd require a new bit."

Grimmet seethes. "Maybe if your methods didn't take so long you wouldn't need special pampering. These damned birds are as hardheaded as ever." His voice tapers off as he grows conscious of the black and yellow orbs aimed down at him. He never approaches Pappu intending to argue. In fact, he'd prefer an amiable relationship with his one and only relation in Promontory. But the boy brings out Grimmet's worst.

"They aren't hardheaded," Pappu says with no emotion. "They just don't respond to being beaten."

Something about his perpetual lack of concern for anything makes Grimmet's blood boil. "You're too easy on them," he says.

Pappu gives a haughty laugh. "You're talking about birds that I trained so thoroughly they're able to train dreadhops themselves. Not that dreadhops have much going on intellectually." He shakes his head. He still hasn't even bothered looking at Grimmet. "Sprakes require a more subtle touch than orcanes. Orcanes are pack animals. It's in their blood to submit. But I bet if you showed them some affection, maybe they'd consider you a leader and not a common enemy."

"You watch your godsdamned mouth." Grimmet takes a step toward Pappu. All squawking, chirping, and rustling of feathers ceases at once, leaving only distant cries of sprakes out over the ocean. Grimmet is now the interest of every bird not capped in a leather hood. And although rusted steel bars separate him from their beaks, his feet plant where they are. Every fool knows that when the young falconer taught the birds vengeance, they took to it like fish to drinking.

Pappu leans back against the table and watches Grimmet calmly. A speckling of freckles across his dark nose and cheeks are all that link him physically to his father. Otherwise, he's the spitting image of his deceased mother. He spends more and more time up here, under the protection of his precious birds. He might as well be one of them, thin-boned and lurking, but without the benefit of feathers or talons. His methods are not Grimmet's, and perhaps they never will be. If only this were a fact Grimmet could accept. Until he does, it is a constant struggle to mask his disdain for this dainty boy who has never broken even the weakest orcane runt. The little bastard has all the rebellious qualities of his mother, but lacks any of her redeeming perks.

"It's not for the orcanes' wellbeing that I train them the way I do, son," Grimmet says. "These are beasts of war. They're meant to kill, like dreadhops, like sprakes."

"They don't need our help doing that," Pappu says, picking at a knot on the table's surface.

"Commanding with a limp wrist is not doing them or us any favors."

Pappu's shoulders lift the slightest bit, as lazy a shrug as Grimmet's ever witnessed. *How does he manage to infuriate me with so little effort?* Maybe because Grimmet came to have an earnest conversation and the boy can't be bothered.

Grimmet takes a deep breath, scans the room for some sort of chair or stool not covered in bird filth. There isn't one. He shifts his weight from one foot to the other, aware of how uncomfortable he probably looks.

"What's the status of the goat hunt?" Grimmet asks.

Pappu eyes him a moment, as if he can't tell it was a question. He rummages in a satchel and withdraws a shiny red apple. "Goat hunt?"

"The uergatas."

Pappu lifts his chin in mock acknowledgment, as if there was some questioning about what Grimmet meant. "Well, not that you'll appreciate this," Pappu says, "but the sprakes have searched the entire mainland." He takes a bite of the apple.

"And?" Grimmet has never wanted to slap an apple out of a hand so badly.

"No uergatas."

"Then where the hell did they go? Are they hiding?"

"I doubt it, considering their size and aggressiveness. But if they are under cover in some old mine, Marshal Zander might scare them up before the sprakes can spot them." He digs at his tooth with a thumbnail until finally adding, as if it's of no consequence, "Personally, I think they're gone from the mainland."

"Gone where? They can't swim."

"Over the Towers to Redemier."

"How would the damn goats even know how to get there?"

"I don't know." Pappu takes another bite of apple. "I'm not a damn goat. Maybe the armorer's assistant gave them a map."

Grimmet is nearly seeing red. His cheeks flush with heat and his fists are squeezed so tight his nails dig into his palms. "Maybe your birds are incompetent and the uergatas are right in front of their blind beaks. Did you think of that? Maybe they have no reason to obey you." He wishes he'd said none of it. Blind beaks? His reservoir for anger is quickly approaching its cap.

A smile crosses Pappu's face. "No. To use your language, I asserted dominance over each one at a young age. Now all that's required is the occasional talk, as you just witnessed."

Grimmet waves his hand at the cages. "You take all of this for granted, like it will always be this simple and everything you want will be handed to you. We have to earn our keep. We have to benefit the war. The day will come when we face the Ausgan monks, and if we're not ready they'll annihilate us." That's the kind of rubbish you hear captains yell at their lieutenants and so probably has no value in this conversation. Unfortunately, that qualifier has never kept Grimmet from shouting a thing at his son.

Pappu perks up slightly, as if Grimmet stumbled on a subject that almost interests him. "How would Ausgan ever annihilate us from across the Faithless Sea? Aren't we the Heathen Tide, destined for their shores?"

"We're at war," Grimmet says. "There are spies of the monks all over, and I'll be damned if you're not acting like one of them."

Pappu settles back against the table and gives an even lazier shrug.

"Pappu," Grimmet says from between clenched teeth. "There is some talking. People think you had something to do with the uergatas escaping. They think that when you coerced the goatmen into being measured for armor, you whispered poison into their ears."

"Why?" Pappu's voice carries no inflection. But the question is a trap, and a foul one.

"Because of your compassion toward beasts," Grimmet says. He's sure his son knows the rest of it. *Because you look like an Ausgan islander, like your mother.* The boy's departed mother is not a subject Grimmet will revive. Not again. Grimmet never intended to love her, but he did. He never intended her to die, but she did. He will never again be questioned by this spoiled pup on that matter.

"Does Vretos think I'm acting like a spy?"

"I hope not." Grimmet can't help but ask, "Is it true?"

Pappu only stares at him.

"Did the armorer's assistant say anything to the uergatas?" Grimmet asks.

"I would imagine he told them to lift an arm."

"But did he act strangely?"

"I wouldn't know. I've never been measured for armor, Father."

Grimmet ignores this stab. "I'm asking because the armorer is Zander's man and I wouldn't put it past him to sabotage me any way he can."

"I think you're giving Zander's presumed cunning too much credit. Besides, he's fifth chair, isn't he? Wouldn't sabotaging you benefit Lanista Udiari?"

"Not if Udiari's prize fighter dies in the process and his second falls off a cliff. Maybe leave the politics to me."

"Maybe I will. But the armorer's assistant wasn't Zander's man."

"The hell he wasn't. Who do you think the armorer reports—?"

"It was Torvald the Tactician, in disguise."

Grimmet's mouth falls open. He stutters for a response. "How can you ... are you sure?"

Pappu tilts his head. "Yes. I realized it, and he noticed that I realized it. And he put a finger to his lips." He smiles at the memory. "So I didn't say anything."

Grimmet's chest tightens so suddenly he worries his heart might explode. His vision is paling. He needs something to hold on to. His knees are all that's there so he grabs them. "You knew that ... all this time ... and you wait until now to mention it?"

"When's the last time you came to talk to me, Father?" Pappu says.

Grimmet's not watching him. He's not risking taking his eyes off the swaying floor until his heart stops thundering against his eardrums. But he hears the boy stroll over to the cage he just shut and lean on the door. "I wanted to see what would happen."

"And what would you say happened?" Grimmet's heart is beating faster and faster. It's making him dizzy.

"No uergatas died."

A fresh wave of nausea courses over Grimmet, followed by a cold sweat. "We are beastmasters, son." His words are forced. He's so angry tears might fill his eyes. "A beastmaster serves his country at the expense of his animals."

"Who said I wanted to be beastmaster?"

Grimmet scoffs. "Then what?"

The boy doesn't say anything.

"Did Torvald give the uergatas a map?"

"Maybe."

"You ... you ..." Grimmet can't put to words the violence that he wishes on the ungrateful whelp. "You're trying to kill me," he manages. "Why am I not surprised that you'd go about it in the most cowardly way."

"I don't want to kill you, Father. But those uergatas should never have been captured. If you can't see that, I don't know how to help you."

"*Help me?*" Grimmet finds his voice like a boiling kettle. "Do you have any idea what it cost to capture those godsdamned things? Do you know what they're worth? One day you have to come down from this aviary and answer for this. There will be no birds to hide behind."

Pappu tilts his head. "Do I?"

Grimmet straightens himself. Tries to breathe deeply. Anger will not avail him. The boy loves animals more than humans. This isn't new. He didn't intend direct assault on Grimmet, even if his actions accomplished little else. "If I take the fall for this, what do you think will happen to you? You think Vretos will keep accommodating you out of charity?"

"If he values my sprakes he will."

Grimmet exhales through his nose, watching the boy. Truth is, rage is never what breaks a belligerent orcane. The whip does. Systematically, as a reward for poor behavior. And while an orcane can handle quite a few knocks, this child cannot. He's as receptive to that as his precious birds are. Punishment must come in a different form.

"Ah, your sprakes," Grimmet says. His tranquility isn't forced. His son has finally given him something he can work with. A stubborn beast always does in the end. He takes a steadying breath. "They are magnificent, aren't they?"

Pappu stands still, not looking at Grimmet but barely looking at anything else.

"The line of communication you've established for this nation is staggering. Your birds can get a message to the Silvercliff Bay in ... how long, three hours now?"

"Two and a half. Unless the wind is right, then ..." Pappu looks up at his father, as if suddenly aware of himself. "... then just over two."

"Amazing," Grimmet proclaims. He pokes his thumbs in his belt, leans back to admire the squawking fowl. "That one you were working with when I came in, is he their leader?"

"She's not, but she thinks she should be. I help her understand."

Amazing, the transformation that befalls Pappu when he discusses the birds. Almost like he's capable of normal conversation.

"Why do you do that?" Grimmet asks.

"Because without my intervention she'd aggravate the leader until she left her no choice but to kill her."

"And your intervention is good?"

"It isn't natural, but it's the only reason she's alive. There are benefits to sprakes not killing each other."

Grimmet nods his head thoughtfully, as if the morals of beasts bears any significance. He strolls toward the bucket of scraps, extends a hand toward it, and addresses his son. "May I?"

Pappu hesitates, then nods his head.

Grimmet takes hold of the driest shred of skin visible in the rank bucket. Treating a carnivore isn't out of the ordinary, but he'd prefer to be wearing gloves. He approaches the crisscrossing bands of the cage wall slowly, his gift extended. Several of the birds are watching him now. Some look from him to the boy, almost like they're asking permission. Grimmet looks to his son as well. The boy's gone pale, fear in his eyes.

The bravest of the birds leaps from a stone shelf to the ground in front of Grimmet, cushioning its fall at the last moment with a single blast of its massive wings. Grimmet draws back slightly as it approaches. He holds the strip of flesh horizontal between both hands. The bird clicks toward him on hooked talons, head low and darting left and right, always watching the scrap.

"A natural hunter," Grimmet whispers.

The bird arrives at the cage, shifting its predatory gaze from the treat to Grimmet's face. "Go on," he says, giving it a jiggle. Blood drops patter the floor. The sprake extends its feathered head through the cage, clicks its beak mistrustingly, gives a tentative lunge, and almost jerks the scrap from Grimmet's hand. "That's a good bird. Try again."

This time the bird strikes confidently, its beak rending fur and locking, tugging. Grimmet grips the snack in his left hand and reaches with his right, snatching the sprake by its neck. It panics, beating its wings in a flurry, screaming.

"No!" Pappu cries, rushing him. He kicks Grimmet's leg. To the boy's credit, Grimmet feels the attack. Pappu grabs Grimmet's arm. Grimmet releases the forgotten snack and swats him away. Pappu collides with his wooden workbench, capsizing it and sending training implements clattering. Now all the sprakes are screaming. Pappu picks himself up and limps frantically for the cage door.

"*Ackk!*" Grimmet's guttural, throat-rending exclamation that can stop an orcane in its tracks works today on Pappu the falconer. "Don't do that."

The bird is trying to get its talons up at Grimmet's arm. He positions so that the cage obstructs it. The boy stands still, wet-cheeked, panting.

"If Vretos *values your sprakes?*" Grimmet scoffs. "Understand this. He values the Heathen Tide. That's it. If I go down, you and I are out of good favor. Zander will inherit this whole quarter. This will be his archery chamber and your birds will be archery practice. First as moving targets, then just as targets." Pappu is as dense as driftwood if he needs this broken down.

His son nods his head, eyes round. Pliable, finally. This gives Grimmet a much-needed moment to reflect on what he's learned. It was suspected that Torvald was involved in the rapist's escape attempt. Irdessa didn't seem to be. She nearly killed the rapist, probably did indirectly kill the skinny convict. Piss Spray, was it? She almost killed one of the goats. But if Torvald was in that room equipping those goats with the means to escape, he wouldn't have done less for Irdessa. He loved that girl.

A talon catches Grimmet's forearm. He flinches, adjusts, ignores the blood running down his arm. There are more raptors gathered around the first now, and Grimmet has to stretch the thing's neck to keep from getting bitten. At least this pressure takes the edge off its screeching and carrying on.

There's a bounty on Irdessa, and until today Grimmet, and seemingly the rest of Promontory, figured Garr's ships or Zander's orcanes would find her corpse bobbing among the Towers or wedged in a cove feeding crabs. But if the Tactician meant to save her, then chances are she is safe.

"I hate you." The boy's whimpering breaks Grimmet's concentration.

"Relax, son. You're afraid because you think I'm angry about the uergatas."

Pappu's lower lip trembles, despite his thin chest pumping to still it. Somewhere deep in Grimmet, he aches at hurting the boy. But, far more present at hand, he is struck by undeniable satisfaction at finding something that matters to his child.

"I am," Grimmet continues, "but I can put that behind me. This is a learning moment. You are my son, and I'm the beastmaster. That means so are you. Your actions put you under suspicion of treachery with His Might. To resolve that, your sprakes have to find Irdessa the Undying. I believe she's alive in Fohrvylda."

Pappu is nodding before Grimmet finishes getting the words said. "If I can have images of her, I can do it. The more recent the better."

Grimmet smiles, feeling optimistic for the first time in this conversation. "Not a problem. There's at least one painted flyer of her for each of her frothing fans."

Pappu seems to be relaxing. "It would help, too, if I could access her quarters. Her scent will be the strongest there."

"Easy." A product of Grimmet's newly elevated seating is increased jurisdiction. Not that Udiari could stop him. Last he heard, the lanista was imprisoned under Keswal, and the remnants of his company of fighters were auctioned off.

"Pappu, I may be coming to understand you better. Not unlike your sprakes, you require a special kind of discipline." Pappu is nodding eagerly, and Grimmet knows his lesson is only half-learned. The boy wants this over and will do or say anything to quicken that result. No better way to cement a lesson than through pain. "But you're young and willful. Despite your lack of wings, you fail to grasp the gravity of our situation. Like you correcting the willful raptor, I must pinpoint this lesson so that you don't forget your place. Our place. I do this for you."

The boy tenses again. "No," he begins. "I understand now. There's no need—"

Grimmet wrenches the sprake's neck against the cage, twisting at the same time to be sure, producing a series of cracks and emptying all the fight out of the bird.

Pappu is upon him, hollering and raining down blows with all the ferocity of a massage. Grimmet snatches Pappu's shirt collar, holds him at arm's length, releasing the limp bird so that its head dangles like a plumed pendulum. When the boy's burst of energy blows out, he crumples from Grimmet's grip. The beastmaster moves away, giving the boy and the bird some space. The surrounding sprakes have gone quiet. Grimmet's never heard so deep a silence in the aviary. Some of the raptors watch him. Some watch their dead companion. Some watch the falconer who they trusted. None come within reach.

"Here's what you need to take from this, son." At last, he doesn't have to yell to be heard. "This is for our good. If the admiral, or the marshal, or even a drunken sheep herder finds Irdessa before we do, plan to watch your sprakes killed and cooked by soldiers."

The boy holds the dead bird's head gently, his shoulders heaving. The sprake's grey tongue is out and its eyes are dull slits.

"Do you understand?" Grimmet asks.

"I hate you," the boy whispers again.

"Of course." Grimmet smiles. Discipline isn't supposed to be easy, and anger is the response of the immature. Pappu should be relieved, considering what he cost Grimmet. This was merciful. Pappu will grow to understand, or they can revisit this event until he does.

Grimmet turns on his heel, happy to be moving, happy about the revelation of Torvald's involvement, happy to be getting away from the sprakes, eager to distance himself from this place and the growing ache in his chest. "I'll get you what you asked for," he calls without looking back. "And once your birds are acquainted with their target, we'll send them out with dreadhops. Do not tell anyone else what you told me."

It's in the falconer's hands now. Grimmet's done all he can. In the end, the best a parent can do is try.

18

Can't Fight Them All

AUSGAN
Obsydia's Tower, Stravhelm

Obsydia is shaken from a dreamless sleep by chitin boots clattering up her stairs. She blinks several times and props herself up among her silk sheets as a sentinel rises into view on her staircase.

"Ausgan had better be under attack," Obsydia says, her voice an unintentional growl.

"Resonations, Magister. I'm sorry. Magus Kalderys seeks audience."

Obsydia squints at him, then at the stars above. It's sometime after midnight. What in all Ausgan is so important it can't wait for the sun to rise? Anyone else would be sent away immediately, possibly after receiving some hard knocks.

Obsydia climbs out of her bed and throws a robe over her bare shoulders. "Send him up," she says. The adherent disappears and Obsydia piles her hair up and pins it in place with two bamboo hairpins. She risks a glance at her looking scale and sighs. This is as good as it'll get tonight. Two adherents approach from the shadows, heading for the glowing braziers with fresh tinder. "No," Obsydia says. "Get out." They retreat silently.

Obsydia arranges herself on the edge of her bed and gazes eastward dully, where the moon paints sparkles over the rippling Faithless Sea. The distant East Rostrum towers over the beach. It is darker than its surroundings and much taller, making it look out of place, like a stranger in a shroud. It's there that Intemrus sings and meditates and observes. It provides the best vantage point in Ausgan, and therefore is the best place to practice supersensory perception of the environment at large apparently. Obsydia yawns. It's in these drowsy moments between slumber and wakefulness that she can best visualize Kalderys, rather than Intemrus, atop that stone tower, singing his song of consonance.

The sound of Kalderys' boots on her stair never fails to make Obsydia's breath quicken. She realizes her crimson robe is as translucent as her blue curtains as the magus rises into view. Obsydia crosses her arms in front of her chest. Kalderys tops the stairs, as always concealing the East Rostrum. But instead of his unbending purpose, she senses anxiety, and is surprised by her own sudden disgust.

"Resonations, Magister," Kalderys says, removing his helmet. He's drenched in sweat and breathing heavily. What appears to be mud is spattered on his boots and gloves and the shins and knees of his armored dele. Not only mud. There's blood. Complications with the cleansing. It's not the first time.

"Yes," Obsydia says. "Bit late, isn't it?"

He hangs his head. "I deemed it prudent to report at once, Magister."

"I'm all ears."

"Hargrim is dealt with. But the campaign wasn't entirely a success."

"Oh? I'd have considered the two mutually inclusive. You put on quite the show from here." Trying to coax him out of his sour mood seems to be doing the opposite. He's ashamed of something.

"I was negated. Cut short mid-song."

"You were *what*? By whom?"

"The offender wore a dele. And when it was over, they fled before I or my primes could get to them."

"Fled? Faster than Selu? After negating that?" Her hand gestures southward. Something tickles at the back of her memory.

"Any negator should have died taking on that much energy," Kalderys says. "Sentinel Arc pursued them. He hasn't returned yet. My expectations for his survival are low."

Arc's survival means almost nothing to Obsydia in this moment. But Kalderys' regret is palpable, like rotten milk. A loss of an exemplar, especially one so strong, is a loss for Ausgan. Nevertheless, Obsydia fails to care. "We can only hope he returns safely," she says. An empty sentiment if ever there was one. "Tell me about who did this, Magus."

"I didn't get a good look. Are there any chaplains, perhaps rogue chaplains, who have abilities ... beyond what I'm informed of?"

"Of course not."

Anger simmers beneath the exhaustion and shame in Kalderys. "That's what I thought," he says. "Someone must have followed me from Erudition."

"Surely not. You'd have sensed them while summoning. A song of that scale? You couldn't have missed them." Again, a niggling tug. Obsydia forces the distraction away.

"I would have agreed until yesterday, Magister. Someone seems to have eluded my pulses." He spits the words as if they disgust him. But it's not the words. It's him. His lips are curled into a scowl. His humiliation is deafening. "When the sovereign hears about this ..."

"Eluded you? Surely not. Who would be able to—?" She gasps. Comprehension, like abrupt immersion in icy water. *The basalt ... Kale.*

"What is it?" he says. Her reaction didn't go unnoticed. Now he's focused his full attention on her. He wants the truth. He's desperate.

"Adherent," Obsydia calls out. Two appear from the shadows once more. She points at the faster one. "You. Bring me Folksteller Tael. Quickly."

The adherent rushes from the rooftop without a word.

"Who else knows of what happened?" Obsydia demands of Kalderys.

"Selu and Arc. Magister—"

"Good." Obsydia fights the urge to reprimand Kalderys. He could not have known. If anyone deserves reprimand, it's her. "Let me do my job, Magus. By the time I bring this before Intemrus, I will have a solution. Don't worry."

"Magister, if you know something of who did this, you must tell me." Kalderys leans toward her. The tone in his voice, while wrought with the same strength she relies on, is aimed squarely at her. As if she's someone he can command. "They interfered with judgment. They must pay, be it spy, native, or exemplar. Someone *has* to pay for this."

"Magus!"

He steps back as if slapped.

"Trust the Triumvirate. We all have our part to play." She steps closer to him, looks into his eyes to convey confidence she wishes she felt. "Trust me. They will pay. They will experience Stravhelm's wrath at your hand."

Kalderys makes no attempt to hide his trepidation. He is not assured. "Include me in this investigation, Magister." His voice is pained. "I know the offender's imprint. I can recognize them without needing to see them."

Obsydia is disgusted by his pleading. How fickle was his pride? He had his chance to prevent this or make it right. So much for absolute. For the first time, Obsydia questions his place in her plans. "Get some rest, Magus. I'll need you soon. In the meantime, don't speak of this. I won't bother Intemrus unless I have to." It's on her to determine the extent of this threat. There are pieces in fragile motion that he doesn't and can't know.

Footsteps approach up the staircase. Kalderys smooths his expression and takes a step back from Obsydia. His rage is nearly boiling over. That, she can admire, as long as it fortifies him. As long as it serves her.

"As you wish, Magister. Resonations." He turns, shoving his helmet into place.

"Resonations, Magus." She doesn't watch him leave.

The adherent has returned, his message for Folksteller Tael passed on.

Obsydia paces, her mind scrambling to contain a damage she doesn't fully understand. Part of her plan, her future, relied on Kalderys being infallible. A ridiculous notion of any single person. So the question becomes, does she truly need him to be all-powerful? If so, what now? And if not, does she need him at all? This line of thinking isn't helpful.

Of course she needs him. For several reasons. Aside from Intemrus himself, Kalderys is the most respected and feared exemplar in Erudition. Without him, her grasp on the highest seat in Stravhelm would become much too hotly contested. Although she believes she can fight off most any individual mancer or rhyolite or andesite, she can't fight them all.

At some length, Folksteller Tael appears at the top of the stairs, straightening his dele and trying to flatten his pitiful hair. Moonlight gleams off his shiny brown scalp where his thinning hair is losing its fight. The folksteller clears his throat, gives a final smoothing pat down of his dele, then offers a lazy, subservient rhystic pose, chin lowered, hands relaxed before him.

"Resonations, Magister Obsydia." He waits for a huge yawn to have its way with him. "And a very good morning. To what do I owe this—?"

"Tell me about last night's count. Was anything off?"

His face wrinkles at her prompting. He doesn't like her. Never has. That is hardly a concern.

"Speak up, counter," she says.

He looks down his nose at her. "Count was in order." He clears his throat again, this time pointedly. *"Magister."* He obviously thinks she has called on him capriciously. That throat-clearing of his failed to remove the shrillness that makes all his words sound whiny.

"Basalt Tier, was it counted?"

Folksteller Tael holds his chin and puckers his lips, eyeing the starry sky. "Yes. It was. The count was in order. As I said."

It takes no deep observation to know those words were based on nothing. Without any other function than to liberate him from this conversation and back to his sheets.

Magister Obsydia approaches him. His eyes fix on hers and his lips part. He's nervous now. Maybe he's considering how high up her tower is. She doesn't stop advancing until her nose almost touches his. "What a simple job you have. One ... two ... three ... and so on. Given a strong enough supersensory pulse, you shouldn't even have to visit the tiers yourself."

Tael is frozen, as if her words have edges that are aimed at him.

"I'd hate to find out you're wrong," she says, then turns and strolls back toward her bed, wriggling out of her robe and throwing it on the floor. She flounces down and looks back at him. Tael stands there watching her. His thoughts are laid bare. No lust or even attraction. *Fear.* He doesn't know Basalt Tier's count. He didn't check it and knows that whoever did gave it a fraction of their attention as they always do. No one inquires about the counts until something goes wrong, which is rare. Tael's about to piss his dele.

"You're dismissed, Folksteller."

He assumes rhystic subservience, this time with immaculate poise, and bows shakily. "Thank you, Magister. Resonations." He makes to flee from the rooftop, as if any action he can scurry off and accomplish will improve his fate.

"Oh," she says.

He freezes mid-step, one foot trembling in the air.

"Bring me Basalt Kale. I'd like to see him."

He stares at her, then nods once. "I'll send for him, Magister."

"No. Fetch him yourself. Do not utter his name aloud. Hopefully you remember how to get to Basalt Tier."

"Of course." He swallows audibly and descends the stairs.

When she's sure he's gone, Obsydia addresses the other adherent. "You. Get my primes up. If Folksteller Tael returns to the gates of Stravhelm alone, they're to imprison him at once. He is not to talk." The adherent bows and leaves her rooftop.

Obsydia fights the urge to sling something off the side of her tower. If Kale is in his dorm, maybe she's wrong. And while that would result in a new slew of questions needing answering, at least none of those would be *How did a basalt negate Magus Kalderys, the Consonant Fist?* This could knock the magus from most feared to most ridiculed in a single breath.

Obsydia kicks her discarded robe into the wind. Imala-damned snooping basalt. He was up to something when she saw him and she failed to get it out of him. She failed to prevent this. Distracted by the might of Magus Kalderys—which apparently isn't what she thought it was.

Obsydia grips a brazier in both hands and wrenches it off its pedestal, throwing char and ash all over the floor and a black cloud into the night. Kale doesn't suffer negation sickness. A fact known to all but acted on by none. First to blame is the Triumvirate itself, because it performs as one entity, each individual responsible for the other, at least in a perfect world. But Sovereign Intemrus, the most passionate about consonance, why would he of all people not collect Kale and take him off to be examined and vivisected? Why didn't he prevent this if he truly sees all? She flops down on her daybed. *Because he doesn't.* The exposing of that fact is this situation's one saving grace.

She should have prevented this. And now it is indeed her problem. She'll have to get to the bottom of it. Everything is in motion and moving too fast to stop. Never again will this chance arise, with all the pieces being as they are. Not in her lifetime. No one can know Kalderys was undone, especially by Negator Kale of the Basalt Tier. If his power and place in the Triumvirate appear to wane, there are named mancers who would pounce on the opportunity like vultures. With resignation, she admits it's time to put her pet ashmancer to work.

19
A More Shameless Strategy

AUSGAN
The road between the Trade and Napiri

Tivali makes her way westward on the path back to Napiri. Behind her Uncle Reilu is pushing their creaking, wheeled barrow. Aunt Mara is grumbling like it's her doing the pushing. In the barrow are five spiralpine sacks of rice. Or rather five three-quarter sacks. All for a whole moon's worth of malva cordage.

It's less rice than she'd hoped. But she's not surprised. Things are getting worse all around. Less rain makes for fewer leaves on the trees, which makes for less shade, which leads to ornery animals, ornery people. Less tolerance for ornery anything. It's a shitty spiral. Today's poor haul is only the latest in a string of disappointments. Tivali hides her discouragement from her aunt and uncle, or tries to. They and all of Napiri benefit from believing that all will soon be better.

The Trade is a half-day hike south and east of Napiri. It's a gathering that occurs at each new moon and lasts as long as goods are selling. The Trade's merchants are born for the life. Impervious hagglers, or so they say. They'd take your haul for a single grain of rice and sleep like babies, smiling while they dream of you and your village divvying that grain thirty ways. Tivali used to try and haggle them down. Play their game. Low success rate, and when it did work it embarrassed them. Then they doubled down. She had to change the battle.

Now she employs a more shameless strategy. She watches them at a distance. Sees where their eyes take them, what they're into, finds the choicest of them. The airy fraction of an outfit she wears to the Trade is a poor choice for the trip to and from, or for protection, or for anything save procreation come to think of it, but it pays dividends in a gritty exchange. Nothing hobbles a horny haggler's defense like a well-timed, accidentally exposed breast. Stick that together with a loose smile and a few barely innocent touches and you can walk through deals that leave merchants contemplating suicide. As long as they don't go through with it, the game belongs to Tivali. Weaving gossip here and there that she is the trollop she pretends to be is enough to make repeat offenders of some of these schmucks. This isn't a strategy that will work forever. But when it breaks, she'll work out a new one.

The merchants are coming together, working in unison with absurd rates. With the jungle drying out, the market's fast becoming theirs, whatever you're showing off. These days the best you can hope for isn't a full sack. It's fresh rice, or at least sturdy woven spiralpine for the sack, so you don't lose what little you got on the trip home. Tivali's not hungry enough to venture further down her chosen warpath. Not yet.

Today the Trade's gossip was the worst sort. Hargrim burnt down, even the stone lodge somehow. No survivors. A monk killed in the jungle, which is unheard of. Tivali wouldn't have believed it. Merchants use any excuse to raise alarm and hike their prices. Then she saw the bloodied scraps of a monk's dele. She doesn't want to believe Hargrim is gone. It's only a couple hours southeast. Sometimes on the way to the Trade, Tivali meets folks of Hargrim making the same trip. Not today. Today's journey has been quiet. The news left her wanting nothing more than to get back to her people and stay there.

Tivali takes refuge in this walk, whatever the tidings. The quiet is a welcome break from the mutterings of the village these days. Napiri feels to be on some downward spiral and taking the village's faith with it. Prayers cease. Cordiality toward chaplains withers. Certain unspeakable subjects gain popularity. *Kidnap the next roving monk and hold them ransom for rain. Feed him to the warthound so the holy city sends help.* Idiocy, all of it. And the fools who blabber their dissatisfaction the loudest do so as if they, too, can't be arrested like Tivali's father was. Apparently some villagers even talk of sneaking off southward toward the Untamed. Seems a sure way of turning the holy city against you once and for all. Tivali is trying her best to quell their unrest and bolster faith, but there's only so much she can do when prayers go chronically unanswered.

Napiri prays for rain, which the chaplains say the sovereign has control over. Then Tivali and her neighbors watch fat grey clouds, so full of promise, squirt a measly pittance and disperse, like they were called off to uninhabited areas of the jungle, leaving the sun to lick rainwater right back up off leaves and earth and collection bowls. *It isn't natural,* folks say, and they're right. If rain's being controlled, then Napiri, and apparently all the villages, are being punished.

Tivali's father, Rathyn, was arrested and taken under Stravhelm. She isn't sure why. No one is. He can talk to the setuar, the floweresque spirits of jungle trees. *Native magic,* the monks call it. Tivali isn't sure whether the monks can't do it or simply choose not to, but it in itself has never gotten anyone arrested. Yeah, Rathyn was grumbling—but who's not? Cautious people are scared to bring up their grievances. Question the holy city's decisions in front of some snitch and you'll be outed as a blasphemer or spy or troublemaker, then it's you getting hauled off. Problem is, he was Napiri's chief. When he went down Tivali unwillingly stepped into his role. She doesn't want the responsibility or the attention, but everyone else seemed happy to wander around like headless chickens. Tivali has chosen to believe that if she can muster the town's devotion to the holy city, she can earn her father's freedom. She can't just do nothing. Meanwhile, she avoids the subject of her father around Napiri. Because the next person who dutifully tells her that he deserved what he got is getting their face clubbed.

But what stripped clean the bones of Napiri's cheer, and nearly decimated its faith, is the warthound. A grown male, probably wandered up from the south because of the drought, made itself a den in the jungle nearby and claimed the whole territory. First it stalked Napiri, snatching chickens or young goats from their pens. They shooed it off. Couldn't kill it. Not with wood or shell alone. Scared it with fire. Reinforced their fences with sharpened stakes. They thought it was gone. Then the warthound made an ass of everyone and came in the middle of the day. Took a little girl. Snatched her up while she played in the sunlight and disappeared into the jungle. A knee-high girl who just figured out how to scamper upright, laughing in one moment, gone forever the next. It was the daughter of a woman named Harla, and it was her only remaining child. She's too old to make another. Something in her broke after that. Broke in Napiri too.

All of Napiri started praying for help from the holy city back when the warthound contented itself stealing livestock. They didn't care what shape the help took, be it armed monks or some miracle. No help came, but Tivali hadn't given up on praying. She couldn't. To her mind, her village's obedience is her father's one hope for redemption and release. She prayed for help until she was the last person doing it. She was her father's last chance. She admonished her people for not praying enough, not giving the sovereign more time, and even as she did, that wild animal took a child's life.

Now the warthound's gotta be dealt with. Tonight, at twilight's gathering, straws will be drawn and three men will be picked to hunt and kill it while it sleeps. Tivali will be the sole willing volunteer. If she is not chosen, she'll go anyway. If she is chosen, maybe she'll have pulled a straw intended for some useless coward, buying him more time to piddle in a dry field or do some farming.

They arrive at the last rest stop. It's a seven hundred-year-old cloud sweeper, or sagacious mahogany as the monks call it, with wall-like roots that wind over an otherwise trodden-bare hill off the side of an intersection of five paths. Travelers pause in the shade here. The paths leading up to this intersection are steep, and with a good haul you'll be out of breath, so you stop and appreciate the burden and your continued ability to tote it. Today, no one's out of breath. Not even Uncle Reilu, who set the barrow down and is rubbing his palms in his oily, grey-streaked hair. Tivali had tried to take a turn at pushing the barrow but he stopped her. Seemed to take offense. He doesn't talk much anyway, so when he told her this was his to carry, she didn't argue.

Tivali pretends to take some water, then passes the skin to her uncle, who takes it with a tired smile. Aunt Mara is busy off the side of the trail, holding her skirt and taking a piss. She finishes and takes the skin from Reilu.

While you're here you have to lay your hand on the tree. The tree's been around longer than the holy city and the monks with all their talk of coming war. Everyone's got their own reason for touching the trunk. Their own desires. Tivali, who never knows how much the sovereign sees, imagines Napiri's residents kneeling in prayer. She has to focus not to dwell on the hope that if the tree existed before the monks, maybe it could exist after them too.

Tivali closes her eyes. Concentrates. Tries her best to swallow down the feeling of futility. Asking for help has never felt natural. But for her father's sake, she has to. She whispers her prayer. "Sovereign Intemrus, on behalf of Napiri, I thank you for your ... your ceaseless bounties. I thank you for the rice we got today, and for the satisfaction it will bring us." In her head she sees Napiri's children with quarter-full bowls. The delight on their faces as they take their time with it, savoring it as if seasoned rice is a treasure. "I thank you for our resilience against the threat of the warthound." She sees Harla, hysterical at the loss of her daughter, fighting the villagers to follow the warthound into the jungle. Fighting to end her own life. Despondent. Sitting alone in her hut. Refusing to eat. "I want ..." Tivali forces back her tears. "... I want to ask you for help. Send someone to take care of the beast. Please. Anyone."

She has no more words. The prayer drained her of energy, left her feeling utterly helpless. She grits her teeth and opens her eyes. The sun is high. At the rate they're traveling, the villagers will be gathering for the evening's fire when they get home. Tivali takes a deep breath and relaxes her shoulders, tries to slow her heart.

"Here, girl," her uncle's voice rattles. He's drawn a tuskshell flask stoppered with a cork. "Have a drink. Napiri isn't going anywhere."

Tivali takes a long pull from the shell and flinches as it burns her throat. Skyseed liquor, and a damn strong batch. She coughs. "Uncle, what did you sneak to the Trade for this? Do I want to know?"

He chuckles and takes a quick pull, sucking air through his teeth but not flinching. "Nothing to bother yourself over." He wipes his whiskers with the back of his hand and gives Aunt Mara the flask. "Don't forget," he rasps. "This isn't our first drought. We've been through worse."

Tivali sighs and tries to be comforted. It's easy for him to say. He's not drawing a straw tonight. He's too old and he can barely see. Best he could do is get stuck in the warthound's teeth while someone else gets a strike in on it.

Uncle Reilu squeezes her arm. His grip is still as strong as a malva snare. "He'll be back, girl. They got nothing on him. Once they find that out, everything will be back to normal. And by then we'll be rid of that old-toothed hog."

Her uncle is smiling at her and she tries to return it. Rathyn's his brother, and maybe it's for her good that Reilu acts so unbothered about his arrest. Either he's unconcerned, or he refuses to believe how serious the holy city is about accused spies.

"We should go," Tivali says. Usually she waits for her uncle to rub his hands some more, for her aunt to break out the plantain cakes, for the sun to slide lower and relent. Today there's not time. Tivali can't miss the drawing.

"I don't know what the fuss is, anyway." Tivali's aunt stoppers the flask and gives it to Reilu, who hefts the barrow. Mara's as oblivious as she can be. Tivali envies her for that.

They've reached the foot of the hill when Tivali senses something amiss. An unnatural lull in the jungle's droning ahead. Probably unnoticeable to her aunt and uncle, but Tivali didn't get this successful at the Trade without making enemies. And if you have enemies, you gotta hit them before they hit you. That's just good sense.

She snatches her bamboo from the barrow and stops her uncle with a raised hand. Mara collides with him, and looks to be winding up for a tirade. Tivali glares at her and says "*Tss!*" Mara shuts her mouth and squeezes into Reilu's shadow.

Tivali prowls on silent feet, remarking on the irony that if she were dressed more for a fight then one might not be upon her. Something's scrambling in dry leaves around a bend. She lowers her stance. Whatever her quarry, predator or prey, surprise is the best greeting. Maybe she'll come out of this with fresh meat for dinner.

Around the curve is a scene that makes Tivali's head cock to the side in confusion. A man unlike any she's ever seen is kicking at the embankment in the ditch off the trail. He's got lighter skin than her and blueish clothes hanging in tatters. He's not even wearing shoes. Seems to be trying to make footholds, but with every step upward he slides back down into the ditch. It's a lot of effort to leave the well-travelled road in favor of impassable jungle, and it's doing nothing to fix Tivali's confusion. He doesn't see her. Barely seems aware of anything. She could sneak over and give him a crack across the head if she wanted to. He's bloodied and gaunt, and although that's the worst kind of person to find in the wild, something stays her hand.

"Hey," she says. "The road's over here."

The man jerks, loses his footing, wobbles and slides down on all fours into the leaves beside the trail. Then ... he's gone? Tivali recoils, blinks. What the hell happened? Did he manage to sink entirely under a scattering of leaves? Did she imagine him?

She approaches the ditch at a low crouch, bamboo first. There is the red sheen of fresh blood. It's on a leg, which is connected to a person. And then he's back, as if he blinked back into existence. There is no rustle or sound from his surroundings. He hasn't moved. Was that some kind of camouflage?

His feet and calves are caked in a mixture of blood and dirt. What remains of his blue clothes is embroidered with scales, not unlike a chaplain's dele. Except, he's no chaplain. This is no fisher, or farmer, or hunter. A gasp from behind tells Tivali her aunt has followed her.

Tivali inches forward, eyeing down her staff, ready to bash this stranger if he looks at her funny. "Turn around so I can see you."

The man is trembling. He's in poor shape. She could end him forever with a clever strike to his neck. Slowly, he straightens his back, clenching his fists over and over. He's either unnaturally bold, leaving his back open like that, or all the way stupid. Tivali is almost within striking distance, and if she gets there before he does as he's told, down he goes. He's not looking like an enemy from the Trade, but she's long since learned not to trust anyone on the trails between settlements, no matter their appearance, no matter the time of day. A loner like this? Might as well be a starving jaguar.

He exhales and his shoulders fall. He turns to face her. "I'm lost," he says.

She stops advancing. He's no older than she is. His eyes are dark and drained, giving him a haunted look.

"Where are you headed?" she asks.

He looks at her, and his eyes are pleading. For mercy? "I'm from ... the holy city," he says.

Tivali's heart leaps in her chest. She's smarter than to assume the best, that he's an answer to her prayer. Been alive too long for that. But what if ... what if he is? She turns to see her uncle standing beside her aunt, both wearing expressions like they're watching a carcass that's risen to its feet. "Uncle, bring the barrow," she says.

"*He's a monk!*" Mara hisses in Reilu's ear, making him flinch and dig at his ear with his pinky finger.

Tivali grabs the front of the barrow and pulls it toward the strange boy. He tries to edge away from her but he's against the ditch. He falls to a sitting position with his arms out in front of him. He is shaking visibly and is covered in cuts and scratches. In that moment Tivali realizes it's the rest of his monk clothes doing rounds at the Trade, bolstering the claim that a monk died in the jungle. She's never been gladder to witness a rumor proved false.

"Come on," Tivali says. "You need medicine." Unless it's too late. Jungle wounds sour quickly without attention.

He looks at her again and his eyes tell a sad story. There is no trust there. He looks like something brutal swept away his will. Tivali has seen that look before, but never on a monk. She'd never imagined a monk in such a state. That's the kind of despair you don't always recover from. Hopefully it's not too late for him. Not if he's the long-awaited answer to Napiri's prayers.

Tivali stashes her staff and rushes to pull him out of the ditch. He raises his hands as if she means to attack. "Calm down, monk. I don't know what you've been through, but you're safe now." It's mostly true. If he is who she thinks he is, she'll kill to protect him.

She takes his hand. It trembles like a tree branch submerged under rapids. She pulls his wrist over her shoulder and hauls him up. He's shaking all over, rattling against her like he's ravaged with fever. He's heavier than he looks, which isn't saying much. He moves reluctantly, but she gradually coaxes him to the barrow. Her uncle and aunt have stepped clear, watching with obvious suspicion. She sets him down among the bags of rice. *Is this why the barrow wasn't filled today? Intemrus' provision?*

The monk casts nervous glances at Tivali, her uncle, her aunt, the barrow. Tivali presses the back of her hand against his cheek then his forehead. He's not feverish. But he flinches away from her touch as if it causes physical pain.

"I'm Tivali," she says. "That's Mara and Reilu. My aunt and uncle."

The monk nods, eyes the dirt path beneath his bloody feet, and does not introduce himself.

She is horrified to ask him who he is, why he's here. Horrified she's wrong. But if she is, best to find out right now. "We're very grateful if you are the answer to our prayers," she says.

The monk's shoulders tighten at her remark, but they don't hold tension long. The tremors return and set him to shivering in the rice.

"Looks like he's got the fever," Mara hisses, as if he can't hear her.

"He doesn't. He's too alert. His skin's not hot," Tivali says. Even if he's not the answer to her prayer, she has to try to help him. This could be a test. Any show of subservience from her or her village might help her father. "Where's the water skin?"

Her aunt and uncle gawk at her.

"Give it. Can't you see he needs it?"

Reilu mutters and offers it to her. Tivali hands it to the monk, who examines it like it's there to drink him.

"Drink up, monk. It won't hurt you." She's gotta work on her manners.

He does, but reluctantly, as if it's the worst advice he's ever followed.

"I'm pushing him," Tivali claims, not that there was any chance of her uncle risking that role now. She hefts the handles and walks. Way heavier than any amount of rice now. His tremors don't make it easier. But it's gotta be done. She won't fail this test.

Tivali wants to find out his name, ask why he's here, what the hell happened to his clothes, end the suspense. But that might indicate a lack of faith on her part. And the idea that he isn't an answer to her prayer is too much to bear. So she hikes and stares at the back of his head in case the answers slip out his ear.

The monk's added weight will slow their trip. But perhaps that's why Tivali felt compelled to abridge their last rest stop. *Intemrus' Will. Providence.* Her heart flutters again at the possibility. She pushes the barrow at a steady pace despite that the monk's feet keep getting tangled in the cart's wheel. Tivali considers tossing out the rice. If the monk proves he is who she hopes him to be, it'll be worth it. Maybe this test of mercy is the final demand to earn Intemrus' favor. The village might not understand this monk's worth, not in his current state. Especially not in the place of something edible. Yes, there's good cause to their doubting. But what's the point of faith if it requires affirmation? That isn't faith.

Mara stares shamelessly. "Least he ain't that big. Don't they feed you up there on the holy hill?"

The monk leans forward, shaking as if possessed by butterflies. He clears his throat. "Um. Does this road run toward Erudition?"

Erudition. The way he enunciates the name proves beyond doubt he's a monk. Something about their deference bordering on fear. Natives don't care that much. They only use the word to look devout in front of monks. "No, it doesn't," Tivali says. The monk's shoulders seem to relax. So, he's not trying to get to Erudition ... Tivali pushes the barrow in growing trepidation. What if he's running away? What if she's wrong? What if she's aiding an enemy to the holy city?

Reilu speaks up, "If you didn't know that, why the hell were you following it?"

"Uncle ..." Tivali says. Except she wants that answer too.

The boy sits there, shoulders hunched, riding along as if he's lost all hearing.

Uncle Reilu snatches the barrow from Tivali and drops it on its rear legs, nearly flipping the monk out the back of it.

"You act like a liar, boy. For all I know you stole those fancy rags. Prove you're a monk or you're getting bloodied up and left."

"Uncle Reilu!" Tivali snatches his wrist and yanks his hand off the barrow. She bends his palm down, making him *yip* and dance backward on his toes.

"I want to hear the boy talk," says her aunt.

"Maru!" Tivali says. She has half a mind to give them both some bonks with the bamboo. This monk might look three-quarters dead but he's still a damn monk.

The boy has risen shakily to his feet and is facing them. His pupils are sharpened now, not so distant. He's taller than Tivali noticed. The black hair framing his face trembles gently. Tivali feels the urge to back away from him, give herself space to swing that bamboo if he turns feisty. But he doesn't look as desperate as before.

He clears his throat. "I am from Erudition, but I don't have answers for your questions or even my own." The words cast a cloud over his face and make his eyes mist over. He addresses Tivali. "You've been gracious to me and I'm grateful. I did not anticipate help, and I doubt I would have survived much longer without it."

Again, her heart flutters. She suppresses her smile. "You're welcome. You'll get whatever help Napiri can offer." And then, prompted by the anticipation in her roiling guts and the liquor having bolstered her courage, she asks him, "Are you here in response to our prayers?"

This appears to catch him off guard. For a moment he shifts his eyes nervously from her to her aunt, to her uncle, and back. Then the emotion vanishes from him. He's changed, without moving a muscle, visually becoming an inert feature of the jungle. If he weren't upright and watching her, Tivali would think she'd just witnessed him die. Chills rise over her sweaty skin, as if she's suddenly come aware she's within range of a viper's strike. The unease nearly causes her to back away.

"I am," he says.

Tivali's heart leaps. She nods her head in response, covering her face with her hand. Tears leak from the corners of her eyes.

The boy turns and sits back down on the rice, chin up as if there's any dignity in his current position.

Tivali wipes her eyes and shoots a smirk at her uncle, who gives her an apprehensive look. She butts him out of the way and proceeds to march forward with the cart at an empowered pace.

"May I ask your name?" Tivali injects as much reverence as she can muster.

"It's Ka—I mean, um … it's Diventae. Mancer Diventae."

"I can't wait to welcome you to Napiri, Mancer Diventae," Tivali says. She's heard of mancers but doesn't know what it means. Doesn't matter. He's the one. "We are so glad to have you."

20

Not Every Study Requires an Arsenal

AUSGAN

The Elucidatorium

Proctor Alika hums while he sweeps the stone floor of the Elucidatorium. The morning air is cool and smells of elima and lehua flowers. A dozen lehua setuar have alighted upon the stone benches and sway gently to Alika's song. They could easily pass for tufts of sedge with a flower sprouting from the middle if it weren't for their synchronized rhythm. Their petals, blooming from their heads like hair, are shades of red and orange and yellow. Their eyes are green orbs. They're content with Alika's song—it is about them, after all—and when he pauses humming, they lean forward, grow watchful, as if they're considering flowery mutiny. He chuckles.

The setuar are his secret. Communicating with them is considered *native magic* and is apparently beneath exemplars. Alika disagrees. Consonance includes the study of everything living and not, and that includes tree spirits. Also, considering the setuar live in harmony with their environment, then they live in harmony with the Imala, studying them should be mandatory. Alika's always assumed the prejudice against communicating with them came from a place of jealousy, since natives are apparently naturally better at it than exemplars. Oh well. The setuar are Alika's respite from Erudition, which feels more and more colorless these days. All everyone talks about is the danger of the Untamed in the south, fierce competition in the ranks of mancers, the pinnacle of devotion himself, Magus Kalderys, who leads the offense against the Untamed. And, of course, Sovereign Intemrus. Usually, when the sovereign leaves tower Syvea and makes himself more present in Stravhelm, he assumes command from the magister and all quietens down. The patience of Intemrus the Timeless puts the trivial matters and flaring ambitions of the city in perspective. Not this time. Intemrus is said to be all around, seeing everything and yet nowhere, watching over nothing. Tensions are high in Erudition.

The morning sun slowly burns the shadow off the mural on the boulder's face. Proctor Alika has plenty of time before the initiates arrive. Today's lesson is on insects, particularly ones that live in symbiosis with flowers. It's not the most riveting subject matter, but the upcoming exemplars could surely benefit from some serenity. Besides, lessons like this let Alika's mind drift while he teaches.

Lately he's been spending more of his time at the amphitheater. When he was younger he resented his place out here, ten miles distant from the holy city, so far away that time stands still and Erudition moves on without concern for him. Over the years, he had to admit, grudgingly at first, this place suits him better than Erudition. Perhaps the time of segregation itself is what caused him to stop caring. In youth, he felt the competitive tendencies of his peers. He was excited to hear of Erudition strengthening defenses against the threat of Fohrvylda. Jealous when a classmate beat him to a milestone in summoning or channeling. Times were simpler then. *The Heathen Tide will invade from across the Faithless Sea*, Intemrus said. But however fresh the concept was to Alika, Intemrus has been saying it for generations, since long before Proctor Alika. Now, the tale of the Heathen Tide has been told for too long. It's stagnated, evidently no closer than it ever was. Far less pressing of a threat than today's tidings of sedition from within Ausgan, and not only from the Untamed. Alika doesn't want to believe the rumors about how those threats are dealt with.

The lehua setuar turn as one toward the path leading back toward Erudition. Students approaching? Occasionally students arrive early to chat with Alika and get insight on the day's lesson. The setuar bounce off their benches, rising like jellyfish on the air, and melt into the lehua flowers in the boughs overhead. The urgency with which they disperse suggests it's no student that approaches. It's probably not a wild animal either. Setuar aren't threatened by those, and there are enough roving mancer-in-training patrols to keep dangerous beasts from wandering this far north.

Ashmancer Haik strolls into the clearing. He's wearing a smile and carrying no fusil. Alika isn't sure which of those he'd prefer. Haik isn't accompanied by his two sentinels. Something about that makes Alika nervous.

"Resonations, Proctor. Singing to the flowers this morning?"

Alika stops sweeping, as much as he'd like to sweep Haik back out of sight. "Resonations, Ashmancer," he says. Hopefully his tone conveys deference. His sentiment does not.

Haik must have sent a sensory pulse over the area to learn of the setuar. That's probably what caused them to flee. Proctor Alika has fallen out of the exemplar routine of exercising vigilance bordering on manic paranoia. Another unfortunate byproduct of his placement out here surely.

Haik saunters around the perimeter of the amphitheater, hands clasped behind his back, gazing up at the trees. He's still pulsing. Looking for witnesses? "Such skittish creatures, setuar. You must be more patient than me to earn their trust."

More patient than the ashmancer, a comparison that disqualifies absolutely no one. Alika demonstrates his patience by saying nothing.

"It's impressive you can garner their attention the way you do. Almost like you're one of them."

It's with great effort that Alika keeps from rolling his eyes.

"Are you one of them?" Haik asks, grinning sidelong at Alika. "A flower with no practical purpose?"

Alika returns a smile. It's like Haik is an overgrown initiate who has stumbled into possession of too much authority and has no idea what to do with it. "If you're calling me pretty, thank you. If you're a named mancer with no notion of the function of flowers?" Alika *tsks*. "Today's education on the subject would serve you well."

"That sounds riveting. I think I'll sit in on your class."

Alika tries to keep a scowl from taking over his face. "You're always welcome. But you might find the lesson tiresome. We're learning of insects, and how their presence and habits predict trends in weather. No fire and destruction, I'm afraid."

Haik chuckles. "I swear, your classes should be prescribed as punishment. Hopefully you have more useful lessons in your arsenal."

"Not every study requires an arsenal."

"Maybe it should. One day whimsical wonderings will all cease to make room for practical purposes, in preparation for the Heathen Tide. Maybe the more frivolous proctors will be repurposed for useful roles. It might prove taxing, though. I know how the elderly abhor change."

"I'll mention that last position to the sovereign in our next talk."

Haik proceeds as if he didn't hear. "But no, Proctor. I'm not here to study bugs. Today I'm more interested in the lessons you're teaching indirectly."

Alika's heart thuds at the implication, and he isn't sure why. He has nothing to hide. Does he? Haik can't read his emotions. He can't discern that Alika has grown skeptical of the Triumvirate. And it certainly doesn't leak out in his lessons. Does it? Alika keeps a level expression.

"I must say, I'm curious what lessons I'm teaching indirectly as well. Should I know what you're talking about?"

Haik dons an easy smile. "Relax. As yet, only Basalt Kale has succumbed to your influence."

Alika's ears grow hot. He's unable to maintain the facade of indifference. "I don't know what you're referring to, Haik, but you'd do well to remember that I'm your senior. And though I tolerate your juvenile banter, I don't take kindly to accusations. If something's happening with Kale, say it. Don't waste my time."

Haik's smile is gone. "Alright, Proctor. Kale is wanted for questioning by the Triumvirate. Either he's fled Erudition or he's hiding well. You know, like he does. And since you act as his personal caretaker, I thought I'd give you a chance to assist the Triumvirate willingly. Trust me, that option is not offered to every suspect. I'm doing you a favor."

"Suspect?" Alika stares at Haik, forcing his surprise down, trying to think logically. There's a reason Haik didn't bring his sentinels. He's not here to arrest anyone. Does he not want witnesses? Perhaps he's been tasked with finding Kale and he wants all the credit. If Alika were truly suspected of something illegal, he'd already be before the magister herself. That is, unless he's fallen further from grace than he knows. More likely, she's demanded discretion. Another intolerable characteristic of the holy city lately is that everything's a secret. Most intriguingly though is Haik's word choice. He said *Triumvirate*. Twice. As if he speaks for them. As if they don't have their own enforcer. Something's wrong here.

"I am concerned for Kale's wellbeing," Alika says evenly. "I try to encourage him and keep him optimistic. But he doesn't share his personal business with me. I'm sorry to disappoint, Ashmancer."

"Optimistic?" Haik says, taking a step forward. "Why would he be otherwise? He's a gifted negator that has never known negation sickness."

Alika nearly laughs. That description is generous to the level of grossly inaccurate. Haik is no doubt trying to provoke some response. But Kale's business is his own, so Alika only says what's necessary.

"Kale carries a lot of regret, Haik. You know that. For Thran."

"Actually, I did not," Haik says, genuine interest on his face. "Kale lashed out in vengeance. I thought he was glad Thran died."

Alika's words spill before he can stop them. "The sovereign tried Kale in the tribunal and declared him to be without malicious intent. I think the father of consonance would know more than you or me about how it works. Stravhelm's court reached this verdict, and yet some refuse to accept it. How would the sovereign feel about you questioning his judgment?"

Haik *tsks*, as if dismayed by Alika's emotional outburst. "I certainly didn't intend to offend Kale's caretaker. Maybe you should be more concerned with how the sovereign will react when you're exposed as an accomplice in Kale's flight."

Alika takes a breath to rein in his anger. His gut reaction suggests the sovereign is oblivious to Kale's flight or else Magus Kalderys would be here representing the Triumvirate, not Ashmancer Haik. "I'll help in any way I can," Alika says. "But I don't know anything about Kale running away. I'm willing to testify that before the magister."

Haik relaxes, easing back and cocking his head. "You've gotten comfortable out here, Proctor Alika. I know how much it means for you to be able to play with your flowers. But don't get complacent. I don't know if you'd heard, but there's an opening for a new folksteller. Depending on how fruitful your assistance is with Kale, maybe I can keep you from being displaced to fill the spot of head counter."

Alika had heard of Tael's arrest. And so, despite knowing no further details, he's able to keep his expression level. "Ah, Haik. You're too young to have already forgotten core precepts. Placement is a product of our contribution. For example, a proctor's placement is not determined by the local spark enthusiast. The day consonance requires you determining what is or is not complacency, we'll all have more to worry about than an errant basalt."

"Folksteller Tael is under Stravhelm preparing for the bath," Haik says, ignoring Alika's response. He announces it as if he's referring to dipping in the ocean, not a forced plunge into molten earth.

Alika bites his tongue. Whatever happened to Tael, he'd prefer to hear it from anyone else. But even more than that, he will not satisfy Haik by expressing concern. He shifts his hold on the broom. "You don't say."

"The magister wants this to stay quiet. Report anything you find to me, no one else. Not even your plants," Haik says, turning on his heel. "I'll be back in time for your lessons."

Alika stands gripping his broom. *Let Haik go.* That would be wise. He's already leaving. But there's a lie here. And the setuars' curiosity has apparently taken root in Alika. "Ashmancer ..." he says. Haik slows to a stop but doesn't turn. "How quiet? To whom?"

"No conversation about Kale ever happened quiet," Haik says, "to anyone."

"Not the magus, or even the sovereign?"

At this, Ashmancer Haik spins back to face Alika, surprised rage showing in his face. His stance suggests he'd prefer to respond in violence. But no response is forthcoming, as if he's torn between blurting the wrong thing or assaulting Alika. As it happens, his silence says enough. Obsydia acts alone in this.

"It won't be a problem," Alika reassures. "Of course the Triumvirate is in unison. To suggest otherwise would be ridiculous."

Haik speaks in a hiss. "To suggest otherwise would be heresy."

"Agreed," Alika says. "And I wouldn't dream of bothering His Presence with something as trivial as a runaway basalt."

Haik is once again without response. But the rage has deteriorated into uncertainty. He seems to be aware that he's given something up in this exchange but can't figure out what.

"As soon as I see Kale, I'll deliver him to you. I'm sure he'll be around soon enough." And Alika makes to return to his brooming.

Haik scoffs, exhaling the rest of the anger off his face. "Well, praise Intemrus. The flower proctor has some sense."

Alika nods, head lowered, having earned exactly that reprimand.

Haik leaves.

Alika relaxes and looks up at the titan myrtles. The lehua setuar won't return this morning. Not before class starts. They are keenly sensitive to less pleasant emotions like anger and fear. A person like Haik will probably live and die never setting eyes on a lehua setuar, only knowing them by pulse and rumor. And although that brings Alika some satisfaction, Haik will also never appreciate what he's missing. Perhaps someday he'll meet a bunch of stirred-up koa setuar. Those are the ones that live in acacia bolds and fear nothing and return hostility in kind.

Ashmancer Haik revealed far more than he intended. Kale is missing and the sovereign hasn't been told. And while it's normal for Intemrus to be spared insignificant details, it isn't normal for him to be willfully left out. If this were truly insignificant, Ashmancer Haik would not be out asking questions and making threats. Magister Obsydia wants to find Kale before the sovereign knows he's missing. Why? What in Imala's name has Kale done now?

Just a few short years prior, Haik had plans to eventually ascend into the Triumvirate himself. Always seemed Obsydia was priming him for the position. Was she grooming him for some other role instead? The ashmancer's attachment to her seems unhealthy at times. Is he her unofficial enforcer? If so, she appears to possess the loyalty of Magus Kalderys and Ashmancer Haik. It's common knowledge Cryomancer Hyrala would kill for the magister's favor. Nothing about Obsydia hoarding that much power reassures Alika. Especially not if Sovereign Intemrus is as disconnected as evidence suggests. Head in the clouds, even when he's down from Syvea Tower, convinced nonexistent heathens will soon rake the eastern coast with weapons made of metal.

Alika shakes his head, proceeds to sweep, too uneasy to continue humming. The ashmancer is tromping out a distant perimeter around the amphitheater at this moment, sending supersensory pulses outward like skipping stones. He's sticking around, like he promised. Alika's shoulders droop. He never thought that showing Kale favorable attention would result in himself coming to dread the ashmancer. It seems funny, but no smile is forthcoming.

Proctor Alika's class will arrive soon. Today's lesson will be a dour one. His mind is elsewhere. Kale's in trouble, and although that's not a surprise, he's in a special kind of trouble. *Secret* trouble. Does Ashmancer Haik know Kale and Culver are friends? If so, has he interrogated the andesite? Surely it's known. But not because Intemrus sees all. There's no way of knowing what Intemrus sees. And what does it matter what he sees if there's no evidence that he cares?

21

Help From On High

AUSGAN

Napiri

Tivali wheels the barrow around the final bend and Napiri's lodge comes into view. It isn't a moment too soon. The monk's trembling is threatening to break apart the barrow. She wonders what he'll think of the village. Everything about him, from the bewilderment in his eyes to his obvious lack of guile at jungle survival, tells her he probably hasn't seen a native village since he was snatched out of one for his infant induction into the holy city.

Napiri is a scattering of thatched huts on the side of a gradual incline, with the dining hall overlooking them all. Uphill of the hall is a grazing pasture for the goats, fenced in with a mesh of tightly netted spiralpine twine, fish-waxed to keep the goats from chewing it, held up in intervals by thin trees.

It takes no time for Tivali to attract attention. Napiri relies on the rice she's bringing, and although they should know to expect little, some folks are bound to express their disappointment, as if it's some surprise. Townsfolk pause from their work, straighten their backs, shield their eyes, peer as Tivali pushes the monk into the clearing. She can only imagine what grim expressions her aunt and uncle are wearing behind her.

The monk's knuckles are blanched from gripping the sides of the barrow. He's not what she expected when she sent prayers up to Stravhelm. His arms and legs are wiry, but they seem solid enough. Tivali's heard of the constant training that happens in Erudition, but this boy does not look like a warrior. She dreads to think what the villagers will say of him, especially Tobas.

"Don't worry," Tivali tells him. "You can rest soon." But first, she has to address the village.

Townsfolk are gathering on the mid-plain between the lower huts. Men pile wood for the fire. Tivali will have to direct the energy here. Hopefully the truth will suffice. She sets the barrow down harder than she meant to, making the monk's head loll back and hit the handle. She steps between Diventae and the gathering mass, chest out. Reilu and Mara back away as if ashamed of the barrow and its contents, maybe of Tivali.

"People of Napiri, our prayers are answered," Tivali calls out. She expects a poor response from the two dozen onlookers, and she gets one. A hiss of whispering rises up to rival the afternoon bugs. Most folks look unimpressed. Jesbr, standing bare-chested in the shade of a hut, spits a splattery clod on the ground. "Those who have spread doubt should get ready to offer their apologies first, and loudest." Tivali holds Jesbr's eyes until he averts his gaze.

"Wait here," Tivali whispers to Kale, who's managed to pale even further. He's watching the gathered townsfolk like they might pounce on him. Tivali's not convinced they won't. Maybe she should get him out from between them and their rice. Her good news requires an advocate. She marches across the clearing, shouldering through anyone not quick enough to move.

Tivali makes her way to Harla's hut. Her breath trembles as she places a hand on the doorway and looks in. Inside is frumpy and disheveled Harla. She sits cross-legged on her mat—as always these days. Draped over one knee is a tiny silksedge smock. She idly kneads its shoulders with her thumbs, staring with unfocused eyes. Her pudgy thumbs are nearly enough to fill the outfit's small sleeves. Tivali has to pull her eyes off it before it saps her strength.

"Harla," Tivali says quietly. "Come see. The sovereign has answered us."

The woman slowly turns her bloodshot eyes on Tivali. Grief has made a wasteland of her face. She doesn't speak, only stares. Tivali takes her arm. Harla heaves a great sigh and rises. She lets Tivali guide her from the hut.

By now the majority of the town is gathered, some forty strong. They're at a safe distance, eyeballing the strange, bloody boy with blatant distrust. Their whispers are growing louder. Tivali overhears remarks as she pulls Harla through the crowd toward the monk.

"What's he supposed to do? He's got no weapons."

"This is our answer?"

"Look at his feet! Probably can't even walk."

"That's no warrior."

"So much for help from on-high."

The monk is trying to squirm into the bags of rice like a ghost crab into the beach. He looks like a cornered animal. Everything considered, Tivali can't blame the people for their doubt. But the same doubt already caused most of them to give up on help coming. A familiar irritation gnaws at her. As if she pushes a boulder uphill and everyone who should be helping is standing directly in her path.

"Quiet!" Tivali barks. "You've complained about the monks forgetting us for so long, you can't even recognize proof they haven't.

Save your griping for your piss-filled huts. If no one else can appreciate him, I bet Harla can."

Harla has dark streaks where dust has caked onto the path of tears on her cheeks. Her hair is like a wild bramble. She hasn't seen sunlight for days. But there's a glint in her eye that wasn't there before as she approaches the monk. She doesn't speak—she hasn't since it happened—but she holds out the dirty smock she's been squeezing. The monk recoils as if it's a dead animal.

"That's just a damn kid. What good can he do?" It's Tobas, and he's stepped forward to aim his tined bamboo pitchfork at the monk.

Tivali snatches the tool from his hands and cracks him over the head with it. Tobas stumbles back. She hits him again and he falls down.

"You monkey's ass!"

Tobas scrambles backward, rubbing his head. Tivali walks in a circle, aiming the tines at every individual in turn, glaring into their eyes. "The next one of you who speaks your poison in front of him will catch the sharp ends. Doubt will be the death of you all."

Behind Tivali, Harla sniffles, stealing her focus. "But it was hers," she whimpers in a hoarse voice, pushing the tiny outfit at the monk's reluctant hands.

Gasps rustle through the villagers. Tivali feels her lips purse, her eyes sting. But this is no time to cry.

"Napiri," she calls, trying to control her voice. "You prayed. You doubted. Some of you spread your doubt to others. And for that, we've had to sit helpless while we were harassed, while our goats were stolen, while our ..." She didn't mean to look at Harla. Now her tears overflow. "While our children were taken."

To her credit, Harla doesn't collapse.

"But today, two miracles have occurred. I found this monk searching for our village on feet unfit to carry him, trusting the sovereign to guide his path. And right here and now, Harla has found her voice."

At last, the village watches Tivali and the monk, no longer muttering, no longer shifting, but quiet. Near reverent. Even Tobas stands with his head hung, his arms slack at his sides.

"Napiri," Tivali says, before the waver can consume her voice. "No one is drawing straws tonight!"

A cheer bursts out, then another. Soon the whole gathering is clapping and whistling. Tivali takes the monk's shaking hand. His palms aren't callused like a farmer's. There's no evidence he's done a day's work in his whole life. But if all the holy city required was skin made rough from hard labor, the warthound would already be slain.

"Tell them, Mancer Diventae," Tivali says. "Tell them like you told us."

The monk looks like he's going to be sick. His wide eyes rove over Napiri. Silence infects the mid-plain. He gives a cough, then swallows several times. He rubs his hands together and stares downward. A cold dread rises in Tivali's gut. Was she wrong?

The monk is shaking his head, as if denying some accusation from the ground itself. Murmurs rise up from the gathering. Tivali is about to give him a hard pinch when he shrugs and clambers to his blood-caked feet. He's taller than the people of Napiri. He brushes dust off the sad remains of his dele and looks around at the gathering. The quiet feels fragile, as if at any moment it could shatter and give way to chaos. Tivali's not sure she can protect him if he is about to disappoint them. Honestly, she's not sure she would if she could.

The monk clears his throat yet again. "I'm Mancer Diventae." He lifts a single hand and jiggles it while he scans them, maybe hoping for a returned wave. When it doesn't happen, he lowers his hand and clears his throat once more. "I am here on Sovereign Intemrus' business in answer to your prayers."

Harla sags to her knees, sobbing quietly. Tivali wipes the tears from her own eyes. She looks at her peers and neighbors. There are still scowls. But there are also wet cheeks and open laughter.

Tivali gestures for Diventae to sit back down on the barrow. "Let's see to your feet," she says.

"I'd appreciate that," the monk says.

The crowd disperses as Tivali wheels Mancer Diventae away from the mid-plain, but it's obvious most everyone is trying to position themselves in ways to keep the monk in their sight. Two boys run ahead of her to the dining lodge. Young Suda and two other girls resume their enthusiastic weaving of a malva blanket outside the far end of the dining hall, though they're utterly distracted. Judging by their giggles and murmurings and the glances they steal at Diventae, the blanket will make fine tinder for the evening fire when they're done with it.

Seducing a monk has long been an unspoken and taboo challenge for young natives. Fact is, if you manage to get a monk baby in your belly, you'll be rewarded generously when the chaplains come for it. Who better to plant one than a monk? It makes sense that monks are more likely to beget monks. Chaplains say that it's not the case. They say a consonant gift is random, given from the Imala with no predictability. There's no point in seducing a monk, they say. Always sounded like goatshit to Tivali, propagated to protect the wayward chaplains from jungle ambush. She's not sure anyone's succeeded at seducing a monk. In her friends' experience, monks thwart all advances, or at least the ones they admit to. She hasn't personally tried. The last thing Tivali wants is a baby in her damn belly slowing her down, much less one that chaplains will take away before she can even get some work out of it.

There are children arranging food and supplies at the lodge. Tivali takes her time wheeling the monk up the hill so they can finish and clear out. Also, her shoulders don't have much toting left in them. By the time she sets the barrow down once and for all on the shaded stone tiles, there's a shallow clay basin of clean water awaiting. The monk stands and hobbles to a stool. On the long table is a platter of sun-dried plantains and salted perch. Those children who acted quickly to get this set up have retreated to a safe viewing distance outside the shade of the lodge. Tivali smiles. Routine chaplains don't even get this service.

The monk scarfs down food like he's never eaten. Tivali warms a mug of coconut ash soap over coals in the hearth and collects a small chitin strigil.

"You comfortable?" Tivali asks.

The monk nods, his cheeks stuffed to bursting. He's still trembling, especially his hands and knees. Tivali had assumed the shaking would relent as he relaxed.

"Good." She sits and begins to rinse his bloody feet. When she applies the strigil to clean the dirt from his wounds, the monk sucks his breath in through his teeth.

Tivali grins. "That's the easy part." She hands him a cord of spiralpine. "Bite this."

He swallows his food and sticks the cord between his teeth. Once Tivali gets the hardened blood and dirt scraped away, she's able to have a better look. Lacerations crisscross the soles of his feet and his toes. There are punctures and gouges. By some miracle, there's no swollen red evidence of flesh bugs. No spiderwebs of dark veins to indicate withering of the wounds. His feet are soft. He's probably never hiked a mile without the luxury of holy city sandals. Tivali wonders why he, of all the monks, was chosen for the mission he's on. Chaplains at least have road-worthy feet.

Once the ash soap is melted, she applies it on the skin of his feet and ankles, cleaning with a tuft from a spiralpear. The monk grunts as the salt in the soap penetrates his wounds. He squeezes his teary eyes shut, making Tivali laugh.

"First time getting a wound cleaned?"

The monk takes a deep breath and looks at her but doesn't respond.

"Bite down," she says, then quickly scrapes away the oil and the dirt it dislodged. Once she's satisfied the tool is no longer necessary, she rinses his feet again and wraps them in several layers of treated malva leaves. She props his feet up on a stool. The monk wipes tears from his eyes, sniffing noisily.

"What did you put on there?" he asks, turning his feet back and forth on their stool.

"First, staunchweed. Helps keep them clean. Then acacia resin," she says. "It will seal your wounds. Those leaves will keep the resin from drying out and stop the wounds from reopening if you're careful."

He pulls his right foot onto his left knee and pokes gently at the sole of his foot, wearing an expression of mild disbelief. "It doesn't hurt anymore," he marvels. "How did you know how to do this?"

"It's … simple medicine," she says. Is he being sarcastic?

He studies her with an air of admiration. "No one has ever ..." he stammers. "I mean, I've never seen this kind of medicine." His cheeks are full of color now. His hair is so black it's almost blue. Tivali is distinctly aware of the glances of the villagers as they pretend to go about their business. She knows exactly what the girls watching are thinking, and is suddenly quite conscious of being knelt right in front of the monk. Her ears burn. She stands, adjusts the strap of her shirt. She should probably have changed clothes.

"Your chaplains taught us herb lore from their books," she says, hoping to shift his attention back to his feet. "The rest was handed down. This is a village of labor, Mancer Diventae. We have no shortage of cracked skin and raw feet here. Yours aren't the worst I've treated."

He nods. There's something off about him and she can't put her finger on what it is. He seems distracted, but she probably would be too if she had his job. He did appear tormented, but that has been declining gradually since she first met him. Ever since he told her he was the answer to her prayer he's seemed guarded, but with moments of vulnerability she's not used to from monks. He handles the smock Harla gave him. "What's this?" he asks.

"It was Elli's. Harla's daughter's." No need to tell him that monks seized Harla's first child ten years ago and she took it poorly. Diventae will surely know that, otherwise what's the point of the chaplains and their tedious counts?

The monk turns the garment over a couple of times and drops it on the table, returning to his food.

"That was all that they found of her in the field," Tivali says, hoping for a reaction. Monks don't make babies in the holy city, as is known. But it's not too far a stretch to assume he'll appreciate the pain Harla and the village are feeling over this loss. Is it?

"Hmm ..." And the monk's eyebrows give a momentary rise. His attention has moved on to food stuck between his teeth.

Heat rises in Tivali's cheeks. Monks aren't this callous. Usually they're all sympathy, even if it's faked. Then again, maybe indifference is necessary for Diventae's job. Tivali clears her throat. "If you don't mind me asking, what's your plan?"

He meets her gaze. His expression is frustratingly void of any emotion. "My plan," he says, "will be to let the sovereign guide my steps, as he has thus far." He throws a plantain chip into his mouth.

Tivali sits back and crosses her arms. He's too flippant about this mission. Maybe he'll make a mess of the beast without breaking a sweat. Doesn't mean he should be a prick about it. "And the warthound?"

"Hmm?" A line of drool leaks from his overfull mouth.

"How will you kill it?"

The monk's eyes bulge and he snorts. He gasps and squeezes his throat as if it has clogged. Tivali hesitantly tosses him a waterskin. It lands in his lap and almost knocks him off his stool. He takes a deep pull from it, sloshing water in the process. He wipes his eyes and flicks the chewed fruit from his dele. For a long moment, he sits with his fist touching his lips, working his jaws on whatever food he didn't spew out. Finally, he places a thumb on one nostril, launches partially chewed food out the other, then repeats the process the other way round. Tivali stares, incredulous.

"Consonance," he says, and continues to eat.

Tivali narrows her eyes and peers at him. Her uncle was right. Although monks aren't liars—they're not allowed to be—Diventae certainly has a damn liar's tells. Napiri has had several chaplains throughout Tivali's life. They each have their own traits, but they're all elusive as hell when you ask them the wrong question. In that aspect, Mancer Diventae reminds her of one of them. *Consonance.* Monk magic, as far as she's gathered. Although the word means almost nothing to her, the feeling of ignorance it produces is comforting. As if monks live and breathe and operate on a level she can't hope to understand. Maybe it reassures her because her lack of comprehension keeps her from worrying holes into his plan. Usually she picks apart all the best laid designs, finding where they'll go wrong and then announcing it aloud. Obviously, it's always to prevent misfortune. It doesn't win her a high opinion from those whose bright ideas she shoots down, but she's more concerned with her village not starving than her reputation.

Soon enough, the monk's platter is clean. He pushes it away and turns to lean back against the table, propping his elbows on it. "How long before I can walk again?" he asks.

"You can walk now. The resin will have closed your smaller wounds already, but it won't be comfortable. I'll give you some hiking sandals that belonged ... they belong to my father. They're fit for hiking in the jungle."

"He won't miss them?"

His question makes Tivali pause. She'd assumed the monks research the state of villages they visit. Chaplains always give that impression, as if they're all knowing. And considering all the notes and scrawling they achieve in their time here, why wouldn't a visiting monk be informed? What advantage would ignorance serve him? Did Diventae ask that because he's clueless about Rathyn, or because he knows Rathyn will be released?

She'd considered asking him about her father. See if he still lives, and if his accusers have reached some verdict yet. Since his arrest, she has been a model of faith, and so have all who fear her, which is everyone who knows her if they're smart. But Diventae doesn't appear to know a damn thing about anyone or anything. What would be the point of asking him? Of all the admirable traits he's presumably been gifted, sympathy and reassurance aren't present. That much is obvious.

"No," Tivali says. "My father's away for a while and doesn't need them just now." It's an invitation for the monk to give a tell that he's aware of more than he lets on. And depending on how it goes, maybe she'll ask him more.

"That's good," he says, picking at his teeth with his fingernail. "I heard you mention drawing straws to your community. Were you intending to kill the warthog yourselves?"

"Warthound," she corrects. Such a question from any other monk might sound loaded. As if Napiri's show of independence is an affront to the holy city, who they're supposed to trust unconditionally. It doesn't seem that way coming from Mancer Diventae. Rather, unassailable ignorance. Tivali's starting to wonder if he's not some impostor who stole the monk outfit he wears. But the way he talks, his light skin, and his childlike naivety, those are proof enough he's from the city. "Yes, we were. Tonight."

"Well, for today there will be no need. Point me in the beast's direction and I'll be off."

She rises then hesitates. "For today?"

His composure slips, eyes widening momentarily before yet again, all emotion vanishes from him. "Correct. Today it's my turn. Intemrus willing, the beast will fall by my ... hand. I didn't mean to imply a lack of faith."

She's stuck staring at him. He has every indication of being an imposter. What would happen if she called him out? *Faith*, she tells herself. *Have faith.* It's easier said than done, which is a thing she's been told by several of her fellows over the past couple of weeks. Tivali shakes her head and leaves the dining hall, heading to her family's hut.

She should be excited. She'd have gone with the hunters to try her luck against the ravenous warthound and now she's off the hook. Instead, she's apprehensive. What if he's duplicitous, even though monks aren't supposed to be? What happens if he fails?

The warthound will persist. The village will be out a pair of sandals and a plate of food. But the last vestiges of Napiri's faith will probably die outright.

And then ... what will happen to her father?

Villagers watch Tivali as she approaches her father's hut. They trust her. Why? She can't weave spiralpine or silksedge into clothes or shoes or mats or even cords. She has no green thumb for farming. She doesn't have the patience for fishing. She can track a boar or a rhinocapy for miles. She can throw a spear with the best hunters of the village, but she's not strong enough to sling a carcass over her shoulders and march through the thick. Maybe they trust her because she's willing to go distances they aren't. Maybe because she hides her fear. Maybe because she thinks about consequences.

Inside the hut, her father's sandals are hanging right where he left them. Tivali hasn't touched them or any of his possessions. Why would she? He'll be back. She takes hold of the sandals but can't bring herself to lift them off their hook. The disparity between expectations and this moment solidifies. These are her father's most valuable possession. He can't hunt without them. It is for his sake that she prays and makes sure Napiri stays devout. Now the answer to her prayers has arrived and it requires she sacrifice the sandals. *Faith.* This cannot be a coincidence. But the trepidation is intense. Exercising faith feels a lot like spitting in the face of lessons life has taught you. If this were guaranteed, she'd have no hesitation in handing over the sandals. More can be weaved. It's just never felt natural for Tivali to relinquish control.

Maybe her expectations were amiss. She's never witnessed the fighting styles of the monks or seen their magic. If you trust the rumors of the Trade, and Tivali makes it a point not to, there's little monk magic can't do. But this boy ... he's ill-prepared to be here, and his behavior marks him as dishonest. No, she didn't pray for an honest monk. She prayed for one to kill the warthound. She keeps circling back to this point—her ignorance is all she has for reassurance. Tivali groans. She will have faith or fake it until she does. For Rathyn.

She snatches the sandals and a strapped goat-skin satchel. She should give him traveling food. The warthound's den can't be a day's walk away. But maybe he'll walk slow to sing or prepare his magic. She stuffs the satchel with leaf-wrapped gingercorm and mullet patties. It would serve her for a week, but that monk has the appetite of a chasm toad.

Diventae is still examining the wrappings on his feet when she returns. Most of the lingering villagers have lost interest and gone back to their business. Harla stands under the shadow of a tree, hands clasped at her waist, staring at the monk with shiny eyes. He seems to be pretending she's not there.

"Here," Tivali says, placing the satchel on the table beside him. He lifts it open carefully and recoils, his nose wrinkling.

"What is it?"

"It's food. Enough for ... it should be plenty. Let me see your feet."

The sandals are a good enough fit, so she carefully wraps the straps up his ankles and calves, making sure to apply only as much pressure as is needed. Too much and his toes will turn purple and go numb. Not enough and the straps will rub his ankles raw, despite the layers of leaves.

The muscles in his legs are more defined than her father's, probably due to organized monk diets and exercise. But his skin, the color of skyseed, made ribbed by fresh cuts and scratches, feels as soft as a toddler's. There are still tremors in his feet, and he flinches whenever her hands touch him. It is known that monks do not make physical contact with one another outside of combat training, but something about his posture, leaning forward as before when she treated his wounds and now as she shoes his feet, tells Tivali that he's not opposed to it, even if it's new to him. Maybe monks *can* have physical contact with natives. Maybe they *do* put monk babies into natives. She glances up at him. He's watching her intently. Her cheeks blaze and she drops his foot, bouncing it off the tile harder than she intended.

"Hey!" he says, flinching, and immediately looks embarrassed. "I'm sorry. You've taken good care of me." He stares at her, looking like he wants to say something more. It's almost a plea on his face and it gives Tivali the feeling he has some confession he wants to make. In fact, it's the most earnest he's looked since she met him. She opens her mouth to prompt him but he interrupts her by pressing his feet against the ground and testing the sandals. Tivali takes his shaking hand and helps him stand. He's even taller in the thick-soled sandals. He seems more interested in her hand than his feet.

"Can you walk?" she asks.

"I think so," he says, turning her hand over in his. "I feel like I could run." He meets her eyes.

Tivali suddenly feels conspicuous and alone with the monk. She releases his hand. "I don't advise running. Let's make sure you can walk. If not, give the sap another hour or so." As the words leave her mouth a nervous energy alights in her belly. And how to pass that hour? For some reason she finds herself simultaneously hoping for more time and dreading it. He hides too many secrets, is too unlike other monks. He's fixating on her but she can't read him and that's starting to bother her.

He strides back and forth. If his feet are hurting him it doesn't show. "I feel as good as new," he says. He wears a wan smile, as if this prelude to goodbye is something significant for him. He pulls the satchel onto his shoulder. "I guess I should ... go."

Tivali nods, swallows irrational disappointment, leads the way up past the north fence. The bleating of goats bounces over the sparse pasture. Cries of birds echo from the jungle. Once again, villagers cease their tasks to stare. Some even creep along at a safe distance. Harla shuffles behind Tivali, watching the monk. Diventae throws an occasional distrusting glance back at her, as if she's conspiring to knife him. Tivali tries to force down her apprehension, treat him as the victor she hopes him to be. This is what she prayed for, a monk who's in a hurry to deal with the warthound. *Have faith*, she reminds herself. She leads him to the beast's tracks, on the edge of the jungle.

"The warthound had never come here in the day," Tivali says, indicating the expanse beside the goat fence. "So the children played in the field."

Harla emits a snuffling whimper. The monk looks startled by it. Tivali wonders if he knows what the word *play* means. Monks don't have children, sisters, brothers, mothers, fathers, families. Maybe he can't comprehend Harla's pain. She shakes her head, annoyed at herself. *He doesn't need to understand death to deliver it to a warthound.*

"There's a hoofprint." She points. Mancer Diventae stoops to inspect it. He places a shaking fist inside one of the twin impressions that make up the hoof marks. Maybe he's not shaking in fear. He was already shaking after all. He has been since birth for all Tivali knows.

He withdraws his fist from the print. Tivali finds herself holding her breath. It's at this point that all others have lost nerve. The accounts of eyewitnesses and the size of the tracks have been enough to make Napiri's fiercest hunters dump their bowels, feign disinterest, poke straw in their teeth, and walk away shaking their heads. "*It's probably long gone,*" or "*I doubt it'll return, warthounds are scavengers,*" or "*If we had a decent rain, I could track it better,*" or "*Just lent out my best spear.*"

"Why haven't you killed it already yourselves?" the monk asks.

Rage flares hotly in Tivali's chest. Where's this monk from? *Because we're not allowed steel. Because we're expected to trust the sovereign. Because we're cowed by the holy city and stripped of defensive means so that we can't keep you monks from taking our babies.* The unexpected anger surprises Tivali. If Intemrus sees all thoughts, she's just failed spectacularly. She grits her teeth. And to think she believed her heart was devout.

"We tried," she says. "Our spears can't puncture it. Shell and rock don't work against a warthound's hide. We're hunters, not warriors."

The monk is watching her. His brow is furrowed as if in deep thought. Troubled thought. Again flashes that hint of melancholy that seems to define him. Or at least whenever he exhibits human emotion rather than a corpse's façade.

"Well," the monk says, standing abruptly, turning his back to her. "I'm off."

Tivali's heart thuds. Mancer Diventae steps into the jungle, plucking the liana leaves away between thumb and forefinger. He has a satchel of food, good sandals, raggedy clothes, and little else. By all appearances, he's a walking warthound snack. Were it anyone else, she'd be sure the beast would pick their bones. She's not convinced it won't happen to the monk, but she will have faith. Or pretend to. Is there a difference?

Maybe if it does eat him, it will buy her village time. Maybe she'll be able to retrieve the sandals. The thought saps any optimism from Tivali. If he fails, then it's on the village once again. Straws will be drawn. Faith will be dead. And when faith dies, so will any chance for Tivali's father.

"Diventae," she says. The monk doesn't respond. "Hey!"

He looks back at her, his face a void.

"Do you need help?" The question erupts before she realizes she was considering asking it. She has no choice but to continue. "I planned to accompany the men willingly—before you came along."

Diventae is visibly taken aback by her offer, his eyebrows lifting and lips parting. He looks hopeful, as if she's offering salvation. Then his eyebrows fall. The twinkle leaves his eyes. His lips press into a line. "No," he says. "But thank you."

Tivali watches him. It's as if he's resigned himself to a fate he wishes to spare her. His earlier words return. *For today.* Does he plan to die out there?

"Just know ... I believe in you," she says softly.

"You ... what?"

Tivali clears her throat. "I believe you can do it." A gust of wind pushes her hair into her eyes. She pulls it back behind her ear.

The monk stares at her a moment. He reaches to pat his bag absently and a stern look overtakes him. "Thank you, Tivali," he says. "It's been ... nothing like what I expected."

"You're welcome," she says, unsure what he's referring to but entirely agreeing with him. Feeling the need to say more, she adds, "Intemrus' Will be done." Monks like to say it. Surely they like to hear it.

He flinches. Turns away. "Resonations," he says, and treks into the jungle.

Tivali watches him go. She doesn't know what sort of magic monks can conjure. Hopefully enough.

22

The Byproduct of a Life Lost

AUSGAN
The Jungle

Kale manages twenty paces into the jungle before the surge of emotions squeezes him like a fist. It's all he can do to keep from collapsing.

"*What have I done?*" he hisses. He minimizes his imprint, telling himself it's from the threat of jungle predators. Surely not because Tivali is still standing there scanning the trees with prying eyes and he lied to her. He can see her but it appears she can't see him.

Of course she can't. Even Magus Kalderys can't see him when he puts his mind to it. She's just a native girl with wiry black hair and barely functional clothes and lively green eyes.

Kale rips his gaze from her and forces his feet onward. *Walk. Don't stop. That's what matters now. Walk and don't look back.* He wiggles his toes in their leafy wrappings. There's not a lot of give in there but that's good. He can feel the shifting of skin where lacerations run the deepest, but all the sharpest pains have relented to a dull ache. He pulls the satchel tight to his chest, involuntarily throws a final glance at Tivali. She's still eyeing the jungle. Her hair is in her face. She pulls it back with her fingers and tucks it behind an ear. Kale runs.

He runs and runs. He slaps leaves out of his way, hurdles over tall buttress roots, ducks under liana vines, dives through malva tangles. Erudition is northward and to the east. He'd know that even without Culver's map. So he keeps the afternoon sun on his left, evidence of it in the diffused light dimly illuminating the underbrush and tree trunks.

Kale runs until the sad state of his feet begins to make itself known once more through the slipping and tearing of the protective leaves. If the resin that girl used on his feet was miraculous, then the sandals are a gift from the Imala. They're like an additional thicker layer of skin and are quite impervious to the roots and vines and thorns on the jungle floor. And he may as well have stolen them.

Why did I lie? He's wondered it ever since he said those fateful words. He told her he was Diventae, who isn't a mancer at all but another negator on Basalt Tier who gets sick after one training session and spends a week bedridden, shitting freely and drinking his meals. Then he lied to her entire village. *"I am here on Sovereign Intemrus' business,"* he said. What was he thinking? Was he only trying to save his own life? Why? He'd planned on ending it. Isn't he still? That's the question that needs answering. Is he finished with life or not?

He knows the answer without having to even contemplate. The prisoner in the cells planted something in him, a seed of curiosity. His experience at Hargrim watered that seed. When he tempted the jungle by spending the night alone, it spared him. Even if that was entirely due to his unerring vigilance and imprint reduction, it awoke a strong desire in him. And so when Tivali unintentionally gave him the ultimatum to lie or die, he had no choice. He isn't done being alive. He wants to live, if only long enough to learn why Kalderys kills children. Why does Obsydia order it? Why would Intemrus want it?

Kale bursts through a basin-shaped leaf, causing cold water to erupt on his face, filling his mouth and shocking him back into the moment. Irritation is fast overtaking his relief and he isn't sure why. Wiping the water away reminds him of Harla's soppy cheeks and bloodshot eyes. Why'd she cling to his presence so? He can't bring back what she lost. Slaying the beast won't *undevour* the child. What a miserable life she has—all of them, living in the dirt in a straw hut, playthings of the weather, plagued by nasties in the forest. They should focus their efforts on a bigger fence. Or take their useless weapons and stab the warthound in its throat. Got no hide there, does it? It's almost like they prefer being harassed by the beast.

Judging by the jungle's unending cacophony, it would appear the birds and bugs are all aiming their creaking and squealing directly at him in some auditory assault. Like the whole world is judging him for lying to Tivali and her village.

"Shut up!" he yells, surprising himself. These emotions, they're too much. His shivering has him too high-strung. Desperation has infiltrated his bones. Relief has made a sweaty, manic mess of him. Guilt ... it's more insidious. Guilt sours his blood and breath and vision. He's guilty of falsely inflating that village's hopes. He's guilty for not reaching that boy in time and trying to shield him from Kalderys' execution. He's guilty for leaving Culver alone. He's guilty for what he did to Adept Thran.

The shoulder of his dele catches on a thorn and it rips all the way to his waist. Loose scale sequins flicker downward in the angled sunlight. He grits his teeth. Guilt, a feeling he'd almost managed to forget. He hurts people. Almost nonstop, he hurts people. Everyone he meets, he lets them down. Proctor Alika, Culver—maybe they'll escape the consequences of knowing him. Thran though ... he didn't deserve what happened to him. Harla didn't either, let alone her child. And now Napiri will relent in vigilance, believing he slew their problem, when the warthound might strike again.

His view of the jungle has taken on a watery sheen. His lungs ache. His feet are slick with more than perspiration. He slows down, rubbing his eyes, trying to catch his breath. Truth is, he's probably undone whatever healing Tivali did for him. As usual, he ruins everything.

The trail is veering to the left, no longer northward. He'll have to vacate it. Ahead and to the right there's a clearing past a waist-high malva bramble. It seems to open up toward the north. Kale picks up his pace to hurdle the foliage. He leaps, clearing it easily enough, but discerns a moment too late that what he mistook for a clearing is a steep drop-off. He stretches his arms for a limb or vine but nothing's in reach. For a moment he's suspended, then sharply-angled jungle floor rushes up to meet him. It makes a jumble of his feet and he tumbles forward, end over end. The jungle is a jolting green blur punctuated by the slap of massive leaves, the bursts of light as his head impacts roots. He careens off tree trunks and heavy vines, grunting, dizzy, trying to protect his skull from cracking like an egg. He's managed to wrap his arms around his head when the obstructions disappear, leaving him falling through open air. He sucks in a gasp. His stomach joins his lungs in his ribcage. His pounding heart forgets all cadence. He crashes to his back.

The canopy is twirling above. Kale's lungs are stuttering, denying him a full breath. New bumps and nicks and bangs are introducing themselves one by one. Kale can only lie there hoping to eventually catch his breath. For a moment his senses are scrambled and he's almost convinced he's back at the spot where he ended up last night, wherever his raging energy deposited him. There are no discerning features to suggest otherwise except the time of day. The pack the girl gave him, assuming she actually did, is gone. He's shaking so hard his teeth rattle. Everything that hurt then hurts more now. The village could have easily been a fever dream.

Kale is torn between formulating a mighty swear that is proportional to this situation and just closing his eyes for good. His self-negation is still powerful, but it's also optional. He could choose to be seen. Then the jungle would do the hard part for him. It's not like he has a chance at stopping Kalderys or even a warthound. How could he?

His eyes slip closed.

Kale is awakened abruptly by a loud snore. It takes him a moment to remember where he is. Another moment of wondering exactly how tired he must be to snore loud enough to wake himself up when the sound recurs. It wasn't him. Something large is slumbering nearby. Bigger than a human. Kale's trembling gains new life, quivering him where he lies. He sits, trying not to grunt. Feels like he's cartwheeled down Erudition's main stairway.

He's in a small clearing, not seven strides across. A rotten odor assaults his nostrils, making his face scrunch inward. There are bones strewn around in piles, remnants of skeletons with little more than sun-bleached fur and skin stretched over them. The snore saws out again and Kale instinctively minimizes his imprint down to near nothing.

It's a sharp ledge he fell off, black basalt that overhangs shadows. Kale shields his eyes, peers into the darkness. Inside the cavernous hollow, a leathery grey mound rises and falls like the tide, in time with the rhythmic, sawing breath. It's obscured in shadow, but Kale can tell it's on its side and that each inhale brings its flank as high as his waist would be if he were standing. It's got to be the warthound. *Of all the luck.* Not for one moment had Kale entertained the idea of actually meeting this beast, let alone dispatching it. Now here he sits on its dinner table.

Run. Live another day, his cowardly guts hiss at him, and Kale agrees.

He rises onto unsteady feet, never taking his eyes off the warthound. He's not tested his self-negation on beasts before, or much of anything besides exemplars for that matter. He may learn quickly how limited his powers are, assuming this monstrosity isn't adequately gorged on native children. Kale's quaking makes his feet skitter on the packed earth as he backs away. Around this clearing are several trodden paths leading out. He picks the closest and inches toward it. He's nearly made it when something dry cracks beneath his sandal. The warthound scrambles to its feet in a storm of dust. Kale's blood runs cold and needle chills race over him, invigorating his tremors.

Minimize, minimize, minimize!

The warthound's tall ears are aimed at Kale ... but it doesn't appear to have spotted him. Its sharp peak of a back, lined with black bristles, is level with Kale's eyes. It scans the den, snorting at the air. Its neck is so thick it has to shift its rear legs to look left and right. Dull protrusions sprout from its cheeks, stubbled and patchy. Discolored saliva oozes from between stained tusks.

Kale stands frozen. *You're a tree. You're a rock. You're the shadow under a rock.*

The beast makes its way into the sunlight, moving in a groggy trot, snuffling as it goes, blasting away dirt, leaves, small bones with each exhale. It approaches Kale but still doesn't appear to see him. Its massive snout bumps into his exposed shin and it hesitates, as if something's amiss. Cold sweat breaks out over Kale's forehead and face. He considers running. Except this shambling stench has twice as many legs as him. It would outrun him, trample him, add his indigestibles to its collection. The beast prods his leg with a tusk the size of a ripe plantain. Kale almost capsizes. It snorts, giving him a shove that could uproot a sapling. Kale reaches and grabs a vine in time to keep from toppling over.

Minimize! You're a leaf. You're a vine.

Kale's legs swing and carom off the warthound's cold gooey snout, leaving a brown smear on his skin. He nearly prays to Intemrus again. It worked last time ... or something. The beast moves on, making a circuit of the clearing. It has the appearance of an oversized lanky grey hog. Its jaws split its porcine face from snout all the way to its tree-trunk neck. Its teeth are exposed, the upper and lower incisors extending several inches beyond its lips, the front teeth flattened like shovels. Its beady black eyes peer from thickly eyelashed pockmarks on either side of its boulderesque head. It appears to have completed its reconnaissance, and Kale loosens his grip on the vine. Then it trots back to him, hikes a leg, and empties its bladder. Kale is deluged in acrid urine the color of honey, the odor of plague and burning teeth. He gags, nearly vomiting. Luckily, his response isn't nearly as loud as the spattering amber liquid. Kale must not have smelled enough like home. He has no choice but hang there and let the beast soak him. His wounds—he cringes. Each individual scratch, puncture, and laceration screams out as the urine infiltrates his bandaging. The leaves Tivali wrapped him in do not suffice. He'll probably lose both feet to infection, if not both legs.

The beast finally runs out of piss, or at least contents itself with the updated state of the stench. It sidles over to its cave and grinds its grey hide on the volcanic rock. *Scritch, scritch, scritch.* Black flecks break off the stone wall and sprinkle the clearing. Kale stands dripping in urine.

The warthound gives a satisfied wriggle, trods a couple of tight circles, then plops down on its flank. It brings up a rear hoof and scratches its ear aggressively. Kale watches, waiting, unintentionally transferring his trembling into the vine he holds, and all the leaves attached to it. If that same scratching were applied to his own ear, it would likely spatter the contents of his skull across the rocks.

At last, the beast stretches out on its side and lies still again. Kale exhales slowly, taking shallow breaths so as not to vomit at the monstrous smell. The sawing snores resume.

"How will you kill it?" Tivali had asked him. And it was a fine question. There's no way. Napiri's best bet is to pack up and move far off.

Kale turns again to his escape path, forcing down irritation. But his feet refuse his command. His teeth grind together. He's trying to do it again. Choosing to live, choosing cowardice to save his meaningless existence. There are only so many times you can do that before it becomes you. He has the chance to live up to the promise he made those natives. A chance to right at least one wrong. Kale's fists clench. What if he had found that lake of magma under Stravhelm? Would he have had the guts to throw himself into it? Probably not. He'd have made an excuse. He always does. He had the chance again on Obsydia's tower right after she reminded him of his worthlessness. The chance to take his first and last flight. And what did he do? *This.* Scurried away.

Kale turns toward the warthound, teeth clenched. Beside its slumbering form is a pale skull, gazing up at him with empty eye sockets. It's no larger than a coconut and is mashed into the ground up to its hollow nasal cavity. There's a crack in the left temple and a puncture mark. It's as if large teeth clamped down on it, perhaps to carry it away from the northern field where Tana's children used to play in the sedge.

The skull stares at Kale and he stares back. Next to it is a tiny, shattered ribcage, the broken bones pointing up like narrow, stiff fingers. Kale's chest has tightened. He'd never considered bones to be the byproduct of a life lost, and feels quite idiotic only making the connection here and now.

The smock Harla gave him has made its way into his hands. He glares at it. How small were the arms that filled those sleeves? How thin was the neck? There's a knot in Kale's throat he can't manage to swallow down.

"But it was hers ..."

That's what Harla had said. Then it became Kale's, not that he asked for it. Then again, maybe he did.

"Elli." Kale doesn't mean to whisper the name out loud.

In Erudition, she would have been an intrant, residing in the nursery in Stravhelm, each day introduced to new concepts of consonance. She'd learn to sing or, like Kale, learn that she cannot. Out here in the wild, Kale has no idea what the children are taught. What their interests are. What makes their eyes light up. Mud, he supposes. Bugs. That little boy from Hargrim smiles at Kale from his memory.

The tiny outfit shakes in his hands. He lifts it to his nose. The garment's sour smell transcends time, pulling Kale all the way back to his own time in the nursery. It's almost too vague to be memory, composed of a hazy fraction of each of his senses. There's a brightly colored window. Soft arms. Soft singing. Warmth.

The hollow eyes of the skull watch Kale, forcing questions on him. How long was that little girl conscious while the warthound dragged her? Did she cry? Was she alive the entire trip? Did she try to fight it? That question tightens Kale's jaw. Because she surely did, even if that means nothing more than resisting. And here he stands, grown, doing nothing and planning to do even less. He blinks until he can see through the stinging tears. There the warthound lies, dreaming of chewing children while Kale stands soaked in piss, devising his next heroic disappearance.

At Kale's feet lies the object that cracked beneath his sandal. It's two halves of a large bone, and where it broke it terminates in sharp points. He looks back to the warthound. It stretches out farther and swats its side with the tuft on its tail. Its belly isn't so grey. More a pale pink, and the hair there is thinner—completely unguarded, the haughty animal. Tivali told him their tools aren't enough to kill it. Maybe she's wrong. He picks up the two pieces of bone, one in each hand. They're not unlike the batons he trains with. *Trained* with. That's over now. He tests the end with his thumb. Sharp. Maybe he can't kill the warthound. But he will punish it for what it did to the young Elli. And Imala willing, maybe it will eventually succumb to whatever wounds he manages to deal it.

He approaches the warthound trying to differentiate his body's chronic trembling from nerves. It isn't fear he's feeling. It's more like whatever made him run for that boy in Hargrim. It's more like ... purpose. In this moment he feels no guilt, as if it can't reach him. That's all the justification he needs. He moves under the overhang's shadow, kneeling over the sleeping warthound. Its belly looks the softest right above its groin. Kale raises the two chisel-like bone batons over his head.

Intemrus' Will be done. The thought makes him smile.

He strikes with both fists. The bone shards puncture the warthound's pale stomach below its ribs with a wet thump. Dark pools seep up around the bones. The beast awakens with a squealing snort, kicking up dust and bones, shattering all tranquility. A rear hoof plows Kale's chest, flipping him backward out from under the overhang. But his grip remains and the bone shards dislodge from the beast's guts with a *slurp*, like walking sticks yanked out of mud. Dark crimson streams erupt from the writhing warthound. It scrambles onto its feet bucking, venting through its snout, churning dusty earth into black muck. Blood pours out of it. Kale tries to retreat. His breath won't come, his arms won't haul him. It feels like that kick broke some ribs.

The warthound's stamping and thrashing shake the ground beneath Kale. Its wild shrieking rattles his teeth. It spots him, hooves wide, beady eyes locked on him, blood misting from cavernous nostrils. Spiky black hackles stand up like a korundite sawblade, from its grey head up over its mountain of a back. Kale minimizes his imprint. If he's lucky, he can get another stab in on it. But the beast is too close for his trick to work. It's too angry. When he failed to kill it, he gave it no choice but to return the effort. It's his fault, but regret is not forthcoming. This, at last, is where he's meant to be. This is where he's meant to die. With as much blood as it's losing, this beast will surely die today. It will not eat another child. Kale smiles, still trembling, here at the end.

"Eat me," he tells it.

The warthound charges, splitting open its tusked mouth wide enough to bite him in half. He has enough time to lift one arm into the path of its teeth. He doesn't close his eyes. The jaws slam shut.

For some reason, there's no pain. Kale feels nothing, not even his trembles. All sound has ceased, leaving a deafening silence. His arm is in one piece. The warthound hangs mid-lunge, hooves hovering, its sand and snot-caked snout frozen in front of Kale's eyes, jaws clamped on his forearm. It seems time has stopped completely, which would be more of a shock if Kale had anticipated anything besides a gory end in the next moment.

Is this what precedes death?

There's an expanding pressure in Kale's forearm where the warthound latched. It's like the pressure in his ears when he swims too deep, like something might rupture. Those shivers that have plagued him all this time are draining from his extremities, rushing toward the bite, concentrating on that point. Even while everything else is locked in place, movement is happening within him. Something infinitely black oozes from Kale's arm, bubbling, expanding, like boiling tar the color of a cloudless night sky. Kale can do nothing but watch.

Time is frozen—as is Kale, the warthound, the dirt launched by its hooves, the hovering drops of its blood, the air itself. But the bubbling blackness accelerates from his arm as if in this static state alone can it exist. And thrive. Energy rushes from him. This is Kalderys' consonance, he realizes, the reason for his trembling, now distorted inside him into some perversion of energy—dense, dreadful, no more logical than lightning inverted—and it's taking its violent leave.

The star-speckled void blooms outward from where the teeth penetrated Kale's skin. It stretches over the warthound's snout, consumes its head. The black mass absorbs its forelegs, shoulders, its chest, waist, legs, and tail. And as abruptly as it all started, the substance follows the tail's tuft into itself and vanishes, leaving nothing.

Time is released from its restraint. The jungle's noise falls back into place like the crashing tide. Kale rocks back and forth with abruptly regained control. Pebbles patter to the ground, some flying past Kale with momentum given by the now nonexistent warthound. Aside from the macabre crimson composition it left on the sand, the beast is gone—as if it was never there.

Kale sits blinking for several moments while unearthly exhaustion creeps into his bones. Feels like he's slipping underwater. He's alive? He inspects his arm, wondering if it's numb because there's no damage or because his senses have gone bizarre. His head is light, his awareness fast waning. He lowers himself carefully, noticing that his trembling has relented, at last. He's alive. He's stopped shaking. The energy he took from Kalderys mutated. And it became ... what did it become?

He's flat on his back. Vision and sound fade away. He's seen that black matter before, long ago, in a similar state. Only when he closes his eyes does he remember it, like a nightmare he'd subconsciously purged, summoned back from the brink. He must have forcefully forgotten it, or tried. The memory resurfaces in frightening clarity, overpowering the present as Kale's consciousness fades.

A clear, blue sky over a flat, twinkling sea provided the backdrop for Kale's last consonant combat training session. The mancers in training were pushing him to his limit and their proctor saw no need to interfere. Sick negators must be relieved. Kale was not sick. And so four exemplars, led by a reedy Andesite Haik, had isolated Kale from the rest. The intent of their song was to concentrate heat and fuse the sand beneath his sandals. Kale negated to keep from burning. He negated until he shook, and he shook until his teeth rattled. The young channelers marveled and laughed—at their power, at Kale's oddity.

Training concluded and the exemplars began their trek back to Erudition. At some point Kale, shaking so hard the ground was a blur, lost his footing and fell down. The adepts laughed, including Adept Thran, who was a promising exemplar with plans of becoming a sentinel. He offered Kale the end of a walking stick to help him rise. He was no friend of Kale's. None of them were. But he wasn't the cruelest. That's always been Haik. And so Kale trusted to reach for the proffered stick. Thran attempted one last prank, maneuvering to crack Kale's knuckles for a laugh. As the staff impacted his hand, time had stopped. Out came the void. Thran was consumed. Kale lost consciousness.

Kale exuded the same devouring mass today after negating lightning as he did then with heat. He's never understood it. Still doesn't. But today one of his simmering suspicions is put to rest. Thran didn't end up someplace else, some other time or plane, to one day pop back up somehow and continue his training and fix Kale's reputation. He's gone. Forever. And so is the warthound.

Kale negated them both.

23
What the Holy City is Missing

AUSGAN
The Warthound's Den

It's past midnight when the monk's snoring tapers off. He shifts where he lies in the nook that was the warthound's. Tivali sits up straighter. The monk's eyes open and slowly focus on the black rock above him, which glows faintly in the light of scattered embers. He becomes aware of Tivali.

"Where am I?" he says, his voice gravelly. His hands aren't shaking anymore.

"You're safe," Tivali says, "for now."

His eyes fall on her and linger there a moment. He attempts to swallow but struggles, eyebrows furrowing. Tivali places the waterskin at his lips and tips in enough to wet his throat.

"I was wrong," he says.

Tivali almost laughs. She'd hoped for honesty. Didn't expect it so quickly. "About?"

"I didn't use consonance."

"Should I know what that means?"

He chuckles, then flinches. "Ow."

"Take it easy. You have some banged-up ribs. Lucky for you, they didn't shift or grind when I pressed them."

"You pressed them?" He lifts his head and looks down at his chest. There's a bruise below his left breast that's nearly black in the dim light, bluish around the edges. "You took my clothes?"

"Yes." She'd considered taking his under bits too, but without any protection down there the bugs would have at him. "The top half of your robe was torn to pieces. Bottom half was soaked in warthound piss. You took that shower well, by the way."

Kale stares at her as if he doesn't understand.

She continues, "I cut it into strips and lined the perimeter. So far nothing's come to eat us."

"Eat us?"

She cocks her head. "You weren't just playing dumb. You are dumb."

"Guilty," he says. "Did you follow me?"

"Yeah. It's a nice disappearing trick you've got. But the blood you left on the way here can't hide. And blood's the easiest thing to track. Everything's after it."

"Why?"

"Why is everything after blood?"

"Why'd you track me?"

"To see if you'd die. If so, I hoped the holy city would send some real help."

Kale smiles. She didn't intend that.

"More to the point, I didn't trust you," she says. "Lucky for you. You can't doze off out here and expect to wake up. I saved you. Again. You owe me some truth."

He attempts to cover his eyes with his forearm, becomes aware of the dressing Tivali applied. He stares at it, turning his arm this way and that. "More leaf wrappings. You're a traveling medic, aren't you?"

"You're welcome. My turn for questions."

He rests his arm on the ground beside him.

"Who are you?" she asks.

"I'm um, Mancer Diventae."

"The truth."

"I already told you—"

She presses her finger against his bruised chest. He gasps, squirms, eyes squeezing and teeth clenching.

"Hmm. Not gonna send me off like you did the warthound?"

"Kale," he gasps. "I'm Kale."

"That's better. What did you mean by *resonations*? You said it to me, but I don't think you meant to."

He takes a slow breath before responding. "It's something we say. Or ... something they say. It means *May the Imala appreciate your worth*. It's about balance and awareness."

His answer means so little she regrets asking. And now she's at a loss. While she watched him sleep she'd thought of a hundred questions to ask—a thousand—getting madder by the moment. He's awoken, and now those questions are nowhere to be found. "You tried to run, didn't you?"

He places his forearm over his eyes carefully. "I did."

"You lied to me," she says.

"I did."

Tivali considers poking his bruise again, or punching his face. "You're nothing like other monks."

He smiles, his eyes shielded by his forearm. "Thank you."

Tivali's face flushes. "You arrogant, soft-footed, songster. Give me one good reason not to leave you to be sucked dry by fanged apes."

He's shaking his head. "There is no reason you shouldn't do that. Not even sure why you saved me."

"Because it's decent. I have no idea why you didn't run away like you wanted to. Imala knows you don't care about us."

He doesn't respond. His smile is gone, leaving a look on his face like he's tasted something bitter. For a while the only sound is the night's song. The jungle's glowing bugs aren't so bright around the warthound's den. Perhaps it's the piss. Hopefully the lack of bugs will keep away bats and night toads. That, in turn, might keep away the cats. Tivali will have to rely on wakefulness to defend from wig spiders. That, and the smoke from the embers. Her chitin dagger is in her belt. Her bamboo is near enough to grab.

"That's not true," the monk says, and his words seem to catch him off guard. "I just ... don't know how to help."

"The warthound might argue that."

"That ... wasn't how I expected it to go. I didn't do that on purpose."

"You stabbed it on purpose," she says. "You were very deliberate about that."

"Yes. But ..." He trails off.

"You took on our pain. That's why you did it."

He says nothing.

"Was your ... magic ordained?"

"What?"

"You provoked it, then you killed it with magic. Was that ordained by the sovereign?"

The monk sits up so quickly it startles Tivali. "Intemrus had *nothing* to do with this," he says, then winces and holds his ribs.

She's aimed her dagger at his throat. She withdraws, sheathes it. "Seems to me like," she says carefully, "we prayed for the sovereign to send a monk to kill the warthound. You came. The beast is dead."

"The beast is dead," Kale says. "But you have no idea what that cost."

"Do tell."

He frowns. Takes him a moment to continue. "The holy city didn't intend this. Trust me."

Tivali scoffs. "Trust you?"

Kale sighs. "Or don't."

"Was it magic you used?" What else could it be? The beast snapped out of existence, swallowed by a hungry shadow.

"I suppose it was."

Tivali proceeds carefully. "I doubt you meant to scramble around lost in a ditch, and yet that's where I found you. Is it not possible you are acting according to Intemrus' Will, even if it's without your knowledge?"

Kale sits in silence, staring at the embers. His eyes are pained, as if he's been tortured. Tivali remembers the look he had when she first saw him. "I hope not," he says.

"Why?"

He looks at her pleadingly. He wants her to stop asking questions. But he also has something to get off his chest.

"We're beyond secrets, Kale."

"Some secrets can get you killed," he says.

Tivali's heart patters against her ribs. That's exactly what her father told her. Shortly after that he was arrested. "What do you mean by that?"

Kale shakes his head. "Nothing. A man told me that. I thought he was trying to entice me. Now I'm not so sure."

She grabs Kale's arm. "Do you know my father? His name is Rathyn. I think he's being kept as a prisoner in the holy city. Please tell me if he's alive."

Kale looks bewildered, either by her touch or her outburst.

She withdraws her hand. "I'm sorry," she says.

The monk turns his gaze to the low fire.

Tivali takes a breath.

"What did he do?" Kale asks quietly, without looking at her. "Your father, that is."

Tivali sucks her lip, uncertain. If this were any other monk, she wouldn't have asked about her father. Answering his question will probably incriminate her. But something tells her to trust him, which is all the odder because he's a proven liar.

"He said he knew Intemrus' weakness. He knew how to make him mortal." That's a thing her father told her that she's never repeated. She wishes he'd not said it, never known it. Until now she's pretended the conversation didn't happen. Saying these words feels like undressing in front of the monk. She has no idea how he'll take it. Maybe he's been fishing for this confession since he arrived. But by saying it aloud, a load is lifted from her shoulders.

"Why would someone want to make Intemrus' mortal?" Kale asks. His voice is soft, as if the idea scares him.

"We're angry," she blurts. There are things you don't say to monks. And yet ... "You take our children away from us. You hold back the rain and our crops die and we watch each other starve. You separate us into puny communities that can't even fend off the jungle's threats. You tell us an army of heathens is on the way but you outlaw weapons that would help us fight them. You do nothing to prepare us. And ..." She's said enough. *Too much.* She doesn't even know this lying monk.

"And what?" Kale's wearing a vacant-eyed expression. As if he's sunk to the bottom of his emotions and there are none left.

"They say there's a monk who uses lightning to destroy villages."

Kale doesn't react. His eyes are focused on something far distant. If Tivali just damned herself and her village, so be it. It had to be said. She hopes Kale denies the claim. Or at least acts surprised.

"It's true," Kale says. "You're referring to Magus Kalderys. He's part of the Triumvirate."

"Why would he do that?"

Kale shrugs. "I don't know," he whispers.

"Then ... why are you telling me?"

He shrugs again. His eyes are gleaming.

"What happened to you, Kale?" Tivali asks.

"My eyes were opened."

A smile curls Tivali's lips. "My father says, '*You can open your eyes or have them opened up for you.*' Sounds like you went with the latter."

"I was doing alright with my eyes shut," Kale says.

"We all were," Tivali says. "But innocence in Ausgan is like fresh water. It doesn't last."

Kale appears frozen. The moisture that gathered in his eyes is gone. "Maybe Intemrus *should* lose his immortality."

A conflict rises up in Tivali. She's tried for so long to bolster the faith of her village so her father could come home. She's dreamed of a chance to prove her people's steadfastness to a monk, any monk. But here she is with a monk and it's going nothing like she'd hoped. The opposite in fact. "Are you testing my faith?"

Kale laughs and immediately flinches. "No. If your faith is based on me, you're in bad shape. I'm the worst exemplar ever."

"I don't know about that. You made short work of the warthound."

"Hopefully your village will be glad."

"Harla will. The rest will complain they don't get to eat it."

Kale smiles. "You'll have to apologize on my behalf. I doubt I'll return there."

"Of course," Tivali says. She figured he'd be leaving. Why wouldn't he? His job is done. "We should get some rest. In the morning, I'll show you how to get back to the holy city."

"Right," he says.

"What will you do when you get back?" Not that it's her business.

He shrugs again. "Hadn't thought that far ahead."

Tivali watches him. He truly seems lost, and not just in the jungle but in his own mind. "Will they reward you for what you did here?"

Kale smiles, then chuckles. Then he's laughing uncontrollably, wincing and holding his ribs. "They might kill me," he says. "I snuck out."

"You snuck out?" Tivali says. "I thought Intemrus sees all."

"If that were true," Kale says, "why would everyone need to say it so often? Surely that's the kind of trait that could prove itself."

Tivali sits shaking her head, feeling as ignorant of monks' ways as Kale is hers. "You really aren't like other monks, are you?"

"Never met another like me." He smiles at her.

She'd not considered her words a compliment. "Well, if you can't get back in, I'm sure a village would be glad to have you. Just tell them you killed a warthound."

Kale is looking at her lips.

Her cheeks flush. She holds up the satchel she gave Kale before he left the village. He'd dropped it in his tumble into the warthound's den. Luckily it and the wraps inside are undamaged.

"You hungry?"

Before he can answer there's a scuffling sound from the darkness, something caught in a bush. Tivali curses her negligence, letting something get so close. It's too clumsy-sounding to be a predator. Too close to the ground to be a fanged ape. And it's too late at night for it to be a peccary or roaming boar unless it's got the foam fever, in which case they're in for a wild fight. Tivali is on her feet, bamboo staff in hand.

"Stay down," she hisses at Kale, and slinks quietly into foliage, out of the ember's light.

A tall man tumbles into the den. He's bound in lean muscle and wearing the ripped remains of a chitin-plated dele that barely covers his torso and legs. His hands are empty and his exposed skin is mottled with blood and dirt. His eyes are round and red around the edges as they fall on Kale.

"Basalt Kale," he proclaims, his voice rising in a sharp lilt. "Why am I not surprised? Thought you could—*ergh!*" He interrupts himself to tear at a wound on his shoulder with his fingernails. "You thought you could outrun justice?"

Tivali backs through the shadows and creeps around the perimeter of the warthound's lair to get behind this crazed man. He doesn't seem to have noticed her.

"Prime Sentinel Arc," Kale says, not attempting to rise. "You're in poor shape. I know a place you could get your wounds seen to."

Arc belts out an overly loud laugh. "You mean Napiri? They served their purpose when they pointed me in your direction. You can't keep me from doing what I came to do, Basalt. I would have killed you for interrupting the cleansing alone, however you managed that. You made me get my hands dirty. You made me chase you. You made me come here. I mean, look at me. *Look at me!*" He's shrieking and trembling, fingers roving over his chest and back, scratching, scratching. The wounds on his skin are puffy and red-rimmed. "Who's with you, Basalt?"

"No one. I was talking to myself," Kale says, holding up both hands.

"Liar. You think I'm blind? I observed two people by pulse. Must be that native bitch they told me about in Napiri." He looks around, but fails to see Tivali, even when his eyes land directly on her. He's deep into fanged ape fever. Makes your eyes play tricks on you. He probably wouldn't notice her if it were daylight. The fever will take his life by morning, but until then he'll get progressively more frenzied.

To his credit, Kale doesn't react or look in her direction. With hands still raised, he says, "How about we go back to Erudition together? You'll get credit for finding me. The magus will reward you."

"*Finding* you? I'm not here to *fetch*." He spits the word. "And I'm not concerned with his rewards. He was negated by *you*. Wait until that gets out. His days are numbered. Selu will, *urgh* ..." He slaps at his back several times, each smack resounding loudly and sending blood spattering out behind him. Tivali takes the chance to inch closer. "No, negator. I don't have that long. The Imala-damned blood monkeys had their way with me before I could kill them. Now something's chewing me from the inside. But I can finish you before this finishes me."

He takes a stride forward, eyes twitching and arms outstretched. Tivali moves quicker, stepping into position, drawing back her bamboo as she leaves the darkness. She plants both feet and swings. The staff catches Arc across the bridge of his nose with a *crack!* It hits him higher than she intended. He reels backward, flailing his arms. Tivali's bamboo is split. She snaps it in half, steps in quickly, and aims a jab at his throat with the splintered wood. Too quickly, he recovers. He dodges and the jagged staff only nicks him, tearing skin, freeing blood from his neck. But the fever seems to have made him impervious to pain. She doesn't see his counterattack until it's too late to react.

His fist smashes the side of her head. Feels like she was struck by a falling rock. She rolls with it, tumbling rather than floundering, tries to spring to her feet but the blow stunned her. The glowing insects skirting the clearing have doubled. Her feet can't find flat ground.

Something impacts her head again and the world leaps at her, wallops her. She's lying on her stomach, breathless on the flattened earth. A weight is on top of her, heavy as a fallen tree. Hands close around her neck. She pulls at them, tries getting between the fingers, but they're too strong. She reaches for her dagger. It's not in her belt. Must have fallen out. The hands are squeezing too hard for her to swallow. *Shit*, too hard for her to breathe. Not many options left. He's pushing her face into the ground, squeezing so hard the bones in her neck click and grind. Something in there is about to break, before or after she runs out of air.

"You first," Arc's voice hisses in her ear. "Then him."

Tivali's mouth is wide open. She gasps for breath, her tongue in the dirt. The grip is too tight. Her vision is fading. She goes for his fingers again. Her heart pounds in her ears. She manages to get one of his thick fingers pried loose and cranks it, snapping it loudly.

"Agh! You jungle cunt! You think—*hurgggle* ..."

Hot liquid deluges the back of Tivali's head and neck and shoulders. The grip fades from her throat. Tivali wrenches her hips. Arc falls away and she scrambles out from under him, rolling to her back, panting, coughing, wheezing.

Kale is standing over Arc with her dagger in his hand. Wide-eyed, Arc squeezes his own neck now but blood pulses out freely. He's shimmying away from them on his back and elbows. His mouth pops open and shut like a beached tuna. Blood bubbles from between his fingers in croaks and gurgles. He backs against a tree. Can't retreat farther. Tivali gains her footing shakily and stalks toward him.

"I'll show you a jungle cunt." She meant to yell it but her damaged throat makes it come out raspy, which only enrages her. She kicks him in the crotch. Blood spurts from his throat onto her leg. She kicks him again. He lowers one hand from his neck, a weak attempt to keep her toe from his groin. Doesn't work. She kicks again, feeling the lumpy contents of his monk clothes shifting. She'll crush them. "Guess you should've squeezed harder, yeah?"

His face is turning grey. His grip on his neck seems to be weakening. She kicks him again, again. She kicks until she loses count and blood has stained his crotch and her toes wrench painfully. She kicks until he stops resisting and she twists her ankle and falls backward onto the packed earth.

Arc is dead. His eyes have a dull sheen and there's no longer a rhythm to the blood flowing from his neck. Tivali gasps, regaining her feet, rubbing her throat and trying to still her breathing. Her emotions are turbulent, tugging her back and forth between laughing and sobbing. Her shirt and shoulders and legs are painted in blood. She leans over shakily and scrubs her hands on the dead monk's sash, straightens herself, tries to wipe the blood out of her eyes and nose and lips.

Kale is frozen in place, watching Arc's dead body.

"Imala abound, Kale," Tivali says and coughs. "You damn near cut his head off."

Kale looks at the dagger. His expression is blank. "This is sharper than it looks."

Tivali snorts. The jungle has almost stopped reeling around her. She squeezes her eyes shut a few times. Not exactly her first scrape with danger, but certainly a nastier one. "Thank you for that," she says.

Kale doesn't seem to hear her.

"This your first time killing a man?" she asks.

Kale lets out a breath and opens his hand. The dagger lingers a moment, its bloody handle stuck to his skin, then drops. "One who deserved it."

"Sounded like you knew each other. Who is he?"

"A murderer," Kale says. "He was with Kalderys. The world is better off without him. But I wish it wasn't me who had to ... do that."

"You mean murder him?"

He winces.

"Will there be more?"

Kale gazes around the clearing. "Probably not tonight. It would be Selu, or Kalderys. They'd be here by now. They're faster than him."

"What about Intemrus?" she asks, her voice nearly failing at the mention of his name.

Kale looks surprised. "What about him?"

"Doesn't he ... see all?"

Kale snorts, as if the idea is ridiculous. As if the single most defining creed uttered by his kind is a joke and it has been this whole time. "How could he?" Kale whispers.

There's more happening behind his vacant stare than Tivali can deduce. "Maybe *this* is his will," she offers.

Kale snorts again, and this time it seems the object of his ridicule is himself. "Maybe it is." His eyes focus on her. "But it's probably best for you and your village if you never mention this. Ever."

"Figured that." Tivali stands up and assesses herself. Her throat is scratchy. There are a couple of knots forming on her skull, beneath her blood-soaked hair. Her ankle throbs. Hopefully it's not sprained. She'll wrap it tight for the night. Might have broken some toes, can't be sure. Aside from all that, she's not felt so alive in a while. "We need to get the body away from us."

She and Kale each grab an ankle and haul Arc's corpse a ways out of the clearing, leaving a black stain at the foot of the tree. They drape the body over a tangle of vines and return to the warthound's den. Ants and flies will get at it first. It's only a matter of time before the corpse draws more unsavory creatures. The body is not far enough away for Tivali's comfort, but she's given up the thought of getting any sleep. She'll have to pass the darkness in other ways. She and Kale settle into their position between the low fire and the black volcanic stone.

"How are your ribs?" Tivali asks.

Kale places his hand on his chest and grimaces. "They hurt. How's your throat?"

She rolls her head back and forth. There's no telltale grind of broken bones. "It'll be bruised. But I'm alright."

"That's good." There's no mirth in Kale's voice.

Tivali touches Kale's leg. He doesn't jump like before, but his eyes plant firmly on her hand.

"Kale," she says. "Way better name than Diventae."

He looks at her. There's a spark of life in his eyes, behind that emotionless void.

"If that monk helped Kalderys kill natives, I'd say you've done some good."

He says nothing.

"Wouldn't you agree?"

His shoulders sag, and he gives an unconvincing nod.

"You shouldn't regret what you did," she tells him. This doesn't break his trance either. It seems talking isn't going to. "We have a way of showing our appreciation. I don't think monks are familiar with it."

Kale's eyes flick in her direction, then away. He swallows.

Tivali reaches behind her neck and unties the knot holding her bloody shirt in place. She watches Kale while the cloth falls away. His mouth eases open. Tivali suppresses a smile. She takes his hand. He's trembling again, but this is more like boyish apprehension. She pushes his hand against her breast, causing the pale flesh to bulge on either side of his clammy palm. He lets out a trembling sigh. A smile is overtaking his face. Tivali loosens the remaining knots holding Kale's underclothes in place. He doesn't stop her.

"Lie down," she says. "Let me show you what the holy city is missing."

24

Onward Despite

FOHRVYLDA

Vim

Irdessa allows Fent to guide her through a town that only vaguely resembles home. Kraus follows her, nervously casting glances as if he's not the scariest looking man on the street. Irdessa has pulled her ratty blanket up over her head once more. She's grown numb to the fishy odor of it. Maybe soon she'll be able to replace it with a proper hooded cloak. One with pockets. But then what? Will there be a day when she can safely show her face in Fohrvylda, or will the cloak become her?

Vim has changed in the two years Irdessa's been gone, and no part of that seems to be for the better. She trudges along in a stupor, marveling over the fact that until this moment she can't recall ever having truly examined the town in which she grew up. The first houses they pass inside the high walls are made of piled stone with sod roofs. The stares Irdessa gets from within these earthen hovels are dark and untrusting. The road, if it can be called that, consists of ruts in mud and smatterings of uneven cobblestone. Was it always like this? Irdessa was sixteen when she was arrested, and although that was only two years ago, she might as well be a different person. Keswal robbed her of what innocence she had left, leaving a grim cynicism in its place. Is that why Vim seems so gloomy?

They arrive at larger buildings, divided by stone-paved streets. Most appear to be storefronts, inns, taverns, and variants of apothecaries. Or they were. Half are sacked, gutted, burned. Some are even smoldering presently and no one seems to care. Brambles and thorns spill over the crumbling walls of what might have been garden beds. Tufts of weeds sprout from cracks between the cobbles, clogging the gutters and holding captive stagnant water where blackened knots of animal bones and offal fester.

"This place smells like a toilet," Kraus notes.

"It wasn't like this before," Irdessa says. "Fent, what happened to the Vanguard? Aren't we … aren't they responsible for the streets and the ..." Her boot squishes into something the consistency of a sponge, the color of brain matter, the smell of a gurgling sewer. "... garbage?"

A smile stretches over his thin lips, embodying more melancholy than mirth. "We were when your father led. There have been some changes since then."

Irdessa nearly responds, *No shit*, but that would be a wildly inaccurate assessment of her surroundings. Seems the maintenance the Vanguard oversaw has fallen to absolutely no one. If there is still a tax collected here, it's winding up somewhere else.

"What kind of changes?" Irdessa asks.

"You'll see when we get to Cornerstone," Old Fent says, warily sidestepping a motionless body. If not for the loosely clutched bottle, Irdessa would swear it's a corpse. She's not entirely convinced it's not.

"What happened to the fields and houses outside town?" she asks.

"Landowners couldn't afford their own protection. With the Vanguard's attention elsewhere, they didn't last."

"What's that mean?" Kraus says.

"Vanguard held back the beasts and the brigands," Fent says. "Now ..." He clears his throat. Irdessa waits. But he says no more.

"Fent," Irdessa says, stopping. "What happened?"

Fent's smile persists, as if there's anything to smile about. "Your father, Irdessa," he says gently. "He did more than collect and deliver the enemies of Fohrvylda. It was charismatic diplomacy that kept the order here. He maintained the fragile balance between Promontory's control and utter ruin. Frankly, I don't know all the details to their relationship. Alderman Dhovoi pretends to know, but I'd be surprised. And for all his complaints about *the old ways*," Fent shrugs, "he lacks your father's diplomatic traits."

"Alderman Dhovoi," Irdessa says, without attempting to mask her sarcasm. "You keep saying that."

The smile Fent wears makes a subtle change. As if he's offering himself to a wrathful mob in lieu of their intended target. "Dhovoi is still figuring out where he fits in."

"I ain't from around here," Kraus snorts. "But I'm not sure how he could fuck it up much worse than this."

"How exactly did Dhovoi come into power?" Irdessa asks. "When I left he was an intelligencer, finding jobs for my father. Seems like you'd be more likely to run things."

Any hint of smile vacates Fent's face. "He and I worked closely with your father. When the three of you were arrested and Andelsior's arrangement with the Domestic Patrol collapsed, the guard moved to inhabit the city, expecting it to be ripe for the taking. They didn't anticipate the anger Andelsior's arrest stirred up within the Vanguard and the population. That felt to me like the time to negotiate a new deal. Dhovoi had different ideas that were, for better or worse, more popular.

He stoked Vim's anger. Against my advice, he led a resistance and drove out Promontory's soldiers."

Irdessa chews on his words without responding. She'd always wondered what happened in Vim after her father and Torvald were arrested. She'd have never imagined that Dhovoi, the quiet thinker who had no skill with a sword, would end up leading. Then again, from the look of it, the role of leader hasn't been filled competently.

As they near Vim's center, the town is more congested. The buildings on either side of the street rise up in masterfully cut timbers with steep roofs that end at sharp angles. Plastered on their walls are parchment notices, thick as wallpaper, flaky as birch bark. Irdessa slows down to inspect them. A wanted face, a missing face, protection needed, grievous stories scrawled in trembling writing that end in pleas for help, advertisements for blade dealers, blade swingers, services of a more intimate nature written out in shameless detail.

Wooden walkways and rafters hang between the buildings like webbing, connecting the upper stories and roofs of each manor and store and tavern for reasons not obvious to Irdessa. Are people frightened to walk on the street? The grey crowd of dour townsfolk thickens as they go, filled with hidden hands and suspicious stares, and Irdessa finds herself unnerved. This may be her homeland, but Keswal is where she became who she is, and right now that seems to be a jittery ball of nerves, wishing for more eyes, more javelins ... one more Torvald.

Why did he make her come back here without him? What purpose is she supposed to serve? And what's she supposed to do with Kraus? Cut him loose? At a glance, it would seem he'd fit in quite well. But he clings to her ankles like a mewling kitten. For her good or his?

Above the street's general din there's a ruckus from a nearby building. Irdessa's pulse quickens. By reflex, her hands go to her belt, where a fisher's knife is hiding. Seeing no such reaction from the people around her, she realizes the life of a Keswal warrior living under a lanista has honed her to be hyper aware of impending conflict. Raised voices first, now the sound of wood splintering. Just as she throws an arm between Fent and the doorway from where the commotion resonates, Kraus steps in front of her.

Two men in full scuffle roll into the street, huffing and grappling. One lands atop the other and, in an instant that lasts long enough for Irdessa's lungs to fail her, lamplight glints off the steel blade in his hand. Irdessa fails to do anything at all. The blade disappears in the other man's gut. Irdessa is frozen to the spot, trying to catch her breath. Her face and palms are frigid. She's back in the arena, at her first fight. Torvald's words are in her ear. *Act quickly, or those who do will get you.* But her body won't respond. The moment cages her and squeezes the air out of her chest. Hot tears fill her eyes, burning her. Kraus is planted between Irdessa and the fight like a knife-wielding wall.

The aggressor punches his blade into the man beneath over and over. To his credit, he doesn't leave the job half done. *Thump, thump, thump, thump*, synchronizing with strained gasps. As quickly as it started, the fight is over. The stabber rises to his feet, pushing off his victim's curled-up body. There is no applause. No petals rain down. The victor does not bow to his audience, which consists entirely of Irdessa and Kraus. In fact, he doesn't show concern for them at all. He cleans his knife on the victim's vest, hawks a slimy wad that impacts his face with a *smack*, offers a couple of swears, then stalks back toward the store.

Old Fent leans against a nearby wall, actively pretending there's not a man bleeding to death on the cobbles. Irdessa's breath returns gradually as the stabber disappears into the building. Maybe he's the storekeep, defending his wares. He could just as easily be a usurper who has claimed the business as his own. No one walking down this prominent street seems to care either way.

Kraus' guard has relaxed. He hides his weapon and straightens his back, but continues to watch the street in either direction, his black eyebrows wrinkled in concern, as if this violence is a sure prelude to more.

The stabbed fellow is trembling and wheezing softly. Irdessa can't see his face. She doesn't want to. This is not Keswal. She may recognize him.

A shifty-eyed woman eases from an unlit alley, approaching the man at a crouch. With expert hands she begins to scour his body, snatching whatever accoutrements he possessed in pocket or on person and stuffing them in her own shabby cloak, like a crab collecting the flesh off a rotting fish carcass. She's quickly joined by others, who alight upon the man like vultures. Not a word passes as they work. When they're finished, they melt back into the street, leaving an unshod body splayed out on his face in an expanding puddle of blood and urine. His trembling and wheezing have stopped.

Irdessa knows that no dreadhops will clean this up. She never expected to miss the birds. However gruesome they were, their motivation was simply hunger. Perhaps hunger motivated the crowd that stripped this body bare, but at least dreadhops didn't have to murder their own compassion as these vultures seem to have, assuming they ever had any.

"This place is a charmer," Kraus says, shaking his arms out and stretching his legs. Apparently, he tasted at least some of the apprehension that seized Irdessa. *Not enough to render him into a boat anchor*, she notes. What good was her time in Keswal, her successes, if she bricks up at the first sign of danger? What good did all those deaths serve? With every fight in the arena, every death of a familiar face, she told herself it would be worth it. It would all amount to something someday.

"Fent," Irdessa says, "where is the Vanguard?" But when such a question as that must be asked, perhaps the Vanguard's time is over.

"Largely at Cornerstone. There's a celebration tonight."

"For what?" she asks.

He sighs. "Celebrations no longer require any prerequisite."

"Then it's not a celebration, is it?" Kraus says.

Fent shrugs.

"And Sura?" Irdessa asks—Fent's personal guard, lacking a better description, or at least she was. "Is she celebrating too?" Irdessa knows better. The woman is as festive as a miscarriage.

"Dhovoi put her to work locally. She'll return by the night's end." Fent recites this distantly, and it's obvious he's not happy about it. "She'll be glad to see you, I'm sure."

Irdessa doubts it. They've never had a conversation. Not that Sura could. She has no tongue. Irdessa considers asking about other members of the Vanguard who she knew before. Magpie and his sister Maudee. Harpold the Hunter. Elaga and Cindie. But there's only so much discouraging news she can handle and she's nearly reached her limit. So instead she forces her feet to carry on. Fent clears his throat and falls in line beside her, refusing to meet her eyes. He looks ashamed.

Kraus assumes his spot at the rear, limping along and offering dirty looks to anybody who glances his way. "I'm gonna need a damn drink pretty soon."

Irdessa shares Kraus' sentiment and is not ashamed to admit it. Her teeth grind as the emotions inside her converge to form a simmering rage. Dhovoi, whatever his title might be, is not doing enough. Simply having the Vanguard patrolling in their colors would be an improvement. As always, her thoughts return to Torvald, and for the first time her response is not utter grief. Did Torvald know what this city has become? If so, godsdamn him for sending her back here without him. Then again, what if Torvald did know ... *and he expected this reaction in me?* The thought weighs on her like a chainmail sheet. *All these years he protected me. For this? To come back here? And do what?* She feels displaced in her own body. Every day in Keswal she dreamed of returning here. It was her first thought when she awoke in the morning, her last before falling asleep. And now here she is. This is not what she hoped for while imprisoned in what she believed was the worst place in Fohrvylda, or even the world.

"It wasn't like this," she mumbles, but the words don't convince her.

"I'd imagine not," Kraus says. "Hell, there'd be no one left."

The Cornerstone is a three-story wood and stone manse that serves as the Vanguard's headquarters. It sits upon a low, brick-built island in the midst of a cobblestone roundabout where Vim's five most prominent streets intersect. It was Irdessa's home for most of her life—as long as Andelsior held power. As she feared, what she sees is not the glowing bastion she remembers. When she was a child, multicolored tents of merchants littered the intersection, creating a maze-like patchwork shantytown where you could sample foreign foods, pet exotic animals, swing bizarre weapons, or pick up a fresh loaf of bread. Today, the vast intersection is mostly empty, aside from mailed individuals with curved bows over their shoulders loitering, watching, lurking in groups.

It's with an unannounced kick in the guts that Irdessa realizes these individuals make up the Vanguard, or what it has become. Her father's colors, the red shield lined with silver embroidery, are reduced to a memory. Instead, all that gives away their like purpose is the suspicion they share and the crimson sashes hanging at their waists like blood-soaked belts. She recognizes none of them. Never in her time away did she expect this welcome home. They begin to notice her and her companions and their gazes stick. Kraus' mounting tension is palpable in the air itself.

Old Fent steps forward. "Vanguard," he calls, smiling, "I bring guests for the alderman."

The attention of all the nearby sash-wearers now converges on the old man and his two companions. One walks out in front of the rest. His face is clean shaven, nose held high. "The alderman's busy, old man. Bring them back in the morning. Get your ass back to the gate." Others chuckle, begin to turn their backs.

Irdessa doesn't know the man, which means he hasn't been Vanguard for more than two years. If Fent's done something to earn such treatment, she hasn't heard it. But she knows Fent. She doesn't know this motherfucker. And she wouldn't have tolerated that disrespect to a friend even before she learned twelve ways to knife a man.

"Is that any way to address one of the Vanguard's founders?" Irdessa demands.

This perks up several of the sash-wearers.

"Well, hello. And what exactly would you know about it?" Clean face swaggers forward, letting his eyes rove up and down her.

"More than you." The venom in her voice halts the man's advance and knocks the smirk off him. "I'm Irdessa, and my father built the Vanguard before you ever cried for a teat or shat your pants."

The man solidifies, unsure.

Kraus places himself beside Irdessa. "From the look of him, he ain't done shitting them."

Clean Face shifts his gaze from him to her and back, anger overtaking his features. Some hissing behind cupped hands among the other sash-wearers. She'd wondered if her name would hold any weight here. Before she left, the name was simply Andelsior's daughter's, and it was enough to earn her a smile at best. Maybe a head rub like she was a puppy, despite all the jobs she'd been on. Now, she has no idea what it means. Enough to stop the so-called Vanguard in its tracks, apparently.

"I think Dhovoi will accommodate a childhood friend," Fent says, and he advances toward Cornerstone. Irdessa follows, before the armed men and women can collect themselves. She takes Fent's elbow as they climb the shallow stairs toward the arched doorway.

"Thank you, girl," Fent says quietly. He has donned a more crippled air. Irdessa approves. Sometimes it's better to appear less capable than you are.

The guards part without word, allowing them through to the door. Although Irdessa's heart is racing in her chest, she is able to keep her hand still as she grips the tarnished brass handle she thought she'd never see again.

The door squeals open, unloosing bawdy, muffled music and acrid smoke from the unlit foyer. The commotion comes from deeper within Cornerstone, on the far side of this dark hallway, and each dampened thump of drums helps nail shut the coffin that holds her definition of home. Her feet push onward despite it.

She's inside. The door has shut behind her, binding her in a gauzy fog, outside torchlight smearing through the opaque glass into the lingering smoke. She glides toward the grand hall in a daze. Her vision tunnels on the glowing outline of the doorway to the grand hall. Inside that room she lounged with friends while her father bent over map-laden tables, surrounded by wise men and women who looked up to him. How utterly naïve of her to think nothing will have changed. A small inescapable voice gnaws at her from within. *Vim is dead. Your childhood is dead. Your home is dead. Your past, present, and future are all dead. Just like your father. Just like Torvald.* A strange numbness has overtaken her limbs, as if she's lying motionless at the bottom of a shallow pool, and in the air above her a violent storm rages. She moves to push open the door and Fent grabs her arm with both hands.

"Irdessa." His lone eye is worried. "You have to understand ..."

"Understand what?" she says. "That I'll find Dhovoi trying to figure out where he fits in?" She jerks her arm out of his hands. *Too late for talking.*

Irdessa kicks open the tall door and strides into the blinding light of the grand hall as if it were Keswal.

She falters, her every sense assaulted. Music and voices, smoke and breath and spilled liquor, dim lighting that throws everything into a writhing, partial dream. Claustrophobia grips her. The first place her eyes focus is the huge wooden armchair across the room. It's painted gold in a tasteless attempt to mimic a throne and is inhabited presently by a pot-bellied lizard of a man with slick black hair. Two mountainous brutes in unadorned armor flank his chair, towering over it. Irdessa can't see their eyes, but their dented steel caps are aimed at her.

You don't have to be the most dangerous person in the room, Torvald's voice tells her. *But know who is and be more ready to strike than they are.* The throned fellow is stubble-cheeked and clad in black leather. Or mostly clad. His trousers are bunched around his shins and there's a girl straddling him. Her gown is nearly transparent and pearl colored, stained muddy at its hem. Her lips are painted red, her eyes shadowy. They're giggling and she's toying with the numerous straps and buckles on his coat. He'd probably do more toward helping her undress himself if he weren't gripping a bottle in one hand and her ass in the other.

Lining the floor are blankets, animal skins, wide cushions, and sprawled upon them are men and women—clothed, naked and everything in between. They're drinking from bottles and steins and crystal glasses, smoking something rancid smelling from stemmed pipes, fucking or being fucked. There's a trio of musicians on a wooden platform in the corner, assaulting a croaking brass horn, a shrieking flute, and a set of tall, thudding hand-drums. The ruckus they're generating would perhaps provide a more festive atmosphere were it not for the forge blazing in Irdessa.

The two brutes guarding the throne seem to be the only individuals in the room aware of the party's newcomers.

"This is more like it," says Kraus. Irdessa readies her most scathing glare and turns to find him chugging down a bottle. Somehow the smile he's able to perform, while shrugging, without interrupting his guzzling, is nearly charming.

Irdessa looks again to the throne. The bottle-wielding man releases the girl's ass and thrusts his hand into his groin, where he appears to be readying his prick.

"Is that ...?" ... *what Dhovoi has become?*

Fent clears his throat. "Alderman Dhovoi," he says abashedly.

Kraus comes up for air. "Looks to me like he's found where he fits in."

Irdessa suppresses a cringe.

"Right in that whore, am I right?" Kraus cackles.

Irdessa ignores him.

"You get it? Because—"

"*I get it!*"

Kraus puts the bottle back to his lips.

Irdessa's shoulders are seized up and trembling around her ears. This is sacrilege. Her father would be disgusted, as would Torvald. If there's a time and place for this, it's not while her hometown circles the drain, and on the same floor where she and her friends learned their numbers and letters.

"Alderman Dhovoi," she calls. Her voice, the same trumpet she used to direct the action over the Keswal battlefield, is lost inside revelry and whores. Irdessa snatches a bottle from the hand of a man blissfully splayed out at her feet. She heaves it at the musicians. It explodes on the wall behind them, scattering their song and making the shirtless percussionist dive for cover.

"*Dhovoi!*" she roars.

The so-called alderman cranes his neck around the whore, who has begun to writhe and bounce in his lap. He grabs her shoulders and pushes her aside, squinting and blinking as if the lamps dimly cutting through the haze are each suns blinding him. The two brutes stir to life, drawing cudgels from their belts and bucklers from their backs. Their arms are lined in scars. For all Irdessa knows they're twins.

Kraus steps around Irdessa. He breaks the ass-end off his wine bottle, spilling its contents, and thrusts it out toward the brutes. "You motherfuckers wanna dance?" he yells.

Dhovoi leaps to his feet, sending the girl to the stone floor, where her bare ass lands with a *clap!*

"Irdessa?" His face is awash with inebriated shock and joy. His arms stretch out like oars. He's as rigid as an overly curious mouse. He flusters with his trousers as he makes his way toward her, kicking over goblets and stepping on fingers and feet. His brutes hesitate, confused by the apparent welcome. Irdessa grabs a handful of Kraus' shirt and hauls him back behind her.

"Thank you, Kraus. Let's forestall murder, shall we?"

Kraus burps. "Sure," he says, bending to procure another bottle.

Dhovoi is closing in, leaving Irdessa little time to formulate a strategy. For some reason, any memory of how they once interacted is nowhere to be found, replaced by a frantic urge to assess. Threat is surely imminent. And if you can't assess, eliminate. Her hands scramble for a knife. But it's Dhovoi. Harmless, surely, if not taller than she remembers and possessing a new fondness for public fornication. He has matured since last she saw him, if only in a reproductive way. Something about that feels a greater threat than anything in Keswal. She knows how to handle violence. Affection on the other hand ...

The turmoil boils down to a primal desire to run. Run out the door and down the street and out of Vim. Instead, shamefully, she freezes, again. Dhovoi is upon her, reaching for her with his long, leather-clad arms. She hoists up a single hand in front of his face. He never sees it.

"Irdess-*hmph*," he says, smearing his trim, black beard into her palm, utterly undeterred. His arms envelop her, and despite the fury that's been mounting within her, all her wrathful anxiety evaporates at once. He's weeping and saying *Thank the gods* over and over and, for some reason, *I'm sorry.*

Her head is on his shoulder, and she doesn't fight it, despite being painfully aware a whore was recently occupying the space. The stale-flower stench of oily perfume attests to it. Chances are she doesn't smell so great herself. Her legs are threatening to fail her and she can't fathom why. She didn't miss Dhovoi. Not particularly. But she missed something. And this embrace feels like somehow, if only in this moment, everything might be alright. She has no tears left to cry. But it is a welcome feeling to think you aren't carrying a burden alone.

Dhovoi rides out his tears and Irdessa realizes she's calculating him, and the two brutes, and the several individuals nearby who've forgotten the party to watch this reunion. She's weighing their worth in a fight, for her or against her. Dhovoi feels to have none. He's tall enough but lacking any fighting muscle. The two brutes are obvious brawlers. Ready to rough a person up, break his bones, teach him a lesson. Less ready to catch a blade to the throat and doubtfully expecting it. Regarding the onlookers, it appears her cover's blown. This impromptu surveying is exactly what Torvald would have done. What he'd have instructed her to do.

And where did that get him?

The alderman holds her at arm's length. "Oh, Irdessa. Thank the gods you made it back," he blubbers.

"Dhovoi," she says, prying his fingers from her shoulders. "You've done a real number here, haven't you?"

His smile is deep, genuine, and suddenly he's aware of himself. Panic washes over his face. He addresses the room. "Clear out!" He claps his hands like he's shooing away chickens. "This party's over."

The revelers begin to rise, those who can, and fiddle with their clothing, help their fellows to their feet, finish their drinks. Some of the more inebriated in the room are hefted up and slung over shoulders.

"I'm sorry," Dhovoi says, his smile back in place. "We're just warming up. There's a hell of a show tonight."

A shudder runs over Irdessa. Perhaps it's the warmth of his welcome. Perhaps it's that she's finally home, a place that part of her never expected to see again. She knows whatever respite she finds can't last. When it becomes known she's alive and here, Promontory will find her. They'll never rest. This is not how she was supposed to return. Alone, on the run. And all because the one she thought was her partner was so convinced she'd die fighting uergatas he sacrificed himself to prevent it. *Torvald* ... Again, the ache fills her guts. Her eyes are watering.

"Oh no." Dhovoi reacts to her expression with his own anguish. Looks like he's about to wail again. "Oh no, oh no, oh no. Poor Torvald."

There's something altogether hollow about his despair. Were Dhovoi and Torvald close? She can't remember them together. Dhovoi falls against her, trying to pull her head back to his shoulder. But Irdessa is sick of crying and this pity is unnecessary. He wasn't this way before. He was shy. And although he seems to be attempting genuine concern, the image of his substandard cock is too fresh in Irdessa's memory. She dislodges herself from his grasp.

"Thank you," she says. For what, she's not entirely sure but it was that or violence.

"Oh, Irdessa," he says, rubbing his eyes and nose energetically. He finishes by slapping his cheeks several times. "Ah, Irdessa."

"Yeah, you said that," Kraus says.

Dhovoi notices Kraus for the first time. He recoils like a snake lunged at him. "For fuck's sake, man. What happened to your face?"

Kraus leans forward, his battered visage aimed at Dhovoi like a haunted ship docking, every ravine-like scar exaggerated by the smoke-drenched lantern light. "I bumped into a cabinet."

"Godsdamn," Dhovoi marvels. "I hope you bumped it back."

Kraus shakes his head. "I forgave it."

Dhovoi's eyebrow has arched halfway up his forehead. "Alright ... well ... Irdessa, is this your ..."

"Companion," Irdessa says. "Dhovoi, Vim is a wreck."

Dhovoi responds by shaking his head aggressively. "Listen. Among other new decrees, the Vanguard is done picking up garbage. We're better than that. Always have been. The town has to manage without. They're figuring it out. Promontory's assault won't stop us. We're getting back on our feet. You haven't seen anything yet."

"But I have," Irdessa says. "I watched a man killed on my way here with no repercussions."

"Nothing like Keswal, I bet." Dhovoi makes to give Irdessa's shoulder a playful punch. He stops just short of her, surely in response to both her and Kraus' subtle shifting of weight. Dhovoi seems to consider at least patting her shoulder, then thinks better of it. He gives an awkward laugh. "Really ... violent place, that."

Irdessa considers how close she was to breaking this childhood friend's arm. "Where is the Vanguard?" she asks him.

"Oh," as if he's forgotten a great surprise. "Some are here. Some working. Most of them are down by the ..." He stops himself, taking on a mischievous smile. "How about I show you? You've chosen a great night to return."

Irdessa isn't convinced anything she's done lately was by choice. But she returns his smile. Part of her is desperate to keep this feeling of safety intact, even if it's a fallacy.

Dhovoi snaps his fingers and his brutes advance. "Sarsen, Visent, get my coach," he tells them. "Fent, stay here. Get this place cleaned up."

Fent solidifies momentarily, his mouth a tight line. Then his single eye twinkles and he nods his head. "Of course."

Irdessa tries to mask her confusion. If anyone's giving orders, it should be the other way around.

The hulking men shuffle through the same door Irdessa kicked wide. Dhovoi aims Irdessa and Kraus after them and toward a side hall. "Why don't you both get yourselves cleaned up and we'll ride out?" He fires a wink at Irdessa that tickles her gag reflex. Judging by Kraus' expression, he'd like to break off Dhovoi's arm and beat him with it. "I'm so glad you're back. You're going to love this," he says, then adds, "Both of you."

Irdessa strongly doubts it, no matter what *this* turns out to be.

25

Not Worth Living For

FOHRVYLDA
Cornerstone, Vim

The chamber Dhovoi indicated once served as barracks. Now it's crowded with wardrobes and chests, each spilling over with dresses, robes, gowns, garters, gloves, stockings. Mostly lace and leather and impracticality. Irdessa's given a basin of water and, frighteningly, privacy. She'd forgotten about it. It's an alien concept in Keswal, no matter your standing with your lanista. You shower and shit at the place where water's running, onlookers be damned.

After a much-needed soaping and rinse off, she finds a pile of garments to settle down on so she can scrub the remaining dirt and blood out of her leather armor and boots. Surely Dhovoi didn't expect her to doll up in this buffoonery. She chooses to assume he did not. Mounted on the walls are scant leftovers of the armor that the Vanguard once maintained, inventoried, and relied on. Hopefully the main reservoir of weapons and armor have been stored, rather than sold or discarded. The absence of armaments suggests the Vanguard's purpose has shifted from violence to something else. While this possibility is strangely rejuvenating, it fails to comfort her. Maybe it would if she hadn't witnessed a stabbing on the way into town. One day things might be different, but in Fohrvylda violence is necessary to survive. Vim's Vanguard isn't doing enough.

Irdessa finds a pair of matte steel bracers bearing some defensive utility, as well as matching lightweight greaves. She finds a green, hooded cloak with several pockets stitched on the inside, and throws her old blanket in a corner. As a final touch, and for no other reason than to celebrate her unexpected, refreshing state of cleanliness, she draws her hair up and clasps it with a simple ruby-studded brooch.

Outside, twilight has surrendered to night and the cobbles and walls have a yellow, torchlit hue. Kraus is waiting with his back to the Cornerstone. He, too, took advantage of Cornerstone's facilities. Someone cleaned up the haircut he began, and now he's got a layer of uniform stubble and a nearly smooth face, ignoring his precipitous scarring. The whore-drobe's offerings managed to compliment him, and seeing him dressed up tugs a smile onto Irdessa's face. He's bound in grey tweed, with a jacket that squeezes his waist and sharpens his shoulders, trousers that cascade straight from beneath his coat to rest on polished black boots. He's donned a shiny ebony pauldron on his left shoulder, lined with black chains of varying lengths fixed to a cloak draped over his right shoulder. A hefty-looking stein occupies his gloved hand. It's made of brass and stenciled wood and presently empty. Maybe he anticipates finding an opened barrel of beer.

"Damn, Kraus," Irdessa says. "You clean up nicely."

She must have startled him because he jumps as if he'd been in deep thought. He tries to turn, nearly twists an ankle on the curb, belches like a trumpet while staggering to keep his balance. Irdessa gives him an understanding nod. It was impressive while it lasted.

In the moat-like courtyard separating the Cornerstone from the rest of Vim, a flamboyant carriage awaits them, tethered behind two long-horned woolly urus. The massive oxen are held captive by a steel yoke that must weigh twice as much as Kraus. Dhovoi's two brutes, Sarsen and Visent apparently, are packed snugly side by side on the coach's rear perch. They're holding onto the thin, shiny railing lining the roof and aiming their steel-capped stares at the alleys between buildings surrounding the intersection. The driver more matches the cart itself. She's thin, straight-backed, sharp-nosed, and wearing a yellow, narrow-brimmed bonnet tailored to contain hair and block sun—not that the sun's out. If it's tailored to mask her utter annoyance, it's failing. The whole picture is as ridiculous an image as Irdessa's ever seen, and when the cart's dainty door swings wide and Dhovoi's slick-backed head pokes out, she is not surprised.

"Shall we?" Dhovoi's smile deepens into a toothy grin when his eyes alight upon Irdessa, and her cheeks burn. She immediately regrets the rubies. This is not Keswal. There is no advantage to drawing attention to herself. But for some reason she doesn't sling the trinket away yet.

Kraus helps himself, lurching toward the carriage in his fancy clothes. After several attempts at throwing his foot up on the step, each punctuated by an innovative string of swears, he hauls himself up into the cart, barely managing to not demolish the frail lanterns swinging wildly outside the cart's door. Irdessa pulls herself up after him. Dhovoi has reserved enough room on the bench beside him, and he gestures to it. She settles in. Her knees have room to shift without bumping Dhovoi's or Kraus', but to call the interior spacious would be generous. The driver clicks her tongue and snaps her reins. The beasts grunt to life and the delicate carriage skitters southward.

"So, I was wondering ..." Kraus' voice is so loud he could just as easily be talking to someone outside the cart, or the city, as Dhovoi, who sits within two feet of him. "Where're we goin' again?"

Dhovoi gives the chuckle a parent might when watching their toddler attempt to form his first sentence. He turns his eyes on Irdessa and smooths his smile away with a gloved hand. "So much has changed since you were here, Irdessa," he says, and his tone and delivery suggest she's in for a script reading. "Since you and Torvald and Andelsior were taken from us." The heaving breath he takes, while focusing shrewd eyes on something out the cart's window and frowning deeply, fails to convey emotion. Irdessa smiles, trying to forestall the feeling that something is wrong and will be forevermore, no matter what. Why is she so suspicious? Is this Torvald's dying curse?

"The old way is gone," Dhovoi continues.

Irdessa clenches her teeth. He's referring to Andelsior's order.

"No one was happy about your father's arrest, least of all me, as you might imagine."

Irdessa is coming to grips with the fact that outside Keswal, examining a person is only half the exercise. Outside Keswal, you must do it without being obvious, while pretending to believe their words, and while offering up your own. Try though she might, however, she's unable to conjure small talk with Dhovoi. Instead, she gives a laugh, as if that's appropriate to the conversation. Being locked up for two years has made her dreadfully awkward. Torvald would have smothered Dhovoi in silence and a stare, extricating the truth from within the act like a surgeon might extract a bloody arrowhead from the ligaments in a leg. At the least, she wants to know why one-eyed Old Fent is among the lowest of the Vanguard's laborers. Then she pictures him trying to mingle among the revelers of Cornerstone's party. Perhaps he was at the gate of his own accord.

"Hey," Kraus says, startling Irdessa. "D'you hear what I asked you?"

Dhovoi flinches. "You'll see soon enough."

Kraus glares at nothing for a moment and gives an exaggerated shrug, pulling his empty, wooden stein tightly to his paunch. A comfortable smile glides over his stubbled face and his eyes narrow and lose focus, as if he has fallen into deep thought or near sleep. Irdessa's thinking the latter. No deep thought of his could warrant so peaceful a smile.

The view from the small window informs Irdessa that they've traveled out of the clog of the city and toward the southern slums, where roads turn back to mud. To the decorative carriage's credit, the ride is smooth, despite that the combined weight of the two brutes clinging to the back has the rear wheels' spring-irons compressed to near uselessness. Irdessa is relieved to not have to witness more of the city than she already has.

Soon, the driver is checking the carriage's pace. Outside the window, more and more villagers make their way in the same direction as the cart. Irdessa begins to hear the telltale murmurings of a large gathering. It strikes her as odd because Vim's south side is barren, made of patchy fields where nomads and beggars pitch their tents, all the way down the hill to the southern town wall. At least, it was.

Irdessa is trying not to dwell on the fact that she has essentially no say over where she's going, what will happen, and that she's largely under Dhovoi's control. Inside Keswal, however constrained she was, there was order, a schedule. On the outside she'll have to learn to make decisions for herself all over again. She'll have to decide whether she's on the right course every hour. Every moment. The concept feels exhausting.

Irdessa is grossly aware of, and trying to ignore, Dhovoi's gaze longingly planted on her. Did he always stare so much? He's different than before, but so is she. She remembers him being a vital source of information to the Vanguard, promising future significance in the high-level planning between Andelsior and other key figures. When Andelsior would take the Vanguard away on a mission, leaving Dhovoi and Irdessa, he gave her his full attention. He treated her like the only person around, even as they dashed through the crowded market. It was endearing, if not somewhat annoying. Now it borders on smothering. Perhaps because Andelsior is not returning, and neither is Torvald or the Vanguard, and Dhovoi appears quite content with that.

The carriage grinds to a halt and Dhovoi's elation springs into full blossom.

"Finally." He exits the carriage and offers a hand to Irdessa. She takes it, unsure what to do with it, follows him, trying not to let apprehension show on her face. Her boots sink into mud. Kraus follows her out. Once they've disembarked, the massive Visent and Sarsent hop down as one, relieving so much strain from the spring-irons that the carriage fairly leaps into the air, almost flipping the driver out of her seat.

They're on a terrace in the hill, overlooking what should be a bare-earth expanse and then the city wall. The scene that greets Irdessa is unrecognizable.

"What happened to the wall?" she asks.

"We needed the space," Dhovoi says, smiling, as if removing a hundred yards of Vim's primary defenses amounts to shaping up some hedges. "Fear not. A replacement is being built."

In the wall's place is what can only be described as an open mine lined thick with an unruly mob. Someone's been excavating stone and left behind a gaping quarry enclosed by a prickly barrier of spiked timber, like a thorny fence. A mass of hundreds gather at the crater's lip, full of raucous cheer. Dread squeezes Irdessa's lungs and she stops walking. Around the pit are several roaring braziers, each half the size of Dhovoi's carriage. On one side is a spidery tangle of wooden scaffolds and supports, forming a crude platform.

Dhovoi situates Irdessa's hand on his elbow and gives a gentle pull until her reluctant feet move again. He guides her down the hill toward the break in the spike-wall fence.

"Dhovoi." Her voice is timid. "What is this?"

Dhovoi laughs. "Oh, come on. I mean, it's no Keswal, but ..."

His mouth is still moving but his words are lost in the rush of blood that floods through Irdessa. They're close enough now to see the pit and its stained floor. How could she have mistaken the crowd's cheers? The look in their eyes? Panic is upon her, threatening to close her throat and stop her heart. Her vision grows pale. A roar from the crowd and in a flash there is Torvald, again, this time holding his guts and pleading with the goatman, who doesn't notice him. Torvald's men fall to pieces soundlessly like spring snow needled to death by rain. There's Jasmin, punctured by an arrow. *Ouch*, she mouths. Her eyes fall on Irdessa as if they should share a final, secret laugh. Then wave after wave of arrows wash over her, each one slowing her until they obscure her entirely. There is Pinprae, tumbling through wind, down toward where Irdessa stands in the hollows beneath the Towers. He crunches into the stone right at her feet. On his face is the same expression he wore the day she met him. *I hope I won't disappoint you.* The rocks chew him up and he's gone.

Irdessa has stopped walking again, instead gasping for air, bent forward, oblivious of her surroundings. Hot tears blind her. She pinches them away. Aware of herself, she shakes her head, blinks until the ground comes into focus. The sound of the crowd swarms back into place. She gets control of her breathing and lifts her head. Dhovoi didn't noticed her reaction. He's scanning the place with hands on hips, proud as a new parent. Irdessa looks back at Kraus.

"I'll be godsdamned." he says, surveying the crowd. There is no humor in his voice. That, and any hint of his former inebriation, has perished, leaving his face as set and hard as a harvested field. "It's a fucking arena."

"Isn't it beautiful?" Dhovoi could not be more ecstatic. "I bet it's a relief to be only a spectator." Then he laughs, as if it were a funny joke and she's the one who said it. Irdessa stares at him. Convicts spectate while they aren't fighting in Keswal. Any idiot knows this. Instead of noticing how flat his comment fell, he guides her into the thick crowd congested at what must be the admission gates, where two red-sashed individuals shout orders and take payments. They look familiar. She probably knows them. But shame engulfs her and she cannot meet their eyes. Dhovoi nods at them as he passes, gives one a quip. They laugh. Kraus and Dhovoi's silent enforcers follow.

Once past the gates, he drags her through the sweaty shoulders and hot breath of the mob. Toward the killing floor. *This is a nightmare I am doomed to repeat forever. I can never escape.* What made Dhovoi think

Fohrvylda needed another arena? Kraus' presence behind her gives her confidence to carry on. He looks as unhappy as she feels.

You will not die in Keswal. Torvald's pale face peers at Irdessa from beneath the black curtain of his hair. There's grave dirt on his cheek. A smile splits his blue lips. *But maybe in some other arena?*

Dhovoi is directing her to a steep set of stairs that ascends the plank-built stands. Irdessa can't muster the cohesion to determine if this is a moment in which she should exercise her freedom, if that actually exists. So she does not resist. *How could you do this?* she wants to yell at him. *Why would you do this?* She wants to grab his neck and squeeze it until he understands what happened to her. To Torvald. To Andelsior. To anyone who catches Promontory's attention.

She doesn't choke Dhovoi. Probably couldn't if she wanted to, what with his two behemoths hounding their heels. Why would she? Why fight Dhovoi for what he has done to Vim? As if he owes her something. As if Vim owes her something. As if she owes anyone anything. *I am damned*, Irdessa concludes as she wipes tears from the corners of her eyes, *and this is hell.*

She follows Dhovoi up the rickety staircase as the familiar weight of grief sinks into her guts once again. *I hope you're happy, Torvald. I'm ready to die now.* The thought brings more solace than before. First she wanted the pain to stop. Then it seemed to, at least while she was distracted. Now it's back and with it, the knowledge that it is here to stay. It will never truly stop. There is nothing for her in Vim. Is there something for her anywhere?

The top tier of the rough seating is Dhovoi's and only here is Irdessa able to catch her breath, high above the suffocating throng. The planks that make up the flooring, uprights, benches, and railing all appear to be recycled from the wall. Something about that fact makes Irdessa feel even sicker.

"Forgive the state of my interim booth," Dhovoi blurts mechanically, as if it's his required welcome and the meaning is irrelevant. He moves to the side overlooking the pit. His brutes take their places behind them, ever alert. On the rail before Dhovoi is evidence oily hands have rested, pounded, and squeezed until slicked grooves exist in the wood. Irdessa questions the word *interim*.

"We're just in time," Dhovoi announces.

From this tower, Irdessa has a good view of the pit. Several individuals stumble from a steel cage, all wearing the blue garb of Promontory soldiers, albeit tattered and stained. The crowd launches a unified roar of disapproval, throwing down soggy vegetables and sodden handfuls of what Irdessa hopes is mud.

"We don't exactly have a *Bloody Portent*," Dhovoi says with exaggerated distress on his face and trembling hands as if this is some laughable state. "But who came to hear talking anyway?" He guffaws at his own wit.

"Why are they wearing that?" Irdessa asks numbly.

"The blue of the Domestic Patrol?" Dhovoi laughs. "Because they're the Domestic Patrol. When Promontory came for the city after your father was arrested, we fought them off. Those we didn't kill, ran. Those who couldn't run, we captured. They were locked up for a while until we figured out what to do with them. I think it's brilliant."

"Doesn't this bring heat down on you?" Kraus says. He is hyper alert, scanning his surroundings with the coals beneath his shaggy brow.

"The arena? No, no, no. Most every town's got an arena these days. Since Andelsior's departure ..." He slaps a visage of grief onto his face as if an afterthought, lowers his head, and places his leather fingers on Irdessa's shoulder, squeezing it gently. "The citizens demanded one. They wouldn't let it go." He gives an incredulous laugh. "And so here we are."

"Yeah," Kraus says, like he's tasted spoiled milk. "Almost too good to be true."

"Isn't it?" Dhovoi faces the pit and grips the wooden edge, elated that his guests share his high spirits.

Now two sand-colored beasts that look like a cross between armored bulls and giant turtles are romping out into the arena from a separate steel cage. Their tails are long and end in huge bony mallets.

"What in Vostuar's name are those?" Kraus says.

"Bludgeontails," the alderman says, leaning forward and placing his elbows on the rail and steepling his fingers. "They're imported from the southern scrub lands of Ausgan. *The Untamed*, as they call it." He raises an eyebrow slyly at Irdessa. He's clearly impressed by this fact.

"How the hell'd you manage that?" Kraus asks.

"A little coin goes a long way," Dhovoi says smugly, as if that's an answer. Perhaps his abridged response is due to the wrong one of his two guests showing interest.

Coin that should have been spent on Vim's defenses and upkeep, Irdessa nearly yells at him. What stops her, she isn't sure. Maybe it's the knowledge that he holds different values than she does. At the time she was arrested, Vim's Vanguard was made up of warriors, be it aspiring, active, or retired. It seemed they had a higher calling, even while cleaning the streets. Maybe even *because* they cleaned the streets. Was she blinded by optimism and youth? Has the Vanguard always served such a frivolous purpose as this?

The soldiers in the pit back away at first, then after testing the bludgeontails with their swords, they apparently determine the beasts are docile. One of the men jumps onto a plate-covered back. The beast doesn't notice. The crowd is losing interest. Irdessa continues to die inside.

"Ain't got much spunk in 'em, do they?" Kraus says. "Do they taste better than they fight?"

Dhovoi winces. It occurs to Irdessa he has no love for Kraus, which ups her opinion of her boorish companion. And to think she wished him dead not two days prior.

"Just watch," Dhovoi says.

On the lip of the bottom tier of the pit, a man with the Vanguard's new crimson sash is emptying a sack of what appears to be red-furred, four-legged snakes into the pit.

"What's he got?" Kraus asks.

"Timber ferrets," Dhovoi whispers, in his most contemplative pose. "Bludgeontails *hate* them."

The ferrets, no taller than kittens but twice as long, sniff the air and scratch at the walls. One of the soldiers points at the rodents and another approaches them with tentative sword lifted. The timber ferrets give a squeal and scatter across the pit. The bludgeontails, who were lumbering around like huge armadillos, visibly panic. They swing their club-ended tails and charge the walls. The thunder of their bedlam resounds from the pit. The ferrets spot the bludgeontails and dash at them, pounce on them, crawl over their armor to bite at their joints. The bludgeontails react in chaos, spinning and ramming, oblivious to the soldiers and each other. The soldier who'd mounted one of the trampling masses of armor is the first to go. His leg is crushed against a wall, making him shriek and drop his sword. His mount seeks escape desperately, smearing the soldier's leg into the side of the pit. The man topples off, disappearing, leaving dark blood on the yellow beast. The bludgeontails' bedlam shakes dust from Dhovoi's rafters. The soldiers make as valiant a stand as lumps of gravy fighting a whisk. The mob loves it. Dhovoi loves it.

"That's what you get," Dhovoi yells down enthusiastically. "For Vim!"

The pit cheers.

Irdessa feels like her body is no longer her own. Her eyes lose their focus. She relents all control, retreats away from the viewpoint of her eyes, back into the shadows in her skull. Life outside Keswal is just Keswal on a more complicated scale. This is not worth living for. But what is? In Keswal, there was purpose. Fight alongside Torvald. The Tactician and the Undying. But without Torvald, who is she supposed to be?

You can't truly know yourself without learning what you can offer to others.

Irdessa's hands squeeze the railing to keep from shaking. How long will Torvald's words plague her? She looks down at the mob. It's of similar hues and energy as the commoners' stands in Keswal. Full of the same people she'd watch from a distance and envy for their freedom. She should have known better. Torvald's insidious influence is coalescing to form a purpose within her, if only her last.

Irdessa steps from the rail and finds Kraus watching her expectantly. He's no happier than she is. "Kraus ..." she starts. His eyes are sharp, as if he and she have some mission left to fulfill. They don't. He's fulfilled his promise. This is goodbye. He can now drink himself to death, or whatever he wants.

"I'm going ... to relieve ..." She doesn't even have the energy for it. And what's the point? She places a hand on his shoulder. His face is ripe with expectation. But she has nothing for him. She's not his problem. Not anymore.

She slips between Dhovoi's two armored men and onto the rough staircase. She'll offer herself to Vim's bloodiest, to let them determine her worth, her reward. Whatever they offer her, she'll accept. Perhaps she will share Torvald's pain. Perhaps she'll join him.

26

I Get to Hit Him Back

FOHRVYLDA
Outskirts of the pit in Vim

Kraus watches Irdessa descend from Dhovoi's tower. If he didn't know better, he'd think she means to ditch him, like he's a stray puppy yipping at her ankle. Best not to give that notion any further thought. Obviously, he's going after her. What's he supposed to do, sit here with ox and other ox and Alderman Dipshit? Hell no. Besides, while Dhovoi stood slavering over how impressively giant cow-turtles can render men to mush, Kraus saw no less than two people in the crowd stabbed and one snatched away and hauled into shadows. If Irdessa's breaching that mob looking for anything besides trouble, she's going to come up short.

Kraus knows one thing for sure. She's not into this arena. That was clear on her face, and Kraus can't blame her. What kind of fucking moron is Dhovoi for showing her this? She's been imprisoned as a fighter in Keswal for years. Dhovoi's clearly got it bad for her. He almost pissed himself when he saw her. And this is how he chooses to show it? Dumbass. Even if she were, for some reason, desperately missing the goofs and gaffes of death matches, this hole doesn't compare to Keswal.

Dhovoi, still fixated on his little pit fight, bursts into laughter. "Did you see that?" he asks. Then he notices Irdessa's gone. He turns his startled eyes on Kraus.

"I must have missed it," Kraus says.

"Where'd she go?"

"I think she's gone to relieve herself," Kraus says. *Of your company.*

Alderman Dhovoi's eyes widen. "That mob is dangerous. I'll send help." He snaps his fingers in the face of one of his two-legged bulls.

"No need," Kraus says. "I'm going."

Dhovoi's eyebrow arches upward, drawing terraces of surprise all the way up his forehead. That seems to be his most common expression. That and distrust. Probably speaks a lot about his character. Thinking of his range of expressions reminds Kraus of the face Dhovoi wore while also wearing that whore. A glassy-eyed, near-drooling, determination. Kraus chuckles.

The brutes turn their helms toward Kraus as he makes for the stairs. They're nearly shoulder to shoulder, directly in his path. Instead of smashing his stein on the left brute's block of a chin, Kraus sets it down. He cranes his head, peering up into the shadow of a helmet. Still can't see the fucker's eyes.

"How do you see out of that?" he says.

The brute mimics a boulder.

"Good talk," Kraus says, shoving himself between the two lumps. He'll have to hurt one of them sooner than later.

Kraus doesn't have the presence of mind to try to find Irdessa while descending the stairs. Rather, he focuses on not causing the contraption to collapse, while putting some space between himself and Dhovoi's barkless dogs before he breaks something that can't be unbroken. Once he's on the ground, in the horde, there's no chance of spotting her.

Kraus isn't comfortable in big crowds and this one is a perfect example of why. It's full of steamy-mouthed, grabby-handed jostlers with dirt on their faces and bloodlust in their eyes. Sharp heels find his toes. Throaty coughs spatter his cheeks. Slippery fingers grope his pockets, disappearing as he swings himself around with heaving chest and squeezed fists. A dull ache in his temples and a sour tongue are all that's left of the sweet mead he found at Dhovoi's party. His hands itch, and itch, and itch. Gotta bleed or make bleed.

There's probably a polite way to move through a crowd. Probably involves lots of inching forward, 'scuse me's and sorry 'bout that's, and so on. But whoever came up with that wasn't half as thirsty as Kraus. He stalks through the throng, employing his heavy black pauldron as a plow, knocking aside shoulders, elbows, ears, chins.

The majority of this stinking, stamping congregation is gathered around the pit's edge. Below it is another stone tier, thick with more people. Rough wooden railing separates that tier from the next one down, where it appears individuals that have to do with the action are sitting, or standing, or yelling. Below that tier is the arena floor. Irdessa probably won't be there. Kraus heads for the perimeter's outer border where opportunists stalk like wolves, watching those who watch the fight, waiting for opportunity.

There's a commotion rising above the general din ahead of Kraus. He pushes in that direction. There, in a space that seems to have emptied of almost everyone, he finds Irdessa. She stands with her back to the shadows, hood drawn. Behind her, a woman is bent over the still body of a man. Two other men stand facing Irdessa. Their posture looks like violent intent. Kraus almost steps in swinging, asking questions never. But something keeps him still. That is as fearless and purposeful a face as Irdessa has worn since she cut his own face open. Kraus places himself in her line of sight, assuming she can see out from under that hood.

The front guy is neckless and toady. His bare arms are overly long and thick with muscle. The fellow behind him has wide hands and a nose like a hook. It seems Irdessa embarrassed them, because the crowd is goading, and toady is fuming. Irdessa's hands are hidden within her cloak, where Kraus is hoping she at least has a knife hidden.

"Who the hell do you think you are?" Toady reaches for Irdessa's hood. She pulls back and smacks his hand away. The ringing slap brings a chortle out of the crowd and a rise in Toady's eyebrows.

"You had your fun with the man. Now let the woman clean him up." Her face is hidden but her voice is strong. "I'm not the one to touch."

"Yeah, Cider," says the sneering man, placing his flappy hands on his hips. "She ain't the one, she said so. Reckon we oughta fuck off with our tails hangin' limp?"

"I got a problem with that, Jin." No-neck's full cheeks are red. "I ain't nowhere near limp."

Jin begins to advance. "Me neither. Reckon we should—"

There's quick movement in the crowd. A flash of a firelight on a busy blade. Sneering man recoils as if punched, and blood spills from his face. A leather-clad woman has appeared in the clearing, her skin the color of a bleached skeleton and eyes like darts. The blade of her polearm is quivering inches over the packed earth, where lies a bit of severed meat.

"Gods ... dab ..." He's not sneering any more. Now he's roving over his bloody face with both hands. His nose is gone. "You fuckigg ... crazy ..." He throws a wild punch at the newcomer. It was well-aimed, all things considered, and should have caught her jaw. But she's quick. Her polearm's dark blade appears where her face was, in time to catch the man's punch on its edge. His fist lodges with a sound you might hear from a butcher's window. The blade is embedded between the bones of his hand, almost all the way to his wrist, blood pulsing down it and staining the wooden handle. The ivory woman watches him with large eyes and a disinterested smile. He opens his mouth as if to scream but only manages a staggered inhale.

Toady turns to see what's the ruckus. Irdessa wastes no time. She throws a weighty jab into his exposed left temple. As it lands with a smack, she swings a left hook, planting knuckles in his eye. He reacts by grabbing his face, shuffling backward, extending out a hand blindly in her direction. Her right hand is in motion again. It hits that same temple with a sound like a mallet on a fish. He's backpedaling. The mob screams in delight. Her left fist clips his chin, throwing saliva onto the crowd's yelling faces. To his credit, he's still on his feet despite the vicious blows. She comes back with the right, thunking his temple yet again. Now there's blood. At this point, Kraus knows her fist must hurt. No-neck plants his feet and Kraus' heart skips. A strike-off against someone twice your weight rarely makes for a good time.

Irdessa reacts to the imminent attack by going on full offense. She lowers her stance and throws all her weight into a flying left jab. His nose bursts like a tomato. His head rocks back and his arms flail but he still doesn't fall. He's preparing to swing. She's moving quickly to get her footing. Not quick enough.

His meaty fist catches her in the mouth. Irdessa reels like her head got knocked sideways. Her hood has fallen, and her eyes roll in their sockets. Kraus steps between her and the neckless bastard.

"That's enough." Kraus' scowl stops the man's advance. Fucker looked too eager to get at Irdessa while she was hurt. Her arms are windmilling, trying to catch something to keep her from falling.

"I got you," Kraus says, grabbing her hand. He raises his other arm to block the inevitable counterpunch. "It's me, Dess. I got you," he says, wincing at the pain in his forearm. Her punch had a surprising amount of force considering how unsteady she is. Then again, the knife wound on his arm screams at every provocation.

Her eyes focus on him. She steadies her feet, touches her mouth, where blood is gathering. Her knuckles shine red in the firelight.

"Your tooth is poking through," Kraus informs her.

She scoffs, and droplets of blood land on Kraus' grey jacket. "Don' trade 'lows with so'eone heavier than you," Irdessa tries to say despite her stuck lip.

"Sounds like a nugget from Torvald," Kraus says.

She nods, and her fingers find the tooth extending through her upper lip. "Yeah, 'ut he's dead so fuck hi'."

"Let me help," Kraus says, eyeing her lip closely. A quarter-inch of incisor is exposed, tucking her upper lip in as if she's saying *Werrr*.

"Do i'." She lifts up her bracer, finds a leather strap, folds it in half, and bites it on the left side of her mouth, leaving a gap between her teeth on the other side.

He takes her top lip between thumb and fingers and pinches it a couple of times, until he's as sure of his grip as he's going to be. He gives the lip a pull. Irdessa's breath catches and her eyes squeeze shut, pinching out tears. The tooth is still poking through.

"It's stuck," he says.

Irdessa is sucking in wavering breaths.

"I'm sorry, Dess," Kraus says. He spits on her face and quickly massages the saliva onto her exposed tooth with his thumb before she can retaliate. She gasps, swings a sharp elbow at his face. He's able to draw back so that it only clips his chin.

"Keep your teeth tight on that strap," he says.

"Fahck yah!" she screeches. There's a stream of red saliva dumping over the leather between her teeth.

She's not the lover of pain Kraus is. Who the hell is? Best do this quick, while she's pissed off. He braces himself and gives her lip a strong tug, hard enough to pull her chin down to her chest. His fingers slip free of her lip. He has just enough time to cover both sides of his head before her responding punches rain on him. As quickly as her attack begins, it is finished. Kraus peers at her from within his guard. The tooth is no longer visible, but left an angry, dark puncture, seeping blood freely.

Irdessa pulls the strap out of her mouth and leans forward to let pink spit cascade silently to the ground, breathing hard for a moment.

"Thanks, Kraus." She wipes the tears off her cheeks.

"You're a tough one," Kraus says, not that it's news to him. This new wound on her face sharpens the edge in her eyes.

Someone in the crowd starts clapping, then another. Then most everyone in the small circle is hooting and cheering. They've barred the neckless man from leaving. His nose is all kinds of broken, and a discolored hematoma has arisen from his left temple as if his head's birthing a purple chicken egg. Blood paints his sleeveless shirt and apish shoulders. Looks like his friend is asleep or dead. The pale warrior stands silently, holding her polearm at her side.

"Can I?" Kraus asks Irdessa, pointing at the bloody-faced man.

"No," she says. "I get to hit him back."

"Ain't he too big for you?"

She turns her eyes and all their fury upon him. "Have we met?"

Kraus raises both hands and retreats a step. She knows better. But the set of her jaw tells him she'll not be dissuaded. Seeing the man punch Irdessa awoke a desire in Kraus to break his bones while he begs for mercy, but it's her right to finish it if she can. Kraus sighs and steps aside. Maybe the best he can do is be ready to patch her up.

Irdessa rolls her shoulders, hefts up her bloody fists, and begins to work a pattern into her steps, bouncing on one foot, the other, both. The crowd is somehow falling over themselves in excitement and maintaining a distinct perimeter all at once. The toady man lifts his fists up and pulls his chin down, making extra chins where his throat should be. That's a shame. She has a damn good throat punch.

The man stalks forward, keeping his left foot in front. If he recognizes her as Irdessa from Keswal, it doesn't show. Looks like he's readying himself to throw another punch when his head snaps backward. Toady pauses, his eyes blinking rapidly. Kraus didn't see it, but she must have jabbed him. Toady advances again. His head bounces again, stopping him. This time Kraus catches the flutter of her sleeve as her arm moves back into guard. Kraus squints. Did she just jab him twice? Both with her left hand?

Toady wears bloody shock and rage all over his face. He neglects his guard and lifts his chin, abandons his stance and makes to lunge. Irdessa steps back as if in retreat, then sidesteps his advance and launches a surgical right hook directly into that poor lump on his temple. His feet almost tangle. Suddenly all his effort is absorbed by the act of standing upright. Hands reaching, feet skittering, eyes searching. She strikes again. That same hematoma. He tries to cover it. She strikes again, maneuvering through his guard like it's not there. The damn lump is turning black. Kraus nearly looks away. He doesn't flinch from violence, but when a face punch sounds more like a melon being stove in, someone's having a bad day.

Irdessa's bought herself enough time to spread her stance and draw back. Her next punch ends the fight. The lump erupts in blood. His hands drop, head bobbles, and he slumps down and plants his ear in the dirt. His rump is aimed at the moon, like a toddler at the end of a summer day.

Irdessa winces, shaking her fists out, slinging blood. Her knuckles are ravaged. Toady's eyes are open but Kraus is fairly certain he's seeing nothing. There's a dark stream pulsing from the black hematoma that was his left temple. Looks like a rotten tomato struck him and stuck. Kraus has the urge to poke it with something. The red trickle paints over his eyeball, spills into his ear. He doesn't seem to mind.

The crowd erupts. Irdessa tenses. They advance on her, arms outstretched. She bares red teeth at them, wide-eyed, a wolf backed into a corner. For a moment, Kraus fears for their safety. Then they're patting her back, rubbing her rigid shoulders.

"Good show," they say.

"He was asking for it."

"Hell of a punch."

Irdessa's apprehension melts, giving way to a look of profound surprise. A small girl stands before her, looking up with admiring eyes. She's talking in a voice too small for Kraus to hear. Irdessa crouches and puts her arm around the girl, pulling her closer. The girl cups a hand and talks in Irdessa's ear. Irdessa is smiling, nodding. She stands. The little girl joins her people and melds into the crowd. Irdessa's eyes fall on Kraus.

"I'm home," she whispers.

"Irdessa the Undying." The woman's voice is brassy and deep. "You always knew how to make an entrance."

"Bravensi," Irdessa proclaims, throwing her arms around the polearm-bearer's neck. The scowl on the warrior's face softens, but her large eyes remain chisels.

"I'm sorry about your father," Bravensi says. "He was the best man Vim ever knew. Maybe Fohrvylda, for that matter."

"Thank you," Irdessa's words are muffled by Bravensi's shoulder.

"And Torvald ..." Bravensi says. "The world grew dimmer with his passing. I'm sorry."

For a moment they only embrace, swaying back and forth. Kraus takes the opportunity to allow his eyes full access to the white warrior. She's taller than Irdessa by a couple of inches, and thin as a rail. Her hair is drawn up in a black ball high on the back of her head, pulling the skin on her pale face tight over sharp cheeks and a cutting jaw. Her attire is made of black leather and steel chainmail, holding her wiry frame tightly and covering most of her skin. Her lips are thin ribbons, almost blue. Her eyes are shaped like bulging plump lemons, with small black pupils and entirely too much white showing.

"You're beautiful." The words are conceived before Kraus realizes they're true. And even though the woman reacts as if his words were icicles against her skin, even if she cuts him for saying it—hell, even if that's the last thing he ever says—he doesn't regret it.

The woman draws back from Irdessa and looks at Kraus. Her nose wrinkles and her thin lips curl into a frown. "What is that?" she says. Her voice is too loud for her body. It's like an anvil wrapped in chains, and with each word she utters, it swings, demolishing Kraus' defenses, his senses.

"Kraus is a friend," Irdessa says. "Without him ... I wouldn't have made it back."

"That's awful nice, Dess," Kraus says, but his eyes are locked on the snow queen, ice goddess warrior.

"So I can't kill it?" Bravensi says.

"No," Irdessa says. "Thank you."

~

They've gotten clear of the crowd for the most part and are standing in the light of one of the enormous, bowl-shaped braziers. Its flickering flames prevent Kraus from seeing Dhovoi's booth, to check and see if he's still hunting for Irdessa or has sent down his brutes. But viewing Dhovoi is not a priority. His eyes have found their home and it will take nothing less than shrieking death to pry them off her. Bravensi proves to be as resourceful as she is mesmerizing. She stitches Irdessa's lip as if wound care is her profession. She slides her thin hook through Irdessa's flesh with deft fingertips, her black nail paint glimmering in the torchlight, sending butterflies through Kraus' intestines. If only he had a gaping wound.

From a vendor on the pit's outskirts, they procured a skin of wine and a meal that resembles a brood of skinned lizards stretched over skewers and burnt to a crisp, tasting mostly of char and salt. Bravensi had a thin bottle of clear, strong liquor she used to clean Irdessa's wound. Kraus enquired and she was gracious enough to hand it to him, but his thirst has lost its influence.

"Why aren't you with the Vanguard?" Irdessa asks Bravensi. Her swollen lip blunts her words.

"Long story," Bravensi answers with a smile. It seems no facial expression can diminish the width of her eyes. She pulls a strip off her skewer and crunches into it. Her polearm is propped against her chest, with the handle against her neck and the blade looming over her head. "You've got some news to catch up on, Irdessa."

For the first time, Kraus is able to get a good look at her weapon. The handle is longer than he is tall, and the blade itself is ornate. It's steel but a dark, matte variety, and when it moves just right its entire surface twinkles with thin crimson whorls. The edge is blindingly sharp, maybe a foot and a half long, curved on its tip. There are patterns cut out of the blade's body, perhaps to reduce its weight. The effect is that the steel appears to have two crying eyes and a sharp-toothed smile, a visage that appears apologetic for how joyful it is. Kraus cranes his head and the shapes transform. Maybe the etchings are supposed to be foliage. Either way, it is the least practical design he's ever seen on a weapon and must weigh a ton. Staring at it leaves him feeling anxious, as if it stares back and doesn't like what it sees. His eyes are happy to return to Bravensi.

"Why'd you come back here?" Bravensi says.

Irdessa shares a look with Kraus. "It was Torvald's dying wish."

Kraus is appreciative of that description.

"His final act was to distract the archers so I could escape," Irdessa says. Her eyes are glossy, but this time her chin does not thrust forward, her lips do not curl, her chest does not tremble. "And he sent this chopping block along to protect me." She slaps Kraus' shoulder, making several of his injuries cry out.

Kraus allows the proud grin free rein of his face. Bravensi doesn't notice.

"Two years in Keswal," Bravensi muses. "You're both legends, you know."

Irdessa shakes her head. "It was all Torvald. I was only ever ... lucky."

"That's not what I saw," says Kraus.

"If they find out you're alive ..." Bravensi's eyes become intent. "There is no hiding from Promontory."

"I know. They'll know soon enough."

"What will you do?"

"My schedule is fairly open, Bravensi." Irdessa gives a dry chuckle. "What about you? Did you leave the Vanguard?"

Bravensi's smile dissipates. She chews a moment, as if the question didn't happen, and takes a pull from the wineskin. A drop of red wine draws a line over her sharp chin. Kraus' tongue flicks over his lips.

"Got kicked out," Bravensi says.

"Oh gods. What did you do?"

There's a surge in the crowd. A new fight must have begun. Bravensi aims her eyes up at Dhovoi's wooden tower. There's pain on her face. "You won't like what I have to say."

Impossible, Kraus barely keeps himself from blurting. She could describe in detail the process by which the gut of a corpse fills with gas and expands until it explodes bloody piss and shit all over children playing in the street and it would be the sweetest poem Kraus' ears ever knew.

"What happened?" Irdessa says.

Bravensi sets her jaw. "If I tell you this, I can't take it back. And if you believe me ..." Her lips pinch together, thinning into a line. "You'll be the first."

"Bravensi, aside from Kraus, you might be the one living person I trust. Cut to it."

"Dhovoi betrayed the Vanguard. He got you captured."

Irdessa does not react, only watches her friend. But Kraus senses the storm brewing.

"Andelsior's last mission was one Dhovoi set up," Bravensi says. "Pick up the admiral's nephew. Seemed touchy, and that's why Andelsior had to be involved. It was a setup. Torvald knew something was wrong. Andelsior ..." She hesitates, reaches toward Irdessa's shoulder but doesn't touch it. "He was such a good man, Irdessa. But he trusted Dhovoi. And he shouldn't have."

Irdessa's eyes are glossy yet again. Kraus will forgive Bravensi for making Irdessa cry, but only if she proves what she's claimed.

"Keep talking," Irdessa says, her face hardening gradually.

"Dhovoi knew the nephew would be murdered before the Vanguard arrived," Bravensi says. "He knew that would be Andelsior's last job."

"But ... Dhovoi loved my father."

"I thought so too."

"Then why would he do that?"

Bravensi gives a sharp laugh. "There are a hundred reasons. And everyone but you could see them."

"What's that supposed to mean?"

"Dhovoi wasn't content. He wanted the Vanguard to be paid for its work. He wanted more sway in the Vanguard, but without fighting to earn it. He's no fighter. He was jealous of Torvald. He resented the favor Andelsior showed him. He ... wanted you."

Irdessa recoils in surprise. "He what?"

"Oh, Irdessa." Bravensi shakes her head. "He was so jealous. Andelsior wanted nothing more than for you and Torvald to be together. And for that, Dhovoi hated Torvald."

"If that's true and he wanted me, why in the name of every god ..." Irdessa's eyes unfocus. For a painfully long moment she says nothing, instead staring and working the muscles of her jaw. Kraus is beginning to wonder if she's finally snapped once and for all, her mind teetering too far off to return. When she speaks again her voice carries a cold clarity. "I wasn't supposed to be on that mission. When they were arrested, I wasn't supposed to be there."

"No," Bravensi says. "You weren't. And that you were caught is what lent authenticity to Dhovoi's despair. That's how he brewed the Vanguard's anger against Promontory."

Irdessa stands with closed eyes for several moments. When she opens them, she's staring at something distant. "How do you know this?"

Bravensi's squared shoulders lose some authority. "I've never liked Dhovoi. You know that. When you all went down, Oekner and I went directly to him. He's never botched a job. Why now? I figured worst case I'd kill him or let Oekner do it." It's Bravensi's turn to go distant. Looks like she's in pain. When she continues, her voice is lower. "I caught him taking payment. The man paying him was in plain clothes, but it was clearly Promontory." She pinches her eyes closed. "Oekner killed the man before I could stop him. Went to kill Dhovoi too but his protection came to his aid. Oekner killed one of his men. One of the Vanguard. He would have killed every last one of them. It was all I could do to stop him."

Irdessa sits silently again, her busted lip shifting slightly as her tongue roves around the inside of the wound. She's not displaying any emotion, as if it's all spent. That doesn't encourage Kraus. "Oekner killed him?" she asks at last.

Bravensi glares at her polearm. "Yes, unfortunately. You know how rash he can be. Got me kicked out of the Vanguard and destroyed the single most incriminating piece of evidence against Dhovoi."

Kraus isn't sure who Oekner is but he sounds a lot like competition.

Irdessa snorts. "Otherwise, he's well?"

A bashful smile takes Bravensi's angular face, pinching the corners of her eyes and making Kraus' heart ache. Her fingers slide up the length of her weapon's handle. "He's perfect, Irdessa." She's blushing. "He's perfect. He hasn't aged a day."

Kraus is about to say *Who the hell is Oekner, and while we're at it, fuck him*, when Irdessa gives him a glare that could silence a waterfall. He closes his mouth.

"If you knew Dhovoi was not content," Irdessa says, "why didn't you say anything before?"

"Because he was pitiful little Dhovoi. Everyone knew how he felt," Bravensi says. "But no one considered him a threat. No one could have predicted he'd do that." She snorts. "No one believes it now."

Irdessa is staring forward with hands on her knees. "How did Torvald let that happen?" The question is aimed at no one in particular.

"I tried to tell the Vanguard the truth. But ..." Bravensi shakes her head. "... you know what they think of me. All Dhovoi had to tell them was that I'd finally lost all senses and was trying to kill him. He told them I was a threat and they bought it."

Irdessa is shaking her head slowly. Her chin juts forward in a Last Room kind of way. "Torvald knew it."

"I'd be surprised if he didn't," Bravensi says.

"That's why he wanted me to come back here."

Bravensi doesn't respond to this. Kraus decides that's probably wise.

"If what you say is true," Irdessa says, staring far past the brazier's flames that light her eyes, "Dhovoi has to pay. The Vanguard must be told the truth."

"Undoubtedly."

Irdessa rises to her feet.

"Irdessa, there's a way to go about this," Bravensi says. "A time and place. Dhovoi's lavish parties have earned him favor, albeit fickle. He won't go down without a fight."

"I was thinking I'd talk to him right now."

"During his prized pit fight?" Bravensi scoffs. "The one he stocked with Ausgan monsters? You'll never pry his attention off it. No. The Vanguard must be involved. There must be a trial."

Irdessa's eyes linger on Bravensi's long enough for Kraus to sense a challenge.

"You're right," Irdessa says.

Bravensi doesn't look convinced.

"I have to return to him though," Irdessa says. "I accompanied him, after all."

Bravensi nods. Her eyes have hardened into black diamonds. "Have patience, Irdessa. The truth will come out. Dhovoi will pay. Don't act without the Vanguard's consent. You know better."

Irdessa turns her eyes on Kraus. "You've paid your debt to Torvald, Kraus."

"That I have," he says.

Please don't send me away.

"But if you'd join me, I'd be honored to have you."

His heart flutters in his chest and his palms itch so bad his fists squeeze into tight balls. "Lead the way, Dess."

"It's time to get back to the booth, wouldn't you say?"

"That I would."

They stalk away from Bravensi.

Irdessa hisses under her breath. "Torvald didn't die for me to settle in like a roosting chicken and abide this treachery. Not after learning that."

"What do you have in mind?" Kraus asks.

"I want to hear the truth from Dhovoi. I need to hear it from his mouth."

"You expect him to confess to you?"

"Yes."

"You don't believe Bravensi?"

Irdessa stops cold. Kraus follows suit. "I do," she tells him. "Bravensi might be batshit crazy. But I wasn't lying when I told her I trust her."

"That's a ... rude descriptor." Something obligates him to defend Bravensi.

Irdessa laughs as she begins walking again. "No it's not. It's the truth. She'd tell you if she liked you."

"Does she?"

"No," Irdessa slings out the word harshly like sand into Kraus' eye. "And she won't, so don't waste your time."

Kraus follows her and his mind dissects all that has been said, all that has made an impression. "Way I see it," he growls as his knee grinds, "I've wasted enough time chasing things that don't deserve the attention. Maybe she's my final chase." Kraus chuckles at himself. "What do you say to that?"

"I say gods help you."

"Why?" he snorts. "You don't think I can be romanti—" A couple has appeared in his path too abruptly for him to alter his momentum. His knee groans with the sudden effort of diverting his direction. They'd be more likely to notice him and move if they weren't tongue-deep in each other's mouths. Kraus swings a back-arm across them, batting their heads and sending them both sprawling. "Outta the damn way."

Irdessa chuckles. "Then again ..."

"So," Kraus says, "let's say Dhovoi confesses, then what?"

Irdessa shakes her head. "I don't know." This admission doesn't appear to worry her. "Bravensi said Dhovoi wants me." She gives Kraus a smile. "Let's find out how much."

27
Her Purpose Fulfilled

FOHRVYLDA
The Pit, Vim

Deception, as a tool in your arsenal, means the difference between life and death in Keswal. In the same way a shopkeep might smile regretfully and utter, "That's as low a price as I can offer," while he scalps you, Irdessa played weak when she was strong. She feinted right before running left. She attacked high when looking low. She puffed out her chest and stamped her foot when scared and wounded. Torvald introduced her to the finer points of deception in combat. Bruises and bleeding etched his lessons into her bones.

But as she climbs the rickety staircase to Dhovoi's wooden perch to slip through a combined six hundred pounds of silent armor and interrogate the alderman under the guise of harmless, hapless refugee, she feels horribly unqualified. Too much is happening too quickly. There isn't time to think—about the state of Vim, about Dhovoi's intentions for her, hidden or otherwise, about Bravensi's words, her warning. It was simpler when her one concern was to be among the last standing. *Never thought I'd miss Keswal.*

Irdessa's boots pad up the rough timbers. Kraus follows with Bravensi's bottle of liquor and a giddy, hound-on-the-hunt enthusiasm. There's something at once heartening and unsettling about having Kraus on your side.

The brutes, Sarsen and Visent, haven't moved since she left, and Irdessa slips between them before they notice she's returned. Dhovoi is gripping the railing, watching the fight with his back to her. His neck is exposed. Irdessa touches the handle of the thin knife against the inside of her wrist, hidden behind her bracer. Dhovoi's hand raises to idly poke fingers through the hair on his neck and give his skin a scratch. Irdessa's mind travels to a memory from sometime before Keswal.

"Do you think they'll make it back?" Irdessa asked Dhovoi while they watched her father, Torvald, and a dozen of the Vanguard's more grizzled fighters filing from Vim at dusk.

Dhovoi took her chin in his shaking hand and aimed her face at his. *"They always do. But if not, I'll never let anything happen to you."*

She'd laughed and slapped his hand away. *"You're more likely to need my sword than I am yours."*

He had not laughed. *"Surviving is not all about fighting, Irdessa. You have to be crafty and clever."*

And then, clueless to the weight of her words, Irdessa had said, *"You mean like Torvald?"*

Only now, looking back, does Irdessa understand why Dhovoi's mood turned dark at that moment. She must find out the depth of truth in what Bravensi told her. If Bravensi was right, Dhovoi has to answer for what he did. But if Dhovoi saw Irdessa talking to her, she may not get the chance to question him. She should ready the dagger—

A gloved vise closes on Irdessa's bicep, squeezing it so hard Irdessa gives a *yip!* She's nearly lifted off her feet. It's one of the brutes.

"Hey, friend," Kraus says, stuffing himself between the walking metal cask and Irdessa. He aims his scarred face up into the depths of the steel helm. "Try grabbing me."

The brute's twin reaches for Kraus.

"What's happening?" Dhovoi turns his highly arched eyebrow on the four of them.

The brutes freeze.

"Seems your guard forgot we're friends," Irdessa says, her toes scrabbling for hold on the floor.

Dhovoi slaps at a metal-clad hand. "Visent, turn her loose. What's gotten into you?"

The brutes hesitantly stand down.

Kraus hiccups and points a finger in one's face. "Ya got lucky, cunt." He turns up the bottle he got from Bravensi. The liquor smells so strong it singes Irdessa's nostrils. *Look drunk, Kraus. Don't be drunk.*

"By the gods, Irdessa, what happened to your face?" Dhovoi holds her chin delicately and inspects her lip.

"Someone in the crowd made a poor decision." She keeps her eyes steel. Dhovoi looks like he wants to ask more. He also looks somewhat disgusted by her stitched wound, which is still oozing. It's swollen so thick she can't speak clearly. To someone outside Keswal, wherein wounds are the way of life, it surely looks repulsive. Especially someone as soft as this man. Irdessa pulls away from his touch and moves beside him to watch the fight. "He won't be making more."

"Who stitched you up?" Dhovoi asks, his alarm having mostly dissipated.

"That'd be me." Kraus raises his bottle. Liquor splashes out onto his shaven scalp. He hisses in pain.

Dhovoi spares him the briefest glance. "I was worried," he says, giving Irdessa's shoulder a squeeze. "But I should have known better. You could always handle yourself, couldn't you?"

It takes all her restraint not to shake his hand off. Instead she forces a smile at him and turns her attention on the crowd.

"Well," Dhovoi says, grinning, "you've had a look around. What do you think of it?"

The crowd surges, in response to some yelled announcement.

"It's ... impressive." Irdessa has to shout to be heard, and luckily that seems to have made her lie palatable, since Dhovoi nods in agreement. Then again, Dhovoi seems tragically unaware of himself or much of anything else. Down in the arena, some sort of salivating, overly tall and long-limbed boar has been pitted against three shirtless men with spears.

"I was thinkin'," Kraus roars at one of the silent brutes, before belching up into his helmet. "Fellow of your talents? Shit, I'm not sure how you settled for a single job."

Irdessa spares them a glance. Neither brute acknowledges Kraus, despite that he, in an attempt to stand still, is dancing around the deck as if it's a ship in a storm.

"Say..." He hoists up his bottle. The lip of it clinks off the left brute's plate armor. "If a fellow half your size ... could do your job ... for less coin than you ... or less food than you..." Kraus takes a break to catch up with his own equation and have a hearty swig. "Hell, the alderman could save himself some coin, couldn't he? On food expenses alone."

Irdessa needs to bring the conversation to Andelsior. She's not sure how, but it'll involve saying something. "Oh!" She feigns fascination. "What is that?"

Dhovoi crosses his arms over his chest proudly. "That, Irdessa, is a warthound. Also originating from beneath the palms of Ausgan. And the men are playing Ausgan natives."

"You have built ... quite an exciting arena here, Dhovoi," she says. It sounds like she's reading the words. Luckily, flattery of any sort seems to bypass Dhovoi's wariness. Or perhaps, flattery from *her*.

"I'm not so hungry," Kraus is telling the brute. He's thrown an arm over the giant shoulders for support. "More thirsty, you know? Bet I could do your job. And save the aldermoney." He hiccups, then squawks a laugh. "Aldermoney!"

The brute could just as easily be annoyed by Kraus or oblivious to him. But soon enough, and with enough liquor, Kraus will get bored with talking. Irdessa needs to get on with it.

"How did you rise so quickly?" Irdessa says. Not exactly a natural segue but she has to put Bravensi's allegation to the test.

Dhovoi's eyebrows hop upward in question.

"I mean, in the Vanguard." She tries to smooth the transition with a smile, and is painfully reminded of the busted lump that is her upper lip.

"Your father's arrest threw the Vanguard into disorder," he answers. "I was the first to step forward. Old Fent argued against confrontation, but the truth is that Vim would have been overrun by the Domestic Patrol if no one had acted."

"Of course," Irdessa says. "I'm glad it was someone who cared for Vim and the Vanguard who stepped up."

"Mhmm." Dhovoi nods, his attention spilling back into the pit. He's essentially absent from the conversation.

The entire wooden floor rocks abruptly and Irdessa has to grab the railing to keep her feet.

"Is that all you got, bitch?" Kraus sputters. He's lying on his back. The brute who'd been tolerating Kraus' armpit has blood leaking from his lip. His head pivots from Kraus to his boss.

"Sarsen!" Dhovoi scolds. The brute shrugs his pillars of arms. Dhovoi looks to Kraus. "Did you hit him? You know he can kill you, right?"

"He can try." Kraus rises shakily, bottle intact, and looks in Sarsen's general direction. "Not a bad throw," he says, drunken discernment wrinkling his craggy brow. "Sometimes size is wasted on a person. Not you. Got a decent jaw too." Kraus stumbles forward, then backward. Either he's mimicking a fighting stance or struggling to stay upright. "Lemme show y'a trick I learned from a Vedorant goblin. Used his smaller size to his advantage. Goes like this."

"That's enough for now, don't you think?" Irdessa makes her words louder than the crowd's ruckus.

Kraus scoffs, launching saliva on the brute's armor. With the same fist that grips his bottle, he points toward Sarsen. "Got lucky 'gain."

"You do care for Vim," Irdessa says to Dhovoi before his attention can escape again. "Don't you?"

He looks at her as if it's a ridiculous question. "More than anything, I do."

"And my father, you cared for him."

"I loved him as if he was my own father."

"And Torvald, did you care for him?"

"Of course." Dhovoi's enthusiasm withers. "He was ... like a brother."

"And me? Was I like a sister?"

Dhovoi turns to her with such a wounded expression that in a single moment Bravensi's words transform from accusation to fact. "No. You weren't." He takes her shoulders and moves his face so close to hers she can smell the scented oil in his trim beard. "There are things I want to say to you. Things I should have long since said. I thank the gods I have the opportunity to do so. I won't waste it again."

His eyes are bright, his primly bearded smile authentic. Such enthusiasm he has, such justification he feels. Irdessa's stomach heaves. This is exactly the direction she wanted the conversation to go. But now that it has, she is physically repulsed.

"Things?" she asks. "Why wouldn't you have told me before?"

Anger flashes over Dhovoi's eyes and he hammers his fist on the wooden rail. "I tried! Torvald was always—" His eyes dart to hers. Fear peeks through. "He was always around you. And it was like ..." He hesitates, no longer confident.

Irdessa turns to the pit, releasing Dhovoi from her gaze. "It was like my father wanted me to be with Torvald," she says, as if the idea exhausts her, as if it plagued her for too long. In truth, it hadn't occurred to her until Bravensi's talk.

"Exactly," Dhovoi breathes a sigh. She's not looking at him but the relief in his voice is thick. "Your father was as in love with Torvald as Torvald was in love with you. I never stood a chance at ..." He trails off sheepishly.

Torvald was in love with me? Even then? It's through every deceptive muscle she knows how to flex that she maintains her facade, prevents her chest from trembling. Even Dhovoi knew it? Irdessa has always prided herself on having at least a fraction of Torvald's gift of perception. And yet she had been appallingly blind.

"But now I'm here," she says gently, inflecting into her voice the despair that is, these days, all too available.

"You are," Dhovoi says, "and when I saw you my heart grew lighter than it has been since you left. Please forgive me for saying this, but it was even lighter since you came alone."

"Alone?" Kraus yells. "What'm I? Chopped ... fucking ... kidneys?"

Dhovoi flinches at Kraus' outburst. "No, not alone. I only meant without..." He gestures indirectly, his lips smacking, his eyes flitting from Kraus to Irdessa.

"I know what you mean," Irdessa says, suppressing a sudden rage. *You mean, since Torvald is dead.* But she keeps her lips sealed and paints on her face a wan, regretful smile as she takes his hand in hers. It is damp, soft. Not like Torvald's. Not like hers.

"I wish you had talked to me then," she says. That is the truth. "Instead of doing nothing." Her final words fall, along with her shoulders, like a dropped dinner platter.

"Oh, Irdessa." He grabs her other hand and pulls them both to the leather on his chest. "I did not exactly ... do nothing." He's breathing heavily. In his eyes is a jittery mixture of terror and anticipation.

Irdessa makes her shoulders small, her eyes round, her lips lusty, however disgusting they might look. She is a smear of cheese on the pressure plate of a sharpened steel trap and Dhovoi is the rat. He need only be himself.

"What did you do?" she whispers, suffusing her gaze with all the admiration she can counterfeit.

A sheen of sweat has risen on his rippling forehead. He wears the face of the boy she remembers, the one whose eyes stared into hers, ripe with trepidation, desperate to say something but always terrified. Now she understands his oddities before. *You never had the courage as a child. Have it now.*

He is teetering on the precipice. She caresses his clammy fingers. *Confess. I'll take care of the rest. I'll do what Torvald sent me back here to do.* "It's alright," she coaxes.

Confess!

He inhales. "Irdessa, I have to tell you something." He swallows noisily. "And I ask beforehand that you consider my motive above all else. And my intent."

"Of course, Dhovoi," she breathes. *Confess.* "Please tell me."

His eyes are wide now and rimmed along the bottom with bulbous tears. "I never meant you to get hurt."

Irdessa's heart punches her ribs. Fire blooms into her cheeks. Her fingers twitch. She's staring into the fearful face of a childhood friend but seeing the surprise in Torvald's eyes as he dies.

Dhovoi takes another breath. "When you got arrested, I—"

There's a shriek from the crowd. Then another. The drunken din is capsized as waves of panic ripple out from somewhere south of the pit.

He releases her hands, releases her stare, releases the moment, and she knows at once it's gone, leaving her shuddering, icy and empty.

There is a flurry of movement on the far side of the arena. Flashes of silver plate, black and white fur—movement too jerky to be absent of violence. Something is tearing through the mob. Several things. Perhaps half a dozen. Steel helmets. Swinging swords. Now Irdessa hears the growls, the barks, the piercing howls. Her heart skips. Orcanes. And the people they're hacking into are unarmed. By the look of it, they're here to kill everyone.

Irdessa's hands ache for javelins, as if two would avail her. She cuts her eyes at Kraus. He has dropped all semblance of inebriation. As one, the two brutes pull forth their bucklers and cudgels, their helmets aimed at the commotion.

"Promontory?" Dhovoi blurts, snatching the railing. "By Lahuvot's great fiery cock, what are they doing here?"

They're ruining your party. Irdessa grits her teeth. *And mine.*

Angry black orbs reflect red fire as darting orcane jaws snatch up men, women, arms, hips, heads, crushing them, tearing them off, slinging them into darkness, into the pit, into braziers. One of the massive fire bowls tips over, spilling its glowing contents down on the lower rows of the arena. Some of the embers cling to clothing and fur, igniting into flames, making the alarmed crowd devolve into chaos.

The orcanes are moving around the pit toward Dhovoi's perch, and behind them come soldiers. Scores of them. Every civilian sword in the panicked throng, no matter how brave, is hindered by its neighbors. People are scattering into the darkness. Some run toward town, some to the black night outside the compromised city wall.

"*We had a godsdamned deal!*" Alderman Dhovoi roars into the fray.

More fire bowls are tipped over as soldiers and their mounts converge on the pit. Embers dot the earth, some lying static on the ground, some clinging to garments and flying through darkness like shooting stars. The tower itself lurches as one of the great bowls collides with it. Fire is spreading. One of the brutes has the sense to take Dhovoi by the arm, pull him away from the rickety rail and toward the stair. Irdessa has no choice but to follow, even though the door to the truth has slammed closed. For now. Survive first, always. Regroup. Torvald visits her, *Just as the oak can topple if erosion compromises her roots, plans that cannot adapt are fated for ruin.*

Their escape from the loft is interrupted as a fully armored captain of the Domestic Patrol ascends to the platform. The brutes advance on him, raising their short clubs high. Irdessa recognizes him at once and lowers her face beneath her hood. It's Captain Jeret, perhaps the most corrupt of Marshal Zander's soldiers, and proud of it.

"Hold it," the captain says, his hand on his sword's hilt. More helmeted guards follow him up, one by one, with hammered steel shoulder-pieces and coats of chainmail. Some bear torches, all bear swords. There are four in addition to the captain, making for a total of ten bodies occupying this horribly under-qualified platform. The floor sways and creaks with their weight. The brutes go still.

"Alderman Dhovoi," Captain Jeret purrs with a narrow smile. His pointy chin and jaw are shaved to a glossy sheen.

Irdessa keeps her head low, shoulders narrow, positioning herself behind Dhovoi and placing a hand on his lower back to remind him she's there, she's afraid. To outsiders, she imagines she looks nothing like Dhovoi's usual company. Too much clothing or too little muscle. But there are too many Promontory eyes up here for her subterfuge to last. Never before has she resented being Irdessa the Undying more than this moment.

Aside from his fine coat, Kraus, with his hacked-up face, could pass for any old pit fighter. Hopefully, between his new scars and lack of oily beard and hair, the soldiers won't immediately recognize him. But he's staring so vehemently at the captain that it's only a matter of time before he draws attention to himself.

With the silent grace of an old tree plummeting to earth for its final rest, Sarsen brings his metal club down on the closest guard's shiny helmet. The helmet crushes inward, lodges in the breastplate and sticks there. The soldier gushes blood, flounders to the deck, spasming. Sarsen lifts his club again but the three remaining soldiers strike first. One sword is deflected off the brute's chest. One buries in the groove in his armor between bicep and armpit. One digs up into that steel cap, in the area of the brute's nose. An eruption of blood is the brute's response. Sarsen's giant, armored body totters back and crashes to the wooden floor. Several planks creak and snap.

"Visent, stand down!" Dhovoi shrieks, grabbing his remaining brute by the arm, not that his weight could have any effect on the brute's momentum. Visent aims his steel cap at his twin. His club quivers in the air but does not fall. The guards regain their line, all swords aimed at Dhovoi's lone armored mute.

"Captain Jeret, we had a deal." Dhovoi's proclamation bears less rage, more despair, now that his guard is halved and he's confronted with so much sharp steel.

"Ah yes, our deal." Jeret paces between the club of the massive brute and the swords of his hard-eyed men. He's smiling, his hands folded behind his back. "You'll be fine. We're here to make sure you don't get any ideas. The Vanguard on the other hand ..." He widens his eyes in anticipation and lets a sly smile complete his sentence.

Irdessa's ears pick up what sounds like termites ravaging a plank of timber. It's Kraus. His fingernails are digging open a scab on the back of his hand, and his eyes, locked on the smirking captain, look like they might vibrate from their sockets.

"My people. Vim's people." Dhovoi flings his hand over the clamor, where mounted orcanes dash back and forth in the scattering mob like marlins taking apart a school of sardine. "My guard," he sputters. "I give Marshal Zander more convicts than anyone in Fohrvylda. This is my payback?"

"Oh, ease up on the charade," the captain says. "Andelsior gave convicts. You sell them. We know who you care about. And it's not Vim, or your guard, or some disposable wench." He aims a smile at Irdessa's chin, hopefully the only part of her face not shrouded in the shadows of her hood. He hasn't recognized her. But now the eyes of his soldiers rove even more curiously.

"You got too comfortable here, Dhovoi," Captain Jeret says. "That little rebellion of yours ..." He *tsks*. "It stung, you know? And now you're using the marshal's men as arena fodder? You knew this wouldn't last forever. As of now, Vim's Vanguard are outlaws. The lot of them. Those who survive the day will be hunted down and eventually fed to Keswal's birds."

"I paid for this," Dhovoi seethes.

"Paid? Or betrayed?" the captain asks.

Dhovoi's eyes dart to Irdessa's and his face pales.

Her blood boils. *Guilty!*

Captain Jeret scoffs. "Judging by your current position, I'd think your little trick did you favors."

"Bastards." Dhovoi is trembling. "Promontory wanted Vim's blood. It always has. If I hadn't fought back, you would have raped this town dry."

"Guess you should have thought of that before you pulled your bait and switch on Vim's old guard, *Alderman*." Jeret's last word is dripping with sarcasm.

One of the soldiers is kneeling. Irdessa was so intent on filtering information from Jeret and Dhovoi's conversation she only noticed him out of the corner of her eye, and thought he was adjusting a strap. He wasn't. He was peering up into her hood. Now he's aimed his sword at her and is whispering frantically at the soldier beside him.

"Before Andelsior," Captain Jeret says, "Vim was nothing. And after him?" He crinkles his eyes, as if delivering hard news. His smirk is immovable. "It's kind of gone back to shit, wouldn't you say? The Vanguard should have stuck to picking up feces."

Dhovoi's jaw is clenching. He looks like he's on the verge of angry tears. "This is wrong," he utters in a wavering voice. "You think everything you see belongs to you. Vretos has no control over you savages. All he cares about is his precious Keswal and his promised war. The *Heathen fucking Tide.*"

Now the captain's smile threatens to deteriorate. "Watch your mouth, Dhovoi. Admiral Garr made peace with his nephew's murder when Andelsior paid for it in the arena. Doesn't mean he can't make peace all over again. Our deal stands. That's why you'll live while the Vanguard dies. Every last member, man, woman, child. But try your luck and you can join the ashes." He scoffs. "As if you're so noble. You destroyed the best thing Vim had going for it when you sold out Andelsior." He waves a black-gloved hand toward the carnage below. "This is your fault."

Irdessa's heart assaults her ribs. Dhovoi looks at her, terror all over his face. The fire rushing through her veins is not to be contained. Her fingers twitch for the dagger at her wrist. There is no abating this. Not until Dhovoi is dead.

A soldier hisses into the captain's ear. Jeret's head tilts toward the whispering guard, then his gaze eases over to Irdessa. His smile turns round, incredulous. His hand finds his sword.

"Dhovoi," the captain says in wonder, breaking into a chuckle. "Oh, ho-ho-ho. Are you holding out on me, Alderman?" Captain Jeret takes a step toward Irdessa. The rasp of his sword slowly being drawn cuts through the frenzied ruckus of the pit.

The alderman's face blanches. His head swivels about. He has no weapon to grab and so he grabs the wrist of his brute, stepping away from Irdessa as if she's a freshly unearthed ghast.

Irdessa sees Kraus' black eyes leap from the captain to her. She swipes a discreet hand parallel to the planks. *Hold!*

All eyes plant on her, burning through her disguise. For the first time since the battlefield of Keswal, Irdessa feels the singeing grip of utter clarity burning away all fear, all indecision.

Assess your goal. Determine the obstacle. Overcome.

There is no possibility of a trial for Dhovoi. Jeret means to end the Vanguard. Therefore, Dhovoi's sentence must be determined and delivered by Irdessa. That sentence is swift death. Here. *Now.* The obstacle is Captain Jeret. His armed men. Maybe Visent, Dhovoi's surviving brute. This isn't the deadliest mob she's faced. But she's swapped Keswal for a narrow deck swamped in the blood of dead men and crowded by their fallen corpses. She's swapped Torvald for Kraus. Although Kraus is as die-hard as a carpet of chokewort, he's no Tactician.

She and Kraus—armed with her thin knife and his liquor bottle— against three soldiers with swords, a cocky captain, a brute with a steel table-leg, and a backstabbing coward with a nicely groomed beard and a hard-on for whores. It would seem they haven't a blind man's chance in Keswal. Fighting against these odds would end her story before she could see her purpose fulfilled.

You've established what is not possible, Torvald whispers in her ear. *So what is?*

Captain Jeret's sword is touching her hood, lifting it carefully, exposing her face for all to see. Crisp night air welcomes her cheeks and neck. The soldiers, even the one who outed her to begin with, all gasp and take a step back. Even as all on Dhovoi's perch have gone silent, the battle below rages on.

"By the gods." Jeret's voice is softened by admiration. "You really are undying, aren't you?" He looks at Kraus now, for the first time. "And you are?" His eyes fall on Kraus' bottle. "Thirsty Rapist? We just keep running into each other. What happened to your face?"

What is not possible, Irdessa answers Torvald, *is that I go on living in the same world as Dhovoi.*

Torvald would understand. *If your goal cannot change,* he offers, *your means of accomplishing it must.*

Irdessa draws in a great, gradual Keswal breath. She takes control of her pounding heart, her rushing lungs. She slowly lifts both hands, palms toward the captain.

"I surrender," she says.

28
There is No Forgetting

FOHRVYLDA
Dhovoi's Booth, Vim

Kraus' ears must have failed him. Surrender? Surely not. *That's the chicken fucker who locked me up!* he wants to yell at Irdessa. He might owe her his life, but surrender is not an exercise he's willing to get familiar with. This is a good moment to hurt people, not go ass-up.

Despite Irdessa's apparent submission, her eyes elicit a calm clarity from Kraus. She's wearing her battle face. Perhaps due to his own curiosity, or a degree of masochism, Kraus cannot help but trust her and see this out.

The captain has aimed two of his soldiers at Kraus, while he and the last confront Irdessa.

"Let's get you both contained, shall we?" Jeret says, so exultant he's almost melodic. Kraus would never have believed the man's taut smile could be any more sickening. And yet ...

The captain holds his sword toward Irdessa's heart while his soldier sheathes his blade and draws a length of rope.

"Before I go," Irdessa says in a small voice. "Please, let me say goodbye. I never thought ..." Her eyes fall on Dhovoi and her chest gives a small seize. "I never thought I'd see you again."

Kraus marvels at her display. It's like she can alter her size.

Dhovoi clings to his metal-clad companion, and wisely so. Bravensi was right. He's a rat bastard needing steel to stir his guts. He stares at Irdessa with round eyes and a bleached face.

The captain shrugs, keeping his sword aimed at her. "Make it fast."

She sniffles, pulls hair from her sticky cheek with limp fingers. "If I hadn't been arrested, we could have been together before now." She sidles toward the alderman. Her meek act seems to warm him gradually to her approach. Perhaps he's emboldened by the swords aimed at her. He moves to meet her with a trembling lip. He wraps his arms around her shoulders, pulling her forehead to his cheek. Her arms tighten weakly at his lower back.

"Irdessa." His shaky whisper is loud enough for all to hear. "If only I had time to explain myself. I will get you out of this."

"Not likely," the captain says.

"Promontory owes Vim," Dhovoi responds to the captain, apparently enlivened by his embrace with the Undying.

The captain scoffs, twisting his thin mouth in a leer. "A reckoning. And here it is."

Irdessa is trembling. If Kraus didn't know better, he'd take it as authentic weeping. Dhovoi pulls her closer.

"Maybe ..." Irdessa's voice is so weak, yet loud enough to cover the deck. "... you could tell me what it is you always wanted to tell me."

"It was my fault you all went down," Dhovoi says quickly, pausing for a rapid breath, "and I never meant it to happen to you. I love you, Irdessa. I always have." Now Dhovoi's cheeks are wet with tears and he's smiling as if a weight has lifted off his shoulders. Irdessa has ceased her shivering, gone fully rigid.

The soldiers are awkwardly flicking glances at him. Jeret taps a toe impatiently, not relenting his aimed sword in the least. Visent watches his master with a deflated posture. Kraus' guts are nearly boiling over in anticipation, and he must exercise every effort to not peel back his own skin.

"Dhovoi." Now Irdessa's voice is lower so that Kraus has to crane his head to hear. "Do you know what happened to the last man who told me he loved me?"

The alderman sniffs, runs his sleeve under his nose while still embracing Irdessa. "Tell me," he whispers.

Irdessa is adjusting her embrace, fiddling with her wrist. She pulls her head back so that her eyes meet Dhovoi's. His face is awash in tears and snot. Hers bears all the emotion of a cliff.

"He fed the birds."

Dhovoi's eyebrow has time to climb halfway up his forehead. Then there's a thump and his teeth bare in agony. Irdessa yanks the knife out of his back, swings the blade across his throat. His tongue flicks out, his eyes bulge, his neck spews red, and she's freed from his embrace. Irdessa's knife flashes again and crunches wetly into the side of Dhovoi's head. The blow knocks his eyes out of sync. It's such a quick and brutal attack even Kraus stands stupefied, blinking, hot blood on his cheek. Then his senses snap into sharp focus.

"Finally!" he roars. He kicks the knee out from under the closest soldier and snatches the man's torch as he falls. Before anyone else can catch their wits, Kraus covers the distance between himself and Captain Jeret in a single hearty stride, clipping the chin of the other guard with his black pauldron and spinning the man around. Kraus stretches wide the torch and liquor bottle like one of Keswal's cymbalists, preparing for the finale. The captain has time only to acknowledge his fate. His sneer sizzles away like butter in a pan as he tries to turn his sword to bear.

Kraus swings his arms closed, clapping Jeret's head with torch and bottle. The bottle explodes in a white blast and the liquor ignites with the sound of a great wing flapping. In a blink, Jeret's clean-shaven chin, his thin neck, his sharp black widow's peak, and his please-fucking-punch-me mouth go up in writhing blue flames.

Kraus shields his face from the heat, and sees Dhovoi drop to his knees, his disjointed pupils searching the night sky and the deck all at once, his mouth working out red sputtering bubbles as one of his skinny fingers digs at the ravine in his neck. Irdessa kicks him off the end of her knife. The remaining brute catches him before his body can hit the planks.

"Kraus, with me!" Irdessa shouts, interrupting his laughter, and throws herself over the railing.

Kraus' heart thuds with the force of a sledgehammer. *Jump?* His hand is on fire. Captain Jeret has gone down squirming, shrieking. One soldier is fixated on the massive brute, who cradles Dhovoi's body pitifully, his chin aimed at his fallen twin. The other two soldiers are coming at Kraus. Their eyes are wide, unsure, and there is no certainty to their steps. As much as Kraus would like to offer them both a lesson in bleeding profusely, he's got no blade. He hurls himself at the railing as they lunge for him.

Like everything in Kraus' life, with the sole exception of setting Captain Jeret's head on fire, his escape attempt goes nothing like he'd hoped. He undershoots the rail's height by a foot. His inner thigh thuds against the railing. The wood cracks, but not before raking up the inside of his leg and giving his stones an indelicate squishing. His gut lurches into his throat and he feels like a large urn teetering on a shaking pedestal—an urn with a plate of steel on its windward shoulder. He tips over and plummets.

There's no time to yell, or swear, or take a breath, or pull his hands off his crotch. Kraus collides with something bony that gives a sharp *yelp!* and flattens beneath him. He clambers up, one hand still cupping his balls, his gag reflexes rattling dangerously.

Down here among the flipped firepits and frenzied townsfolk, it's not so clear anymore what the hell is going on. But at least there's breathing room. The dispersing crowd makes room for Vim's willing defenders to organize in groups against the soldiers, and skirmishes abound. At a glance one might think Vim has a chance turning back these enemies. But Kraus got a good look at the invaders before falling from Dhovoi's stand. A solid mass of soldiers, organized in rows, breaching the fence. There must be two hundred of them, and that's only what Kraus could see. They'll crush this mob. Kraus and Irdessa have no choice but to run. He tries to find her, but is too deep in the pandemonium. To his right, a riderless orcane is nipping at a bludgeontail, which, when you're in range of its tail, turns out to be way bigger than it looks. More like a bale of hay than an ox. The mound of yellow scales spins and gives the orcane a crack on the snout with its club. The barkshark squeals and scampers backward, its lower jaw swinging limp. How the yellow ox got up out of the pit is anyone's guess.

"Let's go," Irdessa calls. Kraus spots her at last, fifteen yards up the hill in the direction of Vim. Seems she's just disentangled herself from an altercation that left a Promontory soldier lying face down in the dirt. The light of the scattered fires illuminates her, highlighting her wounded lip. Another soldier runs at her from behind.

"Check your south!" Kraus hisses through his teeth, prying his hand off his crotch. He can acknowledge pain later. The crick in his knee takes no precedence over a crushed testicle and ribs battered by his landing.

Irdessa turns in time to engage the soldier. Kraus rushes to assist her but something crashes into him from the left. His feet tangle in the body that broke his fall and he flounders down. A figure piles atop him, struggling to rise. Kraus quickly gets his hands around a neck and squeezes. It's a soldier, and his collision with Kraus seems not to have been deliberate. His back is against Kraus, and now that he's being choked, he hasn't got much means of helping himself. Kraus squeezes until the bony throat crunches. This doesn't improve the soldier's mood, instead sending him into a flailing, wheezing panic. Before Kraus can squirm out from under the mailed man, two brown-clad Vim scrappers with short spears approach. Their heads pivot all about as they search the skirmish for opportunity, but quickly converge on the writhing soldier. He seems to be exactly what they were after, and soon they stand over him, stabbing him through belly and breast.

"Quit the godsdamned poking," Kraus yells, squirming to keep his own belly spear-free. "I already killed him."

The men take their blades and move on, even as more soldiers fill the space. Kraus gets himself out from under the corpse and rises quickly, against the protests of his aching body. This fight's looking less promising by the moment, and he's tasted as much of it as he cares to. He scoops the soldier's sword up and rises in time to dodge awkwardly under the swing of a yellow, melon-sized bone mallet. The huge tail thuds into a skirmishing villager's back, crushing him into the soldier he was fighting. Kraus steps away, tries to get his heading. There's Dhovoi's perch, succumbing to flame, and there's the hill. Before he can get to it, an orcane is in his path. It's snapping at a group of three townsfolk waving fiery sticks to hold it off. The soldier on the beast's back, however, sees Kraus and decides he's more worthy of a spearing. Without pausing to think, Kraus lunges forward past the soldier's spear and shoves his sword into the orcane's flank all the way to the handle. The beast yips and rears, throwing the soldier and yanking the weapon away, leaving Kraus empty-handed. Not that he was ever much of a swordsman anyway. He breaks into motion before the flood of soldiers can wash over him.

The remaining people of Vim clash with the orcanes and soldiers. Without the press of the panicked crowd to hinder them, the armed citizens aren't such easy pickings, even if they are becoming outnumbered. In some cases they're forming ranks, giving the snapping orcanes more resistance than perhaps the soldiers expected.

Kraus labors up the hill, swinging both arms for balance, when a bear trap snaps shut on his left bicep, halting him mid-step. "What the—?"

He's yanked from the ground, tossed spinning, watching embers and stars twirl around him. Hard earth punches him and he rolls. Flat on his back with smoke whirling upward, the orcane bite wound on his arm makes itself manifest. His breathing staggers and his vision blanches around the edges. Torn skin. Torn muscle? Bruised bone, maybe even fractured.

Pain'll fix everything.

A spark of nauseating pleasure bores deep into his gut, coiling his intestines around it like an invasive trident. He remembers Irdessa, waiting for him somewhere up the hill. She might need him. *There is no time for this.* He's able to sit up before the pain takes over.

A barkshark is skulking his way, its wide head sitting low on its shoulders, a rumbling growl vibrating the air, orange firelight gleaming off ebony spheres. The man sitting on its saddle has a diseased look about him. His twinkling black eyes peer out from under a sloping brow, and his sharp shoulders hunch forward. His well-fitted armor is of the Domestic Patrol. He is high ranking, a lieutenant at least, not a captain.

"I remember you." The man's tongue flicks over his lips. "From the ambush."

The coiled posture of the orcane gives Kraus second thoughts about standing up, or moving quickly—not that he could if he tried. He extends his ravaged arm, rotates it in a circle. Shoulder's not dislocated.

"Ambush?" Kraus asks, as much to buy time as anything else. He doesn't remember much from his final ambush, assuming that's the one this ugly cunt's referring to. Pirate ale. Puking. That smirking captain. And judging by the screams, that prick hasn't gotten his face fire extinguished yet. This man's gaunt visage brings with it no memories.

"Sorry," Kraus says, squeezing his fist to make sure it still works. "You didn't make an impression." Blood seeps between his fingers.

The man gives a spiteful, coughing laugh. "Didn't I? You haven't paid for your crimes yet, have you? For raping that girl."

Kraus freezes. Some naive, protective part of his mind had convinced him he'd forgotten. But there are her eyes, dull and glassy, clouding over, moist meals for those lucky skittering scavengers who arrive the quickest. Upon Kraus' soul, her eyes are a secret laceration of which there is no scabbing over. There is no forgetting.

"Who are you?" Kraus asks the soldier. Not like it matters. Won't change anything. Won't undo the evil.

"I'm the death of you," the soldier says, flicking his rein. The orcane lowers on its forelegs, tightening like a spring.

Kraus hauls himself to his feet. If he's gonna die, best do it standing. He hasn't got a weapon, but maybe he can throw a punch down the thing's throat. Not much other choice than that besides letting it pull him apart. In this moment, that has its appeal.

The orcane makes to leap. Then a blinding red crescent flickers in the air like the path of a great firefly, intersecting the beast's neck.

There stands Bravensi, the snowy goddess, her polearm returning to her side. The orcane's mouth falls open and blood erupts over its tongue like a wine cask whose spigot broke off. Malice melts from the beast's posture in a single shudder. Its eyes turn lifeless as it hunkers down to die. The man in its saddle spills forward and tumbles down its neck. He lands on his rump with a bark of pain but gets to his feet quickly, slinging his beady eyes from Bravensi to Kraus. He staggers away, his dying animal between him and Bravensi, one hand squeezing at his lower back. Kraus couldn't chase the man if he wanted to, and not just because of his wounds.

"I had to pick one of them to kill," Bravensi notes without emotion, watching the man descend into the fray to summon help. Her eyes could not be more indifferent. But they are still her eyes and they rinse through Kraus' strife the way tincture does a dirty wound. "If I'd killed the man, the barkshark would have gone wild."

"Should'a done it anyway," Kraus says, struck once more by the weight her voice places in his guts. It's prevailing, like pain, but sweeter.

"No." Bravensi doesn't look at him. "I value my life."

"I value your life, too," Kraus tells her.

"Don't bother."

"It's not up to me anymore." Kraus watches her intently. "I owe you."

Bravensi stalks past Kraus, giving her weapon a spin to sling off the blood. "You don't owe me anything. Where is Irdessa?"

Kraus points toward the city. "Last I saw her, she was that way."

Bravensi runs off before he finishes answering. Her lithe frame in motion, her fearful mastery of such a unique weapon, her cold face and eyes and skin, the sheer enigma of her ... it all serves to inebriate Kraus, like strong liquor but without all the effort of drinking it.

He's chasing her and his gimped knee can go to hell. "I do owe you. And I will repay the debt," he calls. There's no indication she hears. Kraus heaves himself up the hill, ignoring the cold air burning the wounds on his arm, the blood trickling down it.

Kraus hears Irdessa before he sees her. She's at the top of a rise directing a handful of wounded Vim citizens to flee the city. There's a spear in her hand. Her face and clothes are more covered in blood than before. She sees Bravensi and Kraus and runs to meet them but pauses when something downhill catches her eye. Kraus follows her gaze.

Dhovoi's tower has succumbed fully to a high, roaring fire, and a river of soldiers is coursing past it, reinforcing their compatriots, ever fighting toward town. Vim's defenders are breaking, fleeing.

"Where is Dhovoi?" Bravensi yells over the tumult.

Irdessa meets Bravensi's eye but doesn't answer.

Bravensi shakes her head in disapproval. "We have to get out of Vim, now."

"The Vanguard has to be warned," Irdessa says.

"You can't go back to Cornerstone. It'll be surrounded. Vanguard had their chance. They lost that when they chose to follow Dhovoi."

Irdessa matches Bravensi's gaze. "This is why I'm here."

Bravensi's jaw muscles work beneath her pale skin. Kraus bends forward, heaving in air and gripping his knees to keep from falling over. Red droplets spatter the dirt beneath him.

"They've come to kill everyone," Irdessa says. "I have to warn them."

"Their captain got his face cooked," Kraus interjects between breaths. "Think the soldiers will still go along with his mission?" It's not that he looks forward to running more. In fact, he hasn't got much running left in him. But Bravensi's suggestion seems the wisest. And if she's leading, and he can run behind ...

"More than before," Irdessa says. "That soldier Bravensi dethroned is the captain's second, Mourt. He'll finish the mission. And without any of Captain Jeret's civility."

Her words bring to mind the man's dark eyes and a shiver rides through Kraus, which angers him. It's the cold air making him shake, not that scrawny vulture. Except it's not cold out here.

"Then we need to go now," Bravensi says.

Kraus clears his throat. "Wherever you go, I follow," he says, taking Bravensi's hand. Her skin is rough, callused, hard.

She jerks it away. "No thanks."

There's a shriek from down the hill. Two orcanes, one manned, one not, have buried their teeth in a grey-clad, red-haired woman, and are tugging at her. Kraus faces the pale-skinned goddess, trying to force down the lightheadedness that has her floating in his vision. The truth must be known.

"You can take your hand back, but know that you've also taken my heart," he says, then adds, "And until I met you, I didn't even think I had one of those."

Bravensi's eyes fall on him, gutting him, making him oblivious to all else until he feels the warmth of blood trickle over his collarbone. Her polearm is against his throat. "It was only disgusting at first," she says. "But it's becoming an annoyance. You should stop. Oekner is the jealous sort."

"Let Oekner know you've stolen my heart," Kraus murmurs. If it costs him all the blood in his neck, it's worth it.

The shrieking down the hill cuts short. The woman's body is in two pieces. The unmanned orcane lurks around, snuffling for a new plaything. Promontory guards are pushing their line up the hill. The final pockets of Vim's resistance break before them.

"To Cornerstone, now," Irdessa says, snatching Bravensi's weapon from Kraus' throat.

Bravensi spits at Kraus' feet, turns, leads the way. Kraus follows her, although he's tempted to kneel and lap up her saliva. He searches his neck with his fingers to see how much more of his blood that cost him. The wound he finds is puffy and tender already. Something about her weapon ... maybe she's applied an irritant to the blade.

"Lay off her, Kraus," Irdessa says, running beside him.

"Impossible."

They're at the top of the hill now. Dhovoi's fancy, uru-drawn carriage is nowhere to be seen. Ahead are shanties. Soon after that, the cobble road starts. Kraus' teeth give an abrupt chatter as a chill rises up from his boots to grip his thighs. It's like he's wading through icy water. He's going to run out of blood. He'd be more concerned about the run all the way back to the heart of Vim if it weren't for Bravensi leading the way, tugging him along on an invisible leash.

"I'm serious," Irdessa says. "People die doing what you're doing."

"Story of my life."

"You don't know Oekner."

Kraus barks a laugh. "You think I'm scared of her man?"

"Oekner's not a man," she says, exasperated. "He's not human."

Kraus' smile splinters and his feet threaten to bunch up, and not only because he can no longer make out the ground. "Then what—?"

"It's her bloodiron weapon."

Kraus' head hangs forward on his neck. *Bloodiron.* That's cursed. Highly illegal. He gapes at Bravensi's figure, surrounded all over by a pale halo which is surely a figment of his blood loss. Her long-handled weapon is tight against her back, glaring down at him, bouncing on her shiny, leather-clad rump as she runs.

"I'll be damned," Kraus says. "I am in love."

29
Vultures Circling

FOHRVYLDA
Vim

Vim is in chaos. Soldiers and townsfolk clash in every intersection. Some of the businesses are being plundered by frantic, wide-eyed townsfolk. Some houses are already in flames. A window explodes out to Irdessa's right, sending an orange plume into the night air, followed by billowing smoke and the smell of things burning that shouldn't be. Beside her, Kraus' pace is dwindling with every lurching step, but he has not fallen. She pulls him along by his right arm, the one not painted with blood. She might as well be hauling a boulder. His bleary eyes are fixed in the direction of Bravensi's heels.

"If you're going to chase her, now's the time," Irdessa hisses in his ear. It's as ill-advised a suggestion as she's ever given, but it seems to do the trick. He grunts in response and struggles on.

Cornerstone looms ahead, solitary in the town square, its high roof black against the night sky. Windows of nearly opaque glass glow golden on both the first and second floor.

"Here they come," Bravensi says, peering backward as she strides. "We could still run, Irdessa. We don't have to die here tonight."

Irdessa follows her gaze to the south, where the orange haze of distant fire smears the dark horizon. Most of the soldiers have formed ranks a dozen across, no telling how many deep, moving at a military jog. Trotting alongside each formation are manned orcanes, tugging at their reins while their shark eyes dig through the shadows. The force is two hundred yards down the wide thoroughfare but closing the distance with the inevitability of the dawn.

"Come on, Kraus," Irdessa urges, squeezing his arm. Her shoulders and legs throb from tugging at him. "We're almost there."

His breaths are ragged gasps, his eyes roving, teeth flashing in the fire's light. "How did I become a ... runner? Should definitely be a striker ... with Torvald."

Bravensi scoffs, her haughty eyes on Kraus. "You haul a dead man, Irdessa. And you'll join him if you don't let him go."

"No," Irdessa pants.

"Just push him into an alley if you care so much about him," Bravensi says. "They're here for the Vanguard, not him."

"She's right, y'know." Kraus' words are slurred. "I'm dead weight."

"Shut up," Irdessa snarls, without the energy to argue.

From the south side, Cornerstone's entrance isn't nearly as grand as the north. Outside a door in the light of mounted sconce lanterns, two dozen Vanguard fighters stand facing the advancing army, their silhouettes black and lined in orange. As Irdessa closes the distance, she sees expressions ranging from grim to terrified. Among them is Old Fent, standing beside a blond woman with hard, narrow eyes and armored in plate and chainmail. It's Sura the Shield, and time doesn't seem to have sweetened her. Fent's battered sword serves as a cane, and his lone, gleaming eye is fixed on Bravensi.

"They've come for Vanguard," Irdessa announces.

This earns their attention. Some recognize her, hissing her name. Irdessa plows onward, not stopping until she's reached Fent. She releases Kraus' arm and exhaustion bowls over her. She doubles forward and grabs her knees, heaving to catch her breath.

One of the silhouettes steps forward. "Where's Dhovoi?"

Irdessa doesn't recognize the voice but she does the face. He's grown since last she saw him. Not as tall as his brother, Dhovoi, but broader. Vyker. Judging by the sash at his waist, he must have come of age and joined the Vanguard since she left. As close as she was with Dhovoi, Irdessa never got to know Vyker. He was boisterous, immature, always piping on about Vanguard fights and fighters or fantasizing about his role in coming missions. In Keswal, he'd have been the wettest of the wets, laughed at, kicked down, eventually fed to birds. Pinprae all over. Vyker's bigger now though, and by the flint in his eye, soberer. Ungainly sprigs of beard and mustache darken his face, muscles ripple on his exposed shoulders. A spear is in his hand. He has the fighter's bearing his brother never did.

"Dead," Kraus says, with all the sympathy of a butcher.

Those within earshot gasp, recoil, turn to each other. There is distress but not obvious surprise. Vyker looks like the wind was knocked out of him. His lips pinch as he tries to hide his reaction behind a façade of disinterest. "How?"

Irdessa clears her throat but her tongue stalls. It's not that she's particularly bothered by what she did. He earned it. But the Tactician whispers to her, *Determine who will be a problem. Remove them before they become one.* Confessing to this lot would force a reaction, and not necessarily a good one. They've got enough trouble headed their way without her stirring up more. Torvald would also say, *Sometimes it's better to treat problems as opportunities.* She can't tell which advice applies, and is drawing a blank on anything someone named Irdessa might do. Indecision freezes her yet again.

"He died at the hands of our enemies," Bravensi says.

Vyker scoffs, shakes his head as if Dhovoi got what was coming to him. The action clashes with the sheen that's come over his eyes. "Probably served him right."

"Undoubtedly," Bravensi says.

Vyker's shiny eyes fall on her. His mouth is a thin line. "What are you doing here?"

"I was wondering the same thing," she says.

"Who's come for the Vanguard?" Old Fent sounds even older, more tired.

"Promontory," Irdessa says. "Do you have weapons inside?"

"We've got liquor," says a woman from among the Vanguard.

"Thank the fucking gods," Kraus says. His face is pale and his eyelids are so heavy his eyes might be shut. It's a peaceful expression. He's wobbling in place with his arms out like a scarecrow with a weasel running through its jacket. "Hey, uh, whatever happened to that one kid?"

"Look," someone cries.

An orcane rider has breached the town square well ahead of the main force. He lurks in his saddle, watching them silently. Second Mourt. Seeing him chills Irdessa's blood. There are too many rumors of his depravity for them all to be false. Seems he acquired a new mount. The thunder of hundreds of marching boots follows him.

"Wha's his name?" Kraus' words are barely intelligible. "Prancer? Whatever happened ...?" His stumbling feet fail at keeping him upright and he pitches forward. Irdessa grasps at him. She manages to slow his descent enough to keep his face from slamming into the cobbles. He spills into a sodden heap. Her hands come back slick and red.

"He's going to bleed out," Bravensi reports without a hint of concern. "As are all of us."

"Get him inside," Irdessa says to a couple of fighters gawking toward the lurking Second Mourt. "He needs to be stitched up. Bravensi."

Bravensi shakes her head gravely. "You've got to be kidding."

Her healing methods are rude and mechanical but undoubtedly efficient. She lacks the finesse of most surgeons or healers, but finesse isn't her priority. If your wound is sufficient to warrant her attention, you're probably at death's door.

Irdessa searches for a good reason. "He helped me," she says. "Please."

Bravensi scowls. "Not sure what good it'll do if Promontory's bound to kill us all." She stomps after the men hauling Kraus into Cornerstone, grumbling under her breath, "As opposed to what? You heard her."

Irdessa's eyes stick on her a moment. Her relationship with Oekner has advanced indeed. "Fent," Irdessa says. "Seems the armory was gutted for dress-up parties. Please tell me there are weapons inside."

Fent pulls his one eye from the south and fixes Irdessa with it. "Enough to turn them back?" He shakes his head. "Not enough able bodies even if we had 'em. That's a battalion, girl. They outnumber us by a landslide."

"Just show me where the weapons are," she says. "And I need all of you inside, now. Andelsior didn't build this place without defensive capacity."

Those of the surrounding fighters who don't ignore her outright give her a confused look.

Fent sputters a laugh. "Irdessa, this town's been dying since Andelsior was taken. You've seen it. Vultures circling. They've come to feed at last."

The streets are emptying of stragglers, leaving only marching boots to be heard, to be felt. Mourt is hunched in his saddle, leaning to one side, peering out from under his jutting eyebrows at Irdessa with dark amusement.

"But ... why? Why now?" Vyker asks, his stare toward Mourt. He's clenching the spear in his hands. Irdessa struggles to get a read on him. In their time together before she was arrested, Dhovoi treated him like a nuisance, but it was obvious Vyker looked up to his brother and wanted his attention. It's possible his adoration for his brother wilted over these last two years, particularly if Vyker has respect and ambitions for Vim's Vanguard, which Dhovoi seemed to utilize only to partake in unmoderated debauchery. It's also possible the boy is putting on a show for the benefit of everyone else. No one else was outwardly saddened or surprised by the news of Dhovoi's death.

"What with the alderman feeding soldiers to the pit?" Fent *tsks*, shaking his head. "Was just a matter of time."

"Who's in command here?" Irdessa demands. "As of Dhovoi's ..." Her gaze veers to Vyker, whose eyes meet hers. "In the wake of Dhovoi's death?"

"That'll be me, I imagine," Fent says, shifting his weight from one hip to the other. At his side, Sura eyes Mourt with distaste. Come to think of it, distaste is all Irdessa can remember of the blond-haired warrior. Fent worked alongside Dhovoi under Andelsior in the old days. Surely he still has some memory of strategy. It hasn't been that long since Irdessa was arrested. He should have been in charge since then. Then again, despite all his pragmatism, he's bent with age, one-eyed, and nearly toothless.

"What will you do?" Irdessa demands.

Fent turns to her with all the urgency of a mortician. "Figured I'd tuck my head between my knees and kiss my one-eyed ass goodbye."

Vyker's chest heaves. "Dammit, Dhovoi," he mutters to no one. He's attempting anger but Irdessa knows his tone all too well. Grief. And once it settles in ...

"We can't just give up," Irdessa shouts at them both.

"Then what?" Fent spits. "If what you say is true, they won't stop 'til it's done. Especially not with that evil scum Mourt at the lead." Fent pauses to spit noisily in the man's direction. "And even if we can hold them off from within Cornerstone, who's to say more aren't coming? Who's to say they're not already on the way?" He rasps out a laugh. "I knew this day would come. Fucking Dhovoi. Best we can do is tear the wolf's throat while it swallows us."

Irdessa is speechless. She can't believe what she's hearing. But even more than that, she can't believe none of the Vanguard is contesting Fent's words. Were they always this flaccid? They sure as hell weren't while her father was alive.

Panic will kill you surely as a knife, Torvald whispers to Irdessa. *And when it stabs, it doesn't stop at only you.*

Fent's right. That force will run through the Vanguard. And in the event of a standoff here in the heart of Vim, the soldiers need only set a spark to Vanguard's tinderbox of a stronghold. *What would Torvald do?* is what her mind asks her. Last she checked, he'd let everyone die to save one. One who didn't ask for it. For some reason, the little girl who approached Irdessa at the pit comes to mind. She'd recognized Irdessa, even if Irdessa did not know her, and said, "*I knew you'd come back.*" That girl ... she may be dead now.

"No!" Irdessa didn't mean to yell it. She finds herself under the stare of all the Vanguard. "I didn't escape Keswal to watch my people die by the same hands that imprisoned me." She points at Mourt. "The same that killed my father. And Torvald. And Dhovoi." Adding his name occurred to her in the same moment it fell out her mouth. She doesn't look at Vyker. "I'm Irdessa. Born into the raids of Vim's Vanguard. Bathed in the blood of Keswal. Sharpened in the school of the Tactician. And I did not come back here to die!"

Her words tear across the square like loose sprakes, snuffing out the Vanguard's mutterings the way a heavy door silences a storm. By the gods, she's ignited a glimmer of hope in some of their faces.

"But we're outnumbered," someone protests.

"We are outnumbered," she responds. "And I've watched less men than you hold off greater forces, in raw daylight, without the shelter of the Cornerstone, *our home.*"

"They have barksharks," someone yells.

"They don't have termites," she yells back. "Orcanes can't get at us once we bar the doors. We'll fill their slippery backs with arrows until they turn savage against their riders." Since spouting off their disadvantages is so popular, Irdessa joins in. "They're also trained and equipped for war. Aren't they?"

Those who watch her have the sense not to answer.

"I know their tactics and their weaknesses. They act with no leader. We took him out and left a shameless maggot." She points at Mourt. "They fight out of fear of a slavering barbarian on the other side of

Fohrvylda. You fight for your fathers, your sisters, your children, your own asses." She draws a breath as a couple of nervous titters ripple through the fighters. "And as long as even one of us breathes, *Vim's Vanguard still stands!*"

Irdessa's last words shake her chest and burn her throat. Hope has infected all the eyes upon her. There's even fire to be seen in some. Fent himself has straightened his back and set his jaw.

"Get your asses into Cornerstone," Fent barks. "Bar the windows. Fill buckets with water. And round up every weapon in the place." The fighters comply. Fent turns a grizzled smile to Irdessa. "That was heartfelt, girl. You've got a bit of Andelsior in you. I'm impressed."

Irdessa feels like an emptied potato sack. The speech left her drained and trembling like no battle ever has. Her heart hammers in her ribs. Torvald never got this winded bolstering the frightened.

Promontory soldiers spill into the square as the last of the fighters clear out. There are hundreds. Outside Promontory, she's never seen that many soldiers in such a disordered state. Clearly Mourt's specialties don't stretch as far as tactical leadership. At least there's that. The front-most soldiers begin fanning out and readying the perimeter with bows, torches, and swords, wary eyes in her direction.

"What now?" Fent says.

Irdessa takes Fent by his elbow opposite the silent blond warrior, escorts him into the strong house. She answers in a voice small enough for him alone. "Looks like we'll find out together."

30

Pretty Things Spoiled

FOHRVYLDA
Cornerstone, Vim

Second Captain Mourt kicks his boots up onto the woodsmith's worktable and leans back in his newly acquired armchair until it balances on its two rear feet. This affords him some semblance of respite from his aching spine while granting a view through the soot-smudged window. Mourt gnaws on a fingernail, spits out the results. *Siege.* He grimaces. Not a task he'd have picked even on a good day. Definitely not after a lengthy orcane ride all the way to Vim, then a bout of crowd control followed by a spill from said orcane. But there's a job to be done and Jeret got himself incinerated. Assuming he even survives, the captain will be no help this evening.

Outside the shop, plopped upon a cobbled expanse in the town's square, is the squat, oaken structure the locals call Cornerstone, although the stones in its construction are limited to the two-foot-high trimming around the building's perimeter. The sharply pitched roof aims skyward like an arrowhead. Mourt is familiar with the building's interior, having followed Captain Jeret inside enough times to meet with Andelsior. It's composed of a large courtroom surrounded by tight halls and smaller chambers. The northern end has larger chambers, including an armory, but Jeret assured him it didn't amount to much anymore. Into that cube of kindling Mourt's quarry has scuttled like so many cockroaches at a lantern's approach. Mourt's directions specifically detail "capture at all costs," but if everything must burn, it damn sure will.

His battalion has split into companies, each guarding one of the five streets that exit the square. The soldiers are busy with the assembly of barricades and battering rams, a labor Mourt has no interest in whatsoever. The thick glass muffles the hammerfalls and the barked commands of their lieutenants, and turns their scurrying torches into golden fireflies on the black backdrop of night.

"Please let us go," comes a whine. "We ain't got nothin' to do with them Vanguard. We'll stay outta your way." It's that stumpy woodsmith, shifting his weight from one knee to the other, with his polish-stained fingers and apron, and his beard as dusty grey as a broom.

Mourt leisurely lifts a single, black-gloved hand with all his fingers outstretched. He meets the sopping eyes long enough for confusion to register on the man's heavy-cheeked face. Then he folds down his middle finger.

First Lieutenant Vernen throws a knee into the woodsmith's back, sending him thudding to the planks. This sets the man's wife and his young daughters to whimpering where they kneel. Their hands are bound behind them, which is likely all that's keeping them from acting on some regrettable notion. That, and perhaps the fact that not half an hour ago they were comfortable under their blankets. Vernen places his wide boot heel onto the woodsmith's left hand, flattening it against the floor. He draws a thick-bladed knife from his belt.

"Wait," Mourt says. Because why not? Without lowering the front feet of his chair, he rummages in the drawers mounted beneath the worktable until he locates the chisels. They're in all sizes, but one leaps out at him in its mediocrity. It has a wide blade, not the widest, but surely good for early in the woodworking process when there's still a lot of waste needing hewing. The tool's got years of use on it, its grip smoothed to a polish, its blade discolored by oxidation. But its edge is straight and true, an inch and a half of shiny, axe-sharp metal.

The sight of the chisel brings a shriek of despair from the woodsmith's wife, which in turn sets the smith's cheeks to quivering, or at least one of his cheeks. The other is smooshed flat on the floor. Mourt holds the chisel out toward Lieutenant Filore. It's high time that boy gets his hands dirty.

Filore takes the chisel with no hesitation. He leans over the table to snatch a mallet. Now the wife and daughters are all bawling. The ruckus of it sets Mourt's teeth to rattling, which makes a corkscrew of pain spiral into his lower back, as everything fucking does. The tumble from his orcane did him no favors. That scrawny rail of a woman, Bravensi the Batshit, will learn his pain well before she feeds the birds. He will fill her with more than steel.

Filore kneels beside the woodsmith and readies the chisel on the thickest knuckle of his middle finger. The smith bares his teeth and squeezes his eyes shut. The wife shakes her head desperately. Maybe she's learned better than to speak out. Lieutenant Filore lifts the mallet high and turns his smooth young face to Mourt. Mourt inclines his chin. Filore pounds the chisel to the floor, causing a thin spurt of red and a crescendo in the choir of agony from all present, particularly the woodsmith's wife. Maybe that one digit was more useful to her than his others. Maybe for her it was a naughty little finger. This makes Mourt smile.

Filore stands, flings the mallet and bloody chisel onto the worktable, then curtly marches back to his place behind the smallest of the two daughters. Vernen lifts his boot off the trembling hand and resumes his place beside Filore, fists at his sides, chin level. The woodsmith's scream has reduced to coughs so deep it sounds like something vital might dislodge and flop out of his mouth. His finger lies in the sawdust and filings, now just another bit of dowel, but redder. The wife's lips and eyebrows are bunched into a wrinkled mess and her shoulders shake with silent sobs.

Mourt nods approval at Filore. It was well done. The kid already surrendered his orcane so Mourt didn't have to walk all the way up here. Truth be told, if he'd had to hike the whole distance from the pit to the square, he'd probably have called it off and let the Vanguard be.

For that, Filore will get to share the wife with Vernen, instead of just watching again. The daughters, on the other hand, they're both for Mourt. No question to that. They're young things. Too young even to have developed the odors and bristles that time plagues upon a woman. Tight skinned. Plump with blood. Pale. So frightened they can't even cry out. Mourt's tongue flicks out past his lips, tasting for the scent of their fear on the air. All he tastes is sawdust. Distant smoke. His own sweat.

When the moaning of the room has returned to a nearly tolerable level, Mourt clears his throat.

"Get him up."

Vernen and Filore hoist the man onto his feet by his arms, return to their places. Mourt waits for the man's red eyes to search out his own.

"It's not about what you *have* done, but what you *can* do. For me. Do you understand?"

There is no legible response, only labored breathing as he squeezes one bloody fist with the other.

"Perhaps you're still feeling encumbered. I can assist with that, to your naughty wife's dismay." He shoots the woman a sly smile. She shudders all the harder. "I have mercy, as you now know, or I'd have taken your hand at the wrist, and with a smaller chisel. Did I have to leave your good hand intact?"

The man is gritting his teeth, eyes leaking tears. His right hand is quickly becoming as bloody as his left.

"Speak up," Mourt snaps. "You understand me, don't you?"

Lieutenant Vernen plants the toe of his boot in the man's back, catching him right below the ribs and drawing out a wheezing *hmmmmph* from spittle-flecked lips.

Mourt is deeply questioning the merits of keeping the man alive when a soldier bursts into the shop.

"They're loosing arrows on the northern barricade."

Mourt's chair slams down and his boots clatter to the floor, sending a fiery vein of agony up his spine.

"What of it?" he chokes out.

"We're thinking ... they may be trying to thin our ranks there. To flee in that direction," the soldier says.

"Perhaps if they've got shit for brains." Mourt hauls himself grunting to his feet, cursing the soldier. There'll be time enough for revelry once the siege is properly set in motion. He swings his torso and arms left, right, left again, slow at first then with some force, until a series of cracks and pops frees his lumbar from a fraction of the tension that grips it enduringly. *Fuck Bravensi for killing my orcane. Fuck Dhovoi for dying. He'd have probably opened Cornerstone's doors for us. Fuck Jeret for putting me in this position.* Then again ... His eyes skim over the two girls once more and an excited flutter takes his belly and his loins, fills his mouth with saliva so suddenly that a sticky strand dribbles from between his lips. He catches it with his fingertips. Vernen and Filore had better keep their hands off.

He hauls his long black coat over his armored shirt and vest and sidles onto the porch, finding a pilaster to lean against. The woodshop is on the southeastern side of the town center. From here he can see the two central highways—the south, to his left, and the north, directly across the square. If the Vanguard means to battle their way past Mourt's battalion, those are their two most feasible choices. They're the widest of the five streets, too wide to support the scaffolding and planks that drape the rest of this town like the work of so many huge spiders. The northern thoroughfare leads all the way to the town's main gate. The south passage travels downhill, back to the pit which is protected by no wall. The Vanguard could split and disperse in any direction from there and disappear into the night. For that reason, the south road is the most heavily guarded, with no less than seventy-five infantry and two orcane riders, not including Mourt.

The eastern street is directly to Mourt's right. It, like the other smaller streets, is guarded by fifty men and a single orcane rider. The Vanguard would be stupid to attempt flight in that direction. It leads deeper into Vim and bogs down into alleys quickly.

On the far side of the square to his left, Mourt has sight of the southwestern road, which is probably a close third option, considering that it eventually veers back to converge on the southernmost road. But since it's narrower than the northern and southern streets, the fifty soldiers there are packed tighter, a knot of swords and spears not to be easily breached.

The only street Mourt can't see is the one leading off northwest. That one is little more than an alley, and the least likely for the outlaws to resort to, as it, like the eastern street, peters off into narrower passageways.

Sure enough, a sparse trickling of arrows is falling among the company on the northern street. Most of the soldiers there are under the cover of awnings, and those constructing the barricades do so under the cover of shields. The arrows are largely clattering uselessly, shot from some place high, probably second story windows, since all the windows of the first floor have been darkened by blockades within. But now and then comes the shriek of a soldier whose cover failed him.

"First Lieutenant," Mourt calls.

Vernen clacks out onto the porch.

"Bring the woodsmith."

The lieutenant ducks inside. There are tooth-gnashed protests, grunting, then he reappears, gripping the hefty man at the armpit. Much of the color has drained from the woodsmith, and his eyes seem unable to focus. There might be less use left in this man than Mourt thought.

"Vanguard," Mourt calls out. "Stop firing or I'll kill the woodsmith."

There is no change in the clattering hail sprinkling on the northern barricades. Another cry bursts forth. Across the square a shield is swinging wildly, its owner stuck through the thigh by an arrow ending in red-tined fletching.

Mourt's teeth clench. He yanks the black-handled knife out of his own belt and holds it to the woodsmith's neck. "Shoot another arrow and this man dies!"

Something strikes the roof of the porch they're standing under with a *thunk*.

"They're firing at us, sir," reports the first lieutenant, aiming his eyes upward and drawing back behind the woodsmith.

"Do you think?" Mourt's teeth grind so hard his hair trembles at the corners of his vision.

Mourt rakes the knife across the woodsmith's throat, spraying blood, turning his apron red in a glossy cascade. The man's tongue lolls out. Blood soaks through his thick beard, steaming in the chill air. He hacks, falls from the lieutenant's grasp. Cornerstone takes no notice; its square eyes glowing from lifeless, internal light. A black pool edges out over the cobbles from the fallen woodsmith. Arrows continue to trickle down on the northern barricades.

"Can't we burn it?" asks the first lieutenant.

"No, jackass," Mourt says. "Irdessa the Undying is in there. She'd be no use to anyone burnt to bits of teeth." *And Captain Jeret, if he still lives, would peel the flesh off my bones if anything happened to that infernal Kraus before he can get at him.* "Also, that polearm-swinging psychopath Bravensi is there. I need to smell her die."

Another squeal from the north. Another shield knocked away and its arrow-pierced owner hauled off the street under an awning.

"Reinforce the northern barricade," Mourt yells, thrusting his finger at it. The gnawing ache nips abruptly at his lumbar, making him grip the column to keep from crumpling to his knees. "Send men," he gasps at his lieutenant.

Vernen shouts the order to his own company on the eastern road, then to Lieutenant Hassand, who sits rigidly in the saddle of his orcane on a porch beside the southwestern road. The man shifts his dull gaze from Cornerstone to Vernen, then to Mourt. It always takes him a moment to catch orders, even plainly worded ones. His expression suggests he's dimwitted. He is loyal, doesn't fear work, has a head of gorgeous blond locks, but is about as clever as dough. He gives his men a command. Soon half a dozen soldiers from either street are marching northward at a crouch, their shields over their heads.

"All we must do is outlast their arrows," Mourt says through clenched teeth. "I strongly doubt they're in there fletching—"

Carpets of torchlight burst over the square from either side of Cornerstone as the shutters on the first-floor windows flap wide. Before the moving soldiers can react, a fierce volley spews forth. The soldiers' shields are held too high to do them any good. The projectiles fly in a concentrated burst. Arrows rip through soldiers, thudding into mail, spinning men and women around with flailing arms, punching through skin and muscle. They're screaming, falling, scattering.

"Return arrows!" Mourt roars. His lieutenant echoes his command in a voice that resounds over the square. The shutters slap shut as the air fills with whistling arrows from all directions. Projectiles thump into Cornerstone, punching the walls and stabbing the windowpanes. Some sail wide, missing the huge building completely, hitting surrounding shops and houses, or skittering across the cobblestones. Mourt draws himself away from the column and back against the shop's wall.

If memory serves, the Cornerstone's spacious courtroom has a balcony lining its second-floor interior perimeter, such that a lucky arrow shot into the upstairs window might still find flesh on the first floor. Then again, the outlaws may have planned for this. Mourt's lips curl downward. The Vanguard could well be trapping the arrows that make it inside. Either way, he's done reacting. He must take the initiative. Siege-craft it is. He pinches at the tight muscles around his lower spine. It would help if he had any experience at sieges.

"Reinforce the northern barricades under the cover of our volley," he hisses at Vernen. "And this time don't broadcast it so godsdamned loudly."

Vernen calls to the nearby lieutenants and conveys instruction, gesturing by hand. This time, when the soldiers file from the eastern street, the southwestern street, and presumably the northwestern alley, they hug the wall of the square, shields close, using the protection of outstretched roofs and balconies wherever they're available. Those soldiers who fell before are dragged out of the clearing to the nearest companies, where they'll get patched up or die, or one then the other. The reinforcements arrive on the northern barricades and join ranks with those huddled therein. They quickly resume work assembling the wooden contraptions. Soon the barricades themselves will offer enough protection, and arrows shot from Cornerstone will mean nothing. Gods willing, the battering rams will be up and swinging shortly thereafter.

"Stop firing," Mourt says.

Vernen issues the command. The arrows cease, leaving little noise but the groans of the wounded, and the muffled weeping of the woodsmith's family from within the shop. This mewling serves to bolster Mourt's enthusiasm and ease the pain in his back.

"Nothing like a snatch made slick by tears of despair," he says, grinning at his lieutenant.

Vernen doesn't acknowledge him. He's casting wary glances around the town outside the square, at the wooden catwalks and planks and ropes connecting the structures. "Some knowledge of the roads would go a long way," he notes.

"Well, we don't have that," Mourt says. "What we have is time. And reinforcements soon enough."

There comes the familiar trickle of arrows once more. Cornerstone is firing on the northern barricades again. Mourt gives a dry chuckle. "That's it. Waste all your arrows. And ours." He grips the doorway. Thoughts of the two girls sprawled on the floor flicker behind his eyelids. "Let them shoot. It means nothing." He turns his back on the square. "In the meantime, find out if they've had to hunt for trees to make those battering rams."

First Lieutenant Vernen gives him a blank stare. "Find out ... what?"

"What the hell is taking so long?"

"Of course."

Mourt's taken a single step when the first lieutenant cries out in alarm. The degree of surprise in his most trusted's voice sends Mourt's head swiveling, which springs a naked demon of pain into his spine.

"Stop them," his lieutenant screams. "Loose arrows! Now!"

By the time Mourt has turned, he's able to catch only the tail end of it. Narrow figures, hunched and hooded, dash from the direction of the strong house over the cobbles. Windows on Cornerstone's eastern wall slam closed. The three sprinters run toward a storefront between the northern and eastern roads. From the Cornerstone's far side, another hooded group, no more than four strong, flee directly into the darkened doorway of a shop positioned between the northwestern and southwestern streets. As quick as that, they're gone, disappeared into the gaping mouths and eyes of abandoned buildings. The arrows chasing them catch only walls, barricades, fellow soldiers.

"Block off those doors," Mourt says, and his lieutenant echoes it. "Give a cover volley."

Arrows spackle the Cornerstone yet again, thudding like hail. Soldiers dash from their cover to nail boards into place not just on the doors the figures escaped into but the windows also, and then those of the entire perimeter. Cornerstone takes this opportunity to shoot at the exposed soldiers. Their arrows rarely strike true. Mourt smirks at his own resourcefulness. Were it not for the covering volley he commanded, the Vanguard would have had freedom to snipe his men. Perhaps he's capable of being more than Captain Jeret's dog after all. Then again, his is the only force present that's taken losses.

"Do they think they can escape by the fours?" The laughter that follows Mourt's question is forced, empty. He knows better. They aren't stupid. One of those shadowy figures could have been Irdessa, and now she's navigating the cellars and alleys and scaffolding of the city, escaping.

His lieutenant's eyes range from the abandoned buildings to the streets beyond the barricades, empty and dark, up to the crisscrossing wooden bridges above the roads.

"Should we pursue?" Vernen asks, not ceasing his scanning.

"No. We'd just be targets," Mourt mutters, suddenly indecisive on what direction his back should be turned. Pursuit is probably what the damn Vanguard counted on, to make even easier pickings of the soldiers who blindly blundered after them through unknown darkness. A nagging fear bubbles up in him, and on its heels, rage. Irdessa the Undying indeed. She's making a mockery of him. And if it becomes known that she was here, and she got away ...

A whistling shriek tears the air, drawing Mourt's gaze upward. There's a flaming wad arcing from the highest window of Cornerstone. Mourt watches wordlessly, ignoring the discomfort his movement cranks into his lower back. The screaming fireball splats on the southern barricade and explodes in a great *thump*. Another flies, then another. Soldiers scramble to get clear of the splashing fire. More of the balls of fire are aimed northward. Some of the masses fly wide and impact nearby houses and shops. There they bounce off, leaving a fiery smear, or break through windows, causing flashes of light from otherwise darkened chambers. Some of the projectiles thump to the ground unlit. A soldier is pulling one of the burning masses from a barricade's sharpened wooden spike. It unravels on the tip of his spear and dangles down to the ground, releasing a flaring cloud of sparks. It appears to be clothing with a length of twine constricting it. Must have been wadded up, soaked in something flammable and stuffed with ...

"Looks like sawdust," the soldier reports. Before his lips close, an arrow sneaks between them, silent until it punches out the back of his neck. The soldier drops his spear and grabs his mouth with both hands, fletching poking from between his fingers, eyes wide like he's spoiled a secret. Blood gushes between his fingers and he falls to his knees.

"They're burning through the barricades," Vernen says. "We have to pull them apart and salvage what we can." He steps forward.

"Like hell," Mourt says. "React again? Play into their hands?"

"Then *what*?" The sharp tone of Vernen's question is dangerously close to insubordination.

"Burn Cornerstone," Mourt says.

Vernen fixes him with an abrupt, emotionless stare. "You said—"

"I know what I said. And now I say burn it to the godsdamned ground. Before anyone else can escape."

Vernen turns and yells out across the square.

"Let's see what goes up first," Mourt says, "our barricades or their skins."

The construction of siege devices halts. All five companies loose arrows on Cornerstone. From each set of barricades marches groups of soldiers huddled under shells made of shields, carrying among them torches, kindling, and gods-willing, oil. Cornerstone returns arrows from windows whose shutters open only a slit. The arrows largely glance off shields, break on the ground, finding skin too infrequently to stop the advancing assault.

Cornerstone's flaming projectiles were concentrated entirely on the northern and southern streets and surrounding buildings, as Mourt can plainly see. The fire was more destructive to barricades and buildings than it was to soldiers. If Mourt had any remaining question as to which direction the Vanguard means to flee, it was just squelched. Next he must determine how to shift the available troops to utterly prevent it.

The soldiers under cover of shields have reached their destination. They crouch, piling tinder, dousing it in propellant, throwing torches on it. Fires burst into life all around Cornerstone's footing and the soldiers break away. Some manage to maintain formation. Those who don't catch arrows in their backs.

On Cornerstone's upper floors, shutters swing wide and outlaws pop from the windows long enough to dump barrels of water on the flames, making them steam and sizzle and hiss. The companies to the southwest, south, and east have the sense to loose arrows on the outlaws as they pop out. More than once, their arrows strike true. Mourt watches a woman take an arrow to the neck and topple from the window, landing on billowing embers. Finally, enemy casualties.

Some of the fires are extinguished. Not enough. The square is lit so brightly Mourt has to squint at it and cover his face. Smoke billows upward on a hot wind, causing drafts to whistle up the streets. The fireballs that landed in buildings on the square's perimeter are now roaring through the windows, reaching for the night.

"This is more like it," Mourt cackles. "Let them burn, let them burn. And if they want their precious Vim to burn with them, so be it."

A final group of soldiers is trying to ignite a fire below a darkened window. Sparks flick from a flint but none are latching to the tinder. Finally, one soldier falls back, leaving a bright red plume gnawing up the wall. The others give a cheer as they gather him up to retreat. The shuttered window above his party swings open and a hefty wooden cask extends, inching out the window like the Cornerstone is giving birth. It plummets. Just before it impacts the heads of the soldiers, Mourt realizes that's no water barrel.

The explosion undoes every shadow in town center, as if the sun peeked from the ground in their midst, and nearly blasts Mourt off his feet. The fire blows itself out quickly, reducing to a smoldering pile, but not before capturing an image that Mourt knows he'll never unsee. Half the soldiers are engulfed in flame, running blindly. One soldier dashes into a sharpened spike on the southern barricade, impaling his face and cutting short his screams. There he hangs and roasts.

"What will Captain Jeret think about losing the Undying?" Lieutenant Vernen asks.

"Assuming she's not already lost?" Mourt scoffs. "That was always second priority. A bonus. We're here to rid Fohrvylda of Vim's Vanguard. At this point, I'm more concerned I won't see Bravensi when she breathes her last."

Vernen turns and barks commands. It's with some distress that Mourt remembers the girls inside the shop. These fires will not be contained, especially with the scaffolding linking all the sections of town like great hanging fuses. The flames crawling the walls will spread quickly, eventually to devour his sweet young prizes. Mourt's heart flutters. Time is running out.

"Make sure none escape," Mourt tells his first lieutenant, dabbing the saliva off his chin with a glove. Surely they can't bungle this assignment. Watch a fire, shoot any rat that crawls out. Mourt pulls himself toward the shop's doorway. "I don't want to be disturbed," he says. "No matter what."

Again, Vernen doesn't acknowledge him, only grimaces, and keeps directing the action—as if he's so high and mighty. Mourt enters the shop and slams the door behind him before anything else can go wrong.

The air inside the shop is cool and stuffy. It takes a moment of blinking for Mourt's eyes to adjust. His hungry hands have already found his belt and are plucking at it, but the sounds of sadness the inhabitants sang has been replaced by silence. He freezes. Lieutenant Filore is gone, as are the wife and the two juicy daughters. Mourt's ears blaze and his shoulders seize up toward his neck. *Filore.* It takes all his strength to keep from breaking into a mad dash at the closed door leading to the back of the shop.

"Filore," he yells. "If I find those pretty things spoiled ..." He snatches for the door's handle but it disappears. The door swings inward without his help. In its place is a lithe hooded figure, two globular eyes visible in the golden light that seeps through those chalky shopfront windows. Chills climb over Mourt's flesh. The figure's arm is wrapped around a polearm tall enough to bump the door's frame. The blade has a red edge, and its surface is scored with openings through the metal, apparently made to resemble a snarling face. Mourt recoils, shuffles backward.

"You," says Bravensi, lifting her chin so her hood falls. She strides into the space Mourt occupied. "Looking for this?"

Only now Mourt notices the object gripped in her other hand. She hoists it up in front of him until he's nose to nose with the silent, staring, clean-shaven, blood-drooling face of the young Lieutenant Filore. Mourt gasps. He tries to call her a psychotic fucking bitch. All that escapes his mouth are huffs and wheezes. *Get to the door.* He backpedals, hands raised between himself and her. She matches his pace, with a hint of amusement on her otherwise emotionless smile. His heel rolls on a loose object and his foot kicks out from under him. He lands on his ass, the severed finger rolling away. Filore's head thumps to the planks between his knees. It seems so much smaller without the rest of the boy attached.

"That looked important," Bravensi says, like the head might have been a rare vase. The pain gripping Mourt's back cannot contest with the dread solidifying his blood. "I'm afraid your pretty things have ..." She holds up a hand between Mourt and her eyes and mimics legs running with two fingers. "... scampered."

"Lieu-Lieuten-Lieu—"

"Are you trying to call Lieutenant Vernen?"

He's nodding his head against his will.

"His time will come. Don't rush it."

Mourt catches a rushing wind of energy. He flips onto hands and knees, scrambles a ways, tries to rise. There's a bright flash of red and his face smashes into the planks as if his hand fell through the floor. Blood seeps over his lip, coats his teeth. His arm is cold. Too damn cold. He lifts it from the hole. Except ... there's no hole. There's no hand. No wrist. Only sharp-edged bones, clean as two cut carrots, and a pulsing black fountain where they protrude from his jacket. Now the scream escapes him. It tears out of his throat like projected vomit, making his eyes bulge and his nose run, clenching his every muscle so tightly he shudders.

"Oh fuck." That's not what he was trying to say. "Oh fuck, fuck, fuck, fuck ..." *Vernen, hear me.* He has to have heard. *Help me!*

"Ooh, yes, Mourt," Bravensi moans at the door, her blank smile and circular eyes planted on him. "Ah, yes." Her face conveys all the passion of a porcelain doll.

Mourt's trembling so hard his eyes won't focus on her. The ache has begun to overtake the shock. "You ... godsdamned ..." He's going to be sick.

She lunges forward and snatches the neck of his jacket, right where it buttons at his throat. He bats at her ineffectively. She yanks him to his feet with one hand, her other holding her weapon outstretched. She hauls him close, until her eyeballs eclipse the blade's leering face and all else.

"Oekner says you taste sweet," she whispers into his mouth. "I'm surprised."

"Who—?"

She gives him a rough yanking, making his words tumble back down his throat. He bashes into the chair, knocking it aside. She's handling him like a gutted elk and he's powerless to fight her. She spins him around, bends him over the woodsmith's table. His arms flail, slapping the surface in time to keep his cheek from impacting the same wide chisel that took the woodsmith's finger. The black on its edge has dried, lost its sheen. Mourt forces his head up to peer through the window. Flames have surrounded Cornerstone and are licking up its walls. The southern barricades are in full blaze.

"I don't find you attractive," Bravensi tells him. "In fact, I don't think I've ever met anyone more revolting. And that's saying something."

"You think I give a shi—*ech!*"

Something cold and thin mashes against his throat, hauling his head up, straightening his back against her chest until he's staring up at the cobwebs between the rafters. She speaks in his ear, "Oekner, on the other hand ... well, he's more open minded. *We're all red inside*, he says. It's gross." She jams her knee between his legs, until he's forced to either spread his feet or fall down with a grievous cut to the throat. "He thinks you both have something in common."

Mourt gasps through gritted teeth. "What ... the fuck ... are you talking about?"

"He made a special request," she continues as if he said nothing, "and he asked so nicely I couldn't dream of turning him down."

The fabric of Mourt's trousers is separating, severing, right at his rump. Something warm and narrow, razor sharp even, touches the soft flesh reserved for matters only he should be a part of. A cold sweat breaks over Mourt's forehead and his heart palpitates. The pressure on his perineum increases, focusing into a single invasive point. Mourt is locked trembling on a horrifying precipice between flailing in utter panic and the terrible realization of what might happen if he does.

"Let's play a game," coos the psychopath, her breath carrying the sting of strong liquor.

His mind reels, barely able to process such an innocent phrase in this nightmarish moment.

"I'll say words to you. Then you repeat those words to your man on the porch."

Mourt is unable to offer more than a wheezing breath. He blinks fiercely, pinching tears from his eyes.

"If I don't like what you've said, or how you've said it ..."

The blade prods into his ass, rending skin and muscle, making his knees wobble beneath him and bile rise up his throat. If it weren't for her knee propped between his legs, he'd surely collapse.

"I've fucking got it," he rasps. "Just tell me what to say."

"Good boy." The words seep into his ear and she begins to direct him. With her knife at his throat, her knee between his knees, and her godsdamned blade in his ass, she guides him to the front door. "Open it," she whispers, "and ..." Her weapon jabs him, making him climb onto the tips of his toes and whimper. "... don't forget what I said."

Mourt's first attempt at grasping the doorknob, which has taken on a glimmering sheen, is with the hand he no longer has. A sob escapes him, and he desperately tries to repress the looming acknowledgment of all he'll no longer be capable of. He cracks the door shakily and Bravensi hauls him away from it.

"Pull all the soldiers from the northwestern alley," she says in his ear.

Mourt tries to gather his breath to issue the command. The wide blade twists, its cruel point digging somewhere deep within his left buttock. When the tip grinds against bone, the shrill cry that escapes his mouth is alien to him. Blood is running down the insides of his legs.

"Pull all the soldiers from the northwestern alley," she hisses.

"Pull all of Lieutenant Narahna's s-soldiers," Mourt shrieks, hoping upon hope that Vernen will hear the distress, recognize it, kick open the door and stab this bitch through her bulbous eye.

"Send them to the eastern street," Bravensi says. He feels the blade shift, begin to twist more.

"Send them to the east. Now!"

"All of them?" The first lieutenant's voice carries a hefty chunk of skepticism.

"Yes. Lieutenant Filore is ..." *Looking at me from the floor.* "He needs reinforcements."

"But the Vanguard is still loosing arrows."

"Just fucking do it!" Spittle sprays from Mourt's mouth.

"Oh, that's good," Bravensi breathes. "I like that enthusiasm."

Lieutenant Vernen gives the command, having to repeat it in parts. *Of all times for the damn lieutenants to question their superior, they choose now?*

For an eternity Mourt stands captive, his sole hand gripping the wrist of hers that holds the knife, his knees trembling, his severed left wrist shoved tight in his right armpit. Tears stream down his cheeks, obscuring his view of Cornerstone, which has flames running all the way up its walls. The damage she's doing to him ... he's terrified to think about. He's lost his hand. He can still bind the stump, keep from bleeding out. His rectum ... it's something besides that now. His mind cannot begin to fathom how he will undo what she has done, how long it will take, if it's even possible. And this cold, psychotic, evil bitch—

"Shhh." Her voice is calm. "It's almost over now."

"Y-you think ... you can get away ... can get away with this?" His teeth rattle as he forces the words out. "You th-think this is the on-only battalion—"

The blade digs at him again, tearing even more flesh, twisting until the point is aimed downward and nearly prying back through his skin. His scrotum grows warm as blood coats it.

"Save your breath," she whispers. "Now send the ones from the southwest to the eastern street."

Mourt's chest is rattling too much for him to speak. A muffled thump shakes the earth, the tremor of what must be a building collapsing, or a good portion of one.

"Mourt," yells First Lieutenant Vernen. "They've burst through the side of the building. It was a false wall. They're running toward the northwest alley!"

A trick wall, of course. A foul little memory had been slithering inside him like so much indigestion, and only now can Mourt conjure it in full. Jeret had told him, *"Last thing we want is the resistance gathering in Cornerstone. Andelsior built that place with siege in mind. He'll have tricks."* Of all the details Captain Jeret had told him, how is that the one Mourt forgot?

"That's probably fine, don't you think?" Bravensi's hair brushes his cheek. Her godsdamned weapon is so deep up his ass he can feel the subtle movements of her fingers flexing on the handle.

"Don't stop them," Mourt wails. "Let them go, let them go!"

The door slams against the interior wall as the first lieutenant barrels into the room. His eyes land on Bravensi and he gasps.

"Thank the fucking gods," Mourt gurgles.

But, rather than help him, rather than engage the woman, Vernen runs back out.

"All companies to the northwest, now!" His voice trumpets over the sounds of the roaring fires. "Lieutenant Narahna, the Vanguard is escaping!"

"You did your best," the woman sighs in Mourt's ear. "It was fun while it lasted, wasn't it?"

Abruptly the knife is gone from his throat, her knee withdraws, the accursed blade wrenches from his rump, drawing a shuddering burble from his lips. Mourt collapses onto his side, racked by weeping, his knees bunching up against his chest. Something is leaking out of him. Or pouring. Bravensi strides for the door, each stamp of her narrow boots reverberating into his torn guts. The ragged breaths he's able to haul jerkily into his lungs carry the aroma of feces. His own, surely.

"Stop the Vanguard," Vernen is shouting. "Charge the—"

A red flash illuminates the front porch, its light spilling through the windows. There's a heavy thud against the floor, enunciated with the rattling of loose plate mail. Bravensi reappears in the doorway holding First Lieutenant Vernen's severed head by the jaw.

"Oekner's got a gift, hasn't he?" The admiration falls off her face and her nose wrinkles. "Smells like shit in here."

Mourt tries to respond but can only weep. "You're gonna pay ... you're gonna pay ... you're gonna pay ..."

Bravensi kneels beside him, her pale, indifferent face cocked to one side. "Oekner told me he enjoyed the game. And to be honest, I'm jealous of you."

"You're a ..." Mourt falls into tremors.

"You taste sweet. Like a child. But he doesn't think you two have much in common after all."

"You're a crazy fucking bitch."

Her eyebrows furrow. A frown encompasses her ghostly face, and her eyes stretch even wider. The room seems to darken. "Be that as it may," she says, "Oekner doesn't tolerate people talking to me like that."

She stands, draws a foot back in a wide stance, raising the bloody weapon high, and for a single, piercing moment, the blade's monstrous scowl harbors more rage than Mourt thought could fit in the entire world.

Mourt sucks in air until his chest nearly bursts. *"You crazy bitch!"*

She swings. The polearm bites his neck in a bright red blast. The woodsmith's shop rolls over, the floor and ceiling swapping places again and again. Dusty planks scrub over his chin, his scalp, his forehead, his lips. Light fades. Feels like he's easing toward her evil weapon. Sounds fade. Mourt can't see but he can taste blood. Can taste sawdust. Can't hear. Can't breathe.

Crazy bitch ...

31

We Remain Vigilant

AUSGAN
Stravhelm

Magister Obsydia rips off the emerald-colored dele and throws it on the gazebo floor. This process goes more smoothly with the help of adherents. Too bad she's sent them all away. It's not often she feels the need to clear her gazebo, but this morning demands privacy. She's not worried that her adherents will speak outside her presence. Whatever they overhear on her rooftop stays with them. But today she can take no chances. Perhaps it looks suspicious when she gets rid of them. Today her excuse is that she's preparing to visit the sovereign. She's never altogether comfortable in Intemrus' presence. Today is worse.

The heavy, starsilk curtains are pulled closed around the north and east off her gazebo, blocking out the sky, the sun, and to some extent the sovereign. She pulls a satin dele from her wardrobe, gives it a fleeting survey, and throws it over the edge of her tower. She needs something respectable, but not something he's seen before. Modest, but not so modest Intemrus forgets she's human. Would be nice if she knew a damn thing that motivates him aside from infatuation with the coming Heathen Tide.

Chitin boots ascend the stairs clacking. The sea-urchin hair of Ashmancer Haik rises into view. There's a smirk on his clean-shaven face and an idleness in his step as if he's deliberately trying Obsydia's patience.

"You should be wearing a helmet," she says.

"What's it matter? *Intemrus sees all ...*" Haik whispers through a crooked grin, looking Obsydia up and down.

Obsydia feels her cheeks flush. Working with Haik is a necessary evil. Hopefully it will soon be less necessary. "Report," Obsydia says.

"Old Alika, flower-lover. He's harmless. I have eyes on him. If he reaches out to Kale, or the other way round, you'll hear about it."

"And the andesite, the basalt's friend. What about him?"

"Culver," Haik says. "I paid him a visit. He doesn't know where Kale is, or so he says. Want me to fetch him? Bring him to the cells for a little question-answer?"

"No. Don't break the snare that catches the hare." Obsydia finds a deep blue dele, one with flowing sleeves, a high neck that will hug her throat when buttoned, and slits up either side that expose her legs all the way to her hips. "Leave eyes on him too. Someone discreet." She pulls the dele over her head and wriggles into it.

"Of course." Haik is distracted.

Obsydia looks at him. Desire is etched on his face. Lust distorts his stance. His eyes are nearly glazed over as they explore her body. Eight years ago, when she first noticed this spiky-haired, fire-obsessed miscreant of an exemplar with his prepubescent eyes shamelessly stuck on her body, she chose not to send him to the bath, but instead make a tool of him. She never intended to form him into a slavering nugget of concentrated lust. That was an unfortunate byproduct. She built of him what she needed, the complement of Magus Kalderys—not remotely as powerful but infinitely more willing to go behind the sovereign at her whim. Blatant lust is punishable by death. Haik is the only exemplar who goes unpunished of this, and he knows it. And it appears the increased risk of his duties brings with it some sense of entitlement.

"There is a reason you pulled your curtains and sent your adherents away." Haik's extending gropy fingers like he's due something. He steps within striking distance. Obsydia attacks before she notices it. The heel of her hand jabs his upper lip, flattening his nose and driving his head back.

He grunts and relents, pinches his nose, trying to stave off the blood.

Obsydia procures a silksedge kerchief and places it against his nostrils, gently pulling his hand away. Can't kill him yet. This is the nature of the arrangement she made with the ashmancer. She explicitly defined the terms: a seat on the triumvirate in exchange for unwavering compliance. Promotions for his sentinels. But the rest of her language told him there's no limit to the available rewards if he commits to her. He has run with that. But being exempt from Intemrus' Judgment does not make him exempt from hers.

"I'm sorry," she says. ... *that I can't kill you where you stand.*

He peers at her sidelong and his mouth cracks into a red grin. His hand slides into her dele and squeezes her bare ass. For the briefest moment, he's wearing Kalderys' face, and Kalderys is wearing his disgusting, lewd expression.

Her elbow ricochets off the side of his head and she rams her knee into his testicles. He grunts, falls to one knee on the edge of the tower. She glares down at him and rubs her elbow, ready to throw the kick that will grant him wings. Luckily for him, the skin isn't broken. Not hers anyway. He groans, pants, and does not look up at her. In this moment, that's the only thing preventing him being knocked off her tower.

302 | David T List

"There will be time for that," she tells herself aloud.

Haik climbs to his feet, holding his crotch. "There better be. I'm not doing all this for nothing."

Obsydia sighs. "A seat on the Triumvirate is hardly nothing."

He leers at her like they both know his *real* prize and what she said isn't it. As if he could ever deserve even what she's promised him.

"Keep your hands to yourself," she says. "That's your only warning."

"Hah." Haik blows blood from a nostril onto Obsydia's tiles. "What about Kalderys?"

Her pulse spikes. "What about him?"

"Have you got him weaned off the sovereign's teat yet?"

Again murder crosses her mind. It takes a moment to trust herself to speak calmly. "The magus is my concern. Worry about doing your own job." She has *never* discussed the magus or her plans for him with Haik. That won't change today.

"Do my job, huh?" He pulls a whaletusk key from his inner chest pocket. "You talking about this?"

Obsydia gasps. "The replacement." She closes the distance and snatches it from him, covering it quickly with her sleeve. *At last.* Relief washes over her. With this she can gain entry to Syvea Tower. With this she can take the sovereign's immortality. She looks at Haik, letting genuine appreciation into her eyes. Judging by the color that ignites his cheeks, her appreciation nearly overwhelms him.

"How did you get it?" she says.

"Had an adherent collect it from the artificers."

"An adherent that could be recognized as yours?"

Haik smiles, his teeth red. "Of course. Who else would they relinquish it to? This is a good thing. There's our scapegoat."

Maybe it's Ashmancer Haik's scapegoat. He himself is her scapegoat. If the key's absence is noticed, she'll personally remove his tongue during what turns out to be a fatal interrogation. He'll be tossed in the magma bath, along with his sentinels and all his adherents. If he has half a brain, he must know this. Doesn't mean she should state it.

"Not that we'll need one," Haik continues. "My adherents would die before talking." Haik spits blood on the shiny floor of the gazebo. His proud expression suggests he's marking some oath rather than making her want to kill him more.

Obsydia paints an approving smile onto her face, purposefully not looking at the pinkish splatter. "You've done well, Ashmancer," she says, sprinkling in as much authenticity as she can muster.

Haik's chest swells and his eyes turn solemn. Gratification. Elation. Neither emotion overpowers his simmering physical craving.

"Let's keep at it. Find Kale."

"Of course."

"Clean yourself up." Obsydia gestures at her basin. "Clean my floor."

He does while Obsydia watches.

"Resonations, Magister," Haik says when he's finished.

"Resonations, Haik," Obsydia says airily. He meets her eyes and she smiles suggestively, injecting a hint of reciprocated attraction. It is a lie, but she has to keep tension on the leash. Seems the promise of power is less effective for Haik than the promise of her body. Lust grips him again and his cheeks redden. He pries himself away and steps quickly down the stairs.

Obsydia smooths her dele, adjusts her hair, swallows down bile, assumes rhystic tranquility—ankles crossed, hands palm-up on her knees, back straight. This dele is not as comfortable as she'd prefer, but nothing worn is. This particular outfit though, did complement her unloading some aggression on the ashmancer. It's earned its place during her visit to the sovereign.

By the time she manages to return to a mentally unburdened state, the morning's shadow has regressed several inches across her flagstone floor. Obsydia hides the key between the mattresses of her bed and descends the stairs.

The floors beneath her gazebo are the residences of her adherents and prime sentinels, each with wooden doors opening to the staircase that encircles the tower. Obsydia makes a stop at the first door. It swings open silently on its korundite hinges. The circular room has lofty ceilings, stacked cots, tall windows. Some adherents are sleeping, others go about their duties, rinsing shellware and clothing, preparing food.

"Thank you for allowing me some privacy," Obsydia tells the room. "You're free to return to my gazebo. Straighten up, but leave my bed as it is." Not an unusual request.

She withdraws and continues her descent. The next door leads to the living quarters of her prime sentinels. Inside, Brel is tightening a strap on Etua's armored dele, while the latter polishes the sea-green scales of his greaves.

"Come," Obsydia says. Her primes follow her, boots clacking.

As they approach Stravhelm's ground level, the voices of rehearsing mancers rise up to meet them, a throng of conflicting melodies. No one's channeling, so there are no direct effects to the songs. But with so many singing at once, despite that it's melody and harmony they practice, not summoning, the potential energy is nearly enough to stand Obsydia's hair on end.

She and her primes reach ground level on the highest street in Stravhelm. The staircase continues down below street level to the subterranean halls. From those fortified passages, one can access the armory and barracks, the entrance to Syvea Tower, the cells, the lava tubes that lead to the magma lake. That route also provides a winding alternative course to the other Triumvirate towers. The path is tempting. Obsydia is anxious to run her hand over the keyhole of Syvea, to compare it with the key she has finally received. On most days she would take the underground path when she'd rather not have to see or deal with her fellow exemplars. But the air outside is cool and the sun is warm and she is in no hurry. Quite the opposite.

Stravhelm's layout, ranging almost to the summit of Mount Adenhelm, is steeper than Erudition. Horizontal streets and terraces rib the mountainside. Connecting them are narrow stairways, switching back on themselves, carved directly into the stone.

Lowermost in Stravhelm, against the inner wall, are the workshops of the artisans, clothiers, architects, and artificers. The nursery is in lower Stravhelm as well, wherein softer exemplars reside over the intrants. Higher up is the library, filled with books from other lands as well as scrolls with collections of writings from the mancers, historians, folkstellers, and the sovereign himself.

Midway up Stravhelm are the squat towers of mancers and sentinels. Obsydia's path weaves between those and the bases of more prominent towers, including the folksteller's. Outside his door, Tael's belongings are being piled, the remnants of his years there. Curtains, paintings, furniture, piles of driftwood-carved boxes and abacuses, all in a heap, with rhyolites coming and going like burrowing crabs, shoveling more of his effects out the door.

Obsydia steps over a wooden box that has cracked open, its contents littering the tiled street. The box held ink quills, parchments, sets of pearl-colored dice, stained dark with age. She wonders what would have happened if Folksteller Tael had simply performed his job and counted the basalt Tier as he was supposed to. He'd have publicly reported a loss and brought the news to Obsydia, no doubt embellishing it and proclaiming it to all who'd listen, in an effort to justify his worth. By then, it would have been too late to stop Kale from interfering with Kalderys. But the news would have spread. Kalderys would have deduced it was a basalt who ruined his song, and Imala knows the lengths he'd have gone to make it right. First and foremost, out of his own sense of obligation, he'd have taken the news directly to Intemrus, who would probably have called a tribunal and tried him for incompetence. Catastrophe. Assuming he survived the tribunal's judgment, he'd have lost his position and all standing with the rest of the mancers. And so when Intemrus finally succumbed to old age or something more abrupt, the scramble to fill that void in power would be impossibly competitive. Too many people resent the magister for her to simply claim the spot, despite that she is Triumvirate.

Obsydia shudders, knowing that threat still looms. It's for the best that the folksteller failed his duties. Now he resides in the cells, with only the baked walls to hear his testimony. Soon he'll swim in magma. Once Kale is silently stamped out and erased, no one will be left to sing of Kalderys' failure.

Too soon, Obsydia arrives at the winding hall leading to the sovereign's doorway. This tunnel, like most under Stravhelm, is illuminated by small oil lamps that are boxed within indentations at the base of the polished stone wall. These insets are closed in behind colored scales so that each flame throws a unique hue over the polished, echoing floor. In the case of Intemrus' hallway, the lights redden as you go, until it seems you're wading through wavering blood. Obsydia has always found it to be the perfect rebuttal to a pleasant mood.

The archway to Intemrus' stairway has no door. Doors are for rooms needing protection, things wishing to hide. The sovereign prefers to be accessible to everyone all the time. He fears no one— not that anyone would ever approach his tower without an invitation indiscernible from command. Obsydia reminds herself that in the years she's acted as magister, she's grown more comfortable with his unsettling characteristics. The intensity of his frigid, pale eyes. His inhuman focus. But his abode ...

Obsydia's two primes will await her return at the foot of the tower. Outwardly, they manage to mask their relief at not having to join her to the top. She has visited the sovereign's home exactly five times. Each time she is surprised by the state of it, and each time the shock is less pleasant than the last. She can't pretend to understand why he does what he does to his chambers. She knows better than to try to plan for what she'll find. Once, he'd arranged bowls of blood on every level surface. For what, who knows? If she tries, Obsydia can still remember the smell. One time he'd collected flowers, piles of them, half of which were dead and rotten and being consumed by slugs. Looking back, that was her most pleasant trip to his tower, not that she appreciated it at the time.

Her bare foot falls on the tower's first stair and the chill from the stone travels up her leg all the way to her scalp. She shudders. There's no point trying to predict what awaits her. *Get this done.*

The sovereign's tower isn't much taller than her own, but the enclosed, windowless staircase traps the sounds of her steps and her breathing. It feels the stairwell is closing in around her, and as it does, so does her dele's collar. How does she always manage to forget this ascent while selecting an outfit?

An odor greets her before any other signs that she's nearing the top. Something sour, putrid. Surely it's something on the stairs. His tower has enough windows to prevent stale air accumulating. Except with each step it grows stronger, sicker. There's a sound like wind rushing, or a waterfall. No. It's flies. Lots of flies.

The light from above pervades the stairway at last, even as the overpowering stench threatens to gag her. Did Intemrus die? Has his absence from Syvea forced his true age on him all at once and killed him like a blow to the head? Is this the smell of his bloated body being feasted on by flies?

At first, the sunlight streaming in through colored-scale windowpanes is all Obsydia's eyes register. The pungent air is so malodorous she sets to coughing. The buzzing of flies is deafening. Above their ruckus comes a greeting.

"Resonations, Magister."

Damnation. He won't die that easily. "Resonations, Sovereign," she says, squinting, trying not to actively cover her ears, her nose. How does Intemrus expect visitors to act? Surely you can't master perception of any sort, much less supersensory, and remain ignorant to how offensive this is.

Intemrus' room is larger than her own and today it's scantly furnished. Only wooden shelves, a skinny cot, several wooden chairs lacking embellishment, a table and a stool. Every flat surface is littered with serving trays, plates, bowls, overturned goblets and cups, all caked and crusted in unfinished food and drink. No surface is sanitary, from the tops of the shelves to the floor itself. Upon the piles of rotten, bitten, mold-covered cheese and meat and fruit are swarms of flies. More flies than Obsydia has ever seen in one place. Fat iridescent flies, crawling over knots of flies, swarming over blankets of flies. Their dead lie scattered by the hundreds. Beneath Intemrus' bed is a crusty jaundiced stain, and at its epicenter a blackened mountainous pile, under a particularly excited riot of flies. Obsydia has observed it before she could stop herself. It's excrement and urine. Days' worth. Weeks maybe. The urine has carved canyons down the sides of it, spread across the floor, dispersing feces like a landslide, dried, flaked, eroded.

Obsydia throws up. The vomit projects out before she can even consider planning for it. She bends forward, emptying her guts until they squeeze. With every inhale, the reflex hammers again. The fattened, buzzing insects ping off her feet, her calves, her hands, her eyelids. They're too engorged and lethargic to even fly straight. Obsydia can taste the filth, feel it in her mouth, her nostrils, her lungs. She gags until she's dry. She notices Intemrus is laughing calmly.

He's standing in the middle of the room, as if this is all some presentation specifically for her. A thick burgundy dele hangs from his shoulders, bunches around his feet. The color is such that an observer at Obsydia's distance can't tell whether the material is clean or covered in blood and shit. She refuses to observe it closer. Intemrus' eyes are as crisp and sharp as the eastern sky greeting the rising sun. Aside from that he looks horrible. His skin, which on a good day is the color of cornmeal, is paler than usual. His cheeks and eyes appear sunken. Veins show on the backs of his hands. In the month since she last saw him, since he announced his hiatus from Syvea Tower, he has aged.

Obsydia is determined not to stand gaping. "Thanks for having me," she says, and spits phlegm. She'll never be wearing this dele again. It's a shame, yes, but a dele's a dele. The sovereign ... *has aged.* "I trust you're ... well."

Intemrus smiles without diminishing the intensity of his stare. "Please don't be put off." He waves a hand to the side, his long sleeve trailing like a curtain. "I'm feeling quite well, thank you. In Syvea's absence, my appetite has returned."

Whether his gesture meant to indicate the unfinished platters or the nearly desiccated feces, Obsydia can't tell. "That is good to hear," Obsydia assumes. She'd not been privy to his appetite. Wishes she still wasn't.

Intemrus' twelve adherents, each as formidable as a prime sentinel, flank the room at intervals, standing tall between the windows. Their hooded deles are dark and long-sleeved, bulky enough to obscure details of their physique. They collectively produce a perpetual hum, even now summoning without cease, their sound faintly audible within the cacophony of insects. Obsydia's never been at ease around his adherents. She outranks them as individuals, but she's aware the collective may represent another obstacle before her. Will she have to remove them, or when Intemrus is no more will they remove themselves? Here in his quarters they are like his soulless extensions.

"I'm glad you came," Intemrus says. "Hopefully the state of the chamber isn't a problem for you. I've been guilty of overlooking ... subtleties others value."

"Of course not." Obsydia's hand is tugging at her collar. It's too tight. So is the entire dele. So are clothes. But the one thing that would make this cesspool less pleasant would be standing in it naked.

"Two days ago, there was a surge of consonance in a southern village. Lightning. Kalderys'. Report on that, please."

It takes a moment before the words register to Obsydia. So it's a regular meeting he called her here for. That's fine. She'd prefer to sneak in an observation of him before their meeting officially begins. At least determine his heart rate. But that's nearly impossible under these circumstances.

"Two months ago, we arrested a native from Napiri. He'd been talking about Syvea Tower in concerning detail. When put to the question, he incriminated Hargrim as the source of his information." Obsydia observes him while she talks. As always there is the hint, below naturally perceivable level, that Intemrus is experiencing attraction. Not Haik's lust, but something else, unique to him. Something she finds flattering. He stands there, lips closed and curled into a slight smile, crystalline eyes on her like frozen water, hands at his sides.

Obsydia continues. "We'd known they trade with the southern marshes and the wildfolk therein. But based on the prisoner's admissions, we deemed it prudent to contain and eliminate Hargrim's population."

Intemrus dips his chin, affirmation on his face.

"Magus Kalderys performed a Campaign of Cleansing, as you observed. His campaign was a success." It isn't technically a lie. And yet the wording makes her heart rate double and her face flush. "The magister returned along with Prime Sentinel Selu. Prime Sentinel Arc did not."

The icy stare is unshaking. "Go on," he says.

She clears her throat. "There were stragglers after the magus' song. The primes dealt with all but one, who escaped. Prime Sentinel Arc pursued them into the jungle, on his own accord. It was dusk." She pauses, shoulders lowered and voice intentionally glum at this announcement. Intemrus has not moved or reacted. "The merchants at the southern Trade were seen with his dele. We assume the worst." She turns her face to the floor, as if this is the detail she'd dreaded uttering. As if she cares what happened to Prime Sentinel Arc.

"Arc is dead." Intemrus releases a sigh. "That is a solemn loss for Stravhelm. I am sorry, Magister."

She had no love for him. He was hotheaded, impatient. But that Intemrus focused on that detail, rather than any other, casts such a relief over her that tears rise to her eyes. She realizes she's mad at the sovereign. Why are they meeting here in these disgusting chambers? How could her witnessing the foul state of this room serve Intemrus or Stravhelm or Ausgan? How much more meaningful a conversation could they have had in a less distracting environment? But then, what does Intemrus consider a meaningful conversation? He has deliberately made her uncomfortable. Best to assume he means to catch her off guard.

"Stragglers?" Intemrus asks. "After the magus' song?"

Obsydia looks up, nearly thrown by his question. She must lie. If she tells the sovereign that the magus was negated, he will cease to be the magus. "As I understand, there were natives nearby in the jungle ... outside his range." As if that's excusable. "Our investigation is ongoing."

A smile is on his lips. "I'm sure you're getting to the bottom of it."

She doesn't trust herself to speak. If only she could observe him deeper. Determine his disposition, not the farce he's presenting with that empty tone and expression. But she dares not. Not with him watching her. Even without deep observation, she has always sensed a calmness over him. A stillness that somehow suggests it is a result of her presence. She can't recall ever seeing him blink.

"What is the status of my replacement key?" he asks.

Her heart lurches. It all comes down to this. On her insides, Obsydia maintains rhystic tranquility. She's fed him one lie. What harm is one more? She'll take advantage of this filth to mask her lie.

"It's delayed. One of the lodestones cracked during endensing. They're having to procure a replacement."

As Obsydia dreaded, he doesn't react. He watches her, as if daring her to add something on the matter. Were it not for the dull roar of the flies, the sovereign's visage might not seem quite so frightening.

It is against her will that she obliges him and says more. "I apologize for the delay. I'll meet with the artificer and expedite the key's construction."

Again, the edges of his lips curl. "No need, thank you. It will be done in good time. Syvea will endure in my absence."

Obsydia carefully considers her words. "And you? How will you fare in Syvea's absence."

The curl in his lips becomes a smile. His gaze sticks on her like a leech. He doesn't have her perception of emotion. No one does. But he erodes her composure. Exhausts her.

"I will endure, Magister. Thank you for your concern." He watches her another moment, his hollow smile lingering stagnant like it forgot how to leave. Then his shoulders visibly relax. Obsydia exhales.

"How is Erudition?" Intemrus asks.

"All our students are on schedule. Administration is diligent," she says simply. Intemrus never requires details. "Except ..."

"Yes?"

"Folksteller Tael proved incompetent. His replacement is being trained presently."

"I see. And Stravhelm?"

"Our mancers grow stronger by the day. And as they grow in consonance, their sentinels grow. We are thriving."

Sovereign Intemrus, standing in fly-riddled filth, at last gives a smile that reaches his eyes. "You're doing fine work, Magister. I'm proud to have you and the magus at my side."

Obsydia bows her head, cheeks flushing from the compliment, not even caring her dele's collar cuts off her air in the process. She lifts her chin and swallows. "I'm proud to serve, Sovereign."

Intemrus begins to move, turning and walking toward a window, navigating the haphazard dish piles, ignoring the clouds of flies he disturbs. "Join me, Magister."

She does, each step deliberate, hoisting up her dele around her knees, well clear of the floor. This may be the last time she ever wears this garment, but for its duration she'd prefer not to decorate its hem in grime. Each motion stirs up an angry burst, sending ripples across the flies like she's wading through a pool. Obsydia grits her teeth. She's stronger than this. It will take more than the threat of sepsis to break her nerve.

The honey-colored scales sealing the tall southern window throw an amber sheen over the distant jungle, dampening the glare of the sun and giving all a golden tinge.

"I enjoy outlandish stories. I recently heard the strangest one." Intemrus' pale hands are clasped behind him. His voice has a bemused lilt and his face wears a hint of wonder. Whether he's experiencing amusement or only pretending to, Obsydia can't tell.

"Yesterday, an exemplar visited Napiri. He went by Mancer Diventae." Intemrus swirls a hand in the air at the fanciful name.

Obsydia holds still. There is no such mancer.

"He convinced the village he was there on my bidding, as answer to their prayers, then he tracked down a warthound and he killed it." Intemrus rotates until, once more, he's gazing directly at her. "... using consonance."

"He *what?*"

Intemrus smiles, gives a sympathetic shrug as if his response was similar.

Obsydia has to make every effort to keep her mouth from swinging wide open. Sentinel Arc? But why would he ...? He'd have to have lost his mind to do that, which may not be a far stretch after an evening in the jungle. But Kale? Slay a warthound? Use consonance? *Impossible.*

Intemrus gazes at his window and sighs. "As usual, the tale is more fiction than fact. The mysterious visitor did kill a warthound. And he was from the holy city. But he was no mancer. He was not there in my name. And he did not use consonance." All humor has left Intemrus, leaving his visage as desolate as Mount Adenhelm's western face.

Obsydia doesn't trust herself to speak. *Intemrus sees all*, echoes in her head over and over. Does he? Is that why she's convinced that her own duplicity has been the actual subject of this whole conversation? Is she merely paranoid? If not, why is he even telling her this? He clearly knows more about it than her.

Intemrus turns to face his cesspool of a room. Obsydia follows the action, embarrassed on his account over the state of it.

"I'd imagine the state of my chamber offends you," he says.

"It's not my preferred ..." *Smell? Sight? Sound? Environment? Company?* She closes her mouth.

"Tell me what you hear."

"Flies."

Intemrus gives a genuine laugh. "A native could have told me that."

She looks at him, his empty smile, the way his eyes pierce her so thoroughly it's as if they don't even see her. He is insane. Whether from studying consonance, exposure to Syvea, or simply old age, he has lost his humanity. His mind is broken.

"The deeper I observe," Obsydia says carefully, "the more flies I hear."

Intemrus chuckles, lets his eyes roam over his chamber with pride as if this is all some impressive construct and not utter pestilence. "Motives have always been your specialty. In all my time studying consonance, there is one lesson above all that grows truer. If one axiom alone could define our song it's that in every moment, the Imala make themselves known."

So, even in the buzzing of flies feasting on shit, Obsydia extrapolates. It's one thing to follow clouds of algae in the ocean or listen to the long-term patterns in cricket stridulation as seasons pass. Those activities don't test your gag reflexes. The sovereign has truly lived too long if this disgusting state is necessary to advance his education.

"The flies have their own song," Intemrus says. "And it, like all, can be interpreted if you slow down, listen."

She tries. The mindless buzz of a bloated horde of flies only conveys to Obsydia that she'd rather be anywhere else. If she's patient, perhaps she'll descend those stairs with a couple of her natural senses intact. She needs to focus on her bathtub, her wine, fresh air delivered gently by fans of her adherents.

"Believe it or not, a fly's appetite is fragile, relying on specific conditions and pressures. See?" Intemrus touches the tip of his index finger to his thumb.

There's an abrupt, painful pressure in Obsydia's sinuses, and for an instant she thinks she's been stabbed in the face. The song of the flies intensifies. Those crawling take flight. Those in the air grow crazed, zipping in tight circles, pinging against walls, diving into the blazing braziers.

Intemrus separates his fingers. The pressure relents.

Obsydia pinches the bridge of her nose, touches her nostril. Blood is on her fingers. "You changed the air's pressure."

"I did," he says. "And therein lies my basis for comparison. With different adjustments under different conditions, the swarm would have reacted differently. Grown lethargic. Grown manic. Died outright. And while that perhaps seems arbitrary ..." His eyes are orbs now. "... it tells me a great deal."

Of all the descriptors that come to Obsydia's mind to characterize a three-century-old man luring flies with rot and stirring them up with his mind, *arbitrary* is by far the most flattering. For the first time since she arrived, Obsydia is not the subject of his attention, which can mean only one thing is.

"The elements and aerology are nearly perfect for the Heathen Tide," he whispers.

Of course. The Heathen Tide. Obsydia opens her mouth but does not immediately voice her confusion. She's familiar enough with the theory of the Faithless Sea, how its unpredictable current is following an immense sea serpent called Tidamora that travels back and forth between Ausgan and Fohrvylda. Even including that feature, she'd never considered that their enemies required specific conditions only insects can predict for their inevitable assault. "Are you saying the heathens are waiting on favorable weather?"

The condescending smile Intemrus uses to dismiss her question tells Obsydia exactly how little she knows about the Heathen Tide. While that pricks her pride, she takes no credit for her ignorance on the matter. Intemrus has had plenty of chances to educate her on the supposed cataclysmic event. But as often as he brings it up, his lessons are rarely even as educational as discussing piss-thirsty flies.

"Not just the weather," Intemrus answers. "This is not the first time I've achieved ideal conditions."

"Ideal? You sound like you're looking forward to the Tide."

He turns incredulous eyes on her. "Of course I am, my child. Of course I am. That alone has become my purpose. For today, it is everyone's purpose." He moves closer to her, and for a horrifying moment Obsydia expects him to take her hands in his. "It is your generation's destiny to witness the Tide. And, thank Imala, I have never overseen a more capable generation than yours."

It's presented like a compliment. Obsydia wants it to be one. But as usual she is not entirely sure what he's talking about or what she did to warrant his flattery. She's planning his overthrow, his demise. Unless that somehow earns his favor, Intemrus does not see all.

The sovereign turns to face the southern jungle, clasping his hands behind him once more. "Napiri prayed for a warthound to die, and with that vengeance for a grieving mother, relief from a stealer of goats." He snorts at the silliness of it. "Imagine if I sent offensive patrols against every dog that nips at our wayward cousins. How dependent would the natives become? How defenseless? Imagine the Heathen Tide arriving and finding them thusly, fattened for the feast, arms held up in anticipation of anything but what the enemy plans to bring." He shakes his head. "Concern for your people should not require that you hobble them. Should it?"

Obsydia doesn't trust herself to immediately answer. She's never fully understood nor supported aspects of the sovereign's treatment of his so-called people. Some might say sapping their rain and leaving them thirsty hobbles them. But he justifies that because he's achieving perfect weather. Some might say restricting their use of steel as tools or defense hobbles them. It is forbidden for any practicing exemplar, and for good reason. But for the songless natives? Why? So they don't rise up against the holy city? The Heathen Tide is bringing steel. And Obsydia has something for them.

She leaves her questions unspoken. You don't climb this high in Stravhelm without capitalizing on opportunities to express solidarity with the sovereign. Truth be damned. "No, Sovereign. It shouldn't."

"It's not my will that they should suffer," he says. "But when war is imminent, comfort becomes a luxury."

Rather than try to work out what someone his age means by imminent, or his definition of comfort, Obsydia simply nods. With the possession of the key she just received, she wagers her imminent is decidedly sooner than his.

Intemrus inhales through his nose deeply and exhales. By the contentedness he expresses, you'd think it was clean air that went through him. Obsydia nearly gags out of vicarious disgust. She has the impression he's always watching, listening, observing, whatever he may or may not see. She rarely considers what he might observe through scent.

"It is for their wellbeing that we remain vigilant," he says. "If we lose discipline now, we may as well open slaughterhouses and blood arenas like the barbarians. Do you understand?"

No. "Yes."

"The village of Napiri will correlate weakness with reward," Intemrus says. "Word will spread that Stravhelm favors the helpless. That complaints earn my blessings."

Finally, something direct. Something actionable. "Not if I can help it," Obsydia says.

Intemrus smiles approvingly. "I trust you to resolve it, Magister."

32
Wasted Size

AUSGAN
Erudition

Sentinel Bronn sits on a flat stone roof in Andesite Tier polishing his new boots. Not much else to do while he waits. Faint singing of exemplars echoes down from Rhyolite Tier, accompanied by the song of birds. Bronn's vantage point gives him a clear view of Porter Culver's bamboo door twenty paces away and, way down at the bottom of Basalt Tier, a view of Sentinel Ilbres sitting on a rooftop with his heels propped up. He's supposed to be watching Basalt Kale's dorm but he seems to have dozed off again. Bronn shakes his head. He should be in a scouring party in the jungle, the ones marching village to village, or patrolling Proctor Alika's amphitheater. Those are the ones who'll find Basalt Kale.

He spits on his silksedge kerchief and rubs it through the grooves on his boot. They're made of bleached carapace plates, mostly from the limulus crab. The main shell encases the toes and the other overlapping scales are sewn and glued onto spiralpine cords that wind up his legs to his knees. He could kick through slate with these. The boots, and his armored dele, are unnecessary for this assignment—sit and wait and watch—but the job gives him time to kill, to polish and inspect them. It's that or run through all the rhystics again.

Bronn's stomach growls. The noon sun burns down on him, making him wish he brought his conch helmet, even if it's uncomfortable to wear for long periods. Prime sentinels get helmets lined with stitched silksedge, so they can be worn for hours at a time without rubbing sores into your scalp. For Bronn to get one of those helmets, he'll need to be promoted to prime sentinel, either by Ashmancer Haik being inducted into the Triumvirate, or by himself transferring to another member of the Triumvirate. Arc is dead, so Magus Kalderys is in need of a replacement. But fat chance of Bronn catching the magus' attention while sitting on a roof, watching empty streets.

He looks up at the eastern towers along the wall. He can make out the silhouettes of the sentinels there, lounging in the shade of their silk roofs. Why they don't suffice for the job Bronn has been given, he doesn't know. Ashmancer Haik told Bronn it's a touchy situation, and that the magister has trusted him to resolve it discreetly.

Keep a sharp eye. Kale is a slippery one.

That's what Haik said, whatever it means. Rumors say Kale knows how to disappear. If that's true, Bronn doesn't know why he or anyone is watching at all.

His boots are about as polished as he can get them. He stands up and paces back and forth. The sound isn't quite the regal clack of endensed chitin, but it's still impressive. He assumes rhystic dominance, clicking his heels and placing his hands, fingertip to wrist, at his sternum. He flicks his shoulder, sending his cape flaring outward. He looks at his shadow. Decked out in full armor, he cuts quite the figure.

Bronn draws his batons and leaps into rhystic aggressor, feet wide, stance low, one baton guarding his face, the other drawn back and ready to crack a heathen. He checks his shadow again. When the Heathen Tide crashes against Ausgan, he'll meet them. He spins, blocks a swing from barbarian steel, jabs their neck, kicks their knee inward. An attack from behind. He ducks just in time, dodging some other Fohrvyldan steel weapon. He throws a kick backward, burying his foot in heathen guts, then gives them two cracks across the mouth with his batons. He turns. There's the heathen king, Vretos, riding on the back of a monstrous Fohrvyldan beast.

What would I say?

Bronn paces, spinning his batons, testing out what message he'd deliver the blasphemer king before bashing him to a pulp. There's a distant snicker. Down on Basalt Tier, fifty yards distant, Sentinel Ilbres is smirking up at him, shaking his head. Bronn feels his cheeks flush.

A sound of bamboo clattering against stone brings Bronn's attention back to Andesite Tier. Culver's bamboo door is open. It wasn't before. Bronn's heart quickens. He didn't see or hear anyone on the streets. It's high noon. There's no way an exemplar could have gotten into Culver's dorm without the sentinels seeing them. Is there?

He should have a closer look. At least to break up the monotony. Bronn stows his batons and lowers himself to the street. He creeps toward Culver's dorm as quietly as he can manage in carapace boots. He's supposed to be discreet. Maybe his choice of attire wasn't exactly ideal. There are voices coming from Culver's dorm. Sounds like arguing. Bronn grips his batons and pauses outside the doorway.

"You said you'd get rid of that." It's the andesite.

"I know. And I'm sorry but I'm not done with it yet, Culver. I have to stop him. I think he'll go for Napiri next."

A brief pause, then Culver speaks again. "Wait. You're returning to Napiri? What are you asking from me, Kale? If you think either of us can stop the magus—"

Kale! Bronn's heart thumps, setting his feet in motion. He steps quickly into the dorm. There are two exemplars. Porter Culver, his big frame occupying an entire corner as if something threatened him, and an individual with his back to Bronn. This one looks like a rogue native, wearing scraps of a dele, his exposed skin striped and mottled in wounds. Culver sees Bronn and gasps.

The wounded exemplar turns to Bronn. It *is* Kale! Bronn acts quickly. He strikes with his left baton, buffeting Kale's shoulder, making him grunt and stagger toward Culver's cot. Bronn swings the right baton. It careens off Kale's head with a sound like a thumped gourd. Kale flops down in a heap. Bronn looks to Culver, who stands frozen, his mouth agape.

Bronn's chest is heaving. He grips his batons, unsure how to proceed. "That's Kale, is it not?" he asks.

Porter Culver looks at the motionless body. He nods his head numbly.

Bronn keeps his elation under control. *I got him.* "What's he doing here?" he asks.

Porter Culver's lips purse and his brow furrows. Bronn can't tell if he's angry, sad, or otherwise. He and Kale are friends. Perhaps Culver's thinking of attacking Bronn. He's a big andesite. But not so big as to shake off some well-placed knocks on the head.

"Speak up, porter," Bronn says. "This is a wanted exemplar. Tell me why he's here."

"I don't know," Culver says. He hasn't taken his eyes off Kale. "He was ranting about ..."

"About what?" Bronn says.

"Saving ..." Culver trails off, looks slowly to Bronn. There is conflict in his gaze. Uncertainty. Bronn rolls his head on his shoulders and squeezes his batons. If the andesite wants to try his luck, Bronn is happy to oblige.

Padded footsteps approach from up the street. Sentinel Ilbres must have worn sandals. He appears in the doorway, batons drawn.

"I got him," Bronn tells Ilbres in as level a voice as he can muster. *And I'll be promoted!*

Ilbres takes in the situation, peers at Culver. "What about him?"

Culver has backed his hefty frame farther into the corner, squeezing the fingers of one hand with the other. He's no threat. What wasted size.

"There's no fight in him," Bronn scoffs. "If the magister wants him, she knows where to find him. Kale is who she's after. And I got him."

"Yes, I heard you the first time," Ilbres says. He's eyeing Culver. "What's your affiliation with him?" He points at Kale's limp body.

Culver stares at the fallen basalt. A hint of anger is evident in his eyes. "None." He looks more likely to kick Kale than Bronn or Ilbres.

"What did he say to you?" Ilbres asks.

"He didn't say anything," Culver says.

"See?" Bronn says. He grabs Kale's feet and drags him out straight on the floor. "Now help me carry him."

Ilbres' gaze lingers on the porter another moment. Then he and Bronn hoist Kale up by either armpit and haul him out of Culver's dorm into the bright sunlight. Kalderys will definitely notice this. Bronn smiles, thinking about his new helmet.

33
Everything Will Change

AUSGAN
Obsydia's Tower, Stravhelm

Magister Obsydia soaks in a hot bath beneath the shade of her gazebo with a damp cloth over her eyes and a sack of frozen sedgenuts on her right shoulder. Thankfully, the cryomancer's adherents in training were able to produce one at Obsydia's request, otherwise the wine would be on double duty. She trained too hard today. Common on days there's too much on her mind. Her meeting with Intemrus left her in need of more than a bath. Carnal release. Katas, rhystic, and limberness went as usual. It was sparring that she overdid, and seems to have injured something. She definitely injured her opponents, some because they held back, some because they didn't, most simply because she could.

A greying adherent finishes sharpening an endensed river clam shell on a flat stone and walks to Obsydia's bath with a silksedge towel and some warmed coconut oil. Obsydia lifts a leg out of the water and rests it on the edge of her tub. Sometimes she regrets the moment in her life when she deemed hair on her body a nuisance, thereby binding herself to this routine forever more. Life would be simpler if she'd never realized it. But she did, and there is no going back. The least she can do is outsource the labor. Get some entertainment out of it.

The adherent rubs oil into Obsydia's calf and begins to shave her leg, starting at the ankle. She uses long, careful strokes, making sure the skin is receptive, the shell is sharp. When she finishes Obsydia's legs, she'll shave her arms. After that, depending on the time, maybe she'll shave more.

The adherent is relaxed and works the shell like a paint brush. Her dark skin is mottled and flecked with age, shiny and loose on her knuckles, but her grip is practiced and sure. Another adherent stands close by to watch and learn. Obsydia is picky about who shaves her. In her experience, women are best. Men can't seem to find the balance between too much force and too delicate a touch. They leave Obsydia with stubble and scratches. And regarding shaving her inner thighs and groin, men are lost. Their heart rates leap about, compromising their steadiness. They fiddle around, not sure which way to run the shell, not sure what skin to press on, what to pull, nerves making their hands quiver. As entertaining as it is to watch them attempt the job, Obsydia prefers not to bleed from her crotch unless nature demands it.

By the time her adherent is done shaving her, the sedgenuts have thawed and Obsydia's shoulder is throbbing. Two other adherents are setting out a platter with seared chevon and cheese and wine. Obsydia rises from her tub as an adherent dressed in messenger orange ascends her staircase.

"Ashmancer Haik is here to see you. He has Basalt Kale in his custody."

Finally. Obsydia sighs. She steps from her tub and an adherent wraps her in a thin towel. When she got wind Kale had been apprehended, she almost cried in relief. Her plan is gradually mending. Her meeting with Intemrus is behind her. Kalderys' failure will soon be buried. Her heart gives a nervous flutter. The pieces are moving.

"Send them up," Obsydia says. She piles her pillows on her daybed and gestures for the food to be brought over. Another adherent approaches and begins to knead Obsydia's right shoulder as she eats. Obsydia would prefer to let the air dry her skin rather than a towel, but if she has to endure the ashmancer's lustful grimace today, he'll die. And she's not done with him yet.

Basalt Kale tops the stairs in a violet-scaled dele that is certainly above his rank. His shins are crisscrossed in fresh scabs. There's a laceration and fresh gouges on his right forearm. But it's his face that strikes Obsydia as having changed the most. His eyes are different. Something's been rinsed away.

Ashmancer Haik follows him up, wearing a smug grin that tickles Obsydia's gag reflex. He's proud of himself. His nose sits crooked and there's a lump near his right temple, highlighted by a large purple bruise. Even as he tops the stairs, his eyes plant on her and explore her toweled physique like she's a banquet he'll soon tear into.

"Resonations, Magister," Haik says. "I apologize for the delay. The basalt had no clothes fit for your presence. I procured this from the clothier. I hope you approve." He's feeling superior for having caught Kale. But he's nervous, insecure because of their last meeting. He's trying to impress her. In his mind, there is a connection between him and her. It's unfortunate. His usefulness is directly proportional to his infatuation. She can't be too annoyed. It's her fault, after all.

"Resonations, Haik," Obsydia says. "No need to apologize. You have done outstandingly."

Elation washes over him.

"Resonations, Kale."

"Resonations, Magister." Kale's voice is level. His black eyes are pits. It's the fear that's gone from them. Obsydia hopes that whatever stripped the fear away left him some welcome honesty. But still his emotions are masked. She watches his eyes while washing down a bite of tender meat with blood grape wine. Kale matches her gaze.

Haik clears his throat. "Sentinel Bronn captured the basalt in the dorm room of Porter Culver, in Andesite Tier. He and Sentinel Ilbres were quite discreet."

As has been reported already. "He did fine work," Obsydia says, not breaking eye contact with Kale. She needs to maintain pressure on him. "They both did. As did you, Ashmancer. Now, if you'll excuse us, Kale and I have a lot to talk about."

She doesn't have to deeply observe Haik to perceive his blooming disappointment, jealousy. What did he expect? An orgy?

"Did you want the porter collected as well?" Haik asks. "I've not had a chance to ascertain his level of involvement in the—"

"None," Kale says, still watching Obsydia.

Haik's mouth curls into a scowl. He steps forward to strike Kale.

"Discretion, Ashmancer, remember?"

Haik doesn't respond. But he stops himself. Kale hasn't budged.

"Is there anything else, Haik?" she asks.

He eyes her. "Assurance that my work will not go unappreciated."

Obsydia's gaze slides from Kale to Haik. That is one hell of a thing to say to a member of the Triumvirate, whether or not you're in front of a damned basalt. She observes him. His pride is hurt. But more. He is prisoner to his bulging, throbbing libido. It throttles his judgment, strangles him the same way he surely strangles it in the dark privacy of his quarters. What fantasies has he conjured wherein Obsydia succumbs to his touch? Or is she even willing in his reveries? Exactly how weak does he think she is?

She has to stop herself observing him further. She cannot afford to know the depths of his lascivious imagination. She'd kill him. *My fault,* she reminds herself, *and temporary.*

"Stand by for my call," she says.

Haik's jaw clenches. "Resonations, Magister."

"Resonations."

He leaves stomping, making no effort to hide his displeasure. His obedience is as deep as a piss puddle on flat stone. Obsydia can't wait for the day Intemrus is retired. Haik's retirement will immediately follow, assuming he remains useful that long.

"Ugh." Obsydia feigns a shiver, smiles at Kale, stands up. "Now that that's over with." She lets the towel fall away and returns to her place on her daybed. "You've been busy since last we spoke."

Kale makes no response. His black hair shifts in the wind.

"Here's what I gather, and you can correct me where I'm wrong." Sunlight filtering through thin silk curtains draws shifting designs over the floor, over Obsydia's bare skin. "You snuck out of Erudition with your disappearing trick and followed Magus Kalderys to Hargrim.

There, you compromised his campaign, somehow. You negated his song and fled."

Kale shifts his weight from one foot to the other. Nothing about her assertion surprises him. So then it's true?

"After that, you wound up in the community known as Napiri."

It's almost imperceptible, but Kale tenses.

"You claimed to be Mancer Diventae." Obsydia cannot help but apply that same storytelling intonation Intemrus used on her, as if the tale is whimsical and intriguing. "And said that you came to answer their prayers."

Kale is frozen. His heart rate is increased. He's making no effort to hide it. But there's something else. Something he doesn't want to expose.

"Then, claiming to act in Intemrus' name, you killed an adult male warthound. *By yourself.*" Those last words she drags out, challenging the truth of it. His heart rate is still increased, but consistent. He didn't expect her to know this and yet he withstood it. It's not the last of his secrets. Not the juiciest. "Is that true, Kale?"

"Yes, Magister."

Obsydia watches his eyes. His heart rate is slowing, returning to normal. That was a close call for him. He thinks the threat is past.

"You understand that's blasphemy, don't you?"

"I do."

"And that is enough to earn the final bath."

"Yes, Magister."

He doesn't fear the threat of death. What does he fear? Obsydia downs the rest of her wine. "Kalderys told me he sent Prime Sentinel Arc after you."

No response. But the beating of Kale's heart intensifies.

"Did you see him?" Obsydia asks.

A lie tempts his tongue. Then he says, "Yes."

"Did you kill him?"

"Yes."

Obsydia scoffs. Well, there's that solved. "Adherent," she calls. Kale tenses. "I'm going to need another glass."

An adherent clears her tray away and scurries down the stairs. Obsydia stands and paces around the perimeter of her tower, hands folded behind her. A breeze explores her body, making gooseflesh rise on skin that's not yet dry. Kale has damned himself. But he was already damned. He was the moment he was captured, and not even for the sins he's confessed. He represents a weakness of Kalderys', and it's Obsydia's job to remove those.

It's reassuring to hear that he killed Arc, if that is indeed true. Perhaps Kalderys' failing had less to do with his own weakness, more with Kale's ... *strength?* The thought nearly makes her laugh. She approaches Kale, stopping a foot from him and gazing into his eyes. Kale stands utterly still.

"What is it you want, Kale?"

This seems to catch him off guard. "I want to understand."

"Understand what?"

His jaw clenches. "Why Kalderys did that to Hargrim."

"I told you last we spoke. Campaigns of Cleansing are sent to villages beyond salvation. This is how we protect Erudition, Stravhelm, Ausgan."

"Children," Kale whispers through his teeth.

"I'm sorry?"

"There were children. Playing in dirt, threatening *nothing*. Kalderys killed them."

Though trying to hide his emotions, this young basalt is nearly shaking with anger. Obsydia cocks her head. He's angry over mud-spattered native youth? As if there's some shortage of them. As if they don't spring up like weeds, spilling out of huts and piling all over each other. "What do native children have to do with you?" she asks.

Kale recoils. "They were innocent."

"Says you."

He goes to speak but doesn't. Furrows his brows, squeezes his fists. His anger seems to be unravelling. *Good.* She's finished talking about native children. "As if you're so much better," she says.

"... what?"

"It's a bad habit you have, killing our own," she tells him.

He blinks at her. "Prime Sentinel Arc was wounded by fanged apes and deranged. He tried to kill me."

"And somehow you stopped him. He's not your only victim though, is he?"

Kale's shoulder sink. He lowers his eyes.

Obsydia's adherent returns with a carapace goblet so large she needs two hands to hold it. *Idiot.* Where did he find such a ridiculous cup as this? She takes a deep draught and offers it to Kale. He shakes his head numbly. Maybe he'd take it if he knew how close he is to his end.

"Place it on the tray," Obsydia tells her adherent. He obeys.

Obsydia wipes the drop of wine from her lower lip with a single finger. There are more secrets in the basalt. She wants to find them. "How did you overpower a prime sentinel?" Obsydia speaks slowly, watching Kale's reaction.

Suddenly the pulse of his heart disappears. His body temperature becomes that of the sky. His stance and facial expression convey nothing. The wind itself seems to blow right through him. Obsydia feels a chill. When she can't observe emotion, she can't determine intent. He's already killed a prime sentinel, supposedly. What exactly is he capable of? She resists the urge to back up. There's a reason he waited to exercise this level of negation. She's close to something. She has to keep pressure applied. "You couldn't have done that alone, however injured he was," she whispers.

Kale's pupils flick to her then away. Aside from that, he might as well be a shadow.

Obsydia smiles at him and turns back to her bed. She walks slowly, adding a little bounce to her step to draw Kale's attention to her ass. Once there, she bends at the hips and slinks onto her mattress on hands and knees. She won't let her aching shoulder distract her from this interrogation. Her looking scale is positioned behind her bed so that she can see Kale's face without turning to look at him. His eyes are on her body. She rolls onto her back and observes him. *Attraction. Lust.* But not for her? She observes closer. Is he experiencing ... *familiarity*?

"Something happened to you, Kale," she murmurs, running her hands over her breasts. "I noticed the moment you arrived. You've changed."

His guard cracks. There's the faint sheen of sweat across his brow. He's exposed, vulnerable. Aroused?

"Plenty of exemplars would be up in arms over what you achieved on your little adventure. They'd want to know why you did it. They'd be fighting to get at you. Make you pay. The magus in particular. But not me. There are two things I want from you." She squeezes her inner thighs in her hands, pushes her legs apart. "Two questions I need answered."

He breathes rapidly, failing utterly to maintain his composure.

"How did you negate Magus Kalderys and live?"

"I don't know," Kale says quickly. "It was the same as other negations, except ... that was the most energy I've ever experienced." He isn't lying.

"Can anyone else do it?"

The question surprises him, but it also seems to relieve him. He need not lie to answer it. "No. They'd die trying. Probably in the same moment. I've never met any other negator who doesn't get sick."

"Nor have I," Obsydia says, sitting up on the edge of her bed. This is good. Better than she'd hoped. She has a drink of wine. Almost too good to be true. "You merely ... negated him? As if he was cooling sand?"

Kale appears as confused by it as she is. His gaze wanders to the shadows of her gazebo. He's hung up on her question. "It should have killed me. But it ... killed the warthound instead."

She shrugs, stifles a belch. Damn the warthound. "Yet here you are. Now, looking forward. I'm the only one who knows the extent of your sins. And although you intrigue me, Kale, your actions can't go unpunished. Perhaps an extended stay in the cells will suffice." *Extended, indefinite, punctuated by execution, same difference.*

He's returning to a level state. This threat seems to bear no significance to him. He must have more secrets. Obsydia's annoyance flares hot. She'll get a rise out of him if it's the last thing she does.

"Napiri is compromised," she informs him. "Your heroic deed taught them that faithless whining earns the sovereign's blessings. A destructive attitude and quite contagious, I'm afraid."

His heart rate spikes. Hers does too. She's struck truth.

"A Campaign of Cleansing is in order."

"You can't," Kale says, startling her. "They worship the sovereign and pray constantly."

Obsydia arches an eyebrow. Outburst, at last. "No they don't. Only one native does. Daughter of the known spy, Rathyn. And her motive is impure. Her faith in the sovereign is proportional to, and reliant on, her belief that Rathyn will return home. And, Kale, he won't."

"That's not true." Kale steps toward Obsydia, desperation in his voice. "Tivali is devout. Besides," he says, face blanching over how forward he's behaving. He lowers his voice. "It's not their *motive* that the faithful should be judged for, it's their acts. Isn't that true?"

His words sound familiar. Obsydia watches him a long moment, sipping her wine, trying to ascertain her own feelings. "Tivali, is it?"

He doesn't answer. Just stands there looking like he wishes he could unsay the name.

There's an emotion stirring within Obsydia, beneath her surprise and amusement at Kale's display, beneath her annoyance at his tenacity and her curiosity about his cloaking. Beneath even her relief at this dilemma ending. It's envy, and that sickens her. She need not envy anyone. Quite the contrary. She's the magister. And yet cutting, filthy envy seeps through her, intensified by her own impatience for getting what she so deeply craves. From within that envy the truth makes itself known.

"You fucked Tivali."

Kale's eyes widen and his mouth falls open. Two large adherents in the red garb of enforcers top her stairs, perhaps alerted by Kale's earlier outburst.

Obsydia flops back on her daybed. Her envy disgusts her. She's done with Kale. Sick of looking at him. "And Tivali helped you kill Arc."

"No!" Kale says. "I did it. Alone. She had nothing to do with that."

He's lying. His heart gives him away. Obsydia gestures at Kale. The two adherents approach him from either side and seize his arms.

"Kale, the negator who feels nothing," Obsydia proclaims sarcastically. She fails to stifle this burp and it's followed by a hiccup. "I have hard news for you."

Fear is etched on Kale's face.

"All actions have a consequence. She will bear the consequences of yours."

Kale plants his feet and heaves against the adherents at his sides. It's no use. Their combined weight is nearly three times his.

Obsydia laughs. "If that's the maneuver you used to slay the warthound, then how pitiful is Napiri for needing your help? Ausgan won't miss them after they've been cleansed."

"It was me, not Napiri. You can't punish them for my actions."

"I can do whatever I want. I need only say this campaign was mandated by the sovereign." The wine has made her lightheaded. She could afford to stop talking. Yes, it was mandated by Intemrus. He told her to handle it. But that's hardly Kale's business.

"Anyone who murders their own people is not sovereign!" Kale's yelling reddens his face.

Obsydia shakes her head, bemused. Now he's done it. She agrees, but that was a stupid thing to shout. So much for an extended stay. He'll bathe in magma tomorrow morning. "Take him to the cells," she says, turning her back. "Gag him. Tie his wrists. If he fights you, break him. I don't care how."

They haul him off. The sound of scuffling continues after they've descended out of view. If Kale's not careful, he and both adherents will take a tumble from her staircase. That's fine. Not preferable, because she'd have to invent a good reason for it. But at least he'll be silenced.

Obsydia glares at Intemrus' tower. There's no way he and half of Erudition didn't hear Kale's words. Unless of course he was too busy listening to flies. Maybe he doesn't care about the tantrums of basalts. Either way, by the time she reports again, Kale will be ash on the surface of the magma lake, unable to incriminate Kalderys or anyone.

Obsydia's plan is aligned and moving toward completion. The lump on her bed where the key is hidden proves that. So then why is she so angry? Why and how was that useless basalt able to negate Kalderys?

Kalderys. Why does he stand out in her mind? Even now? She'll convince him to turn from the sovereign. It'll be easy. Show him Intemrus is weak, she is strong. Promise him ... something.

She looks south, to Syvea Tower. It sways against the distant jungle backdrop, or she's drunker than she thought. The tower's deserted, as it has been for a while now. There is no reason to wait longer. Kale is dealt with. The key is in her possession. It seems the longer she waits, the more goes wrong. So then, tonight?

Obsydia assumes rhystic tranquility, ankles crossed, hands palm-up on her knees. She breathes deeply, lets her meditation wash away turmoil, trying to ignore her throbbing shoulder. Kalderys fills her thoughts to bursting. Why? Ever since she learned of Kale's primal sin, Kalderys has watched her from within her mind. His chin, his eyes, his hands, his strength. "*If it's possible for him* ..." he seems to whisper to her. Butterflies fill her stomach and she's overcome by an urge she cannot deny.

"Pull the shades around my gazebo," Obsydia commands to her remaining adherents. "Make sure the East Rostrum is still visible, then leave." She leaps from her bed as her adherents frantically seal the curtains. Obsydia collects the coconut oil from beside her tub. Her heart flutters as she scurries back to the sheets.

The last of her adherents file down her staircase. Obsydia eases into her pillows. She gazes at the East Rostrum, and pictures Kalderys standing on it with her beside him. Obsydia dips fingertips in the warm oil. Kalderys has called down lightning to destroy the Fohrvyldan invaders, all of them, at her command. Intemrus lays dead at the feet of the East Rostrum, washed by waves and gnawed by crabs. Kalderys, finally free of the so-called sovereign's absurd rules and laws, gazes into Obsydia's eyes. He is intimidated by this sudden freedom but not afraid to take the lead. She touches the warm skin of her inner thighs and a gasp parts her lip. Kalderys takes her waist in his hands, pulling her against his unyielding physique. Obsydia slides her fingers down, down, fondling skin newly smoothed by an expert shave. The gasp becomes a moan. Her fingers explore. Heaving breaths make her breasts pitch like waves on the sea.

The sound of boots ascending her stairs. Obsydia's heart clatters and her legs slap closed. Her remaining adherents most certainly do not wear boots. And she's not scheduled for an audience with anyone else. This afternoon was supposed to be hers alone. A conch helmet rises into view. Obsydia's breath catches. The bright sky casts the armored dele in a silhouette as it tops the stairs and enters the gazebo's shade. It's too thin to be Kalderys. Not even tall enough to obscure the East Rostrum. A scaled sash tight around the waist accentuates a woman's figure. The strut is unmistakable.

Obsydia sighs in annoyance, wipes her fingers on her sheet. "Prime Sentinel Selu, this is a surprise."

"Resonations, Magister," Selu says, pulling her helmet off. Her hair is sweaty and plastered to her head, not unlike Kalderys'. Her eyes are so pale they appear uncolored. "I hope I'm not intruding."

"You are. What brings you?" Obsydia won't bother getting dressed. Whatever situation impelled this meeting will be dealt with quickly. And next time Selu will think twice about barging in unannounced.

Selu saunters over to Obsydia's driftwood armchair. It's cushioned and upholstered in ornately dyed silk. Selu gives it a disapproving look-over, then grabs the back in one gloved fist and spins it to face Obsydia. She plops down on it, making the wood creak, and clacks her helmet down at her side. Selu shifts her hips back and forth on the cushion and frowns, as if displeased with the results. Before Obsydia's irritation can blossom into full-blown rage, Selu clears her throat.

"I want to talk to you about the Campaign of Cleansing to Hargrim," Selu says. She's blunt, always. Not one to waste words or play the games some exemplars play. This is not Obsydia's favorite type of personality. Easier to deal with people who believe their motives are hidden.

"The magus already reported to me," Obsydia says. Sentinels typically have no obligation or excuse to report to anyone besides their own mancer. If Selu is here to be disloyal to the magus, it'll go poorly for her.

"He mentioned that he was negated?"

"What the magus reports is between me and him. If you have a point, get on with it, Selu."

Selu leans toward Obsydia and rests her elbows on her knees. Her mannerisms suggest hostile intent. "The way I see it, Kalderys either admitted to you he was negated, or he lied, which isn't likely. He's too loyal for that. But if he did admit his failing, the sovereign would mandate an investigation to determine if he's still qualified." Selu clicks her tongue, shakes her head. "There's no sign of that happening. I think you lied to Intemrus when you met with him this morning."

Heat fills Obsydia's cheeks. She fabricates a carefree smile and responds carefully. "If you came here to make trouble for yourself, you're on the right path."

Selu continues without acknowledging Obsydia's comment. "I knew it was an anomaly when our lightning failed. The magus' channeling song should have sufficed. Arc and I didn't flounder the summoning. Something else went wrong. I didn't know what, and that bothered me, but Ashmancer Haik just provided a crucial piece of information. He told me Basalt Kale was lost but is found. He's been arrested and is in custody." She pauses, mock incredulity on her face. "Apparently Haik was jealous over the attention the basalt was getting from you, the pitiful dog. He had a lot to say. And while he went on and on, it occurred to me that Kale is the only exemplar who can negate without getting sick." She lowers her voice to a near whisper. "And so I'm thinking, that was him, wasn't it? Down in Hargrim?" She doesn't pause long enough for Obsydia to answer, not that she would have. "I think you failed to report that to the sovereign. Because Kalderys would not still be the magus if Intemrus learned he can be rendered powerless by a basalt."

Obsydia's first thought is violence. *Break Selu's thin nose, smash the goblet on her face, drag her by her hair to the edge of the roof and throw her off. Find Haik. Murder him.* But Selu is armored and at the ready. Obsydia is naked, half-drunk, and has an injured shoulder. Worst of all, she's speechless.

"You must have hurt your ashmancer's feelings," Selu says. "It made his lips quite loose."

"I hope he enjoys his lips while they can still flap." Obsydia regrets saying it at once. Haik's fate, more accurately his imminent death, is not Selu's business.

Selu shakes her head. "If I might be so bold as to remind you a basic mancer's lesson: You can't control damage until you know the extent of it."

"Tell me," Obsydia says through a forced smile. "You've just made enemies of two thirds of the Triumvirate. What good do you think will come of this?"

Selu leans back in the chair and throws one leg over the other. "I want you to report the truth to the sovereign. Kalderys was negated by Basalt Kale, who informed you of it. That explains why he's been imprisoned. If you're wise, you'll report that before he hears it ..." She shrugs. "... from someone else."

"So willingly you betray the magus," Obsydia says, doing all she can to hide her fury. "Why the unfaithfulness? Why now?" It is a weak counter. Not a defense at all. But she has to gain her footing. Selu came prepared.

"*Why now?*" Selu snaps. "Because until *now* ..." Selu blinks several times. A deep grief is surfacing. Perhaps if Obsydia had drank less she'd have noticed it sooner. Capitalized on it. "Until now there have been no casualties," Selu hisses. A tear slides down her cheek before she can catch it. "Why now ...? You hypocrite. What did you tell the sovereign about the magus' other prime sentinel? I doubt you told him Kalderys sent Arc to his death."

Obsydia leans back on her cushions, maintains a relaxed posture, despite this revelation. Selu had feelings for Arc. Now that is rich. Obsydia casually takes her goblet in her hands and sips it, simultaneously regretting drinking so much. A clearer head would help her isolate something exploitable in this situation. Selu's not to be trifled with. Chances are Selu doesn't know Kale killed Arc or she'd want a hand in Kale's death.

A sentinel serves at their own risk, especially a prime sentinel. Arc's death in itself is not incriminating for Kalderys. But compounded with the show of weakness at Hargrim it is. "Enlighten me on how you'll prove this, assuming I don't play along," Obsydia says.

"I can't," Selu says. "And Arc is dead. But the basalt can. And you've sent him to the most secure place in Ausgan. Also, if Kalderys were put on trial, he'd admit to it all. However loyal he is to you, he is more loyal to the sovereign. At least *he* is aware that deceit is a tool of the Deceiver."

A feeling of impotence is creeping into Obsydia, threatening to suffocate her. Her two enforcers haven't returned from delivering Kale to the cells, but her primes are downstairs on call. All she has to do is ring the bell, claim Selu threatened her. The primes would kick Selu to death. Or would they? Selu is a ferocious fighter. She was Kalderys' first pick for a reason. And now she's comfortably selling him out.

"Kalderys has trusted you for years," Obsydia says, failing to produce anything but her pitiful, honest reaction. "He made you. And you turn on him over this, without even speaking to him first?"

"I'm not turning on Kalderys. I'm standing up for Erudition. You didn't see what happened down there. He collapsed. Couldn't even stand. Kalderys is finished, Obsydia."

A knife in Obsydia's stomach would hurt less. Selu cannot say that and live.

"I serve him and will continue to until the due time. But until then Ausgan is at risk. When you report him, perhaps Intemrus will spare his life. He'll be demoted at the least. Then ..." Selu straightens her shoulders and lifts her chin even as her confidence wavers. "... you'll put in your recommendation for Aridimancer Selu as the next magus of Ausgan."

Obsydia cocks her head in surprise. Buy Selu's silence. Obsydia would have thought it was beneath Selu to attempt advancement in such a way. But she'd have thought the same for Selu backstabbing Kalderys. "Promote you to magus? You specialize in ... drying things."

"And what are you? A reader of feelings? What an impractical qualifier for the amount of authority you have. I don't expect you to understand the virtues of aridimancy. Not yet."

Obsydia scoffs. "Aridimancy. As if this place isn't dry enough. My song is my business. Intemrus knows it, and he placed me at his right hand. What does that tell you?"

Selu's nostrils flare but she says nothing.

"When you're promoted, I'll own you," Obsydia says "Has that not occurred to you?"

This frees Selu's tongue. "Of course it has. I aim only to serve, Magister. Our interests are the same. Once the magus is replaced by less of a distraction, I think you'll understand how preoccupied you were. Maybe then you'll ..." Selu gestures as if to pinch together the lapels of a dele. *Maybe then you'll cover those up*, she means.

Again, Obsydia's thoughts become violent. *A distraction.* She grits her teeth but conceals it with a smile. Selu will regret that. Obsydia fingers the indentations on her wine goblet and turns her eyes to the tower Syvea. *Focus on the end.* "I've underestimated you, Selu. I can't help but admire your ambition."

Selu's expression makes no visible change, but some amount of tension eases from her chest.

"You've brought specific demands," Obsydia says. "But not the most realistic. You haven't thought of everything."

Selu nods tersely. "I'd considered that. I don't mean to be unyielding. Woe be to the tree that—"

"Don't preach at me, Sentinel," Obsydia says. "What is it you do mean to do, ultimately?"

"I mean to see Intemrus' Will done."

"And how will that culminate in Ausgan, in your lifetime?" Obsydia asks.

Selu inhales. "In the cultivation and protection of a healthy populace, the selection and nurture of exemplars chosen by the Imala, and in the defense of the holy city against the Heathen Tide, if I live to see that day." Her answers are curt and rehearsed, but there is enough passion to prove she speaks from her heart.

Obsydia places her goblet on the stand and leans toward Selu, pulling a pillow in front of her chest. Clearly Selu finds her nudity a distraction. "Then trust Intemrus, who trusts me," Obsydia says. "We will get to the bottom of Kalderys' alleged weakness. If he proves wanting, we'll proceed as we must. Intemrus' Will is my will, and I won't bother him with issues I'm fit to resolve. He has more to worry about than details of a cleansing." She lowers her voice, caters her tone for this somber delivery, "Even one that ended in tragedy."

Hidden behind the derision in Selu's pale eyes is uncertainty. She is second-guessing herself. Obsydia thinks of Selu's promotion to prime sentinel. She cried, and Obsydia did too. It was a proud day.

"I believe you would make a fine magus," Obsydia lies. *Useless aridimancer.* "And I hope, if you get that chance, that you earn it honestly, in the light of day, as you have every accolade you've earned so far."

Selu looks away. It's the first time she's broken eye contact with Obsydia since she sat down. Shame withers her resolve. She didn't want to ascend Stravhelm like this. She wanted an honest promotion. And now she's tempted to apologize, take it back. But her pride won't allow it and she doesn't trust Obsydia. Doesn't matter. Obsydia doesn't need Selu's trust or an apology. She needs time. An idea occurs to her.

"Selu, Kalderys told me about Arc's death. And of course I told the sovereign."

Selu tenses. She wasn't expecting that. In fairness, neither was Obsydia.

"Tomorrow the Triumvirate will interrogate the basalt, who appears to be the most likely source of information on Arc's demise. We must get to the bottom of what happened at Hargrim. Obviously, when we learn about Arc, you'll be informed. And if the Triumvirate determines Kalderys to be unfit, you'll be on my mind."

Selu's relief is visible, but this new correlation between Kale and Arc has her unsettled. "That is all I ask, Magister."

"I appreciate your honesty today, Selu." Obsydia is wearying of lying. "Until this is resolved, you'd do well to respect the magus, and the hierarchy. No more reporting on the one who promoted you to where you are. You report *to* him. And you're right, he is ultimately loyal to the sovereign and will do what he must. If he is determined to be unfit, he'll step down without the need for a trial."

"Of course, Magister," Selu says. "I trust he will let me know once the interrogation has concluded."

Magister Obsydia's eyes narrow. She relaxes herself once more, takes her goblet in hand. Turns her head as if Selu's already gone.

Selu stands and spins the chair back around. "Resonations, Magister."

"Resonations."

Obsydia is able to hold her composure until Selu's boot steps recede. She smashes her goblet on the floor. Tears fill her eyes, blurring her view of the crimson wine expanding along recesses between flagstones.

Her two primes are on the floor a moment later, alarmed by the commotion.

"Basalt Kale has been taken to the cells," Obsydia says, wiping her cheeks. "He will be executed in the bath at tomorrow's first light." One of her first orders of business when she claims power will be legalizing evening executions. Yet another of Intemrus' ridiculous constraints. "Until then, guard him well. Stop anyone who comes for him."

They leave.

Selu is the only person Obsydia can imagine with motive to try to get to Kale or prevent his execution. For her to pull that off, she'll have to incapacitate both of Obsydia's primes in addition to the usual cell keepers. Regardless of whether she can accomplish that, attempting it would bring down the Triumvirate's immediate and severe justice on her, however spectacular and incriminating her story. She'd get no trial. But would Kale's testimony remain untold?

Selu was right about one thing, Obsydia has been distracted. Never again. She scorned Haik and paid for it. His usefulness appears to be at an end. Maybe she should have eliminated Kale while he was up here. Can't help that now. It'll happen soon enough. No more negligence. No more hesitation. She thrusts her hand between her mattresses and grasps the key. When the sun sets, she will act. She can wait no longer. After tonight, everything will change.

34
The Sovereign Will Die

AUSGAN
The Cells under Stravhelm

Rathyn is roused by the echoing clatter of boots. There's a distinct click, then the rumbling of stone ladder rungs extending in a distant cell. A moment's silence.

"Let's see you slip this one, basalt." It's a monk's distant voice.

Another rumbling. Rungs retracting. The bootsteps recede.

The event brings too much mystery for Rathyn to consider returning to sleep, despite his exhaustion.

He's learned to gauge how long he slept based on the soreness in his back, the strength of the pervading odor of sulfur and his own filth upon waking up. The longer he sleeps, the more overpowering is the smell when he awakens, as if maybe deep in his unconscious mind this is not yet normal. Not how it should be. Not how it will end.

Rathyn lifts his cheek from the stone floor and pushes his gaunt frame to a sitting position. The ache of hunger gnaws at his innards. It usually does when he moves, otherwise he'd move more to combat the stiffness. As is, it feels like his ravenous guts have turned on his own flesh.

"Hey," he calls.

The response is his own echo and that haunting crackle, barely audible, amplified and distorted by this cavernous chamber.

"*Hey!*" he calls again.

Nothing.

The cell keepers must have dropped off an unconscious prisoner. Rathyn shivers despite the sweltering air. Maybe the keepers never came at all.

He's begun to hallucinate. Usually it manifests as tinkling chimes, or indiscernible whispers, or a glowing light just outside his periphery. Or a demon in his head.

He grips the water bucket between hand and wrist and lifts it over his mouth. At length, droplets gather and fall onto his parched tongue.

He holds the bucket until his shoulders can't keep it steady any longer, then sets it roughly on the floor so he can regain strength.

That wasn't enough.

He needs more. He knows too well the pain of running out, and the dark journey that follows. He lifts the bucket again. As he opens his chapped lips, the bucket slips from his stump and thuds into his face. Blood seeps from his lip into his mouth. The barrel clunks to the stone floor. Pain sets Rathyn in motion before he can stop himself. He snatches the bucket and slings it. It collides with unyielding stone and breaks into pieces.

"Oh no." He's on his elbows and knees, scrambling, scurrying. "Oh, no, no, no."

He grasps at the shards of wood, trying to undo what he's done. The twine that held the bucket together is broken. Only thin planks remain of the vessel that sustained him. He fumbles with the pieces, pawing them with his stump, squeezing at them, searching frantically for water he knows isn't there.

You've become a beast, the demon rooted in his mind chuckles. *You're so desperate you'd drink the blood of a child right now.*

Rathyn shakes his head, trying to postpone the truth. The wood that made up the bottom of the barrel is soft, cold, damp. He lays it flat and presses his lips against it, sucking at it.

Try eating it.

He bites into the wood, chews it, gets it wedged at the back of his tongue, gags on it, falls into a fit of burp-choking and dry heaving.

"By Imala," says the sole neighboring prisoner, frightening Rathyn. He's a recent addition. A monk called Tael, and his shrill voice is like a spike. Rathyn had forgotten about him again. It's hard to tell what's real. Whenever time passes without the monk's nagging, Rathyn's imagination begins to convince him he's still alone. Imagination or hope.

"I was dreaming of green blades of sedge ..." The monk's voice bounces over like it's carried by bats. "... stained red by the blood of the magister. If you're going to die, have a shred of decency about it."

"A slinker gave me a bucket of water, but ..." Rathyn whispers, trying to release the shard of wood from his one hand. *I've drunk it all. And now I broke the bucket.* He meant to say some of that out loud. Did he?

"As you've mentioned a dozen times," Tael scoffs. "And if you could get your hands on his throat, you'd strangle him for it."

"Hand," Rathyn says.

"Of course. How could I forget. Evil monks took your poor hand."

Rathyn is struck by a laugh. Instead, he coughs. His gums taste of rotten bucket and blood. For several moments he works his tongue in his mouth, trying to pry the splinters from between his teeth. "It sounded like they brought in another ... prisoner." It doesn't seem likely now that he's said it.

"Oh, did they? Any new prisoners out there?" Tael calls.

His voice bounces off distant surfaces, refracting, dissolving, losing its tinny edge, melting into a dull noise, sustaining, tapering slowly, at last fading completely, leaving only a memory. And for Rathyn, memories have lost their surety. Did the monk say anything? Is a monk even there?

"Looks like it's you and me," the monk says, startling Rathyn. "Guess you imagined that."

Rathyn presses his back against the wall. In front of him is reddish stone. It's always that. But now that there's someone else, Rathyn can occasionally establish some spatial sense, based on the initial jarring screech of the monk's words, before they devolve into muddy echoes. Unfortunately, since the monk was imprisoned here, however many hours or days ago, his every remark has been for the sole purpose of antagonizing Rathyn.

And to think I'd yearned for company, he says. Or no. He didn't say it. Did he?

"You're proof," Rathyn says, and has to clear his throat. "We don't always want what we ask for." He can tell when he's said something aloud because his throat hurts more afterward. He swallows nothing. But ... hurts more than what?

"Exemplars have long known that dirtfeet don't know what's best. Why do you think we're forced to act like goatherds?"

Maybe if Rathyn doesn't respond, the monk will stop talking. *Let me die in peace.*

Faint scratching, scrambling sounds come from the monk's direction. Sounds like he's trying to climb up the cell's rough wall.

"You're wasting your strength," Rathyn mutters. "There's no way out." He swallows. He hadn't meant to say it out loud.

"Maybe if you only have one hand," the monk responds. "I'll let you know when I need a dirtfoot's advice." Tael sounds winded, as if he's exerting himself. "There is a way out, and I know it. Do you?"

"I know one way," Rathyn says. "But it's taking its sweet time."

"I'm not talking about death," Tael says. "There are ancient passages. Escape routes. Unknown to most."

Rathyn chuckles. "More monk lies. You can do better than that."

"This is an active volcano," Tael snaps. "And the fortress has been sitting on it for hundreds of years. You think the sovereign wouldn't have evacuation plans in case of emergency?"

Rathyn considers not responding. The monk's voice whittles away at his dwindling spirit like razorstone against a raw yam. But he can't keep from entertaining the notion of fresh air. "If they're unknown, how do you know about them?"

"I was the folksteller. I kept census of all of Erudition. Can't very well do that if I'm not given rein to wander." The monk's scrambling becomes frantic a moment, interspersed with gulped breath. A muffled thud. Then silence.

When the monk speaks again, it's quieter. "Not that it would help me to get to the passage. There's a locked door at the end. Wouldn't happen to have a key, would you?"

But Rathyn got hung up a moment ago. A word stuck on him like a sandbur in a sandal. *Census.* "No," he says numbly. "Should I?"

"That was sarcasm, dirtfoot. An indication of intellect that your lot are beneath. I imagine only the Triumvirate have keys to such a door."

Something about *census* tugs at Rathyn. Chaplains keep census of villages. Maybe they report to the folksteller. "Did you keep census of the villages as well? Like Napiri?" He tries to keep the hopefulness from his voice.

There's a moment of silence that stretches into several. *There is no monk*, Rathyn's mind informs him.

"No, I didn't keep census of you goats," the monk says. "But I worked with those who do. The Napiri lodge was built some seventy years ago by an old woman of the same name."

Rathyn is on his feet. His stomach cramps, nearly folding him over. He leans against the wall. "Have you heard of a girl there called Tivali?"

"Ah," Tael says. "I remember now. You're the spy from Napiri. I'm surprised they've kept you alive so long."

"Tivali!"

"The acting elder goes by that name," Tael says. "She's a young thing. Is that your mate? You miss romping with her?"

A painful knot rises up in Rathyn's throat. This time it is something besides fear or pain. Of course she's taken over the responsibilities in his absence. Who else would, Rathyn's nephew Tobas? He's got the mouth for it, but Tivali has been kicking his ass since they were knee-high. Rathyn smiles, despite the tears running down his cheeks.

"How is Napiri doing?" he asks.

"I'd say poorly. The strangest rumors are coming out of there. Couldn't say if the stories are true ... but bad rumors never turn out well for a village. They'll probably be visited by lightning soon enough. The magus and his company of death." Tael sounds cheerful to report it.

Rathyn's tears become streams and his smile a grimace. Out of some bizarre concern for his long-extinct dignity, he muffles his weeping with his only hand, fights to stay on his feet rather than collapse. He doesn't know why. The monk finds him pathetic. He is pathetic.

"So sorry to be the bearer of that," Tael says, sounding not sorry in the least. His scuffling against the stone resumes.

It's not dignity that makes Rathyn hide his tears. He doesn't want to empower the monk with evidence of his own defeat. He doesn't want anything to happen the monk might relish. In fact, he wants Tael to die horribly. He will probably accomplish nothing else with his life, but he would sacrifice his other hand and both feet and legs to end Tael's life. He would leap out of his cell and fall into Tael's like a fish and tear the monk apart with his own teeth.

Of course you would, you monster, says the demon.

"Yeah, and then I'd drink his fucking blood!" Rathyn hisses back.

"Excuse me?" the monk says.

Rathyn squeezes his eyes shut, trying to capture the escaping tears, the elusive memory of his daughter's face. Such a pretty girl. He always worried about her, knowing the appetite of boys. He was hard on her, made her tough. But now he knows she's alive. That, perhaps, is as much as he can ever hope for. "Don't ask anything else." It seems he's said it aloud.

The monk is snickering. "Have you finally lost it completely over there?"

Rathyn can't get to Tael. He'll sit in this hole and die of thirst, if starvation doesn't kill him first. But there may yet be a way to ensure the monk dies. In case there was any question.

"Do you know why I'm here?" Rathyn asks the stone in front of him.

"You're a spy," Tael says. "Here's a better question: Do I care?"

"I know the secret," Rathyn whispers. "I know how to kill Intemrus."

The scrambling ceases abruptly, its echoes chasing it away. Only now, on the cusp of saying aloud what those torturers failed to draw out, does Rathyn falter. He's suddenly not alone, standing in his cell. He can hear whispers from neighboring cells, as if they're all occupied and they all have been this whole time and they've been waiting for him to cross this line. What if his admission dooms his village? His daughter?

"Oh, don't stop there," Tael says. "Please tell me how an imprisoned spy can—"

"*Syvea*," Rathyn proclaims. "It's not his tower. It's the crystal inside it." Silence accompanies his pounding heart. He continues over the edge. "And if you steal the crystal, the sovereign will die."

His words echo around the chamber, bouncing back and forth, flying from him, rushing toward him.

the sovereign will die

the sovereign will die

the sovereign will die

Silence stretches on so long Rathyn begins to wonder again if there was ever someone else imprisoned with him. Even his demon has lost its voice. Maybe there's not. Maybe he's still being questioned. Maybe the elapsed time was an illusion, and the bucket, and the guest. Maybe he just earned his freedom, his death.

"Sneaky dirtfoot." There's an edge of irritation in Tael's words. Also fear? "You're trying to damn me too."

Rathyn laughs heartily, falling back against the stone. "Let's hope it works."

"Imala-damn you, spy. What gives you the right to—?"

He's interrupted by a distant *click!* then the rumbling of rungs from an adjacent cell. Rathyn's blood freezes. Bare footsteps, scampering. Pattering. Pattering. Rathyn's stopped breathing. The sound of flesh slapping stone. Running together into a noise like an applause, like wind through leaves, like falling water. Growing closer? No. Quieter now. Growing distant. Fading, fading, until sound is gone, the echo is gone. Next will go the memory.

"Did you hear that?" Rathyn hisses, against his better judgment. Even as he says it, he hopes it was in his head.

"I did," Tael says. Irritation and sarcasm are absent, leaving a frightened squeak.

"It sounded like rungs of a cell extending ..." Rathyn whispers. *What have I done?*

"It was. From within a cell, I gather."

"Do they ... do that on their own?"

"No," Tael says. "You need a key for that too."

"But ... who ... why?" *Why would a prisoner have a key?*

"Must have been that newcomer you mentioned. Maybe you didn't imagine them after all."

Rathyn's trembling. He's not cold. Not particularly afraid. Someone *was* there. And now they've run away. Someone ... *escaped.*

35
Make the Singing Stop

AUSGAN
Stravhelm

The sovereign will die.

That's what Rathyn said. Those are likely the same words that earned him his place here. Chills ride over Kale's arms, despite the humid molten quality of air. Three days ago he'd have placed no weight on a native prisoner's claims. Less than none. He'd have written them off as deceit without a second thought. But now ... it makes too much sense. Kalderys' concern when Obsydia said the sovereign was taking a break from Syvea Tower. The secrecy around it. The fact that the tower has always seemed so vital for Intemrus, and yet he allows no one else in or near it, not even to guard it.

And if there was ever a question as to what a native's motive would be for wanting the sovereign dethroned, in come memories turned nightmares. A child whose smile gives way to wonder at the approaching lightning. A *pop*. Ashes. Kalderys' sentinels braining unarmed natives with chitin-tipped staves.

Go open your eyes, Rathyn said last time. And Kale had. Whenever a village worth of people is flash fried to nothing, it takes no supersensory perception to determine who's at fault. Rathyn also told him he had a secret that would guarantee a swim in magma. Kale had no idea how true that was.

The sovereign will die.

Magus Kalderys performs his atrocities in the sovereign's name. And so maybe Kale needs not confront the Consonant Fist to save Napiri. Maybe the answer is simpler than that. He's in the heart of Stravhelm with a contraband key and an affinity for invisibility. If the prisoner's words are true, the question becomes, will Kalderys still kill in Intemrus' name after Intemrus is dead? Only one way to know. Make Intemrus mortal—take the crystal.

Kale was frisked before imprisonment, and while he did attempt to make the thin disk key invisible, the search the keepers performed was embarrassingly scant. Seemed they were content they had him at all. Pat here, pat there, check his gag, his ropes, now on to the cell. What's a basalt going to have anyway? Kale smiles despite himself. They'd mistaken him for someone less limber. He shimmied his bound wrists around in front of himself, picked the knots with his teeth, then pulled off the fabric gag. The key got him out of the pit.

Kale dashes along the crest of the honeycombed cells. No time for stealth, so his slapping footfalls echo throughout the cavernous chamber. The knot on his head throbs with each step, like that clod, Bronn, is still striking him. The two prisoners, the native Rathyn and Folksteller Tael, are hissing back and forth furtively. Surely about him. Kale doesn't know what the folksteller did to wind up here and he barely cares. Tael's always been an insufferable ass, far snootier than any headcounter has a right to be.

Kale contains his wild sprint before nearing the threshold of the hewn-stone hallway leading from the cells. There is no sound from within, little enough light, and so he proceeds now with as much stealth as he can muster. After a steep incline through the narrow-hewn passage is a small antechamber, the kind of place cell keepers might lounge. And indeed, for the first time in Kale's experience, one keeper reclines within on a simple chair, sandals out, arms crossed, head back, mouth wide. Rattling snores clatter off the walls. He's a new fixture—wasn't here when Kale was brought down—and Kale can't help but wonder if he himself is the prisoner being guarded. If so, they should have chosen a more rested set of eyes.

Cobwebs hang from the ceiling, blowing in the breeze that Kale's movement creates. There is a single oil lantern on a small wooden table beside the one keeper, but it, too, has succumbed to disuse. Against one wall is a pile of boots harvested from prisoners and slung away to be forgotten, not unlike the prisoners themselves as far as Kale can tell. On top of the pile are the hemp and hide sandals Ashmancer Haik procured for Kale's visit to the magister. Kale collects them but does not put them on, instead stowing them in his belt. He can move more quietly without their rigid soles proclaiming his progress.

Beyond the antechamber the tunnel continues to ascend through the mountain. The walls here are smooth, at least compared to the holding cells, and they're growing smoother with each corner he rounds. By the time the floor levels out, the ceiling is high and the walls are polished. Colored lamplight illuminates the path from insets just off the floor.

Kale arrives at an archway much lower than the ceiling. Through it, he can see Stravhelm's main hall, nearly as wide as Erudition's main stair, which serves as the primary thoroughfare for the subterranean sections of Stravhelm. The dimly lit hall is unchanged from when he first crept along it three nights prior. He can hardly believe it was so recently. It feels like a lifetime has passed. As before, the wide hallway is decorated with vases, statuettes, darkness-preferring potted plants, woven rugs on the floor and tapestries hung on the walls.

There's no way to be sure, but if Kale's lucky then it's nearing a count or shortly after it. That would make for emptier halls. He wasn't in the cells long, not relative to some occupants, but he's spent exactly as much time down there as he ever wants to. That his key proved capable of freeing him curtailed real despair. It occurred to him that on his first visit he had the means to free Rathyn and didn't know it—not until he'd seen the keepers extend the rungs of his own cell then retract them. But even if he'd let Rathyn out, then what? Should he have snuck the prisoner out of Stravhelm and down the main street of Erudition to his own bunk? But if the folksteller is right about hidden passages, maybe Kale can do better tonight than he did then.

Here and there, in either direction down the long hallway, orange swaths of candlelight spill from open doorways and stretch across the stone floor. Restrained voices issue forth of exemplars talking, singing, humming. On Kale's previous visit, he had a mind for one destination— the molten pool—and it made itself obvious by the odor of sulfur it excreted. Then, same as now, of all the stone doors in this massive hall only one had the small, circular indention indicating it was locked. Hopefully that is the one he seeks tonight. He could have all night to search, or he may have moments.

Just as before, he avoids the light spilling from the passages and hallways. Before long, he has arrived at a quadrilateral stone slab no taller than himself. At a glance it's unassuming and unadorned, as if it might lead to a lavatory, not that lavatories are locked. Only standing here before it does Kale observe that it's not made of the same stone as the rest of the hall. It's a darker shade, and contoured with age. It's as if this door was hauled from somewhere else entirely.

Kale's palms are clammy as he draws the key from beneath his belt. It's time to learn if it truly came from the Triumvirate. It takes a couple of tries for his shaking hands to fit the heavy disk into the indention, but as soon as he does there's the stone-dampened click of lodestone latches lifting. Kale presses the door with his fingertips. It eases inward. The aged korundite hinges shriek their lament. Kale's heart tries to blast out of his chest. Either that squeal silenced every nearby exemplar or he's gone temporarily deaf. He's shaking as he removes his key from the indention and squeezes into the darkness as soon as he can fit through. The door clicks closed behind him.

He's met with a murky dimness, cold still air, and the sound of his own hushed breath echoing in an obviously enclosed room. For several moments, despite the urge to flee, he doesn't move, straining his eyes to make some sense of the vague shapes gradually clarifying from the utter dark. This is a stairwell and he's at its lowest point. He risks moving his feet, stretching out his hands to make sense of the shapes he's seeing. The stairs begin to his right and ascend steeply upward around a central pillar. There are plain walls, massive block upon block, and the tickling odor of long-disused air. No lamps or lanterns or torches. Maybe windows, far, far above, allowing little more than a dreary haze down here. Kale isn't entirely sure he's not imagining the light.

The tower has every sign of being empty, and yet Kale can barely keep his frantic breathing in check. This could be the wrong door, the wrong stairwell. He'll just have a quick climb to be sure, then proceed to the next if so. It takes some deep breaths and wringing of hands to gather the nerve to mount the first stair. Then he ascends.

Up and up. First he ascends with head tilted back, eyes so wide they're chilled by the air, desperate for evidence he's on the right path, whatever form that might take. That effort quickly proves as futile as it is uncomfortable. So he watches his padding feet, little more than dark impressions on the stone steps, pit-pat pit-pat pit-pat, while his right hand slides up the frigid stone. It takes little time for his wounds to awaken from their relative comfort and remind him how damaged his feet are. No matter. Up he climbs into blackness in a stairwell as silent as death. The damp of sweat spreads over his forehead and cheeks and the chill air bites him refreshingly. His legs warm up quickly. He's no stranger to endurance runs over miles. But the air is suffocating, and these stairs are brutal, and soon his muscles are burning along with his feet.

After three hundred and fifty stairs, it has become obvious he chose the right door. There is no other tower this high besides the sovereign's and Obsydia's. This staircase isn't mistakable for hers. And where this tower has a locked door, Intemrus' has instead a half-dozen armed exemplars. This must be Syvea. He'd take more heart from this fact if he didn't feel locked in place, pushing steps that refuse to stay down, knowing all this stepping will eventually have to be undone.

Either Kale's eyes are growing more accustomed to the dark or there is actual light approaching from above. He was gasping too hard to recognize the hint of movement in the air, as if by some distant door ajar. Kale is too tired to quieten his steps. He can't remember how long it took him to climb Obsydia's staircase. Not this long. But maybe that one seemed quicker because his view progressed as he circled upward round and round.

The wind is not his imagination. The walls are more lit, to the point he can make out the seams between the great stones. This gradual change livens Kale's steps. His chest is so tight breathing is a struggle. He can only hope his descent will require less effort.

The light is bright and cold and stark now, moonlight or Kale's a fool. The air tastes fresher. Excitement and fear are Kale's sole source of energy as he deliberates, finally bothering to still his steps once more. There's a window above and the moonlight pouring in shows exactly how steep this staircase has been the entire time. No railing, nothing to grab. A single misplaced step could result in one hell of a tumble, likely his last, back into the blackness below.

Kale drags himself up to the tall window, panting. The stairwell's outer wall is almost three feet thick and the windowsill, starting wide on the inside with a broad landing, pinches to a narrow opening before allowing in the light of the moon. Perhaps two feet across and seven feet high, the window offers Kale his first open air since before being imprisoned. He sits on the flat windowsill to catch his breath.

Outside, the moon hangs low over the distant sparkling ocean. Down below the tower torch lights wriggling in the dark streets indicate the night is young and exemplars are about. They've not yet had evening count. With a pang of dread, Kale realizes the evening count could easily include the cell he's supposed to be occupying. All the more reason to be quick about this.

Kale pokes his head out the window. To his left and some ways off is Obsydia's tower, with its massive shell above. No curtains are pulled and he can make out the silhouettes of adherents standing at intervals around her gazebo, illuminated by unnecessarily large burning braziers. He doesn't see her. If she's there she must be lying down. Beyond it and higher up is Intemrus' tower, with its shining scale windowpanes. Being at this proximity to it, especially on this reckless gamble, makes Kale deeply unsettled. He withdraws his head, climbs to his throbbing feet, continues upward.

There are more windows on his ascent, and each one faces eastward. Every new window discloses more of Erudition, hidden from the moon by the shadow of the tall eastern wall. A grander view of the jungle beyond that stretches all the way to the ocean, wherein lies Proctor Alika's Elucidatorium. At last, Kale can see the East Rostrum, standing on the edge of the ocean and rising even higher than the sagacious mahoganies of the jungle. Another change his altitude brings is wind, which started as a whisper in the lowest windows but has become an insistent rush. It is not lost on Kale, as he doggedly takes step after step, that despite the solid stone beneath his feet he is nearly as high as the clouds. His unease mounts with every window he passes.

His impending destination makes itself known by sending the echoes of his slapping steps back down at him from above. The ceiling is utterly dark, and the steep steps deliver him to a landing nearly within reach of it. Before him are rungs in the stone wall. They're not entirely unlike the rungs in the cells, except these are permanent. Kale places his hand on one. It's cold stone, or korundite, or maybe something he's not familiar with. Rough to the touch, except toward the center, where something has smoothed the otherwise irregular texture. Did Intemrus' own hands do this work? He's said to have lived and studied consonance for hundreds of years. Has he been climbing this tower the whole time?

Kale ascends the ladder, his nerves racing, sure he's wedging himself in a position from which there is no escape. What if Obsydia was wrong about Intemrus ceasing to visit the tower? What if he's on his way now? Will Kale have to hide above? He slings the brittle bamboo-plank covering off the trapdoor in a near panic, freeing the rushing wind to chill his face and sober him. Dust trickles down into his eyes and nose and mouth, making him sneeze abruptly. For a moment he doesn't move, only listens. All he perceives is wind.

He pulls himself eye-level with a filthy floor in a moonlit room. Just like the entire tower up until this point, there is no splendor herein. It's an octagonal room, with eight total windows lacking shutters or curtains or any decor. Kale hefts himself up until he's sitting on the trapdoor's edge. What appeared to be wooden detritus shoved against the walls of the room are contraptions, or their remains. There's a narrow table with what looks like a frail cartwheel intersecting its surface, and wooden pedals and levers below. Another table-like contraption except its wooden top is intentionally angled and on the lower edge are grooves, as if for holding writing implements. More thin-legged wooden objects are tucked behind those, or under them, none blocking the windows, all of them the inert beige that moonlight turns dusty wood.

They say Intemrus spends days up here. Weeks even. Or he did. Kale expected important volumes of writing, perhaps works in progress. But there aren't even the tools to write, much less a clean surface to do it on. Everything he sees appears distinctly ancient and untouched. Also, the wind up here rushes through the tower's windows like a stream through a poorly woven basket. The tiers of Erudition experience no wind. Neither does most of Stravhelm, including Obsydia's tower. That wind is redirected by Intemrus so as to protect the holy city from the noxious exhaust of the volcano, Mount Adenhelm. It must be to this altitude that Intemrus sends the wind. It never occurred to Kale that just above the silent city's atmosphere was a raging wind, utterly unnoticeable. Well, unnoticeable to anyone as blind as himself.

Kale's nerves are dissolving into disappointment. He's concluding that he has made an incredible effort to visit the most out-of-the-way storage closet in all Ausgan when he notices tracks in the dust on the floor. It's the only evidence this room has been visited in the last century. The faint line of prints runs back and forth over itself in layers on layers, directing Kale's eyes toward the shadows. He rises to his feet slowly. Wind whips sweaty hair into his eyes. The surrounding windows strike him with both a stunning panoptic, and a dizzying sensation that nearly turns his stomach inside out. He is higher than Obsydia's tower, or even the sovereign's.

To the west, opposite the hovering moon, is Mount Adenhelm's peak. Beyond it are the toxic black clouds that rise from volcanic vents. Seeing it this close nearly debilitates Kale in horror. They billow upward in utter silence, slow as flowing sap. The surging westward wind forces the cloud up and away so as not to descend on the holy city. It is said that Intemrus' perpetual redirecting of those clouds is all that prevents acidic rain from falling on the city.

The footprints in the dust terminate at a spindly-limbed wooden chair facing the east. Beside it is a small, ornately carved wooden pedestal, and on that pedestal's small center is what looks like a chunk of quartz holding down a slip of parchment. Kale approaches, his mouth dry and his heart pounding. The prisoner was right. Even in this weak light, he can tell at several paces off it's not quartz. Too pure. Too transparent. This ... is Syvea?

The sovereign will die ...

Kale freezes. What if it's true? What if Intemrus dies as soon as he touches it? What will happen to the black clouds? The wind? The rain that Intemrus diverts, will it fall all at once? Will it rain on the holy city for the first time ever? Will it rain on Napiri? Will there be a scream or sound? Some evidence?

Northward is Intemrus' silent, lightless tower, and looking down at it feels at the same time unnatural and empowering. Suddenly he's not so invisible. Not so helpless. Quite the opposite. Kale steps forward and snatches the crystal.

immortality?

The voice is so near Kale almost panics and flings the crystal out a window. A girl's voice, in a dialect he's never heard. And even as his physical body screams at him to scramble for a hiding spot in all the rubble, he knows it wasn't his ears that heard the voice. It was a memory. And somehow ... not one of his own.

The crystal is warm to the touch. It's small enough to conceal entirely within his closed fist, and when he does, he notices that though it's made up of faceted edges, one side is rougher than the rest, as if this stone is an incomplete fragment.

The wind is still blowing. Kale looks toward the billowing black clouds. No change. Upward they rise like a hooded snake preparing to strike. He looks toward the sovereign's tower. No movement. By Imala, what if that prisoner was wrong?

The parchment the crystal held in place flitters on the pedestal. Kale grabs it before it can fly away. It crackles in his hand, so old that it flakes at his touch. He studies it closer. Only under the light of the moon can he discern the faint writing.

I mean to marry him. I'll be accompanying him when we leave Redemier. I'm going to Fohrvylda, not Ausgan. I'm sorry for hurting you.

I love you, Father. If you love me too, please understand.

Kale's head tilts to the side as he puzzles over the letter. Redemier. The cursed island. Whoever wrote this must have been there before the Split, hundreds of years ago when Intemrus went west and Vretos went east. This was written before the Deceiver's deception. Kale's eyes wander the room again, looking for something to help unravel this intrigue. Is it possible the tools and implements here are all as old as the letter? If so, they meant so much to Intemrus that he saved them all and eventually built this tower to store them. Is this a tower, or a shrine?

Kale shakes his head. There's no time to ponder on that, or anything else. Taking the crystal was what he set out to do and he'll see it done. To protect Napiri. To protect Tivali. He stashes it inside his dele, in his breast pocket, where it clinks against the key. He places the letter where he found it, even knowing that without the crystal holding it down any errant breeze will carry it away. Not his problem.

He flees the room, hardly bothering to lower himself down the ladder's rungs. He's on the stairs again, running, reenergized by what he's done, flinging himself two and three stairs at once as if he can outpace the fact that he has stolen this tower's namesake from the immortal sovereign of Stravhelm. Chills run all over him. He runs faster.

Descending is quicker. He's two windows down and not even out of breath. Once again, Kale reinforces his hypothesis that Intemrus does not see all. Whether or not it's true, it is definitely the preferable scenario.

They're coming.

Kale scrambles to a stop, breath rushing, heart blasting in his ears. Again it was a girl's voice. Again it was only a memory, veiled by a vast swath of time, and yet here, *now*. Was it she who authored the letter? Kale feels he'd be a fool to ignore the voice. He plucks the crystal from his dele. It's of a natural enough design to hide whether or not it was crafted, but it has surely been broken at some point. Kale peers closer. There's color within. A reddish pink pinpoint, the epicenter of the facets, increasing in complexity near the crystal's off-centered core.

He's tempted to shake it, to listen to it, make it say more. Before he has the chance, he hears echoing footsteps. Someone is approaching from downstairs. Kale's blood runs cold. He minimizes his imprint, but on this confined staircase there is no place to hide. He considers dashing upstairs again, seeking shelter in that room of dusty furniture. But there were no nooks that would suffice to hide him, and even if there were, something tells him the person approaching would scour the room, gutting it down to its dusty floor if they were to arrive and find the crystal gone. Are they approaching because he took the crystal? Did he trigger some alarm?

I hoped ... it would take them longer.

Kale grits his teeth, now more tempted to shake the stone into silence. He might have determined that the voice isn't speaking out loud but that fails to reassure that he alone can perceive it.

"*Shh,*" he hisses, squeezing the crystal. He steps into the deeply recessed windowsill, as near to the opening as he dares. The night wind tickles over the breach, tugging the tail of his borrowed dele out the opening, rustling it against the tower wall. Kale panics, seizing at the sheer surface. There is nothing to grip. The footsteps are closer. Sounds like they're running. Moonlight glares in through the window, casting Kale's unmistakable shadow against the inner column. He'd scarcely be more visible if he were shaking a lit torch. The only way he won't be seen is if the person approaching has no eyes.

The clatter of steps is accompanied by hushed breathing now. Whoever it is isn't wearing boots. And they're not on so urgent a mission they've abandoned dignity like he did. There is control to their breathing.

Kale pokes his head out the window, looking for a ledge, or an awning, or an eve, or even a loose brick, something to cling to. The stone edges are sharp and frigid. Moonlight glimmers off Erudition's polished stone roofs and walls over two hundred feet below him, so far away the threat of falling is surreal. The tower's exterior is no more textured than its interior. All there is to cling to is the window's edge. Perhaps he could—Kale drops to his knees—perhaps he can lower himself by his fingertips, wait for the person to pass, then haul himself back up.

Kale tests the edge. Sharper than he'd prefer. Probably edged enough to cut him. He's never clung to anything like this. He's not even sure he'd be able to hoist himself up again once the threat has passed. But what choice is there? He pushes a leg out the window and notices he's perfectly level with Intemrus' tower. A glance in this direction would expose him at once.

Not until this is resolved.

Kale's heart leaps into his throat and he bites back a swear, hauling his leg inside. The crystal is determined to communicate to him, but it's like she's pulling words from a long-passed conversation. Kale welcomes the advice to mean he should not fling himself out the window yet. Instead he flattens himself against the windowsill. No time for anything else. The runner is almost upon him. He presses the warm crystal to his chest, hoping against hope that if it speaks again, only he'll hear it. With both hands he holds the crystal to himself, posed as if in preparation for a burial box. Kale minimizes himself down to a stone's imprint, among thousands of stones. His eyes squeeze close. If he sees his own shadow his concentration will surely shatter.

Abruptly they've arrived, panting. Kale cracks an eyelid to find a tall, slight figure, hunched and huffing with one hand on the wall, hooded despite the darkness and closed air. They too must be intruding. But beyond the figure who has paused to rest is a more curious development. The moonlight casts a perfect window shape onto the interior column, with this newcomer's figure at its center. Kale's own shadow ... is gone. As if light itself finds him immaterial.

The newcomer's breath stops. So does Kale's. They reach their hand to the ground to inspect something. Kale's knees almost buckle. It's bloody footprints. Kale's eyes flicker to his battered feet. The prints are his, from his ascent.

The figure crouches, head turning this way and that in puzzlement. Kale curses himself. He'd forgotten how damaged his feet were, or else he'd have put on the sandals. Too late now. Luckily his feet seemed to have attracted a thick layer of dust, surely from the room at the top, that is preventing further leakage, at least for the moment. Whatever blood he tracked, he did so only on his ascent.

The figure stands, watching the ground in thought, reaches up and drops their hood. Kale's heart stops.

Godsbedamned to Lahuvot's Lake, of all the luck!

Magister Obsydia. Kale cannot imagine a single person, or monster for that matter, more terrifying to face in this stairway. *What's she doing here?* She takes her eyes from his prints and looks directly at him. Her eyes are focused past him. On the moon? She can't see him. Standing at arm's length against a featureless backdrop, she can't see him! But for how long? How long can he maintain absolute invisibility? How is he even doing it?

Kale weighs his options. This is fickle deception at best. He's not capable of consonance or manipulation or any flavor of magic but shallow trickery, never has been. This facade will collapse, and soon. She can sense an exemplar's heart rate across a room like she's got an ear to their chest. She will see him, and when she does ...

He has to do something. He could shove her and dash past. Except she's notorious for combat brutality and lightning reflexes. She'd probably break his arm in a blink, then break the rest of him by throwing him down the stairs. Even if he pushed her off balance and got past her, she'd pursue and catch him.

He could take a leap from the window, hope the crystal is as enchanting as it looks, and bestows wings upon him. Except that's ridiculous. He'd fly like a fish and then splash against rhyolite. His mashed remains would probably cushion the blow for the crystal.

The crystal.

He could hold it out the window, threaten to drop it. Tell her to back up and let him pass. But then what? He and Obsydia would be at a standoff until the sun rose. That's assuming Obsydia even knows what the crystal is. Surely she does, there's nothing else up there. Is she here to steal it as well? The crystal said, *They're here for me.* Did it mean her?

Even if she did come for it, he's struggling to shake any usefulness out of that assertion in this moment. It still puts her at odds with him. Unless she, too, means to end Intemrus' reign. That thought would be more comforting if she hadn't personally commanded the campaign that brought lightning down on Hargrim's children.

Obsydia has gotten her heaving chest under control, deepening the silence and Kale's dread. There is confusion in her eyes as she watches the moon through what can only be an empirically nonexistent Basalt Kale. She reaches out her hand toward his mouth. He holds his breath, clenches his teeth, clenches his buttocks to keep from letting gas slip.

Her hand is so close he can see the individual ridges in her fingerprints, smell the coconut oil on her fingertips. She waves back and forth slowly, as if clearing away cobwebs. Her face, fully illuminated by the moon, is a picture of perplexity. Kale doesn't know what she sees, what made her look, but he prays the illusion holds.

The footprints, he urges. *What about those? Follow them. Up you go now, shoo!*

Was it the crystal's presence that stopped her? Is it helping him hide now? A frightening possibility occurs to him. If this crystal takes away Intemrus' immortality, does it grant immortality to its new owner? *Am I safe to jump out the window?* Without moving his head, he shifts his eyes to the window's edge and beyond. Until recently he's been hunting for an opportunity to quietly die. Or more accurately, to vanish once and for all. And now death is the last thing he wants. He has to live long enough to see this effort through. Maybe he's stolen Intemrus' life and his will. If not he'll have to do something else to protect Napiri. *Tivali.* Her smile visits his memory. The smile she wore after he killed Arc. The one she wore as her clothing fell away. Kale's stomach aches with longing. He doesn't know what he meant to her. He's not even sure what she means to him. It's ... not natural what he did. Or at least not expected. A monk coupling with a native. It changed him. He wants to protect her, even at the cost of the holy city. He wants to save her father from the cells. In fact, he doesn't want to even gift himself with the sight of her again unless he's done everything in his power to help her father. She saved his life. It's the least he can do. If Folksteller Tael is right and there are secret exits near the cells, maybe he'll disclose them if he too is promised escape. But if Obsydia stands staring through him much longer, he'll have a puddle of piss to hide in addition to himself.

Obsydia lowers her hand, her head cocked sideways. She pulls her hood tight, turns abruptly, and sprints up the stairs. For several moments Kale waits, scared to even exhale. Then he dislodges from the windowsill and slinks downward, quietly at first until he's sure his steps will go unheard, then quicker. Long after he hears the last trace of her, he sprints. Three steps at once. Four. No time to think or be careful.

He must have passed the lowest window, because he is returning to the impervious dark. He paces himself. Feeling is all he has at this point. Step, step, step, step, while the fingertips of his left hand rub raw against the wall. He goes for a step and nearly hyper-extends his knee, landing at last on the flat floor of the tower. He grunts, shaking out his leg, taking this chance to pluck his sandals from his belt.

The gods only know what Obsydia was doing up there. But if she came for the same reason he did, she's about to be disappointed. She saw the state of his feet when she arrested him. Once she couples the missing crystal with the bloody prints ...

There is no time to waste. He pulls the sandals on, trying to fashion a story to tell anyone who may be standing sentry outside the door.

Nothing comes to mind. His best bet is to surprise them with a tactical groin kick and run like the wind. *Unless they're armored.*

Kale finds the indention and applies the key. The door unlocks, shifting inward. He grips it with fingertips, pulls it wide open, and leaps out into the hallway, hands ready to deflect or grab a swinging baton. No one's there, only shadows and silence. Magister Obsydia came alone. To Syvea Tower. In the dead of night. If she'd come for Kale, she'd have brought her primes at least. There can be only one reason. She means to steal the crystal. She means to end Intemrus' life, assuming Kale hasn't already managed that by means of his own theft. Did Obsydia plan to supplant Intemrus? His mind races. Has his grand thievery initiated that change of power?

Dwelling on it won't help him. He must free Rathyn. Their escape relies on Tael's emergency passages to escape Stravhelm. Kale sprints back the way he came, this time not even bothering to dodge the swaths of light. His imprisonment, was that even known by anyone but Obsydia? It was Haik and his sentinels who caught him, and they seemed intent on making as little spectacle of it as possible.

Now the oddity of Kale's most recent visit with the magister haunts him. The questions she asked ... they weren't anything he'd expect. She never asked how he left the city or what he'd intended. The city's safety wasn't her concern. She cared more about Kalderys' song being stopped. She asked if anyone else could do it. Does she plan to use Kalderys to take down Intemrus? And if that happens, will native villages be safer or more likely to burn?

The keeper is still slumbering when Kale returns to the neglected antechamber. He pauses long enough to quietly gather an armful of sandals, hopefully enough to find a matching pair. He returns to the massive chamber of cells, where the pore pattern on the floor resembles a great wasp nest. Nothing here has changed in his absence.

Within Rathyn's cell, the native is hunched over, facing the wall, holding his stump of a wrist. He's rocking gently and muttering in a voice too low for Kale to make out words. Kale snaps his key into the indention. The korundite ladder grinds out of the wall, making Rathyn startle, then flinch and shrink back.

"Can you climb?" Kale whispers down.

The man ceases his quivering, turning squinting eyes up toward Kale. "Wha—you?"

He looks even worse than the first time Kale saw him. His cheeks are more sunken. His eyes are deep beneath hairless ridges of brows.

Kale descends the ladder and approaches him. Rathyn slinks backward, as wary as a cornered animal. For a moment Kale has the impression the man will attack—not that he appears to have the energy to do it.

"Can you climb?" Kale asks, holding his hand out carefully, conscious of the fact this man's probably not eaten in days. "I ... I did what you said. I opened my eyes." Kale had hoped for recognition at this. Instead the man's eyes are feral. There is no trust. Quite the opposite, as if he'd prefer to eat Kale than climb anything. Kale is running out of time, but he will not leave Rathyn here. He has to convince the man to trust him. "I met your daughter, Tivali," Kale says. "She misses you."

Rathyn's tension collapses. His eyes become round and shiny. He reaches a shaky hand toward Kale. His shoulders tremble, as if somewhere deep inside he's weeping. His stump is pressed close to his chest. Kale takes his hand, and the realization hits him that outside sparring, this man and his daughter are almost the only people he's ever touched. *Family* is a word that comes to Kale's mind. And he wonders if he could ever end up with one.

"Let's get out of here," Kale says. He pulls Rathyn to his feet. The gaunt man is almost as tall as Kale. He's emaciated and stinks of filth, but his grip is sure and his feet appear steady enough. Kale directs him to the ladder, where Rathyn grabs a rung. His face is lit up in anticipation, as if he's found a secret treasure that will soon vanish. Kale follows him up, pushing Rathyn's bony rump, keeping him from falling backward as he transfers his grip from one rung to the next.

"What's going on up there?" It's the shrill voice of Folksteller Tael, several cells away.

By the time Rathyn has reached the top of the ladder and climbed to his feet, new energy is evident. His eyes are sharp, wild. Exiting the cell seems to have breathed new life into him.

"Can you walk?" Kale asks.

"I can run," Rathyn says. His gaunt face indicates severe malnourishment, but there's a fire in his eyes so intense Kale can't help but believe him. He drops the sandals before Rathyn. "See if some fit you." It's poor payback considering the boots Tivali gave him, but it's better than nothing.

"You can't leave me here," Tael calls.

"Like hell we can't." Rathyn gives a piercing laugh. His eyes are too wide. There's spittle gathered at the edges of his mouth. "Rot, you monk bastard."

"I'll call down the keepers," Tael says. "If I can't leave, none of you can."

Rathyn's eyes bulge and his face flushes and he draws a breath as if to belt out some response. Kale grabs his thin arm to silence him. He follows Tael's voice to the edge of a cell. Tael stands alert in the center of the floor, looking upward with fists clenched at his sides. His cheeks are smudged black. His thin hair is disheveled.

"Resonations, Folksteller," Kale says.

"Basalt Kale ..." Tael takes a step backward, his face darkening. "It's your fault I'm here."

Whatever that means, there's no time for it. "I heard you say you know a way to escape the cells."

Tael's eyebrow arches. "Maybe I do."

"Can you take us there?"

Tael's head cranes to one side. "You'd need a key," he says carefully. "And not just any key." He crosses his arms over his chest. "What are you up to, anyway?"

"No time to talk," Kale says, brandishing the whaletusk key for Tael to see. "You want out or not?"

"Leave him," Rathyn says. "We don't need him."

That might be true. Kale could negate himself to the point of invisibility. But to apply that same invisibility to himself and Rathyn all the way through the halls of Stravhelm, then down the streets of Erudition, especially after the magister inevitably raises an alarm, which she may have already done ...

There are voices from the direction of the exit, accompanied by a faint flickering light, as if someone's moving a torch in the far antechamber. Kale's heart drops. Despite this room's size and its dim light, if those keepers come in here, he and Rathyn will be spotted at once. Aside from the cells in the floor, this chamber is without a hiding place.

Rathyn tugs Kale's dele at his shoulder. "We're too late," he hisses.

"Dammit," Kale mutters. "We have to hide." Except hiding in a cell won't work. This room will inevitably flood with keepers, and they will scour the place.

"Wait," says Folksteller Tael, his eyes wide. "If we take the exit and your key doesn't open the door at the end, we'll be stuck."

"We're already stuck," Kale says, snapping the key into the indention to extend Tael's rungs. Stone rumbles softly, vibrating beneath Kale's feet. Hopefully whoever is in the antechamber can't hear it. "This key will open it."

Tael places his hands on the rungs but doesn't climb. "How can you be sure?"

"Because it opens everything." Kale backs away from the opening. Exposing the crystal might be exactly the proof the man needs. It would also invoke too many questions, waste too much time, maybe even give the folksteller some unwelcome ideas of his own. The far-off voices have diminished, but the light from the hallway is still there.

Tael climbs the ladder, pausing at eye level to give a look around.

"Hurry up, monk," Rathyn hisses.

Tael stands, brushing his hands off against his soot-stained dele and patting at his hair.

"Let's go, Folksteller," Kale says. "If we're quiet, we can make it out of here. If not—"

"If not I'll break his jaw," Rathyn says. He glares up at Tael, daring him. "And I'll enjoy it."

"I'm not the folksteller anymore," Tael says with genuine resentment. "Certainly not now. The path is this way." And he falls into a lope toward the far wall of the cells.

Kale doesn't trust the folksteller, but he trusts the man's sense of self perseveration. They skulk along the precipice of empty cells away from the main exit, toward the far end of the chamber. Kale finds himself stealing glances into the cells they pass, always expecting the worst. Now and then a cell has a garment or strip of fabric. Otherwise the majority are bare. Kale half expected to see skeletons. Perhaps all prisoners eventually do take the bath, before or after starving.

The air grows hotter as they creep along, and Kale has to fight the itch in his throat to keep from coughing. Ahead, through wavering heat, Tael appears to be on course to run straight into the chamber's rough-hewn stone wall. Instead, he blinks out of view. Kale stops, panting in the heat.

"Godsdamned monk!" Rathyn says.

Tael's annoyed face appears, poked out from what appears to be a passage behind a tall outcropping, camouflaged at this angle. "Hurry up," he says.

Kale follows him into a nearly hidden cleft that runs from floor to ceiling, with Rathyn close behind, murmuring under his breath. The floor is rough, merging into the walls on either side, giving the impression this passage wasn't carved by exemplars. The channel closes in above until there is no light, and the hint of a breeze intensifies the smell of rotten eggs. Kale keeps a hand on the wall and covers his mouth with his sleeve. The darkness becomes complete. The uneven floor threatens to trip him. On they go. Kale can only assume that the pattering in front of him is the folksteller, the shuffling from behind is Rathyn.

"Keep your head down," Tael says from the darkness ahead.

Indeed, the walls above are closing in toward Kale's ears, and the stone is jagged to the touch.

"Stairs," Tael calls back.

The warning doesn't keep Kale from stubbing his toe and nearly falling. The stairs are flat and at regular intervals, far easier to traverse in utter darkness than uneven floor. The air cools as they go.

"Here," says Tael's voice. "Where's the key?"

Kale fumbles forward until he accidentally gropes Tael. He stops hunched over on a cramped landing.

"I'll hold the key," Kale says, offering his arm. Tael takes his wrist and directs his hand to what is unmistakably an indention for a key. Once again, Kale is struck with trepidation. Tael blames Kale for being here. He said as much. Kale withdraws his arm. "How do we know this leads out from under the mountain and not into the barracks?"

"Because it does," Tael snaps. "Think about it, basalt. There's no redemption for me in Stravhelm. The bath is my fate. I wouldn't lead us back to those who imprisoned me."

"So you'll escape with us?" Rathyn asks from close behind. "And go where? You'll get no love in the jungle. Your monk friends will find you anywhere you try to hide."

"Same goes for Kale, does it not?"

"As far as I'm concerned, Kale is redeemed, despite any monkery," Rathyn says. "I'll see to it Napiri knows that. And anyone else who'll listen."

Tael snorts at that. "If there still is a Napiri. I can go south, to the Untamed. We don't account for it. Or north, to Redemier. It's cursed. They won't follow me there. I'll do neither if we sit here bickering and get caught."

Kale is not reassured. Tael is surely smarter than to believe he'll fare well in either of those destinations. Maybe he's not. At any rate, Kale can't argue his final point. He places the key in the indention. With a click, a sliver of light cuts through the blackness in front of him, accompanied by a blade of cool, fresh wind.

"By Imala," Rathyn whispers. His voice wavers as if he's on the verge of tears. He heaves himself between Kale and Tael and shoves the stone door. It doesn't budge. Judging by its outline, the door is almost as tall as Kale, maybe twice as wide, and solid rock. Imala only knows how thick it is. Kale joins Rathyn, straining against the door. It shifts, rumbles, inches outward, exposing starry night air above and Mount Adenhelm's craggy face below, which descends in stark moonlight toward the black jungle wall. The door is angled such that without pressure, it will swing closed.

"I ... can't ..." Rathyn gasps through gritted teeth.

Kale places one foot halfway up the doorframe and his back against the door. He lifts his other foot and braces it, hefting the stone door's weight with his legs. It slowly grinds outward over loose shale and shrubbery.

"Crawl under me," Kale says, voice pinched by his straining.

Rathyn removes his hands from the door slowly. Kale doesn't notice a difference in the load he bears, but his legs are starting to tremble. Rathyn crawls under him, scampering out into the bright moonlight.

"Now you go," Kale says to Tael.

"Yes, I could do that."

Only now Kale notices Tael's been lurking back, not helping or even offering to. The sharp edge in his voice sends dread into Kale's gut.

"Or I could do this."

He launches a forceful kick at Kale's hip. The sharp blow hits muscle, making one of Kale's legs seize up and lose all strength. Kale grunts and folds, falling to the stony mountainside, rolling away in time to keep from losing his lower half as the heavy door crashes closed.

Kale leaps to his feet, gritting his teeth at the pain in his thigh. The side of the mountain seems to reverberate from the door slamming. And now there is no sign of it. Kale's key is still inside. Now it's Tael's key. Not that it matters. Kale would be a fool to ever return here.

"Imala's ass!" Rathyn yells, kicking the side of the mountain. "I knew not to trust that snide fucking ... *songster.*"

Kale can't help but smile. "Your daughter called me a songster once. I don't even sing."

The anger washes off Rathyn, making his shoulders relax. "He served his purpose, didn't he?"

"Only other talent I'd ask of him is to taste better than us to the creatures in the jungle."

Rathyn faces the forest and his eyes shine as a smile takes him. Wind makes his limp hair whip around his face. "Leave the jungle to me."

The moon hangs in the sky over Erudition's wall. They're on the mountain's southern face. From this angle the holy city seems a dark, lifeless place. And it is. Kale wonders how he's never noticed. No wind, not even a breeze. No rain. No ... physical contact. His heart gives a kick. *Tivali.*

To their right are the deadlands on Adenhelm's western face. The black clouds rising up are still avoiding Stravhelm. Does Intemrus still live?

Rathyn takes a deep breath, leaning his head back on his thin neck and closing his eyes. "Air," he sighs. He turns his sunken eyes on Kale. "I thought all monks sing. Thought it was required. If you don't sing, what do you do?"

Surprisingly, the question still cuts, even though Kale has been asking himself that his entire life. But he's gaining a shadow of an answer. He plucks the crystal out of his dele and holds it between his face and Rathyn's. "I make the singing stop."

Rathyn arches his nearly hairless eyebrows. "By Imala, boy ..." He fails to produce anything else for a moment. Then he slumps. "That's my fault, isn't it? You took that because of what I said." He looks pained. "I never meant to put you in danger."

"Yes, I do have you to thank. I wish I'd opened my eyes sooner."

Rathyn purses his chapped lips, reluctantly accepting Kale's apparent absolution. "Well ... did it work?"

Speculating on that has done Kale no good so far. "I don't know. We need to get to Napiri. Quickly." Kale looks down over the craggy rocks. It's hard to determine the distance to the forest but it's not close. There is little foliage here. Only angular rocks and hungry precipices. It'll be slow going.

"I can get us there," Rathyn says. A remnant of hope is etched over his bony face. "But it won't be quick. I'm in no shape to run."

They're coming.

Kale nearly jumps out of his skin again. Rathyn shows no sign of having heard the voice, or memory, or hallucination. Kale exhales, gathers his nerves. This mouthy crystal is taking some getting used to. If it did this to Intemrus, no wonder he locked it up.

"We don't have much time," Kale says, as if they're his words. "I might be able to help with the predators. I can make it hard for them to see us. But if we don't hurry there may be no Napiri left by the time we get there."

Rathyn rolls his head over his shoulders, a grimace on his face as if every movement is painful. He examines his wrist. In the moonlight, it looks like little more than broken driftwood. Peering at the jungle, he says, "It's not safe to travel at night. Maybe I can rouse up help from some friends. A little guidance." He gives a wry smile that evaporates quickly. "I don't know how much other use I'll be to you, monk. I've seen better days."

"I told you, call me Kale. Just get me to Napiri. I'll take it from there."

36
A Den of Snakes

FOHRVYLDA
Vretos' Lodge, Promontory

Falconer Pappu clings to the cliff wall hundreds of feet over the ocean, witnessing the march of the morning sun burn Fohrvylda's shadow off the Faithless Sea. In the air around him are his preferred family. The sprakes ride gusts of wind skyward, up and up. Sunlight bursts on their feathers, turning them dazzling turquoise and silver. There they apex, linger, fall back into shadow, grey again. They dive in spirals, navigating the air like playful spears. Some of the birds pull up out of the dive at the last moment. Others hit the sea at full force. The resulting splash is replaced in a moment by the pitching tide, leaving no evidence of the raptors until they burst again from the sea.

"I'm old."

It's Vretos addressing his court. The court meeting must have begun while Pappu was distracted. He pulls himself up the rock face. The cliffs are easy to navigate. You just stick to the deep ridges that crisscross the stone and give it the appearance of huge slabs of bark on a great pine tree. Pappu wedges his rump into the formation beneath the wall-sized window of Vretos' lodge. Here's where he witnesses the court meetings without being seen. He's twenty yards from the five-sided table, but one does not study under sprakes their whole life without obtaining keen enough eyes and ears to conquer that distance.

"I've lived long enough to forget, twice over, lessons I learned in youth," Vretos continues, "even though those lessons were hard won and vital. The problem with being a pinnacle is that you're forever alone. And yet I'm hopelessly optimistic. I see the Heathen Tide on our horizon. I see us riding out with hundreds of ships. Crossing the sea. Combatting the monks on their own beach. I see us silencing the sovereign of monks, taking his island and making it ours." He's silent a moment. "That vision skewed my judgment."

Vretos' voice tumbles alone from his great lodge to intertwine with the rushing wind and the frisking sprakes. Hearing him mention his old age, or time at all, is always strange to Pappu. Vretos is rumored to be over three hundred years old and unkillable. From what Pappu has seen of the man, he's inclined to believe the latter. Regarding his age, one might place him somewhere between thirty and fifty years old. Pappu can't fathom him being older than that.

The five chairs that the court usually occupy—the chairs they lust after and cut each other's throats over—lie smoldering in splintered pieces in the hearths. There is no food served today. Vretos is at his place at the empty table, naked from the belt up as usual. Standing around the table are the admiral, Garr, Pappu's father, Grimmet, and Marshal Zander. Lanista Udiari isn't present. The atmosphere is unusually penitent.

"My expectations for you each were too high." Pappu can't see Vretos' expression, but the threat is audible. "I trusted you."

A frigid silence follows on the heels of his words.

"... when there isn't a shred of trust among you."

The men Vretos addresses express discomfort in varying ways. Garr's mustache roils. Zander averts his eyes. Grimmet shifts his weight, but he does that whenever he stands for too long.

A fervent shriek pulls Pappu's attention to the ocean's surface. Sprakes are attempting to contain a full-grown white shark at the water's surface. Three of the great birds have their talons locked into its tail and pectoral fins. A fourth is making dives at the shark's pointed nose. The shark snaps at the bird each time, driving it off. A fifth bird joins the effort and clenches talons in its dorsal fin. Red trails line the shark and drift out pink over the tumbling waves.

"I've done away with the chairs," Vretos says. "They, and your stipends, aren't being earned."

Pappu looks in time to watch the shoulders of the three other men sag.

"What you *have* earned, I've spared you. But I'm running out of mercy. Justice is inevitable."

The fires in the hearths crackle in response. Their smoke converges and lingers in the rafters, rising to filter through the narrow chimney slit running the length of the ceiling.

"Admiral Garr, are you responsible for the defense of our seas?" Vretos asks.

"I am, Your Might." Garr's bright mustache works rapidly. His broad naval hat sits on the table before him, leaving his flattened, silvering hair exposed. His black coat has squared shoulders and large brine-greened buttons, and ends above his knees, making his already stumpy legs appear even squatter. As usual, he looks as if he just stepped off a ship's deck and he'll return there directly after this.

"Why didn't you catch the Undying and the rapist when they fell from Keswal right into your hands? They are enemies of Fohrvylda, are they not?"

The admiral's response is an angry-eyed, blustery exhale that trembles his mustache. No words are forthcoming. Pappu smirks. No doubt his father is relishing this. Admiral Garr never catches scorn from Vretos. Grimmet will gloat about this moment for weeks. Maybe longer. Or maybe far shorter, depending on how this meeting goes.

Garr lifts his chin. "We scoured the rocks below Keswal and the feet of the Towers. As you know, ships cannot enter the alleys of the Towers, that's Zander's domain, but we went as far south as the Bluffs and as far north as the banks of Redemier. We searched the sea day and night, Vretos."

"We?" says Vretos.

Garr gives a dry *ahem*, as if his throat needs clearing. "My men."

"They might as well have searched their own asses day and night, wouldn't you say?"

Pappu snorts and quickly covers his face with his hand. Grimmet's mustache squeezes into an orange triangle and his cheeks redden. Even at this distance Pappu can tell he's wisely swallowing whatever responses are trying to escape him. Pappu wonders what emotion Garr's lips would give away were they not hidden by the golden mop.

"We searched the places that catch dead bodies," the admiral says at last. "We searched in the direction she'd have gone if she were to run from the mainland. It occurred to me that she might return to Fohrvylda, particularly her own hometown. And so I warned the marshal to fortify Ivolde Bay's defense—"

"You did no such thing!" Zander says.

Vretos punches his table with the force of a sledgehammer, silencing them both. "What will you do to make this right?" he asks Garr.

This seems to be the direction the admiral hoped the conversation would go. A sign that he may survive this meeting. He answers energetically. "Patrols scour all waters surrounding Fohrvylda. The navy has traveled fast, enlisting all able hands in every city. I am holding every port, bay, lagoon, beach, anywhere the water's shallow. We search every ship on the water and sink those who don't comply. If she leaves the mainland by sea, I'll have her." Garr's words are confident, his chin high. He's returned to his usual stately posture, albeit frazzled. For now, no one else ridicules the admiral's assertion, which is surely a first at this table. Bickering usually goes hand in hand with breathing.

On the rocks far below Pappu is the shark, belly up and being eviscerated. Sprakes flock upon it in turns, tearing out flesh. It was inevitable that they would defeat the shark. Pappu's sprakes are resourceful. They work together. They snatch sawtail tuna and silver coley from the deeper waters. Among the sharp rocks in the shallows beside the cliff they drop the writhing fish, to clatter and flop, then throw the battered fish back out in the sea bloody and exhausted. When larger game takes the bait, the sprakes attack as one, each securing its hold so as to exhaust their prey. When one bird tires, another takes its place. They hold their prey until it can fight no longer, a strategy that works particularly well on sharks, even large ones, even if it manages to temporarily pull them below the surface in the process. Then, with claws lodged in flank, the birds haul their catch onto the rocks with the help of the swelling waves. In that way, they feed and sustain even their infirm, their old, those stragglers Grimmet urges Pappu to *euthanize*. He doesn't understand or value the generational wisdom gained and preserved by such endeavors. Obedience alone is the beastmaster's priority.

One time the sprakes managed to flip a great sea turtle onto the rocks. Pappu witnessed the enormous reptile broken into pieces over the course of a month, scavenged until there was nothing but a bleached bowl of a shell, big enough to bed three orcanes. It was during that impressive feat, in fact, that Pappu came to grips with the stark differences between sprakes and Vretos' court. Is it truly such a mystery why he'd prefer the company of the birds?

"Grimmet," Vretos says, and Pappu's heart thuds. His concern for his father immediately confuses him. The man's a bastard. He peers again toward the court.

"I knew those uergatas were too much for you to handle."

Grimmet's not saying anything. Looks like he's holding still. Since his promotion he's positioned with his back to the window. His back to Pappu. He's dressed in the closest thing he owns to formal clothes. Even tucked his shirt in. Perhaps his usual armored training apron and stained yard boots lacked something he expected to need today. Or his new position requires he dress differently. Too bad his crooked back makes him forever artlessly hunched.

"Those fucking monstrosities tore through Promontory then down into Fohrvylda's lowlands. They're rumored to have been seen bounding onto the Towers. Is that what you heard?"

"Yes, Your Might. Marshal Zander's source claims they have left the mainland via the Towers, breaking through any opposition." Grimmet recites the words flatly. He doesn't mask the disgust in his voice.

"What expensive baubles to misplace." Vretos' words aren't as blistering as Pappu would have expected. "But that loss surely can't cut as deep as having a suspected traitor for a son."

Pappu's heel skids out from under him, shifting him down an inch and making a squeal escape his lips. He clamps both hands to his mouth. *Traitor?* His father doesn't respond. Doesn't even move.

Vretos plants his knuckles on the table and leans toward Grimmet. "When Pappu met with the beasts and convinced them to be armored, what did he promise them?"

"He promised them nothing," Grimmet says, his voice loud and clear. "He most certainly did not intend for them to escape. The boy is no traitor."

Pappu is dazed. The accusation was unexpected. It's rare enough that he hears his own name mentioned in the court. It's rarer still to hear any man defend another here. But he's never heard his father speak on his behalf to Vretos. Definitely not with such vigor. He gazes at his father's back. Grimmet's shoulders are heaving. *He didn't mention what I told him about Torvald giving the uergatas a map. To protect me or himself?*

Vretos watches him a moment. "Since he's a child, if your son is guilty, you will be judged as well. Yours will be another head decorating my ship's prow, with your son's head nailed into your mouth."

"The boy is no traitor," Grimmet says. "His sprakes will find Irdessa. They're already flying over the mainland. She cannot travel, not with a group or even alone, and remain unseen to the birds. When they find her, my dreadhops will finish the job Captain Jeret could not."

There's that usual self-ingratiating talk, given at another member of the court's expense. Pappu is still reeling over Grimmet's passion in his defense. He wishes he could have seen his father's face when the words were said.

"We'll see," Vretos says. He turns to Marshal Zander. "And you." He lets a silence draw out while roasting the marshal with his glare. "Do you remember the last promise you made me?"

Zander somehow withers and remains statuesque at once. He does not answer or turn away. Of all men present, he looks the most dismal, despite that nice velvety black coat.

Pappu's gaze wanders back to the shark. The eastern sun scalds the sea, turning peaks into silver. Gulls have arrived near the shark corpse, so have crabs. Sprakes are bathing in the shallows, slinging off water and shark blood in fiery droplets. Those with a brood are flying back toward the aviary, where they'll feed their young.

"You told me you'd burn an arena to the ground. That, you accomplished. And the town."

As always when Pappu stares at the majestic birds, he longs for wings of his own. Birds line the cliff face, preening, plucking at their plumage, cooing contentedly. There is no strife between them more malicious than that of a scorned, would-be mate. What if Vretos' court could cooperate the way sprakes do? What could they achieve? Is there even a limit?

"You also told me you'd set an example. You accomplished that too."

Silence is the marshal's response.

"You showed Fohrvylda that when a Promontory battalion flows valiantly over the countryside to a muddy nest of hovels, they can be trounced by an escaped outlaw with a smattering of shit-picking mercenaries behind her." Vretos' volume rises with each word so that by the end his voice strikes the air like steel on steel, causing Pappu to flinch. He peers toward the table.

"You occupy the lowest position in my court. Your next demotion is death. Tell me, Zander, why should you leave this meeting by the door rather than the window?" Vretos points a finger directly at Pappu, and for a moment he considers throwing himself into the wind, hoping his sprakes will catch him. It's happened enough times in his dreams. But no one seems to have noticed him.

Zander's shoulders rise and fall. "You're all against me," he says miserably. "What hope do I have?"

"Your hope is in your hands, as always," Vretos says.

"Then hear the truth." A knife's edge enters his voice. "Upon raiding Vim with his battalion, Captain Jeret learned that Irdessa was hiding in the town, along with Kraus. Contrary to what Garr has told you, we had no warning of this. She and Kraus were both in the company of Alderman Dhovoi, who, aside from his illegal arena, posed no threat to us. Irdessa, on her discovery, distracted the soldiers, murdered Dhovoi, and threw herself off the side of a building to escape."

"And the rapist?" Admiral Garr asks.

"He ... allegedly set Captain Jeret on fire and followed her to the town's stronghold."

Garr is chuckling under his mustache. Vretos does not look amused.

"The point is," Zander says, "the captain came unprepared for the resistance that could be brought by two survivors of Keswal leading Vim's Vanguard from a defensible position. For that, he paid the price. Perhaps if the admiral had offered us his insight, we'd have been prepared. As it stands, Mourt, acting in Jeret's place, was not suited to lead a siege."

"Of course he wasn't, the maggot," Vretos says. "What became of him?"

Zander chews his tongue a long moment, gazing fiercely at his fists hanging at his sides. "His fatal wound was decapitation," he says through his teeth.

Pappu's father snorts. "That'll do the trick."

Zander aims an intense glare at Grimmet. "I hope you meet the one who did it. They say she carries bloodiron."

"Mourt was killed by a woman?" Grimmet laughs. "That's justice, wouldn't you say?"

"Are you enjoying yourselves?" Vretos' interjection is not particularly loud, but a deathly silence follows it. "Bring the lanista," he says toward the door.

Armored guards file into the room, clanking in their hammered steel plate, arms bared, swords sheathed at their sides. Between them is the old Lanista Udiari, dressed in grey sackcloth with rusted shackles on his wrists and ankles. He hangs from their arms, gaunt, weak. But when the guards arrange him between them, he straightens his legs and stands on his own. Vretos walks to him and places a huge hand on the man's shoulder. The old lanista is no larger than a child beside Vretos. By appearance, he should be the oldest man in the room, and yet Vretos is supposedly five times his senior.

"The rest of my court used to tell me you never should have been allowed in," Vretos says to him. "You should have simply made fights, made money, and paid taxes. They also tell me that you, as Torvald's owner, were in on his plan. If that's true, I don't know how it could have possibly benefited you. Either way, as Irdessa's owner you're responsible for all she's done."

The lanista does not respond or even meet Vretos' gaze. His eyes are fixed on the floor somewhere in front of him. The screeching of diving sprakes punctuates the stillness.

Vretos removes his hand from Udiari's shoulder and steps away. "Do you have anything to say before your sentence is determined?"

The lanista looks at the members of the court one by one, until his bleak eyes land on Vretos. Of all members of Vretos' court, he shows the least fear. He takes a long, tired breath. "I'm here in this court because of my years of service to you, to Keswal, and to Fohrvylda." He speaks slowly to the room. "I vetted Zander's haul and made spectacles to behold in the arena. I turned blood into silver. And with that silver you've equipped Garr with a magnificent fleet, fit to cross the sea and crush your enemies."

His thin voice rattles out over the floor in a storyteller's timbre, and for a moment the stories of him leading battle in Keswal, all those years ago, aren't so far-fetched.

"I didn't know Torvald's intentions, but of course I take responsibility. He had one wish, that Irdessa survive Keswal. Whatever may happen," he pauses a moment, "I'm glad he got his wish. He earned it."

Pappu's mouth falls open. He is no master of politics or court intrigue. But that seems like the kind of thing to say only if you want to die.

"Admiral Garr," Udiari says, "your nephew wasn't killed by Andelsior. He was killed by an assassin paid for by Dhovoi. But you already knew that. You planned it. Your nephew was an embarrassment, and thus expendable. You needed only a reason. Motive."

The admiral snorts. "If you're suggesting I'd turn a blind eye to justice on the murderer of my own nephew—"

"You did." Udiari's words are like a hammer hitting a nail. "For your own gain. Until Andelsior fell, he and the marshal and I had a lucrative relationship. Andelsior and his Vanguard captured outlaws. He delivered them to me on the condition that Promontory leave Vim independent. I turned the outlaws over to Zander, asking for no payment, rather first choice on their purchase. In this way Marshal Zander upheld the law, paid the bounty to himself, then sold his captured outlaws for even more profit. I had my choice of fighters.

Andelsior had peace in Vim. Unfortunately, none of this directly served Garr."

Admiral Garr trembles in anger. Vretos holds a hand up, forestalling whatever outburst he had in mind.

Udiari holds the admiral's gaze. "With Andelsior gone and the Vanguard in shambles, we lost our supply of convicts. Zander's status declined. My status declined. You solidified your place in the second chair at the cost of outlaws running amok in the east. Outlaws who then made a mockery of Promontory." Lanista Udiari leans as far toward the admiral as his guards allow. "You helped build this catastrophe."

Garr aims his mustache from Udiari to Vretos then back. A grimace marks his face. "You've got some nerve," he thunders. He inhales a lungful of wind.

"Garr," Vretos warns.

The air falls out of the admiral.

The lanista is apparently not finished. He turns to the marshal. "Zander, even with the entire army at your disposal, you were never as efficient as the Vanguard at enforcing the law. And so you resorted to fabricating charges."

"And my charges filled Keswal's seats and painted its sand," Marshal Zander retorts. "That's the whole intent, is it not?"

"Was insurrection your intent?" Udiari asks him. He's smiling now. "Because it's here. Common folk take poorly to being burgled, raped, and burned."

"These secrets you disclose carry little significance, Lanista," Vretos says, before Udiari can continue. "It is the ends that concern me, not the means." He aims a finger at the opening again, toward where Pappu crouches. The guards, who'd been static until this point, grab the lanista's arms and turn him roughly to walk toward the edge. Toward Pappu.

"This place is a den of snakes, all devouring each another," Lanista Udiari says, and by the twinkle in his eyes you'd think he's found some peace.

The left guard cuffs the lanista's ear with a gloved fist. "Walk," he barks, as if Udiari can do anything but.

"My only regret," the lanista says amid a chuckle, struggling to keep his feet as he's dragged toward the opening, "is that I won't be here to watch you all finish each other off."

Pappu ducks out of sight, tries to flatten himself against the rock. Gods willing, the guards neglect to look down. But what if the lanista sees him? He hears them approach the ledge until they're directly above him. Hopefully the sun is in their eyes.

Lanista Udiari's dirty feet scuttle until his toes skirt the edge, kicking loose gravel out into blue nothing. Some of the sand trickles off Pappu's shoulder. His heart thunders in his chest. He could reach up and touch a guard's boot if he wanted to. Could he stop this?

"I hope Ausgan monks turn the lot of you into ash!" Udiari screams with manic enthusiasm. He's close enough Pappu can hear the man panting, see up his flared nostrils. "It's no more than—*uhff!*"

A guard punches the lanista's guts so hard his feet lift off the ground, the shackles jangling on his skinny ankles.

"Get it over with," Vretos says.

They hoist the old man like he's a scarecrow to be burned and toss him right over Pappu. Pappu's breath catches in his throat. Lanista Udiari arcs and plummets, eyes wide, mouth wide, sackcloth flapping up around his waist and shoulders, bony limbs flailing with their chains. Lively sprakes dive after him, spiral around him on his journey toward the rocks far below. Pappu's hands grip his cheeks, his ears, his mouth, barely containing a scream. At the last moment, the birds pull away, swooping outward. The lanista does not. Udiari never cries out before abruptly halting on the wave-licked stones beside the gutted shark. Sprakes arrange into a tight spiral above him, chirping and squawking spiritedly, their blue-grey backs nearly indiscernible from the frothy surf.

Pappu watches with a strange void in his heart. Udiari's lying there like he might sit up again, as if he lay down there on purpose. Pappu shakes his head, his eyes locked and unyielding. Udiari is leaking blood, which stains the shallows. He's dead. Still, there's a void. No horror, no sadness. Pappu and Lanista Udiari had worked together at times. The man was always cordial to Pappu, even if he came off like an aging wolf. But anyone who occupies a seat across from your father in Vretos' court could never truly be considered a friend.

Not until the guards turn from the opening and stride back toward Vretos' table does Pappu remember to draw air into his lungs. He drags himself up to peer over the precipice. By now more of Vretos' soldiers have entered the room. They line the walls with shields and spears, armored vests like the others, wearing thick burlap trousers and metal caps. Some stand glaring in the firelight, others lurk in the shadows between the hearths. The mood of the three remaining of Vretos' court has become funereal.

Udiari's corpse calls Pappu's attention back to it. Sprakes scream at each other above the body. It's likely they are determining whether to use the lanista as bait or eat him themselves. Pappu wonders if his sprakes know the shackles will steal buoyancy from the dead man, that they'll pull him down out of reach if he's used as bait. If they choose to eat him, it won't take long.

"Do you know what I need?" Vretos' whimsical question, like a lot about the man, conveys a youthfulness bordering on immaturity. But Pappu is under no delusion that His Might is capable of lightheartedness. "I need fighters filling our ships. The Heathen Tide will rely on overwhelming numbers, steel so deep we can shake off whatever monkly maneuvers they'll throw at us. Irdessa's ongoing escapades threaten this. She reeks of dissent, poisons anyone who hears her story. She presents an alternative to the Heathen Tide for warriors, and she makes it look alluring."

This produces expressions of discerning contemplation from his court, as if they're feeling anything besides relief at not having flown.

"What I don't need," Vretos tells his court, "is Keswal's continued profitability. Udiari's right. Our fleet is constructed and ready for war, after all these long years." Vretos paces between his armored guards and the court, stopping behind Admiral Garr. "I don't need an admiral. I can assume that role when the Tide bears out. Our mariners are ready." Vretos pauses as if tempting Garr to argue the point. The admiral says nothing.

"I need no beastmaster," Vretos says, moving on to stand behind Grimmet. "The orcanes destined for the Tide are already trained. We all know how to feed one, how to tie one up, how to clip their fins." His words hang in the air like an expectant noose. Pappu notices the guards all have hands on swords.

"It is by charity that you both live."

The admiral and Pappu's father both incline their heads in silence. Relief washes over Pappu, and again he's confused by his concern.

"But what I need even less than those is an incompetent marshal," Vretos says. "When I lead the charge over the Faithless Sea, I may not return to Fohrvylda. Arenas, outlaws, false charges, disquiet, pirates ..." He shakes his head as if it's incredulous these were ever worth mentioning. "They won't matter anymore. The strongest alderman can determine the rule of this rock. And the craftiest one can kill him for it. That said ..." Vretos raises his fingers and gestures from the marshal to the opening. Those same two guards waste no time, moving behind Marshal Zander so quickly they may as well be extensions of Vretos' thought. They snatch Zander by the arms.

"Wait!" the marshal cries. "Your ships are ready but who will rally your warriors? It is your marshal's duty to ride the wastelands and the outskirts with your enemies' heads on spears to gather the Tide."

The guards are not impressed. Neither is Vretos. Marshal Zander is hauled kicking from the table. Shockingly, Garr and Grimmet are not gloating. In fact, they don't acknowledge it's happening.

"I know the mainland better than any, the shanties and backroads," Zander says. "The dives and the warrens. I alone can best fill Fohrvylda's ships."

No one seems to care.

Halfway to the opening, Zander's flailing strength concentrates into forceful purpose. One of the two guards drops to his knees, head back and mouth wide, a line of blood spurting from a dagger wound in his neck all the way up to the oak rafters in the ceiling. Zander kicks the other guard's side, knocking the man off balance. It's more artful an attack than Pappu thought he was capable of. With this newly gained space, Marshal Zander wrenches his blade from its sheath. "It's my destiny to ride the Heathen Tide!"

The air tears open with the sound of a dozen swords unsheathing. Chills crawl all over Pappu and threaten his grip on the cliff. Vretos' guards close in on Zander from every direction except the wide window, where Pappu once again wishes he had wings.

"Wait," Vretos says.

The guards pause. Zander's chest heaves as he aims his sword from one face to the next.

"I can undo the damage Irdessa caused," Zander says. "My orcane patrols scour the mainland and the Tower alleys, not just the open water like Garr's boats, and not just in the sunlight like the falconer's birds, but day and night." Zander talks rapidly, his eyes frantic. Pappu scowls. Zander has some nerve slandering the sprakes. Pappu need only give the command and the *falconer's birds* would rearrange Zander's guts. Day or night.

Zander stands panting. Vretos' hand is still raised, his soldiers stayed. In Pappu's observation, loyalty to the Tide is Vretos' most cherished trait. No matter anything else, the deeds it inspires or how barbaric it makes one act. "My orcanes will travel fast," Zander says. "My soldiers will work with civilians. If there is a group of armed outlaws anywhere in Fohrvylda moving in any direction, I'll know it. If they take to the sea within the Towers, I can root them out. I will stamp out this rebellion myself. I will end the outlaws and collect all their heads to decorate your ships. As we speak, soldiers are putting up flyers with likenesses of Irdessa and Kraus and all known members of the so-called Vanguard. Once they show their faces—"

"Alright, alright," Vretos says, exhausted. "Keep your life, just stop talking."

"I will bring you Irdessa's head!" Zander blurts. Apparently his momentum was too much. Pappu reflects that he should have done as advised. Zander's own slapped expression suggests he feels the same. Pappu's only ever haggled with his father but even he knows you don't sweeten a done deal at your own expense. That's just stupid. Recognize when negotiations have concluded. Grimmet taught him that.

Vretos watches him for another moment, entertained, probably curious if the moron will sweeten it further. When Zander continues to mimic a petrified tree, Vretos says, "I take that as oath."

Zander's face is pale. His shoulders heave. "I will," he says. "It is." His conviction now sounds forced.

"Your life depends on it, Marshal. But make sure her head is still attached. Torvald was wrong. She *will* die in Keswal."

The armored soldiers draw back, allowing Zander to be still at last, catch his breath, as the shock on his face teeters on despair. The guard Zander kicked regains his footing, if not his dignity. The guard Zander cut jangles down to the floor, sputtering into his own widening blood puddle, gripping his neck. He gradually stops moving. Zander sheaths his sword shakily, before anyone can change their mind. He flattens his vest and jacket with trembling hands. Pappu wonders how much he regrets that last promise.

Vretos readies himself to depart. "Irdessa is your priority now. Capture her and you'll be above reproach, despite any fuck up you've orchestrated thus far. In fact, you'll get first chair." He strides for the door. "Pending emergency, we'll meet again on schedule. If the Undying isn't captured by then, come with your affairs in order."

It isn't obvious if that last edict is intended for Marshal Zander specifically, or all present. Pappu, already scrambling down the rock face, knows to assume the worst. At this rate, Vretos will kill them all, and quicker if they're stupid enough to return here while Irdessa's free. Pappu's father hasn't earned his affection. The opposite, more times than not. But today Grimmet defended him. And so that beaten-down dream within Pappu stirs and raises its tired head yet again. Maybe there is time for them to make something different of it after all. So long as that pitiful possibility draws breath, Pappu is unable to abandon it. And so his direction is clear. It's time to unite the sprakes to save the man they hate the most.

37
When You Turn

FOHRVYLDA
The Wastelands

Vyker runs, surrounded by the music of ragged breathing and clanking gear. Every inhale burns his throat and lungs. He can only assume the fabric wrapped around his mouth and nose helped protect him. But by the time he'd donned it, he'd taken many a gasping breath of air thick with the smoke of burning buildings. The stench of it is just fading from his nostrils. It's still ripe on his skin and hair and the fabric of his clothes. And every northward gust carries the singed odor of another scorched home, another fallen city block.

Vyker is ever aware of the sun's merciless ascent up over the rolling hills to the east. The bleak morning glow exposes the smoke rising from Vim in frightening clarity. Blackened clouds billow and expand and taint the grey sky.

Most times, when you can see the horizon, you can imagine it continues forever and ever. Something about that has always comforted Vyker. It's as if the world is too big to be known, and he, full of questions, might never stop learning. That changes when you're fleeing your burning village and black smoke holds the sky captive. It feels like the world has ended, at least in that direction.

What remains of the Vanguard is a fraction of its force, yet still too numerous to expect to run unseen under the sun's glare. All night they journeyed at an increasingly crippled pace. They kept the orange haze of burning Vim at their backs, travelling in small groups, no more than a half dozen fighters in each, with the fit assisting the feeble. Among those Vyker would call feeble are a whore named Sevyle and a severely injured man who's bound to a makeshift gurney. Some might consider many of their group incapacitated. Old Fent's pace is nothing approaching perky, even with the help of Sura, nor is Torah's. Irdessa's friend Kraus, whose arm is bound thickly in grey wool, recently abandoned the crutch he'd been using. That man is like a sack of rocks that learned swear words.

Scouts range out from the main body ahead to their flanks and behind, sometimes as far out as a mile. Vyker catches snippets of their reports. So far, all orcane patrols spotted are heading for Vim. Sprakes are starting to wheel about distantly now that the sun is rising. They're not yet close enough to pick out the hooded survivors of Vim making their way through fog-obscured trees, but once in range their presence will make any movement dangerous.

For a while Vyker ran nearby Irdessa—who everyone seems to seek, each with advice on where the Vanguard should go, what they should do. The conversations quickly became volatile. The one thing everyone agrees on is that they can't stop. Some suggest making a final stand. *Rip the wolves' throat!* At least the songs will tell their stories. But Vyker hasn't got much use for such songs, and it seems neither does most anyone else. Other suggestions include splitting up and dispersing into towns in the wastelands, fleeing the country entirely on a ship, going north and taking their chances with the precipitous Towers.

It's nearly noon when the complaints of the bedraggled can no longer be ignored. A scout leads the Vanguard through a dense copse of evergreens until they arrive at a crevasse. A half-dozen yards below the lip, a crystalline stream with mossy banks trickles over smooth stones. The cedars and spruces intertwine their boughs high above, obscuring the glen in shadow.

Vyker plops down beside the creek, dropping his spear, succumbing to the exhaustion gripping his legs, wincing at the rawness of his ankles. He pries off his boots, observes how swollen his feet are. He thrusts them into the stream, massaging his soles against the polished stones. The cool water revives his skin. Drinking it relieves his burned throat. He rubs hardened blood from his knuckles in the gurgling stream, letting his mind wander.

He's always dreamed about riding on missions, maybe even with Andelsior and Torvald. That aspect took a battering when they were arrested, but as long as the Vanguard lived so did the ambition. He swore the oath to the Vanguard on his sixteenth birthday and took Dhovoi's crimson sash. His brother administered the sash himself. What a proud day. That was a month ago. Now Dhovoi's dead, and Vyker is struggling to determine how he should feel. He never saw eye to eye with Dhovoi. He didn't care much for the parties, and certainly wasn't under the delusion that Dhovoi was any kind of leader. Not after Andelsior. But still, that was his brother. His family. And yet he's numb. Is he truly without emotional response to his brother's death? Or is it merely suspended?

Vyker abandoned his sash before fleeing Vim, as everyone did, but his oath remains. This adventure is not like what he had in mind, but by the gods he is excelling at it. Last night, when the Vanguard burst screaming through Cornerstone's false wall, they met roaring fire, snapping barksharks, thirsty steel. Vyker shouldered his way to the front of the charge. He rode the rage of his brother's demise, seasoned with an expectation to join him. He was the arrow's tip leading the charge, thrusting his spear and shouting for death. For a glorious span, bodies fell around him, dropped by himself and his peers. All the hours and days and weeks of training he endured finally proved their worth. His insecurities withdrew until he was forced to admit he isn't just good at fighting. He's damn good.

A grim lieutenant stood her ground before him, not intimidated by his spear or the Vanguard's furious momentum. She wielded her sword with masterful grip, no fear in her eyes, backed by a wall of soldiers. Her grey armor encased her like a cocoon. Vyker relied on his unorthodox stance, the shaft of the spear resting across his shoulders, the blade extending far enough to promise he'd make you pay for a high attack. The lieutenant did as all do, swinging for his undefended legs while protecting her face. Vyker leapt her sword, slashed the inside of her leg with the spear's blade. She fell back, reassessing his range, trying to predict the next attack. But while he kept his eyes on her legs, he aimed his next attack at her unpolished breast plate. No real expectations on it, figuring the armor would stop his spear and maybe knock her off-balance for a neck strike. But his newfound war frenzy loaned him strength. His spearhead crunched through her armor, disappearing to the shaft, and her eyes bulged in profound surprise. He roared in elation, yanked his spear free, kicking her down, blood spraying his hands, his face. She fell in a clattering heap, sword spilling away. The line of Promontory soldiers wavered. His Vanguard brothers and sisters crashed into them and their line broke.

Once an opening was punched through their blockade, Vyker held back and let the Vanguard's main body continue running, heading down back streets Promontory soldiers couldn't possibly know. Vyker joined the rearguard, fending off the surge of pursuing soldiers, darting and stabbing. Beside him were Harpold, Irdessa, others he didn't make out. Each new soldier underestimated Vyker, like their sword was somehow different than all the others. He piled their bodies in the street. When the blade of his spear snapped off in someone's ribs, he snatched another one from a helmeted soldier and paid the man with death. Only when a line of archers formed and Irdessa shouted to fall back did Vyker pull back his spear and take cover. It was just in time. Arrows flitted past as he dove through an open window. As planned, the Vanguard convened south of the pit, circled the city's east side, and fled north.

Thinking about the fight makes a smile nearly split his whole face. *The spear is the best weapon.* He's always said it. Always known it. His beaten fighting partners, limping off with bruised knuckles and bones and egos, always told him he needed to grow up and get a sword. *You'd like that wouldn't you?* he'd mock. He knew better. Forget swords. Even when he nearly severed his own ear training and had to wear stitches and bandages for a week, he knew. Let them laugh. They'd pay in the practice ring. His ear has a notch taken out. No one says a word to him about it.

Vyker has another drink of water, trying to still his racing heart. He leans back, gets himself comfortable on mossy rocks, scans the other survivors. Old Fent is hard to miss, with the sunlight-haired warrior, Sura, standing beside him. He's propped in dewy moss at the foot of a tree with his head back and eyes closed. Dry snores rattle out of him as if all this time sleep was only a blink away. So far this adventure seems to suit him. He must not be as decrepit as he looks.

Vyker sees Caenin the Arrow crouched over his bow performing some maintenance. He stands out because there's no blood on him. If he killed any soldiers, it was at range. That's all well and good, but Vyker wants to see him holding a blade. He wants to get the man in the practice ring. Caenin talks too much, making jokes, cracking people up at someone's expense. Always targeting folks who won't bust his face for him. His day will come.

Irdessa's friend Kraus is up and testing his footing with a bottle in hand. He's so pale he looks like he could fall over dead at any moment. Harpold is with them, offering support to Kraus. Harpold's a good one. Always been nice to Vyker.

There's Bravensi. Vyker shifts uncomfortably. He's never trusted her. And that was before she accused Dhovoi of conspiring with Promontory and tried to kill him. They kicked her out, or so he thought. Why is she back now? Vyker wonders if Irdessa knows about that. What if Bravensi gets paranoid about Irdessa like she did Dhovoi? He should at least warn her. Vyker had hoped Bravensi would stay behind in Vim when she snuck out of Cornerstone to do whatever she did during the siege. Instead, she caught up with the Vanguard outside the city, blood spattered all over her and her weapon.

Vyker looks for Irdessa and finds her addressing a man with his face painted like a performer. He must have followed the party into Cornerstone last night, the unlucky clod. Judging by her confused expression, he speaks a different language or is asking an unusual question. At length, Irdessa pats the man's shoulder, almost like a farewell, and walks away from him. The man turns and looks directly at Vyker. He diverts his gaze to the stream. The damn fellow startled him for some reason.

There are crayfish scuttling beneath the water's surface. Vyker wonders if anyone's discussing what's for dinner. Then again, this is surely just a quick stop. He has his spear, some socks, and whatever was in the bottom of his travel bag. Having only ever taken it to Keswal to watch fights, there's a low chance of being pleasantly surprised by whatever's left in there. Hunger drives him to rummage in it. Loose coins, bits of foliage that suggests a bird tried to nest in there, a sharpening stone, some dirty soap squished in a tin with no lid. There aren't even crumbs. His stomach growls. Maybe Fent has the right idea. Vyker leans back and rests his eyes.

Vyker awakens to sunlight on his eyelids. He stands up and the aches in his stiff back tell him he snoozed longer than he planned to. There's a crowd of hunched hoods gathering in the shadows beneath the bank's over-cropping. Vyker pulls on his boots and shambles over. More people are gathering, cementing their places around something. It takes some squeezing, but he gets close enough to see who's crouched at the center.

Tora the bookmaker is among them. He's rolling a parchment into a tube and stashing it away along with some bits of chalk. Also present, wearing cloaks dyed to resemble patterns of forest shadows, are Maudee and Magpie. The small figures are siblings, twins, both scouts. Useful but hard to tell apart. Irdessa and Fent are there discussing something too quietly for Vyker to make out in the murmur and press of the people.

"Irdessa has authority in the Vanguard," Old Fent says at last to the crowd. "Listen to her."

Whispering ensues. Vyker's unsure how she got authority. Maybe because her father was Andelsior. When he knew her last, they were much younger. She always seemed annoyed by him, preferring the company of his brother. Or more often, Torvald.

"Vanguard ..." Irdessa says. Her eyes sparkle. There's blood spattered on her face and clothes. "You turned back a battalion. I knew you could prevail. Many people died. Some I hadn't seen in a long time. Some I didn't know." Her mannerisms and delivery bring to Vyker's mind no one more than Andelsior himself, and he wonders if Irdessa might plan to fill his shoes.

"We didn't get the chance to tell them what they meant to us. Or even say goodbye." The pause that follows seems unintentional. As if her voice will fail unless she gives it a moment. "There will be a day we can stop, and mourn, and pay our respects or ... or just think about those we've lost." Irdessa's eyes cloud over and her chin juts forward. Something about the expression is so raw Vyker feels it in his belly. He sees his brother's face wearing that wry smile. His eyes are brimming. He wipes them with his sleeve, trying to make the action look like anything else.

"But this fight isn't over." Irdessa's voice isn't diminished by her tears. "There is no future for Vim's Vanguard here." Her words shovel through the whispers, leaving a whistling wind up in the branches, the creek's soft gurgle below. "Not everyone present is Vanguard, and not all Vanguard fighters are notorious enough to be identified. My advice to you lucky ones is to run. Break from our group and get as far away as possible. But for those of us with a name, or a recognizable face, or if you were seen killing any of those Promontory bastards ..." A smile curls the edge of her lips, dimples her bloody cheeks. "Well, we're in this for the ride. Vretos will take the country apart to find us. He'll bribe with rewards, enough money to make mothers sell their sons. He'll interrogate to death anyone who doesn't cooperate. If we're caught we'll be executed, probably in Keswal, and Vretos will relish it." She speaks to every face aimed her way. She's not intimidated by her words or the grim expressions her audience returns. Again she smiles. "I've had enough of that prick relishing me."

A laugh escapes Vyker. He can't help noticing the words *us*, and *we*. Pride fills him. He's one of them. Oath-bound. There's no way he left the mess he did in Vim without being seen. That armored lieutenant. The chokepoint he held. And he'd have it no other way. If only Dhovoi were here to see him. But that's beside the point.

The woman beside Vyker is trembling on her feet. Apparently she can control herself no longer. "Then what do we do?"

"We keep moving," Irdessa says.

"And go where?" says a man.

"East, for now," Irdessa points. "Then, to be determined."

"Don't we have to leave Fohrvylda?" another voice asks. Before Irdessa can address the interrupter there's another outburst.

"Why east?"

Vyker searches for the face of the man who said it.

Old Fent clears his throat. "We determined that—"

"What about our family?" booms a voice from the far side of the gathering. A man there is rising to full height, both hands resting on the head of a double-bladed battle axe at his waist. It's Thiel. His brother, Toma, sits next to him. "Who will protect them if we leave?"

The muttering has gotten its footing. If unchecked, it'll threaten the party's stealth.

"My fate is the Heathen Tide." Toma rises as well. They're both large men with thick arms and shoulders. Both favor axes. Both have stained weapons and are bloody up to the elbows.

"Here, here!"

"That door is closed to anyone with a name," Old Fent says regretfully, shaking his head.

Taut hissing ignites throughout the gathered. Vyker had never strongly considered joining the Heathen Tide. Dhovoi had no use for it, not for the ride over the ocean or the eventual fighting and plundering of a foreign island nation. Vyker is beginning to accept how much of his future was centered around his brother. He'll have to make his own path now, but the fact that the Heathen Tide isn't an option feels insignificant. The Vanguard was always his dream and here he is.

"Maybe we should turn you lot in," someone nearby whispers, intentionally not loud enough to reach the center. "Earn back our place on the Tide."

"Who said that?" Vyker's gripping his spear in both hands looking at the men and women around him. But whoever made the remark has the sense not to admit it.

"I'll ride the Heathen Tide or die trying," Toma growls. "If you think my brother and I will forfeit that just because the half-wit Dhovoi—"

"Shut up!" The command comes from Kraus. His voice scares birds out of nearby evergreen branches. The mutterings fizzle out. "You don't have to come." Kraus glowers at the man, looking every bit like an oversized corpse stitched together from mismatched, leftover parts. "That's what she's trying to tell ya. You're free to fuck off. Go ride the Tide or the wind or your brother's cock."

Toma and Thiel take axes in hand and step toward Kraus. He hauls himself up, empty-handed, grinning at them both as if they're the ones outmatched. "You can try to ride me," he says, "but I'll make ya pay."

Vyker's introduction to Kraus was the man's declaration, uttered not unlike a belch, that Dhovoi was dead. This outburst improves his standing. He's damn sure fearless. Or suicidal.

"I go east," Irdessa says, stepping between Kraus and the two brothers.

"Why east?" It's that same man who asked it before.

"There's better forest coverage in that direction," says Maudee. She's standing but you wouldn't know it. Her head is no higher than the average man's shoulders. Her twin brother's smooth face is turned up to watch her. "East is the opposite direction from Promontory," she says. "It will buy us time."

"Are we leaving the mainland?" someone asks.

Irdessa appears not to hear them.

"We'll be trapped if we go east." says the almond-eyed ranger, Elaga, one thick forearm propped against her massive unstrung greatbow. This comment is met with some agreement. Fohrvylda is almost entirely surrounded by ocean, which is controlled by Admiral Garr's ships. Zander's Promontory patrols range the land. If they are followed eastward, they'll end up caught between their pursuers and a cliff.

"East isn't our final destination." Irdessa spits it out like she'd have rather left it unsaid. The onlookers remain silent for further explanation. Irdessa's glare suggests they've gotten all they'll get. Vyker wonders if she and Fent and Torah even have a plan beyond *go east*.

Old Fent clears his throat, drawing attention. "If you're with us, strap up. If not, if you have family or obligations, go to them. No hard feelings, no accusations of oath breaking. Either way, choose quick."

There's no question for Vyker. The Vanguard is his family now. Where it goes, he goes.

"We leave in a quarter hour," Irdessa says. The crowd's murmuring ignites. Irdessa hushes them with raised hands. "Our priority is survival," she says, and gives as lifeless a smile as Vyker's ever seen. "Trust that I've learned a thing or two about that."

Her final words bring a scattering of muted affirmation from the crowd. The gathering disperses and Vyker goes to collect his pack. He climbs up and perches beneath the shade of a cedar on top of the eastern bank, nestling his back against flaking bark so that he can eye the misty hills to the east and still turn to see who's coming along, who's not.

There are questions digging at him. A lot has changed. Irdessa is taking up the mantle of leader naturally, and without a title, the opposite of how Vyker's brother went about it. Dhovoi came up with *alderman* and focused his attention on getting everyone to call him that. Put more effort into it than it deserved, considering Vim was suffering a lack of direction and breaking down.

Vyker is still in his murky thoughts when people begin to depart. Thiel leads one small group, heading back from where they came. Accompanying him are his brother Toma and the injured man they've carried thus far. Elsewhere, headed north and soon to be out from under the cover of the woods, are the whore Sevyle and another cloaked figure with a bow across their shoulder. If they mean to appear unrelated to this conflict, they might consider ditching the bow, however ill-advised it is to travel unarmed.

"You're Vyker?" asks a soft voice.

Vyker didn't see the man approach. It's the same odd fellow he'd seen speaking to Irdessa before the gathering. There's black paint lining the man's eyes. His dry lips are parted slightly. His head sits forward on his neck and a kerchief is in bunches at his throat. There's no blood or dirt on him. His stare is so unbroken his face could be a mask.

"Who's looking?" Vyker asks. The events of late convince him not to announce himself to any old crackpot.

The mask splits into a smile. "Take this." He proffers a leather pouch no larger than a fist. Vyker accepts it. There's something solid inside, like a block. Too tired to stifle curiosity, he turns the pouch up and dumps a smooth, wooden box into his palm. The surface is riddled with small holes, drilled at an angle so you can't see in. There's no hinge or clasp on it, and it weighs almost nothing. Vyker sniffs it. It's odorless. He'd hoped it was food.

He gives it a shake. "What do we have here?"

"It's a little birdy." The man smiles and flaps his hands beside his hips. It's far more whimsical a gesture than Vyker would expect from someone who looks like he might drink as much paint as he applies to his face. It fails to put Vyker at ease.

"What do you want me to do with it?" Vyker lifts the box to his ear. There is no sound from within.

"Free it," the man whispers. He flits his hands up toward the sky like bird wings, studying them with his black-rimmed eyes.

Vyker's too exhausted for games and intrigue. In a narrow decision, he chooses to pry open the box rather than hurl it against a tree trunk. As he's wedging his thumbnail into the thin line around the cube's circumference, the odd man gasps.

"Not yet," he urges, wrapping his own hands around Vyker's and the box. His palms are soft. "Not yet," he says again with a mischievous curl to his lips.

"When?"

376 | David T List

"When you turn ..." The man hisses through a smile, drawing out the last word like a creaking rope holding a ship at dock.

"Turn what?"

The man only nods. "When you turn."

The words didn't change, but now they hit Vyker like cold water, slapping his mouth open. "Are you suggesting I'll turn on the Vanguard?"

"You'll know the day," the man laughs. "And when it comes, free it."

"Friend," Vyker says slowly, getting a grip on his spear. "I'm afraid there's been a misunderstanding."

A dramatized fear stretches the man's eyes but does nothing to diminish his mouth's leer. "If that's the case, you should kill it."

"What if I kill you?" Vyker says. So far his surprise at the situation might be all that's kept him from doing it.

"No need. I'm leaving." The man wiggles his eyebrows, rounds sharply, and walks away. With his back turned, he's just another departing cloak. "Use fire or water, or stomp it or squish it ..." His voice is sing-song. Would he still be so merry if he knew how close he came to dying?

"It's ... alive?" Vyker asks.

"Of course it is."

"Is it hungry?" Of all the curiosities of this encounter, that's the one to address?

"Already ate. Sleeping now."

Vyker blinks several times at the wooden cube in his palm. Nothing about its feel, appearance, sound, or smell can validate or contradict the abridged explanation.

"Who are you?" Vyker calls, but gets no response.

Vyker is toiling with the thought of returning the box to the pouch and burying both in a shallow hole when Irdessa walks up beside him.

"What's that?" she says. Her proximity unsettles him. Up close, he makes out no less than two stitched wounds on her face. The blood spattered all over her leather garments and fists and tanned neck, coupled with the hawk-like focus in her eyes, makes her frighteningly attractive.

"A box. It's ..." he blurts. In a panic, he stuffs it back in the pouch right in front of her. He fiddles with the strings. "... just something ..." He's stammering. Why? He didn't do anything wrong. "... someone gave me."

Irdessa's severe eyes are pinned on Vyker. He turns toward the departing. "Who was that?" he says. "The one with the paint and the ..." He gestures his hands, trying to convey the man's oddity, and also to shift her stare.

"Oh, him," she says, following his gaze. "Strange one. He keeps birds. Told me he'll be leaving to tend to them." She shrugs, unconcerned. "I don't blame him. Maybe feeding birds has its merits after all." Her sly smile accentuates her dimples.

Vyker can't tell whether he's relieved she finds the man harmless. He suggested Vyker would turn traitor, didn't he? He encouraged it. Seems like he should pay for that, or at least be prevented from wandering into enemy hands and giving them up. But Irdessa ... She's supposed to have Torvald's discretion. That's what they said about her. Two sides of the same coin. And she's letting him go. Is that smart? They said Torvald could measure a man in a glance. What would he have thought of the painted man? Then again, who knows what Torvald could see? Dhovoi always believed Torvald was full of shit. And *they* will say any old thing that'll entertain someone. For all Vyker knows Torvald invented the rumor.

He looks at the pouch in his hand. Doesn't look incriminating. It would be odd to drop it. Especially if someone else finds it and opens it without knowing what it is. Odder yet to stomp it flat with his boot while it squeals.

Irdessa's hand falls on his bare shoulder. Vyker tenses.

"How are you?" she asks softly. "I've not seen you since before. A lot has happened since then."

Her touch and attention are doing his unsettled guts no favors. "I'm not wounded, if that's what you mean." Feels like his voice has risen in pitch.

"I'm glad you're here." She gives him a squeeze. "And I'm sorry for your loss."

He nods. It's all he can think to do. *Dhovoi's death*. That's what she means. But considering Dhovoi tore down Vim's wall for amusement, is he considered ... the enemy? No one's had the chance to discuss such things yet. Or at least, not to Vyker.

"Dhovoi was one of my closest friends." Her voice is subdued. But is that because of the tragic nature of the subject, or because Dhovoi is hated now? "We'll get the ones who did it."

Dhovoi nods his head. He's frustratingly unable to gauge whether she's consoling him or reading him.

"Won't we?" And she gives his shoulder a firm shake.

"Yeah," he says, and finds a deeply buried anger. "We'll kill them all."

She grins, shadowing her dimples and stretching her stitches. "You're fucking right." She slaps his back and rises energetically to her feet. Away she marches, leaving him holding the pouch, with a coldness on his shoulder where her hand was.

The moment to discuss the pouch and box has passed. Telling her about it isn't necessary. He's sworn in, a man. He can handle his own problems. If he told her, she'd probably tell him to destroy it. What else would she say? Don't botch it. Don't go to stomp it and accidentally free the bird, if there even is a damn bird. He shakes his head. At least the unusual man is gone and can't stir up more trouble. Maybe Vyker will burn it or fill the pouch with rocks and drop it in water. For now it's time to go. He ties the drawstring and drops it in his bag.

38
Fuck Birds

FOHRVYLDA
The Wastelands

Shortly after parting with the dissenters, the Vanguard moves out as well. Vyker runs from shadow to shadow, skirting the rocky streambed in the ravine's floor. His boots are tight. His pack is firm against his back. The knife in his belt is secured against his thigh so as not to flail as he runs. He holds his spear at his hip, parallel the ground. Behind him is Elaga. Her greatbow is unstrung and strapped together with the long quiver down her back. Behind her is sharp-eyed Cindie, whose shortbow is in hand, strung, her quiver easily accessible on her belt.

True to Irdessa's word, they travel eastward along the ravine, their party now not even thirty strong. They travel in clusters of three, leaving several bends in their path between groups so that Vyker only sees the other hooded individuals for fleeting moments as they dart around the curved riverbank.

There is no sign of pursuit aside from the high sun itself. At Irdessa's orders, Maudee and Magpie, along with two other scouts, are ranging far enough out to divert patrols of beast or bird before they're a threat. In case they see a patrol, they confound them with false signals or redirect them by heading in the wrong direction. They do not engage.

The team ahead of Vyker's cuts sharply to the left, scrambling up the steep bank some twenty yards ahead, kicking up fallen evergreen needles and twigs as they go. Vyker marks the spot where they ascended. Nearing the foot of the hill, he heaves his weight into a dash, climbing up the crumbling earth soundly. He hooks his arm around the trunk of a thin cedar at the top and turns to look back. Elaga, with the heavy bow on her back, slows as she nears the top. Back the way they came, Vyker spots the following team running hooded in the shade, rounding the bend of the embankment. Vyker reaches for Elaga's hand, grabs it, hauls her up and awaits Cindie. The blond archer springs up the hill like a deer and hops directly over Vyker, kicking off the tree he's gripping. When he pulls himself to his feet he finds her grinning, her cheeks flushed.

"Shall we?" she says, bowing and indicating their path like it's Cornerstone's grand hall.

"It's not a race," Vyker tells her, smiling.

"Says the loser."

The team ahead is nowhere to be seen but can't have gotten far. Soon enough, the forest levels out and Vyker can see farther through the boughs. His position looks down on a recessed valley of tall green grass, naked under the noon sun, glistening like an emerald ocean. There's still a distance of at least thirty yards to the field. Cindie comes up beside him, Elaga on the other side. The closer they get, the more hiding Vanguard members he makes out on the field's edge.

"We're supposed to cross that?" Cindie's voice pinches in disdain for the idea. "In the day's brightest hours?"

Vyker's eyes find Irdessa standing near the edge of the forest, watching the field. She's identifiable because of the tree stump that is Kraus on her right side and Fent and Sura to her left. Next to them is the slim Bravensi, holding the haft of her tall weapon. Vyker closes the distance between them.

"Right there," Old Fent's saying, pointing out over the grass with one hand, leaning on his sword with the other. "Watch the base of that right-most pine."

Vyker can't help but obey, even if it wasn't him Fent was addressing. The valley must be half a mile across. The wild grass grows thick and deep with cottage-sized tufts of it abounding like green beasts. Since leaving that stream, the shadows suggest their new heading is north. After spending so much time under the cover of trees, knowing sprakes are on hunt, Vyker doesn't fancy this new direction or the idea of exposing themselves to be seen. The riverbed they'd been following suited him fine.

Out over the field, at the edge of the distant tree line, there's a glint of light. It's so faint he's sure it's a trick of the sun until it flashes again, then again. Then no more.

"I see it," Irdessa says. "What's it mean?"

"Means north is clear." Fent says.

"And the south?" Vyker asks before he can stop himself.

Irdessa looks at him, then at Fent, who meets her eyes, then back over the field.

"South isn't," Fent says simply, rising and looking around to meet the dozen fighters who've gathered. "We're crossing the field."

"I thought we were going east," Cindie says.

"We were," Irdessa says without turning. "And anyone who's parted ways with us 'til now can report that to our enemies if they're made to speak."

It's not the words that surprise Vyker. Those make perfect sense. It's the way they fall from her mouth like so many dropped stones. Almost like encouraging them to leave the party in the first place was only ever part of some plot to throw off their enemies. It brings to mind something his brother said about Torvald secretly plotting out who lives and who dies. It's one of the reasons Dhovoi didn't trust him. But if Irdessa uses that same guile to preserve the Vanguard, then Vyker's glad to have her. After all, how much courtesy do dissenters deserve?

Irdessa faces the gathered Vanguard. "We'll go single file. Big fellows up front to make a path." She picks several men out of the gathering. Not Vyker, despite how hard he flexes his arms and shoulders. "Hand off your packs and get ready to move. If you get tired, step aside and let someone else pass you. Archers, bring up the rear. Everyone else, get in line. Once we get moving ..." She's enunciating carefully as if this is the most important detail. "... do not stop until we've crossed that fucking field. Now get ready."

The movement around Vyker is so frantic he'd have thought the forest floor became an ant mound. Bows are strung, quivers are stuffed tight and hung in ways most accessible to their bearers. The brawny runners remove their packs, pound and slap each other's shoulders, bounce on their toes. Vyker moves in behind them. Not too close, lest someone mistakes him for the pack-bearing sort. Kraus appears beside him. Must have been of a similar mind. He manages to be even uglier up close. The scant portions of his face that aren't lined in scars are pockmarked by what might have been one of acne's most devastating conquests. His eyebrows are in a perpetual scowl, despite his empty grin.

Torah stands nearby with a mountainous satchel and a troubled frown. The bag is full of loose maps and writing supplies and nothing heavier, luckily, or a fellow as small as him might be crushed by it. Vyker considers offering to carry it, but something tells him he'll need both his hands and all his mobility. Bringing up the rear are more archers, Cindie and Elaga included.

"Hey, kid. You're good with a spear," Kraus says.

"Thanks," Vyker says.

"Ya ain't gonna do me like you did your ear are you?" And he thumps Vyker's notched ear, mischief in his eyes.

Vyker blinks several times. He'd decided long ago to answer that sort of taunt with violence. You let one person get away with it and the gods only know what ideas others will get. But Kraus ... between his own scars and the sarcastic smirk on his face, Vyker can find no malice, and so rage is not forthcoming.

"Maybe stand clear of my head." Vyker tries to keep a straight face but fails.

"Ha! You're alright."

"Hey," Vyker hears himself say. He didn't intend to. But a question wormed its way into his mouth and he is unable to swallow it down. "Did you see Dhovoi die?"

Kraus raises an eyebrow at him, looking annoyed, then smiles at a fond memory. "No. I was too busy torching Captain Cunt's pretty face."

Vyker nods numbly. So then it wasn't Captain Jeret who killed Dhovoi. Vyker had wondered. Dhovoi always hinted at having some source inside Promontory. Vyker had confronted him about the treatment of Promontory soldiers in Vim's pit. Seemed like a bad idea. But Dhovoi was always so sure he'd be alright that he'd managed to convince Vyker. In fact, not until that fateful night, when Irdessa said that Dhovoi had died in the hands of their enemies, did Vyker even question Dhovoi's safety. But if not Jeret, then who? Surely not some damn soldier.

"How did Dhovoi die?" Vyker asks quietly, not wanting to show too much concern in case Dhovoi is taboo to bring up and he'll be marked *concerned for the enemy.*

Kraus glares at him, as if reconsidering any prior approval.

A signal sounds from ahead. The line surges into motion. Kraus turns and runs. With pounding chest, Vyker leaves the cover of the forest, heading out into the dazzling light. He's quickly enclosed between walls of grass on either side. Thorny-legged grasshoppers, leaping spiders, and gnats of all sorts scurry to get clear, pinging off his cheeks and arms in the process. Soon enough the party's pace is halved. Vyker finds himself with no choice but to crowd into Kraus or march in place, stamping on flattened tufts in the hallway of grass.

Their pace reduces to a trudge, as if whoever's leading is scything the entire field as they go. The sun glares down angrily into the high corridor. The claustrophobic hallway of grass closes tighter. The air stinks of sweat and breath and the enclosed rot of grass. Insects are sawing out their melodies at deafening levels. Vyker marks the passage of time by droplets of sweat converging to rivulets that hydrate his ass crack. The fourth time he's jostled into Kraus' back, he nearly begins throwing elbows at whoever is pushing. The whole party is bunching up, despite the hissed whispers zigzagging up the passage.

"Back up."

"Get off me."

"Give me space."

A shrill whistle from behind fractures Vyker's impatience in an instant. All whispers cease. Vyker stands still, stops pushing Kraus, and stops smacking away the hands on his own back. Was that a signal or a bird? How's anyone tell the difference? There's another couple of whistles, or screeches. Without conscious effort, Vyker begins easing against Kraus again, willing the line to move. And then it does. Someone up ahead must have gotten a fire lit under them because now Vyker is running, his feet padding awkwardly on the semi-packed grass. It's almost a breeze he feels over his sweaty cheeks and neck. His bubbling guts tell him a fight's coming. He's ready.

He has just begun to truly appreciate the newfound breathing room when the corridor of tall grass gives way to uneven field, stunted tufts of greenery no higher than his ankle, leaving him and the entire party exposed on the sunny plain like the skeleton of a snake.

The pace quickens, growing nearly riotous. Even Kraus is shuffling quickly, despite that he runs like he's got a wooden leg. Now and then Vyker passes fighters who stand still and hiss encouragement down the line. "Keep running." "Stay in formation." Seems their purpose is to boost the pace, or distract. Something from behind holds their attention, painting varying degrees of unease on their faces.

Trust the line, Vyker tells himself, keeping his eyes forward. *Irdessa's no fool. She knew south isn't clear and will have a plan.* Dhovoi's skepticism attaches to his thoughts. *Her plan will likely resemble one of Torvald's and be decorated by dead Vanguard fighters.*

He hears the unmistakable thumps of bowstrings sending off arrows from behind. *Here comes a fight!* But who? More soldiers? Beasts? Vyker keeps his eyes on the uneven ground. If his feet falter, he'll end up a lumpy mat for many a boot. The alarmed voices are silenced at once when a shrill avian cry fractures the murmuring wind.

"Sprakes!" someone yells.

"Keep running," someone retorts.

There's another bird call, then another. Multiple sprakes. *Do we turn and face them?*

"Guard your eyes," someone says.

Ahead, not so distant now, is the line of trees, with nary another patch of grass to shield the party on their way. *Trust the line.* Except the line is fast dissolving, even as they all run in the same direction. More bird calls rip out from above. Shouts of violent effort from behind. Vyker runs on, trying to convince himself this is not cowardice but strategy. Ahead, the meat block Kraus does not slow. *And neither will I.*

From the corner of Vyker's eye comes a black shape, rushing along the ground as silent and fast as a great cat. He nearly takes a stab at it with his spear before realizing it's a shadow. The huge birds are between him and the sun, and if their cunning is true to rumor, their placement is deliberate. The fighter in front of Kraus runs while looking back over his shoulder, shading eyes with a flat palm. Despair is evident in his contorted face, his gasping breath.

"Eyes forward, unless you're trying to feed the bastards," Kraus shouts at him.

Even as the words are spoken a massive shadow overtakes the man. He throws up a hand. His feet betray him and he tumbles with a yelp. Vyker dashes for him to get him upright, get him moving again, despite the growing shadow.

A blasting downdraft blows Vyker's hood off his head. He falters, shielding his eyes from flying grit. In a flurry of metallic blue feathers, flashing hooked talons, and a storm of dust, three sprakes drop onto the man. Their talons lodge in leather, skin, boots, face. In a frighteningly orchestrated maneuver, the massive birds thrust themselves airborne as one, beyond Vyker's reach before he can even ready his spear.

The man's scream is nearly as high-pitched as the bird's own screeches as he soars higher and higher. Vyker watches, his feet frozen in place. The man's squirming and straining only further rends his flesh, making showers of blood for the wind. Each time he pulls free of a clawed foot it snatches down elsewhere. No arrows chase the birds, surely for fear of hitting the man. They're soon no bigger than Vyker's thumbnail. All at once, the birds release him and bank in different directions. The man plunges, shrieking. He manages to get his feet beneath him by the time he hits ground. He'd have been better off landing on his neck. His legs do nothing to break his momentum, instead flattening like they're made of straw. He flops onto his back with his legs crumpled, his back bent irreversibly. An airy wheeze escapes his parted lips. His fingers give a wiggle. His eyes stare skyward. Kraus hurdles him as he has every yellowed tuft of grass until this point.

"Keep running!" someone calls. Vyker grits his teeth and obeys.

There are more shouts, more cries, more thumping strings and whistling arrows. Vyker can see at least half a dozen of the great birds, spiraling, pirouetting, making arrows look sluggish. They swoop in solo, all unattainable targets, until they converge on a fighter, lift her screaming and dash her lifeless. One fighter employs a tactic that seems to work against the winged assault. He has a weapon in both hands, eyes moving quickly, ducking, dancing. A sprake flies by the fighter so fast Vyker never saw it approach. A red spray erupts from the man's face, and he staggers. The bird tore his jaw off. He lifts a surprised hand to touch his exposed teeth and is wrenched off his feet. His turn to fly.

Vyker can't help but appreciate their efficiency. Even when arrows strike true the birds do not slow. He's heard sprakes fly with injury and will continue their assault despite it. He's also heard they'll draw attention to themselves; distract you while their fellows ambush you. But he knows there is a defense to their onslaught. A counter. There has to be. There's no such thing as a perfect attack. Staying in a line, or at least in groups, seems the Vanguard's best chance.

A shadow falls over Vyker and his blood turns to fire. *My turn.* He squeezes his spear, turns to face the birds with teeth bared and a growl in his throat. But there's just the one above him and it's not diving. Only when he registers the rumbling beneath his feet does he realize his folly.

The roar of sprinting dreadhops makes all other sounds abruptly insignificant. Vyker rounds to find a flock of them closing from the west, noting with a sick feeling they're far bigger than they appear from Keswal's general seating. They overtop Vyker's height by a foot easily. One bears down on him, a mass of brightly colored plumage bounding on long scaly legs, beneath a feathered trunk of a neck and an axe for a face. The emotionless wildness of its red eyes nearly strikes panic into

Vyker. He's never faced a foe like this. It isn't capable of consideration. Has no use for it. Any engagement with a dreadhop will have a simple end.

Vyker grounds himself, steadies his breath. It's just a fight, and not his first. Can't settle for hurting it. Gotta kill it before it kills him. The massive bird launches an attack he's only ever witnessed from on high. It pounces, stunted wings beating as both clawed feet fly at his chest. He's anticipated this before. Any onlooker of Keswal has. He decided then how he'd react now. But he didn't take into account the tangles of grass, his slick palms, hammering heart, the sheer size and speed and bloodthirst of the godsdamned thing.

He dodges, and using the dreadhop's momentum, thrusts his spear at the thickest part of its feathered torso. The attack strikes true, crunching into the plumed flesh. A horrible noise comes from the bird even as it shivers, slumps. Vyker draws back the spear, blood spraying, the dreadhop crumpling, wheezing. He gets the point aimed at the next one just in time. His spear catches it in the chest mid-leap. The curved tip of its beak clacks shut an inch from his nose, making him flinch. The great beak springs wide again and the shriek it utters stinks of rotten blood. Vyker yells from the pit of his guts, forces the bird back, feels its bones separating, pushes harder. The dreadhop croaks at him and he snarls at it, succumbing to frenzied elation. Who knew that dreadhops, so feared by so many, can be defeated utterly by a—

Something slams into Vyker. The world turns sideways. Packed earth crashes against him, knocks the breath out of his lungs. He's pinned under an enormous scaly foot the length of his torso. He squirms, writhes, his roars reduced to gasps. Doesn't help. His left arm is trapped under him. His right arm is gripped in place by the bird's claws. Desperation flares up. He swings his head, his legs, kicking, pushing, panting. Everyone knows once a dreadhop knocks you down, you're done for. Vyker twists, trying to break out from under the dreadhop's grasp, but the way it leverages its weight on him, he might as well be trapped under a fallen tree.

The beak's black, chisel point hacks at Vyker. It's all he can do to thrust his head toward it to try and protect his neck. The point clacks against his skull, so hot and bright a pain he knows at once it at least tore skin, if it didn't scalp him outright. The bird's beak snips and chisels, trying to find purchase, to rip, to pull. Blood fills his ear and runs over his face. His legs scrabble against the stunted grass. In one moment, the birds earned their name. The dreadhop, fed up with his defensive attempts, rams his head with the curve of its beak—which might as well be petrified wood—knocking stars into his eyes and a ring into his ears. It rams again. His head bounces off the earth. His vision swims, going colorful. He has to protect himself. But how? The bird is too savage. If it wanted a bite of his neck, there's nothing stopping it now. Panicking, thrashing, he can already imagine the stab of its beak in his neck, the rip as it pulls out flesh, arteries, bones. This grassy field is where he'll breathe his last, and likely through a new hole.

The pressure is gone. The bird is gone. Sunlight pours down on Vyker. He shields his eyes with a wavering hand, finds Kraus hefting his bloody axe high overhead. Vyker scrambles up onto wobbling legs, falls to his knees, tries to assess the damage to his scalp. His hair is clumped and matted with blood but the skin's not flayed off, which is a nice surprise. He expected to find exposed skull. Kraus' axe falls and crunches into the dreadhop's side like it's feathered kindling.

Before Vyker can gather his balance or his wits, a fourth bird slams into Kraus' back. Kraus tumbles down with a grunt. He releases his axe in time to splay his arms and keep from eating earth. Vyker, gripping his head to try and make it stop reeling, can't help noticing the bizarre disparity between the bird's vibrant colors, flashing in the sun like a child's kite, and its relentless, carnivorous assault.

Vyker needs his spear. He finds it, despite the blood blinding his left eye, reaches for it, misses—if only the ground would stop heaving back and forth. He grabs for it again. It slithers away. He realizes it's stuck in a dying dreadhop that's dragging itself off. He shakes his head to clear the flying stars, launches himself at the bird with an undignified yell. It takes three dizzy stomps to crush its neck. Finally, the spear is his again. He roars down at the dead bird until he's lightheaded.

Kraus is pinned like Vyker was except he's on his stomach. He barks out curses, hands clawing at earth, pinned in place by a single scaled foot. If swearing alone could kill, that dreadhop would be stone dead along with its entire species. As it is, Kraus may as well be a plump squealing pig. The bird has already battered him like the other did Vyker, crowning him with its mallet of a beak. Kraus took it better, still has his senses, if he ever did. But now the dreadhop draws its head back on its neck like a snake tensing at a mouse. It'll chop like a pickax, burying it in Kraus' shoulder or back or neck. It's about to make bloody work of him.

Vyker thrusts forward with a yell. His spear glances off the bird's back, freeing a puff of colorful feathers to descend playfully. He loses balance, falls to his knees. His head won't stop spinning. Feels like the damned bird concussed him. But he bought Kraus time to wriggle onto his back and get one of the bird's huge claws in his hands. He gives it a violent twist. The massive raptor screeches, slinging strands of red saliva all over Kraus. Kraus yells back, "Get the fuck off me, ya murder turkey!"

Vyker stabs the dreadhop's beady red eye, silencing its scream. The huge beak sags open, slackening, grey tongue spilling out. Vyker yanks his spear out of its head, coating himself in bird blood, then kicks the beast off Kraus. He offers Kraus his hand and hauls the big man to his feet.

"Thanks, kid. Thought I was about to feed the birds after all."

The display of teeth that flashes over Kraus' blood-soaked face has none of the cheer that smiles are supposed to have. Vyker can't possibly look much better. A laugh escapes him. "Fuck birds."

"I couldn't have said it better. Let's go."

The party's formation has blurred and scattered. Some of the Vanguard is already at the tree line. Archers under Irdessa's close direction are filling the air with arrows in such a manner that they don't fall on the party. It's keeping the sprakes busy dodging, preventing their approach. A handful of them lie dead that Vyker can see. Several dreadhops prevail throughout the scattered Vanguard. Where fighters band together they fare the best at repelling the ravenous birds. Now and then, however, the long-legged dreadhops catch a straggler and pour upon them, flattening them, hacking until they stop screaming, yanking shiny strands up into the bright sun.

"To the trees," comes Irdessa's command. "To the trees!"

Kraus runs. Vyker follows, trying not to think about the wounded, the fallen. To his right, a dreadhop busies itself with the guts of a fallen body. Arrows appear in its side, thumping it like a drum. The bird falls away. Luckily for the living, the flightless carnivores gravitate toward the bloodiest, least-animate bodies, and make easy targets of themselves. The sprakes squawk and buffet the dreadhops, trying to turn their attention onto the living. It does little good now. Those that run screaming to crash into the Vanguard meet an organized line of sharpened steel. In this way, the remaining dreadhops are dealt with. There's a dreadhop in front of Vyker, limping toward the line of fighters with a bloody leg as if salvation awaits it. Vyker plunges his spear up the bird's ass, dropping it, leaps its feathered form and keeps running.

The remaining sprakes are pulling back. The dreadhops are all dead and the sprakes can't penetrate the forest or even approach the Vanguard's line for fear of arrows. It's interesting to Vyker that they're aware of it. How smart are they? They've marshaled a legion of dreadhops in an organized assault. Now they're retreating. Except one near to him. It hops awkwardly with a bent wing extended. He dashes to finish it off. Reducing his enemy's forces, even one at a time, is his purpose. This sprake has led its last attack.

"Vyker." It's Old Fent, from near the tree line. "Leave it."

This will only take a moment, he thinks, but doesn't bother shouting. Besides, there are still others running for the trees. He readies his spear to thrust into the raptor's side. The bird dodges, flapping both wings and gaining several feet before descending pitifully and continuing to putter along. Vyker dashes again, despite a nagging from within his own head. This time he waits until he's close enough to grab the raptor before thrusting his spear. Again, the great bird flits out of the way as if its wing is whole, watching him sidelong with a single black eye.

"Vyker!" someone else is shouting.

He looks around. The rest of the Vanguard has made it to the trees. Aside from the dead or wounded, he's alone on the field. Vyker stops at once, embarrassment burning hot in his cheeks. The lone sprake seems to learn its trick is up. It gives a rattling sound that may as well be laughter and launches itself into flight, no signs of injury whatsoever.

Vyker runs for the trees, grimacing, trying to pretend a bird didn't make a fool of him. The weight of the small box lashed on the side of his pack suddenly feels like an anvil. Did that painted freak hand him the box because he's gullible? Because he's a fool? He grits his teeth. Maybe the man didn't take him for a traitor but a dumbass. Doesn't feel like much of an improvement. Under the shadow of the forest, he checks his momentum so his eyes can adjust to the dimness. He should have told Irdessa about the box. He should have handed it to her. He slows to a walk, his eyes on the fallen pine straw, his mind elsewhere entirely. Is it too late to hand it over? What will she make of the fact that he didn't do it at once? Was it a test?

"Can't slow down. That's what they want." Irdessa appears in front of him as if she'd been invisible. She raises both hands. "Easy, Vyker."

He's pointed his spear at her. He lowers it awkwardly. "I'm sorry. You startled me."

"Lesson learned." She offers a smile, turns. "Gotta run. They know where we are."

She's right. The carnage over the field is vast. Whatever enemy the departing sprakes mean to alert will have no trouble pursuing them.

39
All Will Go Well

FOHRVYLDA

The Wastelands

Pain comes in a lot of different flavors. And although Kraus seems to have made it his lifelong mission to taste them all, today he would gladly pass that cup along. Pain is better fresh, not stagnant. This lingering sort is apt to rile and antagonize until one's mind comes undone. Well, a weaker mind than Kraus'. It just makes him fucking thirsty. Kraus has never run this long in his life. Surely no one has. Who would? And why? If you hate yourself enough to submit to an all-day marathon, just stick a knife in your neck. There are easier ways to die.

Day is done. Has been. He hauls himself uphill through the forest in some semblance of running, stomping over small trees and tussling with bushes, only bothering to duck under the branches that are more likely to break him than he them. His skin shifts as he runs, keeps him vaguely aware of every scrape, burn, laceration. He's long since grown slick and sticky despite the chill in the evening air. At least under the cover of forest he need not wear the long cloak he found during the siege. Sweat infiltrates his wounds, itching, stinging. He can't scratch the stitches as he'd like for fear of further tearing the wounds, so he has to swat at them. His bones creak with every pounding step, reminding him of bruises, fractures, the arrow wound, his perpetually grinding knee. If not for the necessity to draw rasping, painful breaths as often as his chest will allow, he'd most likely be swearing at the top of his lungs.

What the hell am I doing?

He'd been hoping for a final bloody stand in Keswal. Seemed as good a place as any. Instead he got a final quest. He was ready to die getting Irdessa to her home, by her hand or anyone's. Instead, he fulfilled his quest. And so he was willing to provide knife practice for the lowest thief at that grimy pit in Vim, then lie down and have a well-deserved nap. Instead, everything changed.

Bravensi jogs a ways ahead of him, closer to the front of the party. She bounces on her feet as if they're springs, making the knot of black hair on the back of her head jerk stiffly. He's not so close he can figure out how her lean limbs work to carry her thin body flowing onward. Not close enough to catch any of her enigmatic comments that never regret or even acknowledge the trampled feelings they cause. He is close enough to dash forward in case anything threatens her. In fact, it's imaginings of Bravensi's enemies lying reamed out by his fingernails that drive Kraus' feet. More than any drink ever has. Not that a drink wouldn't be welcome.

Kraus' hollow stomach feels like it's got a wildcat trapped in it, yowling and clawing to get free. He takes water when he has to. The drink rinses dust from his teeth and tongue and throat, cools him as it cascades down his pipes. Then it lands in his yawning guts where it sloshes about, reminding him how long it's been since he was chewing down burnt lizard on a skewer beside Bravensi.

Thinking of her is a welcome distraction from the racking pain of his dilapidated frame. It's not until Kraus plows through a particularly abrasive cedar branch with his face that he decides the sun is too low for this shit. For the most part, his entire body has reached a throbbing state of numbness. It feels like he's held together entirely by the momentum he maintains and if he were to slow, pieces of himself might begin to topple away.

In the hazardously dim light, Kraus can no longer see Bravensi. Not with his eyes anyway. Her face has not entirely left his thoughts since the first time he saw it. Her scent—a blend of a particularly thin, edged musk, worn leather with a lemony oil, and a garnish of rusty blood that's probably Oekner—reaches his nostrils even now and tugs him onward.

His mind is drawn to her weapon, as if the polearm is a drain in a basin and his thoughts are the water being sucked toward it. *Bloodiron*. Kraus never had reason to care why folks call it cursed, or why the distant nation of Halandor devoted an entire agency to bloodiron's extinction. *The Bloodiron Rangers*. He'd never given them a second thought. Just seemed like another variety of killjoy cunts. He wonders what Bravensi thinks of them. One time a man in Ariheim offered Kraus a job. They were supposed to turn over a caravan making its way across the east cliffs from the Silvercliff Port. The man promised Kraus whatever he could find of value. *"All I want's the sangore,"* he'd said, referring to the raw material used to make bloodiron artifacts. Nearly as illegal as the final product. And for a man not discussing food, he looked far too hungry. Kraus had turned him down. Felt wrong. Seemed like too hot a job. Besides, in addition to the man's fingertips being stained scab black, so was his beard and mustache, like he spent equal time tinkering with the ore and sucking at it. Kraus goes to spit, but he has none.

The Vanguard is slowing, checking their pace. Kraus follows suit without hesitation, hoisting his arms up and gripping his hands above his head, walking in circles to cool down, catch his breath, convince his heart not to kill him. If he stops moving, he'll either vomit from exertion or go straight to sleep. And if sleeps, he won't wake up soon. Probably not until the party has gone and left him. He's not so stupid as to think he has friends in this assembly besides Irdessa. Assuming she hasn't had her fill of him by now.

Once he's caught his breath, he ranges through the groups of hunched and resting fighters. The Vanguard are subdued, sitting in shadows, leaning against trees, lying down. Some are huffing quietly. Some are taking water in sips. Some are staring off with glassy eyes that reflect the moon and betray their exhaustion. It's a portion of the same crowd that was partying in Vim last night, now bedraggled and wan.

Irdessa is not to be found. Neither are Bravensi or Fent. Kraus has half a mind to find a good hiding spot and flop down and pass out. Whether or not he wakes is of small consequence. Instead, his feet drag him onward, toward the far end of the gathering. There he sees bright moonlight spilling through an opening in the forest's canopy. The tree that once occupied that space lies rotting on its side, glowing in the moon's light. Several hoods are huddled around, using the fallen trunk as a makeshift table. As Kraus draws closer he recognizes faces. Irdessa, Old Fent and his warrior Sura, Bravensi ...

They've gathered around a parchment that is laid out over the bark. On it are black charcoal scrawlings, illuminated only by what light the moon provides.

"Kraus," Old Fent says, and gives Irdessa a look. It was no greeting. More an announcement or a warning, and not aimed at Kraus himself.

"He can join us," Irdessa says.

Puzzlement crawls over Kraus' face, and more than a trickling of annoyance at the old man. He's protected by Sura, who watches Kraus with an expression that bunches up her lips and her white eyebrows. Her pale hair is dingy with soot and disheveled, several wild strands having escaped their knotted rows. As she is to Fent, Kraus is to Irdessa, as long as Irdessa will have him.

"Maudee, continue please," Irdessa says.

The little rogue, Maudee's, eyes flick briefly between Fent and Irdessa and she clears her throat.

"We're here," she says, tapping the simple X on the parchment with a charcoal-blackened fingertip. "Our path takes us in this direction." Her finger leaves a faint trail as it moves. "Ahead, maybe three hundred yards, the forest narrows, with open fields on either side. Awaiting us in that chokepoint is a Promontory ambush. Six mounted soldiers total. They've got alarm sprakes on quick-release tethers."

Unease drags the corners of Kraus' mouth down into a scowl. He knows the sprakes she refers to. It's a Promontory trick. At any sign of their target, the soldiers cut their tether. The birds soar upward, screeching. Barksharks can hear the sound from miles away and will chase it like it's uncooked outlaw, which in this case it is. There is some murmuring. Kraus looks to Irdessa, who is not surprised by this announcement. She's watching the faces of those around her closely, not betraying any emotion. For a moment, Kraus feels like he's in Torvald's presence.

"Our approach from the south gives them the higher ground," Irdessa notes. "They chose their location well." There is no hiding the appreciation in her observation.

"On our tail ..." Maudee's narrow fingertip taps the map softly, back from whence the Vanguard came. There are several thick, menacing lines here, all narrowing like arrows in the direction of the Vanguard's X. She hesitates, and if the moon's light is no liar, there's a fearful tremble to her lips. "... is an entire battalion, probably alerted by our run-in with the sprakes."

Murmuring spikes into gasps, swears. Seated beside her, Maudee's twin brother whittles fiercely on a bare chunk of wood as if it might be the last bit of art he'll ever produce. Kraus finds himself chuckling softly. One way or another, pain's on the menu. He doesn't say it out loud. No one would get it. Doesn't meet the angry eyes that cut toward him.

After a deep breath, Maudee continues. "They're scouring the forest, led by mounted soldiers."

"How long 'til they're upon us?" Old Fent asks wearily.

"Hard to know," Maudee says. "I'd wager we have less than two hours. Unless they find a definitive trail. Right now they're fanned out, combing the woods as they go. Lucky for us, the barksharks aren't free to track by scent. Their riders ignore their input. But as soon as they hear us, or find evidence of us ..."

"Then we're good and fucked," Kraus offers helpfully. No one's entertained. In fact, those dark glances that do fall on him wear the same displeasure they might at finding a bloating carcass in their midst. Bravensi behaves as if he doesn't exist.

"We cannot stand against a battalion," Irdessa says.

"Then we need to move," says Bravensi. Something about the situation makes her abrasive voice seem overly bold. Kraus wonders if he'll ever not be intimidated by it.

"And go where?" Fent asks. "We can't approach the ambush without them raising alarm, and then the battalion has us."

"Can we sneak past them?" Torah the mapmaker asks quietly, his eyes darting from Irdessa to Fent to Maudee. "I know it's dangerous, but—"

"We'd be noticed in an instant," Magpie snaps without looking up. It's the first he's spoken since Kraus came up. Not an impressive first impression. The narrow scout blows at his carving, then snorts as if he's thought better of it. "Well, you all would, as much noise as you make. The only way past them is here or here." He points at the areas left and right of the orcane patrol, outside the narrow stretch of woods. "Which is moonlit fields. Not enough rocks to hide you all. If the soldiers or their orcanes are conscious, and they are, that's exactly what they want us to do."

Kraus preferred it when Magpie's sister spoke. She was frightened, sure. But something in Magpie's attitude pisses Kraus off. Kid acts like he knows some hard truth that everyone else needs to accept. It's like he hates the inconvenience of enlightenment, having to operate among this incompetent a crowd. Kraus does too, but he's not being a cunt about it.

"The alarm sprakes," Irdessa says. "There must be a way to prevent them from flying." Even when she furrows her brow and studies the map, Kraus has the impression she's more closely observing those who observe her, without even looking at them. As if there's an expectation that this is one big puzzle and the pieces need to be arranged in the correct way. It's enough to convince Kraus an answer is within reach, on the tip of the tongue of someone present.

"The only way to silence them is to kill them," Magpie says. "And that's not happening. We'd have to shoot uphill, in the dark, from a far enough distance that the beasts and soldiers don't notice us, and not miss. It's impossible."

By the sound of his voice, he's checked out. Maybe he gave up before he and his sister reported to the group. If this were the Last Room, the small scout would be cuffed in the face, smacked around, woken up. The choice is to do something or die. And Kraus isn't dead yet. "Can't the archers get close enough to kill the soldiers?" he asks.

Magpie snorts again, looking at Kraus like he might be thick headed. "And risk loose barksharks running berserk? In the dark?" He shakes his head. "I'd sooner take my chance fleeing a battalion through the woods." He lowers the carving he'd been working on and glares around him, his boyish face stopping on Irdessa. "This isn't some simple snatch job for the old Vanguard. And even if it were," he says slowly, in a low voice, "we have no Tactician."

Kraus registers his own sharp intake of breath as he hears the same around him. His weariness gives way to a sudden rage, like a sandbank swept away by crashing tide to reveal sharp stones beneath. "I'll be godsdamned if let some spineless sneak talk shit to Irdessa." The heat in Kraus' words surprises him. Magpie's carving falls from his fingers. Kraus barrels on. "She ain't Torvald, you're right. He died in Keswal. She's Irdessa, the one who didn't fucking die. And from what I've seen, she learned his tricks well enough. If this is all so helpless to you, then fuck off and let those with some fight left in them figure it out."

Kraus is on his feet with a heaving chest. This is probably as good a place to stop as any. But he's never been one to stop when it's time.

"I've opened a barkshark's head with a rustier ax than this." He gives his ax head a thump. "And I've seen her open one's neck like it was made of wax." Kraus dares to point at Bravensi. Her eyes fall on him like boulders sheared from a mountainside, silencing him at once. He's overstepped some boundary, as he does most every time he opens his mouth. He looks at Irdessa, expecting reprimand. Instead, it's a quizzical look that greets him. She's suppressing a smile.

Magpie's jaw hangs open in a mix of surprise and anger ... and fear if he knows what's good for him. Before he can speak, Maudee's hand falls on his shoulder. That simple gesture relaxes Magpie's hackles, and probably keeps his face intact. Kraus has been looking for a way to tell them apart. Magpie snorts bitterly and picks up his carving.

"You're wounded," Old Fent says, as if Kraus might have forgotten the blood oozing from the stitched wounds on his face.

"I'm always wounded," Kraus says. He becomes aware of the kid, Vyker, watching him from the shadows. "What of it?"

Irdessa cuts in as if hers is the only conversation that matters. Truth be told, it probably is. "Preventing six soldiers from launching the sprakes is more complicated than merely killing the sprakes," she notes. Her voice is encouraging, even if her words aren't. Her eyes are hungry as she searches the faces of those gathered. "They all have to die at once."

"Oekner suggests we split into two parties and travel on either side of the ambush," Bravensi says. "Their alarms will still sound, but they probably won't split the battalion. They'll be forced to engage one group, giving the other a chance of escaping."

"That would mean certain death for the party they target." Old Fent spits out the words as if they taste foul.

Bravensi shrugs and eyes her weapon sidelong as if she played no part in the advice. "Any confrontation will result in losses."

Kraus marvels at her. If her intention is to never earn back the trust of the Vanguard, she's picked a winning strategy.

"We will not so quickly throw away lives," Fent says. "Not while I still live."

Bravensi watches him. Moonlight glints dully over Oekner's face, giving his scowl a tinge of sarcastic humor, as if Fent's declaration represents some joke he's waiting for everyone to realize. Sura has tensed, glaring at Bravensi so balefully that Kraus considers stepping between them.

"The Vanguard can't sneak by the ambush," Irdessa says, turning her eyes back on the map and this time appearing to consider it. "At least, not in our entirety. That's what Magpie says."

The skittering scratches of the scout's whittling cease.

"And our archers are not promised clean shots. Not from this angle, anyway." The way her voice lilts and expresses has earned her the undivided attention of everyone present. "What's here?" Irdessa touches the empty parchment on the far side of the ambush.

Maudee exchanges a glance with Magpie. It seems something passes between them, some bit of unspoken communication. Kraus strains his ears to catch hint of whispers, even though their mouths do not move.

Magpie answers. "The same as where we are. Forested hills, steadily inclining toward the north. Enough of a hill to impede our movement."

"Thick enough woods to impede orcanes?"

Magpie answers carefully while concentrating on the map. "Yes."

"Sounds like it looks down on the soldiers," Kraus exclaims, and a quiver of excitement alights in his belly.

Once more a glance is shared between the twin scouts. Are they communicating simply by meeting eyes? Kraus is unsettled by it. This doesn't seem like the time or place to keep secrets. If Magpie has objections, he's welcome to voice them, something of which he's proven himself quite capable. Or perhaps not. Not after Kraus' reprimand. When Magpie turns his gaze from Maudee to Kraus, his eyes no longer bear such a notable hopelessness. "It does."

"Kraus," Irdessa says. "I understand you have some experience with ambushes."

The quiver in Kraus' belly ignites a spark, and his mouth becomes a grin so wide it crinkles the scabbed skin across his nose. "Ambushes are my favorite bushes."

Perhaps it's the dim light, or a stray shadow, or Kraus' hopeless imagination, but some faint semblance of a smile flutters over Bravensi's mouth before she can stifle it. She does not look in Kraus' direction. But that slight, momentary bend in her thin lips pours elation into Kraus like sunshine through storm clouds.

"No good will come of fighting under these circumstances," Fent mutters.

"I have a lot of fight to offer." It's Vyker. He looks troubled but not afraid. A thick silence ensues. One that hardens all the moonlit faces present, turning them into scowls both rebellious and determined. Even Fent has stopped shaking his head, leaving his sole eye aimed at the young Vyker.

From anyone else but the kid, Kraus might have found the comment exactly as compelling as a downwind fart. But the boy's not lying. He's got rage buried in him, whether or not he even knows it, and what he lacks in experience he makes up for in tenacity. Would he be so dedicated if he knew what happened to his brother? Maybe best not to find out.

"I'm always down to fight," Kraus says.

"As if we have a choice," Bravensi says, without looking at him.

"Then fight it is," Irdessa says. Her eyes bear a resolution fiery enough to fit the Last Room.

Irdessa instructs the gathering to disperse while the details are worked out. The Vanguard is to see to their wounds, get themselves prepared, rest their feet, have a quick bite, all in order of their own priority. Irdessa confers quietly with Maudee and Magpie and another rangy-looking man. Kraus finds a wine skin. It's not liquor. Honestly not even strong enough to heat his flesh from the chill kiss of blood loss. But sometimes you have to take what you can get.

Kraus peels back his blood-hardened wrappings to dab more salve on his injuries. So far this has kept scabs from plastering to the fabric of his jacket and pants and cloak. Hopefully kept them at least somewhat clean too. He's never been good at wound care, no matter how injured he was. He always forgets to do it and it takes too damn long, and you have to keep up with little tools and vials, and frankly fuck all that. But his surgery came courtesy of Bravensi, not that he can remember much of it. He considers each stitch as a heartfelt memorial. He won't let her work go to waste.

He's pulling his coat over his ravaged arm when the Vanguard at large begins converging on Irdessa's position. She stands atop the fallen log with a look in her eye like her news will please everyone. Kraus can't imagine that being the case.

"As you all have surely heard by now, we're being pursued by Zander's army, and there's a patrol blocking our escape. We have no choice but to eliminate the patrol, and quietly. Magpie and I will lead two teams that will act as pincers. We will strike from the north, get their attention, and the Vanguard's main body will crush them."

The Vanguard's murmuring ceases. Kraus nearly laughs. One would deduce from her tone it's as dangerous a deed as strolling down a cobbled street.

"Maudee and I will take the left flank, along with you ..." Irdessa points at a man with a smooth-shaved face, chiseled jaw bones. A pretty fucker. "I don't know your name. But I watched you put an arrow through a sprake's heart at fifty paces and I know your feet fall silently."

The man steps forward, his chest thrust out proudly. "You can call me Caenin. The Arrow."

Kraus wonders how well he takes a punch. Something's familiar about him. Kraus realizes it's the same Vanguard prick who tried to shoo them off when they first got to Cornerstone. More like Caenin the Cunt.

"Alright, Caenin the Arrow. We will be crossing a path that a mounted soldier paces. Your stealth is essential. Magpie, you, Elaga, and whomever else you chose, take the right flank. Elaga because she is skilled with her greatbow and can also hold her own in a melee. I suggest Cindie stay back. Same as us, you all will intersect a path they patrol."

"Question," Cindie interjects, moving her shoulder between Elaga and Irdessa. "What happens if they're seen?"

"If one of the two flanking groups is spotted, the patrol will most likely cry out so that the central camp releases alarm sprakes. Then they'll engage us until their battalion can arrive."

Kraus marvels at how matter-of-factly she details their imminent death.

"But if you expect it to happen," she continues, "you will be prepared when it does. You'd be wise to anticipate being spotted." Only now does Irdessa look directly at Cindie. "In fact, a single, silent kill before we engage the camp would thin their numbers and prevent us being flanked by their patrols. Elaga is among the few who can accomplish such a kill against an orcane."

Cindie's response is to furrow her brow, bite her lower lip.

"But we plan to not be seen." Irdessa emphasizes the obvious words deliberately, perhaps so they'll take on a power of their own. "Don't move until you've learned your patrol's route, their pace, their alertness. Determine the quietest path before you try to move on it. Be ready to kill the soldier and his orcane immediately if you are seen." She lets her words linger in the cold air.

Cindie's eyes fall angrily onto Elaga. "What good will it do to ambush this patrol anyway? The battalion behind us will find their bodies and chase us."

"You're right," Irdessa says. "This buys us little time. But if it doesn't succeed, we have none. If we try to sneak over the moonlit field we'll be seen, called out, and rushed by the battalion on landscape they prefer. This plan is more likely to succeed than simply rushing them and hoping to prevent their alarm sprakes." She looks around unapologetically. "Any plan besides this will end worse."

"We're wasting time," Bravensi's voice hammers out.

"Our two teams will achieve the high ground after getting past the patrols," Irdessa says. "We'll maneuver until we have a shot at their sprakes. Our scouts will communicate the word and we'll take out the birds all at once. Three arrows per bird. The alarm will never sound."

Kraus notices Magpie and Maudee share a look that discloses no emotion. Unless Kraus is imagining it, the thin rattle of cricket song buzzes louder with their secret code. Are they speaking cricket?

"You know it's rude to keep secrets," Kraus says at them. *I don't trust you fuckers*, is what he meant but he's trying to be nice to Irdessa's friends.

They hold each other's gaze for an annoyingly long moment, then deliberately converge their matching pupils on Kraus. It's damn near discomforting.

"Seems like a lot of this plan rests on you two," Kraus tells them. "A lot of trust on our part."

Neither of the twins respond. They may as well be porcelain dolls. In the stark moonlight, he has no idea which one's Maudee and which is Magpie. For some reason that pisses him off all the more. "I don't trust you fuckers," he says.

Irdessa clears her throat so sharply Kraus startles.

"With the sprakes dealt with, I'll signal Harpold the Hunter. He'll lead the melee," she says.

That tall, rangy man is standing right before her and there's a proud look on him as he peers around to make sure all heard this command. His attention returns to Irdessa.

Kraus frowns. "Why him?" he says. He himself is perfectly capable of leading the melee. More than capable.

"He can communicate with Maudee and Magpie discreetly," Irdessa says, and Kraus can hear her impatience.

"Not as well as them to each other, I'd wager," Kraus grumbles. "Unless he's a damn cricket."

The twins are still staring at him with dark eyes. A chill climbs over his skin, like a blanket of spiders. Creepy fuckers.

"It's communication between the three of them that drive this entire endeavor," Old Fart spits at Kraus. "That is the extent of our poor advantage. Show some respect."

Kraus gawks. The man's got stones. "You old fu—"

"Kraus." Irdessa's voice is like a slap. "You'll be supporting Harpold with Vyker, Sura, Cindie, Bravensi, and anyone else who can fight."

Kraus forgets the twins and Fent all at once. He looks for Bravensi's eyes, trying to keep a grin off his face.

Sura does not appear pleased by this announcement. She glares at Fent, perhaps expecting him to object. He avoids her gaze.

"The soldiers' reaction to our arrows will be either to regard the dead sprakes or seek cover from the arrows' source." Irdessa's voice has taken a theatric edge. "Either way, their backs will be open to you, Harpold. You'll be able to get deep in range and launch a concentrated attack. Kill the orcanes first, and quickly."

The man gives Irdessa a sharp nod. "Understood."

"Bringing up the rear will be Old Fent and Torah, leading whoever else isn't fighting." There is no judgment in Irdessa's voice, and her eyes seem to urge that acceptance on all gathered. "They'll minimize our tracks."

"We'll do what we can," Fent offers. There is no mistaking the pessimism in his tone. He does not love this strategy.

"Things don't always go as planned." Irdessa addresses everyone now. "But if we're prepared to make a hard choice quickly, all will go well."

Kraus gives an unintentional chuckle. She has a way of enthusing him. And yet, the eerie stares of the twins pulled loose a thread in his tired mind. A thread that caught on Irdessa's words and began to unravel him. *All will go well.* Does she not know Kraus by now? Nothing goes well for him. The thread pulls, trying to disassemble his resolve from the boots up.

The group is disbanding, each individual executing whatever stretch or exercise most readies him to spill blood in the dark. Kraus shakes his limbs, searching for a warmth that is not forthcoming. Maybe he should have spent more of his break eating, less of it drinking. While that notion tickles him, it's not without merit. He trudges off to find a bite. Instead he finds Cindie staring down at her feet. Elaga rests a hand on her shoulder and speaks to her in a low voice. Looks like Cindie is more in need of encouragement than Kraus is. He's never been too good at that, but you gotta start sometime.

"This sounds like a done deal, yeah?" Kraus forces a laugh and makes to give Cindie's other shoulder a pat. Before his hand arrives, Cindie launches into a passionate kiss with Elaga. Kraus' boots grow roots and his attempted smile solidifies on his slack cheeks.

"Stay alive," Cindie whispers after their lips separate. Their foreheads are touching. Elaga's eyes are low. She nods, their brown and blond hair intertwining.

Kraus realizes he's staring. Elaga notices him. "See something you like, rapist?"

The grin Kraus had been trying at shatters like windowpanes hit by stones. Whatever heat was left in him leaks away. He's so surprised by the remark he can't even formulate a response. And what response could there be?

Elaga and Cindie walk off.

Kraus turns his back, longing for a place he can stomp off to. Just when he's pushed it all from his mind. It's with no comfort that he considers the cruel limit of his body's pain. No matter how bright and savage and glorious it can be, it pales compared to what's within. Unlike wounds of flesh and bone, the gash inside festers. His eyes rove the camp, less in search of a thing, more in search of a safe spot to rest. There is none. There are shadows. And in those there are the dead girl's eyes, sticky under a mess of blond hair never to be combed again, if it ever was. Not the only dead eyes he's ever seen or caused. Far from it. Not particularly remarkable either. So why won't they leave him alone? He presses his palms to his ears, lowers into a crouch.

Pain speaks in the language of fear. It says, *Bad things are happening. Do something!* Except sometimes something bad already happened. It happened while you weren't paying attention. It snuck in and ripped part of you away, scarring you like a lightning wound on a tree, not even polite enough to finish the job. And now there's not much you can do about it but grit your teeth, wait to die.

A godsdamned drink would really hit the spot. A real drink. *All will go well*, Irdessa had said. The barking laugh that escapes Kraus is hearty, authentic, and utterly despaired. Nothing has ever gone well. Nothing ever will.

40

What Would Torvald Do?

FOHRVYLDA
The Wastelands

Irdessa runs. All around is the commotion of chaos. Someone's coughing. Someone else is yelling. Maybe her name. Doesn't matter. You can't panic. Gotta run. Even if her ribs jostle and ache and the cold wind is a relentless, rude reminder of the gash on her cheek and the cut on her lip. Torvald said—Irdessa's shoulder clips a tree trunk that yields not one bit. Pain sears through her bones, into the joint in her elbow, making her wrist seize up. Her breath catches in her teeth. Her feet do not stop. Torvald said ... what had he said? Someone nearby is sobbing while they run.

She can't remember anything Torvald said. She can't even remember his voice. She can't picture his face. In fact, she can only remember that he left her. And he made sure she couldn't follow. There is a shriek building up in Irdessa's stomach. He left her. After telling her he loved her. He's gone and he left her all alone.

"Liar!" It erupts without her consent.

Keep your feet. Don't stop running.

Fuck you.

That was Irdessa's farewell to Torvald.

The commotion is fading. She doesn't want to be in control anymore. She walks. Just gotta get away. Doesn't matter where or how. Her heart beats in her ears. She succumbs to the question assaulting her.

What went wrong?

Irdessa's party had successfully snuck past the patrol on the western flank with no incident. With the assistance of Maudee's sharp eye and her intrinsic sense for subterfuge, she, Irdessa, and Caenin passed by the western patrol like shadows. It was exactly as Irdessa had hoped. While Caenin does have feet that fall as quiet as thoughts, he's not built for melee. Too soft for that. Prefers his hands stay clean. In a faceoff with an orcane, he'd probably fill his pants. Placing him in her team was equally important as removing him from Harpold's.

They had circled to the north behind the encampment and waited to approach. Elaga's party was late. Irdessa crept over to the eastern flank to check on them, making sure not to step on anything that might give her away. At the lip of a stony overhang, she arrived in time to peer between branches and watch the soldier there catch sight of Elaga while she was crossing the path in a sliver of moonlight.

The soldier dug his heels into his orcane's sides, making it rear up and claw the air. Elaga immediately rolled onto her back directly in the soldier's path, feet toward the orcane with boots on either side of the greatbow's leather-bound handle. She nocked a javelin on the arrow rest, drew it back until she lay nearly flat on her back with the notched end of the projectile touching her chin. The orcane, not even ten yards from her, leapt into a gallop. But between its second and third step Irdessa heard the punch of the massive string, the faint whistle of something large moving at sudden incredible speed.

The orcane died without warning. The javelin flew between its teeth and out the back of its head. The projectile hit the soldier's chest with the force of a tree limb, throwing him off the orcane and into darkness before he could even yell.

The beast took a few more steps, silently vomiting blood, then eased down and sprawled on its side among the brambles. It drew up in anticipation of a sneeze that never came.

It was as quiet a kill as they could ask for, minus Elaga's grunt of agony after the greatbow's thick string grated a layer of skin off her unprotected shins like two sweet potatoes. Why she didn't put on her greaves is beyond Irdessa.

The two pincer parties made ready north of the chokepoint. They drew arrows and killed the sleeping sprakes so stealthily the rest of the encampment didn't even notice. Based on the soldiers' raucous conversation, they had little faith in the orders that mired them out in the middle of nowhere. It was that boredom that apparently drove them to visit the nearby settlements. Or more accurately, raid them from the sound of it. They boasted of the town that refused them hospitality now lying in ashes.

As the Vanguard crouched in wait, the soldiers resolved their frustrations with copious amounts of whiskey. "Useless orders," one said. "Captain might as well have ordered us to keep watch over a sack of orcane shit."

Irdessa agreed with them on that. A more incompetent group of soldiers she couldn't have hoped for. It took a sprinkling of arrows into the lungs of their orcanes to get the soldiers on their feet. Kraus gave an enthusiastic but quite unnecessary call and Harpold and his party struck them unaware. The orcanes went down, all of them, by one means or another. Mostly hacked and slashed through their heavy necks. At one point, Kraus was on the back of a bucking orcane. He'd chased a soldier up there to stop him from escaping. Irdessa never saw how that resolved other than to eventually observe that Kraus yet lives.

The ambushers proceeded to kill the soldiers until they came to the last two. These had thrown down their weapons. Some of the Vanguard hesitated, unsure of how to treat a surrendered foe. Bravensi did not. She stepped forward and slit both their throats in a single red flick of her weapon.

It was over. Aside from Elaga's self-inflicted wounds, they were whole and once more on the move. Old Fent and the cartographer were among the last to scurry across the encampment. That's when one of the downed orcanes decided it wasn't yet dead. From atop the hill overlooking the last of the group's passage, Irdessa watched the dazed beast stir. The orcane lifted itself dizzily to its feet. Old Fent was right in front of it and stumbled backward, looking up into the beast's black eyes. No one held its reins. It was woozy, certainly due to the gash in its neck. It looked around as if its eyes couldn't focus. Fent stood frozen. Irdessa wanted to yell at him to stay still, yell at someone with a blade to go back to finish the beast. But yelling might attract the battalion. So she only stood there. When the beast made no further cohesive movement, Fent carefully proceeded. The orcane saw him at once and swatted him with a deft paw, throwing Fent into a tree, his head thudding off the trunk. The orcane reeled a moment like it might fall over. Beneath it, Old Fent rocked on his back, moaning insensibly, holding his head with his palms pressed against his eyes. Irdessa could have dashed at it. She could have called for help. But again, the battalion—the need for stealth. Vyker came up beside her, observed the situation in a glance, and made to run in. Irdessa gripped his wrist, stopped him with a glare.

Looking back, she knows what she chose in that moment. She calculated the risk of her call or of Vyker's engagement against the worth of Old Fent's life to the Vanguard. Imminent loss proved preferable. So she did nothing while the orcane wobbled, settled down, reached out a paw and snagged Fent's coat with its claws. She held Vyker in place while it dragged Fent over as if he weighed nothing, placed its paws on his chest, fixed its teeth in his belly, and with a jerk of its head emptied Fent's guts out over the earth.

Fent made a raspy, low-pitched noise. Nothing too loud. Still Irdessa held. *It's almost over*, she told herself, watching one of her last friends die. There was a taut strip, shiny black under the moon's gaze, stretching from the hole in Fent to the corner of the orcane's mouth. Some part of him was already down the beast's throat. Vyker strained against her. *Almost over*. It buried its muzzle in Fent's ribcage and went to work. His eyes bulged and his complaints became no more than a hiss, accompanied by red bubbles. His hands slapped the beast's head, a child splashing a rain puddle.

Irdessa was turning to haul Vyker onward when Sura appeared like an arrow in flight, crashing into the orcane. Echoes of the mute warrior's shrieks draw chills over Irdessa's neck even now. She attacked the orcane's head, its shoulder, its neck. She chopped, chopped, and chopped, screaming all the while until the beast was nearly decapitated. Old Fent was spread over the orcane's feet, and now so was the beast's skull, glistening black in the moon. Sura hacked and hacked until the orcane didn't have a snout, or ears, or eyes. Heavier sections of skull succumbed to Sura's sword, splintering like a driftwood stump. The sword's rhythm underpinned her desperate weeping.

At that point Irdessa had no choice. She'd made her way down and was attempting to pull Sura from the beast without getting herself cut to pieces when Magpie and Maudee dashed off in alarm.

"Soldiers from behind," Harpold hissed.

Apparently, an advance team of the pursuing battalion had been trailing the Vanguard and almost caught up unnoticed while the scouts were busy with the chokepoint. Sura's screams surely helped them close the distance.

A wave of arrows swished through branches and trunks. Two individuals at the rear of the Vanguard yelled in pain. Torah fell down flat without uttering a sound, his fist loosely gripping the arrow protruding from his left ear. Half a dozen soldiers slammed into the Vanguard, swords flying. Unlike the drunken soldiers at the chokepoint, and unlike the war-weary stragglers of Vim, they came primed to fight. Those of the Vanguard who had wished to avoid fighting were the first to die.

By the time Vanguard's fighters engaged, the soldiers had all bloodied their swords. Bravensi and Vyker threw themselves between the infirm and the enemy. Maudee, Magpie, and two other scouts closed in from the side, hitting the soldiers low with arrows and dividing their attention. The soldiers fell quickly enough at that point. Someone from the Vanguard cried "Run!" And that's what Irdessa did.

Too much time was lost. Whatever slim advantage that ambush was supposed to create failed. And it's Irdessa's fault. She weighed a man's life. A friend. And by some metric she can't help but think is a direct influence of Torvald the Tactician, she made a choice. The wrong choice. How many died because of it? The Vanguard killed a handful of Promontory's soldiers. A dozen maybe, out of tens of thousands. The army is closer than ever, and when they discover the carnage they'll increase their pace. Follow the blood. One thing orcanes can do on their own is find what's dying. Help it die.

In Keswal, when the fight was over, you went back to the Last Room and kicked off your boots and leisured barefoot all the way to the lanista's manor. Then you soaked in hot water and drank mead and ate until you passed out. In Keswal, you took no responsibility for your compatriots who passed through the Last Room alongside you, never to return. That burden was for Torvald, who never appeared to have a problem with its weight. Unless he was a virtuoso among liars.

What is the worth of a life that makes Keswal enviable by comparison? So distant a life. She was so childish. So naive. What burden did Torvald carry? If it was as light as he made it out to be, then his sociopathy was of a villainous degree.

Even now, with hot tears searing her face, Keswal prudence insists she value the trimming her party received. A beneficial culling. They're slimmer now. Faster. The survivors are more fit to run. And for appreciating that fact, for even acknowledging it in this moment, she hates herself. Hates what Torvald made her.

Kraus hobbles alongside Irdessa, mouthing something, maybe screaming it. If she begins to trim off the party's fat, sooner than later she'll come to him, whose limping gait is almost too painful to witness.

"Gotta hike, Dess," Kraus says, tugging her arm.

She realizes she's stopped. She's back in the pitch black of the cave beneath the towers, clinging to life by a strand. Where are they running to? Why? The battalion is almost here. And even if it wasn't, the entire countryside will crawl with soldiers soon. Irdessa is losing her grip on the hope that something will give her an idea or expose an opportunity that can save the Vanguard, or even herself. Torvald ... he was the tactician. She's just *undying*. A title the Bloody Portent gave her. A condition she shares with rocks the world over, to no one's admiration. If there were any value to being undying, then all the world's cutthroats could be miners instead.

Kraus is looking behind them, grasping her arm. "Shame about what happened back there. Bad shit."

"Save your breath, Kraus."

"I know," he huffs. "But you two were friends."

She runs, resisting the urge to hit him with something. Even if this were the moment for a valediction, and it's not, what good do words do? Time will bring grief. Or it won't. Keswal taught her to postpone grief. This new life is teaching her to be prepared to postpone it forever.

Irdessa runs. It doesn't matter that Kraus can't keep up. Him or anyone. She can't be trusted to lead. She's done nothing more than maintain the Vanguard's violent descent. Is this all a part of Torvald's plan? Each time the question ambushes her, her perception of the black-haired Tactician warps further from what she thought was true. *You won't die in Keswal*, he promised. Perhaps not. Instead she'll die on the outside, where success is elusive if it exists at all. Out here no one cheers, and rightfully so. By the time the Undying dies, no one will be left to mourn her.

There will be more advance teams before the battalion catches them. The soldiers that assault them will be fresh, unlike the Vanguard. And they won't be dealt with as quickly as the first. There is nothing to keep the battalion from sending out advance teams again and again, until the Vanguard is picked to a scattering of corpses.

Everyone Irdessa has ever known is dying, one after the other. And she recognizes, against all empty reassurances born of self-preservation, that this is her design. As long as she is in charge she'll only kill more. And will their deaths matter? Will they even be noticed? Will anyone's death ever matter? Surely there must be a life in Fohrvylda whose bloody end will change something, will improve the entire nation. She's always thought Vretos filled that role above all. Now she's not so sure.

"Hey!" a woman's voice hisses, from just beside Irdessa. The noise is so urgent and abrupt that Irdessa jerks to a halt.

The hunched woman is wearing a grey animal skin over thick, uneven shoulders, and she is so close she could have reached out and knifed Irdessa had she wanted to. Kraus stomps up, closer on Irdessa's heels than she realized. He stalks crookedly toward the woman, sucking air in great gasps. "How did you—?"

"Did you kill the patrol?" the woman aims the question at them both. More of the Vanguard is catching up.

"No." Bravensi's lie cuts the air.

"We killed the *fuck* out of them," Kraus says. He's baring his teeth at Bravensi in a frightening forgery of a smile.

"Follow me." And the woman turns and shuffles quickly toward what appears to be a knot of foliage. Irdessa watches her arrive at shrubbery then disappear, an act which rouses gasps from others. No one moves. The woman's hooded head pokes from a curtain of ivy interspersed with fallen needles. "You can follow me to safety or keep running. But don't just stand there and ruin our cover."

"Into that ... cave?" Irdessa asks. "There are at least twenty of us." Gods willing there are still that many.

"There's plenty of room," the woman says, "but not if they catch you and find the damn entrance."

"Go." Irdessa points after her. The Vanguard needs no further persuasion. They follow the woman into what appears to be a tall, narrow fissure in the stone itself, hidden behind bushes. Irdessa watches her party's passage nervously, waiting to be the last in. As they disappear, the silence sharpens around Irdessa. Distant signs of the approaching battalion grow evident. Scampering creatures. Bird cries in the night. Her skin prickles, hair rising on her neck. Feels like her enemies have quietly surrounded her already and are guiding her toward this cleft. She shakes the ridiculous idea away, scans the forest. There come the distant reverberations of a mass of marching boots, as if the battalion found the ravaged patrol and increased their pace. She clings to this evidence feebly, uses it as confirmation that sending her people into this unknown cave is the best option, and that following them is a good idea. She steps to the cavern's entrance and pulls the ivy aside. It's a natural-looking cleft, two craggy walls framing a slit of utter blackness. The opening is jagged, slender, no wider than three feet at the base, narrowing as it ascends to converge above Irdessa's head. It's as if a huge stone split in two and the halves spread outward at the base. Godsdamn, she hates caves.

Sound is muffled within, and the air is cool and damp. Irdessa takes a deep breath and holds it, an act which only makes her thundering heart louder. What is it about enclosed earthy darkness that makes her throat tighten and her ears twitch and her palms sweat? All that convinces her foot to breach the blackness is concentration on the fact that she witnessed two dozen people rush in and hasn't yet heard any screams of horror. There is safety in numbers, she tells herself, unintentionally triggering the memory of fifty pirates being slaughtered by goatmen.

The air is thick with the smell of rust and fungus. She proceeds over uneven but solid ground, following light footsteps and skitterings and muttering, with one hand sliding over the cold stone and the other out in front of her face. There's a light ahead, making bouncing silhouettes of the heads in front of her. *They're alive. I'm alive.* Her foot sloshes into a puddle and something frigid seeps into her boot.

Torvald, you son of a bitch, her mind says, as if that specific step was his fault. And maybe it was. For all she knows he planned everything, even after all this time. Her subconscious is not finished distorting his memory and he's not around to defend himself. She's transforming him into a demigod who pulls strings from his grave. She can even picture the curling half-smile on his cold, dead cheek.

She grits her teeth. At some point, she has to take control of her actions. Or has she already? Is it Torvald's ghost that haunts her or her own reaction to his absence? What's certain is that she's responsible for Fent's death. Only her.

The flickering light is from oil lanterns lining the walls of a cavernous chamber, supported at regular intervals by wooden beams. Her people have assembled within and are watching the walls suspiciously. Irdessa's eyes move quickly. Pressed against the hewn stone are individuals with dirty faces and slouched shoulders. A moment's count says there are at least one hundred, and no telling how many more in the adjoining passages. Some wear the same dull grey as the woman who invited them into the cave. Most of them have hoods and capes of animal skin. The floor is freckled with shallow, black puddles. There are openings here and there in the cavern walls, where tunnels lead away from this chamber. Whatever this place is, or was, took a lot of people a long time to form. And now it seems to have died. The wooden tables and chairs lie rotting in mildew-covered pieces, having lost their intended purpose long ago.

The Vanguard has caged itself among these derelicts too comfortably for Irdessa's liking. They're loosening their belts, unstringing their bows, accepting proffered drinks, engaging with these cave dwellers. These people wear forlorn expressions, their eyes wide and vacant. Irdessa stares at them, one at a time, matching their gaze without shame. If they are her enemy, they most certainly have the upper hand. But none of them appear to want a fight, not even those with spears in hand or swords at their side. It's as if they've witnessed something horrific and it rendered them impotent.

"We're not your enemy." The woman who led them into the cave has her arm around the shoulders of a boy who looks no older than ten. Somehow, despite that Irdessa has brought two dozen well-armed, noisy, bloodied fighters into this chamber, the boy's attention is on his own feet. The sigh he heaves blankets the woman's words in melancholy.

"Why'd you help us?" Irdessa asks, her voice searching the room. The woman might not be prepared to attack them, but the hopelessness of her people is palpable. It feels as if it's permeating Irdessa's skin. And if the Vanguard's collective strength is as spent as Irdessa's, this air may well be poison.

The woman touches the boy's head, tousles his hair, whispers in his ear. He rises slowly and walks away, toward other children. The woman approaches Irdessa and sits on a dry spot on the floor. Irdessa can feel Kraus tense as the woman draws near. She gestures to him, *No threat.* He does not respond.

The woman straightens her ragged grey shawl over her shoulder. Somehow, this dismal act conveys how little these people must have. "You helped us first," she says.

Irdessa doesn't respond. That wasn't good enough a reason.

"We're from Adhart. And this here was our mine," she says in a low voice, waving a hand at the cave walls. "Adhart made its living off iron. Until the spring of last year, when the central culvert collapsed due to erosion. Then the mine began to fill with water."

"Promontory chopping down forests for ships," says a nearby man bitterly. "They've stripped the whole mainland. All for the Heathen Tide. Soon enough, Fohrvylda's gonna wash away. Then we'll all be in the fucking tide."

Another man gives a grim chuckle. The Vanguard is silent.

"Little by little the mine flooded," the woman continues in her quiet voice. "Until there was no more iron to be got. But Adhart survived. We hunted, traded. We make cloaks and jackets of animal skins. We were doing well, despite all odds. That is, until a week ago, when Promontory soldiers came."

It takes no gift of perception for Irdessa to know where this tale is going or how it will end. The woman has everyone's attention, even her own people. Maybe it's the first time they've heard this story said. Maybe they're hoping for a better ending than the one they got.

"Six soldiers on six barksharks were stationed nearby. They came to us for food and drink. To be expected, I guess. They took our weapons. Said they needed them. We grumbled. But what could we say?" She's trailed off, distant.

"Then they came for our daughters and our sons," a man rumbles from the shadows.

This rouses the woman. She nods. "They wanted our children. We said no." Her voice is only a whisper. "So they set fire to Adhart in the night."

A knot is growing in Irdessa's throat. Those soldiers were stationed nearby because of her.

"Some of us fought back," the woman says. Her voice is neutral. "They died. But they bought us time to escape to the abandoned mines. The soldiers waited outside, knowing sooner or later we'd have to come out."

"They didn't know the mine has more than one entrance," says a man, smiling.

Affirmation from the others, even laughter. There's a soft burp and the clink of glass on stone. Irdessa turns to see Kraus trying to set down an empty bottle on an uneven floor, oblivious to the hushed atmosphere.

"Then two days ago they left," the woman says. "Something happened. They must've been called away. We ventured out looking for them, went as far as Ingston. There, we heard rumors."

Now some of the survivors straighten their backs, sharpen their eyes. Some even appear to admire their new guests, particularly Irdessa, much to her discomfort. The people she sees are battered. But now she sees something she didn't before. Smoldering in their eyes is hope, if only a spark.

"We heard Vim, too, was attacked," the woman says, "by Captain Jeret himself. But it didn't go so well for him." There is a rebellious strength in her voice. Her people are nodding now, smiling. For some godsdamned reason, Irdessa's eyes are filling. A knot in her throat is restricting her breath. She wants the woman to stop talking.

"Unknown to Captain Jeret," the woman continues, "Irdessa the Undying was there, leading Vim's Vanguard. And she fought and destroyed an entire battalion."

Muted cheers break from the despondent. At the mention of her own stupid name, Irdessa nearly loses control and bursts into tears. *Do not laud me. Do not condone what I've done. I am no better than Torvald.* It is the stretching of the tale that grounds her, angers her. They most certainly did not destroy the battalion. She wants to correct the account. If she doesn't, what's to keep innocent idiots from trying the same, as if she's one to follow? But her throat has closed.

"And now those six soldiers and their six barksharks will never harass another Fohrvyldan," the woman concludes. "Thanks to you, Adhart is avenged."

Irdessa shakes her head, keeps her eyes low to hide the tears. "You saved us too," she tells the woman, just over a whisper.

"It's the least we could do. And whatever provisions we have to offer are yours."

A man with a bandaged arm strapped to his chest rises to his feet. "Word is, Marshal Zander wants you bad."

"Not just the marshal," says another, through a crooked smile. "All of Promontory."

"How bad?" Kraus says.

"You mean in silver?" The bandaged man snorts. "Enough to build a new Adhart and dig a new mine."

Unease ripples through the Vanguard in the form of darting eyes and murmuring.

"Well, now you fucked up." Kraus pushes himself grunting to his feet. "You must know I can't let you live. Witnesses and all that." He stumbles, catches himself, pats at his belt for a weapon that isn't there. He aims a stubby finger at the biggest survivor in the room. "You first?"

"You think we're trying to cash in?" The man looks genuinely amused. "By turning you over to Promontory?" He laughs, as do other survivors. "Let's see how that would go. 'Excuse me, Captain. I'm here for the bounty on Irdessa and the Vanguard. I'll take whatever scraps of that you'd be willing to drop on the floor. Before or after you have your way with us.'" More laughter.

Kraus is not deterred. "Lemme see that." He's groping for Vyker's spear. Vyker looks at him incredulously, slapping away his hands.

"Kraus," Irdessa says, cutting short his attempts.

"We're not stupid enough to try that," the woman says. "Anyone turning you over will end up under a pile of leaves while a captain gets promoted. Promontory's too corrupt. Besides ..." A smile creases the woman's cheeks, taking years from her appearance. "You're a hero. And Fohrvylda desperately needs those."

"I am *no* hero." Irdessa is sharper than she intended. Everyone's looking at her. She looks to Sura, who rubs her knuckles idly and stares at the floor. "Tell yourselves whatever fantasies keep your chins up. But don't call me a hero."

Some of Adhart's survivors look browbeaten at this. The old woman smiles tolerantly. "It hardly matters what you're called. You've begun something that can't easily be stopped."

"And that is?"

The woman's smile remains, even as confusion passes over her eyes. "Your ... uprising." She flits a hand in the air, as if to convey a word she can't think of. Her expression suggests this should all be obvious. The rest of Adhart watches Irdessa intently, and it begins to dawn on her they may have established expectations she knows nothing about. There's an awkward tension in the air.

Irdessa clears her throat. "Please forgive me, but what exactly do you think we're planning?"

"To stick it to Vretos," someone says.

"Hear, hear!"

"Give them what they deserve."

It takes some effort to keep the bewilderment off Irdessa's face. She almost scans the room once more to make sure her party hasn't increased one hundred-fold in size. Because that's the only way these people's apparent plans for her could be anything but laughable. She lifts a hand to forestall the excited chattering. "My ambition is to save what I can of Vim's Vanguard, my people."

Silence grows, encompassing the chamber until drips of water can be heard.

"You mean you won't fight the battalion out there?" asks some child.

"Of course not. We'd be crushed," Irdessa says.

"We'd help," a man offers.

"As would others," says someone else.

Irdessa's mouth nearly falls open. How can this group of people, after all they've already lost, want to pick a fight with Promontory? *What would Torvald do?* is the question that echoes in her mind, except she already knows. He'd presume to decide who matters and who is disposable, and he'd position them in such a way to keep himself in control.

"Promontory has more soldiers than we can count. They have all the orcanes, all the dreadhops, all the sprakes. There's nothing that I, you, or the combined lot of us along with every free city in Fohrvylda can do." Announcing these facts feels a lot like she's doing Vretos' propaganda work for him. She shouldn't have to do it. It's common knowledge.

"Then what are you going to do?" The old woman's face has emptied of expression.

"Run. And I suggest you do too. I can't protect my people on Fohrvylda. I failed them too much already." Irdessa feels the weight of her people's stares. For fuck's sake, did they too think some grand standoff was their destiny?

"Run where?" The woman's sarcasm is evident. Probably because Fohrvylda is a huge island and Promontory owns every inch of it.

"To Redemier. Over the Towers."

Gasps erupt. Irdessa can barely believe she said the words. There were supposed to be more people making this decision with her. Torah, telling the best route, assuming the damn trip is even possible. Old Fent helping with their course. He's traveled onto the Towers before, so he claimed. Someone to tell her this idea isn't utter idiocy. But what choice does she have? The Vanguard has to leave the mainland. They can't use the seaports; Admiral Garr has a stranglehold on those now more than ever. The Silvercliff marauders might have presented an alternate plan. They'd be the ones to smuggle them out of Fohrvylda for an exorbitant price. But after the pounding Grimmet's uergatas gave them, they've largely dispersed into hiding to lick their wounds. And even if they could have smuggled all of the Vanguard away, Irdessa couldn't have afforded their help.

That only leaves the Towers, those innumerable stone landmasses north of the mainland thrusting up from the ocean like fingers. They go on for miles and miles, connected by bridges made of hemp rope, all the way to Redemier, wherein Vim might find safety from Promontory. By Vretos' edict, Redemier is cursed. Visiting it is punishable by death.

Irdessa refuses to meet the eyes of her people. Maybe they're no keener on the idea than these miners. She's probably managed to disappoint everyone. But disappointment won't leave you bleeding out at the feet of an orcane.

"I don't blame you," the woman says at last. "If it were up to me, none of Adhart would have died." The weight of exhaustion has returned to her shoulders. "Maybe we would attempt such a thing if we could." She doesn't need to explain for Irdessa to understand what she means. Among her survivors are children and elderly. Trekking out over swinging bridges to cross treacherous earthen spires hundreds of feet high is not for everyone. "My offer stands. Take what you need. We have more cloaks than we have backs now. They'll help hide you from the ranging sprakes. When you're ready to depart, perhaps we can advise you on safe passage north, toward the Towers."

The general mood has sunk once more into damp gloom. The attention of those gathered frays and they wander away. The Vanguard settles down to have food, get rest, see to their wounds. Irdessa retreats to the solitude of the passage they used to get here. Her mind's eternal inquiry flares up yet again. *What would Torvald have done?* At least the question is coming unglued from the ache it once conjured. Torvald would have sacrificed whomever stood between himself and an arbitrary objective, one that was more a curse than anything else. Irdessa is not him. She will not become him. She will save the rest of the Vanguard even if it costs her everything. She will lead her people off Fohrvylda.

41

Callous Pruning

AUSGAN
Stravhelm

Folksteller Tael scrambles back down the dark tunnel toward the chamber of cells. *Redemption.* He can barely believe it but here it is. It's fitting that the overgrown basalt outcast who cost Tael his life is the same to give him an opportunity to take it back.

He slows before reentering the cells. Magister Obsydia needs to hear of Kale's treachery and Tael's heroism from his own mouth, or else what purpose does he serve? If he delivers himself, and his story, and the key, into the hands of the keepers, trusting them to speak to Obsydia on his behalf ...

No ... trusting his redemption to their incompetence would be a grave mistake. This message is too important. The saving truth too ambiguous. He must be the one.

Keepers are puzzling over the empty cells. They must have already scoured and pulsed the place to their satisfaction. Or dissatisfaction. Because now their attention is on each other, juggling the blame back and forth like it's a molten rock. Tael creeps along the outer wall, staying low. He's far enough away that he may evade capture even if they look in his direction. The air in here wavers. The light is dim. The odor is strong. Even with their supersensory perception, Tael has a chance of eluding them. Keepers aren't known for their perception. Most manage a heartbeat and an appetite, little else.

Tael maneuvers around the chamber, staying tight against the wall. The three keepers have split up, now checking each individual cell in the room, doubtfully for the first or even second time. A dim light still flickers from the main exit. Tael's within five paces of it when the prime keeper emerges.

"Find him yet?" he calls to the room.

No answer from the others.

The prime strays farther from the opening. "Does this seem like a good time to cavort?"

"No," one of the keepers answers from afar, his voice warping in the vast chamber. "Starting to think he's not in here."

The prime steps forward again with clenched fists, gathers a breath, shaking his head at the announcement. "You don't get it. He's here or we're in deep with the magister. Stop wasting time and find him. There are only so many cells." He cocks an ear, anticipating a poor response, ready to swat it down as well.

Tael takes the chance to scurry behind the prime, out of the chamber and into the relatively cool, clear air of the passage to the antechamber. Up he creeps, hopefully maintaining a quicker pace than whoever might follow him. His plan is tricky, delicate. He must execute it perfectly. He makes his way to the keeper chamber, breathing as if in pain, dragging his foot behind him. He throws himself through the threshold.

"Oh, it's terrible," he cries. "The prisoners have ... escaped."

The antechamber is empty save for a torch on the small table. *Useless keepers!* Tael was arrested for much less than this negligence. Then it occurs to him they're all out searching for Kale. He rights himself and folds his arms, pacing. Whatever he's going to do must be done fast. Soon, the news he intends to use to buy favor will not be news at all. He proceeds up the hallway. It's nighttime, so aside from the organized patrols, the random wandering mancer, there shouldn't be much traffic there. This suits Tael fine. Hoping for a levelheaded response from the patrol is unrealistic. They'd probably attack first, not asking questions until he's broken and at the bottom of a cell once more.

Just before exiting into the main hall, Tael stops to give his appearance some attention. It only takes a couple licks of his palm to flatten his hair back down to his scalp, not that there's much up there to offer resistance. Once that's done, he may again pass for any other exemplar if he can keep his head down. He steps through the doorway into the lamp-lit main hall and notices the state of himself. His dele and all of his exposed skin are soiled with dust and soot like he's been wallowing in a hearth. So much for blending.

"You!" Sentinel Bronn is marching toward him, helm first. Seems he was posted here.

"I was attacked," Tael blurts, throwing up both hands, trusting his terror to play its part in this charade. He'd have preferred to let the idea bake longer before serving it. Too late. "Basalt Kale has escaped. I must see the magister." He holds back on revealing the key, his secret weapon. That's for Obsydia alone.

Bronn closes on him at a frightening pace, hand at his baton, boots clicking the floor. He's always been more prone to swinging sticks than speaking. Until this moment Tael found it entertaining, in a rampaging puppy kind of way. Turns out it's horrifying. The sentinel eyes Tael up and down, suspicion all over him. "All right, then. She can sort it out." He takes a step back and directs Tael with an extended hand.

Tael has to force movement into his legs. This is happening faster than he'd like. Walking in front of the thick-headed Bronn, Tael has no time. None to rip his dele or bloody his nose or even scrape his knuckles against the stone wall. Any such adjustment made at this point would mark him a liar or a lunatic.

"You were attacked," Bronn says carefully, walking almost close enough to kick Tael's heels. "And Basalt Kale ... escaped." As if it's taken all this time for him to simply acknowledge Tael's words, never mind consider them. He *tsks*. "I caught that dirty sneaker, you know. How'd you manage to botch that from inside a cell?"

"It's not my fault," Tael snaps. He pauses to turn and glare at the oafish sentinel but catches a sharp rap across the shoulder.

"Save it, Folksteller. This matter's urgent. If I thought your skinny legs capable, I'd make you run."

Tael walks faster, seething, refusing to rub his throbbing shoulder. He'd intended to adopt a limp. Maybe Bronn won't accompany him up the magister's staircase. He isn't one of hers, after all. Then again, he's Haik's, and that's almost the same.

Too quickly the journey is over and Obsydia's tower stands before them, her narrow stairway shining in the moon. Sentinel Bronn advances until Tael is forced onto the lowest step, then plants himself in rhystic alert, feet squared, chin high, hands at his sides, eyes distant as if staring through Tael. Ridiculous lout. He looks idiotic. But at least he's stopped there.

"Tell her I brought you," Bronn says, eyes fixed on a point over Tael's shoulder. "Sentinel Bronn."

"Oh, absolutely," Tael says, barely containing himself. *It's my foremost concern that the ape gets due credit for managing to walk and breathe simultaneously.*

Tael ascends the staircase, rising out of sight of the shell-clad moron. Now he tears the hem of his dele. He scrapes both fists' knuckles on the wall as he climbs, until they're shiny black in the pale light. He put up a fight. Broke Kale's nose even. But the dirtfoot spy got the jump on him. Clocked his head with a bucket. Tael is considering bouncing his head off the stone wall to improve the authenticity of his drama. Only then he realizes he's preparing to present an elaborate fiction to Magister Obsydia, for whom lies are as transparent as her preferred outfit. Tael falters, the urge to flop against the wall in despair heavy upon him. But he places one foot in front of the other, making the surrounding Stravhelm descend into darkness. *Keep it simple.* If he can paint a convincing enough picture, perhaps few words will be needed.

The sovereign will die, said the spy.

Tael nearly loses his footing, his heart ricocheting around his ribcage. "*By Imala,*" he hisses. Shakes his head. Smooths his hair.

He meets no adherent or sentinel on his ascent, which is unusual. Are they, too, out searching for Kale already? He pads up the magister's staircase, rising quickly above the level of the stone roofs and into bright moonlight. Once high enough to see out over the wall, he pauses to peer down the mountain's southern face, hoping for a glance at Basalt Kale or the prisoner. If he can point them out, his usefulness in the matter will be assured. Maybe even redeem him? All Tael can make out of the mountain's feet is a chalky grey mass. Maybe a loftier view will help. He climbs the stairs quicker, now with a sprinkle of hope on his fear. Before he's made a full circuit of the tower he comes face to face with Intemrus' tower. The windows are dark, as always.

The sovereign will die.

Tael shakes his head violently, tries to dislodge the voice. The filthy dirtfoot did *not* damn him. Get this over with. As he nears Obsydia's gazebo he renovates his wounded demeanor. He calls out before topping the stairs. "Magister!"

He arrives clutching his chest in both hands and finds Obsydia, wide awake, standing in the light of a single brazier in a loose-fitting, long sleeved, hooded dele. She's unmoving, staring at him like he caught her at something. She's clothed ... not that Tael had any hopes one way or another, but it seems odd. Unless she's been out. This is not how he hoped to find her. His facade feels terminally shallow, the scaffolding made of straw.

Heavy boots stomp up the stairs after him. Before Tael can react, the magister's two prime sentinels have hefted him off the ground by his arms. They turn neatly, bringing the distant night city into view, dizzyingly far below. Tael's legs unintentionally scramble in the air. They're about to carry him off.

"Let him go," Obsydia says sharply.

The armored fists relent. Tael makes no effort to keep himself from collapsing before Obsydia. He must paint the truth masterfully.

"Oh, Magister, the basalt, he broke out. And he took the other prisoner with him."

A glimmer of relief flits over Obsydia's face, quickly replaced by anger. "Begone," she tells her sentinels. They retreat one after the other down the stairs. Obsydia grabs Tael's dele in both hands and yanks him to his feet with surprising ease. "What happened, Tael?"

"Uh ... the basalt, Kale, he freed himself, and the native that was imprisoned."

"And you."

"Yes." Tael's whimpering is no longer artificial. "I tricked him."

"How did he escape?"

"He had a key. But I took it from him." Tael lifts a hand to retrieve it and finds his wrist locked in Obsydia's grasp. "It's ... it's in my pocket."

She releases his wrist but maintains her grip on his dele, holding him with her eyes. Tael raises the whaletusk key, marking again how heavy it is. Surely this counts for something. It has to.

Obsydia's eyes widen, and she recoils from it. For a moment her grip on his dele loosens. He's almost able to contain his trembling breath.

"Kale had that?"

"Yes."

Her head cranes slowly, puzzlement all over her. "Why?"

It's not obvious she meant the question for him, but he'll take no chances. "He didn't say how he got it. I took it from him." He makes sure his bloody knuckles are visible. "Roughed him up in the process."

Her face has fallen, like she's learned some dark truth. "Who else knows this?" She watches the key with malice, as if it injured her.

"No one. Only me. The prisoner." He feels the situation slipping out of his control. He must fix it. "I saw them escape through a passage. They're ... I think they're on the southern face of the mountain." He points, hoping to drive her attention away from himself.

"They're *what?*" She releases him and storms to the gazebo's southern edge, her hood falling away. By Imala, her hair is magnificent, and without any obvious effort on her part. Tael runs his hands over his sodden dele then his head, tries to smooth out his own wispy hair. He may not be done getting shaken but hopes he is. He'd had open expectations about how this would play out. So far not so good.

Obsydia's shoulders tense and she inhales sharply.

"Adherents," she says without turning. Two blue-deled exemplars step out of the shadows. Tael hadn't noticed them. How many more are hiding up here? "Rouse Kalderys. Send him to me. Wake up the ashmancer. Have him assemble fusiliers on the south wall, there." She points.

They bow. One leaves. The other hesitates. "How many fusiliers should I demand?"

"As many as Haik can quickly muster. *Resonations.*"

He bows once more and moves past Tael as if he's not there.

Obsydia returns to Tael, making his buttocks clench. Her eyes are wide. "What else was the basalt carrying?"

"Nothing. The key is all I ... saw."

The sovereign will die.

All the heat falls out of Tael's face. *By Imala.* Kale ... he fled his cell at the exact moment the prisoner said ... *By Imala.* He couldn't have. He wouldn't have.

Obsydia is observing him, deathly still. He's lost all control of his facial expression. He can't look at her. He's forgotten any shred of the illusion he'd set out to achieve and probably looks a lot like he feels. Like he'd rather be anywhere else.

"Folksteller Tael." Her voice is calm.

He brings himself to meet her eyes.

"The key is all you saw," she says.

Air rushes into his lungs. "That's it." He nearly smiles.

Obsydia does smile. "Of course. What else would he have?"

Tael pushes a sorry chuckle from between his teeth.

"What else, Tael? I can't think of anything." There's a gleam in Obsydia's eyes.

The sovereign will die.

He tries not to react. Obsydia looks frozen, unlockable only by some admission of his. Tael averts his eyes and his gaze flits immediately to Syvea Tower, which supposedly houses a crystal by the same name, and if you steal it—

Tael looks down at once, his cheeks smoldering. *By Imala.* Is she doing this to him?

Obsydia stares at him unmoving, finally taking a breath. Tael does the same.

"Tael," she says in a calm voice. "How did they escape?"

A single shiver rides through Tael, shaking him from ankle to scalp. "The key. I told you—"

"You did. But they're outside the walls. They couldn't have fled through the city. That leaves the lava channels beyond the cells. Except," she pouts, "those are a maze. They'd never have made it through without help."

Tael stammers. "They ... dragged me along. Made me show them the way."

"Made you?" She looks him over, presumably for evidence of what he claims. "You were the folksteller of Stravhelm. You couldn't stop a basalt and a native?"

His composure is melting. "They were working together."

She stares at him. "Do you know the penalty for freeing a prisoner?"

Tael spills words out before she can tell him. "They were going to kill me." His redemption is somewhere in his tale, it has to be. "The prisoner was talking about ... killing the sovereign!"

Her mouth drops open.

On he blurts, words dribbling out like an intrant's slobber. "They were saying ... that Syvea ... it's not the tower's name, it's—"

"*Silence!*"

The way she draws back her hand sobers Tael. Makes him flinch and blink several times. She looked like she was about to strike him across the face.

"I tried to stop them," he says, but fails to expound, lacking an excuse for being jumped by a songless and a one-armed dirtfoot.

Obsydia pulls him close to her, squeezing his shoulder so tightly he fails to blubber further, instead only sucking in air.

"Shut your mouth." She speaks slowly, quietly. Her skin smells like coconut oil, her glossy hair like flowers, her breath like wine. She relaxes. Smiles. Guides him to the eastern edge of her gazebo, where the air rises upward and he can see down over all of the holy city.

"Erudition, though made of heavy stone, is fragile," Obsydia says. "Did you know that? Why else would we devote an entire occupation to counting exemplars?"

Tael can only nod. Something's being insulted here.

"Stravhelm is stacked delicately on the shoulders of an angry volcano. Our work must always please Imala and bolster our defenses against the Heathen Tide. Such an effort requires strategic cultivation, callous pruning."

Gardening metaphors are lost on Tael. He hasn't got much of a green thumb. The breeze drifting up the tower smells faintly of the Faithless Sea, which sparkles distantly under the moon. Obsydia's hair reflects the moon's light in great swaths, shining like silk. Tael's fear is nearly forestalled by the tranquility of it all. He resists the urge to straighten his own hair.

"We should have had this talk before," Obsydia says, turning Tael to face her.

"We should have?" Tael asks. So far, it's felt bereft of substance.

Obsydia's not smiling, but there's a peacefulness. If not for the moving air lifting the back of Tael's dele, he might become entirely relaxed. He's not sure how or why, but it seems his presentation at last forestalled the magister's wrath. What more can he ask for? He's always wanted to compliment her hair. What better time than now?

Obsydia touches his chest with her fingertips. He looks at her hands. It's no attack. Exemplars aren't supposed to touch each other. Some of his contemporaries might overly enjoy such contact from the magister. Haik comes to mind. Is this a test?

"Do you have the key?" she asks.

"I ... do."

If she wants him to hand it over, she could have asked for it. He lifts it for her inspection. She pushes him. It's the last thing he expected. He reflexively tries to steady himself but there's nowhere to set his foot. He reaches for her, his stomach seizing up in his ribs. She's pulled back her arms, crossed them over her breasts, already too far away. He's tilting, falling backward. His foot relinquishes the stone and a *yip!* escapes his lips as he merges with the open air.

She *pushed* him?

He's plummeting. Too fast to muster a scream. Wind rushes past him, through him, stuffing his blustering dele up between his legs, around his waist. His sleeves flap violently, crackling like wood fire. He's panting. Hyperventilating. Still can't muster a scream.

She pushed him!

He's clutching the key as if it might save his life. More likely it did this. Above and falling quickly away, a blue silk curtain whips in the light of the brazier against a twinkling sky. There's Obsydia, watching him, her black hair lifted by the wind, framing her dark face, her dark eyes. Such luscious hair. So thick. It's not fair. He's always envied her hair. Never told her though. Reflex born of insecurity almost has him reach up and flatten his own strands against this wind. She withdraws, unconcerned.

He's upside down. The merciless fall has escorted him into a dive. He looks up. Down that is. A widening rhyolite roof tells him his voyage will soon be over. Forever. There are tears spilling over his cheeks. *She pushed him.* Godsdammit, her hair looked so good.

Tael greets the stone.

42

Protect Him

AUSGAN

Erudition

Proctor Alika has just hung his old hiking sandals over the spikerushes in the windowsill to dry and freshen when a shriek tears through the silence of the night. Chills run over his arms and up his neck, nearly making him tweak a muscle.

"Be damned!" Alika didn't mean to yell it. He kneads at his lower back. His first thought is Fohrvyldan heathens. They've finally attacked. He shakes his head. Surely not. He's too out of touch, out there at the Elucidatorium. His imagination has run wild. This could be any old thing.

Alika pokes his head out the window to peer down the wide moonlit street. Exemplars are shuffling quickly down Rhyolite Tier.

"Hey there," Alika calls to a lone exemplar. "What's happening?"

"Not sure, Proctor." It's Rhyolite Grell, a hydromancer in training. "They say someone fell from a tower in Stravhelm." As she's talking, two exemplars in the deles of andesites run past. One of them calls out, "Or they were pushed!"

"Or that," Grell says, shrugging at Alika. "Resonations." She runs after the others.

It's not unheard of for exemplars to have accidents, particularly off towers that lack the safety of a handrail. But Alika knows it's also not unheard of for death by falling to be deliberate. He hurries to his foyer and sits, not suppressing a grunt, to strap sweaty walking sandals back on aching feet. He collects his staff. For some reason, his heart is pounding and his breath is noisy. It's no longer Fohrvyldan invasion on his mind.

Out in the street he walks as quickly as his stiff legs will let him. Making the daily commute to his classroom keeps him fit, but when the round trip is behind him, there is little energy left. His right hip protests the loudest.

Alika follows the current of exemplars trickling past. Some jostle him as they go, bumping him out of their way as if all discipline has been postponed.

At Erudition's central stairway, he ascends toward Stravhelm. There's a mob of andesites, rhyolites, and even a couple of wary basalts gathered near a large dorm below Stravhelm. Even from here Alika can see their wide eyes, hands covering their mouths. Moonlight illuminates something draped over the edge of the roof. Alika makes out a shining scalp hanging from a limp neck, like a crushed egg in a stocking. A black stain has made a straight path from it all the way down the polished wall. Alika stops, leaning on his staff, wheezing, afraid to go closer. Towering above is Obsydia's tower. Alika doubts strongly this death was accidental.

A large andesite is shoving through the crowd from the direction of the fallen body. Head down, he shuffles against the traffic, directly toward the proctor. Alika tries to get out of the way, but his spent legs don't move quickly enough. The exemplar's shoulder collides with Alika's chest, throwing him off balance. He manages to clumsily jab a stair with his staff, propping himself in time to keep from toppling over.

"Hey," Alika says angrily. Whatever happened here does not warrant this blatant disrespect.

Something clonks to the stone, gleaming in the moonlight. The exemplar gasps and scrambles for the fallen object. Before he's able to stow it, Alika observes it, capturing it with a blink. A bone-colored disk with embedded black knobs. It's a key, and no ordinary one. Engraved by the master artificer, splotched with blood. Then it's gone. Stashed away. The exemplar cuts his eyes at Alika.

"Porter Culver?" Alika says. "Why do you have that?"

Porter Culver frowns defiantly, trying to keep from speaking. He looks pained.

"What are you doing here?" Alika says softly, trying to reassure him.

"I had to see if that was ..." He starts to look back toward the broken body on the roof, stops himself. "It doesn't matter. It's not him."

"Not whom? Kale?" He doesn't know who Culver expected, but he's never known the andesite to have other friends besides Kale.

Mention of Kale's name seems to startle Culver. He clenches his jaw. It looks like he's on the verge of tears.

Alika takes a step toward him, holding up a reassuring hand. "Culver, why do you have that key?"

Anger flashes over Culver. "I never should have given it to him. He was supposed to get rid of it." He looks miserable. "But he didn't."

"You're talking about Kale, aren't you?" Alika says.

Culver's shoulders fall and he gives a wavering exhale.

"Where is he?"

Culver's eyes pinch closed and a tear rolls down his cheek. "They took him," he whispers. "And I did *nothing*." His shoulders tremble.

He's in pain, but Alika is running out of patience. "Andesite Culver, tell me what is going on. Right now."

Culver shakes his head, eyes still closed. "This is all my fault."

Alika considers snatching his sleeves and shaking him. But he's never seen Culver this distraught. He might end up the one getting shaken. Culver's attention is drawn over Alika's shoulder. Alika follows his gaze. The crowd has enlivened. Something high on the southern wall has their attention, causing a stir of excited murmuring. Armed exemplars are lining up, moonlight glinting off faceted chitin helms and tuskshell fusils. They file from the towers, spreading in either direction. Their backs are to the city, facing something outside the wall. Of all the frantic conversations hissing around Alika, one phrase keeps repeating until it snags and sticks. *Escaped prisoner.*

"Fusiliers for an escaped prisoner?" It seems ridiculous. "Who could be so dangerous?" Alika asks, turning to Culver, expecting the young exemplar to share his confusion. But Culver doesn't. All trace of fear is gone from him, leaving determination.

"I know where he's going."

"Where who's going?" Alika demands. "What is your fault?"

Culver gives Alika a shallow smile. "I'm sorry, Proctor. I have to go."

Alika opens his mouth to respond or to stall Culver. Before he can, the porter turns and sprints down the central stair. On Andesite Tier, he rounds a bend and is gone, heading southward. Alika scowls. He has to find out what's happening, however helpless he may be to interfere. He can only hope his legs don't fail him in the process.

He leaves the bloody scene for the nearest tower, at the south end of Rhyolite Tier. Once inside, he collects himself and mounts the stairs. His hip screams in protest. He wants to scream back at it. Is this even worth it? He'll still have to climb back down. Anxiety refuses to let him rest.

At the top of the staircase, he exits onto the wide wall and props himself on a parapet, hunched over and wind battered, patiently catching his breath. With some of the pressure off his hip, it throbs angrily. But throbbing beats grinding.

The wall is thick with exemplars. Some hold torches, their fires dancing blue, whipped flat by the wind. A solid line of fusiliers aim their pale, tuskshell fusils down toward the mountain's feet. Crouched among the firers are their assistants. Some ways beyond, nearly to the next tower, stands Magister Obsydia in an armored dele of orange scales, her black cape and hair levitated by the wind. Beside her is Ashmancer Haik, whose fusil's barrel rests on his carapace-plated shoulder. His black hair makes a spiny shrub. Towering behind them both is Kalderys, a hand taller than any other exemplar on the wall. His helmet is tucked beneath his left arm. He, with his plastered-flat hair, is stillest object in his surroundings, observing the foot of the mountain with severe focus.

"Arm and hold." Haik's command cuts through the wind.

Alika shivers and pulls his dele tighter around his shoulders. No one seems concerned by his presence, if they're even aware of it. In fact, several more nosy exemplars have followed Alika and joined him on the wall.

"He's there." Kalderys points. The magus' selectively targeted announcement is meant for those near him alone. It wouldn't reach Alika if not for the proctor's vigilant observation.

"I see him," one of the fusiliers says. "I see Kale!"

Alika's heart leaps and also drops at Kale's name. It wasn't Kale on that rooftop, thank Imala. But being the target of four dozen fusiliers is not much of an improvement.

Sure enough, there's a speck of movement halfway down the shale between Erudition's wall and the endless jungle. It's too dark, and the figure's too far off for eyes alone to identify. Alika opens his lungs, inhales through his nose, pushes away the distraction of his aching body and his immediate surroundings at large, exhales and sends a pulse. He observes the figure. They're no larger than a grain of rice held at arm's length. And it's not Kale. Not unless Kale has shriveled significantly and gained quite the limp. And possibly lost a hand.

The figure is being supported by something. By the way they're leaning, they should fall over. It's in that cavity holding them up that Alika finds the other figure. It's beside the first, camouflaged to near invisibility, helping them along. Alika almost laughs. He knows Kale's tricks. His abilities of self-negation have improved drastically. But that's him. And he seems to be getting away.

"Mark him," Haik commands.

There's moment of frantic muttering between his nearest fusilier and their assistant. Alika hears numbers hissed back and forth. Distances, wind speed, angles. There comes an apparent accord, and they line up the shot.

"Clear off," the fusilier barks and his assistant falls back, covering his ears. Alika registers a flash, then a *crack!* that echoes thunderously as the saltpeter igniter explodes. A glowing seeker-shell screams, arcs, painting a path in smoke.

Alika leans out over the expanse, too afraid to take a breath even if the stone barricade pressed against his stomach would let him. The ember falls short of the descending figure. It flickers and sparks, illuminating stark contrast onto the craggy landscape while the trail of smoke rises.

The fusilier hands off his weapon, stands, addresses his contemporaries. He's yelling values. Two hundred fifteen yards. Forty-four degrees. Something about the ground they're aiming at. He pauses to cough on the fumes his spent fusil is still generating. "Aim high and left to account for wind," he concludes.

His assistant is already scraping out the barrel to pack in a live round.

424 | David T List

"You heard him," Haik says, raising his own fusil to his shoulder. "Light them up!"

Alika has enough time to slip back and cover his ears before the fusils flash into life. The concussions of the shots crackle and clap, buffeting Alika's chest, slapping the air out of him, resounding off the jungle, making limbs of thick, sulfurous smoke. No longer a glowing seeker-shell, but yucca bombs made from endensed plant-bits adhered with flammable resin, fireballs pounce from the parapets into the feet of the mountain, impacting stone in blinding flashes, rumbling, shaking the wall under Alika's feet. Tree limbs and vines sway in the shockwaves.

Alika releases his ears gradually. What sounds like rain pattering down the side of the mountain turns out to be flaming yucca shrapnel and bits of the mountain itself, the clatter and scrape of stone against stone. These shells need only impact near their target. The resulting spray of endensed, slivered leaf fragments do the real work.

Alika peers through the acrid murk toward a cloud of dust. He blinks rapidly to alleviate the white blobs that the explosions burned into his sight. What could Kale have done to deserve this?

"I can't see him," a fusilier reports. Alika's hand covers his mouth. In the moonlight, the evidence of the attack is a score of black blasts in the stone.

"Reload," Haik says.

Obsydia is leaning out in the wind, scanning the mountainside with her dark eyes. "There," she says, raising a slender arm and pointing. "Both of them."

"I see them," Haik says, sounding annoyed at the thought of a second volley. He hands off his spent fusil for a fresh one.

"Hurry," Magister Obsydia says. "Before he disappears."

Kale and the other fugitive must have taken cover during the blasts and gotten lucky, or else they'd have been mutilated by shrapnel. But now the two figures are scrambling again. If they can break into the leafy cover of those massive acacia bolds, they might have a chance. But the fusiliers are working furiously, and now they've had a chance to better gauge their shot.

If only they couldn't see their target. It seems Kale's negation was entirely disrupted by the first barrage. The next one will kill him unless something happens. An idea occurs to Alika. It's a long shot, considering it's something he's never tried at this range. The likelihood of success is poor. And if it does succeed ... he stops his mind traveling that path. He can't think about that. He has to try. He won't just stand by while Kale is killed by the ashmancer.

Proctor Alika leans farther over the wall, watches the dark jungle until his sight blurs, observing the foul smoke on the air while trying not to choke on it, identifying those fumes as an enemy, the fusiliers as the enemy, and their enemies as his friends. He takes a deep breath, purposefully relaxes his brow, unclenches his fists, swallows his aches.

He hums. It isn't loud, but resonant. The song only has to graduate from thought into kinetic energy. Hopefully those it's intended to reach will receive it.

Protect him.

"I'm primed," says a fusilier, raising his weapon and eyeing down it.

"Prove it," Haik yells, mounting his own fusil against his shoulder, but before the ashmancer can fire, there's a stir.

"What is that?" from another fusilier.

"Did they light a torch?"

"There are two. No, three!"

But the glowing yellow spheres filing from the forest aren't fires. They're koa setuar, answering Alika's summons, and by Imala they seem to agree with his assessment. The orbs bounce on invisible wings, swarming, spreading outward to encompass the two figures and all around them.

"I can't see the target," a fusilier says.

The setuar are bright enough to obscure their vicinity, weaving pale green light into the landscape, a blanket of distant fireflies, each dancing to its own silent song. This is more help than Alika expected. And something occurs to him for the first time. Do the spirits naturally ally with natives? Communication with them is supposedly native magic. Alika has never envied natives, not until that thought.

"Fire," Haik yells, aiming down his fusil. "Fire!"

Alika covers his ears again. This time the shots are sporadic, popping off in twos and threes. Their coverage is even less focused. There's no way the fusiliers can see their target. The shots shriek, drawing lines of smoke, thumping down, bursting apart the earth at the edge of the jungle, slinging up shards, splintering saplings, igniting within the forest in blinks of light as the modified yucca bits return as strangers to their home.

A stray crack and a *whump!* issues from too high, too close. A blast of hot air washes over Alika's face. The explosion gives way to screams, a raspy gurgle. There's a black blast mark on the wall where a fusilier just stood. Two strewn sandals are all that's left of him, feet still within. The firing assistant is flopping on his back, kicking his legs. He's missing a hand and the right side of his face. The gaping wounds are too cauterized to do more than ooze black. Someone else is on fire, screeching, back-peddling into her accomplices, her dele turning red from multiple bleeding lacerations.

Alika's stomach lurches. A misfired yucca shell. He'd heard of their dangers. They may have been understated. The ashmancer throws a cloak over the flaming assistant, as if that will stanch the bleeding. The dismembered exemplar is dragged away. The injured, maybe a half dozen, are removed from the front line.

Once more the spent fusils are reloaded, this time serenaded by the whimpering wounded. The night's grown colder. Most of the dancing lights have retreated back into the jungle. Three aren't moving, only flickering, dimming like they're broken and spilling out. Alika sets his jaw. He knew there would be repercussions.

Ashmancer Haik fans at the smoke cloud dissipating in the updraft. "Report," he commands.

"Look," a fusilier cries.

Another gives an excited yell.

There, unmoving on the ground outside the jungle, is a lone body. All the heat leaves Alika's face. He can't still his heart enough to focus on observation.

Magus Kalderys leans forward, analyzing the far landscape critically. "The escaped prisoner is fatally wounded," he says. He turns to Magister Obsydia, and even at this distance he is glowing with fury. "The basalt has escaped from perception."

Relief runs through Alika, melts the tension from his shoulders and takes the strength from his legs. He steadies himself and inadvertently chuckles. Kale got away.

Kalderys' flattened hair hangs stiffly above his shoulders like a charcoal smudge, only shifting slightly, despite the strong wind. Alika accidentally stares until Kalderys meets his eye. The magus has a scathing expression. Did he hear Alika's laugh?

"Someone hand me a loaded fusil," Haik yells, lips throwing spittle.

"It's too late," Obsydia says, her tone icy. "You failed."

"We what?" Haik spurts. "You saw those damned setuar. What was I supposed to—?"

Magus Kalderys' armored slap resounds off Haik's head, making him reel backward.

The ashmancer stands in shocked anger, blood running down his temple from within his helmet. It could have been worse. The magus could have probably killed him with a punch. That mercy is obviously lost on him. He glares from Kalderys to the magister, chest heaving. Looks like he's trying to decide what to do, or what not to.

Proctor Alika turns to leave. As entertaining as this may be, blame has a way of finding a target. And if someone's to be blamed for the setuar, Alika won't allow himself to be an easy suspect. He maneuvers through the gathered observers, chin down, face solemn in an affectation of disappointment. He'll take the stairs slowly. Tomorrow he'll pay for all this walking.

He'd be more elated at Kale's narrow escape, and at Haik's humiliation, but the image of dying setuar is burned into his mind. His message to them was not dishonest, but if he'd not sung it those setuar would still be alive.

They may abandon him after this. He'd deserve it. They're frugal with their affection toward mankind, slow to trust, as Alika learned over the years, and this act will not have improved on that. His heart sinks at the thought of his betrayal. Whatever Kale is up to, is it worth this?

43
Grant Him Mortality

AUSGAN
Atop the south wall, Erudition

Obsydia squeezes a finger into the collar of her armored dele and tugs. It, more than the press of sweaty exemplars around her, the fusil smoke in the air, the godsdamned catastrophe of the escaped thief basalt, feels the most likely to do her in. It's bad enough when a dele isn't weighted down with scales and chitin. This one has plated straps that burrow deeper into her shoulders with each movement, restricts her arms, squeezes flat her breasts, makes it impossible to inhale all the way. Her armor's black cape is yanked around by the wind, making her feel like a monkey on a rope. She underestimated Kale. Again.

"It was Kale who negated me at Hargrim." Kalderys stares at the jungle. Either he's recently put that together or was informed by someone—Selu if anyone, who learned from Haik—and he will pay for it in blood.

"Clear out," Obsydia commands the fusiliers. Some do, gathering their equipment, collecting the wounded, filing toward the nearest staircase. Others hesitate, looking to the ashmancer as if Magister Obsydia isn't the authority here. "Now!" she barks. With this, they do. She wants to throw the ashmancer off the wall here and now. Not because he failed to stop Kale. These are far from a fusilier's ideal conditions. Firing at retreating, isolated targets was not prioritized in the fusil's design. Their preferred target is a cluster of aggressors charging forward. Particularly the eventual Heathen Tide. She wants to kill him because she can no longer trust him. His discretion and obedience were all he had to offer, and they seem to be spent.

She spent so many years on Haik, building him, tolerating him. She's always known when the day came to dispose of him it may not be easy. She knew her emotions may try to prevent her doing what needs doing. Because of that knowledge, she's maintained her distance. Planned for the day. Every handy tool has a specific purpose, and no tool lasts forever. She'd always thought that while Intemrus lives, so would Haik. That's no longer the case. Thankfully, he's made her task easier.

Kalderys' pulses could tell him everything, even from this distance. Everyone has a signature. If he'd not memorized Kale's before now, before his fateful Campaign of Cleansing, then he shares responsibility for overlooking the basalt.

"Why didn't you tell me? This was preventable." Kalderys sounds hurt. Behind him, Prime Sentinel Selu looks past him at Obsydia. Her gaze serves as a reminder, which is good because Obsydia had nearly forgotten her own lie.

"Kale's interrogation was scheduled for the morning. We'd have gotten to the bottom of it then."

Her words do nothing to improve Kalderys' state. "This was preventable," he repeats. He feels deceived. Untrustworthy. Selu watches Obsydia through narrowed eyes. Obsydia feels backed into a corner. Betrayed by Haik, who then failed to kill Kale. Untrusted by Kalderys, who's come face to face with the extent of his failure. Worst of all, given an ultimatum by Selu the aridimancer, who could have died in the jungle instead of Arc. Heat fills Obsydia's cheeks and her heart pounds. She will not go down this easily. Intemrus told her to deal with it. She will.

"Magus Kalderys," she says. "You failed to prevent this in Hargrim, lest we forget. Make it right. I'd prefer to have waited for this, but now we can't. With the authority of the sovereign, I call for a Campaign of Cleansing on Napiri. Now. If Kale succeeds in getting there, his blasphemy will infect them and spread like brushfire across Ausgan."

Without any obvious movement, the magus' chagrin burns away and he grows intent, primed, a fusil awaiting ignition. By Imala, he does well with instruction. The magus' chest inflates. His chin juts forward. "At once, Magister."

"We're lacking a prime sentinel, Magister." Prime Sentinel Selu's voice is like a rip in Obsydia's eardrums. The magus looks dumbstruck at his sentinel's complaint.

Obsydia observes Selu. She believes Kalderys might fail because he did before. She believes Obsydia planned to cover up Kalderys' failure by getting rid of Kale. Well, she's clever. Courageous. But lacking all sense. Addressing Obsydia rather than him demonstrates an abject lack of respect for Kalderys. No faith in the Triumvirate. It's worse than a punishable sin, it is an insult.

"Magus," Obsydia says, preferring to remain unphased, but also to help amplify Kalderys' rage. "What Selu says is true. Are you still capable of a campaign without Prime Sentinel Arc?"

"*Capable?*" Facing Obsydia now, Kalderys is genuinely taken aback. First she didn't trust him with the truth about Kale. Now she questions his power. This is not how she meant him to take it. "It's *my* song. Arc's contribution was negligible."

Selu's face twitches. "Aside from the song," she says, still to Obsydia, "it is dangerous to travel at night. We all know what can happen out there."

Obsydia doesn't need to observe Kalderys to feel the wave of fury washing over him. Such unadulterated gall the sentinel shows. She will have no place in Obsydia's new holy city. Obsydia never believed Selu was bluffing when she came with her threats. But it seems the aridimancer grew impatient for some change.

"Do you fear fanged apes, Prime?" Kalderys is suddenly looming over Selu. Obsydia has to contain her smile.

"I don't, but perhaps we should bring another summoner, in case someone at the village is expecting us."

"You fear fanged apes ... and *natives?*" As if the thought itself disgusts him. "Since when?"

Selu's face flushes. She opens her mouth to respond. Kalderys doesn't let her.

"We will not stunt our pace so unproven mancers can tag along. And for what, your peace of mind? Where is your faith?" His fury is boiling over, set off by her insult, Haik's incompetence, his own failure. "There's a reason you're my prime, unless something has changed. If it has, tell me. Now."

Selu's eyes narrow. She faces Obsydia. "Magister, we're not enough alone to deliver Intemrus' Judgment."

Obsydia backs away. The heat radiating off Kalderys could ignite green liana vines.

"*I am Intemrus' Judgment!*" Kalderys' voice resounds off into the distant jungle.

"I would agree—" Selu starts.

"Sentinel." Kalderys advances on Selu until she has to turn her head aside to prevent her chin being knocked by his chest plate. "Do you disobey?"

Time is of the essence. But for a moment, Obsydia can only savor this. She watches Selu until the sentinel meets her eyes. It is a grimace of defeat all over the sentinel's face. Obsydia watches her wear it a moment longer.

"Time's up," Obsydia says. "Sentinel?"

Kalderys draws back. Selu sets her jaw and plants her feet, looking up into his dark face. Moonlight gleams off her pale eyes. "If the basalt shows up at the village, what's to keep him from negating you again?"

Obsydia's heart thumps against her ribs. She wasn't even trying to quieten her voice. Kalderys' posture withers. A glimmer of doubt washes over him.

"Kale is indeed an enigma," Obsydia says quickly. "But assuming his aim is Napiri, and he's not stopped by the jungle, he can't outrun you. He will not be present for the campaign."

Kalderys shakes his head. His anger has dissipated, replaced by earnest longing. "Prime Sentinel Selu, I understand your doubt. I don't pretend to know what happened in Hargrim. What I do know is that we make harmony for the gods, who loan us unspeakable power. What the basalt consumed was a mere fraction. I can bring him so much more. I'd rather have my two chosen primes than only one. But I'd rather have neither of them than one who doesn't trust me. You were my first choice, before anyone else. I need you to harmonize with me. Trust my song."

Selu turns her eyes toward the forest. Obsydia reaches up to loosen one of her dele's buttons before the damn thing can strangle her. There's no time for this.

"The sky is ripe," Kalderys says. "I am capable of this campaign. Are you?"

Selu nods. "Intemrus' Will be done," she proclaims. But she is not convinced.

Annoyance flashes over Kalderys' face. Obsydia observes him at once, without moving, snatching a taste of his emotion out of the air the way a mantis would a fly. Kalderys wanted Selu to submit to *him*, not Intemrus. *His* will be done. Obsydia has to suppress her approval. This is progress.

"We're off," Kalderys says, turning on his heel. "Selu, we sing of lightning." He turns on his heel, heading for the nearest stairs. Selu gives a final glance to Obsydia. One that says, *You'll regret this.* She follows after him.

Obsydia almost calls something out. What, she doesn't know. Every time Kalderys leaves on a campaign, she experiences a moment of apprehension. She's never sent him on a mission like this, at night, missing a prime sentinel. Knowing Kale is alive doesn't put her at ease. Selu might be right to worry. It's not realistic that Kale survives the jungle, much less find Napiri, and before Kalderys' direct route takes him there. But nothing the basalt has accomplished seems possible.

"A regiment of fusiliers will be on your heels," Obsydia calls out, before she can stop herself.

"Then they can watch Napiri burn," Kalderys replies without turning, and pulls his helmet onto his head. He disappears into a tower.

Obsydia watches until Selu is gone as well. The spectators have already begun to clear off, and now the last of them file down. Only her entourage and the ashmancer and his fusiliers remain. Haik gazes down on the blast marks. He has not wiped the blood off the side of his face. There's a numbness behind his eyes, as if none of it matters. He's questioning if it's all worth it. Is there a prize for him at the end of his efforts or just more battering? Does he even want to try further? Obsydia grits her teeth. Who is he thinking of running off and blabbing to next? If she asks him to kill himself here and now for failing to stop Kale, will he do it? She's prone to believe he won't. Not after he betrayed her confidence. She could kill him herself. Right in front of his fusiliers. She could shove him over that wall as punishment for failing her. Picturing his body decorating the side of Mount Adenhelm is more tantalizing than she'd expected. But there is one final use she can get out of him, far from anyone he might be tempted to cry to.

"Ashmancer Haik," she says. "Kale is attempting to flee, most likely to Napiri. The jungle might stop him. But this isn't his first time navigating the forest at night."

"He'll never make it," Haik says, without apparent concern one way or the other.

Obsydia observes him, calculating his scant remaining value. "Give us a moment, please," she tells her adherents and primes. "I'll return to my tower shortly." They leave and Haik's fusiliers follow them.

Only when she is alone with Haik does he acknowledge her. He's still browbeaten. But also curious. Like a kicked dog, unable to reject his owner's hand, however hard it's struck him.

"I wish I shared your optimism," she says. "Napiri will burn tonight, at Intemrus' bidding." She lowers her voice. "The more important job I need done is for you."

He doesn't visibly change, but his heart rate spikes. She steps closer to him to take advantage of his mood's upward momentum. Any witnesses are gone. Intemrus' tower is obscured from view by Syvea Tower. "Kale has stolen Intemrus' crystal," she whispers into his ear.

Haik's eyes widen and his posture stiffens. Obsydia moves away, now face to face with him. His heart rate is rapid. She's either empowered him or fed him more rumors to sow. This, she can control.

"Find him. Kill him. I don't care how."

Haik's eyes become distant, his pupils flicking about as a plan is constructed.

"What will you need?" she asks. She'll gather it for him. With his new knowledge, he's no longer trustable inside Erudition's walls.

"A mobile unit. Fusiliers. Sentinel Bronn, Sentinel Ilbres."

"No," she says. "I'll need them."

He snaps out of his formulation and looks at her. "They're *my* sentinels."

Everything that's yours is mine, she wants to tell him. Instead she says, "I'll need them here, to serve while you're away."

"But the jungle ... it may threaten us. And Kale may enlist Untamed help."

"Use Pyroktus on the wildlife. Do you require Bronn or Ilbres to summon it?"

Haik's mouth works and he glares. He's reluctant to say nothing but unwilling to lie. "No," he admits. "For that I need Akoromancer Euphrain."

Obsydia knew that. Pyroktus is Haik's life work. All mancers have one. They must. Pyroktus is a song that generates ash. Only, Haik can't pull off the channeling. He doesn't have the discipline. Never had to develop it. Obsydia saw to that by promoting him to mancer before he'd earned it. And so Haik, employing his cruelty, targeted and domineered a fellow exemplar, a quiet pyromaniac named Euphrain. It wasn't consensual. Haik turned the boy's infatuations and abilities into his own tools, in this case fiery whips that incinerate all they touch.

Obsydia nods. "I'll have him collected, and twelve fusiliers. That should suffice. Cryomancer Hyrala will cover the lapse in Erudition's vigilance in your absence. So long as I keep Bronn and Ilbres here as well Intemrus shouldn't register a concerning deficit in consonance. If you trust them, then so do I." *Besides, one of those two will replace you by my side.*

Haik smirks grudgingly.

"This job is for you alone," Obsydia presses. "You can't fail me again. Do you understand?"

"Yes, Magister."

His guttering purpose is reigniting. Obsydia's confidence mounts. The ashmancer looks directly at her. He licks his lips. His heart is leaping, threatening to burst out of his chest. He moves toward her even as she realizes her mistake. She's given him too much power. Admitted he's inimitable. Now she must make a personal sacrifice and weather his touch. She can't afford not to. She slides her hand to the back of his neck, cupping it, bringing his forehead to hers, hoping to minimize the inevitable contact. It's not enough for him. He lunges for her. His lips are on her, searching, smearing saliva on her cheek, her chin. His nostrils vent against her. She forces herself not to resist. Not to look at him. To get this over with.

His tongue finds her lips, splits them, pries at her teeth. His gloved hands scrape down her armored back. For some reason, the disgust she anticipated is not forthcoming. An unexpected, incendiary craving has eclipsed that. She parts her lips, allows him in, meets his tongue with hers, feels their breath meld, feels heat rising within her, exhales in a soft moan, sees Kalderys' face, his broken trust, his pain.

She wrenches away from Haik, turns her back to him.

"Enough," she hisses. How careless of her. Intemrus could be watching. Contact with a fellow exemplar is forbidden. Carnal contact is punishable by death.

He stands behind her, gasping. Even without seeing him, she observes how strongly the hunger calls him. He wants to snatch her up. Take her. Force her against the parapet and spend himself at her expense. And by Imala she wants it too. At the cost of all her plans, she wants it. Godsdamn Intemrus for outlawing such a thing and damning the population to eternal frustration. Just one more means of control. Basalt Kale, that fateless, songless meddler, tasted it. Look at the strength it gave him.

Obsydia rounds on Haik, who may as well have become sopping desire personified. "Afterwards," she says. "Now kill Kale. Get my crystal back."

His eyes are feral. "Absolutely, Magister. Resonations."

He dashes for the stairs his fusiliers took. She watches him go, wondering if this is yet another misstep. What if he fails to retrieve the crystal? That is a possibility, and more likely than she wants to admit. If she's honest, gaining immortality was only ever second to taking it from Intemrus. Except this feels like compromise, again.

Alone at last, Obsydia rips open the neck of her dele, sending buttons scattering. She stomps to the far parapet. The wind beyond the wall calls her. She looks down. At the foot of Adenhelm, some of the glowing setuar still linger around the prisoner's body. The stones, whose rough surfaces appear smoothed by distance and the moon's light, whisper a promise of release from all this frustration. Each time she progresses her plan, another catastrophe springs up. What good is all the power in the world if it costs what a body truly wants?

Who would Obsydia have become if she'd never been inducted as a baby, instead remaining a native? Would she have starved? Would she have dehydrated to death or been eaten by warthounds? Would she have known carnal bliss? And if so, would she have passed away happy, having experienced pleasure?

Of course not. She'd have taken it for granted, the way the natives do. To truly appreciate something, you must know its absence. This path is the right one. Her fight is worth it. Her sacrifices will pay off. Kalderys will annihilate Napiri. Haik will apprehend Kale. Obsydia will obtain the crystal.

Obsydia loosens the last buttons and drops her armor, allowing the night's breeze to cool her sticky skin. One way or another she must soon answer to Intemrus and explain where his precious stone has gone, perhaps even why she's holding it. She'll have a lot to explain. On that day, he'll be on his back with her heel on his throat. On that day, she will grant him mortality.

44
The Mouth of Dissonance

AUSGAN
South of Erudition

"Get up," Kale cries at Rathyn, tugging his only hand. "We have to warn Napiri." Sulfurous fumes still linger, burning Kale's eyes and his nostrils.

"Get off me, boy," Rathyn croaks out, settling onto his back like the loose scree is a padded cot. "I'm done for."

The dark stains on Rathyn's shirt are expanding too quickly. His eyes rove around, unable to focus. That yucca shrapnel hurt him worse than Kale thought.

"It's a relief," he says. "At least now I can ... barely feel my arm ..." His chuckle turns into a cough.

"I can't go back to Tivali without you," Kale says.

Rathyn yanks his hand from Kale's grip and presses his palm to a stain on his shirt. He grimaces. "I'd have never made it all the way back there. Look at me. All dried out and ... hungry." He closes his eyes. "The monks will burn Napiri for sure now." He's talking quietly, as if to himself. "Murderous fucking bastards."

Kale doesn't want to accept it. But Rathyn's right. Obsydia told him herself, Napiri is doomed. Rathyn looks so comfortable Kale feels guilty trying to revive him.

"I could warn them," Kale says. "But I don't know how to get there." Rathyn lies unmoving on the volcanic stone. He looks dead. Kale fills with panic. He takes the crystal in his hands and shakes it over Rathyn's chest. "Help him!"

There is no apparent response.

Rathyn's chest lifts as he takes a wheezing inhale. "I told you ... I still have friends. Seems ... like you do too."

"Friends?" Kale's heart drops. Rathyn's talking nonsense.

"I didn't think monks knew about this." He's barely moving.

Kale watches him through the tears filling his eyes. If this is some joke to imply exemplars don't know how to die, Kale is not going to laugh.

Rathyn hums. It's so faint that it takes Kale a moment to realize the sound is coming from him and not the breeze rustling through the jungle. The surrounding yellow orbs, which had been milling aimlessly, tremble to life. They hover silently in the air, like smoke in an enclosed chamber. Three of them don't, however. They lie on the rocks unmoving and dull, like melon-sized egg yolks.

Kale has never been so close to koa setuar. Proctor Alika told him they're bolder than lehua setuar. Always gave Kale the impression they're hostile.

"You can communicate with setuar?" Kale says.

"Not just me," Rathyn exhales. "It was someone up there that called them." He doesn't move to indicate where he's referring to, but it must be the city wall. What else, a treetop?

"Who?" Kale asks, but there's only one exemplar he knows who values setuar. Did the old proctor summon them to his aid?

"Just follow them," Rathyn says. The dark stains on his shirt cover his entire torso and glisten under the moon. "Tell Tivali ..." He gives a trembling exhale. Looks dully at the sky. The gleam in his eyes clouds over.

"Tell her what?" Kale whispers. Rathyn doesn't answer.

The yellow orbs bounce away through the jungle. Kale slumps next to the body, gritting his teeth. He didn't just *want* to save Rathyn. He *owed* it to him. Owed it to both of them. Even as he sits trying to register what all has been lost, his mind races, creating a dialogue to present Tivali explaining all he tried to do to save her father. He pictures telling her of his efforts. The image saps all the strength out of him. What did any of it matter? Is she supposed to thank him? Untie that knot on her shirt for him again? As if he could ever deserve her. Kale's head falls into his hands. If he's honest, he *did* have the means to save Rathyn the first time he came to the cells. Instead, Rathyn had saved him.

A chill void expands from Kale's insides, inhaling his pains and emotions the way his cloud enveloped the warthound. *What's the point?* This is not an unfamiliar feeling. He used to feel it all the time, each time he made an effort toward anything or woke up in the night and stared at his unadorned ceiling. Everyone dies. Everything leads nowhere. There's no future for him. There is no future at all. He accepted that and was on his way out. That's when he met Rathyn.

The setuar shiver impatiently. They're forming a queue that leads into the jungle. The last thing Kale wants to do is follow them back into that treacherous jungle, especially considering the news he must bring Tivali at his journey's end.

"I am Intemrus' Judgment!"

Kalderys' voice booms down from the high wall and shakes Kale's bones. It isn't fear that fills him. Feels more like fire. He scrambles to his feet. *Tivali*. His mind clears of the dark fog. What's important is that he delivers his message, not what she thinks of him. He is still Napiri's last chance.

Kale runs in the stream of setuar. They bounce along before him, beside him, behind him. He can't tell if they're running or flying. Their wings, or legs, aren't illuminated like their bulbous bodies. But they collectively generate enough light for Kale to keep from tangling up in vines. Minimizing his imprint has become second nature. The jungle is too dangerous to fail at that. But he has the distinct impression the setuar can sense him just the same.

Kale runs as fast as the undergrowth will allow. The world around him is a limbed, black mass, reaching for him, overflowing with alien sounds. He's afraid to slow his pace, or even glance over his shoulder. Aside from running, there's not much he can do if fanged apes or some other jungle threat catches wind of him.

He can't shake the image of Rathyn lying in a heap in the shadow of Erudition. He doesn't know how natives deal with their dead, but leaving them where they lie is probably not it. Kale has no knowledge of his own father or mother. No exemplar does. Initiation into Erudition severs all outside ties forever. It was a stupid fantasy to think he'd get to reunite Tivali with her father and witness tears of relief wetting her smile. No. He'll be delivering tears of a different sort.

If Napiri even still stands by the time he gets there.

Kale runs till he's slick with sweat. Still the setuar lead him. It's by some miracle he hasn't been caught by vines. That is unless the setuar factored his height into the path they guide him down. There's no telling how much time has passed. Time enough for his mind to examine Rathyn's death over and over. A hundred times, and with each he imagines something he could have done differently. Time enough to grow torturously aware of how poorly Erudition sandals rank at jungle running. These are of higher quality than any basalt should ever wear, but compared to Tivali's father's sandals, they may as well be unpolished bamboo.

It's safe to bet Magus Kalderys has made it out of Erudition and is running parallel to Kale along a road, not hindered by vines and roots, preparing his song of slaughter. Kale increases his pace, ignoring his wounds. He may yet beat Kalderys to Napiri. If so, he'll scatter them, convince them to run. Maybe he can catch Kalderys' song before it claims any lives. The thought of harboring that much energy again horrifies him. And even if he does, will those he saves have their heads bashed in by exemplar staves? It seems like he'll die either way, either finished off by an exemplar as he trembles in a stupor or done in by the jungle after he soars away again. That's fine. It's high time. Ever since he began trying to rid the world of himself, he's only brought down horrors on everyone around him.

Kale runs until his feet are numb. His shoulders ache from deflecting leaves that would otherwise pummel his face. If he could see the sky he might be able to estimate how far he's come. Hours have passed, surely, all to the sound of his barely controlled gasping for breath. He has to outpace the magus. In his dele pocket, Syvea bounces against his chest. There is no evidence the crystal's absence disrupted anything in Stravhelm. Then again, maybe Intemrus died immediately. Maybe Obsydia took over. Would that be an improvement? It's she who commands the lightning fiend. Did Kale take on Intemrus' immortality? His Imala-damned feet think not. What if it was all a lie? The crystal was sitting in an empty, dusty chamber. How important could it have been?

Kale doesn't recognize the clearing he bursts into, but when the setuar scatter away, retreating back into the jungle, and all that's left is moonlight illuminating the stone lodge, the goat pasture to his right, the glow of torchlight from windows of thatched huts ahead, he realizes he's made it to Napiri. *The village still stands.* Relief washes over him, followed quickly by dread. He missed Tivali. And now that he's back, he has nothing comforting to offer her.

"Tivali!" Kale shouts, making for the huts. "Tiva—"

There's a blinding crack and the ground flies out from under him. He's lying on his back, blinking at stars both real and immaterial. His ears are ringing. A stripe of pain permeates his forehead.

"That was clever stick-work," says a voice. "I didn't even see him."

Another chuckles. "Me either. Thought I was swinging at a bat."

Two figures appear over Kale, silhouetted by the night sky.

"You thought a bat yelled for Tivali?" the first says to the other.

"No, gnat brain. I thought that was you."

"Why would I yell for Tivali?"

"I've caught you mumbling it enough times, haven't I?" He chuckles. "Didn't seem too big a stretch."

"Shut your fat gob. You're lucky I ain't holding the stick."

They look down at Kale.

"Shit, that's a monk."

"Shit."

Kale tries to rise, but his vision lurches and he nearly vomits from nausea.

"Reckon it's the one that was here the other day? The one that got the warthound?"

"Nah. That guy was all in rags and corked up like he was gonna pop."

"Huh. What about the one that followed him?"

"No way. You saw the state of him. He's dirt by now. The apes had at him."

Silence.

"Reckon it's that monk going round killing people?"

"I don't know. That one's supposed to be armored. Probably take more than a bump on the head to lay him flat."

More silence.

"Was a good bump though, wasn't it?"

Kale would answer for himself, *Yes, it was a fine bump. No complaints.* But holding his head so it won't come apart is taking all his concentration.

"Still, better safe than sorry," from the one with the stick. He lifts it up to bash Kale's head again.

"Stop!"

Her voice rinses the pain from Kale. "Tivali," he mutters. He tries to sit and his vision rotates, making him career sideways to his elbow. *A respectable bump indeed.* Someone grabs his arm and yanks him to his feet. Kale smiles and his heart flutters. He'd recognize that vicious grasp anywhere.

"You're back," Tivali says. She's a blur, but the smile is evident in her voice. She's holding his arms in a grip that will likely leave bruises. If only she'd never let go. "Looks like you got new clothes."

There are more people approaching with torches. Kale blinks, rubs his eyes, gazes at Tivali. She's wearing a thin smock and sandals. Not much else that he can tell, besides a look of mild curiosity. Those black curls nearly cover one green eye. His guts burble in excitement. Then he remembers the threat. He remembers Obsydia's proclamation. He remembers Tivali's father.

"You're in danger," Kale says. "I escaped Stravhelm with your father. But he ..." Kale's throat closes.

Tivali takes a step away from him, her eyebrows rising.

He swallows several times, trying to push back the suffocating sensation. "He ..." Gods, why him? Why does he have to tell her? Why does anyone? Why does she have to hear this? Kale's throat is too tight for words to make it out.

Tivali shakes her head in disbelief. Her hand grips her mouth. Her shoulders begin to tremble, and tears spill down her cheeks.

"I'm so sorry," Kale whispers. "I thought I could save him."

Tivali turns her back on him and his heart breaks into pieces. It's all he can do to not collapse. Or grab her and try to embrace her. As if that would help her.

She stands for several moments, head down. Sobs leak from behind her hand, each one making Kale's guts twist. In that moment, he welcomes the death that approaches. He's so sick of waiting for it. The others stand silently, some watching her with concerned expressions, some watching him with outright contempt. Kale has never been in such a situation. Erudition has no emotions like this. He is a stranger here, come only to wreak havoc on an otherwise peaceful dwelling. As much as he wants to give Tivali time, the sense of urgency welling in him doesn't allow it. There's still a task to do.

"You're all in danger," Kale says, feeling utterly alone.

At length, Tivali wipes her nose, sniffs, turns to Kale. Her eyes are red and her smile is nowhere to be seen. "What's coming?"

"I'm not sure. But if it's Magus Kalderys, he'll call down lightning on the entire village and everyone in it." Kale is reluctant to say the next words. But they're vital if he wants them to listen. "… like he did to Hargrim."

They murmur amongst themselves. Kale is out of words. His feet want to shuffle. He wants to disappear.

Tivali snorts. "Where's the *bad* news, monk?"

Kale opens his mouth. Was that a joke? Then why did the word *monk* feel like a laceration?

Napiri's villagers watch him. Tivali's expression has changed. It's the way she looked at him when he first met her, when he stood bedraggled in a ditch and she eyed down her bamboo stick at him.

Kale remembers the crystal. He stole it at Rathyn's prompting. Will it make his death worthwhile? Will showing it to Tivali bring some closure? Will it improve her opinion of him? That last question feels so selfish in this moment it nearly stalls his hand. But if the crystal can provide any comfort at all, he has to tell her. As he reaches for his pocket the air drains of moisture, covering Kale's skin with a tingling sensation. His nostrils itch and the hair on the back of his neck stands on end.

Kale gasps. "Run," he yells, startling those around him. "Run! Now!"

No one moves. They must not feel it. Kale makes to sprint to the path leading out of the village, where Kalderys will come from, the same path he rode in on in Tivali's barrow. A villager steps into his path, brandishing a bamboo pole.

"Don't make me crack you another one," the man says.

"Tivali, tell them to run."

"Run where?" Tivali says. She spits on the ground.

"Fuck him," says a man. "And fuck all the other monks too. I'm done being a good dog. What's being tamed ever got us?"

"Thirst," says a woman. "Death."

"*Napiri!*" a voice booms out over the clearing. There, at the edge of the village, standing under the light of the moon in rhystic dominance, is Magus Kalderys, with Prime Sentinel Selu back and to his left. Their armored deles gleam, making them appear chiseled from bone.

Kale shoulders past the man who'd blocked him and strides toward the magus. "Kalderys, don't do this. They're no threat."

"Basalt Kale." Kalderys nods. It seems a hint of smile curls the edges of his mouth. "I was hoping to see you."

Kale stops several yards short of Kalderys with both hands raised. It feels like the damn crystal in his pocket is trying to bore into his chest. "No one has to die, Kalderys. They believe. They pray."

"This village is damned, as are you." His words are a declaration, without emotion. He's preparing his channeling. "Napiri will be different than Hargrim."

The image of the boy Kale failed to save fills his head. Then comes the thought of Tivali meeting the same fate. Impotent anger fills Kale.

He can't physically stop the magus. Couldn't even if Selu weren't right there. But he has to try. "You're right," Kale says. "Last time I stopped you by accident. This time will be on purpose."

"No," Kalderys says. "I learned something that day, when you consumed the tail end of my song. I used to limit energy, using the minimum needed for the task at hand." He shakes his head. "Wasted effort. The Imala does not need me *conserving* their energy. Their energy is limitless. They value my abilities of *conversion*. No matter the cost." The magus' eyes seem to glow. The air around him bends and wavers. "The sovereign's will must be done."

"What about Kalderys' will?" Kale says. "You ever stop and consider that before murdering children?"

"It is the same."

"Magus, let me kill the basalt first." Sentinel Selu spits the words with a ferocity that surprises Kale. Her searing eyes are on him, bringing to mind a puma readying to pounce. What the hell did he ever do to her?

Tivali appears in front of Kale, crouched and eyeing down her bamboo staff at the armored sentinel. "Try it, bitch."

"This is no time for vendettas, Prime Sentinel," Kalderys proclaims. "Focus. Follow my channeling. This night is predetermined. You know I love lightning." His eyes roll back. Kale's ears pop painfully. "For the first time, let's see truly how much lightning loves me." His helmeted head tilts skyward. Selu steps back, joins him in rhystic dominance. "*Intemrus' Will ...*"

A deathly silence falls.

"Get behind me," Kale says, but no sound escapes him. The air is simultaneously arid as sand and dense as water. He grabs Tivali's shoulders. She's stunned, face contorted, holding her ears. He hauls her back, steps around her, shields her, leaving nothing between himself and a glowing Magister Kalderys but hyper-charged air, one spark away from detonation. This is too much energy. Death is imminent. But isn't it always? Kale maximizes his imprint.

"*... be done.*"

~

Tivali's about to shove Kale out of her way to crack that feisty monk bitch when she is thrown backward by a blinding burst. She tumbles head over heels. She's blinking but blind, screaming but mute, fighting to find flat ground.

What ... the hell ...?

It was like a blast of lightning and thunder right inside her head, somehow still ongoing. Wind roars and crackles, dragging her over tossing earth. She lies flat on her belly, braces herself, digs into the dirt with fingertips, eventually manages to focus her eyes. What she sees is beyond explanation.

The entire village is bathed in flickering, silver light. Bolts of lightning rove the earth outside the village's perimeter like huge, glowing spider legs. Everything they touch flares noiselessly into harsh red flames. Trees burn. Sedge burns. The ground turns molten where the lightning claws rake.

But Tivali is untouched. The huts are untouched. As the branches of forked light skitter near the village, they're drawn away violently, converging on a lightless point right in front of Tivali. It's a void, little larger than herself, blacker than darkness. Amid such light as this, darkness shouldn't be able to exist. How can it? The more she stares, the more it takes form. It's human, nearly prone, one hand outstretched.

Kale?

He is reaching toward the magus, who seems to be spawning the blinding energy. Behind the magus, the woman monk mirrors his stance. They're both radiating, and from their opaque white aura comes the assaulting lightning.

But Kale seems to be … engulfing it. Vines of iridescent blue flame spurt to life from the motionless monks, starting small and whip-like, then leaping high, arcing, plummeting to attack earth or tree. They solidify, turning white, growing jagged, edged, hungry. They carve a path for the village, limbs made of light reducing earth to glowing glass ditches, but each one is intercepted, snatched away, inhaled by Kale's outstretched hand. The ravaging light encircles the entire village, burning the jungle all around, but can't penetrate the spherical field Kale generates.

"*How much can one body contain?*" says the voice of the storm itself, roaring out over the gale.

The wind grows furious, ripping and tearing, drawing all of reality toward Kale's hand. Tivali can't see the lightning monk anymore. He's hidden in an opaque flickering white sphere the size of the entire dining lodge. She digs her toes into the ground, grasping at dry earth, feeling for her bamboo.

The huts behind her shake in the wind. People huddle in their doorways, gawking, embracing one another. There's Jesbr, edging backward until it seems he is able to break from the wind's grip. He makes a run for the jungle. A bolt of lightning claims him, squeezes him, pops him in a white flash that is gone as quick as it comes. His ashes rush over the ground toward Kale, peppering Tivali, stinging her eyes. She chokes on the salty powder.

"*More?*"

The tempest intensifies, forcing Tivali's face into the earth. Perpetual thunder fills her ears. Objects tumble over her, pinging painfully off her shoulders and scalp and hands. The earth quivers like a lid on a boiling pot of water.

For an eternity Tivali lies there, unsure if she's screaming, breathing, or even conscious. She presses one ear against the ground, grips the other, squeezes her eyes shut, tries to keep from lifting off into the air. It isn't working. The wind screams from every direction. The ground departs. Tivali is flying, falling. All goes quiet.

She's on her back. The wind is no more. She cracks her eyes. Blinks. Heaves in lungfuls of black air. She lifts her ringing head and finds herself in the middle of a vast plain, trees burning around the perimeter. A blanket of ash covers everything, illuminated by a jungle in flames. Her ears are squealing but she makes out the cries of her people. In front of her, where the standoff just went down, is seared ground absent of ash. From the look of it, everyone there was thrown in different directions.

Her people are in motion. Some flee in fear, carrying children or pulling them by the arm, hefting hastily gathered satchels over their shoulder. Others are pulling tools from ash-covered huts or from scattered piles of thatching. Men and women are assembling with simmering anger in their eyes, brandishing rakes and axes and hoes.

Tivali leaps to her feet, shaking ashes from her head, finally in control of her body again. She snatches up her bamboo from where it fell.

The magus is on his knees, head down, fists planted in the earth, heaving. He vomits noisily. The woman monk is doubled over several feet away, holding her head in her hands, staggering back and forth. Kale is embraced in a wreath of glowing blue vines, vibrating so intensely he looks immaterial. He moves toward the magus on hands and knees, dragging along as if there's an enormous weight on his back, leaving a flattened trail behind him darker than the surrounding grey ash. If he means to attack the monks while they're weakened, his time is short. He needs help. Tivali runs toward him.

"Don't touch me." It's Kale's voice, fractured, multiplied. "You know what will happen."

Tivali stops. She has no idea how Kale knew she was approaching, but she instinctively realizes what he's referring to. *The warthound.*

"Kalderys!" Kale's scream crackles and distorts. "Pay for what you've done."

Kalderys wipes the vomit from his lips with his gloved hand. He gives a tortured cough and smiles, swaying where he kneels. "Impressive," he says. He's trying to stand up. "Have at him, Selu," he tells the other monk.

His accomplice is not in as bad a state as him. She's donned a stave that's tipped on either end with white stone or shell. She lurches toward Kale. She's going to intercept him.

Tivali runs for her, trying to clear the ashes from her eyes and nose and corners of her lips. Her heart thumps, muffled by the ashes in her ears. Selu turns an icy glare on her.

"Back up, native. You're next."

Tivali doesn't know how monks fight. Aside from her encounter with the monk who almost killed her, she's never witnessed their style. But if they swing their sticks the way the wildfolk do from the southern peninsula, then Tivali won't be entirely unprepared.

She aims a jab at the monk's shoulder to gauge her range, her reflexes. Selu knocks it away and counters in a single fluid motion, striking at Tivali's face. Coupled with an abrupt lunge, the attack is too precise for Tivali to avoid. Tivali ducks but the stave's vicious tip grazes her head above her ear. She grunts, grits her teeth. It feels like the stave peeled back her scalp.

It's all Tivali can do to roll backward and grip her bamboo with two hands to block the monk's next attack. Selu's stave hits Tivali's bamboo so hard both Tivali's wrists bend backward and her staff cracks.

"Wait your turn," the monk commands. She's gained her footing and strides toward Kale, who's crawling so slowly he may as well be scaling a vertical wall.

"Stop her," Kale says raggedly. "I have ... to get ... to him."

Tivali doesn't have the strength or skill to stop the monk. Hot blood seeps through her hair down her temple, trickles from her earlobe. Her wrists throb. She's barely able to keep her grip on her bamboo. But it serves to give her the appearance of a threat. She places herself between Kale and the sentinel once again.

"It *is* my turn," she tells the monk.

Selu cocks her head to one side and her eyes narrow. Her curved lips indicate amusement. "You'd die for an exemplar? What has he ever done for you?"

"He saved my life," Tivali says. "Last time one of you monks tried to kill me, he cut the fucker's throat wide open. Did the world a favor."

The monk stops dead. All semblance of smile is gone. Her pale eyes glisten in the firelight and a shaking inhale trembles her plated dele. "You're right," she says. Her wavering voice has lost all command. "It is your turn."

She's airborne, her stave drawn back for a ferocious attack. Tivali can only brace herself. Hopefully she's bought Kale enough time to kill the one who brings the lightning.

There's a *thump* and the woman monk's leg juts out sideways. Her attack is compromised. She lands crookedly on her ankle. Her shoulder bounces off Tivali and she crashes to her side.

There is Tobas, wide-eyed, bamboo in hand, inching backward. He must have swept her leg. Selu climbs to her feet, takes up a defensive stance, her feral eyes darting from Tobas to Tivali. A stone glances off her helmet, then another off her breastplate. Villagers are approaching with staffs, stones, tools of shell and chitin.

A retching sound comes from the magus. He's vomiting on the ashy ground again. Kale is within seven paces and creeping steadily closer. His frame is flickering, snapping in and out of visibility, making the hum of rapid insect wings. Tana's people are converging toward the lightning monk.

"Selu," the magus calls, spitting out a grey glob. "Help."

Selu's stance tightens, her fists grip her weapon, her eyes deaden, as if his call triggered something primal in her. She springs to motion. Before Tivali can register what happened, Selu is wrenching her stave out of the side of Tobas' head. She twirls her weapon. Something warm slaps Tivali's cheek. It slides off and lands in a puff of ash—Tobas' ear.

Selu carves into the villagers before Tobas' body can finish falling. She smashes open heads, caves in ribs, stamps forward, drives through Tivali's people like they're stalks of sedge.

Tivali stares. Her tongue is bone-dry. Selu is a white blur in a red mist.

But there's another monk approaching her now, come from gods-only-know where. Broad-shouldered, brightly dressed. He throws himself at the murdering monk. Selu's stave stops abruptly, shivering against his. The monk is young, with gritted teeth and a sweaty face. And although he's a hefty one, Tivali can tell at once he won't stop her for long.

"Porter Culver?" Selu backs up, confused. Her expression hardens. "You meddling andesite. We should have imprisoned you with Kale."

She assaults him with a barrage of strikes. His stave holds up better than Tivali's bamboo did. But he's losing ground. What she lacks in size, she makes up for in ferocity. Tivali's eyes can't keep up with their combat.

The ground is piled with Napiri's parents and brothers and sisters. Tears burn Tivali's cheeks. Her hands have lost the will to hold her bamboo. Each time she blinks she sees Tobas' empty eyes as he falls. Bodies lie in ruin. Fires have overtaken the tallest trees. *Why is this happening?* A glimpse at Kale turns her stomach. He's on hands and knees, creeping, shimmering like something leaked from a nightmare.

A massive acacia groans and creaks, leaning over the village. With a wrenching crack its trunk gives way. It plummets, showering burning leaves, crushes the dining lodge in a deafening thud. The tremor rattles Tivali's teeth. Napiri is gone. It's hard news but the truth usually is. Her neighbors who've escaped are running into the jungle in the dead of night. They need her. With Tivali's help, they might stand a chance. If they are destined to die, she'll share their fate. Whatever these monks are fighting over, they can have it.

~

The world is a smear. An ocean of energy scours Kale's insides, flushing throughout him and filling his senses. It is relentless. He's dimly aware of his body, in that he's struggling to push it forward. His skin, bones, teeth, ears, hands, feet, are a unified basin of raw motion.

His eyelids no longer matter. Feels like he's looking in every direction all at once, hearing the roar of a thousand fires, smelling the blackness between stars, tasting electricity.

He drags his hand forward one inch and slips fingers into the earth. It parts for him like sand. Like water. But the closer he gets to Kalderys, the harder it is to proceed. He drags his other hand. The chaotic energy inside him is desperate to be freed but it's repelled by Kalderys, like two similarly polarized lodestones.

The last time Kale cradled energy, it ignited his feet like the explosive powder of a fusil. Would he have moved this slowly then if he'd tried to move toward the magus? And now, if he releases this wall he climbs, will he simply fall away like a leaf on the wind? If so, no one can catch him. But if he doesn't stop the magus, Tivali will die. Before he explodes, or implodes, or simply ceases, he has to rid the world of Kalderys. That's all that matters.

Tivali is nowhere to be seen. Prime Sentinel Selu has torn through Napiri's people to get at Kale. And somehow, for some reason, Culver is here. He's fighting Selu to Kale's right. He shouldn't have come. He's no match for Selu. There is only death here.

A grunt from Culver. He's been laid out in the ashes, gripping his ribs. Selu dispatched him. Now she's coming for Kale. She's going to hit him with that stave.

"No!" A dozen voices issue from Kale's throat, layered like a summoner's song. "It's for him."

"I don't know how you've done it, Basalt, or what consumes you right now." Selu's voice is deafening. She's at ease. Maybe rampant murder is her usual precursor to clarity. "I don't know what you have in mind for the magus. But *your* will is not my priority and neither is his."

Kale drags his knee forward. It feels like Mount Adenhelm sits on his feet.

"Despite all you've done, I have to thank you." Selu kneels beside him and roars in a hushed, conspiratorial voice. "I was distracted too. By Calomancer Arc. That is behind us, for better or worse. Tonight is Kalderys' undoing. It's a necessary purge. You've brought to light a sickness in the Triumvirate that can't persist. When Kalderys is exposed ..." She leans in close to Kale's ear. "I'll be the new magus."

"Not ... if you ... touch me." Kale's mouth is wide but his teeth are clenched.

"Insect," Selu says. "Look at me."

Kale pulls his knee, but it refuses to advance. Kalderys is ten feet away. It may as well be miles.

"Look at me, you failed negator." The chitin on the end of Selu's stave hovers in front of Kale's chin. "Don't die a coward."

Kale grunts, pulls harder. Reaches out with all his might. Fails to advance. It's no use. It's as if the energy protects its origin, striving only to propagate Kale away violently.

"Kale," Selu says. "*Look at me!*"

Kale relents, defeated.

"Fine." He turns his head toward Selu, gives in to her pale eyes. "Have it."

In one motion Selu draws back and launches a strike that should puncture Kale's head. Time grinds to a crawl. Kale watches the gore-caked chitin tip approach him at a slug's pace. His eyes travel up the length of the stave, over her red knuckles, her wrists, arms, shoulders. Her bloody face. By the time her attack lands, Selu's expression registers her mistake.

Everything is shaking. Kale is still. Unmovable. The burnt ground is a grey blur. The blazing forest an orange haze. Selu is a violent statue, carved into a confused mid-strike. Her stave is almost against Kale's temple.

Send her away. The concept terrifies Kale. She will disappear forever, leave no explanation, leave nothing. The only evidence she existed will be the accounts of others. What will happen to her? Will she die? Worse, will she survive? Not that Kale can influence any of that. All he can control is whether it happens before or after her attack kills him. Until now he hadn't realized he had any control. But he does.

The energy he harbors doesn't explode like Kalderys'. It condenses to a point under his skin, hungry for her touch. Selu's stave contacts his temple like a fallen feather. He releases. His ear belches a black smoke ring. It billows outward and obscures, a window to a starry sky. Nothing is vibrating anymore. Time has stopped, almost. Kale aims the void at Selu by simply thinking, *Be gone.*

The starry essence rushes up the stave's length, expands to absorb Selu's fists, her arms, and then, accelerating as it expands, it swallows her. She's engulfed. *No more.* The black window hisses as it snaps out of existence. Vision returns to normal. Kale gasps. Feels like he was doused in cold water. His ears ring.

"Scourge!" Magus Kalderys has ceased trying to rise, swaying instead with fear in his eyes, blowing spittle off his lips. "You are the mouth of dissonance. I thought I had seen evil ..."

"You have." Kale exhales steam and collapses onto his back. Syvea the crystal rests on his chest, lucid, the same way Tivali's hand did that one night. He'd sent a void then too, and slept. Tivali had protected him. But now she's gone and Kale doesn't blame her. She survived. That's the best he can ask for. Did Culver survive? He should never have come here.

Kale will lose consciousness soon. Anyone with ill intentions can have their way with him after that. Kalderys will eventually manage to stand up, and surely has all sorts of ugly death in mind for him. None he hasn't earned. Short of the Heathen Tide itself, Kale is probably Stravhelm's worst enemy. He smiles. Whatever plan Erudition had for him when he was taken on as an intrant, this couldn't have been it.

Intemrus sees all.

Kale imagines the look Intemrus will wear when he hears of this. He would laugh if he could. Maybe the sovereign will die. Maybe the crystal will protect Kale. Maybe it made him immortal. Maybe not. It doesn't matter.

"*What is it?*" the crystal says. It has a feminine voice. Curious, otherworldly. That odd, unrecognizable accent.

A man replies. His accent is too thick for Kale to make out words, but he understands. "*It is your future.*" Lovingly, like he's showing off something he worked hard to present.

It's a conversation happening somewhere else. Kale wants to do more than eavesdrop. He wants to go where they are. It can't be worse than here. His eyes slide close as he grips the crystal. He exhales, listens.

45
Those Who Would Imprison You

REDEMIER

Kale's waking vision is hazy, made entirely of pale light. It's like a dream but becoming gradually more substantial. Objects are taking shape, as if a thick fog is lifting. He's unable to move and yet the body he occupies is somehow moving freely. A breeze travels over his skin, through his hair.

He's standing. The crystal is in his hands. Except those aren't his hands. They're smaller. The fingers are thinner. Wrists are smoother. A girl's arms.

The crystal is different. It's larger. Kale realizes it's whole, unbroken. This must be a memory. But whose? Large hands appear, so dark grey they're nearly black, encompassing hers and the crystal.

"And it will protect you," the man says.

"Protect me from what?" The words come out of Kale in the girl's voice.

"Sickness. Harm. Forgetfulness. Age."

"Age? Does that mean ... immortality?" Now she looks up at him.

He towers over her. His black mane defies gravity, rising upward like fire. His eyes are violet, with black points for pupils. His bare chest and arms and smooth face are like a burnt, polished granite, reflecting sunlight blindingly. This man is portrayed on a window mosaic in Stravhelm. He's depicted on the cursed island, all grey and black with amethysts for eyes, surrounded by four-legged monsters with shark fins on their backs. This is the Deceiver.

"No human can achieve true immortality. But you'll outlive those who would imprison you."

The girl pulls her hands from his, examines the brilliant pink stone. "You're talking about people I love."

Kale can't tell what sort of relationship this is. There's affection but she doesn't seem to feel physical intimacy toward him. Kale's less sure about the Deceiver's feelings. There is a deep trepidation in the girl. She doesn't think of this man as a deceiver. And she doesn't want to hurt him. Not him too. She can't keep hurting everyone forever.

"I know," he says softly. "Their passing will be painful to bear but only for a time, then they will become merely a chapter in a grander life."

He steps back, turns slightly away. Kale feels the girl take a breath.

"The Great Beast doesn't give away her blood idly." His voice is a deep purr. His eyes are jubilant. "This is a rare gift. The Great Beast has seen something in you worth preserving."

She hesitates. To reject him is to return home. And she can't do that.

"Please consider it at least," he says. "I'll understand if you return the stone to me. But know ..." His eyes glitter like they're jewels. "... there is much, much more to this world than their selfishness."

Kale's surroundings are growing clearer. They are in what appears to be a ruined stone-built temple, long since taken over by creeping vines and moss and rock-splitting shrubs. Columns are all that remain of the walls. Beyond the columns are more block buildings in a similarly derelict state. The stone structures that still stand are tall. They're etched and chiseled with runes and writing Kale has never seen and can't decipher. The greenery that has devoured this place is foreign, no myrtles or mahoganies. Trees are thicker trunked, their leaves smaller and darker green. Their rough grey bark is lined with vertical fissures.

"This is not what I wanted," the girl says, turning away from the tall man and walking toward an arched doorway. Either she is abnormally short or the doorway is some fifteen feet high. In the distance, descending a forested hill are more ruins, evidence of houses and streets, long neglected. No roofs are intact, and judging by the size of the trees that have grown up where they once were, this place hasn't been inhabited for many lifetimes.

Beyond the ruins the forest continues to descend, steeply at first, then shallowly, for as far as Kale can see. Miles off, trails of smoke rise from the forest's canopy. Somehow he knows, maybe because she knows, those are civilizations of man. It's from one of those that she fled and does not want to return.

The Deceiver approaches, stands beside her.

"You're young. Your captors have influenced you. That, along with the tendencies of your kind, has made you lost. I offer you something they cannot. Something they wouldn't if they could. Your own choice."

He means to reassure her.

Immediately past the massive archway is a broad stone landing, baked by the sun, carpeted with flowering vines. Beyond are stairs that descend into the trees, and from that direction comes a commotion, voices in distress calling out, and a clattering, ringing sound, clear and bright. Kale feels the girl's chest tremble.

"They've found me," she says. "They're coming."

"You knew they would. Your betrothed is a peerless hunter. Your father uses sight beyond sight."

"I hoped it would take them longer."

"As had I. But soon enough, time will cease to be a concern. Would you like me to be here, or do you prefer to confront them alone?"

She looks at him and again Kale is struck by his appearance. He must be nine feet tall, not that there's much basis of comparison other than the crystal the girl and Kale both hold. His violet eyes sparkle. His broad jaw and high cheekbones are sleek, like they're carved from volcanic stone.

If he stays, violence will ensue. Kale knows it because she does. "They are my people. Please don't hurt them."

The Deceiver does not immediately respond.

"Promise me," she says.

"Pain is the only language they know."

"If you hurt them ..." Her voice is small, frightened. She's searching for a threat that will matter against this giant. "... I'll never forgive you."

"Very well. I will leave them to you."

She turns back to the stairs, sees an individual ascending. Kale doesn't see or hear the Deceiver leave, but he knows the man has gone.

"Syvea!"

The familiar voice strikes fear into Kale's heart. Or is it her heart? Her fear?

A lanky man is shuffling up the stairs gripping a wooden staff. He's wearing a simple dele. His mouth is twisted into a panicked scowl. His eyes ... Kale knows him, and if he could run, he would.

Behind the first is another figure, not as tall but twice as broad. This one wears the silvery fur of an animal across his shoulders, with its head draped over his own. He's muscle-bound and laden with implements on his belt that click and clang against one another as he bounds up the stairs. They catch the sun, reflecting light like crystal tarpon scales. Kale knows the material at once though his eyes have never seen it. *Steel.* He's imagined it a hundred times, but none of Erudition's images do it justice. It is portrayed in murals to be matte, dull, like a corpse's bones. But no. It's bright, pristine. Surely too beautiful to be an abomination. Is that claim another of the holy city's lies?

The one wearing the dele arrives first, out of breath, hunched over and gripping his knees.

"Oh, Syvea. Thank Imala."

Syvea takes a step away from him. She is hesitant to welcome him or the other man. Favoring one will exclude the other, as time has proven, and nothing will be gained. She's happy they're together. They must have worked side by side tracking her. If so, it's the first time they've cooperated on anything in a long time. That's no small accomplishment. Perhaps it's what they needed. Perhaps this marks some change.

The fur-clad man tops the stairs in a massive leap, his steel accoutrements jostling on leather belts and straps, on his waist, his ankles, his back. He's an energetic youth, perhaps no older than Kale himself. Straw-colored locks encircle his face, scruffy around his chin and lips where a dark beard has not yet filled in. His light hair contrasts his black, piercing eyes. Whatever creature gave up its skin to him, with empty eye sockets and lifeless fangs, makes for a disturbing avatar of death.

Although the boy strikes unease into Kale, the girl is not afraid. In fact, his presence instills a calmness within her.

"Syvea, let's go home," the fur-clad boy says, reaching for her hand. His gravelly voice makes Kale think of the warthound.

"No." She pulls away from him as well. "Not until this is resolved."

The man wearing a dele straightens himself until his face is visible in full clarity. Kale's fear is visceral, even if Syvea is merely intimidated. The man's hair, his eyes, his posture ... Kale's gut demands him to flee despite that he's not in control of this body. That is Sovereign Intemrus. Only younger. Perhaps not yet sovereign? There is passion on his face. *Pain.* Kale would never have believed it possible.

Intemrus steps between the girl and the fur-clad boy.

"Vretos, for Imala's sake, relent," he says. "It's you that drove her away. She wants no part of your insatiable bloodlust." He turns his crystalline eyes on Syvea. Kale, though distanced from this event by miles and years, reels in terror. Somehow, there is compassion in Intemrus' eyes. Perhaps even love. *Impossible.*

"*My* bloodlust?" the boy says. "She ran from the prison *you* made. I set her free, monk, from your cult." The boy, Vretos, steps toward Intemrus. His hands twitch at his sides where the grips for his steel weapons await. He appears to be beast and man all at once. Kale had imagined Fohrvyldan heathens. Who hasn't? But he never thought of them being his age.

"Stop!" Syvea says. "If you can't stop fighting, I won't go with either of you." Disappointment squeezes her throat, makes her voice high, which frustrates her. The two who have come for her are oblivious to it.

Kale is aware they're talking about leaving Redemier. Today is the day a population split and journeyed to the west to Ausgan or east to Fohrvylda, according to their preference, or perhaps more accurately, their allegiance. As many times as he's heard Alika or another proctor recite the event, Kale barely gave it a moment's thought. It never seemed relevant.

Intemrus drops his staff, places his hands in rhystic dominance. "Back up, heathen. I'll not say it again. Syvea will accompany me to Ausgan."

Vretos grabs the handle of one of his steel devices and pulls it from his belt. It rings harshly, like chitin sharpened on stone, but brighter. So much brighter. It's so thin, so sharp. Like a blade of spikerush, no longer than his fist is wide. It's still ringing.

"Heathen is it?" the boy says. "Better that than jailer. She's not yours to control. None of us are."

"Look at me," Syvea tries to scream the words. As if it would matter.

Intemrus snorts. "I never intended to indoctrinate you and your rabid supporters, Vretos. That would serve no one. The best I could hope for was to prevent you turning your depravity on the population."

Vretos scoffs. "Staring at clouds has left you senseless." His voice is low, threatening. His stance is tense, like a coiled snake. "She's flown the nest. Fohrvylda is her future. She can do what she wants there, not live in a cage as another of your loveless mages. Why would you want that for your own daughter?"

Intemrus is shaking his head. His face is a vicious scowl. "Treacherous animal. You've plagued us far too long." His eyes shift in color, the pupils turning pale. Vretos draws back his glinting weapon.

"Stop!" Syvea cries. Kale knows it's far from the first time. They won't hear her. But this time will be different. She will cry no longer. She will not choose one of them over the other, or a prolonged life with neither.

Before Intemrus can launch his song, before Vretos' blade can strike, Syvea lunges in between them, against anything Kale can do to stop her.

The pointed steel in Vretos' hand punctures Kale's chest, sliding through his ribs, stealing his breath and his voice, driving him against Intemrus. Immediately Kale experiences the absence of consonance. He'd never known it was there. He doesn't sing, or summon, or channel. He'd grown to believe those who'd deemed him susceptible to consonance, plucking him from his birth mother and initiating him in Erudition, had made a mistake. They didn't. With this heathen device embedded in him, consonance has abandoned him, and there is a frigid expanse where it was.

Behind, Intemrus cries out. Vretos stands frozen in shock. Syvea, unable to draw breath, looks down at the weapon's handle, grabs it. She tries to pull it out while her dele reddens. She can see the blood running down her hands, her wrists, but she can't feel its warmth. She falls, releasing the crystal. It bounces once, rebounding high, a crack on its surface distorting its ring. She cannot arrest her descent, only try to slow it. The world turns sideways. Her bloody hands smack against stone. Her cheek eases down onto cool moss.

"Syvea!" Kale is aware of Intemrus' hysteria, his terror. It is not as satisfying as he would have expected. Quite the opposite.

Before her eyes the crystal strikes stone again, this time breaking in half in a burst of sparkling splinters. Breath eases from Syvea's parted lips. A chill rides over her. Kale's pain grows dim. Somewhere, Vretos is roaring like a wounded warthound.

Just as Kale's vision of this memory began in a hazy cloud, to there it is returning. Syvea is dying. Her eyes are losing focus. The Deceiver approaches, an obsidian monolith, flanked on either side by enormous shapes, black beasts walking on all fours, the fins on their backs rising nearly as high as his shoulder, just like in Stravhelm's mural. The Deceiver comes to a stop, as do the beasts. A grimace of disgust is etched into his dark face.

"What have you done?"

Kale's vision fades to nothing.

46

A Shittier Job

FOHRVYLDA
The Northern Seaboard

On some nameless, wind-blasted cliff, Recruit Loran brushes down Lieutenant Azri's orcane. He hums softly, shivering in the salty sea wind that rushes up over the precipice. The wind's cold, but at least it keeps at bay the rusty-blood stink of the animal's wiry, oily coat. His humming and brushing puts the orcanes at ease, if only a bit. It's said wild orcanes bathe themselves, but there are no wild orcanes in Fohrvylda, so who the hell figured that out? These ones still tug at their reins. They would still make a quick meal of him if they could yank free of those leather muzzles. But that's not likely. Of the few skills Loran mastered thus far as a soldier of the Domestic Patrol, securing orcanes came with ease. The steel anchor screws are buried five feet in the earth, and the attached harnesses' rivets and buckles are all tighter than Lieutenant Azri's ass. Otherwise he'd not dare to stand amongst the beasts. A recruit learns first and foremost to respect the ferocity of orcanes, usually by witnessing the consequences of a neglected harness, or an ill-established anchor screw.

Behind him is the precipice, and hundreds of feet below it, is the Faithless Sea. To the west, the sea stretches indefinitely, melding into the blue-grey horizon, its surface flashing white peaks at him beneath the brilliant late-morning sun. Ausgan's out there somewhere, with its musical monks.

To the north are the Towers, sea stacks rising up from the ocean like an endless army of earthen spears. Those formations stretch northward for miles and miles, all the way to Redemier, the cursed island. Most of them crest in forested peaks, as if their sharp tips were dipped in the blood of green giants. Some stacks are relatively narrow, and if you peer hard enough you can make out impossible-to-access, blade-thin footpaths hewn around their rock necks like delicate necklaces. Other stacks are large enough to accommodate mountain peaks and forests— and feral communities, if the rumors hold truth, people with no love for Promontory, or Vretos, or soldiers. From where Loran stands, there is no evidence of human civilization out there on the Towers, not even a hint of smoke rising from the forested spires.

Creaking in the wind nearby is one of several suspension bridges made of hefty hemp cables as thick as Loran's calf, and massive planks of ash or cedar. It's this isolated chokepoint that Loran and his party are here to guard for some reason. The lonely apparatus looks out of use, easing back and forth in the wind. Supposedly, the bridges are to transport valuable hardwood from the Towers to the mainland— hardwood needed for ships, which are vital to the Heathen Tide. Each time Loran tries to work out how tree trunks would be toted over so frail-looking a bridge, it ends with him imagining the inevitable plummet of all involved.

The bridges connect the Towers in a maze-like net, the way vines are said to choke the jungles of Ausgan. Loran's heart flutters at the thought of that distant, ripe, sunny land. The Heathen Tide will feast on it without consequence. They say Ausgan monks attack with not steel but song. Loran has always appreciated a good song. Never comprehended why he might fear one, however off-key it's yelled.

Over by their wind-licked campfire, Lieutenant Azri sits on an exposed stone, endlessly poring over maps with a magnifying glass pressed against her left eye. Shovel and Hound sit amongst the weapons, the supplies, the saddles, pretending to provide maintenance. They're actually doing little more than sneaking swallows of that blackberry brandy they got from the last mire of a village they visited. Visited, sacked, whatever. If the lieutenant knows of their subterfuge, she doesn't appear to care. Loran snorts. Gods forbid he cease his brushing even for a blink.

Azri's orcane vibrates with a growl so low it trembles Loran's guts all the way down to his feet and halts his humming. He's strayed too near the raw flesh of the beast's throat where the leather muzzle grips the tightest. He moves away. Don't brush them there or their white bellies, no matter how mud-speckled. Not unless you've got a death wish.

"Stop tickling the dog, recruit," Shovel calls, without bothering to look over. "And quit your damn humming."

"It settles them," Loran mutters.

"Are you singing, recruit?" Lieutenant Azri has looked up from her maps and removed the glass from her eye. The glass left an indention on her otherwise featureless, puffy face. Her flaxen hair is bound tightly in a knot on the back of her head, but stray strands flick about like the branches of a dead tree. Her squinting gaze is aimed at Loran but not quite fixed on him.

"No, Lieutenant," Loran speaks loudly.

"That's good," she says. "'Cause you know who sings? Ausgan monks. You're not a damn monk, are you?"

What a stupid question to ask. Why's everyone always talking down to him? "No, Lieutenant," he repeats. Clearly this patrol has spent too much time out here in isolation and grown sick of itself. What Loran wouldn't give for a recruit greener than himself.

"I'll tell ya how to settle them beasts," Hound says, his words sounding like they had to crowd past some sort of wad in his mouth to get out.

Loran cringes. Nothing good has ever come of Hound speaking.

"You could reach down tween their flanks and give 'em a good jostle round the hindquarters."

Shovel belches a laugh, shakes his head.

"Or hold them steady while I do it." Hound's attention falls on Loran. He's joking no longer.

"Shut up, Hound," Azri says, returning to her maps.

Loran says nothing. The second lesson he learned as a recruit was to never speak unless demanded to do so. Easily enough he could earn a less enviable job, one that'll make him wish he was still brushing an orcane, like digging a new latrine, burying the old, or feeding the alarm sprakes, which is a good way to lose fingers. Or, and his heart lurches at the thought of it, scouting out over the Towers, for no other reason than because the others are bored and would like to see him topple off the rickety suspension bridge.

If he thought there was a chance of being commanded to collect firewood from the forest down the hill, on the other hand, maybe he'd speak up. Admit his shoulders are throbbing, his palms are split, and his fingers ache from gripping this damn brush. But collecting firewood is a job that belongs to Stubbs, and he's taking his sweet time at it. Probably napping under a tree.

The sun is nearing its highest point. Soon the orcanes will be hungry enough to grow restless, adding significantly to the inherent danger of Loran's current preoccupation. Although he himself dare not remind Azri of the time, perhaps the orcanes might if he can manage to safely prod one. It's just as likely though that he'd rouse the beast into action. And however tightly he's fastened the straps, however deep the anchor screw is planted, he'll not take those securities for granted.

Maybe Stubbs' return will trigger lunch. Loran aims his gaze southward, back over the mainland. The tree line is some hundred yards down a shallow hill, and the forest it introduces rides the lumpy land away south, punctuated by enormous grey boulders that peek over the treetops like turtles poking their noses out of a green lake.

One of the alarm sprakes gives a splitting shriek so abruptly that Loran spasms and slings his brush out over the cliff into the wind. The brush descends toward the sea into blue obscurity. Loran observes that it's the bird not currently hooded, and the damn thing's only preening itself. Its neck is craned so that it can thrust its sharp beak deep into its silver breast feathers.

Loran's mishap is taking shape and setting his heart to galloping. "The brush ..." His words hiss out. That was his only protection against a shittier job. A dozen strides off, the hemp bridge purrs out its taunting acknowledgment.

His eyes fall on Azri, whose squinting gaze snatches him.

"What's that?" she calls sharply. "What's the matter with that sprake?"

"Yeah," Shovel says. "That bird see something?"

Loran places his back toward his companions and reflexively continues brushing down Azri's orcane ... with his fingernails.

"The bird's just cleaning itself. Look and see."

It's true enough. The other bird, the hooded one, perches motionless. Its silvery-cerulean plumage enshrouds its shoulders like a cape of royalty and its long tail feathers ripple in the breeze, reflecting every shade of blue. A warn-smooth leather cap, large enough to fit both Loran's fists into, is snug on that raptor's head so that only its hooked beak is exposed, like a gutting knife.

Loran feels no need to clarify again to Shovel that alarm sprakes don't ever *see* something. If the lesson hasn't taken by now, then he'd be the dumbass for reiterating it. Alarm sprakes don't look for anything. You're supposed to be the one doing the looking. They register that either they're secured to a perch or they're not. "I think the birds are hungry," Loran risks, without stealing a glance at his fellows.

"Then feed them," the lieutenant says.

"I'm hungry too," Shovel offers.

"Eat something dry from your pack," Azri answers.

"I don't got nothing dry left."

"I told you not to eat your rations so fast."

Loran pretends to focus on brushing orcanes. Their exchange feels awkward to observe. There's been a bickering quality to the rapport between her and Shovel lately that does not feel fitting for either of their stations.

Shovel angrily studies a leather sheath for a moment. "I'm hungry right now," he decides.

The lieutenant huffs out an immense breath. "We wait for more firewood before cooking anything. If Stubbs fell off a cliff or got eaten or stabbed by something, this wood has to last us." Azri returns to her maps and presses the magnifying glass to her eye socket, satisfied with her assessment.

Shovel lurches to his feet, apparently not at all satisfied by it. "I'm done waiting for that fucker to finish wanking in the woods. I'm boiling water for porridge."

"Shovel ..." Lieutenant Azri again lowers her magnifying glass. This time she deliberately sets down her maps. She puts the glass upon them to hold them in place, then spends several moments rubbing her eyes. "Tell me, soldier, what have you done to warrant another meal since the last time you stuffed your face? Not including drinking yourself inept?"

Shovel opens his mouth and gives a small, wet noise. He closes his teeth, downtrodden, and returns to his seat among the leather and steel. Then he looks at Loran, who barely has enough time to hide his smile. "Well, he's been brushing the dogs this whole time. You're hungry, aren't you, recruit?"

Azri turns her plump face at Loran, eyebrows furrowed.

Loran's smile flees. Seems any response will polarize him against one or the other. But before he has a chance to determine which of them he'd prefer for an enemy today, Hound rises to his feet, extending his long neck toward the forest intently. His shoulders are hunched forward, elbows thrust out behind him. Such an awkward looking person. He suffered a grave head wound years back when a house collapsed on him. It should have killed him. Instead it left him with unusual fixations and characteristics, and earned him a new name. He produces a thin whine, so high pitched it wavers in and out of Loran's hearing. Down the hill and exiting the forest's shadows is Stubbs, so far off he's no taller than a bean. He's brought someone out with him.

"Look," Loran says, pointing.

Azri and Shovel rise as well.

A small-framed figure in sparse leather armor clings to Stubbs like he might fall over without support. Hound's whining takes on a whistling, saw-like quality. It seems restraining himself takes quite the effort.

Loran shields his eyes. An unease he can't quite identify creeps through him, holds his feet where they are. The figure's leather armor is snug and his long, dark hair cascades around his shoulders. One thin arm is thrown over Stubbs' steel-plated shoulder. Stubbs' arm is around the figure's narrow waist. Stubbs is bent forward, perhaps under the effort of keeping the person upright. His helmet is aimed at the uneven ground at his feet.

"It's a woman," Hound mutters thickly, between his whines.

"A woman?" Shovel says, the upward-darting pitch of his voice perfectly exemplifying Loran's surprise.

"Ho, Stubbs," Lieutenant Azri calls out, squinting and advancing to the campsite's perimeter.

Stubbs gives no response. Now Loran can make out the pained grunts of the person Stubbs is supporting. It's definitely a woman's voice. Nothing about this makes sense. Stubbs was gone for at least two hours. And now that he's back he's got no wood to show for his time away, but instead a wounded woman. Loran's head tilts to the side, as if all his thoughts and observations will tumble into a deep enough pool for him to fetch some sense out of it.

"This is weird," he determines.

Shovel has claimed his sword belt and fastens it around his waist. He throws Hound his belt. It bounces off Hound's shin and lands in a heap at his feet, utterly unnoticed. A line of saliva has crept over

Hound's gaping lips and dangles in the wind. His whining is more insistent.

"Hound," Shovel snaps. The man returns to awareness long enough to notice his weapon at his feet. He bends to collect it, running the back of his gloved hand noisily over the peppery bristles under his chin then securing the belt clumsily at his waist. Loran considers, not for the first time, the advantages of an actual dog in their party rather than this individual.

"Get ready to free the sprakes, recruit," Shovel says.

Loran draws his knife, but the lieutenant shoots him a glare over her shoulder. "Do no such thing," she says, then back to Stubbs, louder, "Speak up, Stubbs. You're spooking the animals. Don't make me shoot you. What do you have there?"

"Don't shoot." Stubbs' voice is rough, as if he might have gargled pinecones while he was away. He speaks without lifting his head. "I caught Irdessa."

Loran gasps. *Irdessa the Undying.* This is it. This is who they're here for. Oh praises be, they'll get to leave. Damn the brush and damn the towers and godsdamn the bridges. He runs to the alarm sprakes, knife in hand, grin on face, ignoring the urging from his guts that insists, *This is weird.*

"Stop," Lieutenant Azri barks at him, this time rounding to face him from across the camp. "If you cut that tether you better cut your own throat while you're at it."

"Why?" Shovel says. "She's dangerous." He points his sword at the pair gradually creeping up the rock-strewn hill. "What'd you think we brought the birds for if not this?" His outburst is certainly motivated by his own self-preservation, but Loran's glad to have someone come to his defense for once.

The lieutenant turns to Shovel and stamps in his direction, making him step back. "We free the sprakes only if we're in over our heads. Does that look like a threat to you?" She points her own sword at the approaching pair, but as usual doesn't give anyone a chance to answer. "If we cut those birds free, this hill's gonna swarm with soldiers. Up comes Captain Rale and his patrol, or Captain Alcus or some other captain, all wanting a piece of the Undying as if there's enough of that skinny bitch to go round. Then you know what happens?"

Shovel glares at her, then at Stubbs and the woman, then back.

"They take the damn girl," Azri answers herself yet again. "They get the reward. We get fuck all and I'm stuck with you lot."

"Something's ... weird," Loran hears himself interject.

"Then get your bows up and ready arrows," the lieutenant commands. "Are you scared of Stubbs and a wounded Irdessa? Everyone knows she's nothing without the Tactician. Look at her. Looks like Stubbs already kicked the shit out of her."

Loran doesn't have a bow, so he shifts his grip on the knife instead. It feels quite inadequate in this moment, however maimed Irdessa appears. If Stubbs hurt her, then why's she leaning on him? Why aren't her hands tied?

Shovel claims his bow and nocks an arrow. Hound does not, instead snuffling loudly and making a wailing sound, as if his stasis causes physical pain. Lieutenant Azri stalks directly to him, draws back a mailed fist, and punches him full in the side of the head. He gives a sharp cry, stumbles for footing, then blinks several times, rubbing his ear and looking sulkily at the lieutenant.

"Raise your godsdamned bow," she yells in his face.

Hound scurries over to fetch his bow and scrabble for an arrow, as obedient and void of dignity as his name suggests. Even standing with bow and arrow beside Shovel, the faint, shrill whine is soon leaking from his lips again. His unease has infiltrated the orcanes, drawing their focus on the approaching pair. They're fully alert, hackles standing tall across their black shoulders, massive paws planted wide, heads low on taut, trunk-like necks and their eyes bulging like shiny black eggs. They're beyond appeasement by any sort, and frankly, Loran's done being anywhere near them.

He moves up behind Shovel and Hound. Hound is muttering under his breath. "Just need me those stems. Or the bottom half. The bottom half. The bottom half. Or the stems. The stems. The stems." He doesn't even seem aware he's doing it. Loran considers retreating back among the orcanes.

Stubbs and his baggage are halfway between the tree line and the camp when he loses his grip on the woman. Her arm slips from his shoulders and she slumps down in a heap at his feet. Stubbs kneels to lift her.

"Stubbs, leave her," Lieutenant Azri calls. "Get up and show us your face or Shovel's putting an arrow in you." She reaches back to gesture at Shovel. He draws his arrow, grimacing in distaste at it all.

"Stubbs, say something," Shovel calls. "I don't want to shoot you."

All has gone still, even with the wind ripping its claws up over the cliff, the orcanes rumbling their warning, Hound chanting in his whistly whisper, and Loran's heart banging at his ribs. Why won't Stubbs raise his face or give a damn shout or a joke? He's full of wisecracks. Usually can't stop talking. He's not obviously injured, so that's not what's got him acting odd. There can be only one reason.

"I don't think that's Stubbs," Loran declares.

"Shovel, shoot Stubbs, now," Lieutenant Azri commands without taking her eyes off the pair.

"The hell with that," Shovel says, throwing his bow down. "I'm freeing the sprakes."

"By Lahuvot's fiery cock, if you free the sprakes I'll kill you," Azri says, striding over to his bow and snatching it up. It looks small in her thick hands, but when she draws the arrow to her cheek and levels it at Shovel, there's no questioning her proficiency with the weapon. "I give you one damn fling out of boredom and you decide you're above my command. Maybe I'll stick you and repay the favor, except I'd wager you'll like my arrow more than I liked yours."

"Alright, alright!" He backs away from the birds, both hands held high.

"We all done talking about alarm sprakes?" she asks him. One of her eyes is pinched. The other sights down the arrow at his chest.

"Yeah, I'm done. For fuck's sake." He pulls his knife out and tosses it away.

"Good." She lowers the weapon.

"Not gonna be me explaining why the Undying died in custody," Shovel mutters.

"It sure as hell won't if you don't stop that tongue." Azri throws his bow at him. "'Cause I'll cut the useless fucker out."

Loran lets out his breath. His hands are trembling. His appetite has taken its leave. In this moment, he's unable to determine which of the two he pities more for their rendezvous. And to think, he found Hound to be the most disgusting. This isn't the first time he's appreciative that his cot is arranged closer to the orcanes than his fellows.

"Hound, go help with that girl," the lieutenant says. "If Stubbs is up to something, kill him. I've got your back." She collects her own bow, squares off toward the pair.

Loran knows Lieutenant Azri can't make a shot from this distance, whether or not she'd admit it. She has to squint and lean forward when looking down the hill, or even across the camp at Loran. Her eyes are bad, perhaps from years of studying and writing maps. But chances are Hound doesn't know it, nor do Shovel or Stubbs. Not the kind of thing they notice.

Hound could not be more excited to finally have at the woman. He sets off at a canter, eyes glistening, the bow dangling uselessly at his side.

"Leave the girl whole," Lieutenant Azri says. "Don't try to take her apart."

Hound lopes down the hill, eventually bothering to lift his bow.

"Tell him to give her an arrow in the knee," Shovel suggests to Azri. "Just to be safe."

"No," Azri responds. "She'll have to walk back to Promontory between Hound and the recruit, barring whatever injury Stubbs already gave her. Not gonna damage her further unless she gives a reason." Azri watches Hound's path with the vigilance of a nearsighted hawk. "Unless you want to share your orcane with her."

Hound nears the struggling pair. Must be within fifteen yards, and he's slowed to peer at them, holding an arrow not quite at the ready. He's saying something at Stubbs that Loran can't discern. One of the damn sprakes has chosen this moment to violently beat its wings and apparently never stop. Loran is about to check the bird's tether when he sees Stubbs' helmet fall off. For some reason, the hair on Stubb's head isn't rusty red anymore but dirt brown and sheared nearly to his scalp. For some reason, there's a bow in his hands and a murderous crouch to him.

Hound leaps backward, his arrow clattering against the handle of his bow as he tries madly to get it nocked. "Not Stubbs!" His voice is shrill with panic. Loran's guts fill with ice. "Not Stubbs! Not—"

His head rocks backward, abruptly adorned with an arrow sprouting from his cheek. He backpedals stiffly. His arms wave, flinging his bow away. The noise coming out of his face now is a prolonged nasal grunt, and somehow sounds even less deliberate than his canine whining. Not-Stubbs draws back another and looses it into Hound's chest, knocking him off his feet. Not-Stubbs runs over him at a crouch toward the camp. Irdessa the Un-fucking-dying springs up, healthy as a buck. She runs alongside him, brandishing a knife.

Lieutenant Azri gives a startled yelp. She launches an arrow, as does Shovel. She's drawing another even before her first is done flying. "Free the sprakes," she yells. "Free the sprakes!"

Loran spins to make a dash at the birds but stops short.

"I'll help." A small man with a dirty face is holding the hooded sprake by a strap on its leather cap. The man's dressed in a dark grey animal skin the color of the cliff he's standing on. The sprake's massive blue wings are beating violently, forcing the man to fight for his footing. Loran watches in horror as the man drags a long dagger across the bird's feathered throat.

"Now you're free," the man says, as the sprake's blood sprays out. A figure that could by all appearances be the man's twin is struggling to kill the other sprake. It has leapt into the air and is flapping at the end of its tether like a kite in a gale. It's shrieking, but not at the peak of its capacity, certainly due to the energy it's expending to escape the flashing dagger below it.

Loran paces backward numbly, entirely bewildered. This is not how it was supposed to go. He forestalls panic by gulping great lungfuls of wind and squeezing his knife's handle in both hands like a solution might squirt out. The two figures, both with thin fabric wrapped around their wrists and ankles, concentrate their efforts on bringing down the second sprake. They must have snuck around the encampment by scaling the cliff wall. The girl, Irdessa, was a distraction. They planned it all out. Heat is rising in Loran's cheeks. He even saw the signs of it. He tried to warn his companions. If only he weren't surrounded by incompetent, idiotic—

"Free the damn birds, you useless clod," Azri orders. Seems she and Shovel are unaware of their cliff-climbing guests. They've had no luck with their arrows either and now Not-Stubbs is returning arrows, giving

Irdessa the opening she needs to rapidly close the distance to the camp. Down the hill at the tree line, a dozen figures wearing animal skins have appeared and are advancing toward the camp at a run. Loran's mouth falls open. *Vim's Vanguard. How did this happen? We're done for!*

It is the grim spark in Irdessa's eyes that sends Loran into action. *Free the sprake at all costs.* That's what he has to do. It's all the hope they have left. He dashes at the two climbers come to kill the birds. They're smaller than him, even if there are two of them. He'll knock them aside. Surely they're tired from all the climbing.

The first one drops the dead sprake and moves into Loran's path. The compact man is still smiling, and now he's spinning his dagger masterfully and spacing his feet out into a bouncing combat stance. Loran needs no further display to know he is outmatched, despite the man's slight build. He'll have to rush the man, knock him back, cut the tether, even if he takes a wound. Even if that wound is fatal ...

Loran's feet betray him and stick to the earth.

The small man laughs. "What's the matter? Don't want to dance?"

The twin is still tugging at the live sprake's tether, jumping and cursing. "A little help, Magpie?" It's a woman's voice.

"Just a moment, Maudee," says the man, not taking his eyes off Loran or the smile off his face. "Listen, orcane boy. Go stand over there. We won't lay a finger on ya. Got no reason to."

Loran frowns and his brows knit together. Everyone talks down to him. Even complete strangers. This man is probably telling the truth. Loran could take the easy way out. Let them go. And tomorrow he'll loathe himself that much more. If there is a change in his rank because of this, it won't be for the better. His knife devises a new strategy and drags him along behind it, toward the nearest orcane. He's sick of being talked down to.

"How's this for an orcane boy?" Three fierce hacks at the taut leather, against all better judgment, and Azri's orcane is free.

The beast, aware abruptly of a freedom it's probably dreamed of its whole sad existence, bucks into life. Loran falls flat, wondering if this grand design of his will end with him flung off the cliff by raging claws. The small man who killed the sprake has lost his smile and apparently all desire to dance. He grabs his twin's arm, heaving her toward the creaking hemp bridge. The orcane ceases its celebratory frenzy long enough to claw madly at the muzzle holding its jaw shut. The muzzle is secured by harnesses behind its head and the effort takes more patience or thumbs than it has to spare. The orcane darts at Loran, leaping over him just before he voids his bowels. It slides to a stop at the edge of the bridge, its whole body racked by muffled barking at the two invaders. Red spittle flies from its sealed lips. It's trapped the two climbers on the bridge, and judging by the terror in their eyes they're not too thrilled about it.

The other two orcanes, witnessing their companion's freedom, go berserk. They spasm and yank so vigorously the ground shakes. Loran stumbles away from them. Either the leather straps, the buried anchor, or their own necks will have to give, and soon.

Loran dashes for the abandoned sprake, giving the orcanes a wide berth. The disgraced bird rests once more on its high wooden perch. It surveys the scene, ruffled and disheveled, with wings outstretched, beak ajar, and an avian scowl in its golden eyes. Loran dives, grabs the thin tether, folds it over and jerks his knife cleanly through it. The sprake is freed but it doesn't fly, either too exhausted or traumatized.

A piercing squeal from Azri's orcane. It flees from the twin climbers on the bridge, thumping past Loran and directly through the campfire. One of them must have hurt it.

"You're free. Fly!" Loran flaps his hands at the sprake. The bird eyes him threateningly, like he's come to finish it off. He throws a glance over his shoulder. Outside the camp, Azri's orcane reaches an unaware Shovel at full speed. Without slowing, it thrusts its massive snout between his knees and throws its head, sending Shovel cartwheeling with a surprised scream. He impacts earth at a sharp angle, his leg bending so that his knee strikes the back of his head. His weapons forgotten, he flops on his back, shrieking through his teeth, gripping his hip, legs twitching.

With a noise like a stray thunderclap, one of the other orcanes breaks a crucial tether, at once freeing itself of the leash and the muzzle. It throws back its head and howls in frenzied delight, its voice trumpeting down the hill, bending higher and higher in pitch until it pinches into a deafening squeal. Loran flattens himself on the earth again, hoping beyond hope the orcane will remember his brushing and humming fondly if it spots him. The beast makes a break toward the approaching Vanguard, its shark-like eyes ripe with bloodlust.

The last orcane tears at the earth and whines, desperately jealous.

"Fly!" Loran screams at the wary sprake. "Go on, go! I thought you damn birds were supposed to be smart."

Arrows thump the ground at Loran's ankles. The Vanguard is trying to kill the alarm sprake. And him. It's all the validation he needs. He lurches forward and grabs the bird by its thick, scaly ankles and tries to wrench it off the perch. In a flash, the thing darts its beak at him, stinging him and sending hot blood over his hand, down his wrist. He flinches. That was no flesh wound. Too bright a pain. Loran squeezes his eyes and tugs. The sprake flaps its wings for balance, cries in protest. Loran's able to suppress the pain, but his hand, now slick with blood, loses its grasp on the bird's foot. He can no longer forestall the knowledge that the godsdamn sprake snipped off his pointer finger.

He falls back a step, squeezing one hand in the other, swearing through his teeth. He'd not noticed that Shovel had been screaming this whole time until the screams become guttural grunts, over and over, each quieter than the last. Loran looks and spots Not-Stubbs systematically stabbing Shovel's belly with a short sword. Raspy growls and shouted voices come from farther down the hill where the Vanguard has engaged Azri's loose orcane. It's all happening too close. He has no time. Loran acts in desperation. His maimed fist *thocks* against the living sprake's head, slinging it backward too far to maintain its balance on the perch. It gives a squawk of disdain and pumps its massive wings, gaining fifteen feet of altitude in a single windy blast. Now its freedom becomes plain.

"Fly, idiot," Loran yells. "And scream."

And the bird does. Its azure wings pump the air with no obvious effort, lifting it quickly to a dizzying height. Arrows chase it with all the luck of children snatching for haddock in a deep river. The bird ascends, reclaiming its elegance and wonder as the sun coats it in a silver bath. Its brilliant, flashing display of metallic feathers is no larger than Loran's outstretched fingernail when it elicits the call.

Nothing could have prepared Loran for the sprake's scream. A noise like a massive sword rending open a mountain made of plate steel. The sound drives Loran to his knees where, even while clamping the sides of his head with his palms, it's so piercing he starts to wonder if the ground itself isn't shuddering in reply.

When he's able to pry his hands off his head and open his eyes, Loran finds the final orcane lying still with dark blood oozing from its ears and nose and mouth. Whether that's due to its own frenzied escape attempts or the sheer volume of the alarm sprake, he hasn't a clue. Azri's muzzled orcane is scampering off like a pudgy wolf, barking and whimpering.

Far to the south, Loran sees the luminous fleck of feathers that is the next alarm sprake relaying and responding to his own. Soon after, the bright echo of its cry resounds over the rolling hills.

It's only a matter of time now. A giddy grin comes over Loran. He'll earn a promotion. He heaves in elated breaths, even while cutting fabric to stem the blood flowing from his sheared finger. He's done it. Now he needs to survive until help arrives. For all he knows, a battalion is camped out of sight in the woods, awaiting exactly the sprake call he sent up. Loran flees down the hill, away from the bridge, hopefully out of sight of the vicious Vanguard.

Lieutenant Azri has ditched her bow and drawn her longsword, with which she is considerably more skillful. She is engaged with a tall thin outlaw woman with bulbous eyes and a bladed polearm. Several of the other outlaws have surrounded the loosed orcane, including a frighteningly ugly man with a pickaxe. Even as Loran watches, the man rushes the beast, shouting insults all the while. The orcane bats him away, sending him rolling, and several spears and arrows find purchase in its heaving flank, bringing it down. Nearer, Irdessa runs past Azri's back, swinging her dagger at the lieutenant's ankle as she passes. Loran doesn't see the wound, but it must have hurt because the lieutenant screams, faltering. The tall Vanguard woman's polearm flashes out as if they planned it. Lieutenant Azri's head topples away and blood fountains as her body drops.

The Undying has reached the swaying bridge and turns to call down to her people. The fur-draped outlaws follow her. Loran gets a rough count of them and almost laughs. A mere two dozen strong? That's considerably less than the rumors tell of the formidable Vanguard. Some move quite slow, as if they aren't fit for combat at all. The big ugly man has regained his feet. He brings up the rear, running as if one of his legs has broken bones in it.

The whole Vanguard is oblivious to Loran, which suits him fine. Except he needs to stall Irdessa or this will all be for nothing.

"Hey, Undying," he calls at her. Her eyes flick over him, pausing long enough to deduce that he's unworthy of even a response. Her people file onto the bridge and she ushers them.

Black birds erupt screeching from the forest to the left of where the outlaws felled the orcane, directly in front of Loran. The earth rumbles. Mounted orcanes rush from under the limbs in a flurry of branches and leaves. Six of them, running at a murderous pace. At their lead is a figure in a captain's helmet. He doesn't have Captain Rale's blond beard, or Captain Alcus' jiggling girth, or the markings of any captain stationed nearby. This man's helmet is blackened with soot. His cape and the cloth of his shoulder appear to have been ravaged by flames. He stands in his stirrups, bent forward intently, riding out his orcane's mad pace with the expertise of years of practice and the fury of some unforgivable personal vendetta. His face is made awful by rage. Loran moves himself into their path and leaps up and down, waving his arms. He can leave no questions as to who sounded the alarm, lest some corpse steal his glory.

"Here," he cries. "It's Irdessa, I have her here!"

The patrol did not need his announcement, but Loran is sure now that they've all witnessed him. Behind, Irdessa's commands pierce the wind. Most of her people are either spanning out over the bridge, which creaks and squeals under their weight, or waiting their turn, casting anxious looks back at their pursuers. Irdessa herself appears to be waiting to be the last to mount the bridge. How tragically noble. That hefty, limping barbarian is slowing with every lurching step. If she's determined to wait on him, the reinforcements have a chance.

"Hey, Undying," Loran yells again. This time she gives him her attention, perhaps only because awaiting the struggling brute leaves her with a moment to do it. "Remember my face," he says, elated to near breathlessness. "I'll be the one looking down from Keswal's front row while you die in the arena." She expresses no emotion. He wasn't cruel enough. "Just like Torvald," he adds.

The reaction she gives him is not what he predicted. Even at this distance, he sees her lips draw tight and her brow wrinkle. He hurt her.

She's ... just a girl. Maybe no older than Loran. It renders him speechless.

"Check your south, dipshit." The shout comes from the ugly one staggering ever closer to the bridge. His display of teeth makes him even more ghastly.

Loran turns back to his reinforcements and finds the wall of trampling orcanes closer than he expected. He gives them a wave to ensure they see him. This closer vantage of the captain's face knocks the wind out of him. The man's skin is a shiny, crisp mask, taut and disfigured. His leer appears less of his choosing, more a result of the flesh not being sufficient to seal around his teeth. The orcanes, mad with the chase, stay their course despite Loran standing in it. It's as if they haven't noticed him, which is highly unlikely.

"Hey," Loran yells with a wave. His stump of a finger is starting to throb. The captain spots him. Or at least, one of his eyes does. The other eye has no pupil. The exposed eyeball is a wrinkled milky sphere, set deep in a grey fissure lacking any distinguishing features or hair a man's face should have.

"Hey," Loran murmurs. It's too late to get clear of them. The orcanes are bearing down too fast. They're so close he can hear them huffing for air. The damn things probably wouldn't slow down if they could. In the air above soars his alarm sprake, probably making its way home to the aviary at Promontory for a nice meal. Loran's stomach grumbles.

The moment stretches into a facade of infinity, leaving Loran to wonder which of his choices specifically landed him here. Punching the sprake? Cutting its tether? Volunteering in Azri's patrol? Enlisting? Or maybe—

47
Something Wrong With Him

FOHRVYLDA
The Northern Seaboard

Kraus watches the skinny soldier fall under the charging orcanes, giving all the resistance of a corn stalk.

"Dumb shit," he roars in laughter.

Ahead, Irdessa does not mirror his amusement. "Kraus, hurry!"

He tries. Feels a lot like wading through gravy except it hurts. Those reinforcements came out of nowhere.

"Go," he pants at her, squeezing his knee to make the thing stop antagonizing him for a damn moment. He wants to throw down the pickaxe. If Irdessa thinks there's any sense in linking her death to his, she's as stupid as she is stubborn. He spits out a swear and tries to push his legs to life again, using the pickaxe to row the earth. A godsdamned drink would be more than welcome right now.

"Not without you." She runs for him, stowing away a knife that could barely threaten a cooked potato.

She is upon him, yanking his arm, nearly making him break down laughing. How many times has she yanked his arm or he hers?

He tries to push her off. She must've anticipated it because her shoulder disappears and his hand slips past. She hauls him by his own momentum. His feet are just able to kick into motion to keep him from flopping down on his face. Her fingers bite his triceps like wolf teeth, not an entirely unwelcome sensation. He nearly feels guilty enjoying it.

"Go on," he says. "I've made my peace."

"Liar," she grunts. "You're as peaceful as an orcane."

He snorts. It ain't false.

The bridge is right in front of them, a one hundred-yard-long rope conglomeration wide enough for two to walk abreast, draped over a nauseating expanse.

"Looks like your captain friend found us," Irdessa notes.

"Saw that. Fuck him. Where's Bravensi?"

Irdessa expels a breath in what might be a laugh. "She's waiting for you. Naked. Come on."

Kraus cackles. "Now who's the fucking liar?"

And yet the thought of it, despite being an empty fantasy, invigorates Kraus like liquor down his pipes. He plows forward, unwedging Irdessa from his armpit at last and giving her a shove. "Cross the damn bridge, Dess."

She snatches the hemp rope and aims an arched eyebrow at him.

"I'm right behind you. Go."

She does. And true to his word, he follows. Except, one boot on the sun-bleached plank and his resolve turns to bile in his throat. The whole shitting thing is no more than neatly squared lumber held together by braided hemp. The fighters on the far side appear no larger than maggots, well outside spear range or even arrow. How the hell'd this bridge even come to be? Hemp fucking ropes and the Vanguard fighters sprint over it like it's a highway. A million miles below, the Faithless Sea gnashes her teeth on iron-colored stone. Kraus squeezes the rope to his left, but his palms are slick with cold sweat. He stretches out his arm, but the bridge is too wide to reach both sides at once. He takes another step and the contraption jounces beneath him, angling to eject him. He throws his arm over the rope and squeezes his eyes shut. Seems he's lobbed his pickaxe into the wind.

"Kraus!"

Irdessa has stopped before him, not a third of the way over the bridge, which drifts in the sea's wind like the tail of a kite. The rest of the Vanguard is across and gathered around the far anchor poles. They seem to be writhing, yelling, gesturing for him to hurry and die so they can have Irdessa. Their voices are lost in the wind. If it weren't for her, they'd have probably cut down the bridge. In fact, that might be what they're working on right now.

Irdessa looks so small, clinging to the opposite railing, pulling herself hand over hand toward him. Kraus grits his teeth. She's bound and fucking determined to die with him. And here he stands, gripped by a fear of open air. Kraus slaps his cheek roughly. *Swallow your fear. It's just the Faithless Sea. The worst it can do is not kill you.*

He proceeds toward Irdessa as mad barking erupts behind him. Can't look yet. If the soldiers have bows, Irdessa is in range.

"Go, Irdessa, you stubborn ass!" he yells, dragging himself forward as quickly as his feet will scrape over the old wooden planks.

She's no longer approaching, but the look on her face is far from relieved. "Kraus, *hurry.*"

"Yeah, you keep saying that."

He tries to hurry, but he can't. He's not like those skinny scamperers Maudee and Magpie, who could probably cut cartwheels over the hemp hand ropes. He's the stalwart oaf with a cracked kneecap and a healthy thirst. Can't help but throw a look over his shoulder. All six orcanes have halted panting between the anchor poles not twenty yards behind him. They're within a spear-throw's distance and Kraus will be godsdamned if they don't all have spears. The bridge is wide enough for the orcanes to cross, if only single file. Maybe the reason they haven't is because he's there. Nothing else is stopping the fucking barksharks from running across, crashing into the fighters on the far tower and throwing them to their death. Kraus isn't sure what's to keep them from cutting the bridge. If they did it in this moment, it would be the end of him and Irdessa. How badly does Vretos want Irdessa back?

Kraus shimmies awkwardly, gaining distance all too slowly. The farther the bridge gets from its hold on land, the more it heaves in the murderous wind. He's wearing his newly acquired chainmail, and it's probably all that saved him from that most recent nip from the orcane. But if he's tossed off this bridge into the ocean the heavy gear will only protect him from breathing. The puncture wound in his forearm throbs from squeezing the rope. He is exhausted of the ache in his knee. It's not getting better. His shoulder hurts, as does his bicep, and his nose, and his guts. He's getting nowhere.

"Halt right there!" Captain Jeret's high scream rides over the gale. Kraus recognizes the voice at once, even if it sounds like the man's gnawing a pork rib.

Kraus almost ignores the captain. But if he tries to run, they'll fill his back with steel and orcanes will catch the Vanguard before they can escape. Then again, if he halts, so does Irdessa, and then they both probably die.

Kraus' eyebrows and lips scrunch inward. Making hard decisions has never been a strength of his. Seems he's most likely to choose wrong. But when the whole damn world is wrong, the wrong choice is all there is. He ain't about to get killed running. Definitely not by that captain.

He yells at Irdessa. "You already saved me enough, girl. Now save yourself. Save the Vanguard."

She looks distraught. The Vanguard is calling to her—not to Kraus, and so he doesn't spare them a glance. He grins at Irdessa with as much calm as he can inject. "Go, Dess. You aren't taking this away from me."

Irdessa's hair whips in the wind. Her lip juts forward. An arrow thuds in a plank at her feet. Another arcs past her into the open sky. She backs away, her face a conflicted mask.

Kraus nods at her and turns to examine the captain.

"By the gods," Kraus marvels. The captain's ruined face ... Kraus' masterpiece. It is a work of art. "Looks like a hungry scrotum got at your face."

Irdessa gives a yelp that spins Kraus' head on its shoulders. Bravensi has grabbed her up and is hauling her toward the Tower, despite her protests. *Good.* The Vanguard will destroy the bridge. Then his pain will be over. If sprakes can tuck their wings and still control their plummet, then maybe he can too. His last heroic act will be a passionate kiss with a seaside rock. He'll picture Bravensi's face on it.

Kraus turns back to the soldiers, but not in time to see the spear coming. Doesn't hear it shear the wind on its way to him. He sees it land though, right in his thigh, like a hearty slap. Kraus' face breaks into cold sweat. His vision narrows on the spearhead, embedded in pale flesh that peeks through newly rent trousers. There's no blood. Was he already out of blood?

"You were saying?" The captain stands in his saddle empty-handed. It was his spear. He chuckles with his men, who are smiling, laughing. *That's what the damn rapist deserves*, they're probably saying. And it's true. Three soldiers eagerly offer the captain their own spear.

The bridge sneaks up from behind and crashes into Kraus. Seems he's taken a seat. And that motion apparently jogged his flesh's memory because now the wound pulses red. By some unfortunate reflex, Kraus snatches the spear's handle. White searing pain shrieks through his leg, tickling his bones until his toenails dig into the insides of his boots, making his teeth grind and his guts shudder. Clever spear to choose his leg. Wouldn't have bitten so deep where his mail is.

"Oh gods." The moan escapes him. His vision succumbs to white haze, bereft of sky or sea or bridge. The wind's scream becomes a sigh. Kraus wants to lie back, revel in this sweet dish. He could push the spear, see if it's stuck. Thump the haft. Or just let the wind continue shivering it. Pain has crawled throughout him. His leg feels utterly flayed. He gulps down a breath of wind, eager to know how much more this spear can give him.

Pain'll fix everything.

Kraus can't remember who told him that. He pushes the spear's haft with both hands. A sensation of lightning bores into his femur and stops his breath. The white haze glazes over, as if clouds are tightening in the sky. Before his eyes can slide shut, a thought catches on his fragmenting consciousness. Nothing's to stop the captain and his men from stamping over him and having at the Vanguard. Nothing except, perhaps, the captain's desire for long, drawn-out vengeance. And for that to happen, Kraus has to stay alive.

He blinks his eyes. Heaves air in through his teeth and swings out an arm until it finds the rope railing at his side. Not done yet. *Soon enough.* For now, swallow it. He hauls himself up to a sitting position without allowing his leg to bend. His eyes regain their sight slowly. The hemp rope creaks beside him, smelling of sea salt and neglect.

"You want another one, rapist?" The captain's tone suggests that under that burnt mask, he's still smiling. But his charred lips make it sound like "rafist," which Kraus finds funnier than is appropriate in the moment. He chuckles, while trying to wiggle the first spear loose. His hands quickly slicken. His trousers are soaked black. Maybe he should leave the spear alone. The captain has another spear in his hand. The sight of it simultaneously fills Kraus with dread and thrills him. That first one is surely doing irreversible damage.

"Yeah, cunt," Kraus calls, "this one's stuck. Bring me that one." The words are hard to pronounce. Almost like he's drunk. A shiver runs through him. He's gonna bleed out. Finally. So, why not wrench the spear loose and have some fun with it?

The captain is not getting off his orcane. Spineless shit. He's not throwing the spear either. He's addressing one of his soldiers and his command carries to Kraus. "Ride out there and collect that *rafist*."

An orcane noses ahead of the others. Kraus pries the spear out of his leg with a gargling roar. A fresh pulse of blood finishes the job of staining his pants leg.

The orcane mounts the bridge. Kraus pulls himself to his feet, testing his unbending leg. However much this height dislodges his bowels, it looks worse for the orcane and the soldier atop it, sitting high above the hemp rails. The beast's shivering vibrates the entire bridge. That the soldier is able to make an orcane trod out onto such a contraption is a testament to the beast's discipline. Or at least the persuasiveness of its mouthpiece.

It places its paws slowly, each step forcing the braided cables to creak and clang like pebbles impacting a sheet of tin. The orcane whines with every exhale, the sound wavering between a low hum and a thin, high squeal. The whites of the soldier's eyes are round within the shadow of his helmet. He grips the orcane's reins so hard his knuckles glow. His spear seems to serve only as an impediment to his hold on the reins.

Kraus bounces his new spear on his palm, finding where the weight is centered. His blood flicks off the blade in droplets, catching the sun like rubies. He's never been much of a shot with an arrow or spear. But he's always had a gift at hurting people. He smiles in introspection. Must be something wrong with him. People aren't supposed to hurt each other so easily.

The spear thuds into the soldier's right breast, below his stitched leather pauldron. He spasms, jerking his shoulder up reflexively. This drives the orcane's bit so hard into its jaw that its head bends perpendicular to the bridge. The beast rears, yipping in pain and kicking, its splayed claws like sharpened bits of coal raking the wind. The bridge bobs, sending out a wave that scoops Kraus' feet out from under him. The roped planks snap taut beneath the orcane, sending one of its hindlegs scampering off the bridge's edge. It regains its footing violently, launching the soldier sideways over the hemp framework. The soldier topples so slowly he seems almost frozen in a handstand, watching the rope that could save him as it passes, the rope he does not release his reins to grab.

His mailed torso claps against the outside of the bridge, sending lines of dust off the hand rope in either direction. The orcane's snout bunches up against the woven supports as its soldier dangles from the far side, kicking his legs above the yawning drop.

Kraus laughs from the pit of his stomach, even as the bridge bucks yet again. It disappears beneath him, giving his stomach time to flip, then the planks ram the bottom of his boots, bending his knees into his chest. He flounders onto the wood, wrapping both arms around the nearest rope. The orcane squeals, wrenches against the handrail, jostles that poor soldier, and does a good job of making the whole bridge writhe.

"Kill hi*ng*," commands the captain.

There's a thump, and another. The hanging soldier jerks and bounces as arrows invade his ribs, giving the spear some company. Without uttering a complaint, he releases the reins and is gone. A gift to the wind, and eventually the sea.

The orcane recoils off the handrail, flusters about, throwing its snout and working its mouth in great licking chomps as if it's got feathers stuck between its teeth. It gives a blasting sneeze. The bridge rocks beneath it, but the orcane's stance is wide and its feet shift to compensate. Without the soldier sitting on it, it seems to have found its legs and some amount of confidence.

Kraus pulls himself up in time for the orcane to lock eyes on him. Two pinpoint voids, one in the shadow, the other reflecting the sun's light, unite on Kraus. A guttural growl rattles out over gleaming red teeth. Looks like that bit in its mouth did a damn number. Kraus balls his fists. "Come on, you slippery ass licker."

Agile footsteps sound from behind him, clicking over the planks, sending shivers up his leg. Hands dart under his armpits, threading a rope around his chest once, then again. And then, against all odds, the heavy, dizzying scent of Bravensi crashes into him. His guts soar. *It can't be.* Her face appears beside him. *It is.* His inhale catches her smell in his lungs and he holds her there. "If this is my very last breath," he squeaks, "It's worth it."

"Shut up."

The orcane plods forward, undeterred, blood from the corners of its mouth soaking into its dingy white chin and drawing wavering lines to the planks. Kraus is trying to focus on his fists instead of everything he should say, everything he shouldn't. The bridge gives a shudder beneath him, lowering by several inches. A splintering crack from the Tower echoes off the mainland cliff walls. Bravensi's arm fishes around him once more, pulling the rope tighter, and this time her hair tickles his neck, giving him chills.

"What have I done to deserve this?" Kraus sighs.

"This isn't about you," she says flatly. "They're going to cut the bridge. Be ready."

There's a whistling, whipping sound. The left handrail slackens, along with all the support lines attached to it. Vanguard must have sawed through it. The orcane is a single leap away when it tenses, sprawling into a low stance, its growl snuffing out.

The entire bridge drops away, rotating to its side. Kraus' guts and lungs and bowels stuff into his ribcage as he, Bravensi, and the orcane plummet into the wind.

Kraus shrieks. Bravensi clambers over his shoulder like a spider over its prey and throws her arms around his neck. Her face is so close he can see how chapped her thin lips are, the tiny blue veins on her pale nostrils, the sheen of her enormous eyes. She's so close he could kiss her. Oekner is nowhere to be seen.

Wind is rushing past, cementing his dry lips onto his exposed grin. Kraus curses himself in the midst of his euphoria. Even if he'd ever had the stones to fantasize about Bravensi, he'd never have had the imagination to dream of this. If he had, maybe he'd have planned something to say.

Kraus clears his throat and yells over the wind. "To what do I owe this—*hurrrrggghh!*"

The thick rope beneath his armpits snaps taut, crushing his ribs and extending his spine, squeezing flat his lungs and making his lips flap in exhaust. The orcane plunges out of sight, and the mainland cliff wall before him ceases rushing upward, instead now soaring away.

"That's better," Bravensi says. The wind narrows her eyes and throws every loose lock out behind her head like streaks of black lightning. Her long legs are tight around his hips. And although her face is a glacier there is a curl on the edge of her lips. "How'd you know the barkshark had a slippery ass?"

Kraus rasps in a painful breath in lieu of a laugh. Doesn't help his ribs that she was hanging on him when the rope caught. But he'd have had it no other way. *You're perfect*, he wants to tell her.

"Why do you always do it?" The brass of her voice pierces his eardrum.

"Do what?"

"Get your ass kicked."

Kraus frowns. "Did you not see the other guy?" He'd point down if she could see his hands—if his fingers weren't thick red sausages, plump with blood.

Above, the bridge breaks loose of its Tower side, freed by Vanguard blades, and drifts slowly, splaying out as if it's underwater. Crowded on the mainland side, distant now, are the soldiers with their gleaming helmets. Probably shooting arrows or throwing spears or kicking dirt or crying. *Fuck 'em.*

Kraus eases his hands up Bravensi's back and clasps his arms, inhaling her scent and ignoring his wounds. She flinches, solidifying into a trunk of driftwood. "Enjoy it while you can," she says through gritted teeth.

"As you command." The smile on his face is chiseled in cedar. But this moment, like all, must end. Nothing lasts forever. "How far off's the Tower wall?"

"Funny you should ask," Bravensi answers even as she turns sideways and tenses against him. Her hip presses firmly into his groin, likely making it impossible for her to ignore his current state of attentiveness. "I don't know which of us will enjoy this more."

"Oh, easily me," he tells her. "But I can make it up to—"

48
Citizens of Fohrvylda

FOHRVYLDA
The Towers

Vyker shifts his foot along the inches-wide path until the toe of his boot contacts the heel of the other. Here he pauses, adjusts his grip on the gurney's rope handle to relieve his aching knuckles, and gives his sweaty hair a shake, enough so that some of the droplets fly off but not so much that he loses his balance and follows the sweat. To his right, the vertical rock face, along which he has dragged his shoulder for so long his shoulder is scraped raw. To his left is nothing— yawning, hungry air. There are more Towers out there, some paled by distance, some so close that an idiot might think he has a chance at jumping to one. None are close enough to do him any good, so Vyker keeps his eyes on his feet. He slides his foremost boot forward. Ten inches, always. Eleven, if he's feeling—

"You alright up there Vyker?" says Harpold.

The outburst rattles him, snapping him out of his focus. Wind screams from below, lifting his shirt tail and hair. His feet tremble, which makes his shoulders reflexively seize, which makes him rebound faintly off the cliff wall out toward the expanse. And then, for a single infinite moment, he's locked teetering at the gurney's mercy, feet toe-to-heel in a uselessly unstable line, breath leaping in his throat. Any movement could shatter his balance.

A hand on his chest, flattening him to the cliff wall. All he can do is squeeze his eyes and try to stop hyperventilating. Harpold was behind him. Surely it was his hand. For a moment Vyker stands with eyes closed, breathing slowly so his heart doesn't rupture.

"Satuavo's winged balls," he exclaims at last. "You scared me."

"Sorry," Harpold says. Sounds like he's smiling. "You don't like heights, do you?"

Vyker likes Harpold well enough. Or he wants to. But then Harpold says some shit like that. "What exactly is there for any person to like about heights?"

"Promontory can't reach us here."

"I bet their sprakes can."

"Now that would be a fix." Harpold's quiet a moment, then he laughs. "Shit. They'd have their way with us, wouldn't they?" As if he's only now considering it.

Vyker's been considering it since Irdessa first announced they'd be traversing the Towers. And now he pictures it as if it's happening, massive birds swooping in, nipping or clawing or maybe blasting the party with wind until everyone's flying. He's never known much about these unlikely earthen columns. As a child he once travelled far enough north to view the windswept pillars at a distance. They looked impossible. They don't seem any more possible with him perched on the side of one. Back then he'd heard wild sprakes lived all over them, as did a tribe of people who may or may not be hostile toward Fohrvyldans. *Catchers* is what they're called. *Fallers* seems more likely. Vyker, whose experience of the Towers is limited to a mere handful of days, can't imagine how anyone could survive out here. Maybe they give birth to larger litters to compensate for those they inevitably lose to fatal topples. It's said their archers' arrows are huge enough to sink Admiral Garr's warships. What if they're above the Vanguard right now, looking down with harpoon-sized arrows drawn? Vyker's scalp itches. His heart is pounding again, harder than before. "Must you?" he hisses at Harpold.

"Sorry," Harpold says. He's still smiling. "We're almost through this. One step at a time."

With a deep breath, Vyker gets his pulse under control again. He wants to ask, *As opposed to what? Hop like a rabbit?* But he needs to focus, not whine.

Kraus the Rapist lies on the gurney. He's unconscious, or dead, and wrapped snugly to a narrow framework which hangs between a few ropes, held aloft by a total of four unlucky clods. At this moment, that includes Harpold and himself. Kraus saved his life before while they fought dreadhops. Then he placed himself between those orcanes and the Vanguard, buying enough time for the bridge to be cut. This man is a new addition to the Vanguard, but Vyker can see his worth. Any fighter should be able to. He fears nothing, will fight anyone or anything. But there's something else about him holding Vyker's fascination. It's the face he made when Vyker asked him about Dhovoi's death. He knows something he has yet to say.

Vyker anticipated eventually feeling closure about his brother's death. After all, he dismantled the wall to make pits for soldier execution. That was Vim's deathblow. So ... he got what was coming to him, right? The farther they get from the razed Vim, the freer the scorn flows. People spit when Dhovoi's name is brought up, no longer masking their disdain even in front of Vyker. A greying woman in a vest and sword belt said, *Vim died when Andelsior was arrested. But it stood, like a dead tree, as if it had some brighter future than an inevitable plummet.* Vyker has had to defend his brother in the past, sometimes with words, sometimes with fists, sometimes with a spear. All this open scorn is giving him the desire to defend his brother in death. It's bringing the opposite of closure.

Vyker's foot is in motion again. Then his other. It's impossible to gauge progress out here. The cliff wall never changes. His view of the Towers doesn't change. Not in value anyway. This knife-narrow ledge will inevitably lead to yet another hemp bridge. If all goes as it has these past days, the next suspended path will be even thinner and flimsier than the last. And it'll lead to an even more treacherous trail where they'll stuff their asses in nooks for some meager shuteye. By that point Vyker will have passed gurney-duty on to someone else—assuming Kraus isn't dead. Vyker spares him a look. Judging by his face, he's not waking up anytime soon, if ever. His skin is an arid grey canvas, with sunken eyes and black ravines held closed by zigzagging, blood-clotted stitching. He might already be dead. He's been unconscious since they dredged him and Bravensi up after cutting the bridge. He was out when she sewed him back together, again. That was two days ago. Or ... three days? By the gods, surely not four. How long until they return to flat ground? Will they ever? Was going this direction smart? When Irdessa told the Adhart survivors the Vanguard would be leaving the mainland via the Towers, Vyker assumed it was a ploy, a diversion, much like when she'd declared to the dissenters they'd head east. But here they are.

Thinking of Adhart recalls the ambush they performed on that Promontory patrol. It was nearly flawless. Then Irdessa had made the decision to let Old Fent die. Poor Fent. Vyker could have killed that orcane, and probably silently. It was half dead. He certainly would have been quicker and quieter than Sura. Thinking of her hurts his chest. He can convince himself the reason Irdessa stopped him was to keep noise low and protect the Vanguard. Because why else? Vyker grits his teeth. Since the event, he's been avoiding that inquiry. He can almost hear what his brother would say. *Because she learned from Torvald, and he would have gladly let the old die so the party can move faster.*

Vyker shakes away the thoughts, scoots his foot forward. A chunk of the ledge dislodges from under his boot and tumbles away. His guts run circles inside him at the sight of it plummeting frictionless, rolling through nothing.

"Fucking hell," he groans. "It could not get worse."

A sharp crack of thunder abruptly draws Vyker's attention to the wall of black storm clouds creeping across the ocean from the west.

"Hey." The gravelly voice is Kraus, who's opened his eyes. "What's there to drink around here?" He jerks and the gurney wiggles.

Behind Vyker, Harpold scoffs. "You had to say that."

~

Irdessa stalks through a bright green forest. It's the first regular, solid footing the Vanguard's seen since leaving the mainland, several days ago. Not even the alcoves and crevices they've rested within were level. Flat ground arrived not a moment too soon. Rain is pounding down, drumming against the wide leaves of the understory and the top of Irdessa's scalp. Rich black dirt has spattered halfway up her legs, covering her boots. This is not so chilly a rain as she's used to in Fohrvylda, probably due to the vine-laden trees blocking all the wind, or perhaps the lower altitude. When viewing the Towers before, Irdessa always expected the green stubble spattered over their tops to be little more than sparse shrubbery and moss. She would never have believed it was entire lush forests covering mountainous peaks.

The scouts claim that the Vanguard is alone. No spies, no sprakes, no orcanes. Whatever mountain cats, constrictors, and raptors stalked them hang lifeless and gutted, stripped of fur and feathers, skins and scales, on shoulder-mounted racks between grinning fighters. Despite dumping rain, spirits are as high as they've been since before Vim was assaulted. Gone entirely is the shortage of water and meat. A fire to cook that meat, on the other hand ...

Irdessa appreciates the scouts' reassurances, for the sake of her people. But she maintains tense vigilance. This forest is like none she's ever seen. Nothing here bears needles or cones. Everything wears leaves. They sprout from tree trunks, grey vines, the earth itself. They stick to her legs and arms and hair. Anything could be hiding within striking distance and she'd never know it in time. The squeaks and chirps and calls, most barely discernible from the rain, tell her they're surrounded by living creatures, threat or no. If this were Fohrvylda, beggars would be climbing the trees to eat whatever's making all that noise.

Some of the Vanguard insisted this particular Tower was Redemier itself, because of its immensity and the striking difference in the plant life. Irdessa knows better. She, like her father Andelsior and Torvald, was educated by Torah, whose maps showed that Redemier is nearly fifty miles from the mainland, and is significantly lower in altitude. Though Vanguard has struggled out here for days, there's no way they've covered that much distance. This Tower juts up from the ocean like all the others they've crossed thus far, and is pinned around its rim with rope bridges. Redemier, supposedly, is ringed in sand.

Farther down the line, somewhere behind Irdessa, a song has broken out, sung by voices gruff and shrill. It's an old Vanguard song that recounts and surely embellishes the tale of a ferocious, exotic sword fighter, wanted by Promontory for violent crimes. He carried a curved blade in each hand and laid low a dozen fighters before a thief was able to get in close enough to navigate his ribs with her rusty knife. Before Irdessa realizes it, she's joined in, shouting the words upward in defiance of the muttering rain. The song's tragedy, of course, is how fine a Vanguard fighter the bladesman would have been had he not attracted the attention he did. As most Vanguard songs go, this one ends with profuse drinking at the Cornerstone. Perhaps for the first time Irdessa feels the pain of the stronghold's death as if it were one of her own people. A good thing about rain is that an observer can't differentiate it from tears on your cheeks.

She is proud of her people. They are as organized under her command as they were with Andelsior before her, never mind Dhovoi. They make steady progress despite their losses, their hunger, their wounds. Then again, the brunt of this party's wounds are borne by a single individual.

Now and again Kraus is conscious, for better or worse, and swears he can walk. She's not letting him. Not letting him drink either. Nothing besides water and tea, much to his profanity-laced disapproval. Luckily for all in earshot, he can only complain in short bursts. He tires himself out quickly, struggling at his bonds, and falls asleep again, at which point his bonds are reinforced. The fighters have taken to calling him the ogre. Not to his face. Not while he's conscious anyway. The duty of hauling him has cycled throughout every able member of the Vanguard, giving each person equal chance to hate him, and maybe Irdessa. That's a price she is willing to pay. She knows what Kraus contributed. Without him, there'd be no Vanguard.

The rain ends and the searing sun knifes through rusty clouds to illuminate a watery haze hanging in the air between the trunks and the leaves and the vines and the sopping fighters. The animal calls are naked and edged and threatening to drive Irdessa crazy. Her heels burn where they've rubbed raw against her boots. The songs sung behind her are less melodic now, more griping, if they're songs at all. It's time for another rest. One that, for some reason, Irdessa has been dreading. She passes the word along to the scouts.

The party's path soon brings them to the edge of a hidden pond of crystal water stretching some thirty yards across and lined with massive chunks of smooth-edged granite.

Several people have already stopped at the pond's edge and are prying off their boots to dump out water. They settle themselves and inspect and oil their blades. They unstrap their layers of leather and mail, stripping down to undergarments or less with no regard for modesty. It takes a collective effort, but a meager fire is brought sputtering to life as daylight wanes. Flasks of liquor and wine are produced and passed around. Kraus sleeps through it all, a fact which perhaps contributes to the merriment.

Irdessa, finally freed of her boots and every other bit of stifling leather, accepts a bottle and has a deep draw from it, or pretends to, for the sake of those watching. For her, this newfound comfort goes only neck high. There are quandaries demanding resolution, and if she doesn't resolve them they'll continue to pile up.

The Vanguard needs a destination, and the Towers are not it. They need to know for sure whether Promontory is following them, or worse, somehow anticipating them. Despite that they severed a large bridge connecting Fohrvylda to the Towers, there could be other paths leading from the mainland to this very lake. In fact, Irdessa would be surprised if that weren't the case.

Maudee and Magpie have seen none of the falconer's sprakes. That should be a relief but Irdessa only registers suspicion. So far, all that suggests Promontory has not given up on them entirely are the orcane patrols circling distantly in the waters around the Towers' feet. Where are the sprakes? Are Pappu's birds crafty enough to blend with the native sprakes nesting on the vertical cliff walls? If so, have they already spied the fighters and returned to the mainland to somehow report the Vanguard's position? Irdessa fights the urge to leap to her feet, to strap her sodden clothes back on and demand that the Vanguard move on. But to where? Redemier? She'd assumed that was their destination, but knows nothing of that island. No one does. It's full of monsters, so they say. Does that mean soldiers won't follow her there?

Her people need rest. They deserve it, whether or not Irdessa can have any. Let them celebrate their victories, however empty. What is strife worth if its only reward is more of the same?

They left Captain Jeret alive and pissed off. How far will he go to get revenge? Will he bring orcanes onto the Towers? And if not, what about soldiers? This foliage makes for excellent cover. Maudee and Magpie are perceptive, but only human. And right now they're nowhere to be seen.

That mining town said Vretos is offering riches for Irdessa's capture. Will anything stop Marshal Zander from charging over the Towers with an entire army while Admiral Garr's navy awaits their plummeting bodies in the ocean below? Vretos will invent threats against his court that inspire even the most unimaginable strategies. He does not age. Not like normal men. He could hold a grudge for generations. In fact, they say it's a grudge that makes him immortal. If that's true, there is no outlasting him. Irdessa could hide out here on these sea-stacks for ten years, or a hundred, only to then be crushed by an enemy just as spry and pissed off as he is in this moment. The thought of it exhausts her more than miles of hiking already have.

Every question her mind demands returns the same conclusion. If Zander dies, a new marshal will replace him. Same for the admiral and the beastmaster. As long as Vretos lives, there will be no peace for her or the Vanguard. The Heathen Tide is supposed to sail soon. Maybe it will. Maybe Vretos will charge across the Faithless Sea and never come back. Maybe he'll die there, killed by the songs of monks or drowned by the sea or stabbed in the back by one of his own court. Even as she considers it, the image of Vretos flipping a uergata onto its back flashes before her eyes. Her head is shaking in answer to a question she did not ask. He will not die on his own.

She sits up, angered by her restless mind. Is this what it's like to be Torvald? Her anger flares. *I didn't ask for this, you son of a bitch. No wonder you killed yourself.* But he's not here for her to punch. And he's never coming back. Wherever he is, is he happy?

Tears sting her eyes. The pain of his absence is no longer sharp as a dagger's tip, but dull and mottled, like a clod of frozen mud stuffed in her ribcage crowding her lungs and heart. The pain makes no sense, and she is realizing that it never will. Of course she misses Torvald, even if she's losing the memory of his voice, his face. Of course she loved him. But ... was it the same way he loved her? She never imagined being intimate with him, or anyone. In the years of her life that other girls might seek a trade or hook a man to make their own daughters, Irdessa learned how to spot weakness, exploit it, hold her weapon aloft while her enemy bled to death under her boot. The only intimacy she had time for was the sort only one party survived. She's never considered that a bad thing. But she's so alone. A little company would go a long way. A little guidance.

Daylight is long dead. The fire rages and the scent of cooking meat fills the air. Scanning her people, Irdessa meets eyes with Vyker, who looks away at once. He's surely not happy about what happened to Old Fent, and Irdessa doesn't blame him. She's not either. To her chagrin, Kraus has somehow freed himself from his gurney and is stalking the encampment looking for liquor with all the poise of a three-legged dog. As yet, it seems the Vanguard is obeying Irdessa's command that he is given nothing stronger than a cup of wine, but preferably water. He responds to their generosity with spittle-coated swearing. Irdessa's anxiety comes to a boil. Kraus' wandering presence stokes her anger like straw on a fire. Can't he control his damn thirst long enough to stop bleeding? Can *she* control nothing?

Irdessa is cycling through choice insults to yell at him when she notices Magpie. The small, hooded man is weaving toward her with obvious purpose through the half-dressed, half-inebriated fighters. His jaw is clenched. Irdessa's pulse spikes. Is this it? Are they surrounded by Promontory? Is this pond the final stand for Vim's Vanguard? If so, she regrets not having a deeper pull from that liquor bottle.

Magpie walks past Irdessa, gesturing that she follows. Once outside the range of anyone who might overhear, he offers her a flask with one hand and gestures discreetly with the other, a quick swipe of his palm, flat, parallel the ground. *Be still.*

"There are people watching us from the forest. Five total, in two groups. They're not soldiers."

Irdessa blinks several times, fights the urge to look around or let her surprise show. She has a drink. "Sent by Promontory?"

Magpie shakes his head. "I don't think so. They look too familiar with the land. And too curious, like they're surprised to see us. Promontory would only venture this far to locate us or to kill us. Five men aren't enough for the second option. And if their scouts are meant to watch us so their companions can report back to the mainland, any Promontory soldier should know that by now we've spotted them and could've already killed them if we wanted to."

"Then who are they?"

"Maudee and I think they're from the north, deeper in the Towers."

"Catchers," Irdessa speculates. "Where is Maudee?"

"Observing them. They haven't seen her. If we're lucky, they don't know we're on to them."

"Are they armed?"

"Not by any standard we could deduce. They don't wear armor or even boots. They're wearing sandals, and they carry staffs of polished wood."

Irdessa's prone to believe the instincts of her two finest scouts. "Tower dwellers," she mutters. She wondered if they'd cross paths. Having minimal information about the people, she'd not devised much of a plan if so. She'd been relying on one of their rumored characteristics being true. Tower-folk left the mainland because they had no interest in riding the Heathen Tide. If that is the case, perhaps it is enough common ground to precede welcome.

"We need to make contact," Irdessa says.

"I agree. I can ..." Magpie trails off, his eyes still on Irdessa but unfocused, as if he's listening to something Irdessa can't hear. He looks over Irdessa's shoulder. "Dammit, Maudee."

And there she is, strolling from the darkness alongside two figures, both old, both wearing sandals and bearing staffs, just as Magpie described. The main difference between them is that one has a thin grey beard sprouting from a wrinkled chin, and the other's face is clean, even if its sun-kissed skin is sack-like with age. They are not warriors. Maudee shrugs at Magpie. "Sorry. You were taking too long."

Irdessa's initial impulse, the reaction Keswal taught her, is to debilitate both strangers at once. Throw a kick into the bearded one's groin, punch the other's throat and take the staff. Finish beard with stick to the face, then finish wrinkles. It's a far stronger urge than she would like, and it sets her fingers trembling at her sides. There's no emotion attached, only a command from her survival instincts to put these two down, now. Whatever consequences ensue do not compare to losing another member of her Vanguard. What stops her hands is a fleeting inquiry, that same one that's been embedded in her for some time, now rolling over to be reexamined. Is that what Torvald would do? If so, she won't.

"Irdessa the Undying." The bearded man smiles disarmingly as he says it. His eyes are so pinched they may be closed.

Irdessa's mouth falls open before she can stifle her surprise. She glares at Maudee, who she trusted until this moment. Maudee flinches backward and throws up both hands defensively.

"She didn't give you up," the man says. "We've been expecting you." His accent is distinct from the mainland's, as if his throat is more used to yawning than speaking.

Irdessa, in dire need of properly assessing this situation, employs the best tactic she knows to make a person say more. She says nothing.

"I'm Capper. This is Rowan," the woman says. Her smile crinkles the edges of her eyes. "We'd like to invite you to our home."

Irdessa stands silent, giving the truth another moment to make itself known. When it doesn't, she asks, "Why?"

The man works his jaw, perhaps taken aback by Irdessa not reciprocating their good cheer. The woman places her hand on his wrist. Her smile holds. "There are safer places to talk," she says.

"Are we not safe?" Irdessa asks.

"Relatively," the man says. "Not to alarm you, but the jaguars are braver at night. Your people are ..."

"Getting shit-faced, I know," Irdessa says.

"We consider ourselves citizens of Fohrvylda." His voice has gained more steel. His grey eyebrows converge. "Promontory does not agree. Surely you, of all people, can relate."

"Talk to your people," the woman says, before Irdessa can determine whether that assumption was merely intrusive or insulting. "We are offering rest and food, in a safer and more comfortable location than this."

There's no need to ask her party. Safety, rest, food. It's not even a question. But her restless mind ...

What will this cost? Torvald whispers.

Irdessa grimaces. *Didn't you die?*

He's not deterred. *Nothing is free.*

Death is, she tells him. Then, to the two strangers, "Alright. Lead the way."

~

Kraus stumbles between dreams and nightmares. He's been stuck for days, or weeks, or forever? He's wearing no clothes, only a body-sized scab that fractures with every movement. He's searching for something. A face? A friend? Something to godsdamn drink? But behind every door, around every corner, there are shadows. And within them, chalky glass—the kind you have to peer into up close to see what's on the other side, and when you do, it turns your stomach. Two sightless eyes staring. Framed in blood and mud and tousled yellow hair. They chase him, rolling over the earth, flattening stone towers into the sea, stirring up massive waves in their wake, somehow remaining locked on him and yet vacant.

He frees himself from the cocoon of bandages that encaged him but regrets it almost at once. Now the seizures are restrained by nothing. His every joint rattles, and he grips himself, crossing his legs and squeezing his chest, freezing to death in a puddle of his own sweat.

Every time Kraus awakens, or thinks he does, he himself is a stalking nightmare. Smiles turn to scowls at his approach. Conversations become wind before he can make out a single word. His muddy, roving fingers find bottles, force them to his chapped lips, but within is empty fluid, tasteless, bland as liquefied air like some sick joke. Occasionally it's sugary fruit water, and even then just enough to send him back into nightmares.

He awakens to the stench of food. Seared gristle and bone, simmered grain with chunks of plants in it, blocks of rank cheese or powdery loaves of bread that stick in his teeth and lodge under his tongue and clog his throat. His roiling guts resent this offense above all, and their eruptive protest is a thing of violence.

It is dusk. Kraus crawls toward consciousness but it flees from him down a cavernous maze. If he's not diligent he'll never catch it. He must have been asleep for some time, but now is not. He's lying flat on his back, as opposed to curled on his side. Above him stars are just twinkling to life from a deepening dark. It feels like he's noticing them for the first time. He watches the glimmering blanket they're weaving over the sky and lets the salty breeze wash over him. Aside from the pinching pain in his temples and the cramps in his guts he almost feels ... well.

"Back with us, rapist?" A man's voice. Familiar. Some Vanguard fighter.

It takes several attempts at clearing his throat and swallowing chalk, but Kraus is eventually able to turn his head and croak out a response. "Unfortunately."

It's that pretty fellow from Vim who tried to send them away. Cave man or Cunt nun or whatever. The one who always looks down his nose as if the world is his to fuck. The one who shaves his cheeks and chin and neck every day to show off that dainty jawbone, as if it amounts to shit. Fucking sop.

The man snickers, his smile bringing dimples to his shiny cheeks. "I'll say." There's the scrape of a small blade unsheathed. "Got something for you."

Kraus closes his eyes again. It's as much effort as he cares to put toward anything. This must be some old enemy who's found his perfect opportunity for noble vengeance. Pissed off about some horrible deed or another that Kraus committed drunk and failed to notice.

"Go for it," Kraus says.

"Irdessa won't admit it, but you're an anchor. You drag us down. You're a scourge on the Vanguard. And you stink. You scare off women. I'm not entirely sure your condition isn't contagious. We'd be better off without you, and she would be too."

"That bad, huh?" All the blathering is fanning Kraus' headache. "Why talk me to death if you've got a damn knife?"

The man snickers again. "Oh, not me. I can't kill you. Irdessa the Angry would have that evil bitch hack me to bits if I did. I'm offering you the chance to do it yourself. If you care about Irdessa, you will."

Kraus is struck by a burst of hacking laughter. "You fucking sop!" He's straining at the guts, nearly crying. "A fighter who's scared to use a knife ..." He's seized by a series of rattling coughs. "... and *I'm* the anchor." He laughs so hard tears squeeze from his eyes. His ribs hurt, and his forearm, and shoulder, and face, and pretty much all of him hurts, and he knows for a fact that he is, regrettably, alive.

Finally he manages to subdue his giggling with deep, wheezing breaths. "I needed that." Kraus bends his stiff arms, wipes his eyes, squints at the man. Fellow's not snickering anymore. His pretty frown suggests he's stepped in shit.

"Do I know you, sop?" Kraus asks. "'Cause you're about to regret what you said about Bravensi."

"Caenin." It's Irdessa, and her voice is as sharp as winter wind. "Leave us."

The man flinches at her voice. His anger dissipates to annoyance. He stows his dagger and brushes past Irdessa, knocking her sideways in the process. She snatches his arm, stopping him. He turns to her. For a moment they're at a standoff.

Irdessa speaks first, and slowly. "You can't know who I am and believe I'll tolerate that. Maybe I haven't properly introduced myself."

His cheeks flush. "It was an accident," he mutters through his teeth. She releases him and away he stomps.

"Caenin, is it?" Kraus calls. "We'll talk later. Ya godsdamn sop."

Irdessa sits down beside Kraus and fixes him with a motherly concern. Her stare is too serious for him to match so he uses the opportunity to take in his surroundings. He does not attempt to sit up. Not yet.

"Making friends?" Irdessa says.

Kraus smiles. He's laid out on a blanket. To his right, what he'd at first taken as walls of vertically piled rocks turn out to be houses, some with thatched roofs, some with roofs of sod. It's not entirely unlike the residences and buildings on the terraced landscape above the Bay of Ivolde, but leafy vines climb this stone, and instead of drab wooden doors and shutters these all have brightly dyed canvas or fabric blocking the openings. The vibrant blues and yellows, far more garish than any decor on the mainland, are almost enough to hurt his eyes. To his left, not twenty yards off, beyond vine-wrapped trees, the ground disappears and there, like always it seems, can be seen the Faithless Sea. Otherwise, they're surrounded by an airy forest dominated by light shades of green. The air smells like earth and ocean, and somewhere, a wood fire.

"Where are we?"

She offers him water and he sips enough to rinse his pipes. "A village of Rain Catchers, way out in the Towers." Irdessa speaks softly. Maybe she knows how much his head hurts. Seems like she has more to say. Instead, she tucks her lip and starts laying out food on an intricately stenciled porcelain platter. Soft white cheese, raw spinach leaves, greasy links of sausage. Kraus flinches at the smell.

"Go on," he says.

"It seems like ... we're safe for now?" she says carefully, as if announcing it might undo it.

Kraus meets her eyes. "How long are we here?"

She shrugs, shakes her head. "They've asked us to stay."

"Why?"

A laugh spurts from Irdessa. It's gone just as quickly. "They want our help making bows. Their elder, Rowan, was their bowman. Now he's too old. Hands can't do it anymore."

"Sounds like he should've taken an apprentice."

"He did, long ago. The boy died. Fell off a cliff. He didn't take another."

"Why not?"

Irdessa shrugs.

"By the gods, tell me one good thing that's ever come of soft feelings."

"I wish I could. They claim their cliff archers are formidable, and I'd heard the same thing. Well, once they have bows in their hands. Apparently that's been a glaring lack for some time. They've got fishing arrows, used to feed themselves, and finishing arrows, used to feed the fish."

"Clever," Kraus says, and burps. Nearly vomits. Probably would have if there were anything left inside him. He pinches his eyes, swallows several times. "Tired of puking," he says.

"Good. We're all tired of listening to it."

He chuckles.

Irdessa shifts where she sits. "Apparently violent types have been sneaking over from the mainland and threatening these people."

"Violent types," Kraus says. "Like us?"

She gives an empty smile.

Kraus watches the newborn stars. *Violent types* ... The idea to stalk the Towers for easy prey crossed his mind in the past. Always seemed like too far a trek to snatch something perfectly snatchable from any sun-beaten highway or damp alley in Fohrvylda.

He rubs his eyes again. The wind brings the cooked meat's zest to his nostrils and his stomach yowls. Maybe he is hungry. He dabs at the cheese with a finger so grimy he first mistakes it for a stick. As soon as the pungent cheese touches the tip of his tongue, his mouth erupts in saliva. Must've been starved nearly to death. He knows better than to gorge himself. Doesn't keep him from doing it.

"Why would they trust us?" Kraus asks her, covering the spatter from his mouth with a cheese-smeared palm.

Irdessa's eyes are distant. Her head is shaking. "Because they've heard of Vim, and our ... *rebellion.*" The way she enunciates that word is as if it's her first time trying to pronounce it.

"How in Satuavo's sack did they hear that?" Kraus asks.

"They stay up on news from Fohrvylda using scouts. Riots are springing up all over the mainland. Apparently because of us. Towns are tired of getting attacked. So they're doing the attacking. They call us heroes." Irdessa sighs. "Even Kraus the Thirsty."

Kraus looks at her, his face stretched long. Irdessa mirrors his surprised expression, then they both break into laughter.

"I'd nearly forgotten Kraus the Thirsty. Kind of leaves a lot to be desired though, doesn't it?"

"Do you prefer Kraus the Rapist?"

He shakes his head. "Folks must be sick of Promontory's shit if I'm a hero. They've clearly been lied to."

"Clearly."

Kraus slurps up the last half of a sausage link and grinds the skin thoughtfully, savoring it like a cud. "Well," he swallows, "you want to stay here a while?"

Her expression turns studious. "Our stories have strong enough legs to set fires all over Promontory. We're probably on more than a couple shit lists. Vim's Vanguard throwing off the marshal's battalion sparked a nationwide revolt. I don't expect Vretos is taking it well. What would you do about that if you were him?"

"Dess." Kraus can't help but smile. "You sound and look exactly like Torvald."

"Fuck you."

Fair enough. He probably should have known better. "I'd execute my marshal publicly. Or throw him in Keswal armed with a spoon and a bowl of orcane shit."

"Or at least replace him," Irdessa says. "With someone proficient."

Kraus picks his teeth with a fingernail the color of an acorn. "Then I'd crush those rumors. I guess by crushing you. Hell, I might postpone the Heathen Tide for it. Might cease everything to throw all my weight at getting you back in Keswal."

"Same thought I had," she says. "According to Rain Catcher scouts, Promontory has removed most of the bridges to the mainland to control traffic and is using the rest to dump soldiers into the Towers. We're in no danger here yet. This Tower is closer to Redemier than Fohrvylda. It took us four days and we went a direct route. The village is quite hidden." Her expression suggests there's a hitch.

"So what's the bad news?"

"Scouts also report more activity from orcane patrols in the sea below. Lots heading north. I'd wager they're going to the border between the Towers and Redemier to cut us off, whether or not they can legally set foot on the cursed island. Eventually, the soldiers infiltrating the Towers will find us. Might take weeks, might take days. They'll flush us north. Then it's only a matter of time before we're stuck between them and whatever awaits us."

"Aha. So we can move on and eventually meet the barksharks on our way to Redemier, or wait here and try to hold out with our new friends." He waves a hand sarcastically, in case Irdessa mistook his use of the word *friends*.

"That's my thoughts. Except I bet soldiers aren't all they're sending onto the Towers. There's no reason they won't send assassins too. Or envoys to bribe the Catchers or whoever they might find out here. Point is, we can't stay. And we'd be smarter to move soon."

"Damn, Dess. Sounds like you've got it sorted out."

She glares at him, goes to speak, stops herself, huffs. "I'm not qualified to decide all this on my own."

Kraus shakes his head. "You're at a low point if I'm the best you've got for advice."

She acknowledges with a twitch of her eyebrows and thinning of her lips. "Rub it in, won't you?"

Kraus winces at his choice of words. It occurs to him that her predicament came at the cost of a lot of lives. And all he's got is jokes. Then again, no part of that can possibly come as a surprise to Irdessa. Kraus furrows his brow, which makes his head throb anew. He reaches for the bottle she brought and has been protecting, all the while trying to quell the expectation that it's more than water. He raises it and the hairs of his arms stand up at its bitter smell. The froth of hot, pungent ale cascades over his tongue. His eyes widen and he elicits a guttural exhale out his nostrils. He sucks at the bottle until it sucks back at him, pulls free with a thick pop, sucks it again. Then it's all gone.

"More," Kraus says. Foam speckles Irdessa's cheek and he realizes he screamed it at her.

She wipes her face with the back of her hand, watching him flatly.

"Sorry," he says, embarrassed.

She shrugs.

"Sooner or later, the soldiers will find this village whether or not we're here," Kraus says, setting down the bottle. "What then?"

"The Rain Catchers will cut the bridges. Or, at least, enough of them. They've already begun. That'll slow the soldiers down."

"Then what's keeping us from staying here? They can't reach us."

"If they believe we're on a Tower, they'll find a way. They might teach their sprakes how to fly guy lines over and start new bridges. We can't shoot down all their birds. And when the birds come, there is no hiding here."

"Then it sounds like our new friends are gonna die either way," Kraus says, although he's unsure if that's a condition that he personally opposes, or one he doesn't care about but expects the Vanguard to.

"Maybe," Irdessa says. "But I don't think Promontory will focus their energy on the Towers if they know we've left," she says. "This is too defensible a position to try and make an example of. They'll aim all their wrath at us. We'll make them."

"You mean if they know we've left and gone to the cursed island?" Kraus says, feeling a chill.

She nods. "As soon as we're known to be heading for Redemier, the soldiers should pull out of the Towers. If all goes well, that will happen before they learn the Catchers are complicit, but after we've escaped their grasp."

"*If all goes well.*" Kraus shakes his head. "Please never say that."

She ignores the comment. "We can't be sure soldiers are waiting for us on Redemier. For all we know, they won't even go on land. And if they're waiting, it's a long stretch of coast they'd have to patrol. Rain Catcher scouts can watch and provide a route to avoid them, hopefully."

Kraus flinches. "*Hopefully* is as bad as *if all goes well.*"

She ignores this too.

Kraus rubs his shoulders with his ragged palms. Feels far chillier out here than it seems to be. "Take our chances with the cursed island." Maybe saying it aloud will loan it some appeal.

"Oh come on, Kraus. Don't tell me you're scared of a curse."

"It's not what's there that I'm scared of. It's what isn't."

She puzzles at him a moment, then rolls her eyes. "Liquor. You're hopeless."

"Hmph." Kraus observes the blue paint on the door of the nearby hut, letting his mind roam. He's not offering any insight she hasn't already considered. Did she just need to have him probe the idea? Her apparent trust is flattering. But he can't help pitying her if he's her best auditor of ideas.

"For what it's worth, you are qualified to lead. I've never met anyone more qualified."

She shakes her head, staring over the Faithless vacantly.

Even Torvald, he wants to say. *Because he died.* Instead he says. "What do you want to do?"

"Carry on to Redemier. Take our chances."

"Then we carry on," Kraus says.

She's nodding. "Not everyone will be happy about that."

"Can't please everyone." It seems more productive than *Fuck 'em.* "Blame me. They all hate me anyway."

"That's not true."

"It's fine with me, Dess. Someone's gotta be the most hated. I'm good at it."

"I'm not going to blame you for my decisions, Kraus. You don't want that." Irdessa's hand has idly moved to the stitches on her lower lip. "I'm trying to keep everyone alive."

Kraus is unable to contrive an honest response that doesn't involve laughing. "When do you want to leave?"

"As soon as we can. Harpold and Elaga have been working with the Catchers, helping them with bow design. We'll give them another day at least. The Vanguard could do for more rest anyway. Also, Rowan and Capper, the Catcher elders, have asked for a meeting to discuss our plans tomorrow. I think most of the village will attend ... maybe even present a case to convince us to stay." She rubs her face with both hands, groaning.

"Then we leave?" Kraus says.

She looks out over the ocean. Her eyes are distant, shiny. She heaves an enormous, shuddering sigh, looking like no more than a young girl. It's like they're standing in the shadow of the Towers again and her wounds are fresh. Next comes the part where Kraus accidentally incites her to violence. He grimaces at the memory.

"Hey, tell me this," he says. "What did the Vanguard do in Vim after a mission?"

For a moment it seems she didn't hear him. When she answers, only her lips move. "Probably have a fire. Sing. Drink a lot. Talk about the dead. Some people ... celebrate in different ways."

"Well, I'm not sure what our food and drink stores are looking like. But do you wanna have a fire like that after tomorrow's meeting? I bet there are some goodbyes needing to be said."

She looks at Kraus with a blank expression. He notices her state for the first time since he woke. Her face is gaunt, her cheekbones sharp. Dark bags weigh down her heavy eyelids. The sight of her makes Kraus' thirst feel petty and selfish. How much of that fatigue is his fault? His guts sour. She gives her life for him.

He clears his throat, trying to alleviate the tightness. "How about we weather the Catchers' meeting, stay the night, leave the next morning."

"That sounds good," she says numbly, then adds, "Don't kill Caenin."

His face falls. Feels like she stole something from him. A shiny bottle of whiskey, snatched right out of his hand. "You heard what he said about Bravensi, didn't you?"

Her eyes narrow. "I didn't, and I don't care."

A half-dozen complaints occur to him. They all die on his tongue. He's fully capable of making horrendous choices. Starting a fight with Irdessa is not one he'll make again. Not soon anyway. She's not helpless, however this moment portrays her.

"Fine," Kraus says, and begins the process of standing up. It takes more than one lunged attempt to achieve a kneeling position, and after getting his boots under him, several moments of balancing to be sure they'll stay there. Short on blood ... makes him dizzy, heavy, shivering. He spares Irdessa a glance and makes his way slowly to the cliff's edge. The moon sits low above the far horizon, making the Faithless sparkle.

"Either way, we'll take some time," Kraus says carefully, "to acknowledge everyone who's fed the birds."

Irdessa follows him. She moves close enough so that her hair tickles his arm and sends chills up to his scalp. "To tell them goodbye?" she whispers.

He drapes his arm over her shoulders. "To tell them goodbye."

49
How to Impale the Gullible

FOHRVYLDA
Rain Catch, the Towers

Caenin the Arrow sits among the Vanguard facing the so-called Rain Catchers, in prelude to some meeting Irdessa has asked the Vanguard to attend. They've been at the village for days, and don't seem to be in a hurry to leave. That's alright. There's no rush. There is a relaxed feel around here that Caenin could absolutely learn to love. No soldiers. The air is fresh and the surroundings are verdant and exotic and exciting, what with the lush plant life and the sheer cliffs. Caenin himself is probably in even less of a hurry than his companions. He could find a suitable wife here. Testing out the potentials has proven worthy of his time. The Catchers invited the Vanguard to stay indefinitely, and Caenin can think of no reason not to. Running does not compare to fucking.

These people treat the Vanguard like war heroes, giving up their cozy homes for the fighters in the scenic western side of their village, temporarily moving themselves out in accommodation. Those who offer their residences all squeezed into homes farther up this rock formation's side. Up there, the houses are piled higher, sometimes atop each other, where expeditious vines blanket the walls, helping secure the chipped stones to each other. The families with young children were the first to offer up their homes and find shelter with other Catchers on the far side of the village. Seems everyone wants to keep the young away from the fighters. Stupid objective, as far as Caenin is concerned. Those children could learn a lot of lessons no one here seems to be teaching. It's never too early to get ready for combat. Combat's always ready for you. Learn to shoot a bow and you may not have to learn to catch an arrow.

Among the Vanguard housing, Cindie and Elaga fill one home. Not that they matter. Caenin hasn't the prerequisite equipment to appeal to either of them, never mind that Cindie is a captivating little thing with piercing eyes and bouncing blond locks. Elaga, while black-haired, dark-skinned and gorgeous, is even less of an option. Caenin has strict edicts against pursuing women that match or exceed his bulk.

Bravensi got a hut all to herself and she can have it. She's there now instead of at this meeting, doing gods-know-what to that weapon of hers.

The Catchers offered Irdessa a large home, what with her being the unofficial ringleader of this circus. She shares it with Vyker and Harpold.

Kraus' cot was set up on the outskirts of the village, where he could roil and vomit without emotionally scarring anyone. The Catchers gave him a tincture for blood loss. Made him sleep for three days. Seems to have worked though, because now he's conscious and thirsty. Maybe Caenin should have stabbed him while he was out and been done with it. Who would've known? Not like any wound fresh to Kraus' skin will stand out. And if it did, he could've rolled the ogre off the cliff. Who would have missed him?

Caenin was offered a house. He refused. "I'm more of a nomad," he told the Catchers. He's found warm beds each night. Their occupants were nothing to complain about either.

Irdessa stands up to address the Catchers, indicating the meeting commencing.

"Capper, Rowan, Rain Catchers, on behalf of the Vanguard, thank you for your hospitality. You put yourselves at risk helping us. I won't forget that."

The pause that follows stretches into melodrama, making Caenin anxious for some reason.

"Capper, you graciously invited the Vanguard to stay here for a time."

Caenin makes eyes across the gathering at a red-maned girl with dark eyelashes and freckles on her arms. In reaction to Irdessa's words, he raises an eyebrow at the girl and shrugs and smiles as if the rendezvous he has in mind is not even up to him. An inevitability. Her cheeks turn the color of her hair.

"As much as we appreciate the offer and wish we could ..."

The heat falls out of Caenin.

"... we cannot. You all know who I am. And I imagine you know who's after me. Vretos will stop at nothing."

The girl across the camp must taste some of Caenin's chagrin, because now she leans toward him, hands unsure, concern on her face. He makes no effort to hide the disappointment in his silent sigh.

"It is only a matter of time until they learn we're here. Destroying the bridges won't stop them. They'll use sprakes to run more lines and make new bridges. They'll find narrow expanses and swing across on long ropes. They'll mount the bases of the Towers and scale them progressively. They'll train their birds to carry the soldiers across. They will squeeze in bit by bit until they've infiltrated the Towers. And if all that fails, I wouldn't put it past Vretos to concentrate the navy's efforts on chipping through the base of this very Tower and felling it, burying us all in the ocean. He has the time."

Whether or not Irdessa intended to murder the mood, she's done it. The girl across the gathering seems to have forgotten Caenin, focusing instead on hyperventilating.

"To accept your invitation would be the pinnacle of selfishness. We'd buy ourselves some comfort, but inevitably doom you. For your sake, we refuse. The Vanguard will continue on to Redemier. Once we arrive, we will make ourselves known, in one way or another, to draw attention away from your settlement." She amplifies her voice to keep it above the rising clamor. "We plan to leave in the morning."

Caenin has a sour taste in his mouth. The girl's attention has returned to him, and she is trying to communicate sympathy from across the gathering. She's resorted to loosening the straps at the neck of her blouse, letting sunlight explore her collarbones. She's a pretty thing, sure. But she's only one. And now time has grown sparse. There are so many girls. If this is his last night here, what qualifies her to hold the monopoly on his attention? Then again, does it have to only be her? A smile finds its way back onto his face. The girl takes this as encouragement and frees enough skin to let the sun warm the pale gully between her breasts. Caenin yawns.

"And what if the diversion doesn't work?" Rowan responds. "Suppose you merely draw them here faster, full of rage?"

Irdessa addresses him. "That isn't likely. But you knew who I was when you invited us here. You knew what's at stake. If Promontory insists on destroying your village because of that, the Vanguard is hardly responsible."

The old man has lost his tongue, even as many around him spring to their feet. Caenin's pulse leaps. Vanguard's fighters tense. So far, the Catchers are smart enough not to let their actions be mistaken for threats.

"If Vretos wants the Catcher village destroyed," Irdessa says, "there's nothing I could do to prevent it whether I'm here or elsewhere. I promise we will try our best to prevent it."

"Then you'll leave with our blessing," the old woman, Capper, says. Rowan's tense shoulders hold their rigor for a moment, then he slowly deflates. "You're right," the old woman says. "It was our decision to take you in. Let me tell you why we did it."

Caenin scans the potential village girls. When his gaze touches the cherry-haired girl, he displays disinterest. The hungrier she grows, the sooner he can have it, leaving more time for the rest.

"We are not helpless. Satuavo have mercy on any who land under our finishing arrows," Capper says. The Catchers nod agreement, some elbowing each other with wry smiles. "And with your help soon we should have regained the means to defend ourselves, fish for food, and train, all at once. So, thank you. All of you."

Irdessa tilts her head in a slow nod. Her face is impassive but Caenin can tell she's uncertain of the woman's intent.

"We came to the Towers for peace," the old woman proceeds. "To live as we like. To not rely on, or live in fear of Promontory. For most of Fohrvylda, migrating here is not possible. So they survive at best, under Promontory's shadow."

That rings true to Caenin's ears but he fails to care. He's caught the attention of a woman he'd overlooked before. Older. Sand-colored hair made of tight springs. Those curls and the twinkle in her eye suggest she's got a hidden energy, despite the age that the faint lines at the corners of her mouth betray. She's close enough to the man beside her that they must be together. But he looks tired and pudgy, and his thin, black hair is half grey. She deserves a sturdier man than that. At least for a night.

The woman has noticed Caenin's attention now and the strategy begins. He must demonstrate careful appreciation. Too much hunger and he looks like a starved dog, willing to lap up anything. Not enough and the thought of their naked bodies clashing will never even cross her mind. He paints an unexpected wonder on his face as their gazes meld. Girls cherish attention, which is cheap. Women ... they're complicated. They know what they want and they know how to relish it. Caenin's eyes wander her lithe arms, her fingers. The stirring in his guts does not lie. She is the one. But the redhead's stare is bright and inescapable, like he's trying to hide from the sun under a tree with no leaves. He'll have to be deliberate, indirect, lest he lose them both. He takes a moment to stretch, flexing his bare arms above him. Pudgy-man doesn't have arms like his. He concludes by running a hand through his hair and slinging it out of his face. He doesn't meet her eyes again, instead aiming a thoughtful squint at the old woman, Capper. He is vital, after all, and clever, and the Vanguard will need him to weigh in on her words after they've all been said.

"We began to hear stories," the old woman says. "People under Promontory's shadow daring to fight back, and on a grand scale. We heard of a woman named Irdessa the Undying, who escaped Keswal. She breathed life into Andelsior's Vanguard and took down three hundred soldiers, maiming a captain and killing his second. We heard stories of a man who fears not soldier, sprake, nor orcane. A collector of scars who cannot be killed, Kraus the Carcass."

"Hah," Kraus bursts, spraying the foam of the beer he'd been sipping. "I love it."

Capper continues, "We heard of Maudee and Magpie, who outwit their foes by sharing a twin mind." Capper turns to her people. "Who else?"

"Cindie the Surefoot," a young girl calls. She's only a child.

"Harpold the Hunter," says a man.

"Elaga, whose greatbow can puncture an oak." It's an overly excited boy with the precursor of a black mustache darkening his lip.

"Sura the Shield."

A child stands, gripping the hand of what may be her father. "Bravensi," she squeaks. "the Batshi—" The father's hand claps to her mouth so brutally she flips over backward, her bare feet cartwheeling. His round eyes dart across the Vanguard, as if the psychopath might leap out at him.

"Bravensi the Beautiful," Kraus says.

The girl gains her footing and returns to her spot, oblivious to the assault. Seems nothing can quell the admiration brimming in her. "Yes. Who knows no equal on the battlefield."

"Caenin the Arrow," says the red-haired girl with claustrophobic breasts. Her voice is bold. "Whose stamina knows no equal ..."

Caenin, taken aback, appraises her once again, a smile dawning on his face. He'd not heard—

"... off the battlefield," she finishes wryly.

Other girls titter. Men's faces grow dark. Heat rises in Caenin's cheeks. That's irritating news to announce. A girl is more receptive to a boy if she's under the delusion that she alone holds his attention. But the redhead is not put off by her own announcement. In fact, her claim is concentrated in the smile she levels at him. Does she think to mark him? Pudgy man has shifted obnoxiously close to spring-curls, and he's placed a thick, sun-leathered hand on the woman's knee. Caenin might have underestimated the redhead.

"Indeed." Capper's face has lost its smile. "And now, amid riots and disorder, in the height of opportunity to strike Vretos a wound he doesn't soon shake off ..." The old woman pauses to catch her breath. Her gaze on Irdessa doesn't falter. She proceeds wearily. "Those legends cower before us. Planning to run away. It shouldn't come as a surprise. Things are rarely what they're promised to be." Her eyes fall on Caenin. "Life is full of disappointments."

Derisive laughter snorts from some of the Catcher men. Caenin's mouth falls open. Did she call the Vanguard cowards in one breath and question Caenin's virility with the next? Maybe she doesn't know it, but he would have no problem laying her dusty ass horizontal and reminding her the value of a healthy man's vigor. Spring-curls looks down her nose at Caenin and runs her fingers up pudgy's arm.

"Truer words I've never spoken." Irdessa's voice slices through the murmurs. She doesn't appear deterred by the insult. "While flattering, your rumors omit the practical details. We didn't destroy that battalion. We merely survived Promontory's assault, and not by a boast-worthy margin."

Caenin fights the urge to hiss at her, give her a *pst!* Silence this self-degradation. Lowering your perceived worth serves as an excellent exit strategy, but he's trying to do the opposite of that at the moment.

"My obligations are to my people," she says. "We have suffered irredeemable losses. I will save what is left of the Vanguard or die trying."

"And what about us?" asks a round-shouldered Catcher.

"You made it this far," Kraus says. "You'll do fine."

The Catcher leaps to his feet in a huff. One of Kraus' eyebrows imitates the man's ascension, marking his face with a morbid challenge.

"If I might ..." It's old Rowan, and he appears even more tired than Capper. He rotates where he sits and gestures at a nearby boy, maybe five years old, who'd been crouched, playing, oblivious to the conversation. The boy reluctantly stands and walks to Rowan's outstretched arm. "This is Makan. He, like many his age, is second-generation Tower-born. He's never known the Fohrvylda we're from, where the only greater danger than hooded villains with hidden knives are the soldiers tasked to stop them."

The boy, aware of the sudden attention, sidles behind the man and eyes the Vanguard nervously, pulling at his fingers. Something about the old man's words has stirred to life a probing curiosity in Caenin. Enough to distract him from the individual women present, broaden his focus. If fresh-baked children are in demand, Caenin might have more usefulness here than he first thought.

"I know where your thoughts would go. He is ill-prepared. He needs to harden his hands, take some wounds, learn a weapon. To that I respond with a challenge. If your imagination allows it, consider a place where that is not the case. Children would not need to forgo youthful curiosity for training, because here the villains are dealt with by the just. That's the intention for our village, and it's our dream for Fohrvylda. But it's only a temporary condition for a place like Rain Catch," he draws out his words, demanding all ears, "as long as Vretos holds Fohrvylda by the throat."

The pause that follows allows the man's words to tumble around within Caenin's head. You would never hear such words as that on the mainland, and something about that is refreshing. But what exactly is this old man proposing, the Vanguard's supposed to up and murder Vretos? Caenin would scoff, but seems he'd be alone. Everyone else is acting touched by the words. Maybe Caenin is too. Would it be so bad for the Vanguard to take off on said quest and leave Caenin here to fertilize the field?

The little boy has grown uncomfortable. Rowan gives his back a pat and releases him from the gathering's attention.

"What are you suggesting?" Irdessa asks. Despite her brevity, a question seems to have fallen over her conviction. For a man like Caenin, this may as well be a direct invitation. Whatever the old man's selling, now's his chance to hook her.

Kraus, who apparently takes Irdessa's softening as a direct threat, does not give Rowan a chance to respond. He clears his throat so loudly it sounds like flesh rips. "What's your fucking point, old man?"

"I suggest that you consider a Fohrvylda with no Vretos," the man says to Irdessa, paying Kraus no mind. "With no Marshal Zander or any corrupt captains murdering citizens and oppressing them into poverty so they'll murder each other. A place fit for a child's wonder."

Kraus gives a cold laugh. "At the rate Vretos is dying, might as well imagine the Faithless Sea is made of beer while we're at it."

If only, Caenin thinks. *Then would you jump?*

"No one lives forever," Rowan says. "And until now, no one's ever challenged Vretos and lived."

"Not due to a lack of invitations on Vretos' part," Irdessa says. "He maintains that whoever kills him takes his place. Is that what you're suggesting the Vanguard does? That I do?"

He shakes his head wearily, maintaining his smile. "I mean only to plant a seed of hope. As far as I'm concerned, any force that can accomplish what yours has should welcome such a hope."

Caenin has to appreciate the old man's tack, because his damn seed planting seems to have propagated indecision. And judging by the uncertainty in the faces of the Vanguard, it's working on some of them too. Not Kraus. He looks like he wants to strangle the man.

"We did not *kill* three hundred men," Irdessa says. "They almost killed us. That's one battalion, under one captain. Do you know how many captains Marshal Zander has?"

Something about Irdessa's tone sounds ... whiny. She's making excuses. Caenin can't quite put his thumb on why, but this is not improving her attractiveness. Quite the opposite.

"Irdessa," the man says, not without some condescension. "If I had the answers, I wouldn't be sitting here. You're the Tactician's protégé. Your father was Andelsior, who I believe would share this dream. I've heard what you're capable of. Deeds no one else has accomplished. How many times have you outsmarted Promontory? If you wanted to stop him, I believe you could. And you would have our help."

The old fellow has struck silence into the gathering. Anticipation. And it's ripening as moments of staring ensue. The Catchers watch the Vanguard, feigning disinterest. No apparent expectation. The fighters, however, appear far from unified. The man's stirred forth a range of emotions. For Caenin there is anxious unknowing. As long as the Vanguard stays here, so does he, with his own seed and plow at the ready. If the Vanguard keeps going toward Redemier or charges back toward Promontory, they'll demand he accompany them so they can benefit from his bow skills. In such a case, Caenin might suffer an untimely debilitating injury. One of his own design if need be. He smiles. An injury like that would serve dual purposes. Nothing like a slice of sympathy to help moisten a field.

"In any case ..." The man rises to his feet with a strained exhalation. He helps Capper stand. "We appreciate the expertise your archers have bestowed. Food and drink are on us tonight."

Apparently this meeting is over. Most of the Catchers file from the clearing after Rowan and Capper. Spring curls is a lost cause, clinging to her man's arm like it's the mast of a ship. The red-haired girl deliberately tightens her blouse and follows, not even bothering to look back. Caenin finds a frown hardening on his face. Those are his tricks, meant to incite. Not to be used against him. He approaches Irdessa before his mood can sour further.

"So, Dess ..."

She executes a brisk march toward her cabin. "Don't call me that."

Kraus calls you that. But there's no point in saying that. "The old man made some interesting points."

"Sure."

He nearly has to run to keep up with her. "I think we should stay here longer. Don't you think—"

"I don't. I'm not going to damn these Rain Catchers, however ungrateful they are."

"You don't know we'd be found here."

Irdessa stops walking and gives him her full attention. "Don't I?" The look in her eyes illustrates exactly how little consideration he gave his words. "Caenin, the day I tell you how to impale the gullible, I'll accept your guidance on any matter at all, strategic or otherwise."

Caenin's temper flares. "The old man's right and you know it. This country is a murderous wreck, and it will be as long as Vretos is in charge. The Vanguard doesn't have to confront the entire army to resolve that. There are riots on the mainland. We could use that to our advantage. Should we not stay here a while longer? Let conditions of the mainland devolve further, ascertain what help these people are capable of? Surely their contribution changes the field." Sounds strategic enough. And who knows how wet he can get his cock while the ascertaining is underway?

She turns and walks again. But there was a moment's hesitation. And this time her feet aren't as fast. He moves closer to her, glancing his bare shoulder off hers.

"I'd do anything to prevent another of our people dying," he says in a low, deadened inflection, to convey that the world holds no greater terror than his wrath.

"Besides fight?"

Her words slap away the rest of his improvised monologue. He glares at her. On she marches, jaw locked and chin forward. It's like there was never an opening. He is failing utterly at reading her. But the challenge is tantalizing. He needs a new tack.

"Irdessa, you should make room for love."

She halts, her eyes stretched wide. Caenin second-guesses saying it, but now it's out there. Best he can do is try and smooth it over.

"What I mean is ..." He bolsters courage and places a hand on her shoulder. It's sturdier than he expected. Her eyes follow his hand, disbelief solidifying on her features. She does not immediately knock his hand away. Good sign. Maybe she's curious why someone like him is noticing someone with a face as hacked-up as hers. Maybe she's curious why he's not placed his hands on her before.

"Torvald is dead," Caenin says softly, and as he hoped her gaze now finds his. She isn't any more readable. He narrows his eyes in appreciation of her facade, makes his cheeks sallow and presents a show of wetting his lips. "But you aren't. Let's pause here a while, in the easy company of these Catchers. Open yourself to affection. Sometimes, all love asks is that you relent." He squeezes her shoulder and slides his hand down to her triceps. Solid as an exposed oak root. She's stronger than she looks. Pursuing her would violate another of his edicts; *Don't fuck a woman who can kill you with her bare hands.* Luckily, he's not interested in pursuing her so much as persuading her. "Sometimes love requires less than that." He gives a wink.

That wink usually elicits response in girls, voluntary or otherwise. But Irdessa only looks back to his hand as if she can't tell what it is. She's locked her feelings deeper than Caenin expected. He rubs her shoulder's smooth skin. Her muscles are immaculately defined, even if her skin bears more mementos of violence than he'd normally forgive. But if it is up to Caenin to help her discover her passion, it won't be his least savory pairing. Not by far.

He is considering moving his lips nearer to hers to make it easier on her when his charm inevitably breaks through when she plucks up his hand like she's snatching a frog. She folds his palm toward his forearm, forcing his arm straight. A squeal leaks out of him.

"Put this on me again and it'll never pinch another tit." She releases him and he draws his hand to his chest, involuntarily cradling it. "The Vanguard leaves in the morning. Stay here if you want."

He squeezes his aching wrist, forcefully stifling further whimpers. There don't seem to be broken bones in his hand, however much it hurts. *Fucking barbarian.* What kind of depraved prude scorns him with such finality? What sort of sexless, jealous ingrate? The answer reveals itself to him like mist clearing out of a valley. Kraus ... she must have feelings for him. Caenin tries to ignore the throbbing in his wrist and forces calm condescension into his voice. "I doubt your ogre will be in any shape to travel by the morning."

"He'll be fine," she says.

"Why are you babying him? He slows us down. You say your loyalty's to us. That ogre will get one of us killed."

"My loyalty is not to you, it's to the Vanguard. Kraus has earned his place half a dozen times over. You shot a dreadhop and diddled the locals."

"That's how you justify protecting a rapist?"

She grows static all at once, taut as a spring. Her eyes are lifeless like an orcane's, and harboring at least as much threat. The hairs stand up on Caenin's neck and he fights the urge to back up.

"I'd better not hear you call him that again," she says quietly.

However unsettling she has become, Caenin can't fathom relenting just because she threatened him. The words come out against his better judgment. "I don't know why. It's true."

She continues to stare at him, long enough for his mouth to dry out. Long enough for him to gather she's probably contriving a quiet way to kill him. It takes effort to keep from fleeing.

"Go find Bravensi and any others who missed the meeting," she says. "Tell them we're invited to dine with the Catchers. Tell them we'll be recognizing those who've died." She turns her back and leaves him standing there.

He does not respond. *Do chores*, he mouths at her. Like hell. It's time to salvage the night. She's several feet away before she looks over her shoulder and meets his eye. His feet ferry him off.

On his way to Bravensi's hut he finds Sura watching the ocean while the setting sun melts into it. She was absent during the meeting too. Not that anyone would notice. Caenin's never heard her say a word. He always assumed she was fucking Old Fent. Her new surliness at the old man's absence does nothing to disprove it.

"Hey," he says. "We've got a get-together happening shortly. Mingle with the locals."

If she responds at all, it's with a brief flick of her pupils in his direction. He's never gotten a good read on Sura and this encounter is no exception. Not that it matters. She breaks the bulk edict anyway.

"Probably saying a few words for the dead," he says. "You want to come?"

Now she solidifies, leaving only the non-plaited strands of her yellow hair free to lift in the wind. There's no indication she's going to respond.

"Alright. Well, the offer stands." Caenin takes his leave, starting to wonder if *pariah* is stamped across his forehead.

He slows as he approaches the stone cabin Bravensi occupies. He's not comfortable around her, and not because she is utterly immune to his charm. She's high-strung and unhappy, as if behaving normally without attacking everyone in sight requires some tremendous effort.

The slow rhythmic scrape of a whetstone grinding on a blade's edge comes from within. Barely audible beneath it a conversation is taking place. He hears Bravensi's voice, and the intimacy it harbors is so alien to Caenin's ears it forestalls his impatience and piques his curiosity. And so, instead of making his presence known, he does not.

"I handled it," he hears Bravensi say. "No need to get worked up."

Then there's a pause, and a *shhhhwhip* of a weapon growing sharper.

"If he tries me again I'll tell him the truth," she says, as if answering some inaudible question. "He doesn't compare to you. He never will."

Another pause. Another *shhhhwip*.

"No. I'm not turning you loose on Irdessa's dog."

Another frustrating pause and Caenin deduces he's only hearing half the conversation. Whoever she's talking to must be whispering. He risks sliding the fabric away from the doorway enough to peer into the small chamber.

A low fire in the earthen hearth provides the only light. Bravensi sits straight-backed facing it, entirely naked, cross-legged with her black-red weapon across her bare thighs. This discovery, as these sorts inevitably do, brings an excited flutter to Caenin's guts. He has no choice but to appraise her in a way he never expected to.

"I didn't say he was untouchable to the blade. No one is. I'm not touching him. And you aren't either."

She's bone thin. Hungry looking. But unquestionably fit in a wiry kind of way. Her skin is as pale as porcelain. Can't see her breasts from here, but unless that tight leather she wears has hidden compartments, they're not feeding many babies. Her hair is fixed in a knot high on the back of her head. The bun is more relaxed than it usually is, so there are loose locks drifting down to explore the delicate curve of her neck, the hard line of her shoulders. As she runs the stone over her blade, her back muscles and triceps ripple. Now and then she shifts her weight, making one buttock bulge as the other lifts, accentuating the dimples above her ass. Caenin cannot help but admire her musculature and relish this stolen intimacy. In fact, he'll be damned if his unexpected appreciation isn't tightening his pants.

"According to you, everyone's done damnable sins." It sounds like she's smiling. "Surely I have." The way she's cradling the burnt-crimson blade of that weapon, staring down at it, holding it still with one hand and sharpening with the other, it's almost like she's talking to a lover laid across her lap while brushing his hair.

"Then how many sins has Kraus committed?" Playful sarcasm is in her voice.

This time it's only a brief pause before she visibly recoils, sits straighter, the whetstone faltering.

"I'll say whatever name I choose, including Kraus. Especially if you're making a demand like that." There's the harsh tone Caenin recognizes.

She sits frozen a moment as if scorned. "Do not kill him, Oekner."

Caenin's mouth goes slack, his eyes wide. Everyone knows Bravensi is batshit crazy. Hell, it's her name. He had no idea how bad. She's trying to convince an inanimate object not to murder. Caenin is catching a sight he'd have thought only Kraus could ever appreciate, while witnessing firsthand that she is fucking unhinged.

Bravensi carefully wipes the weapon's face with a clean white cloth, then tests the weapon's edge with the tip of her thumb. She inspects it with loving deliberation, pressing the edge then shifting her hand, bit by bit, all the way down the blade's length. When she finishes, she sticks her red-tipped thumb between her lips, watching the weapon thoughtfully. The faint trails of blood her thumb left behind disappear into the dark metal, absorbed. She takes up her whetstone and makes fine adjustments.

"Do we have to talk about this now?" she asks quietly. There's a pleading quality Caenin didn't know she had in her.

She finishes with the whetstone, places it to the side, wipes the blade again. From a small, ornate box beside her, Bravensi takes a vial of honey-colored liquid and an object wrapped in fine animal hide. She unfolds the skin to reveal a square-cornered object. It is a strip of wheat-colored leather folded over a length of polished wood maybe two inches by seven. The leather is fixed to the board with hammered silver rivulets. She unstoppers the vial, places a fingertip to the opening, flicks it over and back. She rubs together finger and bloody thumb until they both glisten in the firelight then leans forward and places her shiny fingertip against the weapon's face. Her fingers begin to perform a circular massage. Caenin, mouth ajar, is so enrapt he imagines her touch on his own skin.

All of this she does with such passion, Caenin can think of nothing more than a girl he knew in Vim. Rina, the only girl to ever hold his heart utterly captive. Such a passionate lover she was, and so meticulous with her slender hands and fingers. So talented. Unfortunately, her passion was not exclusively Caenin's, and so his unkempt, boyish jealousy resulted in the end of their time together. Of course people warned him that's the nature of a whore. But how was a boy to understand that?

Judging by the time elapsed since Bravensi's last inquiry, Oekner had much to say in response to her question. Or maybe he's said nothing because he's a stick with a blade attached and Caenin is catching the lunacy.

Bravensi gives a small, tired sigh. "Fine," she says. "How many sins?" Cold again, emotionless as the whetstone.

A moment passes. Then she speaks. "I will take one hundred lives, one for each of his sins, if that's what you want."

Caenin takes this opportunity to gently slide his head out of the flap and, as quietly as he can, run the hell away from the cabin.

50

Collateral Insult

FOHRVYLDA
Rain Catch, the Towers

Vyker stands alone. The terraces on which the festivities are arranged are probably the closest to a gathering place this village has to offer. They're nearly level, or at least the scattered plateaus of this Tower's shoulder are less angled, aside from one steep mound that could serve as a stage. One of the plateaus is reserved entirely for a roaring bonfire. The Catchers have collected limbs to burn and stumps and logs for seating. They've also set out cooked fish and fowl and steaming vegetables on several tables, and an entire wall of beer barrels. Seems they specialize in brewing. If their feelings were hurt by the Vanguard's rejection of their invitation to go murder Vretos, or whatever that old man was offering, they appear to be over it. That, or they poisoned the food. But they're eating as much of it as the Vanguard, so probably not.

A lot of the younger Catchers are falling over themselves to get near the named members of the Vanguard. Vyker's unaccustomed to the admiration. A boy several years older than him lingers nearby. Rather than passing on his way as Vyker would prefer, he stands several paces off, sneaking glances as if an introduction is in order. Vyker looks at him. The boy turns his head, hiding his face. Vyker pretends he isn't there. The boy stares at him harder. Vyker turns to his fellows for direction. Most simply ignore the Catchers, even while basking in their attention. Some fighters lap up their reverence, as if this is all perfectly natural. Chief among those is Caenin the Arrow. He's a man Vyker watched kill sprakes and dreadhops at a distance, but during the chaos of their skirmish with the six-orcane patrol, he'd scampered away when a soldier came too close, leaving Vyker to skewer the soldier alone. But judging by how Caenin beams and boasts in the company of teenage boys and girls, he led the charge.

Vyker drinks beer from a shell cup, wondering where Harpold got off to. A Rain Catcher introduced the food and drink as these festivities kicked off. The details about their beer stood out to Vyker. He found it overwrought but unique. Apparently there are two competing brewers here at Rain Catch. The primary difference they claim is their choice of water. One captures rain of the storms that come from the west, out over the Faithless Sea. His lager is dubbed Skyside Pale. The other uses rain harvested from the tangle of Towers to the east and named his product Highwater Husky. Those titles were a natural evolution of the competition between these otherwise amicable brewers. And while it all comes off as the antics of the bored, Vyker can't deny that the two brews taste as different as night and day. The Skyside is lightly golden, nearly transparent, and has a hint of melon rind. The Husky is darkly opaque and nearly thick enough to chew. If you hold it aloft you can see a purple coloration, evidence of the grape skins that went into it. Vyker has no use for beer education, but there is comfort to be had in a place that has the luxury to prioritize beer the way they do here.

The Catchers and the Vanguard idle about, consuming at differing rates and with varying dispositions. But as the sun retreats, the mood at large grows ever less reserved. The Catchers each have their preferred brew and they pitch their choice emphatically to the Vanguard, who will never complain about endlessly proffered beer. Now and then someone climbs that stage-like mound, calls for the gathering's attention and says some words for the fallen. Torah, Fent, and others have gotten their dues. An older woman named Lissa takes the mound to bring up Andelsior. The crowd affirms the weight of his death, him being the *last real leader of Vim*. She seems to have been attracted to him. Each of his mentioned merits is paired with her wiping her shining eyes, inhaling to say more, then losing her voice and pursing her lips, shaking her head. Finally she relents.

It stings, the omission of Vyker's brother, but he doesn't want to show it. There's an unspoken consensus that Dhovoi got what was coming to him. Unspoken around Vyker anyway. Harpold told him. That's well and good and maybe even true, but Dhovoi also liberated the town after Andelsior's arrest. Seems like that should count for something. Vyker heaves a sigh. Someone thumps into him, jostling his thoughts and sloshing beer onto his leg.

"Look at 'em," Magpie mutters, pointing a bent finger. Vyker deduces he's referring to his sister, Maudee, who's pressed firmly against a Catcher villager in the light of the fire, faces close, deep in a private conversation. By the look of them, an exchange of bodily fluids is in order.

"That son of a bitch think I won't poison his damn Catcher beer?" It dribbles off Magpie's tongue like a single word.

Vyker's surprised Magpie can even recognize his twin sister considering how chaotically his pupils are dancing. Magpie *harumphs* and continues on his shambling way, stalking his sister from a distance.

As food and beer run free, the gathering grows louder. Songs are shouted, beer is spilt, clothing gives way to indecency in a shameless way, and a confusing anxiety mounts in Vyker. He hasn't seen revelry like this since ... since his brother's parties in Cornerstone. Vyker sighs again. Dhovoi would love this.

"How you feeling?" It's Harpold, approaching to join him, and in a looser state than Vyker's seen him in some time. Seems he favors the Skyside. He settles down on the log beside Vyker.

Vyker struggles for a response that won't out him as a mood murderer, which also reminds him of awkwardly attending his brother's parties. "Glad to be off my feet," he says lamely.

"You and me both." Harpold always seems more relaxed than Vyker. It's comforting. Something to aspire to. "You don't strike me as the attention-hungry type," Harpold says. "But I'd wager you've got some things to say for Dhovoi. He was your brother after all."

Vyker forces a smile onto his face. *He is my brother. He didn't undo that by letting down Vim. Or dying.* The words are fighting to come out of him, but he holds them back. He shakes his head and makes a dismissive noise, glad Harpold is too drunk to see the conflict he feels.

"Everyone's cheery. Bringing up Dhovoi would ..." His words have caught in his throat. When's the last time he said his brother's name aloud? For a moment he can only commit more effort to forging a smile, shaking his head. He has a drink of beer.

"Cheery?" Harpold snorts laughter. He grabs Vyker's shoulder, his eyes bleary. "You miss the point, boy. Look over there." He aims his cup across the gathering. Lissa, who commended Andelsior so freely, sits hunched, face in her hands, rocking with sobs. A younger woman is rubbing her shoulder companionably while sipping her own beer. "She look cheery to you?"

Before Vyker can answer, Harpold shifts his cup to another. "And him." It's a man staring into the fire, beer cup resting on his paunch, eyes shining like stars. "That's Torah's nephew. Adopted, but the only family he had left." As they watch, the man shifts his gaze to the mound, then averts his eyes nervously. "That ain't cheery."

"Alright," Vyker says, "you've made your point."

"Not yet I haven't." Harpold shifts where he sits. An earnest expression comes over him. "I know you grew up in Vim and the Vanguard's your family. But you're new to this part. Loss. Death." He shakes his head. Goes to speak. Stops and shakes his head again.

Vyker leaves his attention on Harpold, unconvinced the man will come to a point.

"Don't let anyone tell you how to grieve," Harpold forces out at last. An intensity simmers in his expression. "Don't let them tell you shouldn't, or to get past it, or to move on, or any other ignorant shit. They might mean well but they're dumbasses. And if someone tells you not to mourn your brother Dhovoi, you tell them to go fuck themselves."

Vyker's eyes pinch closed and tears roll down his cheek. For a moment he doesn't trust himself to respond. "Yeah?" he says.

"Damn right," says Kraus, approaching from Vyker's other side. He settles down on the log, grunting mightily with the effort. He's got a bottle of the dark Highwater Husky. Makes sense he'd favor that one. "Now, who we telling to go fuck themselves? I'll tell them for ya. Just point toward them. You need some asses kicked?"

His craggy smile is softened by drunkenness.

Vyker pats his back. "We're good, Kraus. Thanks. Are you supposed to be ... that drunk?"

"I ain't drunk." His smile broadens further, squeezing his already narrow eyes to slits. "Shhh. Don't tell Dess."

Vyker decides he's probably the soberest person present. He downs the rest of his Skyside. To his left, Harpold squeezes his shoulder then uses it to stand up. "Give it a thought, Vyker." He flicks his eyes toward the mound. "Might be good." And he goes to refill his cup.

"What's that hunter going on about anyway?" Kraus asks.

A moment ago, Vyker might not have admitted to Kraus that his brother occupies his thoughts. But maybe Harpold's right.

"He told me I should go up there and say something about ... about Dhovoi." The name still tries to stick in his throat, which suggests he needs to refill his beer too.

"Ah." Kraus rocks back, eyes ajar. "That's right, he was your brother." He extends his bottle toward Vyker's cup to refill it. Vyker lets him. For some reason, every time someone tells him that Dhovoi *was* his brother, a drop of anger adds to what feels like a limited reservoir.

"Dhovoi *is* my brother," Vyker corrects. "And whatever he did to bring down Promontory on us doesn't change that." His heart thunders at his words.

Kraus nods, smiling comfortably. "Fucking right," he proclaims, and has a drink. It's like he didn't notice the words, let alone the storm of emotions they brought out.

Vyker exhales some tension. Will the rest of this gathering be so understanding?

"I didn't know Dhovoi so well," Kraus says. "Just met him."

Vyker's heart leaps again, which frustrates him. Can't he discuss his brother without feeling defensive? He needs more beer.

"But in the short time I knew him," Kraus continues, "he displayed a wide range of facial expressions."

Vyker gives that a moment to make sense. When it still doesn't, he looks at Kraus. "What?"

Kraus doesn't acknowledge him. "He may be gone, but I see his influence in you. You both like stabbing things. Just in different ways, you know what I mean?" He hacks laughter, elbowing Vyker roughly and almost sending him sprawling. "But you've got a bigger spear than him."

Heat rises in Vyker's face and his hands turn into fists. He knows in that instant he's in no shape to say anything on the mound. He takes a deep breath to regain control of himself. "Thanks for that, Kraus. I guess."

Kraus dips his chin, clicks his bottle off Vyker's cup, cracking the thin shell. "I'll tell you this. Dhovoi knew how to party. And *that* I can appreciate."

Vyker nods numbly, wishing he could.

The guttural noise Kraus elicits in an effort to stand up puts his previous grunt to shame. "You reckon I oughta say some words about Piss Spray?"

It takes a moment for Vyker to deduce the question was intended for him. "I think pissing will do the job."

Kraus bursts into giddy laughter, surprising Vyker. "You're alright, kid." And off he shuffles toward the beer kegs.

Hollis, a greying fighter who was in Andelsior's advisory, is taking the mound with a cup of the Highwater. He clears his throat for attention. Once he gets it, he lets his rich voice deliver the story of how Torvald came to Vim, all those years ago, with no family but with a glint in his eye, a knowing smile, and more confidence than any thirteen-year-old boy deserves. Hollis tells how the outsider boy interrupted a dispute in the streets, placing himself between two men arguing with drawn steel and somehow managing to mediate until they came to an agreement. Andelsior caught wind of it and sought out the boy, to thank him. This young black-haired boy from Halandor made such an impression that Andelsior took him into Vanguard employ at once.

"But ..." and Hollis smiles at Irdessa, "for all the boy's poise and self-control, he was smitten at the first sight of young Irdessa, then and forever more."

There are warm chuckles at this. Across the way, Irdessa maintains a steel expression, but a sheen overtakes her eyes. She deals with that by downing her cup. Vyker can't tell which brew she's drinking and has the impression she doesn't care which it is.

He'd expected to see her climb that mound and address the gathering. She's the leader here after all. But she doesn't appear to have any interest in it. If he didn't know better, Torvald's name does to her what Dhovoi's does to him. Considering she alone shared his company for his final years, maybe she's convinced no one else knew him like she did. If so, anyone else talking to her about Torvald would inevitably get it wrong. Vyker suddenly wants to approach her. She and Dhovoi were friends after all. She surely has stories about him. She would understand how Vyker feels. He remembers the words she said to him. *We'll get the ones who did it.* But will they? Does she even remember saying that?

He watches Kraus attempt to ascend the mound. Walking up it proved impossible for him, between his gimped knee and the fact that he's staggering drunk. He gets on all fours. Now he's splayed on it like he owes it marital duties. Caenin the Arrow is snickering, pointing, all for the benefit of the Catcher woman holding his arm. She's easily ten years his senior and not striking. Muted face, a blushing forehead, and a smile that exposes her teeth but fails to shift her slabs of cheeks. She's too happy to have the attention he's giving her, as if Caenin's attention is some rarity.

"Better make sure it's consensual," Caenin calls at Kraus. "We know how you are."

Kraus either ignores him or doesn't hear. The woman at Caenin's side is far more entertained by Caenin's cleverness than it deserves. And in a self-perpetuating loop, her laughter inspires Caenin to continue antagonizing. He throws an apple. It bounces off Kraus' boot heel, which is enough to make him slide back down the hill. "What's the matter, ogre?"

Kraus still doesn't respond, instead positioning himself again as if the hillock is vertical.

"Hey, ogre," Caenin says. "When someone around here says *ogre*, they're talking to you." He turns to the woman. "One must forgive the collateral insult it levels at actual ogres."

She reacts as if that was the pinnacle of comedy. Kraus has yet to acknowledge Caenin, despite that Caenin is effectively preventing him from doing anything more than hump the hill.

"Ogre!" Caenin calls, his voice nearly cracking. The woman flinches. Looks like Caenin's not getting the response he expected. Vyker doesn't know a lot about Kraus, but is astute enough to have learned that whatever you want out of him, expect the opposite.

Vyker can hear Kraus muttering to himself. "Don't kill him." He chuckles, teetering on both knees and one fist, trying to climb up the hill while maintaining his grip on his bottle of Highwater. "Got something to say ... 'bout a boy named Piss Spray," he sings. If it's a real song, Vyker's never heard it.

Caenin is finished being ignored. He unlocks himself from the woman and saunters to the hill, where he energetically pulls Kraus' boot, making him flatten and slide down the incline on his belly. Kraus flops onto his back with a sigh, has a drink from his bottle.

"What's it like to always be confused for an ogre?" Caenin asks down at him.

Kraus burps, wipes his mouth, rises to his feet, sways like a lone pine tree. "Didn't keep me from fucking your mother."

A squeak of laughter escapes Caenin's date before she's able to stifle it with both her hands. Caenin's cheeks turn purple.

"Drunken idiot."

Kraus moves forward with bleary eyes and a carefree smile. Caenin moves backward, synchronizing with him like they're dancing. Kraus looks the man down and back up. "Fucking sop," he proclaims.

Caenin clenches both fists. "Rapist," he hisses.

Kraus' eyebrows furrow and his shoulders slump. You'd think he'd been punched in the gut.

Irdessa appears, striding toward the hill as if summoned from the shadows. Before either man notices her she throws her full weight into a punch that impacts Caenin's face with a meaty *thock!*

Caenin's head jerks sideways, feet skittering beneath him. He topples. Irdessa stands above him. Confused rage paints his face, but it's bereft of any threat due to the tears spilling down his cheeks. His chin sits sideways and his teeth won't quite line up. Vyker cocks his head, considering. Funny how the most defined jawbones can be the most brittle.

"I fucking told you." Irdessa dumps the words down on Caenin. She's drunk too. And she's gripping her hand like she might have broken it on Caenin's face.

Caenin's date springs into life, rushing to his side and taking his head in her hands, craning his neck, peering at his jaw, mouth, teeth. The studied ease with which she examines him tells Vyker this is not her first time assessing injury. She's certainly a mother. Caenin initially reacts by recoiling, out of surprise or pride, but then falls limp in her arms, flinching as her touches produce pain. He looks like a child being dusted off after a fall.

"Damn, Dess." Kraus has a look on his face that resembles disbelief.

Irdessa places a hand on Kraus' shoulder, either to help his balance or hers. She squeezes her fist, grits her teeth, draws a breath. "Hey!" she yells at the procession in general. The din declines to accommodate her. "Anyone else want to call him rapist? That's fine. But if you do ..." and she points at Kraus, even while leaning on his shoulder. Blood drips from her hand. "... you're challenging him to a fight. And I'm not stopping it. Fight ends when he's done with you."

The skepticism on Kraus' face gives way to a wide grin, even if his eyes are inebriated slits. "I'm in." He faces the crowd. "Who's first?"

Vyker has walked away from the clearing. He needs something, and whatever it is he's lost hope of finding it here. He follows his feet until realizing they're taking him toward his temporary home, wherein lies silence and his bag, and strapped to it that damn pouch. He falters, hesitating. Why would he seek comfort there? He needs to be rid of it.

He collects the pouch from the dwelling and heads for a cliff. He'll throw it, as is. Let the Faithless take it. So long as the box remains in the pouch, no hidden birdies within can do whatever it is they're intended to do.

Tree limbs and vines give way to starry sky as he nears his destination. The sun is long gone and a cool breeze rises up over the lip of the cliff. Vyker draws back to hurl the pouch and notices Sura sitting alone on the precarious ledge, staring out over the glittering ocean. She's still, like a pond in a cave, imbuing a serenity he immediately envies. It takes a moment, but he's able to huff in enough air to slow his heart. He stashes the pouch away.

"May I?" he asks her, pointing at the ground.

Her shoulders rise then fall.

Vyker sits beside her. She doesn't speak. For a moment, all he's aware of is his rushing breath and his efforts to abate it. Sura offers him a bottle. He takes it, has a drink. It's the Highwater.

He's always felt a kinship with Sura. There's comfort in the company of a person you know will never pry at you. Especially if said person is a peerless warrior, like Sura. And now he feels a closer bond. She lost Old Fent, who according to Dhovoi saved her life years ago and gave her purpose. Apparently Fent found her as a tongueless child, starving in an empty home. He took her in. Raised her. Protected her from the world. Now she is alone. Does she know that Irdessa might have been able to prevent Fent's death? It doesn't seem wise to bring up.

Whatever the Vanguard had to say about Fent from atop the mound, Sura obviously didn't care to hear. Vyker understands. They didn't know him like she did. But seeing her here, suffering as she is, Harpold's words start to make sense.

"I am sorry," Vyker says. "about Fent."

Sura nods without looking at him.

"Are you alright?" he asks.

She turns toward him with watery eyes then away again, as if even that small effort was nearly too much. She lays a hand flat against her chest then makes a gesture like she's breaking a stick.

Vyker sighs, and for the first time doesn't fight back his tears. "Me too."

~

Irdessa thought she'd composed herself pretty well, until Hollis started talking. *Torvald loved her. Now he's dead.* Thanks for the reminder. Needless to say, she got thirsty after that. East beer, west beer, who gives a shit? Then she found herself standing over Caenin with what felt like a broken fist. Now she and Kraus are seated and he's examining it, pinching and bending.

"Nothing's broken," he says.

"You sure?"

He laughs. "Nothing in your hand is. Can't say the same for that fucking sop's face."

Irdessa watches the gathering and sips her newly refilled cup. She hopes this respite has served its purpose. A few scuffles sprouted up but were dowsed before significant injury could occur. Mostly. There's a camaraderie among the Vanguard. A unity founded in exhaustion and loss, cemented by mutual near-death experiences. Her fighters needed rest. They needed closure.

Some want to stay here in Rain Catch. Some seem to want a piece of Vretos himself. Inspired by that old man's sermon no doubt. Those who want to stay are free to. In the unfortunate event that a battalion falls on the Vanguard again, five or ten extra bodies will only prolong the suffering. Then again, if they escape to Redemier and find peace, assuming it's there to be found, this scant party will need to become a functioning colony. The diversity of skills a larger group can offer would avail them. Irdessa huffs. This chain of thought is too slippery to even try to grasp at the moment. She hasn't drunk enough to mute the Tactician inside her yet. This must be remedied.

"Why'd you stand up for me?" Kraus asks. "You think that spineless fucker can hurt me?"

"Not half as much as you hurt yourself."

He raises an eyebrow in consent.

She gives the question deeper consideration. "Because sometimes it's better to treat a person as they're attempting to be rather than what your eyes tell you. Eyes tell lies."

"That gem come from you or Torvald?"

The laugh that escapes Irdessa surprises her, leaving her feeling empty. "I can't tell anymore."

He's quiet a moment, has a drink. "What am I attempting to be?" He sounds entertained by the thought.

"Not a rapist," she says. "Any fuckwit can regurgitate your charges. I think they're sprakeshit. You're not like the others."

"I'm not like the other rapists?" He bursts into hacking laughter. "Gods' shit, Dess, you know how to butter a boy up. I'll be naked in no time."

A smile cracks her cold cheeks. "In that case, I take it back."

"Hell no. Can't unring that bell."

"You didn't rape me when you had the chance," she says.

Kraus is surprisingly silent, clenching his jaws. It's the same look he gets when you offer a compliment he can't refute.

"You've been through a lot for me." Irdessa says the words without knowing where they came from or where they intend to go.

"Yeah." He smiles. "It's been wild."

"Why'd he do it?"

Kraus looks confused. "What?"

"Torvald. Why'd he leave us?" She didn't mean to say it. She certainly didn't mean to start crying again. At least she's reached a point in her grief where tears can escape without distorting her face in the process. "Son of a bitch."

Kraus plucks at his lip, studies the ground. He opens his mouth, then thinks better and has a drink.

"Sorry," she says, taking a moment to expel loose snot from each nostril. "Every time I think I'm past it ... I pretend to be, because everyone's watching. Then something blindsides me and everyone's still watching and I ... I ..."

"You break someone's fucking jaw." Kraus cackles.

"Glad you find it funny," Irdessa says.

"Someone's got to."

The festivities are diminishing. Catchers and fighters have broken off into smaller groups or pairs, wandered off, laid down flat on the ground. The once-blazing fire smolders orange, neglected.

"You're mad at him," Kraus says.

"No shit."

"You know what they say about forgiveness, don't you?"

Irdessa looks at him, incredulous he even knows the word.

"It only takes one." He's looking all sagely, nose high, mouth thoughtful, eyes drunken slits.

"Does that not apply to you? You can't even forgive yourself." The words clatter out before she can catch them.

His brow furrows and he looks away. "It's just a thing I heard. Probably sprakeshit."

His offended reaction is the perfect capstone to Irdessa's dismal mood. She's hurt his feelings. Amazing how easily she does that, considering he's tougher than orcane steak.

"You know why Torvald chose you?" she says.

His eyes are distant a moment longer, then he gives a *hmph*. "'Cause I'm hard to kill?"

"You're fearless."

"Am I?"

"You are," she says. "You're the bravest person I know."

"And the brave dodge the grave." He says it with a mocking flourish of his hand.

"Hah. Keswal." She clinks her cup off his bottle. "Those were the days."

Kraus snorts. "You're drunk."

"Yes." She downs the rest of her cup, in case there was some question about her resenting the fact, then rises onto unsteady feet.

"You're braver than me," Kraus mutters.

"Shit," she tells him. "I'm not brave. I'm pissed off."

He laughs, rising to his own feet. "Well, I'm not brave either. I just don't mind dying."

"Then we make a fine pair."

Kraus smiles, sighs. "I wish Bravensi had come out."

Irdessa shakes her head, unable to imagine that having gone well. "Get some sleep, Kraus the Carcass. Tomorrow's going to hurt."

51

All Things Have a Season

AUSGAN
The Tribunal, Stravhelm

The late morning sun glares down on Obsydia. It feels like the focused, condescending attention of some judgmental entity. *Look what came of your laughable ambitions.* She shifts her weight on the hard bench. The silksedge cushions stitched into the mahogany seating of this booth might have, at one time, provided more relief than bare wood. That time is long past.

There is no shade here, not even for the Triumvirate's booth. The air is barely moving, surely stunted by Intemrus' efforts to ensure no one misses any detail and to maximize discomfort for all. There aren't even fanners on hand. Obsydia's dele is among the thinnest she has, best for flowing in a breeze and allowing heat to escape. Not as comfortable as wearing nothing.

The auditorium where the tribunal meets is crescent-shaped, carved into the northern face of Mount Adenhelm. Rows of concentric steps hewn from the mountain itself serve as seating. They overlook a bare expanse, maybe a dozen strides in diameter, that serves as the stage. Off the north side of the stage is open air, so that a panoramic view of the islets and lagoons north of Ausgan make a backdrop for whatever unlucky soul is being tried. Today, that honor belongs to Magus Kalderys. He stands center-stage wearing an unadorned rhyolite dele and a vacuous expression. Obsydia refuses to observe him. She cannot.

Stravhelm's court meets rarely, only a handful of times since Obsydia became magister some fifteen years prior. Ausgan justice is simple, straightforward, with seldom confusion on who's guilty and how to deal with them. Usually Obsydia acts as judge here. But today, with the magus, the Consonant Fist standing trial himself, Intemrus' alleged sovereignty is required. The auditorium is stuffed to near bursting. There are probably five hundred exemplars squeezed into the stone benches and Imala only knows how many crammed into the hallways to listen in. Named mancers fill the lowest, front-most seats. Behind them are their sentinels, then mancers in training, proctors, chaplains. The next rows seat rhyolites. Behind them, most numerous of all, are andesites of all ranks and professions.

The Triumvirate's booth is for the sovereign, the magister, the magus, and select members from their respective entourages. It is stage-level, facing the tried, partitioned off from the other audience, and today a third of it is empty. Intemrus sits straight-backed to Obsydia's immediate left, immaculately clean today, his crystalline eyes planted on the horizon like his mind is not even present. Obsydia always assumed his failure to emote was a result of an elongated life of disciplined self-mastery. A byproduct of his preference to the company of gods over mortals, or the future over the present. Knowing now what she knows of Kale's emotion-canceling abilities, she's less sure of that. Maybe Intemrus is simply masking his feelings. Maybe he does care what is happening here today. Despite his clean clothing and astute, controlled posture, the blunt sunlight exposes him as downright vulturine. The glossy skin of his cheeks and wrists and hands is webbed with branching veins, nearly stabbed through by sharp bones. It would appear the crystal's absence is bringing his decrepitude to light. This is the intended result, and it's granting Obsydia the strength to endure the day.

Abvelt the Crier takes the floor leisurely. He's in a floor-length violet dele made largely of shimmering parakeet feathers, with swirling designs embroidered in pearl-colored silk at its wide cuffs and hem and neck. He's had his face freshly shaved and his grey-peppered black hair trimmed to a clean quarter-inch. He stops, facing the Triumvirate, with Kalderys behind him. If ever an exemplar fit his position perfectly, it is Abvelt. His face is sopping with cheer, as if it's not sweaty exemplars his beady eyes perceive but playful puppies. Despite his obvious ownership of all attention, he patiently aims his chin this way and that, rooting through his audience, proving to everyone the stage is his. Experiencing his utter satisfaction at today's bulging audience is making Obsydia's temper rise toward boiling. He clears his throat, and even that feels like part of his grand melodrama.

"Resonations," he says, in his rich voice. "We congregate today to address events momentous to the fate of Ausgan, of Stravhelm, of the Triumvirate." He patiently lets each point linger before moving to the next. "And of course, of Magus Kalderys." He extends an arm behind him without looking back. There's another excruciating span of naught but distant waves, gull cries, and the sound of sweat creeping out of Obsydia's pores. Abvelt's enjoyment of the silences he inflicts is inversely proportional to hers. And of course it is. When else does his life have purpose?

At some cue only the crier notices, he proceeds, drawing a thin scroll from within his dele. He opens it, peruses it a moment. It is so quiet Obsydia can hear the breath wheezing through his nostrils. He turns his pinched eyes toward the upper seats.

"To recount the events of the last several days in a succinct manner: Basalt Kale has betrayed Stravhelm and amassed a staggering quantity of criminal offenses. At present, the charges he owes answer to are—and this list may not be comprehensive ..." Abvelt takes a breath, clears his throat again. "The interruption of the ordained campaign on Hargrim. The murder of Prime Sentinel Arc. Aiding the escape of a prisoner from Stravhelm's cells. The interruption of the ordained campaign on Napiri. The murder of Prime Sentinel Selu."

Abvelt concludes with a grave expression, looking around like this is all his audience's fault. The crowd reacts with shocked silence. Rather than fabricating her own expression of appropriate concern, Obsydia shifts her weight from one aching buttock to the other. He didn't mention the crystal. She didn't expect him to, but relief fills her nonetheless.

"Never before has an exemplar of Erudition gone so wrong. The inciting incident was a single conversation between him and the imprisoned spy he eventually freed. Sovereign Intemrus has warned us in no uncertain terms the threat our enemies pose, explained why we must harden our hearts to them. Does exposing ourselves to their lies prove our faith? Do we improve from such a test?" He scoffs and shakes his head. "Does breathing molten earth strengthen your lungs? No. That will kill you. And discoursing with liars only expresses our distrust in lessons already hard-earned by our timeless sovereign. What a tragic waste, to insist on relearning a time-tested maxim ... again." His shoulders plummet, a testimony to his personal and profound disappointment.

"For even one of these charges, Basalt Kale has earned death. He has earned a place below that of our enemies, the Fohrvyldan heathens. At least they, though little better than animals, do as they promise to. They behave as expected. Basalt Kale resided in the holy city, basking in the enlightenment of consonance his whole life. He was, by merit of his residency here if nothing else, obligated to return the blessing. Alas."

Some of those details are debatable, and surely inventions of the crier himself. While Kale the songless did enjoy benefits of dwelling in Erudition, he never showed the slightest interest in consonance. Toward the end, in fact, it seemed he preferred the jungle.

"After the murder of Prime Sentinel Selu, the basalt escaped with the help of ... Porter Culver."

At this, the crier's disappointment is authentic, a first for this monologue. The announcement produces unhappy murmurings from the audience. Kale was odd enough to warrant aberrant behavior, especially after the incident years ago with Adept Thran. But no one expected such deviance out of smiling, stalwart Porter Culver. Physically imposing, but no more threatening of demeanor than a gorged tapir. He had a mind for pristine clothes and how to earn more of them. Promotion was his priority, as it should be. What was it about his

1518 | David T List

friendship with Kale that turned him against the holy city? Why did he throw everything away? The last time his advancement test was scheduled, Intemrus was unavailable and so the test was postponed. Upon scrutiny in this moment, Obsydia realizes that might have actually happened twice. Surely that alone wouldn't have damaged Culver's loyalty. Then again, were those the only times his promotion was postponed? Obsydia pinches the bridge of her nose in frustration. She should have questioned him immediately after learning of Kale's offenses. She should have had him brought in when Kale returned to him.

Culver was Kale's only friend aside from Proctor Alika. The proctor is not in attendance today. His absence isn't out of the ordinary. There are no flowers here. And Alika shies away from conflict, competition, even raised voices. His social lethargy makes him a fine fit for the overgrown Elucidatorium. But it certainly doesn't explain why he mounted the city wall two nights prior to crane his old neck, snooping on Haik's fusiliers while they failed to bring down Kale. Their shots were confounded by setuar—flower sprites. The proctor's relief that evening was palpable, but with a hint of shame. He's had more than enough time out there in isolation to make bonds with the spirits. Surely he didn't call them ...? He couldn't have, could he?

Obsydia squeezes her temples, trying to fight back the looming headache. Exactly how distracted has she been? How right was the late Selu in her accusations? Obsydia feels the need to break something.

"This brings us to the here and now," Abvelt says.

The magus' body becomes rigid. Obsydia's heart thuds. Dread runs through her. The crier will embellish Kalderys' charges. Everyone knows it. That's his job. She shifts her weight again, trying to hide her unease.

"Magus Kalderys was incapacitated by Basalt Kale."

Truly, a more unlikely sentence has never been spoken. Kalderys' eyes slide closed. Abvelt's eyes glow as if you couldn't ask for cheerier news.

"In the process, the basalt allowed most of the spies who had infiltrated Napiri to flee into the jungle. The full extent of the damage has yet to be ascertained. Guaranteed containment may not even be possible."

Abvelt rolls the scroll and swings it round behind his back, where he clasps it with both hands, but doesn't yet relinquish the floor. Of course the sack of air isn't done. That would be too much like mercy. Here comes his long-winded take on the matter.

"Calomancer Arc and Aridimancer Selu knew the hazards of the occupation when they sought to become prime sentinels for the magus himself. And when he picked them, tested them, accepted them, he obligated himself as their protector and mentor. He ..." Abvelt's voice wavers. A sheen of sweat glistens across his forehead. His eyes flick to Kalderys. Most likely the rest of the audience doesn't have the means to observe what has affected the crier. Obsydia does. An intense blast of emotion radiated out from Kalderys at the mention of his two primes. A cloud of pure shame and disgust, regret and disappointment, all compressed into a scalding rage.

Obsydia revels in Abvelt's discomfort. Inciting that reaction is as close to power as he will ever come. Overgrown andesite. His masterwork is to entertain an idle mob with polished words. Glorified bloviator. The exemplar behind him animates air into omnivorous energy capable of disintegrating all it touches. Kalderys' each exhalation means more to consonance than Abvelt's entire legacy.

The crier draws forth his scroll once more and scrutinizes it. He arches an eyebrow as if unsettled by what he finds. As if it was written by anyone besides him.

"Magus Kalderys failed his sentinels, and he failed us," he mutters, rushing to get the words said.

The magus shifts his weight. His boot scritches against the dirt. Abvelt gives a start and the scroll leaps from his hands, falling in a heap. He collects it, attempting to do so with some amount of dignity. Once composed, he does not turn his back to Kalderys again.

"If anyone can defend the magus by speaking on his behalf, do so now." The crier blots at his brow, stepping aside to leave the accused as the stage's only occupant. Judging by the deep breaths he's gulping down, he couldn't be more relieved the ordeal of accusing the magus is behind him. What a hero.

The calls of gulls rise up over the northern lip of the stage, cushioned faintly by the whisper of distant crashing waves. There is a muffled cough from high in the seats. A clearing throat. Subdued shifting. Aside from that, Obsydia's pounding heart is all she hears. Of course no one will defend Kalderys after that condemnation.

The power seekers won't speak up, despite that Kalderys' personal advances in consonance were integral to their own journeys. There is too much at stake for them. Charges like these have never been leveled. If Kalderys is indeed weak, then standing up for him would sully their name, in the eyes of their peers and competition, maybe even the Triumvirate for all they know, or what remains of it. Helping him would hurt their chances of scavenging his title. As if anyone here is worthy of it.

The cunning incompetent, those who know better than to think they can carry Kalderys' mantle, are all attached like thirsty lampreys to someone more capable than themselves. To defend Kalderys, prevent his removal, would betray unspoken arrangements. *Fucking ticks.* Thank Imala Selu isn't here to further besmirch the magus. *Dead bitch.* Hopefully her absence is marginally less incriminating than whatever vitriol she might have spun had she not been negated out of existence like Adept Thran.

Kalderys is a statue, moving less than even his shadow. Obsydia's gritting her teeth. How can the gathered mass understand a thing about consonance and still mistake him as weak? He's a pinnacle of consonance. How can anyone misread his silence, his control, for anything but power? *Ingrates.* How can the sovereign allow this farce to proceed unless he himself is threatened by Kalderys? That's proof Obsydia's plan is just.

Surely Intemrus knows what his disapproval is doing to Kalderys. The pain it causes. The blessing of Obsydia's gift of emotion perception is also its curse. Secrets are laid bare before her. None can lie to her. She is and will forever be alone, surrounded by people impervious to glaring truths.

Sunlight glints off a tear on Kalderys' cheek. It's more than Obsydia can take. She stands. Kalderys' eyes fall on her immediately. Buried deep beneath his shame there is an ember of hope, and that itself nearly crushes her. She didn't want to speak first because it's likely no one will follow her. But Kalderys must be defended. The Triumvirate is expected to speak, either on behalf of the accused or to damn him further. Her words must target the up-and-coming mancers, those most immediately affected by this potential gap in Stravhelm's leadership. Those who ascend ranks must respect Kalderys, even if they don't serve him directly. And they must do so while retaining the respect of their peers and followers. It is her duty to make this their conclusion as well. Her title, even as one of the Triumvirate, does not alone secure her as sovereign's beneficiary once he's gone. She needs Kalderys.

"Resonations, exemplars. Thank you for your presence on this unfortunate but important occasion. Abvelt has stated the magus' charges, and even saw fit to grace us with a crier's perspective on the allegations." Obsydia pins the crier with a sweltering glare. "We appreciate your insight."

Now it's Abvelt's turn to tug at the neck of his dele. She spares him and explores the faces of the exemplars gathered. There she finds indifference. Skepticism. Mild bemusement. Most experience feelings of being insignificant under her gaze, which, compared to Magus Kalderys and a scant few others, they are. Perhaps over the years she's made her position on that too obvious. But why wouldn't she? The ladder of Erudition is fiercely competitive. Stravhelm even more. Obsydia knows it perhaps more than any other. No one reached down their hand during her ascent and she never expected them to. Everything she has, she took. She expects no different from them. But standing here now, with the gulf between her and her peers so bleakly exhibited, she can't tell if she's a product of Intemrus' holy city, or its precedent. The majority of the gathered would fall on her like vultures at their first opportunity, a fact that makes her equal parts proud and unnerved.

This audience will take her words with a grain of salt, expecting little more than to be entertained by a groveling magister trying to save her right hand. They will inevitably mistake Kalderys' humility for weakness and underestimate him. She has to surprise them.

"The crier merely scratched on a crucial point. But who can blame him? This is all in regard to consonance, not crying." Obsydia smiles disarmingly and is rewarded by some tittering from the haughtier exemplars.

"He said, *Never before has an exemplar of Erudition gone so wrong.* What an understatement. Basalt Kale is indeed an anomaly. He was brought in as all were. Chaplains witnessed him showing resonance with the Imala and he was inducted, while his birther and her village were rewarded. Like some of us, he went on to express little innate musical ability. No ear, no timing. He was designated basalt and destined to serve the holy city negating as basalts do. Nothing extraordinary about that."

If any basalts were present today rather than cot-bound and moaning, they'd surely agree.

"But that's where similarities ended. He never experienced any familiar ailments as a result of negation. Never before or since has an exemplar reacted to negation the way Kale does. It was *decided* ..." This wording is important. "... that he remained in place, be observed, tested, utilized. It was our mission to watch him and learn more about consonance in doing so, and hopefully one day devise a calling and title worthy of his unique abilities. At the least, an exemplar who experiences no negation sickness could benefit our training regiments. But one day something went wrong and Adept Thran, a classmate of Kale's, was taken from us." Also important wording. A pause to emulate reflection. "After much deliberation, the Triumvirate concluded his actions weren't malicious. Our sovereign's judgment was such: We don't punish individuals for anomalies in consonance. We would continue observing him, preferably without placing anyone else in danger."

Here she pauses. Looks in their eyes. Her next point must transcend their opinion of her, of Kalderys, of Intemrus even. It must be as precise as a viper's strike, and so she delivers it plainly.

"We knew the liability Basalt Kale presented. Our acceptance made us all complicit."

She pauses for them to ingest it. For Intemrus to ingest it. Hard words, considering they incriminate the sovereign. She feigns relaxing before proceeding. Less somber, equally earnest.

"The defining nature of any subject worth studying is that we cannot yet predict it. We must strive to. Consonance is not a rehearsal of established concepts, it is an adventure. And those have risks."

She's not looking at Intemrus but can tell his attention is on her. She will not observe him, but the pride he emanates at her words is evident.

"Kalderys is the greatest adventurer this nation has ever created. He was inducted just as Kale was. He, too, was an anomaly. He sang before he spoke. His devotion to consonance is rivaled by one alone." *If even one.* "The title of magus was invented for him, a means to try and encapsulate an exemplar whose discipline and mastery towered over any who came before him." If the crier can embellish, then she can too. Kalderys isn't called *maester* like his predecessor because Maester Kasm the terramancer accidentally killed himself with quicksand and jinxed the title. There's hardly been an earth-based mancer since.

"The work he's done in defense of the holy city, in preparation of the Heathen Tide, and in opposition of the Untamed cannot be overstated. You all know this. You've seen it. And the simple fact is that there isn't a rhyolite, andesite, or even basalt alive today that doesn't have Kalderys to thank for their education." Not that a living basalt would thank Kalderys for anything. Negating for the magus is a death sentence unless you're a freak like Kale. "That includes me." She will leave to their imagination whether the sovereign is included as well.

"Working together with his prime sentinels, Kalderys pruned away infection in the south wherever it sprang up. And in all his years, only twice have missions been anything aside from absolute success. As Abvelt said, our sentinels know what they take on. We could all benefit from this sobering reminder. We are at war with Fohrvylda. Our enemy sneaks through our borders in the south and seeks to dismantle our defenses in any way possible. We may die for our faith. And when it happens, we should hope our lives were as productive for consonance as those of Calomancer Arc and Aridimancer Selu."

Time to bring it in. Attention wanes. A thrill of trepidation arises in Obsydia. Her final words must work toward stealing the sovereign's power while blaming him for this mess.

"I'll spare you after this final thought. Today we ask ourselves ... if we'd known the consequences of leaving Kale in place, would we still have done it? Looking back, one might assume the advances Kale indirectly brought on do not excuse the tragedy he sowed directly."

She smiles, despite the conundrum. Clasps her hands in front of her.

"To those of you suffering such a dilemma, allow me to remind you. *Intemrus sees all.* He knows no surprises. For those of you intent on condemning consonance's most devout student over this incident, I ask that you bear that in mind."

She is finished. She sits down, spending the last of her energy to do so gracefully. This bench was designed for discomfort and achieves it masterfully. In this moment she relishes it. What she wouldn't give for her adherents' fans. Her speech seems to have accomplished its purpose, inasmuch as it could have. There's a squared quality to the magus' shoulders once more, despite his plain sack of a dele. The eyes gazing at Kalderys exhibit reverence, their murmuring hints of deference, even from the named mancers who yearn for his position. A general pulse of the audience reveals an increased admiration for the magus. She has changed some minds.

Abvelt returns to the floor, cheer anew on his face. "Thank you, Magister. What profound points. Anyone else? If you'd offer words for Magus Kalderys' defense, do so now."

Obsydia can't even manage to hate the crier. It's not his priority that Kalderys be condemned, only that he himself be seen and heard. Although, watching him hung up by his heels and slowly dipped in magma would be quite the treat. She leans back, picturing that while idly fretting at the neck of her dele.

A hush falls over the gathering. Intemrus is rising to his feet. Obsydia's heart pangs against her ribs. It's too soon. Something was supposed to happen first. Absolution? She clenches her hands together to keep them from ripping open the throat of her outfit. Buttons will truly be the death of her.

"Magus Kalderys, those who have spoken ... spoke truth." Intemrus' voice is neither loud nor soft, not angry or glad. Without inflection. His eyes are neutral, windows to a barren sky.

Kalderys watches the sovereign without fear, and for a single moment Obsydia imagines him challenging Intemrus. She imagines him striding forward and lifting the ancient exemplar by his neck, wringing him like a chicken, and throwing his body over the stage's edge. It is an idle fantasy. Today, anyway.

"Time moves differently for me," the sovereign says. "I expect I sometimes appear inattentive, absent even. But I assure you, Kalderys, your devotion and sacrifice are known." His lips curl slightly. On anyone else, that would be a warm smile. "Obsydia is right. Consonance has advanced more steadily in your lifetime than ever before. That even includes any point in my own life. You are truly gifted by the Imala. Thank you for your service. Resonations, Kalderys."

"Resonations, Sovereign."

"Do you intend to defend yourself from the charges set forth?"

The question hovers like a raised baton. Kalderys' shoulders lift and fall. His eyes do not waver. Obsydia sees what's about to happen. He won't speak. His life work is unambiguous. His deeds unquestionable. His devotion unwavering. But if Intemrus himself cannot see Kalderys' worth in his actions, then his words would be no more than excuses. They would mean less than nothing. Normally, that would be a respectable sentiment. Commendable even. But Intemrus isn't the only one judging him. That has never mattered to him before and it certainly doesn't now. But now, above any other moment, it should. Would he speak up for himself if he knew what was at stake? Then again, would he still be the Magus Kalderys Obsydia needs if he did?

Kalderys' voice is steady. "No, Sovereign."

"Very well." Those crystalline eyes. That lifeless smile.

Obsydia grips her seat.

"All things have a season. Yours is over. You are no longer the harbinger of my justice."

A collective gasp rises from the audience.

"You no longer have a seat on the Triumvirate or a tower in Stravhelm. You will no longer teach consonance in Erudition. Ausgan cannot afford to spread a discipline of failure."

Kalderys' mouth tightens. His eyes gleam. Someone somewhere gives a sound of despair and it almost sends Obsydia over the edge. The sovereign's words may as well be slashes across her heart. It's all she can do to remain straight-faced, and she expects she is failing at that. She needed Kalderys to lose respect for the sovereign. But not like this. Intemrus' utter rejection will crush him. And Obsydia can only blame herself.

The sovereign continues, "Obviously, we've yet to analyze the situation completely. Basalt Kale is still at large, being pursued by Ashmancer Haik and Akoromancer Euphrain. Once he is apprehended we will learn more. In the meantime, you may continue your training, alone, while dwelling in Rhyolite Tier. You are no longer magus."

Kalderys' chin dips. Tears spill over his cheeks. His shoulders shake gently. A miasma of scorn rises from the named mancers. Obsydia can almost taste their contempt at his display of weakness. She rips her eyes away before the image can sicken her.

"In the meantime, we must appoint an interim magus," Intemrus says. "Magister Obsydia, who will you put forth for the honor?"

Obsydia's presentable face is spent. But having known this may happen, she's not entirely at a loss. She rises to her feet again. The audience's collective amusement falls on her. Abject contention hasn't managed to kill her yet, and hopefully it won't today. Chances are her selection will not surprise many who have been paying any attention. Thankfully, the ashmancer isn't here to throw a fit at her choice.

"Yes, Sovereign." Obsydia swallows the lump in her throat. "Cryomancer Hyrala will make an excellent magus, interim or no." An outright lie. Kalderys is the only magus. And Obsydia cannot even look at him after saying those words.

Hyrala stands at once, faces Obsydia in rhystic subservience. Her grey-streaked black hair is braided tightly and knotted high on her head. The broad smile splitting her olive-toned face does little to dampen the harsh black pinpoints of eyes, her curved hawk-beak of a nose. Her movement belies the controlled elegance of one who, although far past their youth, makes special efforts to remain fit. "Thank you, Magister. Intemrus' Will be done."

"Cryomancer Hyrala and I will convene to appoint her prime sentinels," Obsydia says, trying to infuse enthusiasm in her voice. She may as well be talking about the ingredients of bricks. "They will be announced once the ceremony is scheduled."

"Resonations," Hyrala says, still in subservience, still beaming.

Obsydia offers her as authentic a smile as she can muster. "Resonations, Hyrala."

Hyrala sits back down, folding her hands in her lap, to revel in the hushed congratulations of her nearest contemporaries. She is proud, excited, a little nervous. Obsydia only registers loss. She should be happy for Hyrala. That's hard considering discovering Hyrala's fortune involves shoveling dirt over her own dead dream. But why is it that way? She needed Kalderys for his power, and if that was only ever a product of his confidence, then it has truly expired. Hyrala is as devoted to her as Kalderys ever was. More so maybe, if she's less enraptured by Intemrus. And she is quite powerful. The gargantuan seashell on Obsydia's gazebo is testament of that.

The sovereign tips his head, releasing Obsydia from the audience's attention. Obsydia flops down. The crier speaks again, about the different sorts of responsibility, be it shared or individual. He mentions the position of folksteller. Obsydia wishes she cared. Kalderys hasn't looked at her since Intemrus' sentence. He is molten shame. It's a miracle he's remained upright. He believes he disappointed her. Probably he did. She's too numb to tell.

The audience stands. The tribunal has concluded. Obsydia is vaguely aware the Triumvirate is released. Except it's not a Triumvirate any longer. Not without Kalderys. She, Intemrus, and their entourages rise. She follows his lead from the auditorium into the shade of the upper hallway. Her hands move, at last, to undo the top several buttons of her dele in preparation of its coming retirement into the hottest burning brazier on her gazebo. Intemrus slows his pace to walk beside her in the hallway.

"Any word from Ashmancer Haik?" His voice is flat. If he knows Haik seeks not only Kale but his stolen crystal, he doesn't indicate it.

"Yes, Sovereign. The porter and the basalt have fled to the Faithless Sea and taken to canoe. They departed from a fishing village south of the East Rostrum. I received Haik's report early this morning. He acquired a vessel in Midharbor and is in pursuit. It's just a matter of time, surely."

Intemrus is quiet a moment. "Taken to the Faithless by canoe," he speculates. "Bearing east? Toward Fohrvylda?" His tone is more curious than concerned.

"That, I don't know. Haik expects to catch them with little difficulty. He reported, and this detail may have been mistaken in the report, that the basalt was still unconscious when they stole the canoe. I gather the porter simply meant to escape, by any means and toward any destination."

"Unconscious?" The sovereign's thin eyebrow rises. "So the porter ... ported him? The entire way from Napiri?" Intemrus looks like he's holding back laughter.

Obsydia is devoid of cheer. "As I gather."

Intemrus has his hands clasped behind his back. There is a glittering thoughtfulness in his eyes. "Hm. A basalt, able to negate our strongest channeler, turned corrupt by an imprisoned spy, in turn corrupts an andesite porter." Now the sovereign does chuckle, as if this is all some joke he alone gets. "How refreshing. That basalt does not get nearly enough credit."

Obsydia's mouth falls open. If she didn't know better, she'd think Intemrus is impressed. Anger is rising in her, and all the accusations she didn't yell during the tribunal are threatening to boil out. This is his fault for being captivated by the meddling basalt. She expected her speech's suggestion of his negligence to be subtle, not lost entirely.

"Yes. Basalt Kale makes a fine weapon against consonance." She doesn't even attempt to dull the sarcastic edge.

Intemrus is not taken aback. Judging by his distant, mirthful expression he's still basking in Kale's glory. "Basalt is no longer an accurate title. Nor is negator. No, he's something more."

Of all the titles that come to Obsydia's mind to describe the one responsible for ruining her dreams, murdering fellow exemplars, and fucking natives, none are as pretty as basalt. This is not even mentioning that Kale stole Intemrus' crystal. Is the sovereign trying to goad her into screaming that aloud? Because it's almost working. While she roils in the grief of losing her near-invincible right hand, Intemrus puzzles over a fitting word for Basalt Kale's catastrophic achievements.

Intemrus can't possibly know Kale has the crystal, or surely he'd be more concerned that it's heading out over open sea. Why did Kale steal the crystal? What was he trying to accomplish? To save that one filthy native who hiked up her vine skirt for him? If that crystal bestowed Intemrus immortality, then why is he still happy? And if it didn't, why is the claim punishable by death? Surely not to simply confound spies.

Obsydia doesn't have enough wine in her. Her glaring ignorance of the crystal has been bared, making her grand plan seem like a child's ploy, lacking any functional forethought. What truly motivated her? If power, then why is she seething? Hyrala could prove more useful than Kalderys. But thoughts of his punishment possess her mind.

"The cleansing of Napiri," Intemrus says, jarring her from her contemplation. "How is it progressing?"

"Poorly. There is only so much we can do to apprehend the scattered natives. The daughter of the spy we captured is fleeing south toward the Untamed. Seems she is spreading rebellious propaganda as she goes." This admission reflects poorly on Obsydia, even if Kalderys has already taken the fall for it. But she doesn't have the energy to pretty up the truth. Also, Intemrus is entirely too happy. He deserves a slice of misery.

"This confirms the fleeting nature of her faith," Intemrus says. "You were right to order their cleansing."

At that, for the first time, Obsydia comes face to face with the disconnect Intemrus suffers. This girl's behavior could be a direct result of her father's imprisonment and death, her town's destruction. What is the advantage of forcing an action on a person then punishing them for it?

Intemrus gazes up at the mosaic murals in the windows they pass. His eyes linger on one particularly disturbing depiction labeled *The Infernal Deception*, featuring a grey beast of a man with purple eyes devouring a pale young girl. It's the Deceiver, purportedly responsible for the strife between Ausgan and Fohrvylda. "Traveling south, sowing discord," Intemrus says. "That will be to her own detriment if she winds up a guest of the cannibals."

Intemrus doesn't actually seem to care. He is still disconnected from this conversation. She'd have sworn that this, surely, would rile him up. Is he no longer concerned with corralling blasphemy? She always gathers that the sovereign is more interested in her demeanor than her report, as if nothing is news to him except her reaction. But now that she's dying inside, he's entirely untroubled.

"Our first priority, Magister, is the defense of Stravhelm. You know that, don't you?" Intemrus doesn't look at her, but there's been a shift.

"Of course."

"The Heathen Tide will crash on our shores soon. Are you prepared?"

"I was." Another response that would have benefited from a lie.

"Yes," Intemrus says. "Hyrala is no Kalderys."

Obsydia almost stops in her tracks. One hundred unspeakable responses rise to her tongue. *You've crippled our defenses. You rewarded his fealty by stripping his title. This is your fault!* Except, that isn't true. If any single person is to blame for his demotion, it is her. She could have stopped Kale. She alone saw there was something wrong. And she was distracted, as Selu accused. She could have imprisoned Porter Culver after learning he was an associate of Kale's. She didn't, because she was afraid tying up too many loose ends would draw attention to her. And so instead of yelling, Obsydia sighs in defeat.

"Don't mistake me," Intemrus says. "You made a fine choice promoting Cryomancer Hyrala. She is devoted, powerful, eager to learn. Her song, while not as shocking as Kalderys', is beautiful. It need not be electrifying to render my will."

"Thank you," Obsydia says, conscious that her voice conveys no enthusiasm. It occurs to her the sovereign attempted humor.

"Have you put any thought into her prime sentinels?"

The thought of it thumps Obsydia's heart like a mallet. She'd been grasping to the idea of Kalderys' reinstatement, however stillborn that possibility is. She isn't ready to move on yet. Does this conversation have to happen now?

"I'd planned to meet with Hyrala, take into consideration who she'd recommend, although I'm sure it will be Rotiv the glacimancer." Obsydia watches her bare feet as she walks. Her toenails need maintenance. Sometime thereafter she'll have to shave her legs. Again. "And if Rotiv is elected ..." Obsydia is struck by another deep sigh. She needs sleep. "... it would make sense to also put forth Sidna, an aspiring hygromancer. She's only recently been promoted to andesite but ... in the spirit of a cohesive unit ... it's, um ..."

Intemrus stopped walking several paces ago and stands watching her. Their entourages hang back a dozen yards. Obsydia feels the tears on her face. Her cheeks flush with heat. She wipes her eyes. "I'm sorry, what did you ask?"

"I hate what happened to Magus Kalderys." The vehemence in Intemrus' words chills Obsydia, steals away any response. His face, for the first time today, reflects disappointment. He moves to an eastern window that overlooks Stravhelm. The sun nears its highest point, eliminating shadows from even the narrowest alleys. "You and he work together flawlessly. You divine my needs, the needs of Stravhelm. He executes them without hesitation or regret. It is a travesty that this has befallen you both."

Obsydia can scarcely believe her ears. A moment ago she hated Intemrus for the sentence he doled out. In a handful of words he's transformed into a more kindred soul than anyone in all the world.

"Do you think that he ... um ..." Obsydia stammers. "Is there a chance ...?" Maybe she should have considered her words before letting them dribble out like diarrhea.

Intemrus turns to her quickly, with eyes so earnest that she is nearly fooled into thinking him capable of sympathy. "Ausgan has never had so fierce an exemplar as Magus Kalderys. Not in three hundred years. And I doubt we ever will again. Never has a disciple been so in touch with the Imala." His voice is full of passion. "He hasn't even plateaued in consonance. Not even close. It would be the ultimate shame if this were the end of his journey."

Obsydia's heart flutters. Now the tears that threaten to dislodge are of a different sort entirely. She can barely control her rapid breathing.

"You want to know if there is hope for redemption?" The question is rhetorical, and yet Obsydia nods frantically. "Yes, Obsydia, I believe so. Surely you understand the sentence he received. Our exemplars are fiercely competitive. They follow strength, despise weakness. You know it. Part of an exemplar's strength is the respect they demand. Kalderys is humble to a fault. He's been marked weak. You and I know better. But I'm afraid we may be alone. Now even Kalderys believes the lie." Intemrus steps closer to Obsydia, lowers his voice. "And a lie it is. Even *I* would think twice before challenging him."

Obsydia is at an utter loss. What did Intemrus just admit? That he fears Kalderys? He is a meteomancer who can control wind and rain on a ridiculous scale. But is that even a weapon? Kalderys can call down lightning. Nothing survives him. Well, almost nothing.

"I will not make excuses for Kalderys, or anyone," Intemrus says. "But who in their right mind would believe any basalt could undo Baromancer Kalderys' Litany of Lightning?"

Laughter bursts from Obsydia. Tears spill from her eyes. She'd had no idea the extent of the weight sitting on her heart until Intemrus lifted it with these spoken sentiments. He continues walking and she matches his pace, with a spark of hope she did not expect.

"Stay the course, Magister. Convene with your new magus. Don't fret on the unrest in the south. The storm will not hold much longer. The Tide is almost upon us. I tell this to you alone: the spies of the Untamed couldn't threaten us now even if they all amassed. There isn't time. Our truest threat is Vretos and his bloody army. And I firmly believe Kalderys has some role to play in their defeat."

They've reached the foot of Intemrus' tower. He offers her an apologetic smile. "I know how hard Kalderys has taken this. If you see fit, please speak to him. Lift his spirits. I will not. It isn't my place. One day Kalderys must thrive independent of my approval. His priority must be consonance alone. No time like now to begin that transition."

Obsydia beams at the sovereign as he turns and ascends his staircase, followed by his adherents and prime negators. His odd, parting words off-balanced her, which isn't uncommon for him. She never observed him. Didn't even consider it. And not only because of how sensitive she imagines he'd be to such an intrusion. But because his implied promise was too good. If she didn't know better, she'd translate his final point to be empty motivational platitudes, meant to lift her spirits, not incite action. But the sovereign doesn't lie. He has no need to.

She quickly makes for Kalderys' quarters, which are surely being cleaned out at this moment. Her intention had been to retreat to her tower, strip off her clothes and burn them, then drink wine in her tub until daylight died or she did. But a flame has resurfaced in her heart, and with it a purpose and lightness of step.

Kalderys can earn absolution. Regain the respect of the mancers and himself. Redemption is in his grasp. It won't be easy. But nothing worth having is. He'll need to do something he alone can do. Something impossible for any other exemplar. Easy. He is, after all, the once and future Consonant Fist.

Intemrus wants Kalderys to be independent. So does she, even if it's for different reasons. There has always been a part of Obsydia's master plan that needed work, and that was removing the sovereign's approval from among Kalderys' priorities. He has freed her to do just that. For the briefest moment she pities the old man. But he's led a full life, and his decisions brought him here. His death will not result in the collapse of consonance. Just a restructuring. Inspiring Kalderys has always been her strength. She need only do it in the name of consonance and of Ausgan, not the sovereign. Never again the sovereign. Her words must once more rouse action. And that action must result in either the death of Vretos or his permanent inability to launch an attack against Ausgan. Obsydia lacks the imagination to devise the specifics of such an order, but barring interruption from the consonant freak Kale, Kalderys has never failed a mission she gave him. He must prevent the Tide from crashing down, even if that involves severing the heathen's head.

52
No Love for the Holy City

AUSGAN
The Jungle

The sun weighs on Tivali's shoulders like a blanket of molten stone. Her ankles are swollen and bleeding from rubbing her sandals. Her wrists throb unbearably unless she holds them over her head, due to her run-in with the pale-eyed monk. She can no longer close her fingers around her bamboo. She, and everyone following her, have hiked all night since they fled Napiri. Even when harsh sunlight finally dawned to expose how much of Napiri they'd lost, Tivali did not slow. The monk who came to help Kale told Tivali more of his sort are on the way, and with more of their monk weapons, so she'll keep heading south toward the sinksand and fierce winds of the so-called Untamed, until there is no chance in hell they're still being followed. If any of Napiri's survivors following her have any complaints about their pace, they haven't voiced them. Not to her at least.

It took Tivali the better part of an hour scrambling in the dark to collect the scattered villagers after the lightning monk did his work. Grouping up is decent repellent to the beasts that stalk the jungle at night, second only to lit torches. But Tivali wouldn't allow torches, not with the holy city in pursuit. And so, during the night, her party diminished, picked off one at a time by the ever-watchful fanged apes. With each scream cut short, sobs sprang up, useless advice was hollered, the party's pace quickened.

Surely by now the survivors have figured out she has no idea how to help them. Then again, the survivors have done so thus far because they lack the means to defend themselves or run. Tivali, and her father before her, spoiled them. Today it is to their advantage. Included in that group are her uncle and her aunt, who is uncharacteristically gripe-less. Maybe witnessing violence would always have been the cure for Aunt Mara's incessant mouth. If only Tivali had known.

It's before noon when they reach the south crossing, where another path runs east to west to intersect this one. Traveling farther south has never even occurred to Tivali. As many times as she's been here, this is the first time that road unsettles her. It's as far from Napiri as she's ever been. In a few hours' time, they should reach the borderlands beyond the chaplains' reach. But what new threats will they find on the way? The blaring song of the jungle, the screeches and creaking and whooping and calling, has never felt safer. As far as Tivali is concerned, any jungle song, no matter how carnivorous, is preferable to a song from a monk.

At the crossing, Tivali stops to rest. Her aunt and uncle need no invitation to follow suit. As soon as her pace falters they find a shady tree. Tivali eases her pack off her aching shoulder and turns to face those who follow. Napiri's survivors trickle in by threes and fours. There are so few. There's a stillness in the gathering unlike any Tivali's ever seen in this lot. Eyes are red-rimmed and forlorn. Faces are haggard and dirt-specked. The survivors huddle back-to-back like mice in the middle of a burning field. How can these be the same people who were celebrating the dead warthound just yesterday? They dart their eyes at Tivali then look away, like she's the one who fucking called down lightning. Do they blame her for this? If so, why the hell are they following her? Tivali settles in beside her uncle, as eager to be out of sight as she is to be off her feet.

"Is this everyone?" she whispers.

Uncle Reilu works his jaws, the grey bristles on his leathery skin shifting over his sharp chinbone. He doesn't meet her eye. "Lost some good folk. You know that."

"Not that many. There were more this ... morning." And the reality is upon her. *They left.* They did blame her, as well they should've. They didn't say goodbye. They must have veered off at some point and never come back.

It's hard for Tivali to understand why that hurts so much. She's doing the best she can. Did they think she'd try to stop them if they paused to at least say goodbye? She's not Napiri's leader. Her father is. *Was.* Tivali heaves such an exhausted sigh it feels like it takes some of her bones with it.

Whoever left didn't owe her some explanation or excuse. Her masterful guidance has gotten Napiri massacred and scattered. What's that say about the sense of those who remain?

It takes three tries for Tivali to voice a question to her uncle. Her damn throat is squeezed up. Breathing takes more effort than it should. "Why haven't you and Mara left yet?" She tries to follow up that *I'm only going to get you killed.* But her throat pinches closed. Tears are filling her eyes.

"And go where?" Mara snaps. "Dumb girl."

Tivali snorts. Mara's got a point. Chaplains count heads for a reason. There's no escaping them. They're probably up there in the holy city drawing up individual warrants right now. They'll start with the neighboring villages, then expand from there, tracking down every loose runaway. Didn't those who left know that? And still they left? Tivali sighs again.

"What's the plan, girl?" Uncle Reilu says.

"Plan?"

He offers a tired smile. Places his rough palm on her shoulder and gives it a squeeze. "Best think of something. They're in your hands now." He juts his chin toward the assembly. More and more of them are stealing glances at her.

A surge of anger washes over Tivali. She still owes them? Are they truly not content with the catastrophe she's brought them so far? How exactly did she earn the honor of steering Napiri into extinction? Because her father knew a dirty secret? Kale didn't even tell her what happened, why he died or how. She doesn't want to hate Kale. But what if he'd never shown up? Maybe she'd have led the party that killed the warthound. Napiri would have regained some faith. The lightning monk wouldn't have come. Her people would be hungry, but alive. Should she have killed Kale in that ditch?

"They're not in my hands," Tivali whispers. "I've done enough to Napiri, wouldn't you say?"

"No," her aunt says. "Now quit your damn crying and say something."

Heat rises in Tivali. Before it can culminate in a scathing response, she takes a good look at her belligerent old aunt. She'd always thought Mara was socially crippled, oblivious to expectations or manners. But is she? She's callous, sure. So is the jungle. So was the warthound, the lightning, the holy city. And now, she's right.

Tivali stands up abruptly. "The way I see it ..." she blurts. The hush that follows tells her they were waiting desperately. The entire clearing is focused on her. If expectation had its own face, somehow all of Napiri's wearing it. Too bad Tivali hasn't worked out how she sees it and is under threat of just standing there staring back. All she knows is that she's not leading these people another step. She won't get another soul killed. They need to stop trusting her. That's the way she sees it. But the words are stubborn. Why? She delivers hard news all the time. Her eyes fall on a woman clasping two frizzy-headed children to herself. Nina is her name. One of those is hers. The other is likely newly orphaned. Godsdamned monks.

"The holy city aimed their war at us," Tivali says. "Tried to kill every damn one of us. They're our enemy." She didn't plan to say any of that. But no one argues or even flinches. They watch her, jaws set. She realizes she's fidgeting with her wrists. She stops.

"We'll die if we try to fight them. And I don't want to see any more of you die. Too many ..." Damn throat tightens up. She tries again. "Too many have died ..." *And I'm done being the cause.* Why can't she say it? Does she have to say it? She could take off at a sprint. They can't keep up. Except, her aunt and uncle stuck by her ...

"I'm continuing south," Tivali says. "Out of their range."

This is met with head shaking and hostile huffing.

"There's man-eaters down in the Untamed, everyone knows it," someone says.

"You think cannibals are better than monks?" says someone else.

Of course. Cannibals. Untamed. But are those even real? It had never occurred to Tivali until now that these may be more methods of control for the monks. Monks don't produce their own food. They need natives for that. So they make the south sound uninhabitable. They don't want natives gaining a combative edge, so they say steel is cursed.

Tivali raises both hands to silence the arguments. "The monks are the ones who said there are cannibals down there. You still believe everything they say? Because I don't."

"Well, I ain't going down there," says a woman who obviously trusts monks over Tivali. She continues under her breath. "Tired of all this walking."

Tivali responds before she can stop herself. "I don't give a severed monkey cock what you do. I said *I'm* going south. *Me.* You can sit right there and eat a hot pile of—"

Someone gasps, and for a petrifying moment Tivali thinks they've been found by monks.

"Hey." Her uncle taps her arm, points.

There are two strangers approaching from the east. It's a man guiding an older man, both wearing the dark green silksedge common in the southern villages. The younger one has a thick black beard and looks capable of defending himself. There's a staff with a leather strap slung over his shoulder and a sheathed knife on his ankle. Napiri has few left like him. The older one has patchy remnants of a beard on sagging skin and a patient authority in his beady eyes, despite the milkiness of his pupils. They part the ragged gathering in a beeline toward Tivali.

"Are you Tivali?" the younger one says.

Tivali doesn't answer. Her right hand rests on her knife's hilt. This couple doesn't appear to be a threat to her or her people, but Tivali's lost all faith in the concept of safety.

The old man clears his throat. "It is against the council of my people that I have traveled to find you." His voice has a tired waver. His eyes are aimed at nothing in particular. Probably blind, or close enough to it. "But when I heard that someone took a stand against the monks, I had to know. Is it true?"

Tivali would prefer not to react, especially considering how intently the younger one is searching her face. These people could be anyone and she'd be surprised if they're friendly. If she attacked the two, would Napiri follow her lead? Or would they scamper like squirrels? Tivali contains any reaction, glaring at the one with the working eyes. Disappointment overtakes his features.

"It's not her, Father. Let's go."

The old man's shoulders droop unevenly. The light in his sightless eyes sputters. He allows the younger one to turn him back toward the east path.

Father ...

"Who are you?" Tivali says.

The old one turns back. "I'm Gwin, chieftain of Gwal. This is my son, Venjir, my heir."

Tivali knows of Gwal. She's dealt with traders from there. They produce sugarcane and hogs. It's as far south of the Trade as Napiri is north of it. Or was.

"I'm Tivali," she says. "What do you want?"

"We offer our strength," says the young one. "We'll fight alongside you."

"Fight?" Tivali can't help but scoff. "I don't know what you heard about our valiant stand, but unless you want Gwal burnt, crushed, and scattered to the wind, I don't advise throwing in with me."

"You killed a monk," says Venjir.

Tivali scowls at him. "No. I didn't."

"She killed two!" one of her own people yells. It's followed by more rampant affirmation than Tivali has the energy to shout over. Instead, she glares harder at Venjir. The ruckus fades and a Napiri voice sneers at the newcomers, "How many monks have you killed?"

"Not enough," Venjir says.

"What's your problem with the monks?" Tivali asks him.

The old one answers, "Gwal has no love for the holy city. Too long they've kept us unarmed while choking us dry. Maybe up north you can get by with wooden weapons and shell blades. Not us. Not this close to the wild. That magus of theirs has been warring with the border for a long time. Napiri ain't the first village attacked. But it may be the first to fight back."

Fight back. Tivali thinks of Tobas. She touches her cheek where his ear slapped her and finds dried, crusted blood. She thinks of Jesbr turning to glowing ash. Thinks of the pale-eyed monk bashing in the heads of her people. None of that felt like fighting back. "How did you hear about any of that? How'd you find us?"

The blind man cocks his head as if confused. "Your messengers. They're spreading your word. Inviting any who'd join. Said you follow this road."

At this Tivali does lose control of her expression. Messengers? Spreading *her* word? She has a word? Are those the ones she thought had abandoned her? It must be. Who else could it be? They didn't flake. They sought to help, and to strengthen Napiri, and in the process to pile more responsibility on Tivali, and for some unexplainable reason that thought rinses away some ache from her chest, some exhaustion from her shoulders. For the first time, Napiri's destruction does not feel like a total loss. Tivali's eyes burn.

"This might surprise you," says Gwin. "It's not a thing northerners can discuss. But the south has had enough of Stravhelm's rules. Done with them. And it seems all we needed was an example. Besides, that war they're always preaching about. It's coming. Soon. And if Ausgan's native children stay spread all over, if we don't unite ..." The old man's jaw is tight. He shakes his head.

"The Heathen Tide," Tivali says. She has no idea what to believe anymore when monks are the source. Ever since she met Kale, her faith has been in steady decline. But the descent didn't start there, did it? "How do you know it's close?"

"Spies," Gwin says, and laughs. "The holy city can't catch them all."

Tivali watches him and his son Venjir. She's skeptical of any talk of spies. Seemed like an excuse for the monks to deal with insubordination or inconvenience. Her father was no spy. Was he?

This pair seems authentic, which scares Tivali. If they're telling the truth, more will come. Uniting may be their best bet, unless the magus' lightning prefers them clustered, in which case death will be quick for them all. But will the magus still murder citizens of Ausgan when their promised war is finally at hand?

Tivali thinks of Kale again, how he protected her and the village. He seemed to mean well. Maybe not at first, but after ... after the night they shared. Not that it matters. It's not likely she'll ever see him again. If the holy city is after her, then they're definitely after him. That big monk, his friend, was carrying him off toward the ocean. Maybe they'll escape. She hopes he does.

And yet ...

There are more individuals in the clearing now. Some are returned Napiri villagers, "messengers" she thought gone forever. Others she doesn't recognize. As validating as it feels, she's too well aware that if the monks are hunting them too, they're not making it a challenge. They've lingered too long. Tivali needs to put more distance between them and the holy city.

"I agree. United we're stronger than spread apart," Tivali says. "We should keep moving. Any who would join us are welcome."

Gwin smiles in apparent relief. Fire flashes in Venjir's eyes. "I'll return to Gwal, get them mobile. We'll meet you at the border, at the south end of this road. When we meet again, I'll not be alone." He squeezes his father's shoulder, then runs.

Tivali stashes her water skin, pulls her pack over her shoulder, pushes her hair out of her face, tests her feet. They hurt like hell. She sets off.

"You able to keep up?" she asks Gwin.

"Needn't worry about me," he says, falling in beside her. Looks like his feet are better off than hers.

Tivali wants to ask him a question but isn't sure she wants the answer. *Better to have it now than when we get there.* "Monks say there are cannibals down south. That's a lie, right?"

Gwin smiles and at first she's reassured. "They're not as bad as the holy city makes out." The smile fades. "But they don't like being called cannibals."

53
An Indicator of Ill Intent

AUSGAN
The Faithless Sea

Kale awakens to ocean spray on his face. He's bobbing on waves and being cooked by the sun, and for a moment he wonders if he's dehydrated driftwood or a corpse. He tries to swallow. Throat's too dry.

"Finally, you're awake. You'll be thirsty, I bet. Water's beside you." It's Culver's voice, and it has a manic eagerness. His gushing relief at Kale's consciousness suggests panic wasn't far off.

Kale shades his face, manages to get his eyes open and focused. Everything appears barren and bleached, as if he's had sunlight on his eyelids for a long time. He and Culver are in a rough wooden canoe surrounded by endless ocean. Culver is holding an oar, wearing an expectant expression, and looks less kempt than Kale's ever seen him. It's unsettling.

Kale carefully clears his throat. "Where are we?" he hisses.

"On the Faithless. Heading east."

A modicum of consciousness is enough to validate each of those facts. Kale tries to formulate a more useful question. "... what?"

Culver juts his chin in a direction over Kale's shoulder. Kale turns to look back. First he sees nothing, has to blink and rub his eyes. There's a grey peak no larger than a ghost crab's claw thrusting up from a beach. It's the East Rostrum. Kale's never seen it from this direction. Between it and their canoe is a white speck atop the glittering waves. A sail.

"We're in trouble," Culver says.

This deadpan understatement hits Kale so abruptly it looses a harsh laugh from him. Feels like scouring his throat with a scrubbing sponge. He coughs. Takes some water. "What tipped you off?"

A smile crosses Culver's face but quickly succumbs to the anxious expression he'd been wearing. "Most recently? Ashmancer Haik chasing us with a gang of pyros."

Kale groans. "It would be him."

"I would've considered raising my stave against Selu pretty offense worthy. That is, until you did whatever it was you did to her."

Dread courses through Kale at the memory. "Probably stopped any further complaint from her, didn't I?"

"Quite." There's an intensity developing in Culver's eyes. "Before that, my only sign something was amiss was Sentinel Bronn clubbing you unconscious in my dorm, then you being the target of a wall of fusiliers like you yourself were the Heathen Tide!"

Kale shields his eyes, not from the sun this time but from his friend's increasingly scathing glare. "I suppose that's an indicator of ill intent," he agrees.

Culver is silent for several moments. Probably doing the mental exercises he relies on to keep from strangling Kale.

"What is going on?" Culver says at last.

Kale straightens himself up to a sitting position. He owes his friend answers. If only he had them. *The Triumvirate incinerates native settlements with such regularity they had to devise a friendly name for the process.* It wasn't so problematic before Kale watched it happen. He pats his dele. There's the crystal. He withdraws it so that Culver can see.

"I was trying to stop the Triumvirate," Kale says. "But I failed. This was supposed to have Intemrus' immortality inside it."

The oar clatters against the canoe in Culver's slack hands and he sucks in a breath, rocking backward. "Imala above, Kale, why? What did that prisoner say to you?"

Kale shakes his head. "It wasn't him. Kalderys kills children. At Obsydia's command. *That* is Intemrus' Will."

"Kills children? You mean exemplars?" Realization washes over him. "No. You mean *natives.*" He utters the word like it's rotten. "You mean spies."

Heat surges through Kale. "No. I mean *children.* Does it matter what side of the wall they live on? Obsydia sends him off, and down he runs and doesn't come back until a village is dead. He calls down lightning and *poof!* Spies, blasphemers, heretics, sinners, old men and women, children, doesn't matter. *Poof, poof, poof.*" Kale's wild gesturing probably isn't adding to his credibility. "And if the lightning fails, out come the staves to knock holes in their heads. It's barbaric."

Culver lowers his gaze, looking troubled.

Kale takes a breath to collect himself. "You would have tried to stop them too if you'd seen that."

"I would have?"

"You're here."

Culver bites back whatever response he'd intended. He's quiet a moment. "So you stole the crystal." His shoulders droop. "... using the key I gave you."

Kale turns his attention on Syvea. The memory it made him relive is still so fresh he has a hard time discerning it from reality. Under the glaring sunlight, the crystal is only faintly off-white, on the outside cloudy like quartz but pinkening toward the center of its most jagged face, where there's a bead of dark crimson, as if a drop of blood froze while diffusing into water.

What exactly happened all those years ago when this crystal broke and Syvea's body died? Surely Intemrus and Vretos weren't immortal before that. Does Vretos have the crystal's other half? Was part of Syvea trapped inside? Or maybe a thin sliver of her memory, starting when the Deceiver handed her the stone, ending when it broke in half? Does the other half contain the same thing? Can the two halves be reunited? If anyone has the answers, it seems to Kale like it could only be one individual. This is assuming the Deceiver from a three hundred-year-old memory still lives. And murals in Stravhelm seem to suggest he does, whatever that's worth.

"You saved my life," Kale says. "I owe you."

Culver doesn't react to this, instead gazing wide-eyed at the canoe's deck. He's probably trying to work out his place in the crimes Kale has committed, his level of guilt. He's probably wishing he could take it back. Kale doesn't want to voice what he's thinking. *You saved my life and threw yours away.* Culver speaks without looking up and it's as if he heard Kale's thoughts.

"How much trouble am I in?"

Kale almost laughs, which confuses him. Nothing's funny. *All the trouble. It couldn't be worse. You are an accomplice of mine, and I'm well-damned.* He looks in his friend's face. Culver looks exhausted, like he's put on ten years. Maybe it's the derelict quality of his attire that Kale's not used to, his unshaven cheeks. Maybe it's deep concern that weathered him, becoming a permanent feature of his face. But in Culver's eyes is a hint of hope, as if Basalt Kale the failed negator and scourge of consonance will deliver some good news. As if he could ever. Nothing worth saying is coming to Kale. He shakes his head.

Culver gives a quiet sigh. "That bad?"

Kale says nothing. He doesn't want to speak again until he can find something redeeming to say. But will there ever be? They're probably both done for. "Why'd you come, Culver?" Frustration sharpens the question and he regrets it. He didn't mean it like that.

"That's a funny way of saying thanks."

"You shouldn't have left the holy city. I was ..." Kale bites his tongue. Then he thinks better of it. "I was ready to die." With those words, the dam breaks. "I've been ready to die a long time. It was planned out. I got the key from you so I could jump in Lahuvot's Lake. I'd have disappeared. You would have ceased to be held back by the Imala-damned basalt. You'd have gotten promoted, moved up to Rhyolite Tier, eventually made mancer and moved into Stravhelm. It ... it didn't exactly go as planned."

Kale runs out of words. He's failed in every endeavor he strived for. He failed to kill himself, then after finding something worth saving he failed at that too. He didn't save Rathyn or Tivali. He didn't stop Intemrus or Kalderys. He did manage to damn his friend.

"This ..." His voice cracks. "This is the last thing I wanted."

Culver's silent a moment. Kale doesn't look at him. "And what about me?" There's heat in Culver's response. "What about what I want?"

This takes Kale off guard, makes him feel even more selfish. "I doubt you wanted to be on Stravhelm's bad side."

"Doesn't mean I wanted you to die. Is that not obvious by now?"

Kale closes his eyes. "I was trying to help you." It's true, but it sounds pitifully misguided now that he says it aloud. "Not involve you."

"If that's true, you shouldn't have come back at all. When Bronn came for you ... when he did what he did and I did nothing to stop him ..."

Kale looks at his friend. Culver doesn't meet his eyes, instead sitting and shaking his head in disgust.

"You were smart not to interfere. They'd have arrested you too. Maybe you're right, I shouldn't have come back. I'm sorry, Culver."

Culver scoffs. "I don't want your damn pity. I'm here now. Let's get on with whatever you had in mind."

Kale smiles, despite himself.

"On that subject ..." Culver smiles too. "Exactly what might that be?"

Kale considers the crystal. Its source, his flashback, the girl, the Deceiver. He considers Hargrim, Napiri, their people. "Stravhelm kills innocent people and claims it's to protect us from Fohrvylda and the Heathen Tide." He shakes his head, unable to even pretend there's suitable defense for what Kalderys does. "If something has to become a monster to save itself, then it's not worth saving."

Culver watches him. He looks analytical, and maybe even proud. "I'm in."

Kale takes out the crystal again, watches the light glitter across it. "I thought stealing this would take Intemrus' immortality. I guess there's more to it than that. I intend to find out."

Culver nods, less certain now. "Still in, but this is getting convoluted. Maybe just tell me what you know so I can keep up."

So Kale does. He recounts the imprisoned spy's proclamation, then his own theft and the state of the tower, and finally the vision the crystal showed him. He doesn't mention meeting Obsydia in Syvea Tower. He's still unsure why she was there but is almost certain she meant to steal Intemrus' immortality for herself. While that does lend credibility to the crystal's supposed purpose, it also indicates strife within the Triumvirate. If it turns out Obsydia is responsible for all the rampant murder, and Intemrus was holding her back from even crueler tendencies—no, it does no good to even theorize on that.

Culver digests his words thoughtfully. "It sounds like only two people aside from the sovereign can shed light on this. Vretos the Fohrvyldan is one."

"He is," Kale says. "And although I've proven to be an excellent weapon against consonance, I'm in no hurry to meet him."

"You sure? He may welcome you as a hero," Culver says. There's mischief in his voice.

Kale pictures the beastly youth from Syvea's memory that stabbed his own beloved. "I'm sure."

Culver nods. "That leaves the Deceiver. You think he's still in Redemier? It's been a while since all that went down."

Kale sighs. "It's been three hundred years, if the stories are to be believed. As unlikely as that seems, I'd still prefer to risk the cursed island for him than Fohrvylda for Vretos."

"Me too, if those are our options. It's cursed, we're damned. We'll fit right in."

"Redemier it is," Kale says.

Culver collects a second oar from the hewn floor of the canoe and throws it to Kale. "Then help."

Kale does. A thick silence blankets them both, despite their attempted optimism. Kale manages to postpone his dread at the entirety of his trouble by ignoring the white sail still following in the distance. But it's there, and relentlessly keeping up. Maybe if he can keep from looking at it for long enough it will cease to be. *Focus on rowing.* The quiet is a glaring, encapsulating thing. It may as well be an entity occupying space in the canoe with them, enunciating every interrupting wave that slaps the craft's side, every distant gull's shriek. Eventually, Kale's mind wanders. Judging by the drained, disconnected quality of Culver's eyes, so does his. His every stroke is less effective than the last.

"Hey," Kale says, getting his friend's attention. "Get some sleep. I'll row."

Culver doesn't respond, instead relinquishing his paddling immediately and wedging himself in the canoe's nose. What Kale had thought was a dilapidated blanket tucked beneath his seat turns out to be an old fishing net. It does suffice, however, to block some sun for his friend's face. He is snoring in almost no time, mouth wide and expression at peace. Kale smiles, despite the guilt stabbing his gut. Culver should never have gotten involved. He had a future in Erudition. More than Kale, anyway.

The entire horizon belongs to the ocean, save for the grey-green toothy line marking distant hills and keys to Kale's left. The East Rostrum is long gone. They're far enough offshore that nothing else exists to visually mark the passage of distance. All Kale can do is have faith that the Faithless is moving beneath them. He's soon soaked in sweat. It spills from his hair down his eyebrows to the corners of his mouth, down the back of his neck, his chest, his armpits, the crack of his ass. He'd like nothing more than to deluge himself with the waterskin.

It's against his will that he occasionally checks for Haik's sail. Each time he hopes that something has happened to remove it from the horizon. Each time he's disappointed by that looming, twinkling white peak. His thoughts cycle through patterns, first building arguments asserting that his craft can outrun the ashmancer's, for any number of unlikely reasons, then breaking said argument down and accepting that the opposite is more likely. Then the process starts over. The fact is, there's nothing to deter or undermine Haik's pursuit. If the ashmancer were going to catch up or fall away, he already would have. Kale's only respite is to ignore his surroundings, focus on breathing, rowing.

North and west are the islets and keys north of Ausgan. They're close enough to make out differences here and there. Kale can spot the white lines of their beaches, see the naked boulders littered here and there at the feet of forested hills. He can even make out the odd thin plume of rising smoke, narrow lines indicating an organized fire. A stove in a dining lodge maybe, if the keys are anything like mainland Ausgan.

On the waters between the land and the canoe are small fishing vessels. Kale considers the possibility of infiltrating those boats and hiding before the ashmancer can catch up. Except it's not with simple human senses that the ashmancer and his forces track them. Also Haik would interrogate the natives and likely resort to horrific means to gain their cooperation in rooting out the perceived criminals. Kale and Culver would be found, and they'd probably cost even more natives their lives. They'll proceed to Redemier. Maybe Haik won't follow them onto land.

"Hyrala's Lagoon is beyond that islet." Culver's voice startles Kale from his thoughts. He's stretching, rubbing his cheeks, collecting his oar, his sleepy gaze westward.

"How do you know that?" Kale asks. Hyrala's Lagoon was named after the cryomancer managed to exhume from it the mammoth translucent shell that wound up adorning Obsydia's tower.

Culver works his mouth a moment, spits phlegm into the ocean. "Maps. Never seen it from this direction, but there's only one spot where the hills are that spiked and barren of trees." He points and Kale follows but is unable to discern whatever stands out to Culver. "The natives on that islet cut down all the trees for fishing vessels. You can get a good view of exactly how much they cleared out from on top of Erudition's northern wall."

Culver picks up his oar and proceeds to row. Kale's never been on the northern wall. But the mention of industrious natives brings Tivali to his mind. The memory he conjures has her distorted by her tears. He'd rather carve out his own heart than relive that. It's probably for the best that he put Tivali entirely out of his mind. Except now, with little to distract himself, she owns his thoughts—lying beside him in the jungle, their hands aloft, fingers intertwined; he himself is sticky, sweaty, cut-up, blood-drenched, aching, spent, and wanting nothing to ever change so that he can dwell in that moment forever. He feels her hair on his chest. Smells her. Sees her eyes by the light of scattered embers. They're the greenish-grey of steam rising off the morning jungle after a night's rain. She's searching his face curiously. Reaching toward him.

Kale's eyes burn. He squeezes them shut, turns away from Culver and rows. Kale rows until rowing becomes him and it hurts more to stop than to keep on. If he pauses to rub his palms, his hands tremble and cramp and his heartbeat resonates throughout his spent muscles. He tries not to think of Tivali, instead watching the bubbly spirals his oar weaves into the indifferent waves.

Hours pass. Kale feels the passage of time in his hands, his biceps, his shoulders, his back, and his sunburned skin. If he focuses, he can retreat into a state of numb near-sleep, a state exemplars are taught to reach to overcome repetitive, mindless tasks. The monotony of the ocean—the white water slapping the canoe, the unbroken wind pushing at his grimy hair, the stagnant expanse of barren blue sky—serve to proclaim that he's getting nowhere, only stirring a vast empty pot with an insignificant spoon.

"Redemier." Culver's voice reaches Kale as if through a veil of liana vines. He'd nearly managed to fall asleep while rowing. It was such an all-consuming trance he'd achieved that upon snapping out of it he finds a good many noticeable differences in his surroundings.

Firstly, the sun is behind them, hanging low in a fiery sky. When did it get so low? There can't be more than two hours of daylight left. Haik's triangular sail is a dull beacon against the amber horizon. So much for losing him. The northern sky is slowly succumbing to a blanket of puffy clouds. The landscape has changed as well. It had been white-beached and largely flat, interrupted here and there with the symmetry inherent in human-built artifacts. There's no trace of artifacts anymore. And all the land is taller. Wider. Those aren't islets anymore but an unbroken mass, and Kale will be damned if the trees there aren't the exact same hue as those from Syvea's memory. There is no sign of humanity at all in those dark green hills.

"Let's get closer," Kale thinks aloud. The thought makes him uncomfortable. He'd hoped this distance would best afford him some advantageous vista to maybe spot a recognizable feature. That idea has proven ridiculous. Assuming this is even the same landmass from the memory, he didn't experience it from the ocean but from high forested hills. Redemier spans the entire horizon, and at this range lacks any discerning features.

"You looking for something in particular?" Culver eyes Redemier as if it's cursed.

Kale chooses not to immediately answer. If the murals in Stravhelm's windows are accurate, Redemier is four times the size of Ausgan. He and Culver could wander the island for the rest of their lives and never find the location from the vision. Especially considering how old the memory was.

His shoulders slump. "Shit," Kale says.

Culver turns his wary gaze onto Kale. "Shouldn't be a problem. I've got a mean one in the works."

"Let's keep rowing for now," Kale says. And wait for what exactly? Maybe skipping Redemier and making for Fohrvylda *is* their best bet.

"Oh, terrific," Culver says, "I was hoping you'd say row more."

Kale chuckles. They push eastward, gradually approaching land, and the green peaks rise even taller and wider, taking the place of the sea and sky entirely. The island looks to be made exclusively of heavily forested mountains. These green spires aren't bare and edged like Mount Adenhelm. In fact, they dwarf any mountain on Ausgan. There's a cold wind rushing over the water as if Redemier is trying to blow them away. Kale abruptly remembers the black-furred, shark-finned beasts from Syvea's vision. A chill runs over him.

"I hate to rush you," Culver says, "but we're running low on daylight. Is there something I can help look out for?"

I'm looking for the ruins of a city halfway up one of those mountains, although I probably won't recognize it seeing as my memory is from before Stravhelm. Kale doesn't say it. Not a good way to benefit morale. Instead he bolsters a concentrating expression and veers yet closer to the cursed island.

They're two hundred yards off now, close enough for Kale to make out the jagged brown rocks that make up the landmass' unwelcoming shore. Clouds stretch out from over Redemier, attempting to overshadow the canoe. Given the hour, the steep terrain, and now the overcast sky, Kale knows darkness will embrace them abruptly. He's almost desperate enough to simply aim for a point on land and take his chances when he spots a deviation along the bank. Within an indention in the dark wall of green is a recessed cove, its banks steeper than those of their surroundings. Kale makes for it, trying to keep his expectations in check. It's doubtfully related to his quarry but it may provide cover, which in this moment is more valuable. He scans behind them for the white sail. There is only choppy water. At this moment, Haik's ship isn't visible. If there will ever be a perfect time to discreetly make for land, this is it.

The steep banks of the cove are sheltering a hidden lagoon, already shrouded in late-afternoon shadow. On its northern side, opposite the entry, is an outcropping aimed out toward the open sea. The object is the same dark green as everything surrounding it, but unnaturally squared and extending some ways into the ocean before it appears to have crumbled away.

"There," Kale says, his voice startling even himself. This is what he was after. Signs of civilization, however ancient. If they're lucky, some semblance of a road yet connects that object to the location of Syvea's death. Even if they're not, they'll make landfall here.

At the lagoon's mouth, the land walls on either side point toward one another, coming within thirty yards of pinching closed and sealing the cove off. The sea enclosure blocks wind and waves, creating an ominous silence. Within the cove the water is no longer choppy azure but shimmering turquoise and nearly flat. Submerged below the canoe is a vibrant coral bed that stretches over the entire entryway, enclosing the bay and likely helping to break surf. As Kale gazes down, fish begin to appear, weaving in and around the corals. Some of the rainbow of species are numerous, swarming in schools. Some are larger, wide-finned and cruising alone. It's impossible to tell the size of any of them. Given the clarity of this water, the seabed could just as easily be ten feet away as it could a hundred.

"Eerie feeling, isn't it?" Culver's voice, though hushed, is amplified by this place, echoing off the green walls. Kale can't escape the impression that the forest is looking down on them.

As they paddle closer, it becomes obvious the outcropping once served as a pier, made of huge, smoothed blocks that are now enveloped in pillows of moss and sheets of flaking lichen. Once under the shadow of the cove, it's easier to make out details in the forest wall above where the ancient pier meets land. What Kale sees gives him hope that they may be in the right place.

Peering out from behind great, grey-barked tree trunks are the faces of buildings, long stripped of life, with square, black eyes and gaping doors. The closer Kale gets, the more building skeletons are revealed, hiding, waiting for nature to engulf them. The remains of the civilization span the entire northern bank, squat stone houses with skin of vines and ferns and algae, slumping upon one another as far as Kale can see up the forested hillside. This visage makes him think of an alternate Erudition that has spit out its inhabitants and lost a war to a rough-skinned forest. There's the sound of dribbling water nearby. Fresh, drinkable water, Imala willing.

Kale and Culver mount the stone pier carefully, trying to disturb as little as possible despite their utterly stiff joints. Tugging the canoe up the uneven stones is no small task, but it's that or sink it. Leaving it tied up and clonking about would make it an unmistakable beacon for even empirically sensing pursuers. When the craft is safely a dozen strides within the forest, Kale relents and lowers himself beside the chattering stream. Where the stream meets saltwater there's a pool of smoothed stones, home to brightly colored crustaceans and darting fish.

"Dinner?" Culver says, plucking up one particularly angry, golden-shelled crayfish.

"Breakfast," Kale says. "We need to get well inland. Away from the dock and the fresh water. Some place to hide out the night, just in case."

Ausgan's jungle comes to Kale's mind. Hopefully this island isn't as hazardous, despite the alleged curse. "If we're lucky, there's a visible enough path to follow from up into higher ruins. Then it's a matter of picking a safe nook."

Culver drops the crayfish into the shallows. It scoots backward under the shelter of rocks. "Lucky for you," he tells it. As he goes to stand, something catches his attention. He sticks his hand into the shallows, wrestles a plant from the earth. Once he's rubbed the soil from its surface, it resembles a wild potato.

"Dinner," Culver says, with considerably more enthusiasm than Kale feels.

"It's all yours."

"No, it's safe. Trust me. Just gotta boil it a while first."

"That's tough with no fire."

Culver sighs heavily. "Fine. Breakfast."

"I'll leave it to you."

Culver gives him an insulted look. "You think I don't know yams?"

"I didn't say that. We've never been here is all. That could be—"

Culver scoffs. "Unbelievable. You think I don't know yams."

Kale raises both hands. "The last thing I'd do is question your yam lore."

"See that you don't. You've got no yam lore." And he thrusts it into his dele.

They take their fill of water, stretch their legs, and get moving. Insect noises rattle from within the emerald shadows. Nearer the derelict residences are the remnants of a road, several yards across at its widest. It appears to have once been flat and paved in flagstone. Now it winds upward like a trampled snakeskin. The tiles are, more often than not, upended by gnarled roots, cracked into pieces, or missing entirely. Regardless of that, it's still their best avenue to infiltrate the island.

Kale minimizes his imprint as they go, ever aware Culver has no such talent. He could maybe hold Culver's hand, expanding his invisibility onto his friend. As if either of them has the energy for it.

Redemier's forest is markedly different than Ausgan's. In a word, it's drier. The air, the sounds, the flora. Even the bird calls resonate down with a hollow arid quality, as if produced by an emptied gourd. There are no vines draped from the limbs. Not the kind Kale's used to, anyway. Instead are scratchy-armed brambles, puny, thirsty-looking leaves, crunchy undergrowth, bark that snags your clothes and surely breaks down Culver's resolve one thread at a time.

Melding into the somber canopy that ascends before them are more buildings, all roofless, none entirely intact. Kale and Culver climb over collapsed houses and under thick, grey boughs that have no place looming over a road. Daylight retreats as quickly as Kale feared it would and soon there is no choice but to call it for the night. Veering off the road they find a flat expanse, spacious enough to have once served as a marketplace or gathering grounds. From this elevated position, Kale can view the entire shadowed bay and the evening sea beyond it. There is no white sail to be seen.

"This place was huge," Culver marvels, turning a slow circle and taking in the dilapidated surroundings. Indeed, even as far as they've come they've not strayed from within the limits of this once-enormous city. Kale tries to focus on the scenes from his vision so that if they find the location, he'll recognize it. But three hundred years of plant growth ... Once again he thinks of the beasts that flanked the Deceiver. Are they watching him and Culver now? Are they part of the curse? Is there a curse at all? These are issues for a more rested mind.

They'll split up so that Kale can maintain some semblance of a watch, at least for a while. Culver inquires once more about a fire, a small one made only of sticks so that it doesn't smoke much but can at least heat up a small room and *get his tuber toasting*. He informs Kale that even if Haik follows them into the cove and makes his way up that broken road in the darkness, he and his lot have low chances of finding this exact ramshackle clearing. It's safe. Culver presents his case with such earnest concentration that Kale almost feels bad when he says, "Absolutely not, for any reason, for any length of time, for any circumstance whatsoever are you to ignite even a single spark." Culver agrees quietly. He picks an abandoned building, arranging a pile of dry leaves to act as bedding. Kale mounts the roof of a structure across the clearing. It's cold but the nearby walls block the breeze.

When they are settled at last, Kale stares through the meandering boughs at the stars. Again the crystal weighs heavy on his chest. There's always the impression that it's more aware than any mineral should be. Doesn't help that he's learned its story. Is this why Intemrus hid it away? Is the stone capable of somehow spying on him? Kale stuffs it into a pile of rubble and lies back down. The flat ground beneath him pitches like the waves he rode for so many hours. This sensation does wonders at weighing down his already heavy eyelids. He fights it, propping himself up to remain vigilant in case the need arises to fight or flee.

"It wasn't only for you that I stepped in front of Selu." Culver's disembodied voice floats to Kale's ears like a lone specter. "I saw what she did to those people. Whatever she and Kalderys were meant to accomplish, there has to be a better way than that."

Kale smiles, despite the pain in his chest. Culver acknowledging it aloud makes his failures feel less sharp. He would thank Culver for saying it, but his throat is too tight. Tomorrow they will continue upward. In time, they'll find the place from his vision. The place where the crystal split in half. Kale's eyes slip closed. He relents, letting his thoughts drift. If he tries, maybe he'll dream of Tivali.

54
A Larger Part to Play

AUSGAN
Syvea's Tower, Stravhelm

Obsydia pauses and adjusts her dele. It's a unique design, merging formality with functionality, bright and decorative but cut and bunched so as to maximize mobility. She could spar in this dele, maybe even kick someone out a window if need be. Refined silksedge, the gentlest material in Ausgan, but for some godsdamned reason abominably itchy. The clothiers will answer for this. In her lifetime, she vows either to invent a new fabric that can evade being felt entirely, or normalize nudity for everyone. These are hardly pressing concerns at this moment though. She's reached the top of Syvea Tower's staircase for the second time in as many days—for the second time in her life. This time is at the summons of the sovereign, who awaits above.

Standing below the trapdoor, her chest is tight with anticipation. The messenger who delivered the summons wasn't urgent or even excited. There was no armed escort. She's taking heart in that. This calling is certainly in response to him finding his crystal stolen. And yet she is not as horrified as she might have thought. More intrigued. Because he's shriveling and dying? *Maybe.* Worst case, she is outed for her part in the crystal's theft. Depending on the company he's brought with him, advancing her plan to the step where Intemrus dies is entirely on the table. It's not like he can physically stop her.

The success of her recent visit with Kalderys bolstered her shattered morale. She offered him the promise of absolution lying on the far side of some critical blow to the Fohrvylda heathens. She explained that Intemrus understands Kale alone is to blame for the botched cleansings, not Kalderys' supposed waning strength. She told him that while Ashmancer Haik captures or kills the basalt anomaly, it is Kalderys' unspoken obligation to deal Fohrvylda a blow from which they cannot recover. She'd been anxious to deliver such a vague ultimatum, relying on the knowledge that every mission she's ever given Kalderys, he has accomplished, Kale's interference notwithstanding. As she talked to Kalderys, she witnessed a spark reignite in his eyes, felt his hope rise from the ashes. He set his jaw and promised her he'd prevent the Heathen Tide. She didn't ask him how. She never has. The details are his business. What's important is that he's never made her a promise he couldn't deliver. Mostly.

Obsydia cannot linger here. No doubt Intemrus has sensed her already. Either he knows she has a secret or he doesn't. No sense in prolonging suspense. She ascends through the trapdoor. Intemrus is alone in the room looking out an eastern window. His dark blue dele hangs from narrow shoulders all the way to the floor, where it bunches around his feet, making him look tall and thin. And old.

"Resonations, Magister," Intemrus says without looking at her. He isn't excited or frantic. *Good.* She won't have to pretend to be.

"Resonations," she responds. No honorific. Just to test the water.

Oddly, the place is exactly as she left it two nights prior. Nothing's been tossed around in frenzied reaction to the missing artifact. In the light of day, Kale's bloody footprints, while faint, stand out like beacons. His visit is laid out as clearly as if written in text. He entered the room, paused while looking around, smearing two parallel blots, moved toward the now-empty pedestal, paused again—for how long, who can say? He took a step, took the crystal, turned to face Intemrus' tower, then fled. Meanwhile Obsydia's footprints, written by sandals much too large for her feet, tell a shorter story. A story of disappointment. She reduced those sandals to ash after returning to her tower in defeat. But standing here now with Intemrus she considers how thin her deception is. There are only two keys that would grant access to this tower. She cannot claim ignorance of both keys while remaining an effective magister. Will she have to kill Intemrus today?

"I'll miss it." There's a bleakness to Intemrus, like he's about to climb his own funeral pyre.

"I'm sorry?" *Miss the crystal? Because you're going to die?*

Intemrus takes a shallow breath and glances back at her. Despite his waxy pallor and his careful movement that hints of physical frailty, his crystalline eyes are as sharp as ever. The soft smile he gives suggests comfort, but remorse. She observes that somehow he's arrived where he's standing without disturbing the dust on the floor. That would feel less notable if it didn't trigger a chill in her.

"Ausgan wasn't always so orderly," he tells the window. "When I arrived, the whole island was Untamed. Stravhelm was born as a collection of stone-built huts halfway up a volcano the natives feared. In time, I learned to tame it, and then they feared me too. I put them to work. We built Erudition gradually. I continued to uncover consonance. Across the Faithless Sea, the heathen Vretos built arenas for bloodletting."

Obsydia feels the urge to yawn. She wasn't prepared for a history lesson and has zero expectations of this information ever becoming relevant. Best not to interrupt though. He's probably just losing his mind further.

"He and I were at each other's throats then." Intemrus smiles at the fond memory. "Spies were everywhere. I launched no less than a hundred assassination attempts in as many years. None returned. Eventually we tired of it, he and I. There are still spies, but far fewer. And those who can't be controlled or misinformed are dealt with decidedly, as you know. *Cleansed.*" The word brings a twinkle to Intemrus' eyes, as if it's the name of some old friend. He sighs. "Someday there will be no Untamed. The war with Fohrvylda will be done, and outposts will be erected throughout Ausgan. Exemplars may even ..." His mouth sours. "Integrate with the native population. Thankfully, I won't live to see that."

Obsydia nearly scoffs. What would he say if he learned Basalt Kale's gotten a head start on the integration? His last words delve up more questions than she can untangle in this moment. They also fail to even scratch on the one topic she anticipated dominating this conversation.

"You won't?" she prods softly. *Because I'm going to kill you?*

He shakes his head. His eyes harbor melancholy. Has he written off the crystal so quickly? Accepted his own fate without even putting up a fight? She cannot be that lucky.

"I won't. And that's what I've called you to talk about. Our future. Your future. If you will indulge me, however, first let's talk about your past."

He extends his hand toward the only chair in the room. Obsydia pads toward it, anxiety flaring, conscious of the bloody footprints, unsure how she should react to them. Avoid them at the least. She sits down on the flimsy wooden contraption, folds her hands in her lap. She feels like she's in class again, but on a day she's meant to present a thing she failed utterly to prepare for.

"Do you remember your childhood?"

She doesn't answer immediately. She remembers hating clothes, hating classes, boys hating her, beating up boys, girls fearing her, beating up girls. She remembers the other children never including her. She remembers outperforming them all. She remembers trials, competition, singing, sweating, bleeding. As if she could forget.

"I remember Erudition."

"I mean before that."

Obsydia is taken aback. There is no such thing as before Erudition. Induction happens before the exemplar's first birthday and intrants begin their consonant training in the nursery. Nothing before that matters.

Intemrus gives an apologetic smile. "You were born Dyana and determined to be exemplary at four weeks of age. But because of your circumstances you weren't yet inducted. Your mother didn't know who sired you. There were a half dozen potentials. That's not uncommon considering her profession. She gave her body to native men for carnal pleasure in exchange for barter privileges. At times in exchange for nothing. This isn't unheard of. But such preoccupations have their hazards, especially where the emotionally driven are concerned."

He pauses. His face is unreadable. Her mind is a storm. The tone Intemrus uses is so matter-of-fact, Obsydia can hardly accept it's her story he's telling. But the name Dyana strikes a chord in her memory. A woman calling it in distress. Over and over. Croaking like a bullfrog. She remembers crying in response.

She's familiar with the exchange he refers to. It goes by many names. His condescending tone indicates how little he thinks of it. And knowing the rules in place here in the holy city, that doesn't surprise her. But Obsydia can't deny a twinge of curiosity. A half dozen ... spread out or all at once? And if all at once, how? For how long?

"You were five years old when we retrieved you. Nearly starved, lying beside your dead mother. She was killed by a fellow native. In the wild, such a thing is written off as a crime of passion. Some might call it a just wage. Consequences of depravity. But who am I to judge?" The smile he pairs with that question suggests he's in on some joke. As if judgment were not his modus operandi.

"It was then that you were inducted. Too old for the nursery, you were never an intrant, beginning instead as initiate. You had much catching up to do, much to prove, and in the company of initiates who didn't know you, didn't trust you."

Obsydia shifts in her chair, more irritated than surprised at this revelation. No wonder she didn't get along with anyone. It seems like he expects her to care about the natives in his story. Maybe she'd care if she could remember. Do others remember what they did before their fifth year? A better question is why in Imala's name did he take it upon himself to dredge all this up and recite it today? What's the point? She adjusts her sleeves, her cuffs. Comfort eludes her.

"Refined silksedge ..." Intemrus says, in a tone suited for introducing a bit of trivia. He's peering at her sidelong. Obsydia stops moving. "... is incredibly soft. Thinner than worm silk. More porous but smoother. Fashioned and perfected specifically for such an environment as Ausgan. Blocks the sun but not a breeze."

She'd love to appreciate these helpful details but at the moment the miraculous fabric is about as comfortable as tree bark. How does this have any bearing on anything? She'd ask if it weren't for a blooming sense of foreboding.

"Except sometimes it doesn't feel so refined." His eyes are twinkling again. "Maybe the fabric ages poorly, succumbs to aridity and develops rough patches that irritate the skin endlessly. Sometimes the fabric attracts the skin's oil, then smothers, bunches up in the most inopportune ways, catching hairs at the base of your neck, plucking them out one at a—what are you doing?"

Obsydia's fingers have undone the top three buttons on her dele and they're working on the fourth when she catches them. She stops herself. Clasps her lapels back together. She looks up at Intemrus in surprise.

He raises an eyebrow, smiles. "Getting warmer?"

She is. As if the ceiling vanished and the sun is bearing down on her, but somehow from inside her dele. She has to fight herself to remain clothed. The truth sets in.

"Wait ..." She doesn't trust herself to say more. Takes a deep breath. Exhales. Now her dele is comfortable, like she's reached the eye of a storm. She speaks slowly. "You're not saying ..."

He nods. "Your propensity toward nudity. It isn't happenstance."

Obsydia stares at the sovereign. "You ..."

"I can't take all the credit. Your bloodline plays a part, instilling shamelessness or promiscuity or ..." He waves his hand like that detail is beside the point.

"My bloodline?" she says. "We sever from those at ... induction." Unless that was a lie.

"If only," Intemrus says regretfully. "Our environment ever competes with our blood at carving our identity. But that inconvenient fact has been known to push wayward exemplars toward notions of wanderlust, or undue curiosity of their origins. And so, some time ago, an alternate truth was invented. It's better this way."

Obsydia can only shake her head. "You tried to make me ... a whore?"

Disgust flashes over his face. "Of course not. Nothing so vile as that. I made you powerful. When your gift of empathy was discovered, I capitalized. You understand the longings you incite because you share them. To minimize the chance of you being ensnared and succumbing to those base desires, I positioned you to have any inherent sympathy phased out. Thank your rigorous upbringing for that. The alienation cemented in ruthless competition. Therein you also developed your motivation: reach the pinnacle, take my seat. After that, I armed you with the strongest consonant mancer to ever live."

Obsydia has taken her head in both hands to keep it from spinning off her neck. *Intemrus sees all*, echoes in her head like a starving bird's call. *Intemrus sees all*. Of all the lies she believed, of all the truths she didn't. *Intemrus sees all*.

"I expect you're upset. But don't pretend not to understand. You've done the same for Kalderys. Build him up. Make him invincible. Tell him he is, show him he is, instill in him immutable purpose. A purpose that is, in fact, yours. You did the same for the ashmancer, not that his power compares."

Obsydia glares at him, starts to yell that he's a liar. He's wrong. Kalderys isn't some tool. He's more than just ... utility for her. Except if so, then what? Her mouth fails to produce rebuttal to Intemrus' allegations.

"At this moment," Intemrus says. "Kalderys is preparing to swim all the way across the Faithless Sea. From there, he plans to scale the bluffs of Fohrvylda, then find and assassinate the heathen king. All thanks to you."

Obsydia's mouth swings open. She pictures Kalderys, at night, paddling up a mountainous swell in an endless expanse of ocean. "Fohrvylda is a hundred miles away," she murmurs.

"Indeed it is. And if anyone can swim the distance, our magus can. He'll have help. Tidamora will cycle eastward, creating for him a steady current. After all ..." and Intemrus fucking winks at her, "it's only Faithless for the faithless."

She looks at him, capable of nothing more. It feels like this conversation has slipped and tumbled away from her down the side of Mount Adenhelm. She can't stop it. The damage isn't over.

"Kalderys can't kill Vretos," he says. "The heathen has honed his body for centuries in the same way I've honed consonance. For all I know, he can't be killed."

"Then what will happen?"

Intemrus looks down at Obsydia and speaks with a voice as clear as a tide pool. "Kalderys will die. And his failed assassination attempt will set off the Heathen Tide."

Obsydia's face feels hot and cold at the same time. "You ... want that?" But her concern is not the Tide.

"As much truth as I bend for my purpose, I've never lied about the severity of the Heathen Tide. It must happen now, or consonance will not survive it." His eyes soften, going roguish. "Do I want it?" A corrupt smile stretches his mouth. "The heathen king will bring his clattering horde to our beach. We will meet them with music. We will kill them all. I will take *everything* from him. Just as he did me."

His words whip her back and forth. A shiver runs through her and she trembles. *Kalderys.* "What have I done?"

"Try not to blame yourself, Magister." Intemrus rises, steps backward, giving her space. "I've been weaving this tapestry for longer than you can comprehend. Generations. You're not the first ambitious, whore-bred sociopath I've groomed. Kalderys isn't the first mindless consonant slaughterer. No. What set this instance apart from all previous attempts was a new variable. One I didn't anticipate. One Fohrvylda's spies didn't know to watch. An anomaly."

Intemrus has stopped directly beside the empty pedestal. He places his fingertips on its dusty surface. Excitement radiates off the sovereign. Obsydia knows what's coming but is incapable of feeling anything.

"The consonant vacuum. The first entropomancer, he who made all this possible by hobbling Kalderys and foiling your plan. Relinquishing Syvea to him was the hardest thing I've ever done. But at least when I lost her this time, the choice was mine."

"Relinquishing Syvea?"

"The crystal."

Obsydia scoffs. And to think, she arrived in a good mood. "By Imala. Is there anything you don't see?"

Intemrus laughs. "It is by Imala that I see. Some say I was given the name sovereign by the souls of the dead who learned its truth too late."

Obsydia groans.

"By now Syvea will have told Kale her story," Intemrus says. "The origin of my curse. It's her favorite story to tell. The one story she remembers." His smile wavers. He takes a breath. "The Faithless will carry Kale to Redemier, where he'll be killed. Haik too. That island is overrun with beasts and Imala knows what else by now. The crystal will be lost. Or it will return to the hands of its creator, the Deceiver. It always did call out to him."

She feels numb. His words have become as meaningless as drops of rain in a river. On he goes.

"It's taken me a long time to accept this is for the best. The benefits of possessing that crystal are no longer worth the cost. You shouldn't fret. Ownership of her wouldn't have done anything but confuse you. Possession of the crystal doesn't stave off the effects of time. That affliction was tailored for myself and Vretos alone. I'm sorry to disappoint. We're not meant to live forever. And maybe the Deceiver, in his timeless wisdom, has accepted this as well."

He's gone distant, as he does, no longer aware of Obsydia, who he filleted and left lifeless. He couldn't care less what he has done. His absent smile attests to this. She's a tool. Another whore-breed that happened to work out this time. All the concern she'd brought with her, all the fear, it's immaterial. All the hesitation, the indecision. Something inside Obsydia snaps. This skinny, ancient, pitiful man and his horribly intricate schemes and plots, what are they to her? Nothing more than what she is to him. Maybe less. She'd never been certain how Intemrus would die. That part of her plan had always been hazy. No more. He dies today. And he will see her first. He will fear her.

Obsydia leaps from her chair, sending it clattering. She grabs Intemrus by his collar, hefts him up. He weighs almost nothing. She slams him against the stone wall, producing a thin grunt that inflames her rage. She draws him back, bunching his dele at his throat to keep the narrow weasel from slipping out of her grip. Slams him again, this time thudding his head against rock. He doesn't stop her. Because he can't? She'll find out. The fear isn't in his eyes yet. It will be.

"What's to keep me from stopping Kalderys?" she hisses in his face. "What if I prevent his little suicide swim before he can ignite your war?"

He laughs, despite his awkward position. "Stop Kalderys? There's no stopping him. He *believes*. If you tried, you'd only weaken him. Make him resent you. You would assure his failure. After all—"

"We'll see about that." She drags Intemrus to a window and stuffs his head out, making him flinch in the sudden sunlight. "What's to keep me from throwing you to your death?"

"A fall wouldn't kill me. Besides—"

"Liar!" she screams at him, pushing him farther until most of his weight is outside and the sun looks down on his pitiful, sickly physique, and her grip alone stands between him and rapid descent. That bemused smirk is still written on his brittle face. His bright eyes are like shards of sky. "Intemrus sees all, does he?" Obsydia says. "Did you see this?"

"Our goals are the same," he says.

The words stall her. In her hesitation he continues, "Kill me and your plan is truly done for. Stravhelm will not accept you. Mount Adenhelm will poison the holy city. No one will survive the Heathen Tide."

She shakes her head to keep out his lies. Kalderys was her plan and he's en route to death. "What do you know about my goals?"

"I fear you will try to prevent Kalderys' sacrifice. If you could see the grander picture, you wouldn't. You have a larger part to play, Magister, and it's the one you've been working toward. Ausgan needs you. That's why I summoned you. To remove the veil from over your eyes."

She draws him inside, lets him go, steps back. "You can't control me. Not anymore."

"I won't presume to." He straightens his dele, rolls his old head on his thin neck. He doesn't appear put off by her assault in the least. Amused at best. "I will present your available paths, and the one I'd prefer for you happens to align with what you want for yourself."

"There's nothing you can say that will keep me from going to him."

"Hear me out, then decide." Intemrus' smile wrinkles the edges of his eyes. "People who understand the consequences of their actions tend to prefer Intemrus' Will."

55
So Evil a Sin

AUSGAN
Rhyolite Tier, Erudition

Intemrus' Will be done.

The creed comes as naturally and often as exhaling. It's been Kalderys' defining purpose for as long as he's had conscious memory. And now it brings nothing but pain, anchoring him to the moment of his greatest shame. The tribunal. Where Intemrus' Will deemed him useless.

In a dusty rhyolite manse by the light of a single oil torch, Kalderys runs the yucca-sharp shell up his oiled calf, shearing away all hair. He's done the same for his head, arms, chest, and stomach already. He rinses the shell in a clay bowl and runs it against the sharpening stone. He's filled himself with rice and steamed goat and fresh fruit, and has procured a streamlined knapsack, designed to flatten against his chest or back while swimming. He commissioned it from the malva clothier of Stravhelm. A parting gift of sorts. It is packed with the barest of necessities, and nothing that will spoil in the sea. Enough for his trip there. Not enough for a return.

The shell bites into Kalderys' skin, behind his knee. A red line of blood draws a lightning shaped path down his leg, intermingling with the glistening oil. Kalderys pauses to stare at it.

If only there were a specific event or action that he could pinpoint, identify, blame for this all. But there isn't. More like a mixture of unfortunate events, all of his creation. It started at Hargrim. He shepherded the damned town into a tight proximity and dealt them clean justice. All was the same as every time before, except one thing. An unnamed basalt came and stole his song. He'd noticed the peculiarity before beginning. He should have paid it more attention. Should have examined it. He didn't, because it eluded his perception and therefore the Imala's. Instead of that dignifying a deeper examination, he'd decided such an anomaly, one that exists outside his awareness, couldn't possibly matter. *Pride.* Kalderys neglected due process ... because he was distracted. *Did* it start at Hargrim?

Magister Obsydia stirs something inside Kalderys. Her eyes, regardless of what might be happening, convey an appreciation that seems to transcend their positions and even his utility. She believed in him. She knew his heart for serving Intemrus. For consonance. For Ausgan's efforts against the Heathen Tide. Even if she had never voiced her confidence in Kalderys' purpose, which she did frequently, her gaze alone would have inspired him to fight this fight.

But her eyes ... they also confuse him. They hold him captive, muddle his thoughts. He always wondered, were her gazes a test? It is a common practice in Erudition to offer a challenge to those you're mentoring, not intending them to succeed but instead to gauge their efforts and ability, to give them a goal. The magister wears little to nothing in the presence of most exemplars. Kalderys has always assumed it was to put their resolve to test. She spares Kalderys her temptation though. In his presence, she remains clothed. He'd decided it was because of his position in the Triumvirate that she spared him the threat. But is that truly why?

Another line of blood runs down Kalderys' leg. This train of thought always leads to the same regrettable place, scrambling to distract himself through meditation or song or sparring. Only now he's alone and trapped and his failures are laid before him under harsh light. Kalderys is confronted with a curiosity he will never admit, will always fight to suppress, but can no longer flee. Some deplorable part of him wishes she didn't remain clothed in his presence. Some hidden, evil, envious part of him wishes to see her undressed, and it wishes bloody, violent ruin on anyone who has. This evil bores through his being, usually while he lies in the dark awaiting sleep. It examines his memories of her, attempts to see through that thin dele. It marvels at the smoothness of her skin, her hair. It imagines her skin against his. Her lips ...

Kalderys throws the shaving shell against the bare stone wall with such force that it shatters. A shrill scream dislodges him forcibly from his thoughts. Magister Obsydia is standing in his doorway. She's wearing a featureless black hooded robe that is clasped at her neck with a single bead, and descends almost all the way to her bare feet. Her reddened eyes suggest she's been weeping. *How long has she been there?* Kalderys quickly pulls a towel over his lap, trying to do so without drawing attention to his engorged state. He would stand, but ...

"Don't go," Obsydia says, taking two tentative steps toward him and drawing back her hood. "Please."

"Resonations, Magister," Kalderys says to the floor, his cheeks glowing. He can smell her hair. Smell her tears. He's all too aware of his lowly place, sitting naked on a cubed stone in an otherwise empty rhyolite manse. Surely she can detect the stench of his shame.

"Intemrus told me you plan to swim to Fohrvylda." Her voice is wavering. "You can't. That's not what I had in mind when we spoke."

Kalderys' head tilts to one side. She didn't stoop to detail his plan when they spoke. She has never needed to. As always, he did. His trip will be difficult, but he has enough experience in the sea to know what he can and can't swim. "Magister, with respect, I was demoted, not hobbled. My mastery over consonance is untouched. I wouldn't embark on a mission I cannot complete, even in my absolute disgrace." The words ring hollow. Did he not make an identical promise standing atop the wall while Selu yet lived? His teeth clench. What's the point of talking when your words have no meaning?

"No." She's taken his hand, holding it in both of hers. He's never noticed how small her hands are compared to his. "You will fail. Intemrus foresaw it. He's using you. You can't kill Vretos. You'll only enrage him and make him launch his ships against us."

Kalderys' eyes narrow. *Can you use the willing?* This mission was his idea, not Intemrus'. Obsydia has never told him what he is not capable of. He pulls his hand away from her. Touching like that is not allowed. "Why would Intemrus want that?"

"He says he and I are ready to face the Heathen Tide, here in Ausgan. But you ... you won't survive to see it."

Kalderys had considered that he'd not make it back. Apparently Intemrus truly is done with him. So that's it. This mission is his final purpose. And to think, he'd always imagined the Triumvirate at a time of peace, furthering consonance together freely, without fear of spy or heathen. Kalderys snorts. His imagination was a tragically naive fantasy.

"So be it," he says, mustering resolve, trying to quell the encroaching flood of despair. "Intemrus' Will be done."

"No," she says, angry now. "You don't get to just leave."

He considers pushing her out of his way. It wouldn't take much. "My mission has your blessing, Magister. The wind itself testifies to the validity of this quest. It will carry me east across the Faithless, and I will sing and summon the entire way. I will climb the cliffs of Fohrvylda and deliver my life's work to the heathen king. He cannot survive the song I have in mind." *My final song.* "Nothing can. Not wind, not rocks, not water." Kalderys stands, securing the towel around his waist. "You have good reason to doubt me, as I am well aware. But when I tell you I have a song for Vretos, the likes of which the world has never known, believe me."

"I've never doubted you!" Obsydia delivers a stiff push that's nearly a strike, knocking him back down onto the cot, where he sits stunned. "I was wrong, Kalderys." There are tears on her face. His words have hurt her. "I was wrong about *me*. Intemrus gave me a choice. I choose this." She falls on him, straddling him, her dark skin peeking from within the robe. Her face is almost touching his. "If you refuse to hear the truth, feel it."

Kalderys is too shocked to resist, and in his hesitation she locks her ankles around his calves. Her attack would render his legs useless if she were heavier. For him to escape, he should turn his hips, lifting her, then pin her leg and roll on top. From there he could pummel her face with fists or elbows or his own forehead. Except his body doesn't obey, because she is not an enemy, and this is not an attack. His hands scramble against the stone cot, in fear of touching her. The robe has parted enough to reveal that she is stark naked beneath it. All that separates his skin and hers is the towel at his waist.

Say something!

It's not experience that warns him what she is attempting. The feeling she's awoken is unmistakable. A roaring heat rises up from deep within, where a long-repressed, unappeasable appetite lurks.

Do something!

His hands are at her waist, where they should be lifting her off, throwing her aside. Instead they range to her robe's collar and they rip, sending the bead clasp bouncing away. He peels the robe back, allowing her to wriggle free of it, exposing her bare shoulders and arms and breasts to his torch's flickering light.

"Don't go," she moans in his ear, sending chills over his neck and down his arms. She takes his hands in hers and kneads them into her breasts. His breath releases, sending a shudder up his spine. The fire down below becomes a point, intense, painful. Before he can stop her, she manages to rip away his towel, leaving him poised without defense.

"Don't go." Her lips smear the words into his ear, and her teeth close on his earlobe. The feeling hammering through his veins is like breathless dread, and yet his body will not cooperate to prevent it. She grinds her hips against him, making him dizzyingly familiar with how closely she has shaved even her most intimate region. She pushes her mouth to his. Her tongue roves over his tongue. Her heat is infectious, summoning his hips to hers. His will is powerless, his body invincible. This is a test. A test he is failing. Her hand snakes downward, past his stomach, groping, sending up sparks with each touch of her fingertips. She finds what she seeks and squeezes, making the pressure triple, his teeth clench, his eyes roll back.

"Imala ..." he says.

Her other arm drapes over his shoulder and around his neck. She pulls herself up until her breasts flank his cheeks and adjusts Kalderys, as if righting a wooden dowel to be pounded into place, then eases down onto it. Resistance, slight and painful, and then at a wiggle from her behind, he is engulfed. Lightning is upon him, inhaling him, surrounding him, making him gasp for breath. A cry escapes her, full of pain, and something else more akin to the euphoria consuming him. Her head falls back.

You have to stop this!

Why? roars the repressed evil, as Kalderys' hands grip her thighs. *I'm Intemrus' spent song, useless to all the world. I will be damned by every god if I can't serve some purpose yet.*

Kalderys forces her hips against his. She cries out louder. Something is dripping. His hand runs up her arched spine, beneath her raven hair, gripping the back of her neck. Her fingernails bite into his back, a pain that provokes only deeper yearning. Holding her neck and her thigh, he accelerates her gyrations to a violent grind. They're becoming one in a way he'd never known possible. Until now, harmonizing in song felt like the pinnacle of intimacy. How wrong he'd been.

Her bare behind slaps against his lap. Something's wetting his inner thighs. A clammy sweat frosts her skin, and his, and on they go. Flashes of her eyes, languorous, entranced. Her body, so soft and so hard all at once. Her breath, pained, craving, enraptured. A smell of coconut oil, vitality butter, sweat, blood? His perception, stunted so absolutely that he's nearly forgotten where he is, aware now only of her breath, her heat. She surrounds him, consumes him. He fills her, stretches her. Their union rides a blade's edge, teetering on chaotic collapse and yet entirely inescapable. As natural as the storm waves that pound the stones. Despite how dangerous their entanglement has become, how loud and oblivious and enslaving, he craves more. This is not evil. Can't be. This pace must endure. No, increase! A carnal apex looms before him, made evident by the concentration of energy rushing through his body toward his groin. She is close too. He can feel it. Tighter she grips him, harder she grinds, hungrier she cries. This yearning has become his most vital mission, and if he slows, if he looks away, if he acknowledges what is happening, what he is sacrificing ... He looks down. There is the unmistakable sheen of blood, glistening at the vertex of her legs, where he and she connect. At once the spell shatters.

He stands, throws her off. She falls in a naked heap, all limbs and black hair, a spider in the corner. He's backing away with hands outspread. His gleaming weapon of choice bears crimson evidence, betraying him for all to know his evil. There are no words he can say. She's rising, she's reaching toward him, her face is a storm of fear, of hunger. He has the presence of mind to fling her aside with his forearm, grab his knapsack, flee the manse into the golden twilight of upper Erudition.

He hears her contact a wooden stool, take it clattering down with her. "Kalderys!" It is a shriek of the purest torment and infects his feet with a relentless vigor.

What have I done?

Intemrus surely saw it. He probably heard it. Smelled it. Kalderys' feet slap the stone staircase, ringing out with the sound of her skin against his.

Oh Imala-be-damned, what have I done?

This is the sin he was meant to avoid at all costs. This was the test. All else was preparation. This will cost him something, and he dreads to know what. Everything? But what else was there to lose? You don't ask that.

The smell of her hair rushes through his lungs, torturing him into running faster. He can taste her skin on his lips, feel her tongue with his. He is passing Andesite Tier. Straight ahead, beyond Basalt Tier, are the shut gates of Erudition.

"Open the gates," Kalderys roars.

The two rhyolites leaning on staves against the wall were in conversation with one another. Now they're slack-jawed and spellbound by what Kalderys imagines must be a truly shocking image: a hairless, naked, once-magus wearing the blood of his latest adversary in the unlikeliest place.

"*Open the gates in Intemrus' name!*" Blasphemy. There's only one more task he'll ever do in Intemrus' name.

The exemplars jerk to life, prying the heavy korundite beam from its place and frantically pulling both doors wide.

"*Kalderys!*" Her cry tumbles down the tiers of Erudition and rakes at him. The pain in her voice nearly causes his feet to deceive him, nearly causes him to return to where he was, within her grasp, between her legs, inside her. So evil a sin, to clad itself as an emergency, to reward so deeply for your slightest indulgence. *Why?* Why would such a sin even exist if not for torture's sake? Kalderys' grasp on his purpose has never shaken. Not until now. Now, at a single shameful encounter, he almost lost his entire identity.

He's past the gates, free of Erudition, and on level packed earth he hits his stride. His feet punish the ground. His fists squeeze like collapsing stars. She can't catch him. No one can outrun him. Selu could. But she's dead. He will run to the ocean. He will swim. Come Fohrvylda or death, he'll swim and he won't look back. No matter what truths or lies or evil came with Obsydia's visit, it is on one revelation she brought that all of Kalderys' hopes now rest. Once he leaves, he will never return.

Intemrus' Will be done.

56
The Daunting Landmass
That Awaits

FOHRVYLDA
The Towers

Morning greets Irdessa with all the courtesy of a kitchen fire. Her tongue is caked to the roof of her mouth. It feels like tentacles have invaded her eye sockets and are expanding. She doesn't brave cracking her eyelids until several moments of temple massaging and deep breathing. When she is able to achieve a cross-legged slouch, she rubs her neck and her eyes, trying to recall the last time beer treated her so poorly. Or she, it. Last night's festivities seem at once a single blink ago but also a different lifetime. West beer versus east beer. The way to determine a winner was drink more of both. Irdessa had several opportunities to stop drinking and failed to take advantage of each.

After ingesting a couple chunks of hard bread from last night, made harder by an evening's dew and the morning's sun, then a swallow of hot beer, she's up and moving, carefully. It's time to go. Past time. She makes a circuit of the Catcher settlement, rousing her companions as she walks. The provocation to get the Vanguard up more resembles punting than prodding. But after a dissonant symphony of groaning, griping, and vomiting, the fighters are on their feet. Practice at being nomadic has made the party quite mobile, even in its alcohol-ravaged state. It's good to see that running for your life has advantages.

Today, they will follow Catcher scouts north, in such a direction and to such a destination as drunken Irdessa agreed to. Shortly after last night's meeting, Catcher scouts went ahead and roved out across the northern Towers, studying for optimal routes. Today's scouts will simply act on their findings. Meanwhile, Catcher villagers will conspicuously make their way eastward, noisily filtering throughout distant Towers to misdirect pursuit. Having local help was a parting favor Irdessa asked of the elders, and the best gift they could offer.

As the Vanguard assembles to leave, Irdessa observes that her party has swollen. First she mistakes the increase in hooded heads for hungover double vision. It's not. A good many Catchers stand among them, and judging by the packs slung over their shoulders, they plan to accompany the Vanguard. This observation brings an annoyance so sharp Irdessa nearly demands the extras go home. Then memories swim back to her from a far more comfortable state.

Last night at the fire Harpold had informed her there were some adventurous Catchers who wanted to volunteer their services. Rather than asking why, or anything for that matter, she'd immediately agreed under the condition that they pass auditions. That's the way Vim guarded the Vanguard after all and vetted its recruits. "We have fucking standards!" her throat remembers shouting.

Harpold had rounded up those Catchers who were enthusiastic to join. Even after Kraus foretold that they'd all probably die by orcane, their enthusiasm held.

"Can't eat us if they eat our arrows first," one said, to his fellow Catchers' roaring agreement.

"You'd be surprised," someone answered.

Irdessa found herself utterly unable to devise any sensible means of testing. Kraus suggested they fight to the death, the last Catcher standing earning a name in the Vanguard. "It'll save us all time and food," Kraus explained. The volunteers insisted on something less terminal. Kraus proceeded to berate their cowardice profanely, and at a volume that shook pebbles from distant Towers. When no more reasonable examination was forthcoming, Irdessa had them compete to drink the most beer. By this morning's bloated count, it appears that whoever did the judging let on anyone with a functioning gullet. Hopefully, the active threat of the coming journey was enough to dissuade any who can't hold their own. That, and Kraus' verbal assault. It's enough of a struggle to try to keep her own people alive, without unproven spire-hoppers mucking around. One thing's for certain. Catcher baggage will not get special treatment or priority. May as well be wets.

"We're off." Irdessa's announcement comes out more a grumble, and it intensifies her headache. She pulls her hood over her eyes to thwart the evil sun and marches. She'd wanted to thank the Catchers for their hospitality, but Capper and Rowan are nowhere to be seen. They must have said as much as they cared to before last night's festivities. That, or maybe after witnessing the shameless debauchery the evening devolved into, they're still busy amending their notions of Vim's heroic nature. Doesn't matter. Soon enough, Vim's marching boots fall back into rhythm and the calluses around Irdessa's ankles warm to a pliable state.

Cindie and Elaga are in high spirits. They were noticeably absent from the gathering last night. Whatever activities consumed their evening were evidently less destructive than profuse beer consumption.

Bravensi didn't attend either. This morning there's a distinct vigor to her stride, but also a hint of unease in the clench of her jaw.

Caenin ... well, there is no Caenin. After the woman from the fire proved her worth at mothering his cracked jaw, he fell madly in dependence. He means to remain at Rain Catch, which is fine with her.

She squeezes her puffy hand. The pain is sharper now, but still not so sharp as a fracture. "Worth it," she tells herself.

Kraus walks beside her, now limping on both legs, but as energetic as Irdessa's ever seen him. Of everyone who quenched too much last night, he bears his residual damage the lightest. All his practice pays off.

"Do you need help?" she asks him, as if she's in any state.

Kraus takes in her question with a face scrunched in what appears to be thoughtful consideration, then responds with an extended fart.

"I'm done being a burden," he says.

"I'll leave you if you fall behind," she lies.

"Smartest thing you could do."

Vyker is impassive, striding alongside Sura. She knew he probably wouldn't climb the mound and speak for his brother last night. A fierce warrior he may be, but that requires a different sort of courage, particularly considering Dhovoi is partially to blame for all this. She wondered if someone else would mention him. He had his merits. It couldn't be her speaking for him though. Not with any authenticity. Perhaps Vyker and Sura found some closure last night. Perhaps they provided some solace for each other.

As they venture farther from civilization, Maudee passes Irdessa to take the lead, and Irdessa makes no complaint. She was up before Magpie, working alongside Catcher scouts to ensure a clear path. A tall Catcher named Otto walks beside her and seems to have trouble keeping his eyes off her. When Maudee notices, her cheeks glow. Then his cheeks glow. Then Irdessa stifles a gag. Magpie, oblivious, is sulking along behind with a dripping compress across his forehead, blocking all but a thin slit so he can see his feet.

Leaf-laden vines curtain the trees and cliff walls and obscure the path, occasionally reducing marching into grunting and hacking with knives and hatchets. As the sun heaves itself up from the east, the emerald leaves slow-cook dew, creating a sweltering humidity. Trees sprout here and there in the path, their roots buried in vines, barely clinging to crumbling stone, giving the false sense of ground where there is none.

Soon enough the Vanguard skirts around Towers, no longer navigating established trails but merely opportune outcroppings. Once more they journey over treacherous hems of stone, flanked by a cliff wall and a gasp. These locales bring to her mind their first miles onto the Towers, but are made less familiar by the wall of thin, hairy vines cascading down and draping over the walkway, entombing it and the cliff like a blanket of green spiderwebs. The path takes them over dry-rotted planks secured on wooden rods protruding from the stone wall itself. It is by some miracle that none of Irdessa's companions, who shamble with vacant stares and comically matted hair, have taken a topple. They make better time here than on their first miles on the Towers, only pausing to drink water. Irdessa is struck with pride again at the Vanguard. They are resilient and adaptive. They don't complain. What the Catchers have to offer is yet to be determined.

Each successive island tower in their path is less tall than the one before, each closer to the tossing waves. It's as if these Towers, distant from Promontory's strict eye, have shrugged off their sharpened edges like unnecessary formalities, leaving fallen stones heaped in the ocean below. This gradual decline in altitude makes a change so subtle it sneaks up on Irdessa. Viewed from Rain Catch village, the ranging orcanes below were little more than points at the head of thin white chevrons on the blue-grey swells. Now they're close enough for her to make out glinting steel and the black tails coursing behind as patrols carve through the waves.

The fighters once strolled across suspension bridges with no concern other than falling. Now they must await the signals of high-perched scouts then sneak across in pairs, timed so that neither they nor their shadows below alert the lurking orcane patrols. Until now they've taken no heed to the volume of their voices. They've not needed to, being so far up and in the company of such raucous sprake clamor. But the predator birds appear to have no use for these alleys, what with the boulders and aquatic shrubbery clogging the waters below. The sprakes Irdessa does observe are always distant, riding forceful upward gusts in the open air, their azure plumage as dazzling as tumbling sapphires. The Vanguard must limit communication to the necessary. Now when a voice rises above the others, its echo resounds off nearby Towers for far too long. When displaced pebbles trickle off the path to click resonantly on every outcropped stone between the Vanguard and the Faithless, Irdessa plasters herself to the spot, dreading that some decrepit, girthy boulder will awaken and come loose to punch the water like an explosion, alarming every patrol for miles.

By her estimation, if the Vanguard is spotted the alarmed orcane patrol would split up. One part would ride out to alert all nearby. The rest would gather below the Vanguard like hounds under a treed cat. Each patrol they signal would do the same, splitting, branching out. Every passing moment would bring more soldiers. More eyes, more orcanes. However stealthily Irdessa's party attempted to retreat from view and navigate a new route, it wouldn't be enough. While they pushed through the thick vines over treacherous footing, possibly dodging Promontory arrows and eventually sprakes, their enemies could keep the pace by merely treading water.

What the Vanguard does have going for it seemed an impediment initially. Those leaf-laden vines shroud everything, flowing down the sides of the dilapidated Towers like chunky green manes, not just hindering the party but hiding it. Even the few remaining suspension bridges have succumbed to the viridescent locks. The thin strands inundate the planks, the hemp rails, and all spaces in between, to the point that it's unclear where one Tower's creeping vines end and the next one's begin.

The sea-bound orcane patrols below are irregular and wander listlessly. The soldiers all appear bored, which presents advantages and disadvantages. On the one hand they never look up, evidently having lost all confidence in spotting the Vanguard. When they're boisterous with one another, they're impossible to miss, even from this high up. But sometimes they're static, like barnacles. They lurk in coves and alleys between Towers, drinking, or gambling, or crabbing, or dodging their superior officer. Sometimes a soldier finds a flat enough rock to stretch out on, interlacing fingers behind his head to gaze at the blue sky while his orcane is tethered to a tree trunk. In the moments before sleep takes them, they are the most dangerous, watching quietly from the shadows.

Fading sunlight forces the party to make camp, which tonight is a fireless and largely foodless respite. Irdessa wedges herself into vines for well-needed sleep but her mind keeps marching. What if the Vanguard was already seen, miles ago, and the indifference of the patrols is a façade? Maybe they were instructed to behave lax but are tracking the party's every step. In that way they could simply wait for when the Vanguard inevitably descends. When sleep eventually welcomes her, it's fitful and gone too soon. She rises before the sun, and on they march.

The distance between the Towers grows. The walls here are brittle and porous, largely succumbing to the combined efforts of gravity's merciless tug and the vines' insatiable ambition. Fallen stones decorate the feet of these Towers, lying in ancient ruin, slick and blackened by years of shadowy tide. Witnessing this unlikely and untamed landscape, Irdessa loses herself in thought as her feet mimic those of the person in front of her. Stories say that hundreds of years ago, when Redemier was initially cursed and all were forced to leave, Vretos led the future-Fohrvyldans southward over these same spires, while the monk Intemrus took the easier route westward toward the verdant, indefensible islands. Some of the stories claim that at that point the Towers weren't separately formed yet but a single mass of land that proceeded to crumble to seal Vretos' escape from the curse. Some say Vretos destroyed the land as he went, leaving only the Towers.

Irdessa is so preoccupied with what's beneath that she doesn't immediately register the enormous landmass that has been vying for her attention from gaps between the Towers. The green behemoth comes as such a jolt because part of her doubted they'd ever reach it. But now it's unmistakable. Still miles off, appearing hazy and purpled by the distance, it has consumed the horizon—a jagged green line visible between the vine-shrouded spires. There's no confusing it for other

Towers or the mainland. Fohrvylda's landscape is all scrub land, evergreen gatherings, and fractured boulders scattered around like great broken dice. The green backdrop lurking on the far side of the Towers is made of soft hills and gullies. Green swells roll away into the distance with pools of mist creeping upward from the valleys.

What had been the silence of stealth within Vanguard's ranks gradually becomes a different kind of speechlessness altogether. While the landmass is in view, the fighters are reverent, hesitant to rush or even take their eyes off it, as if it might dissipate like a smoke ring. While the land is eclipsed by Towers, they whisper excitedly to one another, contrasting what they saw, stepping more carelessly, anxious to be back within view of it. Irdessa, too, is struck by unease, but is in no hurry. Traversing the Towers has its risks, but she's familiar with those risks now. She's comfortable in this set of perils. But perils inevitably forsake you, making room for new ones, sometimes preferable—usually not. Every moment that she's exposed to the daunting landmass that awaits, her imagination creates new dangers to ambush her and her people, hiding within that unending forest.

Before she's ready, the Vanguard has run out of Towers. There is nothing more between them and Redemier. Those in front of her shamble to a stop, bunching up on each other over piles of vine-knotted rubble. Irdessa elbows her way to the front of the line, where Magpie and Maudee and the Catcher, Otto, perch, tensely watching the landmass like it might open eyes and watch back. Irdessa is still too struck by the sight to demand a report. She's never imagined such an island as this and now here it is, awaiting them across a one-hundred-fifty-yard sheet of flat water glittering above white sand.

One of the first details Irdessa registers is that Redemier has no cliffs. It's like the whole green mass has melted, slouching from its highest peaks down into accessible slopes that welcome the ocean. This sight is at the same time intriguing and deeply unsettling. Redemier offers an invitation to breach its shores from any direction, discriminating against no man or animal. Those placid inclines make the step-like terraces climbing up out of the Bay of Ivolde seem like vertical cliffs. Irdessa has survived long enough to be wary of such an invite, and her mind sets to work digging out the hidden threats. If the land has no natural barrier, any beast or bastard could be lurking just out of view with knives or claws at the ready. This land is as accommodating to her foes as it is her. Without a single damn cliff to keep your back against, would there be any peace of mind on such a land? Also, who's to say how high the Faithless Sea climbs on her highest tide? What if she swallows half the island? What's to keep the ocean from wrapping her grey lips around the lowest perimeter, then spitting it back out crawling with thunder crabs or sea salamanders or leap sharks or wilder orcanes? Even as the thoughts are born, Irdessa snorts laughter at her own ignorance. Her idiocy. She's never spent much time wondering what sorts of beasts would climb all over Fohrvylda if the land's legs weren't so long. Redemier threatens to answer that for her. It is cursed, after all. The unease and anticipation whirl in her, making her heart race and her hands clammy.

A white border frames the great green land against the ocean. Irdessa cranes her head in several directions and deduces that it's all sand, as if a single beach encompasses the entire mass. Something about this sends a fresh wave of terror crashing over her. Not only is there no defensible position, there is no hidden entry point for her people. They'll need to make landfall at a sprint to quickly reach the trees' shelter, making their way around the massive piles of rock and earth that litter the sand. Enormous broken flagstones checker the beach. They cluster the thickest at the base of ruined stone stumps and boulders. Some of the ruins retain evidence they once had smooth stairs that led to piers or maybe to platforms meant to reach up and access the Towers. They're all so ancient and rundown it hardly matters what they were made for. Now they're obstacles in Vim's path. Perhaps they'll provide some use.

It never occurred to her until now that not all of the world's land masses tower above the ocean the way Fohrvylda does. This leaves her feeling as clueless as a child. The Vanguard trusts her. Why?

"Too bad Piss Spray isn't here to tell us that's Redemier." Kraus is beside her staring at the landmass. It does Irdessa some good to see him and others wearing expressions of perplexity. Till now she felt alone in her naivety.

You can reach your journey's end, Torvald whispers, *but if you don't take the final step, you may as well never have stood up in the first place.*

"Shut the fuck up." She doesn't realize she's said it out loud until Kraus chuckles awkwardly.

"Sorry," he says. "Just a joke."

Irdessa doesn't have the presence of mind to attempt explanation. "I guess we ought to get over there," she says blankly.

Kraus frowns down at the ravaged rocks below, then out at the expanse of shimmering ocean, then squints toward the shadows under the dancing green boughs beyond the distant boulder-littered beach. He rolls his head on his thick neck, making a crackling like burning kindling. "I'm right behind you," he says.

Magpie clears his throat. "Orcanes patrol the shallows in groups of three." He indicates the expanse of water between them and the beach.

"How long between patrols?" Irdessa asks.

Maudee answers, "No obvious rhyme or reason to their frequency. It appears random, same as how they weave throughout the Towers."

"So you know," Otto offers in his airy Catcher inflection, his words in no hurry, "we chose this particular location to infiltrate Redemier not because this Tower is the closest to the beach, but because it's close enough while still unassuming. Also the water's shallower here."

Indeed, to the left and right are more Towers, each as collapsed and green as the one the Vanguard occupies. The closest sea stacks to this one are about as distant as the beach itself. None intrinsically draw attention to themselves.

"What's the state of the soldiers as they pass?" Irdessa asks. "What do they watch?"

"They watch the beach with some suspicion," Otto says, "which makes me think there are still no soldiers on Redemier."

"Still?" Irdessa says.

Before Otto can respond, Magpie speaks. "We can't know that for sure." There's more of an edge to his voice than Irdessa thinks the comment deserved.

"But it would be nice if there aren't," Maudee says, shifting her eyes apologetically toward Otto.

"Yeah, well, hope in one hand and shit in the other ..." Magpie says, glaring at his sister. "See which one fills up first."

"Why would you shit in your hand?" Maudee asks flatly.

"Have Catcher scouts ever seen soldiers on Redemier?" Irdessa asks Otto.

"No."

His answer fails to reassure. There's too much uncertainty. Too many hiding places for Promontory. Hell, there could be hundreds of soldiers behind nearby Towers, waiting for the Vanguard to try and swim to the beach. There are too many fighters and Catchers to be displaced subtly.

"We need more information," Irdessa says. "Need someone full time watching the patrols, how many there are. Need to know how deep that water is and how low we have to climb to keep from breaking our legs if we jump. We need more time. But with every passing moment, we risk—"

Maudee silences Irdessa with a raised palm and a terse hiss. An orcane patrol drifts into view from the left. The stillness provoked by Maudee's action spreads over the perched fighters, turning them silent and vigilant. But as hidden as Irdessa would like to believe they are, there must be forty people up here clinging to rocks. Forty opportunities to be spotted by a single soldier's wandering gaze and this game is up before it starts.

The three soldiers are passing by. They're sitting in their saddles, submerged from the hips down, rather than standing upright like tall shark fins. The cut of the wake they produce is transparent, lacking the white foam that haste generates. Their pace is leisurely. From this lofty vantage point, their orcanes appear as wavering black masses just beneath the surface. True to Otto's word, the soldier closest to Redemier mainland throws regular glances at the beach, from which his orcane is no more than fifty yards away. It appears his comrades find his fear entertaining. The soldier on the right mocks him, false shivering and whipping his helmeted head to and fro, prompting the one in the middle to turn up her face and give a high, raucous laugh that echoes up to the Vanguard, cementing their silence. The soldiers maintain their plodding course, massive orcane paws pulling them lazily through the clear water, while their shadows slide over the white sand below. Judging by the position of the shadows, that water isn't more than twenty feet deep.

"They don't care how much noise they're making," Maudee notes.

"They don't expect to see us," Otto says. His nonchalance suggests this is not the first time he's watched orcane patrols from on high.

Irdessa peers at the soldiers, trying to absorb as much knowledge as Torvald would. They're inattentive, which could mean several things. Maybe the waters are so saturated with patrols that each individual soldier feels useless. Maybe they've been out here a long time, days even. Maybe the Catcher diversion to the east is working and the brunt of the expectations are with the soldiers chasing shadows below uninhabited Towers. Maybe these are just sorry soldiers. None of those possibilities is inherently bad. But none are certain. Irdessa swears under her breath. Torvald would not sit frozen, overanalyzing the situation.

Soon enough, the soldiers have drifted away to the right, behind a far Tower and out of sight.

"We should have rained arrows on them," Kraus says. "Or rocks."

"That's the stupidest thing we could have done," Magpie says. "If blood spills in that water, we're done. Barksharks will smell it for miles. You mind letting the smart ones talk?"

Kraus raises a scar-dented eyebrow at Magpie. "Enjoy this distance between us while you can."

"I am, and so are my nostrils," Magpie says, inhaling deeply through his nose. "May we perch on this crumbling cliff forever."

"You cheeky fucking halfman—"

"Kraus," Irdessa injects enough edge to silence him. A fleck of stone glances off her shoulder from above. Paralyzed, she watches it fall until it disappears silently in a patch of shrubs. Above, Harpold is scrambling down, far hastier than stealth demands.

"Heads up," he calls.

"Thanks," Irdessa says, rubbing her shoulder, but the fear on his face forgoes her sarcasm.

"From the south," he wheezes, pointing, unable to continue without gasping for air first. He'd been scouting from several Towers back. Whatever he saw scared a serious spring into his step. "They're coming."

"Who is?" Irdessa demands.

Harpold heaves in a great breath, exhales. "More orcane soldiers than I could count. And at their head, Marshal Zander's banner. They're tearing over the damn water like they know exactly where we are."

"How long till they're here?" Irdessa asks.

"Nightfall."

Suddenly the sun seems to be in quite the hurry. Irdessa squeezes the bridge of her nose between her eyes. Nothing is easy.

"Why would it be Marshal Zander and not Admiral Garr with the navy?" Maudee's voice is pleading, as if any answer might undo the situation. As if Garr's warships are preferable to Zander's orcanes. "Shouldn't he be ... I don't know, burning down towns on the mainland?"

"Ambition," Harpold offers. "Probably wants a higher chair."

"Retribution," Kraus says. "Probably looking pretty stupid after we shat on his battalion and blade-fucked his henchman."

"Just because we haven't seen Garr's ships doesn't mean they're not out there somewhere," Irdessa says. The two factions are probably competing to capture the Vanguard, same as how Vretos' court competes for everything.

"It hardly matters why," Magpie says. "We need a plan."

With a clench of her jaw Irdessa extinguishes a budding thought. Never mind what Torvald would do. It's on her to turn disorder into decision. *Now*. A deep, silent breath clears away the clutter.

"Harpold," she says, "Search our ranks for swimmers and archers. I need to speak to anyone who can do either."

His face is blank for a moment as the instructions set in. Then he dips his chin in a nod and scrambles away.

"Send me Bravensi," she calls after him. "And Vyker and Sura."

"I could get Bravensi," Kraus offers.

Irdessa ignores him. "Otto," she says, "you know this area better than us. Gain some altitude and do more recon. How many patrols are nearby? How much time can you guarantee us from the moment you spot one? Gather the Catchers. Put their eyes to work. Plan to put their bows to work too. I need to know how many orcanes are coming. Can't make a strategy until then."

"Of course," he says in his carefree way and turns to climb.

"I'll go with you," Maudee says, a little too eagerly.

Magpie snorts. "I'm sure you'll both be incredibly attentive up there *alone*."

Maudee widens her eyes at him and her cheeks flush. Otto's back is to them both so only Irdessa is privy to the hint of a smile that flickers on the edge of his lips.

"It's a good idea," Irdessa says, before the siblings fall to bickering. "Magpie, I want you with me, relaying what they're seeing."

"Not sure I want to relay everything she sees up there."

Maudee pokes her tongue out at him and follows Otto upward.

"Kraus," Irdessa says, and draws a blank.

When assigning pieces, play to their strength, is what Torvald would say.

Yeah, no shit.

But do not overlook their shortcomings.

"You can't swim," she tells Kraus, embarrassing herself. What a useless observation. She is immediately flushed with an irrational anger at the long dead Torvald.

"I can too." He exhibits a perfunctory squat. His knee gives a grinding creak, then noodles under him. He flails his arms, nearly topples off the cliff. Irdessa grabs him by his sleeve and rights him.

"Don't be an ass. We've got to figure out how to get the non-swimmers across."

"How?" He asks from between clenched teeth, pinching his kneecap between thumb and forefinger.

"They fly, genius," Magpie scoffs.

Kraus turns a dark look on him. "You're closer to that than you know, you shaved cunt."

"Gonna tie feathers to me and throw me?"

"I was thinking rocks."

Irdessa's pulse thumps angrily in her temples. She is reminded of goofing off while Torvald assembled strategies to save her life. She grits her teeth. There's no time for distraction. She knows the obstacle. Now she must identify her resources. Pare out the useless. These are methods Torvald taught her. But now they're all empty words clattering around, further complicating.

"Irdessa." It's Bravensi, large-eyed, leather-clad, and utterly composed on the ragged cliff with Oekner strapped at her back. Kraus is admiring her in unadulterated approval. Magpie is watching Kraus with mounting excitement, clearly working up the humiliating quip that will likely beget his own demise.

"Magpie," Irdessa says, "make your way down to the ocean without being seen. Bravensi, you, Sura, and Vyker go with him. Collect wood and vines. We need rafts. That's how we'll get the non-swimmers across. Surely in all those sea laurels down there is some sturdy deck wood. Gods know there are enough vines to connect them."

The young scout scoffs. "The Catchers already have vines. Miles of it. They turn it to fiber and rope while they walk." He smirks like he's dodged duty.

Irdessa's eyebrow raises in approval. They're wise to collect those vines. That's surely the most versatile commodity this land produces. And if the Catchers have as much as Magpie says, they've proven their worth.

"Perfect," she says. "This gives us options. Bravensi, take Sura and Vyker and get harvesting wood. Only hit it with an axe if you have to. Stealth is the priority, then speed. Magpie, talk to the rope makers. Have them bring it down."

Magpie looks crestfallen. "Collect vines? What do you take me for?"

"The one for this job. Communicate with your sister, and through her, Otto, to expedite this. By the time you get the vines down we'll all know more."

He's still staring at her, shaking his head slowly.

"Get climbing or get flying," she says, and turns to Kraus. "Find him his wings."

Kraus' feet spring to life, slinging gravel down the cliff face.

"Alright," the scout says, scrambling away. He ascends in the same direction Harpold came from. Bravensi, Sura, and Vyker descend toward the sea. This leaves Irdessa with Kraus, who can't scout, shoot, swim, or shut his mouth. But he's good at hurting people. And he can drink. And he makes her laugh.

"Kraus," she says, drawing his attention from the departing Bravensi. Perhaps between his experience as an outlaw and her time as Torvald's protege, they can cobble together a strategy to thwart organized orcanes attacking on their preferred battleground. "Tell me ... if you were Promontory, here and now, how would you ambush us?"

57

Zander's Education

FOHRVYLDA
Below the Towers

Captain Jeret sits his orcane on broken, sea-licked stone rubble under the shadow of the northwestern-most Towers, awaiting the marshal's signal and trying to ignore the pain in his face. To the west is the sea, glistening in the sunset, sending its wind rushing over him. Bobbing about are the orcanes that make up his force. Or rather, the rest of Marshal Zander's force. His own orcane would prefer to be among them in the water, pitching with the waves. His orcane-leather breeches and boots would prevent his feet from becoming sodden. But each spray of salty sea to hit his cheek reminds him of the fire.

His godsdamned face hurts. Hurts too bad to move the skin.

Kraus...

Jeret squeezes the reins in his fists and closes the one eye that still obeys him. He wants Kraus so bad it hurts his chest, tightens his throat. It's worse than being scorned by a hateful lover. A longing so deep it throbs in his marrow.

Ever since Captain Jeret's defeat in Vim he's had the same nightmare, an eternity stretched across a single moment. Forefront is Kraus' pockmarked, cut-up visage, eyes like a demon, mouth a-snarl. The sharp punch of glass dicing his ear. A frigid sensation of saturation, the liquor's chemical burn. The thump of ignition and the blast, then the pain, which has yet to relent. Swatting his face, feeling the fire spread, the disastrous reflex to bat and rub his cheek and ear with his gloved hand, knowing the flesh would tear but unable to stop himself. Feeling the skin separate. Feeling the fire chewing deeper. Watching the horror in the eyes of his own men, who did little more than back away.

It was the hush that saved his life, administered by the marshal's own medics. There was no saving his left eye. Hush courses through his veins yet, fighting rot and revitalizing the wasted flesh. No one warned him that when hush is used for a burn the remedy hurts worse than the original injury. Each time a briny ocean breeze washes his stiff plank of a cheek it feels like liquid fire again.

Funny, he'd never been too concerned with his looks. As a ranking soldier, looks have never factored into his pursuits of the finer things. Those are given. That said, he'd always wanted a beard, to confer width onto his chin. Never managed it. Now the opportunity for a symmetric beard is gone and his face is permanently disfigured. The shameless stare of even his sole remaining lieutenant, Hassand, attests to this. Jeret cannot undo what that bipedal boar did to him. The best he can do is invite Kraus to join him in suffering.

Lieutenant Hassand, newly promoted to first lieutenant, is pitiful consolation for the losses suffered in Vim. He's a dull-eyed youth, sloppily dressed and accident prone, more eager to work than to think. At least he's tireless. Jeret would have preferred to promote almost any of his lieutenants to first over Hassand, the foremost being Narahna.

Narahna was twice the lieutenant as Hassand. It is a genuine tragedy she fell in the siege on Vim. They tell Jeret she met the escaping Vanguard head-on and that her blockade was hit by the brunt of their force. After his hush dream wore off, Jeret was shown her body. They'd not finished preparing her for the fire and she was naked, lithe as a maple branch, fit as a dancer, dead as shit. Her auburn hair was combed and arranged behind her shoulders. Her eyelids weren't fully closed but no life twinkled from within. Her knuckles and hands were scraped and torn; fresh wounds crisscrossed over old scars. The rest of her was whole, a testament to her battle agility, aside from two cleaned wounds that seemed almost too insignificant to consider. One was a straight laceration near her knee. Not grievous. Hardly more than a scratch. Enough to get her attention. The other was a perfectly placed puncture directly between her breasts. They say the strike maneuvered between her steel plates like a needle through a button, piercing leather, sternum, heart. They say she died without a sound. They say it was Dhovoi's brother who administered her death. A fearsome strike for someone so young.

It's interesting to Jeret that the boy would fight for Irdessa, considering it was she who murdered his brother. Hell, she murdered him thrice over before he fell. Did that tiding fail to travel beyond the booth of Dhovoi's death? If it had, wouldn't he prefer to kill Irdessa than kill for her?

Mourt ... well, his death is a damned inconvenience. A foul mongrel perhaps, but ever intuitive of Jeret's needs. Never needed to be told twice. Sometimes not even once. Never hesitated. Something was broken inside him and it manifested in his cravings. Truth be told, it was only a matter of time before that caught up with him. Captain Jeret's contingency plan was Lieutenant Vernen eventually taking his place as second. But Vernen, Filore, and Mourt were powerless against the batshit murderess who shortened them all. Fucking Bravensi.

So many outlaws Jeret wants to kill today, but Marshal Zander is set on *capturing* Irdessa. What an idiotic notion—a prime showcase of his ignorance. For him to capture Irdessa, he'll have to kill every outlaw loyal to her first. But to reach even one of them, he'll have to kill her first. Captain Jeret eventually feigned compliance with the marshal's strategy. But when the fighting starts and the air is loud and the blood is free, who knows what will happen? Jeret's priorities are simple. Kill Batshit. Kill Vyker. Catch Kraus. Cage him, break him, take his tongue, his feet. Make an animal of him.

The tension in Jeret's baked cheek has been growing as his jaw tightens and tightens. Too late he feels the flecks of broken tooth along the side of his tongue. He has to forcefully release his jaw muscles. This quiets the thrum that had been building inside his head but sends a fresh pulse of blood throbbing into the strangled arteries hush is knitting into his bark-like face. With each beat of his heart a sledgehammer wallops his head. It's all Jeret can do to clench his fists and long for distraction.

"Think we should move?" Hassand's voice is barely audible over the thumping in Jeret's face.

"For what reason?" he asks without opening his eye.

"To hear the alarm. We might have missed the marshal's signal."

"It'll be relayed," Jeret hisses out, pressing knuckles against his one smooth temple. "There'll be no missing it."

Besides, the marshal gave explicit instructions not to engage hastily. Jeret intends to follow them to the letter. Zander's briefing was not limited to instructions on today's mission.

Marshal Zander had summoned Jeret early this morning, interrupting his breakfast of briny bread gruel. When Jeret arrived at the sea cave wherein Zander and his officers were camped, he found the marshal positioned over a keg-turned-table with maps of the Towers laid over it. He had a cluster of grapes in one hand and a sprake quill in the other to mark the parchments. Nearby, a black skillet was heating on a lard stove fueled by smoldering, fat-soaked pineheart. The heated iron made Jeret uneasy. A recruit laid out thick strips of hogback upon it. They sweated and sizzled immediately, popping out hot grease to shine the recruit's gloves and stain his blue sleeves.

"Today's important," the marshal had said, with a mouthful of fruit warping his words. "It's our last shot at redemption, you and me."

Jeret had never paid much attention to campsite cooking. Even of bacon, which he used to love. Never concerned himself with the process. But this morning it commanded his attention.

"You've not only failed me once ..." Zander had chewed a moment. "... but twice."

It wasn't the first time Zander had told Jeret this. Surely won't be the last. And it's frustrating. As if no one can even entertain the notion that maybe Irdessa prevailed because of her own capabilities, not Jeret's perceived shortcoming.

Marshal Zander stabbed the map with a finger. "You'll take the majority of the force and approach from the west, from out of sight so our prey doesn't flee. Linger in the open water beyond the Towers so you can navigate fast and react to our alarm if it's sent up. Trap them if they flee in that direction." He swallowed, had a gulp of milk. "Though I plan to deal with them in short order."

Jeret failed to contain his snort of contempt at the idea.

"What's that?" Zander said. "You thought I'd trust you with something more integral? Again?" He scoffed, had a grape. "Can you even speak normally yet to command troops?"

"I'm getting better," Jeret said, and it was mostly true. No need to explain to the marshal that he's making a grave mistake if he expects to find Irdessa a pushover. What would be the point?

The bacon was browning, sizzling, filling the pan with a puddle of grease and filling Jeret with anxiety. His hand strayed to his face, for no other reason than to create a barrier between that skillet and his cheek. "You'll find more challenge in the Vanguard than you expect."

He said the words before considering them.

The marshal laughed, spitting bits of grape skin. "Well, there it is. *Fear.* You fail because you fear, Captain. What happened to make you so cowardly? Was it your face? You weren't always this way." He shook his head, wiped his mouth with a cloth, watched his maps. The question was clearly not meant to be answered. Not by Jeret. And so he kept quiet.

"You used to be ... well, effective, if not messy." Marshal Zander spoke in introspective longing.

Jeret could not pull his gaze from the cooking bacon. The recruit who placed it was nowhere to be seen, and so the strips of hogback smoked, darkened toward black, toward ruin. No one seemed to notice but Jeret. The sizzling grew higher-pitched, raspier, as the moisture baked from the meat. The sound assaulted his ears from every direction. Jeret fought to remain motionless, fought to convince himself they weren't burning it to get in his head, fought to stop himself from kicking that flesh off the skillet. How could they know his nightmares? How could they know the sound his eye made before it burst?

"I request the honor of avenging my slain lieutenants by killing Bravensi the Batshit," Jeret had said, locking his eye on the featureless cave wall. "And the honor of avenging myself by killing Kraus the Rapist."

Marshal Zander shook his head vigorously before washing down his grapes from his wooden stein. "Don't make me laugh."

Jeret's teeth had locked then. He expected a poor response but had to ask. Sometimes the regret of not having tried outweighs the shame of the rejection.

"We capture Irdessa first, foremost, and only. I will not lose more men to her."

Jeret took a silent breath. "With respect, Marshal, we don't know the size of the Vanguard's force. They've recruited Tower dwellers. We don't know how many or what they bring." The marshal began chewing rapidly, in a rush to spit out some contradiction. Jeret felt the temptation to slap the food out of his mouth. Instead he pushed on, "I have learned the folly of rushing into confrontation with the Vanguard. That's why we're here. We need not make the same mistake two—"

"The size of the Vanguard's force?" Zander had not quite finished swallowing and so a purple trail of juice decorated his chin. "What happened to you, Captain? Their *force* is unpaid ruffians. Men who must forfeit offensive capacity to traverse from the Towers to the shore. Whereas our force excels at water-borne assault." He dabbed at his face, glared at Jeret. "Size of their force indeed. Tell me, does an increase in gristle avail the defenses of a steak on a platter?" He delivered his question with the slow condescension reserved for recruits who must be told a thing twice.

"You underestimate Irdessa," Jeret said. "And her followers' devotion. They won't let you take her."

"Then I will kill them all!" Zander thumped his hollow table with both fists and came to his feet. "I am Irdessa's fate."

With that, the mood had changed. Despite all the sarcastic responses Zander's outburst conjured, Jeret said nothing. Zander's face had lost its color and his chest heaved, as if he was plagued by some threat. He looked like a trapped animal.

"I swore to deliver her to His Might," Marshal Zander said. "I swore it. If I don't deliver her to Vretos ..." He trailed off, frowning, eyes elsewhere.

Jeret kept his silence, reevaluating the situation.

Marshal Zander cleared his throat. "This is our last chance. If she and her cohort reach the cursed island and brace themselves, it is over for us."

"What are my orders?"

"There is one thing you need concern yourself with, and I'll make it as simple as I can. We don't have exact whereabouts yet, and by the time we do speed will be key in intercepting them. I will take an agile but sufficient strike team to the location our scouts indicate. Once the outlaws are in motion, at an opportune moment I will engage. At my sprake calls, approach and gain a vantage point. Create a barrier and observe. Do not engage. If, by some freak blunder, I require assistance, I will alert you with my own sprake. Otherwise, stay back. I cannot afford more incompetence from you. Do you understand?"

Captain Jeret frowned. In other words, sit out. *Spectate.* Despite Jeret's knowledge of this foe and his own experiences, to the marshal give the glory. Then, when the dust settles, ride home empty-handed with only the memories of his slain lieutenants and an unslaked thirst for vengeance. Back to wastelands patrol or some asinine pit-burning mission. It was through gritted teeth that Jeret answered the marshal. "Yes."

"Your concern for me is touching," Zander said, entirely mislabeling Jeret's chagrin. "Nothing bad will come of this if we play it as planned. Your spear—" and Zander gave Jeret his full attention "—stays sheathed until I personally launch a bird."

"Understood, Marshal."

The marshal settled himself again and returned his attention to the maps, as if this conversation and life in general were all going just as he'd hoped. The hogback, reduced to ruin, was indistinguishable from the iron.

"This situation is your fault," Zander said, solidifying Jeret's notion that lacking other topics to discuss, criticism always came readily. "If you and that disgusting animal, Mourt, had done your job, this would never have become a situation. You had her in Vim."

Wouldn't that have been convenient? Jeret thought. *Your captain, while on a mission to pointlessly destroy an arena at your behest, happened to capture Irdessa the Undying, creating a hero of you.*

The marshal continued, "You should be glad for that psychopath, you know. If she'd not killed all your worthwhile lieutenants, one of them would be captain now. And you'd be ..." He flicked his fingers vaguely, leaving Jeret to imagine what he'd have been.

Jeret lacked interest to engage further with the marshal, but failed to prevent himself from provoking. "Our mission was to destroy Vim's arena," he said. "The pit burned. It was a success."

"A success?" Zander reacted physically, rocking back on his stool with rounded eyes. "I imagine the ensuing riots have been part of your design as well? You wouldn't know success if it laid itself naked in your lap."

Jeret had stifled his enjoyment of the man rising so easily to the bait, and mentally vacated the conversation, leaving Zander to be his tirade's sole audience. What an unfit marshal—reactive, emotional, shortsighted to the point of blindness. Every little setback demolished his poise. If he was truly that inconvenienced, he should have executed Jeret and been godsdamned done with it. *He didn't because he is weak.* Gods know Jeret would have executed a subordinate for less than catastrophic failure. But no, the marshal keeps Jeret in a position of some semblance of power. That way, he can unload the abuse he's surely receiving from Vretos' court—wherein he occupies the lowest seat—onto his captain. It is a self-destructive strategy to perpetually berate those who answer to you.

Jeret finds himself examining deeper. It's possible the marshal has only ever contributed to Fohrvylda vicariously, through the late Andelsior of Vim. Meanwhile, Zander takes no credit for his failures, giving that exclusively to those he relies on. A successful officer knows to seek guidance. That's not Zander. Captain Jeret takes all lessons taught by Zander and strives to do their opposite. Jeret may be a notorious hardass, but at least when he punishes his subordinates it's their fault.

The scream of a distant alarm sprake pulls Jeret from his thoughts and sends lightning through his veins. The call is little more than a thin whistle at hearing's edge, riding against the wind from the northeast, among the sunset-reddened Towers. Jeret's heart gallops. Beyond those Towers is Redemier's wide beach. In that instant, his honest reaction reveals to him a shameful truth. Some part of him had hoped this wouldn't happen. The coward in him had secretly wished they'd return home empty-handed, and from Keswal's shaded seats he would witness the marshal's violent demotion.

Jeret guides his orcane into the tossing froth, gritting his teeth in anticipation of the salt water. It's not that he opposes conflict. He doesn't. He yearns for it. But on the ocean? Miles from home? Facing off against the Vanguard? A distasteful combination all around. If he wanted to splash in the fucking water he'd have joined Garr's navy. A wave kisses his cheek, lighting up his face like the original burn. Jeret clenches every muscle to keep from crying out. He is sickened by his weakness. Sickened by this new fear. He is no coward. This is Kraus' fault. And to conquer Kraus is to conquer it.

"We ride," he tells Hassand, "but with stealth." He'd yell the command if he could trust his mouth to form the words, but hush hasn't finished repairing him. Lieutenant Hassand can do the shouting.

Hassand relays the command to the orcane riders in a pinched but loud, plainly worded command. The soldiers snap to attention and fall in. Captain Jeret leads the way, his orcane coursing beneath him like a great black shark.

Rather than taking a faster, direct route northward first, circumnavigating the obstructing Towers entirely then skirting the beach, they wind between the Towers. It's the best way to prevent their force from being seen and sending the Vanguard back up into a defensive position, thereby ruining the ambush. If anything goes wrong this day, the marshal will blame Jeret. And Jeret can little afford more blame.

Their path quickly takes them out of the setting sun's reach, into the shade within the Towers. Where the sunlight does strike the water, its rays are nearly parallel to the ocean's surface, so that gullies of shadow dance below golden, blinding peaks. If Marshal Zander is approaching the Vanguard from the east, aimed toward the sun, he'll be nearly blind. Irdessa probably planned this. Jeret smiles. *But did she expect reinforcements approaching from her west?*

Another sprake call. This one sounds closer but tumbles about through the massive earthen columns, obscuring its source. Captain Jeret slows his pace. The anticipation is suffocating. His breath is fluttering and his hands are trembling, leaving him no room to worry about the digging ache in his face. *Jitters.* He fights the urge to slap the shit out of his whole cheek. *Kraus, you fucking bovine, what have you done to me?* He must steel his nerves. The sprake call tapers as it tires itself out, and once again that cowardly hope ignites in Jeret's pit. Then Hassand speaks.

"There." He's pointing a gloved finger up toward the deepening dusk, where stars will soon make themselves known. First Jeret sees nothing. Then a silver flicker, unmistakable sprake plumage.

"Ride," Jeret commands, forcing himself forward.

To Hassand's credit, despite the utter monotony of his commands, he arranges the orcane force into a narrow column, three soldiers across, communicating the need for stealth.

The sprake is gone and Jeret has to trust the direction he's chosen. Redemier's beach is visible now and then between the ranks of passing Towers. The cursed island looks like a slumbering behemoth beneath a green blanket, glowing in the dying sunlight.

Distant shouts. All human. Captain Jeret must be close to his quarry. He raises a fist to halt the column and his first lieutenant ensures the command is followed.

"With me," Jeret tells him, making for a navigable bit of stone detritus beneath a particularly stepped Tower. He drops from his orcane, taking a moment for his legs to adjust to straddling nothing and secures the orcane's reins to a half-submerged, hefty-enough sea shrub. Once his lieutenant has stopped the force and dismounted, Jeret begins scaling the Tower's stone face, reflecting on its similarity to his own.

As altitude increases, the volume of the waves gives way to more shouts. Jeret and Hassand angle their ascent to round the side of the Tower and gain a vantage of Redemier's beach.

Out over two hundred yards of glittering peaks and caps is the marshal's banner, streaming against the wind. The marshal has arranged his force—thirty-two orcanes strong—into a charging wall two deep and sixteen across, with him near center. The charging wall is an efficient, haste-conscious formation. While not particularly imaginative, it wastes no spear or tooth, relying on decimation in one fierce pass. Ideally, their speed is such that they arrive on their targets airborne. This doesn't work on larger ships.

Their wild pace tells Jeret they've found their prey, but it takes a moment for him to spot them. From this height, he'd first mistaken the smudge on the sea for a submerged cloud of seaweed or perhaps another lost boulder, remains of an ancient Tower. It turns out to be a long makeshift raft, fashioned of crooked limbs with leaves still attached, and bloated with outlaws.

"They aren't even holding oars," Hassand scoffs. "They aren't moving."

It's true. But that tells Jeret a different story than it apparently does his lieutenant. *The Vanguard was not caught unaware.* If so, they'd be panicking, scrambling, swimming, seeing their imminent death on the

582 | David T List

horizon. They've got a plan, and whatever it is clearly has them under the impression they're not all about to die. By all counts, Marshal Zander should ride through that pitiful contraption like a flaming broom through a web full of spiders, cementing Jeret's perceived inability once and forever. Jeret hisses a swear. Has he overestimated her? There's no secret that poor contraption could be hiding that will change the truth.

He's one frantic heartbeat away from scrambling down the cliff and leading his force into a premature flank so as not to be entirely useless in this crusade, when the outlaw raft begins to break apart.

Hassand barks out a laugh. "They ride trash. This will be over before it's even started."

Jeret squints. The breaks in the raft are too symmetrical for this to be accidental. That's their plan? Forfeit structure? Jeret nearly fumbles the longglass, trying to get it to his good eye. Once the tube is pressed against his eye socket, the scene presents itself with enough clarity to confuse him even further. Fur-clad outlaws are deliberately breaking the raft apart at apparent seams. It's in three pieces now, each bearing several bodies, and a single thick rope straddles them all. A closer look reveals the effort at play. That line runs the length of their path, from Tower to beach, and where it's not draped over their crafts it is submerged. It's holding the segments in a rigid line.

Jeret's head cocks to the side. "How the hell ...?" The answer is on him before the question escapes. Those rafts aren't the first to cross. Someone must have gone before, submerged so as not to be seen, dragging the line. The water's shallow enough for it. His eyes follow it to the beach. Sure enough, the late sun glints off steel, hiding behind boulders on the sand. Archers probably. Impossible to know how many.

By now the marshal's charging force is within forty yards, and the orcanes, in their insatiable bloodlust, are alternating diving beneath the surface and leaping like dolphins. Their blue-clad soldiers stand crouched upon their saddles, reins in one fist, spear in the other, sun flashing on steel helmets. When their mounts dive, they stand straight, buried nearly to their hips in rushing ocean. When the orcanes fly, the soldiers crouch low against their saddle. They're the ones yelling, made crazy by their impending victory.

The sections of raft are spread far apart now, perhaps ten yards between each third, and the passengers who tugged the line to situate them thusly have all picked up pointed steel. It's no longer a prime target for a charging wall sixteen across. While the central raft will undoubtedly be obliterated, the other two are outside range of the formation's outer wings. At this rate unnecessary losses will ensue. The Vanguard has forced a decision on their enemy mid-charge. Jeret can't help but appreciate the strategy.

The marshal sees the folly of staying his course. In an effort to respond to his foe's new shape, the driving force falters. At the pace they were approaching, there'd have been no time to break into three patterns, as would now be the cleanest strategy. And so the pace is halved, the war cries silenced, as a wall of thirty-two scrambles to become three untidy chevrons. Marshal Zander still maintains the lead, aimed at the central raft. Had it not been for that maneuver, the orcanes would have had the momentum to leap clear onto the rafts. No more.

The longlass has become slick against Jeret's sweaty face. His eye itches from refusal to blink.

"What are they trying to pull?" Hassand's dull voice floats from nearby.

"Trying, hell. They neutered the godsdamn charge." It's known Torvald the Tactician passed on his uncanny intuition of battle strategy to Irdessa during their time in Keswal. Jeret never assumed that would include strategies outside the arena, but the idea surprises him less each time he encounters the Vanguard. They always know too much.

Collision is imminent. But, as quickly as the rafts initially transformed, the outermost rafts close in again, with the burliest bodies on hand tugging that submerged line, closing the gaps under shouted orders that reach Jeret's ears like distant seals barking. The marshal cannot hope to adjust his force again in time. They never finished the first adjustment. The chevrons bunch in on themselves, forming a knot, effectively disabling every charging spear except for the front line, which is now no more than seven orcanes across. The outer rafts are separated from the central one by just several feet, so that any orcane navigating between them must defend itself from two directions. Jeret marvels. That was Irdessa's idea: split the rafts, pull them back together, move the target. So simple it's idiotic. And yet it worked. Only a person intimately familiar with orcane strategy would have ever dreamed it or expected it to work. And in this situation, considering what the Vanguard has to work with, Jeret cannot think of a better tactic.

As the marshal's orcane is about to ram the central raft, the outlaws aboard all shift to its port side. The raft tips upward, begins to capsize, rotating with the line on its deck acting as its axis point. Jeret's position makes for poor viewing of the raft's exposed underside that will meet the orcanes, but he catches the unmistakable glint of steel.

From his vantage point, witnessed at his elevated excitement, the clash unfolds at a muddy pace, the black orcanes flowing against the contraption like a pile of crayfish against a trap in a stream. Voices yelling. Steel scraping. Orcanes squealing. The mallet-thump of snouts impacting rafts. The central raft bucks as no less than three orcanes crash into its underside, including the marshal's. The outlaws who can't keep a grip on the line are thrown into the ocean. The wings of the charging wall clash with the outer rafts, meeting flashing spears and responding with the like. Behind the orcanes' front line, soldiers disentangle their bunched-up mounts, urging them either left or right or both at once in confused attempts to get into the melee.

Captain Jeret has no control over the booming laughter that escapes him. "I fucking told you," he roars at his marshal, despite no chance of the bastard hearing him. "They won't go down without a fight!" He is giddy with relief. Irdessa may die today, but not without validating Captain Jeret first. He slaps his lieutenant's shoulder merrily. "The gods are generous, Hassand. All I wanted was to watch Zander's education. Here we are."

Hassand attempts a chuckle. His drab face bears no trace of Jeret's elation. More like concern.

The marshal's orcane is impaled by the snout and stuck so that its wild thrashing echoes in the upturned raft, making a treacherous ride for the outlaws still clinging to the vertical deck. Clearly whatever snares they rigged on the underside of the craft served their purpose. The marshal yanks his reins this way and that, his yells lost in the tumult. The two orcanes pinned to his sides are within range of the more ambitious outlaw spears, and while packed as tightly as they are, the beasts make perfect recipients.

The first orcanes to circle round the outer rafts pour upon the tossed outlaws, who stand no chance. They're chomped or stabbed tidily, unable to defend themselves. One man is sinking even without injury, maybe due to his armor's weight. Maybe he can't swim. His flailing hands reach for salvation but catch a spear's thrust. The soldier stuffs the man down until he's only red bubbles. One of the orcanes has a screaming man by the arm and is twisting back and forth, slapping the man against the surface, then under, then up again. Damn orcanes. They do love to play. The soldier is trying to spear the man to silence him. Before he manages it, fletching appears hovering in front of his belly. Another arrow hits his face. His playful orcane notices only the freed reins.

The next soldiers engage the outlaws holding their place on the outermost raft sections while their orcanes tear at the rafts like minnows on a heel of bread. The outlaws are focusing all attacks on the orcanes, ignoring the soldiers' spears as best they can. The orcanes, even though each alone probably has the girth of any one section of raft, are held at bay. But more and more are dislodging themselves from the unsuccessful charge to join in the flank. The outlaws are quickly losing any advantage. Soon the orcanes will surround them utterly and squeeze like a fist on a robin's egg.

"Well ..." Jeret gives his eye socket a momentary relief, taking a bolstering breath. "It was a valiant stand. Better than I expected. Hopefully the marshal has had the chance to accept I was right." *Unlikely.*

The sun is low, half-consumed by the horizon, and grey has washed over the scene. A fitting mood for Irdessa's end.

"Should we join in?" Lieutenant Hassand asks, failing utterly to mask his disappointment that it hasn't happened yet.

This question requires weighing the marshal's commands against Jeret's own priorities. What would be his penalty for joining in at this point? He'd not compromise the mission; there's no escaping for the Vanguard now. On the contrary, he'd hasten their success. And if he manages to dispatch a famous outlaw, he could gain at least some standing. He's yet to spot his quarries individually, but then he hasn't searched them out. Kraus, Bravensi. Maybe the boy Vyker. He returns the longglass with such urgency that it thunks dryly against his brow.

"I suppose we ..." The response melts in his teeth as he surveys the scene. Something's wrong. The flanking orcanes on the Tower side have failed to surround the outlaws. Instead they're thrashing like maggots on a hot plate, and the surrounding sea is reddening. White tufts of water erupt throughout their ranks.

"What the hell?" Hassand says, even as Jeret cranes his neck for a better view. Then he sees movement. Something barely perceptible descending from on high, visible only while its backdrop is open air. It disappears, flight obscured by the cursed landscape rushing behind it. But Jeret approximates its path down to a hapless orcane whose rider is drawing back his spear to skewer an outlaw. The object hits the orcane's head with such force it dunks it beneath the surface. The unbalanced soldier falls forward, lending velocity to the outlaw spear that welcomes itself to his mouth. The spear tip punches out the back of the soldier's neck and he oozes bonelessly off his saddle.

"Arrows," Jeret exclaims, jerking his head to scan the Tower from which the submerged line begins. Sure enough, perched on the cliff wall like featherless sprakes, are long-limbed archers, gilded by the sunset's failing grasp like some desperate last hope.

"By the gods." Hassand has followed Jeret's gaze. "Those are Rain Catcher archers. I've always wanted to see them."

"You sound impressed. Did you always want to see them annihilate your fellow soldiers?"

"Of course not." Despite his obvious awe, the concern on his face hasn't diminished. "I'd just heard they're brutal. You don't want to be caught under them."

Indeed, the arrows they're loosing may as well be spears. Those that miss soldiers punch water like hurled stones. Those that hit their mark reduce targets to screaming messes. Even as Jeret watches, a soldier catches an arrow in his left shoulder. Despite his thick leather vest, the projectile hits him so hard his entire torso distorts, warping as if his spine snapped. He drops his reins and his spear.

Some of the orcanes dive, seeking shelter beneath the rafts or simply beneath water. Neither option helps. The water's too clear, too shallow. Those that descend beyond the range of the outlaw spears are still prime targets for Catcher arrows, which chase them like kingfishers.

High above, the Catcher archers slouch on precarious overhangs, draw back hefty arrows with little obvious effort, release without contemplation. Below, their stew simmers nicely, punctured beasts and soldiers kicking the water into a bloody froth.

"Look there," cries Hassand, pointing.

On the white sand of Redemier, the cohort of outlaws that first crossed the shallow expanse to drag the line has made itself known. They creep out from around chunks of Towers and bend bows toward the unaware orcanes.

Jeret blinks his eye several times, squints. Maybe ten archers total. At that range they're enough to get someone's attention but little more. Then out marches a stocky outlaw with flowing brown hair, exposed muscular thighs, ornate greaves on her calves, and a ridiculously large bow. Even as Jeret muses on what the hell she's planning to do with it, the archer drops to a prone position, leveling a harpoon of an arrow on a string hoisted up to her chin, her boots at the bow's grip.

The massive projectile springs forth. It would be harder to follow if its path weren't so destructive. The harpoon flies twenty yards uncontested, then reduces a soldier's head to flowering strands. It punches into another soldier's chest, ripping him from his saddle.

Jeret marvels. "I'll be godsdamned."

The other archers loose arrows. Over the water, several orcanes twitch in response. One bucks its soldier and turns to rush the archers.

"Should have strapped himself in once they engaged," Jeret comments.

"They need armor." Hassand tries to be nonchalant but panic tinges his heavy voice.

Jeret scoffs. "Of course. Steel sheets and plates while perched on the ocean. Sure way to decorate the sea floor and breathe water."

Hassand flinches. "If they're dismounted, they're fucked either way."

Jeret can't argue that. "Fucking Catchers. They've been tolerated too … long." His longlass falls on the marshal and the sight makes his breath falter. Marshal Zander, still wedged atop his thrashing orcane, is struggling with a hefty wicker container. It's the cage for his personal alarm sprake, which had been mounted on the saddle behind him until now. Younger and smaller than standard alarm sprakes, it's intended as a last resort. It can't cry as loud as its contemporaries, but shouldn't need to.

Has it gotten that bad down there? The marshal is trying to free it. Jeret's throat squeezes, his heart pounding. Witnessing the act is the same as hearing the call. That's the law, punishable by death. He must act. The marshal's least anticipated outcome is at hand. Jeret is validated and now obligated to engage. But … now that the moment is on him, Captain Jeret pauses. Aberrant thoughts cloud his mind. Who else is watching the marshal try to send up his sprake?

"We have to help," Hassand says, sending a fresh jolt through Jeret. But Hassand isn't looking at Marshal Zander. He's still watching the Catcher archers.

Jeret looks back at the marshal, experiencing a similar feeling as spying on a stranger undressing. It'll be over too soon. Zander's frantic fingers manage to lift the clasp. He rips the cage door wide and the wad of blue-grey feathers inside wriggles, shifting into a position to escape. Alarm sprakes are smaller than attack sprakes, and personal sprakes are smaller still, but they're wedged in their cage until needed like a shoe in a boot. Once this one pops free, climbs the air and yells, Jeret will be forced to ride out to save Zander from his own stupidity—the fuckwit marshal, whose idiotic plan prioritized special circumstances over an efficient solution. The captain will save the marshal, despite that their roles should be reversed. In fact, for the good of this battle and all of Promontory, Jeret should be marshal. Zander should be retired. But once the bird screams for all to hear, that possibility will be out of Jeret's grasp. No consideration or strategy, just mindless reaction. And by the time this tale makes its way back to Promontory, it will bear little of today's truth. Pressure builds as Jeret's teeth tighten. This is not the first injustice of his career. Won't be the last. But right now? Right here? It is the worst.

Jeret makes a conscious effort to unclench his teeth and prepare himself. Leading his force directly under those raining Catcher arrows has no appeal. He'd do better making landfall on the beach west of the archers there, charge at them over land, dispatch with minimal effort. Even with that gargantuan bow, they'd put up small enough resistance. Then the marshal's force can freely circle around the north of the bramble raft, where Catcher arrows won't reach, and hasten the conclusion of this colossal clusterfuck. Jeret exhales a string of swears.

The sprake has its head out of the cage. Marshal Zander shakes the wicker contraption vigorously. A wing is freed. The sprake squirms and out pops its other wing. But before the bird can fly, a thrown spear punctures Zander's spread hand, intersecting the cage and its contents. The feathers deflate. Blood spills onto Zander's lap, pain overtakes his face, and his mouth stretches in a scream Jeret cannot hear, only feel in the pit of his gut. It feels like exultation. Zander pries the cage off the spear and throws it at the closest outlaw. It bounces off the man and plops into the ocean. Jeret is afraid to exhale. A smile crawls over his face. Is injustice ... averted?

"Shouldn't we stop them?" Hassand demands, still fixated on the Catchers.

All at once, Jeret is in no hurry. Moments like these ... hell, he's never known one. He aims his desiccated face at the young dullard, locking his gaze long enough for the lieutenant to cringe in discomfort. His smile is surely lost in his crispy face's translation. "What do you propose? Scale that Tower with our fingertips?"

Hassand's eyes lose focus as his pig's brain scrambles for a solution. "They have to be stopped."

Jeret shakes his head, pitying himself for the lamentable support he's left with. Fucking Bravensi. "That will require an entire campaign, Lieutenant, to root out those dissenters, or to chisel down their Tower itself and drop it into the Faithless, if that's what you're suggesting. And perhaps you're the mule to haul that load. But not today."

Several orcanes are belly-up, forelegs curled at their chest, sleepily riding the choppy surface outward from the turmoil. The bloody water has expanded well beyond the fight.

The marshal's orcane isn't bucking, still adhered by the face to the halfway-capsized central raft. Two outlaws balance atop its edge, engaging the marshal and preventing him from doing anything more useful than flail atop his likely dead mount. At least he got the spear out of his hand. A soldier in soggy blues makes his way up over the lodged orcanes and defends Zander. Jeret watches in apt wonder. His aches are forgotten, his frustration washed away. Anticipation has turned his guts molten and is brimming out of his ears. These moments feel stolen, fragile. Jeret wants to grip them and hold them, not let them slip by.

If Hassand could see what Jeret's seeing, he'd know they must ride to defend their marshal at once. Captain Jeret has transcended that notion. Prolonging the marshal's command is detrimental to Promontory. Any tactician would agree. Vretos would surely agree. There is an opportunity waiting here. He'll watch until it reveals itself.

There are far fewer dead outlaws bobbing about than dead orcanes and soldiers. That is a piss poor ratio by any measure, but quite on par for Irdessa the Undying and Vim's Vanguard. Arrows are still claiming soldiers and orcanes. More outlaws have been thrown from the rafts. Three orcanes have lost their riders and roam freely, no longer chasing their original purpose but whatever human appendage they can get into their mouth and shake until it comes loose. There's nothing a wildened orcane loves more than playing in the water.

"What a mess," Captain Jeret says. "The marshal should swallow his pride and send up his alarm. They're losing too many men."

Hassand, squinting at the turmoil, hesitates a moment before responding. "Can't we engage? It looks like they could use the help."

"Sadly, no. Our instructions were clear." Jeret did not anticipate how much he'd enjoy saying that. "But climb down and ready the soldiers. Surely he'll make the call soon."

Hassand obeys, and if he's aware of Jeret's subterfuge, his slow, deliberate descent does not suggest it. Perhaps he does know what's happening. If he does and his ignorance is a facade, he could have a future as Jeret's second after all.

When Lieutenant Hassand tells the soldiers the time to engage approaches, they respond by cheering and hollering, clashing spears on helmets. Jeret takes heart in their enthusiasm, wondering if they'd still be so excited if they could see what he's seeing.

Distantly, poor Marshal Zander is wielding his spear in one hand. His other hand is tucked under an armpit, red all the way to the elbow. He's tugging his spear free of one of the two outlaws who'd been perched on the sideways raft. The figure falls, and now it's Zander standing off against one final enemy on the upper edge of the piecemeal plank. From their posture and concentration, the surrounding skirmish doesn't exist. The marshal's spear lunges, misses. It lunges again and the outlaw punches the blade away with a bare fist. It's a large man with close-cropped black hair engulfing most of his head and face, twice the marshal's girth, and despite being unarmed displaying no fear. Quite the opposite. Chin up, chest out, like he's energized by the possibility of injury. A chill runs over Jeret.

The marshal has expended all poise, and throws a desperate attack, swinging his spear like a club. It wouldn't have had sufficient force even if he'd used both hands. His enemy lifts an arm, catches the haft against his ribs, traps it there. If that attack was meant to entertain the outlaw, it's a shining success. Zander releases the spear and reaches for his belt, where he keeps his knife. The outlaw doesn't give him time, snatching him by his chin and the back of his helmet. Jeret's guts churn and tumble like mud under marching boots. He numbly removes his glove and touches his burnt cheek. The assaulter's mannerism is unmistakable. The outlaw bares his teeth and flings both arms outward like he's opening a huge jar. Jeret's imagination fills in the sound of bones splintering. Marshal Zander teeters. His head bobs and flops on a broken neck. Jeret wants to look away but can't. Zander slumps down, splaying out over his mount with unseeing eyes. All that keeps him from spilling into the ocean is his belt, snagged on the upright raft. The outlaw throws his head back, his mouth wide, and the gravelly roar that climbs the wind all the way up the Tower to engulf Jeret sends chills running out his ruined ear and down all the way to his toenails.

Kraus.

The surrounding soldiers recoil as one, collectively pausing long enough for the truth to make itself known. Their marshal has fallen. The outlaws take Kraus' cry and add their own, escalating the noise until it overpowers waves, wind, and all.

Marshal Zander's force fractures into pieces. Mounted orcanes are reined away by the snout to flee to the south, back toward Fohrvylda, as if they've got a fifty-mile trip left in them. The outlaws among the rafts yell after them.

Kraus.

Jeret stashes his longlass with shaking hands. His teeth give a rattle, immediately disgusting himself. This time he does slap his cheek.

Whack!

The sting gives way to that relentless throbbing burn. Again he hits himself.

Whack!

He gasps at the pain, the pain that belongs to him alone, whoever its author. Again he strikes. Again the burn is made irrelevant. This is his pain. And this is his moment. *Finally.*

The outlaws are working to dredge up their wounded, free their rafts, haul themselves toward shore. Jeret's leer lets salty tears into his mouth. *They think they're going to get away with that?*

Over and over he attacks himself—the whole time he descends the Tower—until bloody spittle flies from his lips, riding out on a guttural growl that's just this side of vomiting.

"We ride!" His voice is shrill, hysterical. His soldiers look at him, silenced surely by the outlaw upheaval they heard but couldn't see, then further by Jeret's outburst. "We ride!" he screams, thrusting his spear high. Some match his gesture, shouting but without his luster.

"Our marshal ..." Captain Jeret nearly scoffs at the man's embarrassing legacy, now complete. "... commanded we sit by while he and those thirty riders take all the glory. He commanded that I hold you back, tread water, until he called for aid. I obeyed. And now, despite greatly outnumbering a nearly defenseless mob, he is *dead*. Murdered by his own pride."

A grave silence blows over the soldiers. Lieutenant Hassand does not meet Jeret's eyes. Jeret feels balance shifting, their loyalties coming under their own scrutiny.

"I suffer no such pride. I want a decisive end of Vim's Vanguard, here and now, as I suggested to him. I want an equal share of glory for every soldier who has sweated and bled for His Might."

Nods. Grunts of approval. A cheer sparks another cheer. Jeret's always had a gift for invigorating bloodlust.

"Irdessa has believed she cannot die for too long."

Louder cheers. The orcanes champ at their bits.

"She and her Vanguard die today."

Jeret yells to be heard over their response. "All of them." The last words he roars are enunciated, isolated. "By our spears!"

The responding choir of shouts makes him feverish. Blood runs down his chin. He leaps atop his orcane. Hell can have his aches. "*We ride!*"

With thunderous cries, they burst from hiding. Captain Jeret and all those he leads stand in their saddle, flying over waves like skipping stones, even as the rest of Marshal Zander's beaten force retreats. Jeret soars for his destiny, his glory, his vengeance. The sea kisses him, electrifying him. The chills that climb over him are elation. *Purpose.* There is no room for fear and no need of it. Where Zander's thirty orcanes failed, Captain Jeret's sixty will not.

58
Refuse to Fucking Die

REDEMIER
The Beach

Irdessa bobs in a red sea. She stands straddling Marshal Zander's dead body, draped over his dead orcane, which is still impaled against the underside of the central raft. After the terminal improvement Kraus administered to the marshal's neck, his force lost all enthusiasm. They panicked, disengaged, scattered, leaving just a few riderless orcanes, wounded or about to be, nipping at the remains of the rafts and the floaters.

The Vanguard is burning off the last of its energy roaring at the retreating Promontory in case there was any questioning whose ass got kicked. Irdessa's not so confident. There was a reason the marshal sent up that earlier sprake, and it's taking its time revealing itself. Yes, she prevented an additional alarm with her own spear. But there must be another force out there, or else that was quite the desperation move on Zander's part. Besides, Harpold said there were more orcanes than he could count riding under the marshal's banner. This was thirty at the most. There must be more. The question is, where did they break off? How far away are they? Are they still en route, despite that she prevented the call? What if the Vanguard's celebration becomes their enemy's beacon?

They must make landfall on the beach, which is still too distant for comfort. It's the only chance of surviving another attack. Their rafts are all but demolished. Too many of their force toss about lifelessly, adding red to the waves. The Catcher archers, once again showing their worth, proved integral against the marshal's charge, but probably have little further use. The Vanguard is nearing the edge of their arrows' range, and are too scattered for the archers to snipe enemies without sniping friends. Especially not as dark as it has become. Besides, from the look of it, the Catchers have all begun to descend from their vantage point toward the Tower's feet.

"Vanguard," she yells, cutting through cheers. "To the beach. Save your strength."

Luckily, she's caught them before the battle frenzy can burn out. The fighters snap back into purpose. Some, however, seem to notice their fallen floating companions for the first time, and the idea of abandoning them paints scowls on their faces. They do not move.

"I don't relish leaving our brothers and sisters pitching on the waves," Irdessa says, less sharp, just as earnest. "But it's that or join them. This isn't over yet."

Magpie is squinting toward the Tower, where archers, and Otto and his sister, make their way toward the water.

"Magpie," Irdessa says, "tell your sister to maintain altitude, keep an eye out. I don't think we're alone."

"I did," he says.

Irdessa and a couple fighters try to free the central raft from the full-grown dead orcane helplessly impaled on its underside, but several of the blades must have entered the beast and bent at opposing angles. She'd have to nearly dismantle the raft to free the corpse. It wouldn't survive being hauled through the surf to the beach. The central raft is lost, but the raft behind it is not. Her party is decreased in size, perhaps so much that they can fit on two meager sections of improvised raft.

They haul the third section out from under the submerged line, pushing it through the cool water around the jumbled mess that is the central raft. With hardly a word, they kick and paddle until the two surviving craft are in a line, as close to a single flotilla as they can become. These hastily assembled plank-crafts started their life unattractive and the orcane attack did not improve them.

Irdessa directs them to help the wounded on deck first, spreading them across the two rafts. By the time that's done and all the living are accounted for, the overburdened rafts strain under too many bodies. Irdessa, Vyker, and Harper man the line on the rear raft. On the foremost Sura, Kraus, and Magpie ready to haul the rope, until a heavy Rain Catcher gestures Magpie to get out of his way. Magpie obliges. The man is easily three times the scout's girth.

"Haul!" Kraus yells from in front. And they do, pulling that vine rope hand over hand. The raft was sitting so low that Irdessa's boots were submerged, but as the line-tuggers develop a strenuous rhythm, the ocean nearly inhales them all. Waves crest at Irdessa's hips. Those wounded who seemed to expect to ride this out lying down have a rude wakeup as they're submerged entirely.

It feels excruciatingly slow. But the water courses beneath them. The beach inches closer. Upon it, Elaga and her archers are holding their end of the line, calling out. Irdessa understands immediately.

"Cut the line behind us," she orders, and someone does, freeing it so that the beach archers can assist by pulling their end. Those of the fighters who can swim do so, nearly as fast as the raft is being pulled.

Magpie has frozen, gripping the big Catcher's vest to keep his footing in the rushing water, staring north of the setting sun as if trying to make out a distant conversation. A grimace takes his face. He shakes his head, shifting his eyes to Irdessa. "You were right."

"There!" cries a fighter, pointing her soggy sleeve westward. On the far horizon, where the dying day bleeds out on the sky, is an unmistakable charging line, as uniform and spiny as a fortress wall. Irdessa does not relent hauling the line. There's the backup she anticipated. They're too far away to determine much, but that line is wider than the one they barely turned back, and it's consuming the distance like wildfire blown over a dry field.

"By the gods," someone whispers, and their dread washes through the wounded. Cries of anguish. One fighter dives off the raft and tears off in the direction the other orcanes fled. But now some of the vanquished orcane soldiers halt their retreat, peering toward their wayward companions and pumping spears in the air.

"We're done for," a man says.

"Haul the fucking line!" Kraus roars, planting his feet wider in the rushing current, heaving the rope with his entire weight. Those nearby brace him and the other pullers, shoulder to chest, leaning against them. Irdessa's arms are weakening, her hands numbing. The only indication they're doing a damn bit of good as they slap against the sodden, fibrous rope, is that water continues to tug her legs. The sun forsakes them, leaving the cursed island a lifeless grey. *Got to keep pulling. It's that simple.* Whatever awaits, right now she must pull. Her companions pull as well, grunting. The wounded are mercifully quiet despite the dread on their faces. Those who swim do so without looking back.

They're within thirty yards of the beach when the foremost raft begins to break apart, shedding branches and dumping its load. The passengers scramble like flies from a kicked corpse. Some break into frantic paddling, or desperate attempts to. Some cling to the line with a barnacle's grip even though without a raft acting as bobber, it sinks below the surface. Among them is Kraus, who hauls himself fist over fist even as he plummets toward the ocean floor. The water can't be more than ten feet deep here, but that won't console anyone trying to breathe under it. Hopefully they have good lungs.

"Keep pulling," Harpold yells, so close to Irdessa's ear she's convinced the intensity is aimed solely at her. But with the bodies anchoring the line in front of her, the task is impossible. She would tell him it's no use, but the Vanguard cannot afford more desperation. Some of the newly submerged fighters free themselves from the detritus and paddle toward the surviving raft, as if it even has room for the bodies already occupying it.

"To the beach," Irdessa tells them, pointing over their heads. "Swim to the beach!"

They don't listen. She'd have to kill them to stop them. The instinct to thwart drowning has set their minds to stone, made them oblivious.

As the jumble and panic of it all crests to crash down on her, Irdessa takes a deep, clarifying breath. A Keswal breath. Never mind that this is what Torvald would have told her to do. She does it because it works, not because she's his sheep. As experience has taught her, chaos greases the gears of her mind, slowing time to allow possibilities to formulate once she dislodges her emotions from the immediate. Somewhere at her disposal is a means to coerce her enemies into their own failure. It always has been before. Irdessa's never faced odds this poor, but that's nothing new.

This raft is done for. Promontory's backup will catch up soon. Fohrvyldan orcanes don't thrive at night, but there are enough of them to make up for any disadvantage the dark brings. The Vanguard will have to be out of the water to stand a chance. For that to happen, the line and everyone gripping must be hauled onto the beach.

Irdessa yells, "Keep holding the line," and abandons the raft in a dive, sucking in a breath before plunging into the sea.

The frigid water slaps her, reviving her spent muscles. Hopefully enough to get her to sand. Between gasping in breaths and clawing the sea, Irdessa observes that some of the late marshal's scattered orcanes have regrouped on the beach, and one among them, a lieutenant at least judging by his spiked helmet, is pointing at Elaga's archers. If Elaga's force doesn't defend itself or scatter, it'll be run down. But if they cease pulling that line, every fighter in the water will likely die there, including Kraus.

As soon as Irdessa's feet can keep firm sand beneath them, she plunges down and hoists the submerged line out of the water, up over her shoulder.

"Pull," she yells at the archers, blinking away salt water, toes digging sand with all her strength.

Elaga spots her. Any indecision vanishes from her face. "Haul!" she calls.

That larger approaching force is close enough that their faint cries tear over the waves directly into Irdessa's bones. They're fresh and bloodthirsty. And if that force isn't twice the size of the marshal's, she's a fool.

The tense line digs into her shoulder like the backside of a chef's knife. How the damn Catchers made it so strong so fast, she hopes to live long enough to learn. Between the tugging archers ahead and the resistance from behind, the tension is such that she may as well be trying to uproot a Tower. At least the fiber is rough enough to grab without her hands slipping. She ascends from the surf's pull gradually, fighting for every soggy step as her shoulder muscles feel like they're separating. She's assisted by Elaga and her archers, and now that Irdessa's on dry ground their momentum builds. They haul up fighters who wriggle like fish on hooks as they gain air to inhale. With each new fighter washed up comes more hands to haul the line. The beach is quickly decorated with dredged-up bodies. Soon they no longer need Elaga or her crew, who are now just twenty paces up the beach from Irdessa.

"Stop them," Irdessa points at the late marshal's orcanes, led by his last lieutenant. Her legs fail her. She falls into rattling seawater coughs, crawling out of the path of those who continue to haul the line up behind her.

Elaga and her archers have enough time to draw bows, ready arrows, and launch a concentrated attack against the marshal's unorganized, charging orcanes. Her greatbow throws a harpoon that thuds into a beast's shoulder, eliciting a pained squeal and sending its snout carving into wet sand. Its soldier tumbles over its head, impacting a rock, getting up stunned and catching an arrow in the guts. Two more charging orcanes trample him on their way to get to Elaga's warriors. The archers make hasty shots, doing little more than earning them the beasts' anger. Their time is up.

Elaga, left with no room to prepare another shot, lifts a spear-sized arrow toward her enemy. The charging orcane surges forward, closing the last two yards with its toothed maw wide. Elaga's arrow and her arm disappear between teeth. The beast yanks her, never even slowing its pace. She flies into a nearby boulder like a thrown rug, crumples unmoving. The orcane slings its head, hacks out Elaga's severed arm, hacks out blood, does not hack out that harpoon-sized arrow. Its rider yanks the reins but its new preoccupation of vomiting blood has taken precedent. That massive arrow must have lodged in its throat. More orcanes replace the fallen. To their credit, the archers continue firing until they too are thrown or crushed or skewered by soldier's spears.

Irdessa's legs and shoulders feel as boneless as candles in an oven. Her people lie snorting out seawater on the sand or hunched over gasping for air. Death is closing in on the Vanguard from all directions. *But maybe not yet.* Irdessa sucks in a burning breath, forcing out exhaustion. She draws two knives from her belt and aims them at the straggling orcanes.

"Go for the soldiers. Free the orcanes." She tries to take energy from her order. Maybe it works. Either way, she charges. An exhaustion-dampened roar is the Vanguard's response. She hears them struggling to join her. One archer remains intact, and he strafes toward the forest, keeping the Vanguard out of his line of shot while pelting the foremost orcanes. This serves to disorient them, if little else, but between that and the scattered boulders hindering the orcanes' mobility and visibility, Irdessa finds an opportunity. The lieutenant suffers momentary indecision, snapping his orcane's nose from the soggy fighters to the single archer. In that moment, Irdessa acts. She picks an opportune outcrop on a boulder, leaps at it, stomps off it, throwing herself high enough to clear the orcane's rows of teeth and the point of the spear. She collides with the mounted soldier, splits his cheek with her dagger, cranking his bearded mouth wide to match the surprise in his eyes. The other dagger plants in orcane flank and is all that keeps her from tumbling off its back. Not a killing blow but maybe enough to enrage it beyond control. She hurls herself off the beast's opposite side with a grunt, severing the lieutenant from teeth to spine to free her knife, landing on the packed sand on exhausted legs, rolling sloppily and colliding with a boulder. A new pain radiates from her hip. It doesn't prevent her throwing herself to her feet and clambering up a rock.

"Kill them all!" she yells, quelling the knowledge she's probably killed her last and it's her turn to be killed. Her bedraggled force presses the momentum, acting in pairs to pick the disoriented orcanes apart. Leaderless soldiers on spent orcanes stand little chance, and by the time they come to grips with it, it's too late for them. This time when they try to run, the Vanguard dresses them in their own spears. There's no celebrating their enemies' second defeat. Instead, there's a frantic collecting of all the functional weapons on or embedded in the marshal's decimated force.

"Regroup!" The command erupts from Irdessa like a frog's call. Her throat's giving out. Doesn't matter now. Not much yelling left to do. She jumps off her boulder, tugs a spear out from under a dead orcane. Pulls another one out of a moaning soldier's stomach, giving his song a tortured squeal.

"I need arrows," says an archer.

"Get them from the dead," someone responds.

Over the water on the Tower, the Rain Catchers have returned to a high enough altitude for their projectiles to reach the fringes of the advancing force. But their contribution is negligible. That can't be less than fifty orcanes, fresh, tearing over the water like they're sliding downhill. *Too many. Too fast.* Irdessa throws a glance back at the silent wall of the forest, which may as well be one of Keswal's. It's even farther away than she realized. It might be possible that some of the Vanguard could busy the front line of orcanes while others flee to the forest. But those who could make such a dash over that much beach in such little time are the only ones still capable of offering resistance. The wounded would all die either way. And Irdessa will not be the sole survivor. Not again.

The Vanguard doesn't stand a chance. Do they know it? Maybe they're ready to die. Irdessa decides that she is. She's cost Promontory a marshal and a chunk of orcanes. Gave Vretos a split lip. And if she can accomplish that with a smattering of outlaws and no plan, maybe the nation can unite in an uprising that will hit him harder. Maybe they'll finish him off. She has to convince herself they will after she's gone.

The freedom of welcoming death inspires her. Freedom from fear. Now's the time to tear the wolf's throat, like Old Fent said so long ago. She was a different person then. Haunted by a ghost who refused to be silent. She wonders where Torvald has gone. Maybe he noticed her proximity to the grave and is off preparing her place. Maybe he doesn't contribute because there are no options left. He doesn't fight fights he can't win. He's all but said as much. Irdessa smiles. He broke that rule once. *Died.* He haunted the last of her days, then he left. *Again.* Maybe he was only ever an illusion. Certainly was a godsdamn distraction.

She shakes her head. "See you soon, you son of a bitch."

She'll do her best damage from on high, so she returns to the top of a boulder. These large irregular rocks are better than nothing and the orcanes are too clumsy in the dark to benefit from them. Even while she tries to take hope in that, the vantage from atop her half-buried boulder offers so desperate a scene that Irdessa cannot help but laugh. This flat beach probably submerges entirely during high tide, and the stone detritus with it. But at the moment it's an exposed, pale plateau and the tree line is impossibly far off. The orcanes are closing and their riders are nearly as frothing mad as they are. The last of her people clamber out of the water. Some lie still on the beach, having been dragged ashore but in need of resuscitation. They may already be dead. It occurs to Irdessa to place herself between the wounded and Promontory's charge. Spare them what she can. Create one more chew toy for the orcanes, one less leader for the Vanguard. Maybe she can aggravate her enemies. Call them to her. Create opportunities for others.

Every moment is someone's opportunity, Torvald whispers.

"No shit," she responds. She'll die here. And she'll take the ghost of Torvald with her.

"Come on!" she screams at Promontory, at the three-deep rows of dashing, shark-eyed orcanes, their steel-helmed soldiers crouching in the saddles. There's another lieutenant at the point of the charge, and he's directing the orcanes to spread over the beach like a carpet.

"Here I am," she roars, shaking her spears in the air. Get them to focus on her. And when they do, refuse to fucking die. Deep behind their front line is the unmistakable helm of a captain, and Irdessa can guess who it is without even seeing his burnt face. She thinks of Kraus and smiles. He's wanted to die for some time. Maybe he'll manage to get something sharp into that man in the process.

"Come on!" she yells, and her voice gives out. No more shouting. Promontory has seen her. Now to give them what they came for, Irdessa the Undying.

~

Lieutenant Hassand's orcane shimmies off a spray of seawater and dashes up the beach. It's time to work. The first soldier he encounters is belly down on the sand. He takes Hassand's spear in the back without a sound. Might have already been dead. He is now. The next is running, exhausted, trying to get to one of those boulders. Hassand's orcane lunges. His spear glances the man's shoulder, spinning him. His orcane flattens him with both forepaws, snaps his head off with its teeth. An arrow flies at Hassand, missing his face by inches. He lowers his chin, presses on, heat surging through him. The soldier to his left roars in elation, hoists his spear, catches an arrow in his stomach with a grunt and crumples in his saddle. Hassand tucks his elbows, grips his spear, his reins, presses on. Work, don't yell. The job's not finished. Celebrate when it is, if you must.

Behind him and flanking on either side, come the rest of the soldiers. They're yapping mad with war frenzy and bloodlust, hollering and screaming at the soon to be crushed outlaws. Hassand refrains from adding to the tumult. Maybe an intimidating war cry would give them the edge. Break the foe's resolve. But it's not a matter of resolve. The enemy is already defeated. This is only a matter of time and effort. Hassand works better without needlessly winding himself. Besides, the ones making all that noise are attracting archers and spear throwers. *Just do the fucking work*, he wants to command.

Captain Jeret held back in the shallows to direct. On their way here he told Hassand, "Spread over the beach so the orcanes don't knot up on land. Don't try to climb the boulders. Course through them like a river. Find Irdessa. Cut a path to her. Silence her and the rest will surrender."

Simple, like Hassand prefers. Captain Jeret should have been leading this mission from the start. The marshal let politics and pride determine his strategy, or lack thereof. This could have been over by now if not for him. He never understood the value of hard work. Shortcuts and trickery are no substitute. Jeret was right to let the marshal die. The man was unfit, not that Hassand would admit it aloud. That would suggest His Might erred in promoting Zander and relying on him. *Unwise.*

He navigates between two of the cumbersome rocks, both topped with outlaws. A spear thrusts toward him and he ducks, never slowing. It's a pitiful advantage those tall rocks give the Vanguard. Once Jeret's force surrounds them, they'll fall easily enough. Some of the outlaws are fleeing up the beach, scrambling toward the distant Redemier forest. Not Irdessa though. She's standing tall on a stone, rallying her troops, yelling at the orcanes as if death has kept her waiting. Nearby outlaws are electrified by her voice, by her fearlessness. They seem challenged by it, expending the last of their energy toiling against impossible odds to ensure her cry never ends. They struggle as if there is some hope for them when it's obvious there's not. Jeret was right. Ending her will end this.

Hassand grinds heels into flank, whips his reins, aims his spear and lowers his chin. *Undying.* He'll see about that. He surges toward Irdessa. To his left and right orcanes join him, slinging outlaws aside, crushing them. The outlaws atop the jagged stones are making a nuisance of themselves, assaulting the slower orcanes with spear and sword. They should have broken and run by now. Can't they see they've lost? Hassand planned to tear through them like a comb through a tangle, but the closer he gets to his target the more ferocious the outlaws become.

Nothing hard work won't fix.

He stabs at an outlaw, misses. The outlaw yells, enraged, leaping onto the orcane on Hassand's right and hacking at the soldier with a short sword. Ahead, Irdessa hurls a spear. The soldier on Hassand's left catches it in the breast, falls from his saddle. The persistent bitch is going to fight till her last breath. Hassand grudgingly admires her work ethic. She'd have made a peerless soldier. But the end is upon her.

There are two outlaws between Hassand and Irdessa. He watches one, aims his spear, gives a battle cry, then yanks his reins toward the other. His orcane doesn't hesitate. It pounces, catches the outlaw in its teeth, claws him. The outlaw's body opens up, releases guts black in the moonlight. The other hesitates, surprised, and Hassand jabs his spear into the man's face. The spear's tip lodges in his eye socket. Hassand jerks his weapon free, pulls his reins to pry his mount from the loose guts, meets Irdessa's eyes. He thought he'd find terror. There's only rage. No matter. The work's almost done.

Hassand springs forward to skewer her, but his orcane falters, squeals. The strike falls short. Hassand's mount lowers to its haunches, whistling through its nostrils. Hassand snaps the reins, digs in his heels.

"Get up!" he shouts.

Irdessa is moving, leaping to another rock out of his range, carrying on as if Hassand isn't even there. His orcane refuses to budge.

"Stubborn beast," Hassand yells, digging his heels deeper. Fucking orcanes. So wild they're nearly useless. His orcane squeals again, and this time it yanks its head to the left so hard it pins Hassand's leg. Irdessa is slipping farther away. He grits his teeth, draws his dagger to give his mount more motivation.

"Your dog's got a spear stuck in it, you dumb shit."

The voice comes from behind Hassand. He twists in his saddle and finds a hulking, black-haired outlaw with a dark glint in his eye and a lopsided grin on his face. This can only be one man. Irdessa looked fearless. This man looks like he's enjoying himself.

"Kraus the Rapist," Hassand exclaims. He hurls his spear, except his orcane's whining gyration ruins his shot. The unarmed brute smiles at the spear as it passes by him.

"Too bad," he says. "Got another one?"

Irdessa is the target, but Hassand is not turning his back on this man to chase her. Horrible idea. His useless mount is too injured to salvage, and if he dismounts, it may turn on him. It may turn on the captain. Not worth the risk. Besides, it's still got his leg stuck. He stabs the orcane behind its right foreleg and rakes his knife upward. The cease spot, as it's referred to. His mount stops whining and exhales in a huff, easing down to bleed out.

Hassand hurls himself at the unarmed rapist. "I'm bringing your head to Jeret," he yells.

The idiot stands there grinning. Hassand stabs his dagger into Kraus' chest. Except the blade stops at his shirt, bending Hassand's wrist so severely he loses his grip, drops the weapon. The brute throws his head back and laughs.

"Two layers of chainmail. To think, I almost took it off. You unlucky fucking cunt." And the man's enormous hands close around Hassand's throat.

Hassand tears at the furry knuckles. They may as well be chains. He swallows the encroaching panic. This is nothing hard work can't resolve. He digs with his fingernails, even while his face swells. His tongue pushes itself out of his mouth and rattles. Kraus the Rapist hauls him up close, so close Hassand can count the individual scars running over the outlaw's crooked nose. "I'll bring my own head to Jeret. And here's the last thing he'll see."

Hassand's airway is being crushed. His heart is pounding in his head and his eyeballs feel like they're about to pop onto Kraus' face. He can't manage a kick with either of his dangling legs. His mouth is as wide as he can get it but there's no air coming in. A closed window would do him more good. He's not trying hard enough! Hassand tries to yell for help but only serenades the ghastly outlaw with gargling hisses and spittle.

"What's that?" Kraus' hot breath assaults him even as the world fades.

There's a bright red flash and a distinct ringing, and abruptly the pressure in Hassand's head is gone, replaced by the curious sensation of spinning through the air while still locked in this man's grip. He licks his lips, bounces off a rock, splats to the sand. All light leaves.

~

The man's head bursts so explosively Kraus is momentarily blinded. Did he squeeze too hard? Choking a person to death has never ended like that. It's not until his eyelids can shovel away a sheen of gore that he observes what happened.

"You're wasting time," Bravensi scowls at him, slinging pink matter from Oekner's face. She leaps atop a rock, agile as a cat. "Stop playing with that and get a damn weapon." And she's off to follow Irdessa.

Kraus stands with mouth ajar, still holding the limp lieutenant by his neck. The man's newly shortened head ends in a clean cut from the bridge of his nose to the back of his skull, offering a tidy cross section of brains, bones, and bubbling ducts. The helmet and its contents are nowhere to be seen, and yet the damn corpse is hanging there dancing with its tongue roving around like a severed lizard tail. Kraus slings it away.

Bravensi springs from rock to beach and back, surrounded on all sides by her enemy's spears. She flows through her enemies like smoke through grass. Her fearsome partner leaves a trail of their body parts in its wake. Kraus' heart is so filled by the sight it might just burst. He barely knows the woman. Has had no part in her upbringing or training. And yet he's never been prouder. That he's on her side. That he could ever even witness such a beautiful thing. Old scholars croak about the seven pinnacles of creation. As far as Kraus is concerned there is but one, and he's looking at it. Everything else is barfed-up bones.

Kraus has eaten a mouthful of salty sand before he realizes there's a barkshark standing on him, and something's prodding him in the back and shoulder like he's slept through a wake-up call. He's able to crane his neck enough to see it's a spear tip prying at his chainmail.

"Two layers," he snorts, spraying sand. *What an idea!*

Seems the spear's next intended destination is the side of his head. By some freak athleticism fueled by a fear of never witnessing Bravensi kill another human, Kraus maneuvers his neck, lets the spear punch into beach, showering his face in sand. He tries to call the man a dumb cunt but only growls and slobbers. The orcane pinning him down shifts enough for Kraus to free an arm, and with it the knife at his belt. He makes like a pinned mackerel and bucks until, at last, he can plunge blade into barkshark belly, haul it diagonally, free some steaming innards to paint his shirt. The orcane springs off with a howl.

By the time Kraus has his feet under him and his back against a rock, the beast's bloody guts are a prominent part of his ensemble. They smell like shit. The clamor of battle surrounds Kraus, and though this one is not as chaotic or populous as the skirmish at Vim's pit, it's way fucking meaner. The Vanguard's backed against a wall, fighting, killing, bleeding, all while yelling like animals. They're outnumbered two to one, worse maybe, and without a saving grace.

To his left is Sura, who's covered in blood, limping and groaning like at least half of it's hers. She's surrounded by spears. She grunts and swings her great sword in an arc. The orcanes are too sprightly to be caught by it. A soldier takes the opportunity to impale her through the back. She cries out. Another soldier springs forward, stabbing her thigh. She grabs the spear, falling to her knees. An orcane rushes in and snaps its jaws on her neck. It flicks her body away like a full tissue and spits her blond-haired head on the sand.

"Shit," Kraus says, looking away before her lifeless eyes can find him. But it's too late. The blond hair. The girl. "Fuck," he says, and his legs quiver. This is no time to go back there. Not now. He grips the sides of his head, squeezes so the memory can't crawl back in. "Ah, fuck." *Please not now.* He'll die if he goes there now. Then again, hasn't he been waiting for death? He didn't expect to survive this long. But he could say the same thing for most every moment of every day. This time,

602 | David T List

though, the possibility needs no self-loathing to pass as legitimate. Barksharks are eating through the Vanguard.

But Bravensi ...

"Not yet," he tells himself, and slashes his knife at a passing orcane, opening a red stripe across its haunch that the beast fails to notice. "Come back here, you coward!"

A fighter is batted to his knees by the butt of a spear. An orcane sinks teeth into his back and launches him, keeping a disturbing amount of him locked in its mouth as the rest pirouettes away. Another fighter draws back his sword in preparation for an attack that should cost a soldier his hand. Before his stroke can fall, a spear tip bursts from his chest. Down he goes.

Kraus is smashed against the rock by a riderless orcane that appears to have lost the tip of its snout to a sharp weapon. It keeps sneezing, backpedaling, painting red blasts on the beach. He heaves it away. Something cracks off the side of Kraus' head, causing him to duck uselessly. He feels the wound. Hurts like a bitch but isn't bleeding bad. One of the archers resorted to throwing rocks. To no surprise, it doesn't protect her from Promontory spears.

Kraus lashes out again and again, aiming for their saddle harnesses when he can. If he can't kill the beasts, maybe he can at least sever their usefulness. But the opportunity to exact unimpeded swipes at nearby orcanes and soldiers is getting disturbingly more frequent. The Vanguard is being rendered to spare parts, leaving Kraus feeling mighty lonely. The soldiers can't occupy the rocks with their great bumbling mounts, definitely not while still pressing forward. And so the boulder at Kraus' back is vacant. He hoists himself up it, unable to do more than maintain a jittering crouch without falling off.

This elevated view is nothing to cheer over. He's on the fringe of the conflict, presently unnoticed since what remains of the Vanguard has bunched into a cluster twenty yards away toward the forest, mostly occupying a single massive stone plateau. There's no sign of Bravensi or Irdessa. In fact, he can't pick out a single recognizable face. Is everyone else dead? Promontory's soldiers are still pouring onto the beach from the water, rushing over the dead and dying, encircling the last stand like sharks on wreckage.

"Come at me!" he yells. But no one hears him. They're too enlivened by their inevitable victory. Standing in his saddle on the edge of the water is Captain Jeret, exercising one-eyed vigilance as his soldiers course past him. The moon's light illuminates him, making his roasted cheek shine like waxed cheese. His mouth is shut, which strikes Kraus, because last he saw there wasn't enough lip left for that. It's as if it's healing. And—Kraus cranes his head to be sure—it looks like the motherfucker is smiling again. At this rate, his entire face scorching will soon be little more than some rumpled skin. Kraus' work of art will be for nothing.

"Hell no," Kraus whispers. He throws himself off the rock, intent on another masterpiece. His feet contact the sand and his godsdamned knee chooses that moment to remember it's cracked. Kraus falls, rolls, swears. He gets up and limps toward Jeret. "Hey, ya fucking cunt!" His yell does not travel over the clamor of dozens of barking, growling, howling orcanes. Kraus has a knife and that's it. And although you can get creative with a knife, maybe he should find a spear on his way to Jeret in case anyone else objects. But who knows how long he's got? The bastard hasn't seen him yet. Cannot afford to waste this opportunity. Probably his last.

He's on the captain's east and closing, unnoticed, despite his knee's efforts to sling him down and make him squeal. If he were a knife thrower, he could probably murder the smug shit from here. But he's not. And he doesn't want the man murdered peaceably. This ain't gonna be a long-distance exchange. He wants to pull the captain's ribs open with his bare hands and splatter shit in his lungs while they still wriggle for breath. Maybe piss in his mouth after that.

There's a spear protruding from behind a soldier's dead body. Kraus doesn't want it, but he still might need a spear. What he doesn't need is indecision. He crouches to grab it. Something wallops him across the back of the head, making his skull ring like a clubbed coconut. Stars dance before him and he joins them, slipping into the black of a night sky.

~

Recruit Manjer stands over the unconscious outlaw, unable to believe his luck. That there's Kraus the fucking Rapist. It has to be. Who else is so huge and ugly?

When Captain Jeret promised a promotion to anyone who could capture the lout alive, Manjer barely registered the words. He knew it wouldn't be him. He's only been in the damn service for three months.

What a turn of events. He's had a shit day until right now. His orcane fought him from moment one, finally failing to even tote him to the beach, thrashing and misbehaving so violently Manjer had no choice but to hit the cease spot with his own spear. After that and a near-death swim in waterlogged seal-leather, he had piss-poor expectations for the evening. He trudged unarmed over the beach toward outlaw forces too stubborn to admit they'd already lost. His mounted companions rushed by him like he was standing still, bedecking him with sand.

But now, this blundering oaf threw himself in Manjer's path and bowed down to be brained by any old length of driftwood. Once the damn brute fell over, Manjer snatched up the spear he'd been going for. Now all he needs is to wait.

He could kill the man. He could stab him right through the liver. If rumor holds truth, liquor will pour out. But the captain wants him alive.

Manjer may have to get pokey if the big man wakes up feisty. But how much longer could this all take? Half the outlaws are dismantled corpses, and the rest are about to be.

"Lieutenant Manjer," he whispers, trying out the name. It sounds damn good. This is far from the first time he's imagined it. But by the gods, he'd never believed it might come to pass. He's tempted to stick the big outlaw in the legs a few times, hobble him to prevent any drama. But that might wake him up. And after all Manjer has heard, he'd rather rouse an orcane.

He considers dragging the big fellow behind a rock before another soldier sees his catch and gets ideas of their own. But Manjer doubts he could move this hefty fucker if he tried.

That only leaves burying the brute under sand. It's the one sure way no one else will see him and try to take him. This way, if the rapist decides to wake up, Manjer will have time to club him or stick him or, worst case, run.

"Lieutenant Manjer," he says again, smiling, shoveling sand over the outlaw's boots with his speartip. Like burying a treasure.

All of the captain's orcanes are landborne now. The conflict must be nearly concluded because haste is no longer a priority. The final orcanes are milling about while their soldiers stab the wiggling wounded to death. This doesn't bode well for Manjer's catch. He shovels sand with renewed vigor.

A few soldiers converse with Captain Jeret, who is scanning the beach with a single, sharp eye. Manjer's tempted to wave at the captain, to hail him and call him over, show him who he's caught. But again, that might attract unwelcome attention. Besides, for all he knows there are more outlaws creeping around even as their main body is reduced to scraps. *No.* Can't call attention to himself yet. Burying is best. No wonder the pirates do it so much. Once the conflict is over he'll find the captain and bring him here.

"Captain Jeret," he practices. "I bested a famous outlaw and restrained him under sand. I think you'll want to see this."

He's got the boots and lower legs covered, now for the hips.

The captain in Manjer's imagination nods sharply and tells Manjer that he did well. He's promoted. He will get a better uniform. His pick of orcane. A squad of soldiers. A new name.

"Lieutenant Manjer." He imagines how the whores in Promontory will say it while they pour his wine and loosen up his trousers. He can't control the excited flutter in his loins.

Something trickles down the boulder behind him and he spins around, thrusting with his sand-caked spear. The tip clatters against stone. No one there. Heat blanches his cheeks and he forces out a chuckle, to no one's benefit. He's so jumpy. No need for that. Just bury the rapist.

"What the fuck?" The rapist has awoken. He's trying to gather his fists beneath him to rise.

Manjer starts, accidentally pitching the spear. He snatches his driftwood club and bats the brute in the head. Nothing happens.

"You pocked orcane fucker. Wait 'til I get—"

Manjer cracks him so hard the driftwood breaks into thirds. Kraus the Rapist crumples into a snoring heap. Manjer's chest is heaving, and his heart threatens to break his ribs. He collects the spear, resumes his shoveling, wonders if he's cracked the man's skull. He's not about to reach down to check and see.

More pebbles rattle against stone. This time Manjer notices an accompanying rumble beneath his feet, barely audible behind the cries and clashes of the conflict. It's like the earth itself gave a shiver. Manjer recognizes that feeling. Chills ride up his skin. Maybe a foreign land such as Redemier finds such tremors insignificant, but the nearly buried memory the quake dusted off is disturbingly specific. Manjer continues his labor but slower, unwilling to relinquish his gaze on the boulder before him, trying to imagine an alternate culprit than the one memory is unearthing.

Another tremor, as if a tree fell, and this time Manjer watches the thin trail of sand cascading down the boulder. It was like that one time in the stands of Keswal …

Manjer's eyebrows bunch and he turns his full attention to the forest wall, forty-five yards distant but suddenly way too close. Birds are taking flight, which would already seem odd at this hour. Coupled with the tremors, it's enough to nearly cause concern. This island is cursed. How'd he forget that? He's transfixed by the forest wall, made dull and flat by the night. He's identified the memory, but it makes no sense here. Yes, those demon beasts escaped Keswal, but they were surely caught by now. Weren't they? How would they end up in—?

A shape too big to be a bird explodes from over the forest wall. Manjer freezes. The figure ascends from a plume of leaves against a star-punctured deepening dark. It rises until the moon itself is pierced by its two horns. There it crests.

"No." Manjer's throat's gone so dry he hisses the word. By the time the horned shadow's descent has begun, there is no question. "No!"

The uergata lands amongst milling orcanes in a blast of sand, flattening two soldiers under hooves the size of battering rams. Its halberd flashes out, disappears down an orcane's throat, emerges in a black splash. A soldier draws back his spear but the goatman bats his helmeted head clean off. A spray of blood chases the flying helmet.

The soldiers forestall their fighting to stare upward at this new combatant. The towering uergata, standing dark against the night sky, returns their gaze. Moonlight glints off shoulder armor, glints off a bladed halberd that's twice Manjer's height. Plumes of steam vent from the devil's nostrils. A soldier spurs his mount into action, coming alongside the uergata in a flanking attempt. The goatman throws a kick into the galloping orcane's ribs, snapping the beast's back and severing its rider's leg at the knee. A shriek rises from the mass of soldiers, and the terror of it makes Manjer's arm hairs stiffen enough to pierce his shirtsleeves. The uergata hefts up its weapon and swings a broad arc. Sparks and bits of soldiers tumble through the air.

Blood slaps Manjer's cheek, reviving him from his stupor. He's running, empty-handed, heedless of the direction. *Away*, that's all that matters. Run away. Another thump. Elsewhere. Another uergata has landed. A chorus of screams rises up and is hacked short, crushed under the sound of mashing steel and rending limbs. Another thump and a third uergata appears, bouncing from impact into a murderous stalk directly toward him. The thing must be ten godsdamn feet tall. They were supposed to be growing weak. Do they thrive on curses?

Manjer screams, falling onto his rump. He crab-scrambles away from the towering goatman, who doesn't seem to have noticed him. White stripes run up the otherwise black coat of the beast's legs and arms. Its chest, torso, and shoulders are armored with layers of steel scales. Manjer scurries back among the rocks even as the uergata launches over him toward his fellow soldiers. It lands in a cacophony of screams and squeals.

Manjer grips his ears, squeezes his eyes shut, presses against a boulder, wishing he could make like a ghost crab and disappear. How do they do it? The half-buried Kraus comes to mind.

"Maybe ..." He tries stuffing his fingers into the packed sand. A wet smack against the rock. Something bounces off Manjer's shoulder and lands in front of him. Against his better judgment, he looks. There's the bottom jaw of an orcane, tongue included, teeth up, lying there like half a bear trap. His stomach roils. Even while enjoying the fleeting comfort of hot piss filling his sodden trousers, he realizes the object could probably work as a shovel. Better than his fingers.

The ground and everything attached to it has been rumbling since the beasts landed. But now the tremors punctuate into even stomps. One's coming toward him, fast. Manjer is up and running again before he even decides to, this time in the direction he hopes Captain Jeret to be. Surely the captain will focus an attack, or preferably call a retreat. The marshal is dead. The orcanes are being trounced. Maybe there's a spare orcane for Manjer. If not, he'll drop his clothes and swim naked and never look back at the cursed fucking island.

There's Jeret alright, already afloat on his mount some ten yards out, yelling at his soldiers. Looks like he is calling the retreat. And it looks like Manjer's not the only soldier, mounted or no, making a dash for the ocean. Manjer runs faster. This fleeing crowd will draw the beasts' attention. He has to get in front of them, give the goats an alternative back to skewer. Lucky for him, some of the other soldiers are wounded and moving at a slower pace. Manjer slings his belt away and with it his spear scabbard. He flips the sodden leather anchor that is his armor off his shoulders and into the path of a fellow soldier. It's enough to trip the man, securing Manjer's place in the race. A thump erupts to his left. A scream is cut short. Manjer rips the neck of his shirt and wriggles out of it without slowing down. There are soldiers already diving into the ocean in front of him. Men, women, some armored, some bare-assed. What if he's last?

Panic showers Manjer, makes his fingers too shaky to undo the knots holding his trousers up. A couple of whore fingers would be handy. One of the uergatas thumps down at the edge of the wet sand off Manjer's right shoulder, landing in the path of another sprinting soldier. In the beast's same plummeting motion, it rams the soldier, horns crushing helmet like a hammered bell, laying him flat with a caved-in head and still-scampering feet. Manjer abandons the effort of ditching his trousers and tears toward the other fleeing soldiers. There are six mounted orcanes in the water now. Maybe a dozen mountless soldiers swimming. Another uergata has landed nearby. This one's also on the water's edge, as if unwilling to get wet.

Manjer's waist-deep, trying his damnedest not to rejoice. He's alive. The beasts fear the sea. But the expressions of those treading water before him do not reflect his elation. They're watching the beach in horror, as if some new nightmare approaches.

Something's dashing up behind Manjer, thumping through the shallows with lightning-fast feet. Manjer doesn't have time to turn. A growling, four-legged shape flies over him, eclipsing the moon. Then another, and this one piles atop a mounted orcane, clamping it by the neck and shoving it below the surface. It looked like an even bigger orcane.

Manjer's feet falter. Two more black flashes rush past him, spraying sea water in his face. One of them snatches a soldier in its teeth and throws him aside. Yet another flies over Manjer, impacting the water in a booming splash. Moments later, a soldier's mount is plucked downward, and her along with it. She gives a yelp that becomes bubbles.

"Fuck this," Manjer rasps, and turns to seek safety among the murderous uergatas.

Then, all of a sudden, he's looking down at the beach from far above. His entire left side has been crushed. It becomes apparent he's been thrown. The scene unfolding on the beach is no less mysterious viewed from on high. It first appears the unmanned orcanes collectively turned on the others. But no. The new beasts are enormous and they have no saddles. And they have dorsal fins, like sharks. These orcanes, tall and thin like battle axes, are largely ignoring soldiers, attacking Promontory's orcanes. Manjer must have been in the way.

He's cartwheeling as if gravity doesn't matter, transfixed by the sheet-like design his blood makes as it abandons his gaping torso, anticipating the tidal wave of pain that has yet to crash against him. But gravity does matter and it's calling him back to the ocean. His vision is failing, starting to go dark. His limbs aren't responding, probably due to his spine being mangled. He'll drown when he lands. In two feet of water. This day could not be more shit. Manjer spirals, plummets toward bloody surf, and as his vision gives out he accepts that he'll not be making lieutenant.

59
Peace Is An Illusion

Redemier

The Beach

Vyker is suddenly without obvious targets, leaving his red spear thirsty and his hands itchy. There are three enraged goatmen wreaking havoc on the Vanguard's enemies and stealing his momentum. They're so strong they may as well be battling children. Promontory orcanes are not equipped to deal with them. Vyker watches a soldier's orcane spring forward to latch teeth into one of the goat's ankles. The uergata thrusts his halberd into the path of the jaws. The orcane clamps onto its handle. The goatman throws a kick, sending the mounted soldier flying with a crushed chest, then cranks his weapon so hard the attached orcane flips onto its back. Another uergata falls from on high, impales the orcane's white belly while it paws the air, then launches skyward again in a fountain of blood. At this rate, those three fighting uergatas will end this conflict in moments.

But Vyker doesn't want the fight to be over. Killing soldiers relieves him in ways nothing else does. His mind demands something. Vengeance? Justice? His own death maybe? Ever since Old Fent, invasive thoughts have been sprouting out like the vines that strangle the Towers, stretching down and blotting out his judgment. They make no sense, suggesting things he doesn't understand. Like, *Irdessa has to pay for all the chaos she's created.* Was Old Fent's death where these thoughts originated? Was it the painted man?

Before the uergatas arrived, this had been a chance to purge that clutter. A real fight at last, albeit one he had poor prospects of surviving. There at the end, Bravensi alone matched his combat vigor. That's until the goatmen arrived. Now he and she are left to dive for soldiers like beggars lunging at fallen coins. Whenever he gets in her range, her actions suggest she cares nothing for his wellbeing. Quite the contrary. It's become a competition to kill as many soldiers as possible, and Vyker is an obstacle to her tally. More than once he tests her space, seeing if she'll rein in her weapon to accommodate him. She doesn't. He barely parries attacks that she seems oblivious she even launched at him. She can't be contained. And her fervor whispers a challenge to Vyker. *Try me.*

The tide has turned in the Vanguard's favor, but Vyker is determined to maintain his productivity despite Bravensi's wild dance. He's exhausted. Maybe more than he's ever been, even counting back when he first laid hands on the spear and he'd practice until his hands bled and it felt like a mountain perched across his shoulders.

He aims a springing stab at a soldier, knowing before the blow lands that it was sloppy. The spear misses the hefty woman's eye, stabbing crookedly through her chin bone up out the back of her head, lodging in her steel helmet. The woman slings her hands up as if to retrieve something off a high shelf. She's vomiting blood and snoring at the same time, her eyes vacant. Her reaction entertains Vyker, saps the urgency from him. She's dead on her feet and Vyker holds her rigid leash. It's a distraction that should cost him his life. He should kick her off the spear or release it for another one. Except his foes are thinning out and taking his clarity with them.

Fight. Fight while you can. Fight till none stand. It's a piece of a Vanguard song he's hummed a hundred times, longing for the day it would apply to him. Now it does. And the price it cost him feels too high.

He wrenches the spear downward, twisting it, sending the soldier flipping to her back where she continues to snore and bleed. The spear is freed and Vyker finds a retreating enemy to chase.

"Hey," he shouts.

The man never looks back. He doesn't want to fight anymore. But he forfeited the choice when he and his lot came down on the Vanguard. When they killed his brother. Vyker launches his spear. It embeds in the man's back, knocks him down in shallow water, steals whatever sprint he had left. Vyker steps on him, unwedges his weapon, metal scratching ribs, leaving the man blowing red bubbles out of his back for the sea to fill him up. There will soon be no one left to fight. Not unless he wants to fight his own people. Should he try to contain Bravensi?

A new growling is emanating from the forest, where branches tremble and leaves are trickling down. Seems the cursed island might address some questions Vyker preferred to remain unanswered. Rushing black shapes file from the shadows of the forest at a frightening pace. Five of them. Now ten. They're like orcanes but bigger, more wolfish, tall and thin and wild. Vyker faces this new threat, simultaneously clenching at the death they'll bring and exhilarated that the fight is not yet done. But the pack rushes right past him, ignoring him and the Vanguard and the standing soldiers. Seems these orcanes' blood thirst is quite specific. They target Promontory orcanes, mounted or otherwise. For every Promontory orcane still breathing, no less than two of their larger, wilder counterparts assault them.

Until now, Vyker had found this battle to be the pinnacle of brutality, without even a close second. Promontory meant to end the

Vanguard and the Vanguard resisted with bloody teeth bared. But the savagery of these new orcanes is stunning, like rabid wolves tearing into a flock of sheep. They lock teeth into throats and tug and rip, planting feet and pulling until their prey lies flayed and twitching with exposed vertebrae. The squeal of orcanes having their thick hide ripped away is enough to still Vyker's spear.

The wild beasts quickly clear the beach, silence the orcane death throes. But they aren't finished yet. Promontory orcanes are escaping over the water. But they cannot hope to match the speed of this new enemy. Wild orcanes dash after them across the beach, pounce into the surf. Any soldier unlucky enough to find himself in their path is trampled, launched, thrown. Their tall dorsal fins carve the water like knives, congregating on Promontory orcanes, plucking them down below the surface one by one, to a fate Vyker can only imagine.

Kraus is standing at the ocean's edge among the three statuesque uergatas. He's screaming at the retreating soldiers.

"What's the matter, you fried fuck? I thought you wanted me. Come back and let me fix that smile for you, ya spineless cunt!"

Farthest out among the soldiers is the leader. Judging by what Vyker overheard from Irdessa and Kraus, that's Captain Jeret, who led the assault on Vim. Not the one who killed Dhovoi, according to Kraus. Maybe the one guilty of that died on this beach tonight. Vyker scans the littered bodies, as if there's some way he could tell. Irdessa promised they'd get the ones who did it. He looks back to the captain. As he watches, the high-ranking soldier abandons his orcane, the last one, just before it's pulled under like the rest of Promontory's orcanes. The captain swims toward the distant Towers and a handful of soldiers follow. Vyker searches for the rage to fill his blood, incite him to swim after the man and finish him. But exhaustion is smothering his rage.

Even as the sounds of war have reduced to the whimpering and moaning of the dying, Kraus still rants. There's no way the soldiers can hear him, but on he goes.

"Yeah, run, ya sop!" Kraus says. "That ain't surprising no one. You skinny-chinned do-boy. Fucking head looks like a block of cheese. Better bring a damn backbone next time you challenge Vim's Vanguard."

The night is quickly taking on the silence and stillness of any other. A chill crawls over Vyker. The spear in his hand weighs too much to hold. He drops it. Maybe someone will make rounds and grant mercy to the dying soldiers. That's not a job for him. But there is something he must do.

Sura's head has been kicked around since it first came loose. Sand covers it, mercifully obscuring some of her ravaged neck. Vyker lifts it carefully, cradling it like there might still be life within. Ignoring the dripping, he carries it to the water, staring at it. She looks restful in death. It's the first time since Old Fent died that she seems to have relaxed, her eyebrows entirely unfurled. He rinses her off, letting her blond hair drift outward in the shallow water while he uses his thumbs to remove the sand from her ears and nostrils and eyes. He gently tries to close her eyelids, but they separate again. Nothing about this feels right. The Vanguard won. But what? This beach? The uergatas and native orcanes might argue that. Sura didn't win. She couldn't have lost more. First, she lost a friend when Irdessa let a wounded orcane open up Old Fent. Then she lost her life. Maybe she wanted to die.

Vyker exhales miserably. He's got no brother. No home. He's just lost a kindred soul, someone he hoped would become a friend. He holds Sura's cold face below the surface, unable to take his gaze from hers. Not that her cloudy eyes notice.

Someone on the beach is wailing at the top of their lungs. It's Cindie, and from the sound of it Elaga did not survive. Vyker remembers her teasing him as they progressed over Fohrvylda. She's so lighthearted. Or she was. Vyker wonders if she regrets doing this. Will she develop the same resentment that's threatening to take root in him? Will hers be more abrupt?

Vyker absently caresses Sura's cheeks with his thumbs. Although he's been near her his whole life, he didn't know her well. And yet here in her absence he feels crushed by her passing. As if another of the few sources of light in his life is gone now. Like Dhovoi. Clumsy, excitable Dhovoi, with his wild smile.

Tears burn Vyker's eyes. Dhovoi was no fighter. He never cared about joining the Heathen Tide. *I'm more suited for fucking*, he'd say. But he encouraged Vyker. He had Vyker's back. In fact, the only times Dhovoi fought were in Vyker's defense. It was one particular walloping that Dhovoi endured in those efforts that motivated Vyker to defend himself, and his big brother. Watching Dhovoi have his ribs broken by vicious boots meant for his own ribs is what drove the spear to Vyker's hands. It was a natural fit. *You're going to be a fine heathen*, Dhovoi told him once through a bloody smile as Vyker collected him from the street to get him back home. It was all the validation Vyker needed. Looking back, he never fantasized about the Heathen Tide the way some do, but now that the path has closed to him, it feels like more of his life is lost.

Vyker sighs again, shakily, and releases Sura's head. This whole trip feels like walking toward darkness, pressing himself tighter and tighter into a lightless corridor. He blinks away the tears. Sura's head rests on the ocean's floor. Her hair, pale in the moon's light, whisks over her face like the finest seaweed. And somehow, in a defiance of logic, that damnable little box is in his hands. His entire pack didn't survive the swim from the Towers. The pouch must have, because there it drifts. How? It's as if the thing swam after him. Moonlight illuminates the box's slick surface. He rotates it and water drips out.

"For when you turn."

What an evil little box. Evil for the questions that coil out of it. Evil for chasing him down and not letting him go. Vyker has entirely forgotten the face of the man who bestowed this curse upon him. Was he an enemy? Certainly didn't seem well-intentioned. Maybe he gave everyone these boxes. Maybe they're a test to separate the loyal from the ... Vyker looks up, searches the beach with his eyes until he finds Irdessa, leaning on a spear and breathing heavily, watching those silent uergatas at the water's edge. She probably doesn't even remember her promise to him. And why would she? There are more important things at play. In fact, avenging Dhovoi can't possibly be a priority of hers. Not really.

Vyker settles lower on his heels until he's slumped in the shallow ocean. Maybe this emptiness is the aftermath of violent conflict. His hands are turning the box over and over. Maybe if he cracks it open, it will alert Irdessa that he is no friend of the Vanguard. His heart gives a muffled leap. Maybe it has a fight in it.

Abruptly he's on his feet, drawing back, and before he can stop himself, he's flung the box with all his strength. It's too dark to see its path. But out there on the waves a splash punctures the ocean's surface. That effort utterly drained the last of his strength. He staggers out of the waves and plops down on soggy sand, gutted. Only now that it's gone does he notice the companionship that box offered. It, too, was full of questions.

~

Irdessa watches the wild orcanes skulk back to the forest one by one, some pulling dead Promontory orcanes with them. They skirt the people scattered on the beach—living, dead, or somewhere in between. These bristling orcanes are quiet, whether by nature or having sated their bloodlust on what must be their cousins. They are stoic, almost contemplative, as their black orbs drift over the battered men and women.

The sight of unmanned, oversized orcanes offers no comfort to Irdessa. That towering dorsal fin on their backs doesn't help. She grips her remaining spear tightly, clinging to it like she's rappelling off the Towers and it's her only line. These aren't the Fohrvylda variety—the kind she's killed. Those orcanes weren't a pack. Hell, they weren't above turning on one another at any provocation. The unity of these island orcanes unsettles Irdessa nearly as much as the uergatas' battle efficiency. Their deliberation belies cunning. That is evident in their eyes and their calmness.

Survivors watch the beasts depart warily, all clinging to weapons or remains of weapons until the orcanes have disappeared through that dark forest wall. The uergatas stand at the ocean's edge looking at that distant scattering of soldiers escaping over the night sea. The clash of battle still echoes in Irdessa's ears. She expected it to be the last thing she'd hear. Now it's the waves and rushing breeze mixing with the suffering of broken bodies.

She must tally the living, assess the survivors, deal with the dead. A defeated sigh escapes her. She must make a plan, get clear of this beach, set a course ... toward something. The weight of exhaustion drives her shoulders down, nearly flattens her. She wants to lie down.

Bravensi is in a hostile debate with Oekner, discussing numbers, totals. She's arguing over whether orcanes count toward some quota. Irdessa has long since decided to keep out of their business. Largely because she's never personally benefited from conversing with the inanimate and has little to offer on the subject. Ghosts, on the other hand ... She shakes her head, before her mind can even whisper his name.

Out of nowhere, Cindie falls into Bravensi, weeping clamorously. She pleads at Bravensi, tugging the tall warrior's arm. Seems Elaga is still alive, for better or worse, but in desperate shape. Bravensi reluctantly follows Cindie to where Elaga lies propped against a rock, eyes closed, skin pale, missing an arm. Bravensi gets to work on the large archer while Cindie nervously hovers behind, pacing, gnawing her fingernails. She'd been holding a torch, but her fretting makes the light more a hindrance to Bravensi's attempts. Another of the Vanguard gently pries it from her and crouches beside Bravensi, offering what help he can.

It's not that Bravensi's medical expertise is unsurpassed. She's just clean. And she has a disturbingly thorough knowledge of people's insides. And she doesn't mind hurting people. During such surgeries she sets Oekner aside, which has a varying effect on her general disposition. Sometimes it makes her short-tempered and snappy. Other times it unfurls her angry eyebrows and puts a smile on her face. Perhaps it was for the best this time.

Vyker kneels in the shallow water with his back to the beach, shoulders slouched and trembling. She saw him carry Sura's head with him. He treated it with such care that Irdessa couldn't bring herself to interfere. What he's doing at this point is his business. She knows better than to get between a person and their grief. Just because she can't imagine the good that comes from battle-shocked introspection while holding a severed head doesn't mean there is none.

Magpie stands beside Irdessa. "Should the Catchers follow the soldiers? Finish them off?"

"No," Irdessa says. "Either the Faithless Sea will handle them or they'll live to tell Promontory what's waiting for them here."

"You think it'll stop Vretos sending more soldiers?" Magpie says, his voice full of skepticism.

"No," says Irdessa. "But maybe it'll fill their pants with shit."

Magpie arches an eyebrow and nods.

Irdessa proceeds, "We need Maudee here, and the Catchers. We need all the help we can get." Her mouth goes quiet, but her thoughts do not. *I need to know we're alright. I need to see Otto together with Maudee. I need Elaga to pull through.*

Harpold approaches. "We're seeing to our wounded. But what of the wounded soldiers?"

Magpie answers with no hesitation. "Chop them up for chum and mount their heads on sticks."

Irdessa's first reaction is to agree. But the thought of more killing, more death, the thought of even picking up another blade feels like downing poison from a flask. And although she is surely poisoned already by her deeds, she refuses to accept it's irreversible. A public mass execution is the last thing this party needs.

"Spare them," Irdessa says. "Once our people are seen to, help those soldiers you can."

Harpold doesn't immediately react, instead leaving his eyes on Irdessa a moment longer as if her actual response hides within the one she stated. Magpie glares at her like she suggested sharing steak with an orcane.

"Mercy?" he says. "After what they've done to us?" He waves a hand over the body-strewn beach like Irdessa needed some reminding. He steps toward her, lowering his voice. "The man whose barkshark took Elaga's arm is over there. If she dies ..." He shakes his head, lowers his voice further. "If she dies, then *you* try to keep them from killing him."

Irdessa keeps her expression stone and he stops there. But he's left more unsaid. Nothing she hasn't considered. She damaged his trust with that order. And maybe that's for the best. Maybe she's had the monopoly on the Vanguard's trust for too long. How many people have to die before the trust in her is fully spent?

"It's not mercy," Irdessa says, utterly calm. "We're decimated. We don't know Redemier. We may be attacked again, from any direction. You saw what lives here."

Harpold does a better job of hiding his displeasure than Magpie. But now those near her have quieted to hear her words.

Irdessa continues, "I'm not asking you to trust them. But they're not Promontory's any longer."

More watch her. Skepticism is rife in the looks aimed at her. Irdessa addresses them. There's no time like this moment. "Promontory soldiers!"

Those capable turn to her. The rest will need it relayed by someone else.

"You're at a crossroads. You can swim after your captain ..." She aims a finger at the night sea. "... or stay on Redemier. If you survive the swim, maybe you can earn forgiveness and regain your place with the Heathen Tide. Knowing what I do of Promontory, I doubt it. If you remain, you are giving your allegiance to the Vanguard, to me, and I'll hear it sworn by each of you."

Judging by their surprise, this is a better opportunity than the soldiers had expected. The same can't be said for her own people. Narrowed eyes. Mouths fall open. Until moments ago, they were working hard to kill each other. Irdessa stalls the rising muttering with a lifted hand.

"If you stay, you'll keep your blue uniforms on. You'll forfeit all weapons. You'll get medical treatment as it's available, and by volunteer. I won't demand any of ours to treat you against their will. Those of you who are able will carry the wounded and our packs."

Irdessa takes a breath. Surely she's appeased someone by now. "We don't know you. We don't trust you. Maybe that'll change in time. But if you commit violence toward any of my people, it's execution for you."

The soldiers, segregated from Vanguard by a mutual distrust, aren't unanimously relieved. Some freeze midway through disrobing. Others do not yet acknowledge her command. Not until nearby Vanguard warriors display eager willingness to spear them if they go through with undressing.

Harpold speaks to her quietly. "So far their enemies have been able to tell us from them and spare us. What if their next enemies aren't so discerning?"

"All the more reason to keep them in blue," she says.

"And if that's not enough?" Harpold asks.

"I guess we'll have to kill them ourselves. Will that be a problem?"

"Fuck no," Magpie says.

Harpold leaves his eyes on her a moment. "No," he says with finality.

Hopefully it's enough consolation to her people. It is a compromise between betraying the Vanguard and massacring the defenseless. *For now.*

Kraus has been yelling after the retreating soldiers for so long his voice is as ragged as a battle's last flag, torn and flapping in the sea wind. He's winding down, shoulders relaxing. The chirps and calls coming from the night forest will soon overtake his ruckus. The soldiers he addresses are too distant to be seen. Maybe they'll make it to the Towers without falling prey to Catchers, which is unlikely since Catchers own this entire stretch and little goes unseen to them. Maybe they'll somehow make it all the way back to Fohrvylda. Irdessa can't imagine they'll receive a warm welcome if so.

"I'll see you in hell, Captain jerkoff!" Kraus concludes. He spits a grey wad, contented at last with the state of the conversation, whips around toward the beach, and crashes headlong into the leg of a motionless uergata. He falls into the shallows with a swear. The goatman inclines its head slightly, resting its eyes on him. Its goat face reveals no emotion. It could be amused, annoyed, or oblivious.

"Hey, ya goat," Kraus growls from where he sits, running hands down his sea-logged chest as if somehow he came out dirtier in the exchange. The uergata turns and walks. The other two goatmen follow it. They approach Irdessa, marching between the dead and dying, and a reverent—if not horrified—stillness radiates over the fighters. Despite the beasts' placidity, they are an imposing trio. They pass through the people like walking trees, with the moonlight stretching their shadows out over upturned faces. Their hooves leave platter-wide craters in the damp sand, crunching as they settle. By the time the apparent leader stands before Irdessa, she has to crane her head to her neck's limit to see its face.

The uergata squats down onto both knees, settling into the sand. It's still a head taller than her, and that's not counting its horns. One of the others kneels as well, giving a pained grunt that transcends language. That one is exhausted, and now Irdessa sees the streaks of blood staining its leg. The third uergata stands tall, wary of all its surroundings, its monumental weapon acting as an additional leg. This feels like a trial, and all Irdessa can think of is the uergata she wounded, perhaps fatally, in Keswal. But these beasts don't seem like the type to waste words or draw out a sentencing. If they wanted her to pay for what she did, she'd already be skewered.

The beast's voice is deep but piercing in timbre, too loud and in an unfamiliar accent. "It was by your efforts that we escaped our captors." It's the first time she's heard one speak since Keswal. It's no more comforting up close, when the thing is looking down at her. "This does not make us allies." It waves its long arm over the beach, over the dead. "Those wanderers met the same fate as would be fitting for your entire nation."

Irdessa doesn't know how to respond. She's still not convinced the uergata is talking to her. But the thing paused. And Irdessa is unable to keep her words in her mouth.

"It wasn't my efforts that freed you. My ... friend—" a piss-poor description "—didn't fill me in on his plan. I tried to kill one of you." This admission seems unwise and potentially disastrous. But considering the state of things, why break a streak?

The uergatas do not visibly react. Irdessa is out of her depth. She cannot read their body language. They don't share humanity's emotive expressions. There is a faint humming vibrato accompanying their exhalations, and for all Irdessa knows they're communicating by it, conspiring to kill the rest of these puny things once they catch a breather.

"You succeeded," the uergata says. "His wound proved fatal. Etz is what he was called. He was responsible for our capture. The fate you administered was predetermined."

"It was ... what?" A chill wind brings goose flesh over Irdessa's arms.

"Your beast catcher met Etz in our homeland. He tricked Etz into trusting him. Etz led them into our home. Once inside, the beast catcher fed us poison to sedate us and take us. The entire Gygus tribe suffers for what Etz did. When the time came to face you, he accepted his fate honorably."

"His *fate*. He ..." Irdessa does not want to say the words. "He let me kill him?"

The uergata's head cranes ever so slightly, horn-tips scratching the night sky, in a gesture that can be nothing but incredulity. "You believed you killed a uergata singlehandedly?"

Her cheeks burn. The standing uergata snorts. "*Jaetmi*," it rumbles, disgusted. "What use is such relentless delusion?" It continues ranting in its own language until the oldest of the three, or at least the most tired, silences it with a huff.

Irdessa shakes her head, powerless to the blanket of truth descending down to suffocate her. Even that detail. Is there no end to Torvald's manipulation? Standing off against that uergata was a defining moment. A turning point. Now it, like battling caged and broken orcanes, feels empty. What ignorant pride she suffered. She must move this conversation past her facade of accomplishments before they're all revealed as charities.

"Are we safe here?" she asks.

The standing uergata directs a bleating growl at the leader, takes an impatient step toward the forest. The leader responds in the same animal tongue, abating.

"I know why you came here," it tells Irdessa. "The same reason we did. Your enemies are our enemies. This island belongs to orcanes. They haven't removed you yet. That doesn't mean they won't. Perhaps battling the abominations earned you their favor."

"They didn't attack you," Magpie notes.

The standing uergata snorts again, glares down at Magpie, as if it's weary of all this patronizing.

"Of course they didn't," the crouched uergata says. "We're kin. Vostuar's children do not turn on one another."

"They killed the other orcanes," Harpold interjects from somewhere behind Irdessa.

The leader uergata looks at him for so long that Irdessa questions whether it understood him.

"Those mongrels from your homeland are not orcanes," it says at last. "They are a disgrace to the blood of orcanes. Mankind, for all its misguided efforts, regressed them into a fate worse than death. Cancer. Vostuar rejects what they have become."

Kraus has approached. He's found a spear. And the way he's gripping it concerns Irdessa.

"Hey, ya goat," he says again, pausing to catch his breath. He addresses the standing uergata. "One of you knocked me down back there." It's undoubtedly a challenge, despite the grin wrapped around his face. The uergata doesn't acknowledge him. The kneeling one continues addressing Irdessa.

"I am Ber. And until I was captured I was *teezh* of the Gygus tribe."

"I'm Irdessa. Of Vim. What does ... *teezh* mean?"

"I was to be chieftain." This exclamation is noticeably quieter and suggests regret, shame, anger. "The Gygus tribe will be leaderless."

Kraus, miffed at being ignored, sidles up closer to the standing uergata, eyeing it, circling it. The standing uergata glares down at him.

"So is this your ankle, or your knee?" Kraus gives the uergata's leg a rap with the butt of his spear.

The response is so fast Irdessa only retroactively perceives what happened. The uergata snatches the spear and throws it in a single motion. Its hoof lifts up, leg tensing in preparation of a kick that would surely annihilate most of Kraus' bones. The crouching uergata, Ber, gives a sharp command, seemingly just in time to save Kraus' life. The hoof hovers midair a moment. It descends. Kraus gathers his footing. He had tried to hold on to the spear and almost flew away with it. He's not deterred. If anything, the smile on his face widens. He'd braced himself for the kick.

"I liked that spear."

The standing uergata vents a blasting exhale through wide nostrils. "A *jaetmi* who attacks a uergata values neither his weapon nor his life."

Kraus shrugs. "Got me there." He looks the uergata up and down, and Irdessa realizes the idiot is about to take a swing.

"Kraus." She hopes her voice is enough.

His grin has grown menacing. "Go get my spear, you fucking goat." He lets the words drip out like syrup.

The uergata has grown entirely still.

"Kraus," Irdessa says. "Stand down." Of all the uergatas for him to antagonize, why the angriest?

Kraus shakes his head at the goatman. "Plenty of other spears out here." He takes a step backward.

The third uergata, which Irdessa had almost forgotten until now, rises slowly from the sand. It gives a slight growl as it stands, holding its weapon with both hands. The crouching uergata lifts itself up, turns toward the forest. The standing one follows.

"Wait," Irdessa says. "What will you do now?"

The annoyed uergata and the injured one proceed toward the dark forest wall. Ber pauses, half-turning back to her, one large black eye fixed on nothing if not the darkness itself. "Go home."

"How?" she asks, and she realizes she's stalling the goatman to contrive some pitch to enlist him. "Maybe we can help each other."

The other uergatas have departed. Ber's gaze centers on Irdessa, and again that incredulity afflicts his posture. "Help me?"

Irdessa is abruptly aware of her scattered Vanguard, who will be helping nothing but the crabs and the birds.

The uergata snorts. "*Jaetmi,*" it mutters. Irdessa knows an insult when she hears one. But there's a fondness in his tone. "They say foolhardiness is a byproduct of your short life. Moths, who throw yourselves at open flames. They say Alesuariil erred when he encouraged you to wander. But they mention nothing of your resilience. Your ambiguity. You manage to both forge and reject your fate."

Irdessa has no response for that. Again, it's not clear the uergata is directing his words at her, even if he is watching her.

"What will you do now?" the goatman asks.

The question catches her off guard. And the silence of the night reveals itself as a collective inhale from everyone nearby. Perhaps from the entire company. Everyone present probably heard the uergata's strong voice. Once again it comes down to her. But she doesn't have an answer, not a complete one anyway. What she does have is a wish.

"I want to protect my people. Find them peace."

Ber watches her another moment. "We're not so different," he says, and turns away. "If you want peace here, you'd best seek out the resident Balvred. The orcanes obey him."

"The resident what?" Irdessa says.

Ber pauses, head tilted down as if he's scouring his memory for a word. "The statue in your arena. Your leader called him *Deceiver*."

"He's here?" Irdessa says. "Where?"

"North and west. Find the ruins of a human civilization, then continue north. He'll introduce himself. One way or another." The goatman leaves.

Kraus is beside Irdessa, eyeing the forest the beasts disappeared into. "So what are we really going to do?"

"Rest," she says, and means it. "Wait for dawn, then move inland. Off this beach and farther from Promontory."

Kraus gives a chuckle and Irdessa deduces his meaning. There is no *far enough* away from Promontory. Not so long as the one in charge is without death. Vretos' grudge will never expire, only marinate. The Vanguard could feasibly find a comfortable glade high in a Redemier mountain, build a new life, forget the old. But no passage of time will free them from the possibility of Promontory falling on them like a flood. And when that happens, Promontory might even attack from the east and the west, depending on how the Heathen Tide resolves. Perhaps by then Vretos will have control of Ausgan's monks. She shakes her head. Peace is an illusion. For Irdessa to truly protect her people, Vretos must be stopped.

"We need help," Irdessa says.

"I'll say." Kraus is spitting away the cork from a freshly unstoppered bottle. It's miraculous how he tends to come into possession of those.

"May as well seek out the one Ber mentioned," Irdessa says. "The Deceiver."

Kraus has a swallow from the bottle. He lets his head fall back and sighs. "Ber said he's a Balvred. They're supposed to be mankind's predecessors, you know. Immortal. Demigods."

"I didn't know that, actually."

"Now ya do," Kraus says. "I've always wanted to meet one of them."

Irdessa takes the bottle from him. "You mean *fight* one of them."

"Well, yeah."

She takes a pull.

"Then what?" Kraus' voice, as gravelly as ever, is quieter than before. Deliberately dampened. And if Irdessa didn't know better, she'd take his tone for sympathy.

I don't know, is her gut answer. But that's not the truth. She does know.

What would you do? she wants to ask Torvald. But he's dead. And he's been dead this whole time. She's relied on what he taught her. What he made her. But however painfully bound to his methods she finds herself, she is truly independent of him.

There is only one answer, and it sits patiently before her. The Catchers knew it. And this time, try though she might, Irdessa cannot skirt it or ignore it or even see past it. Cannot run from it or bend it into something prettier.

"I've gotta kill Vretos."

Epilogue
It Shouldn't End Like This

REDEMIER

"Wake up, Andesite!"

Culver sits straight up, blinking rapidly. It's dark. Still nighttime. The gripping soreness in his shoulders is not enough to keep him from immediately noticing his guest. The silhouette of a deled figure fills the doorway of the ruined home he'd sworn was a clever hiding place. They've been found. Culver knew it might happen, but not like this.

"Come on out here." The exemplar in his doorway isn't Kale. The voice is crisp, alert. Culver forces down his dread and pushes himself drowsily up to come on out there. What else can he do? It appears he's about to find out exactly how much trouble they're in.

The derelict city square has taken a nightmarish turn since Culver last saw it. A chorus of exemplars lines the perimeter, producing a low song that accompanies a sharp breeze. The choir surrounds the clearing, summoning. Their torch light makes the encroaching forest and gutted buildings large and ominous. The decrepit masonry resembles skeletons melting into the earth. In the center of the clearing stand Ashmancer Haik, two rhyolite sentinels, and between them Kale, looking unhappy but not afraid. He's alive and unrestrained. Maybe that's as good a sign as Culver can hope for.

Haik is talking to Kale. "Your native plaything is wandering through Ausgan, rounding up traitors to join her insurrection."

Kale's mouth turns down at the edges, but he doesn't respond. Haik shakes his head and paces. The exemplar who found Culver clears his throat pointedly, calling Haik's attention to him.

"Ah." The ashmancer smiles. "Resonations, Culver." He sounds so nonchalant Culver is almost convinced they're not actually in trouble. Then he remembers standing off against Prime Sentinel Selu. He remembers seeing her get eaten by a starry shadow that came out of Kale's head. He remembers that they're on the cursed island, which is punishable by death. Are he and Kale about to be executed? However cruel Haik is, he just doesn't seem capable of that.

Culver clears his throat. "Resonations, Ashmancer." His voice is a groggy growl. He's never cared much for Haik. Always so smug, even now. Hateful to Kale. Haik used to approach Culver when Kale wasn't around to question him about his choice of associates. He'd throw some slander at Kale, trying to convince Culver that consorting with the *"useless basalt"* would stunt his progress. As if the ashmancer has any say in Culver's education.

"Now we can get somewhere," Haik says. "Come here." He points at a rough-spun sack on the ground. "Open that. Take out what's inside." Haik gives it a kick. It clinks, not unlike shells. But thicker, heavier.

Culver tries to ignore the hooded, humming individuals lining the entire square. Last night, as the fading sunlight let the shade slowly deepen, the place felt eerie. Now in the golden flicker of so many torches, with the tension of a dozen summoners preparing for Imala-knows-what, it feels even less inviting. The exemplars holding the torches aren't looking so confident. None hold still, aiming their eyes back and forth at the forest's every sound. What are they summoning for? Surely it's for protection from beasts. They can't be preparing to summon Consonance on Culver and Kale, can they?

Culver, still attempting to rouse his sluggish wits and assess the situation's danger, pats at the bag, feeling for the opening. He hefts it up, loosens the drawstring, shoves his arm in. The sack is woven of thick malva twine. Whatever's clinking about can't be in small pieces or they'd fall through. His hand touches something scalding hot.

"Dammit." He recoils, glares up at Haik.

The ashmancer grins. "It's perfectly safe."

Culver chances it again, carefully. Turns out the object isn't hot. It's frigid. So cold it feels wet. The coldness seeps into his fingers and all the way to his chest, leaving him with a suffocating anxiety. The texture is like rough bark, but sharper. The pieces are too regular to have occurred naturally. Too circular. He pulls it from the bag, consciously fighting an inexplicable urge to drop it or throw it. Two twin semicircles connected by a joint on one side, rough textured, the color of mud, and as he turns them over in the torch's light the hinge conjoining the pair gives a thin squeal.

"This ... isn't korundite," Culver says. His abilities of enhanced observation are gone. He's never been the most gifted in supersensory perception. But at this moment he feels blind. It's not only the fog of drowsiness still clouding his awareness. Something else. The chill in his chest is deepening. "What is this?"

"It's called a manacle, and it's harmless," Haik says.

"It doesn't feel harmless," Culver mutters. "It feels like ..." *It can't be.* Steel is grey. Right? It is in all the images. Why would the ashmancer have such a thing? Unless to contain a fellow exemplar's power. The heat drains from Culver's face. "Steel."

Haik's lip curls into an appreciative smirk, giving Culver an answer he'd rather have not gotten. Steel is cursed. You can't own it. Where would Haik even get it? Fohrvylda? The Untamed? Culver searches the faces of the surrounding exemplars for some sign he's not going crazy. Judging by their expressions, most of them are as surprised as him.

"Why isn't it grey?" Culver asks.

"Rust," Haik says grandly. "The Imala's effort to undo the curse. Given time, it will reduce to dirt what human hands can't hope to break. Take it over to Kale."

Culver hesitates. If he shackles Kale, then Haik channels an attack, Kale won't be able to negate it. "Are you planning on hurting him?"

Haik looks amused. "Oh, you are too thoughtful. If only the basalt cared as much for you. You wouldn't be here now, would you?"

Culver doesn't respond.

Kale speaks up, "Do it, Culver. It's fine."

Culver obeys numbly. He's eager to be done touching it. It's heavy, as if endensed. Supposedly, you can't endense steel with consonance. You don't need to. For every moment he handles the cursed object it feels like his core is suffering irreparable damage. Kale's expression is unreadable as he looks down at the discolored contraption.

"Place the binding on his wrist," Haik instructs.

On some inspection, Culver manages to spread the two halves, creating a brittle croaking noise so unhappy it makes his teeth clench. He holds it out toward Kale, who at last meets his eyes. Now he looks afraid. Haik must have some idea of what Kale did to Selu. What he's capable of. It makes sense why he'd contain Kale, but Culver wishes it wasn't him enforcing it. "I'm sorry," he says. But the truth is, containment is better than execution. This could be far worse.

Kale extends a shaky wrist. Culver tentatively places the frigid object on his friend's arm. At contact, Kale hisses in through his teeth, chills riding out across his skin from the ugly device. Culver closes the manacle, tightening it to Kale's wrist.

"Secure it with this," Haik says. Culver turns to him in time to see him toss a small dowel. He catches it. It's polished wood, perhaps endensed, about half the length of his thumb, flared on one end like a fishing arrow's tip but with flexible flanges. Flat on the other like the head of a korundite nail. There's a circular opening on either end of the manacle, and when they're squeezed shut, the holes align. Culver presses the dowel into the opening with his thumb until there's an audible snap. Kale shudders.

"A cruel device," Haik admits, like he regrets the situation. "Made by our enemies, for our enemies. And a perfect fit for you, Kale."

Culver is still holding the manacle, now firmly affixed to his friend. This feels wrong. He's hesitant to release Kale's arm, knowing once he does this burden will be Kale's alone. "I'm sorry," he says again, although unsure he had any say in the matter.

"Well done, thank you," Haik says. "Step over here, please." He indicates a point several feet in front of Kale, facing him. Culver does as he's told. Despite the solemn setting of it all and the implication that his and Kale's excursion is at an end, Culver feels some relief to see his fellow exemplars. However this ends, at least they won't be alone in these woods.

"Now ..." Haik says sharply, his voice clashing with the reverence of the murmured summoning song. "Let's continue. Basalt Kale, I warned you. Remember? I told you all threats will be eliminated."

Kale stands perfectly still, watching Haik. His skin is pale, as if that bracelet is draining the color from him.

"You thought your disappearing trick could solve all your problems, didn't you? You believed you could negate your presence and this andesite's from the scrutiny of everyone." He laughs. "Why don't you give it a try now with your new accessory?"

Kale still says nothing. If he is attempting to drop from view, it's not working.

Ashmancer Haik nods knowingly and turns to Culver. "Where's the crystal?"

The question startles him. His urge is to look directly at Kale. But he's been in this position before. Only, the last time was in his own dorm. The questions came from Haik's sentinels. The last time, he failed his friend.

"Where's the what?" he asks innocently.

"What do you have there?" Haik points at Culver's dele. In almost the same moment both of Haik's sentinels are upon him, restraining him and forcing their way into his clothes until one produces the object that caught Haik's eye. They release him to catch his footing and smooth his dele. One holds the procured object up in the torchlight. It's the yam he dug from the stream.

Culver can't hide his amusement. "Did you forget to bring food? It's yours. Just boil it before you eat it."

The sentinel drops the dirty yam, giving Culver a malicious look. Haik's smooth face wrinkles into a momentary scowl. He recovers, fixes his smile, takes a relaxed step toward Culver. "Do you know what the natives are saying about our Basalt Kale here?"

Culver doesn't. Before he can state as much, Haik answers himself. "They say Kale killed Prime Sentinel Arc with the help of some dirtfoot girl."

Culver stands strong rather than letting an honest reaction take place. He wants to ask if Arc earned it the same way Selu did. She was behaving like a rabid wolf among rabbits and, he tells himself, deserved what she got. That doesn't mean Culver wants to remember her being inhaled by an inky void of Kale's creation. He'll need Kale to explain what happened to Arc. But Haik never has to know that. So he keeps his face free of emotion.

"He is damned, Culver," Haik says. "Destined for the bath. But you don't have to be. If you help us, you can be redeemed. You're not the first exemplar Kale has used or hurt for Fohrvylda's gain. Not the strongest either. The tribunal will show mercy if you cooperate."

Culver looks from Haik to Kale and back. Maybe Haik's lying. Maybe he's not. Maybe the deal he offers is the only way Culver can be redeemed. How could he know for sure? Haik is a petty prick who's not above lying. What Culver does know is how it feels to do nothing while Kale is being attacked. He won't let that happen again. Despite the charges leveled at Kale, he'd hear Kale's side before passing judgment. Haik's been out to get Kale forever. Or at least since Thran.

"The crystal," Haik prompts. "Just point in its direction."

"First I'm hearing of it," Culver says.

Haik *tsks*, shakes his head, looks at the two sentinels he brought. They don't react. One of them is Euphrain the akoromancer. Weird fellow who refuses to shave the patchy stubble off his upper lip. Large eyes. Has a fixation on cuttlefish. There's something unsettling about him. Where are Haik's own, Ilbris and Bronn? Why aren't they here?

The ashmancer paces, head down in thought. The forest's insects buzz. The gathered exemplars hum. The initial surprise of the situation is wearing low, leaving Culver's eyelids heavy. Could this conversation not wait until the morning? The ashmancer abruptly strides over and faces Culver. He's not smiling anymore. Doesn't look happy at all. In fact, Culver wonders if Haik is about to take a swing at him.

"Last chance, Culver. Don't force my hand." It's the same earnest tone Haik used to employ when Kale was out of earshot. It nearly convinces Culver Haik is concerned for him. But he's observed too much cruelty from the ashmancer to believe that. He cocks his head to one side, weighing Haik. He's no match for Culver at martial arts. If it's a brawl he wants, Culver can indulge him. Educate him even, since Bronn and Ilbris aren't here to back him up.

"I can't help you," Culver tells him. And this time his resolve speaks for itself.

Haik doesn't attack. Instead he snorts, looking authentically disappointed. After a moment's hesitation, he addresses Kale. "Tell me, why do you kill your own kind?"

The forest's song is his reply. As uncomfortable as Kale looks, Culver is glad the attention is off him. While he'd love to pound the ashmancer, there's no way it would end well here.

"What's your count up to? Three now? Soon four?"

Kale says nothing but Culver gets the feeling Haik will demand a response soon enough.

"Your friend from Napiri, the village girl, she's preaching your deeds across the land. She says you took a dagger, not unlike this one." He pulls an immaculate chitin dagger from within his sleeve, showing it to Kale. "And ran it across Arc's throat, not unlike this."

Haik springs toward Culver, bounces on the balls of his feet, sweeps the dagger in an arc at Culver's face, making him flinch, and is back where he started in a single moment. The swipe came so close Culver felt the wind on his skin. He swallows. His neck feels warm. Haik is watching him with a mischievous expression. Kale's eyes are round. The sentinels at his sides have taken hold of his arms, restraining him. The summoning song stills. Culver swallows. Haik shakes something off his dagger. Kale is struggling against the sentinels as if breathing has become a labor. Culver swallows again. There's a lot of saliva gathering in his mouth. And it tastes like blood. Some of it travels down his windpipe, making Culver cough abruptly. A red spray bursts from his mouth. He touches his neck, where something seems to have stung him, and pulls back a hand glistening red. He gasps, immediately drawing more liquid into his throat, and falls into a hacking fit. He grips his throat with both hands. Blood is pouring freely from a gaping ravine. Imala above, Haik cut him! Why didn't it hurt?

He's fallen to his knees, trying to catch his breath, keep blood from running down his throat, but with every cough comes a gasp and with every gasp he inhales more blood.

"You ... you ..." Kale is digging at the ground, trying to break free of his captors. "*Why him?*" he yells. "He didn't do anything!"

Culver finds a position in which blood doesn't gag him, bent over on his knees with his chin forward. But this seems to be a perfect way to empty all his blood, despite that he's clenching his throat tightly. He needs to wrap something around it. A shiver takes him, makes his teeth rattle, shakes red spittle from his lips. The temperature has plummeted.

"Oh, praise Imala," Haik says. "I get it now. That is much more satisfying up close. Fire is cleaner but this is *exciting*. If only you could sense my pulse."

Culver feels his own pulse as it ejects measured spurts of blood.

"One less traitor," Haik says. "Now, where is that Imala-damned crystal?"

Culver tries to talk but only gives a raspy boiling sound from the crevice. It seems like it should hurt a lot more.

"I'll kill you!" Kale screams.

Culver grips his dele to shift some of the fabric up and bind his wound. But his fingers are numb and uncooperative as if they're made of driftwood.

"I'll kill you."

Culver has gotten his breathing under control. Now to stop the bleeding. He shivers again, harder. Soft white light is overtaking his periphery. There's a gentle tinkling sound in the air.

"I'll kill you ..." It's not a scream any longer, more a sob. Kale is hanging from the sentinels' grasp, staring at Culver.

Only upon seeing the desperation in his friend does Culver understand. He's going to die. *Why didn't it hurt more?* He searches the faces of his fellow exemplars. His vision is too blurry to see their expressions. Did they know Haik would do that? Why would they let him

628 | David T List

do it? He risks swallowing so he can say something. Anything. All he manages is a whispered, "Why?"

There's a thump like a log hitting earth, then a gasp, the sound of someone who's taken a blow to the guts. An exemplar topples over, pounding face first into the ground and lying still. Another thump. Another exemplar grunts and falls. There's something thin extending from his back.

"*What are you waiting for?*" It's a booming voice, deep and ragged, in a dialect Culver's never heard. "*Kill the fuckers!*" A shape that appears to be a bear charges from the forest in an explosion of leaves, hefting an object that flashes brilliantly silver in the light of the torches. Another figure follows closely behind him. "Godsdammit, Kraus." It's a woman's voice.

Culver blinks, swallows, tries to contain his shuddering. More animals spring from the forest. They're shedding their skins, exposing human shoulders and legs and arms, all bearing bright weapons, surely steel. Culver's head feels heavy.

This is what it's like ...

"Exemplars, on me, now!" It's Haik and he isn't half as cheerful as he was a moment ago.

Everyone's running around as if it's all so important. Culver places his cheek on the red puddle on the ground. It's not as cold as he expected. Warm, actually. Still, he can't stop shivering.

... to die.

"I'm sorry, Culver."

It's Kale. His eyes are soggy. He's lifted Culver's face off the ground. Apparently the sentinels restraining Kale found more important obligations. Culver can't feel much. Can't see much either.

"I'm so sorry."

It's alright, Culver mouths, *I had nothing better to do.*

Kale doesn't laugh. The large bear with a man's face swings his massive weapon and an exemplar opens at the waist, a splashing red blast. Shiny entrails gush out.

Is this real?

The bear's face looks like a man's, albeit disfigured by scars. His steel is shinier than in the murals. So shiny Culver's eyes can't release it. Ausgan's artisans probably couldn't replicate so bright a thing if they tried, which may be why he always expected steel to look like clay. It flares while it flies. *Gleaming.* Glittering even as Culver's sight blurs. How dazzling would scales of such material look on a dele? They'd probably look like stars. Constellations, even. Oozing blood trembles on Culver's lip.

"Euphrain ..." Haik's voice wavers from somewhere dark. "Pyroktus formation!"

"I'm sorry." Kale is weeping, pulling something around Culver's neck. Maybe he'll stop the bleeding. It would really help. Culver can't feel anything on the outside, but inside he's finally starting to warm up. His shudders are subsiding. He draws in a slow breath, so as not to cough. If he's careful, maybe he'll be able to say something. Getting sleepy though.

"Turn them all to ash!" Haik's voice is distant, irrelevant. The summoning song magnifies. Bright whips of fire spring up, writhing against the stars like tentacles, making everything orange. Culver watches while his fading vision allows it. Pyroktus. He'd always wanted to see it. Kale is talking to him. Culver can't hear him. The bright red light exposes their attackers. They aren't bears or beasts. They're rough-looking people who wear the hides of animals. Some are on fire.

Culver wanted to say something. Doesn't matter now that he thinks about it. His head rests in Kale's lap like a boulder. Kale is so distraught, snuffing and wheezing. No need for that. Culver wants to reach up and comfort him somehow. He tries but the action feels unfamiliar. Can't tell where his hand is or if he even managed to lift it. He lets the warmth overtake his vision, his coldness, his feeling. He's so tired. He remembers what he wanted to say but doesn't want to bother Kale with anything else. He tells himself.

"It shouldn't end like this."

Acknowledgments

To my wife Bray. Thank you for supporting me and helping me break out of the grind.

To my children – Donavon, Simon, Evie, Rowan. Thanks for inspiring me constantly and making me aspire to be better.

To my writing group: Story Time. Ben Credle, Matt Smith, and whoever else randomly joined us for lunch at the Mexican restaurant on Fridays from 2017 until whenever. You guys, particularly Ben and slightly less particularly Matt, created for me the deadlines and critique and approval I needed to finish this at last. Thank you.

To the editors, John Jarrold and Lee Burton. Obviously, the piles of money I heaved at you should in itself indicate my gratitude, but I'd rather you know for sure. You accepted an enormous job from a nobody with no credentials and you both delivered above and beyond expectations. Thank you.

To LE Brooks. As ARC readers go, you are the pinnacle. I don't know how many typos and errors you pointed out to me, even after the story had been scoured by professionals and unprofessionals alike. This book is truly better because you reached out to a stranger and offered to ARC read. Thank you.

To Drew Cochran, Brandon Duncan and anyone else I've accosted with blabber about this story for the past ten years. Thank you for tolerating me.

To those I've neglected to mention here. You knew I would. I'm the worst. But thank you.

Author's note

Dear Reader

You are an absolute hero for making it this far. Thank you for reading or skimming all the way to this remote location. If you heed no more of my words at all, hear this: Please go rate or review this book at the place where you purchased it. This will tremendously help the second and final book of Turesia Untamed:

THE HEATHEN TIDE.

On that, I'd love to tell you the release date of book 2, but that would require a level of prescience I haven't mastered. Follow my blog, Regarding Silexare, or social media because I'll probably not shut up about it until it's in your hands.

See you soon.

dtl